GABRIEL'S LAMB

by Martin Sparks

Contents and cover copyright © 2013 by Martin Sparks
ISBN 13: 978-0615716237
Revision 3

Dedication

I remember when, as a boy, I read my first real novel. In the front I discovered the dedication, where the author showered praise on his wife. "That's boring," I thought. "When I grow up, I'll dedicate my book to someone cool." But at nine years old, one doesn't know what an author and his family goes through in preparing a work. Likewise, at nine years old, one thinks highly of oneself, and doesn't yet know how cool the person is who will spend his or her life with you, despite your flaws and obsessions.

Now I do know. Honey, this book is for you.

Prologue

Hosts

Rosie sat up in the bed. The texture of the quilt under her arms and palms drew pleasing pictures in her mind, and the creak of the carved wooden bed spoke of long service offered to many sleepers before her. Dim light from the stars outside reflected off the silver fringe of the thick rug, the glass knick-knacks in the window, and the gilded edges of the picture frames that adorned the unfamiliar room. The smell of dust and the elusive sweetness of old, dry wood told her she was the room's first occupant for some time. She turned in the bed, trying to remember where the light switch was before she got up, so she could find the door without knocking into any of the fragile and old things in the room. The motion made the bandages on her back crinkle. The itching of the burns these covered intruded upon her consciousness, becoming the only irritant in the room's quiet midnight welcome.

After a second she found she had no need to visit the bathroom. She wondered why she had awakened, but as she paused to think, she realized he was in the room. Comfort changed to delight and wonder.

"Beloved," she thought. *"Did I call you? I am sorry if I did, I must have been dreaming. I am safe: you don't need to be here."*

"BELOVED," he answered in kind, his voice carrying that strange whisper, a whisper in which she imagined she could hear a multitude of other conversations.

Rosie smiled. She lowered her arm, no longer needing the light switch, as the room was suffused already with the awareness her beloved brought with him. There was still only starlight in the room, but now, joined with him as she was becoming, she was aware of every object in the room. She could see the collection of glass paperweights in the drawer of the old writing desk and the store of memories that clung to them, and feel the coolness of each particle of the plaster right to the point where it ended around a metal box which in turn enclosed wires. And these wires coursed with energy, thrumming sixty times a second with the vibration that was the universe waiting for her to turn on a light. These moments of oneness with the world were to treasure, but to be kept secret. Even trying to explain them prompted normally loving and helpful people to send her to therapists. So despite the joy of the moment, she knew this wonderful visit would become one of the secrets she kept.

"YOU ARE MENDING FROM THE FIRE. I AM SORRY FOR YOUR PAIN. I SHOULD HAVE TAKEN GREATER CARE, FORESEEN MORE," he said regretfully. "I WAS ANXIOUS FOR YOU, AND I HAVE NOT YET MASTERED THE LAWS OF THIS WORLD. FOR ALL THE TIME I HAVE WATCHED IT, THE MOMENTS WHEN I HAVE BEEN ABLE TO ACT IN IT ADD UP TO MERE CLUMSY HOURS."

Since the moment she had gotten the burns, she had understood that they, however painful, were proof of her beloved's love and protectiveness. But this understanding mingled with harrowing recollections of the violence and energy which had created them. Like the itches which diminished her comfort, her memories of the voices, and the screams, diminished her peace. But she pushed the thoughts out of her mind to comfort her visitor.

"Do not heal them. Save your energy, and let my body heal on its own. I

want to spend with you the moments we create by saving that energy. I will heal when you have left." So they sat together, touching in the way that he touched and was everything in the room. Through him and his thousands of arms which radiated from him, she could even feel multiple points of her own body in a strange iteration of what her computer savvy brother, Devon, had called "recursion." She could feel her beloved feeling her feeling him feeling her down to infinity.

This entwining of senses continued for long happy minutes. But as she explored the world through his senses, she felt embarrassment. She could feel him noticing that she was wiggling her toes as she often did in excitement. A moment of self-consciousness emerged as she noticed him noticing her noticing the twitch all the way down the levels of inter-consciousness they shared. Their connection collapsed like a house of cards gone a level too high. Her senses abruptly became her own again and she felt sheepish. But his voice and reassurance was comforting. "THE DAY OF OUR UNION APPROACHES, BELOVED, DO NOT WISH OR WAIT FOR IT, IT IS INEVITABLE. BUT I HAVE BEEN SENT TO DO A THING IN THE MEANTIME. YOU MUST COME WITH ME."

Disappointment filtered through her, but she knew all good flowed from obedience and surrender to their Friend. As her beloved obeyed him, she would, too. *"So now He sends you. Why does He not talk to me as he used to?"*

"THIS IS NOT FOR ME TO KNOW," came the reply. "BUT I CARRY A STORE OF HIS LIGHT AND INTENT. WE MUST GO."

"Take me," she said, reaching out with her arms to the empty air full of him. She knew how to travel with him. When he had first come to her, he had taken her to Maisajeh Hill. In resting there with him and watching the animals in the Lame Burra game reserve, she had first understood the world and her ties to everything. So she knew these trips were important.

She cleared her mind and imagined emptiness. The wind-up, folding clock Faith had left on the night table ticked once and the journey began. Her vision folded, and as it folded in on her, it was as though she passed through a plane like the surface of the water. Inside this plane, she could see how everything alive had "tails." David sleeping in the other room, the trees outside her window, and the fish in the gorge, all had a part of themselves which extended away, nearly parallel, to a point so far she could not see. But at that point, she knew, they would touch. Everything living touched at the same point: they were all connected. It was the fate of all that lived to journey along these lines until it was reunited with itself, God.

After a second of this, she stood at the bank of a river. The grass under her feet ran down to the water, but to her right the bank was covered with boulders and chunks of concrete rubble of such size the river could not have put them there. That meant, she supposed, they had been moved there with the labor of many men and machines: they had been moved by power. The willow tree beside her rustled in the night breeze as she climbed up the grassy bank.

At the top of the slope was a road, flanked by an asphalt sidewalk still warm on her feet from the day's sun. Beyond it was a field of short grass, and an ocean of buildings she did not recognize. They were of many different types, but they all shared one thing: they were not homes of people. They were grand, important buildings, buildings with names and not numbers. At this time of night, she could feel few people amongst them. But even when they held people, they were not homes or schools or even wholly workplaces, but storehouses of power.

"Why do we always journey at night?" she wondered aloud. Her companion did not answer, and she understood from his silence that the ration of energy he held would not be enough to answer the question and do what he had been sent to do. The starlight, and the wasted light from the many lamps which illuminated the buildings around her, glowed off a piece of paper on the ground that was out of place. As her nanny had taught her, she reached for the waste paper, and sought a trash can to put it in. She saw no can, but she did notice a wooden fence blocking the road further down the riverside marked "President Santorum Memorial – Closed Due to Flooding."

"IT IS THERE," he said, interrupting her search for a trash can. She looked up and saw the middle and top of a gleaming white tower standing far over the roofs of the other grand buildings. It had more light and more importance showered on it than anything else by what could only be hundreds of enormous electric lamps. The light brought to mind a tone in her ear. She exhaled, humming the tone, and flew with the light up and to the side of the tower. She ran her hands over its grainy white surface and pressed her fingers into the joints between the stones. In the edges of the stone blocks she could feel workmanship a century old, and see both the errors and triumphs of men and chisels. It was odd, to feel stone and earth beneath her fingers, but not beneath her feet.

"It's beautiful," she said as she floated.

"ALL OF CREATION IS BEAUTY," he answered. "WHAT IS MORE FASCINATING TO ME IS WHICH PORTION OF BEAUTY YOU CHOOSE TO SEE. THIS NAMING AND SEEING BEAUTY IS THE PURPOSE OF YOUR KIND." Whether it was because his reflection made him drop his guard, or because she was having a moment of awareness, in the corner of her eye, she caught sight of him. His arms extended from him like rays, touching all, and he regarded the tower with her. But he was not to be seen when she turned her head. He always eluded her thus. "I MUST HOLD YOU HERE, IN THE AIR. I WILL USE ALL MY OWN ENERGY, AND DRAW WHAT I CAN FROM OUR ENVIRONMENT, TO KEEP YOU HERE AS LONG AS I CAN."

She pressed her back against the stone of the tower, letting air blow beneath her feet as her toes warmed in the brightness of the sea of lamps. Shielding her eyes with the paper made the images and words on it stand out against the glow through the page.

"Welcome to the National Mall!" it read, and it featured an image of a panda bear standing with one arm around the same tower before which she now floated. It would have to be a giant panda bear, she thought, to stand upright beside this tower as it was in the picture. She folded the paper and clutched it. She had no pocket to put it in, as she was naked except for the huge T-shirt David had given her to sleep in. She closed her eyes against the light and smelled the vapors of the river, the grass which filled the open spaces, and the oils and spilled food on the web of asphalt running through the dark city.

"This is the place?"

"YES."

"What should I see?" she asked.

"I CANNOT KNOW THIS. IT WAS FOR ME TO BRING YOU TO THIS SPOT, AND THIS TIME AND PLACE. ONLY YOU, THROUGH YOUR CONNECTION TO THIS WORLD, CAN INTERPRET WHAT NEEDS INTERPRETING."

She relaxed and reached out with their shared senses, looking and feeling for whatever it was she was supposed to see. Nothing caught her attention immediately, but she kept sifting through the impressions of sight, smell, and empathy with determination. She hoped that understanding might help explain the mystery God had made of her life by taking away her language.

After a few moments, she began to sink toward the ground. It meant her beloved was slipping from the world. The array of lights surrounding the tower dimmed as he consumed their power to buy her a few more seconds. She cleared her thoughts and reached out again, touching the surfaces of all the hearts in her reach, looking for the sign she was supposed to see. Desperation tinged her actions and blunted her perceptions, however, and she knew she would not find her goal.

She was still in the air, slowly falling, when she passed again through the folding plane and saw, for an instant, the "tails" of everything living extending away to a distant point of union. She pictured the world of people as a community of monkeys with invisible prehensile tails they didn't know were all clasped together! People were this close, like they were all holding hands at every moment, but they didn't know it.

Then she was sitting back in the bed she had been sleeping in, enclosed in a darkness made opaque by the brilliance of the lights which had been in her eyes moments before. Her beloved was gone without warning. He had used his last jot of energy to keep her where she had floated, but even so, she had not seen or understood whatever God had intended. And now she would not be able to say goodbye to him, and there would be no gentle letting go. There was only the shock, the loneliness, and the repetition of her failure to grasp her own purpose.

She curled up into the quilt and sighed in frustration and loneliness. "I name you, beloved. Maybe you are but one of a host, but you are everything to me. Goodbye, Gabriel."

After a moment of this, she corrected her thoughts. Gabriel was not gone; he was just not perceptible any longer. He was still there, all around her, but without the energy to manifest and speak. And the best way to show how much she loved him was to love the world that contained him.

Chapter 1

A Foundling

May 5th, Year of Our Lady 11.

Doctor Hildegard Teschke watched her office clock. It was an unremarkable clock, the same cardboard and plastic twelve-hour wall clock which had been on the wall when she'd moved into the office decades before. It had a white face and black tick marks for each minute. When both her inner office and the teaching assistants' outer office were quiet, it ticked a trifle loudly when the minute hand moved. But the clock suited her, or she would have replaced it. It matched the worn oak veneer desk and green vinyl furnishings of a 70's era. She and the room were aging well together: much of her own hair was now as gray as a worn coin.

It was the fashion in her adopted homeland, the United States, to believe time was money. This was also noted in her birth country, Germany, but was not the prevailing use of time. There time was life. She was glad her accomplishments had exempted her from the awful necessity of equating time and money and allowed her to focus on time's other merits in a way which would have made her watch-making grandparents proud. Unfortunately, as she had no children, this success on behalf of her family could best be described as modest. She had never made time for children, manifesting a choice she had never been able to say out loud. Time had spoken for her.

Her doctoral thesis and several succeeding works (all received with acclaim) had explored time and language. At first, she had studied time as an element of the Schwabian dialect of German. Timing and syllabification combined to make Schwabian a beautiful language, whereas many forms of German were seldom described by a non-native listener as beautiful. But this research was now dull to her, merely the cataloging of the characteristics of yet another language soon to be dead, as she feared many European tongues would become.

Though sounds and grammar had lost their luster after long study, time had not. She had done a comparative study of how quickly different languages could impart information. One of her peers had once surmised, based on some ignorant stereotype of why Germans did what they did, that Hildegard was trying to determine which language delivered the most semantic meaning the fastest and was therefore most "cost effective" for humanity to use. As if such a statistic could ever be derived, or if it were derived, would ever be anything but trivia. As if anyone who loved a language, its poetry, its spoken melodies, its idioms and double meanings, would ever surrender it on being informed by a clipboard-carrying linguist that it was "semantically inefficient."

No, time and the spoken word were woven into songs far beyond her bygone critic's grasp. The study of time and efficiency had been instructive. English, as spoken between Americans who did not know each other, was semantically slow: Americans talked slowly, and focused (particularly among men) on the messages imparted by the words. But in the openness and the lack of social and emotional information it imparted, it reflected American society. It was egalitarian, with fewer assumptions and bits of information about rank, station, and power.

German had embedded social information in it, so while slower than English, one could swiftly get an idea of who in a conversation outranked whom, by virtue of age, position, or gender. You would have to understand German culture to interpret this additional information, but once you did, you could learn a lot more bits of information over time by listening to German than American English.

But the languages most dense with meaning were the Asian ones. Since for all of her early academic career China had been behind a curtain of communism, she had studied Japanese. It was still her greatest challenge. So much information was embedded in the spoken language, the choices and uses of the different alphabets, and the careful shell games of hidden and displayed emotions that she had long ago admitted she would never master Japanese. This fact was proven anew to her whenever her Japanese research assistant burst out laughing at a joke Hildegard never noticed in a recording. In this sense, Japanese could impart much more information between speakers much faster, but then, it took a lifetime to learn the social trick of "being Japanese," so the language could not be regarded as "efficient" to anyone but the Japanese.

Most fascinating, though, was the use of time itself as a form of communication. One need only watch people to conclude time was a language. Subordinates given orders by superiors often went to work with needless bustle and haste to express with their use of time the esteem or fear they felt for their superiors. Judges, bureaucrats, and professors, in contrast, often did things in a deliberate way, either to express their power to others, or because they subordinated time to the disciplines of regulation and deep thought. They suggested these things were timeless without ever saying a word.

Hildegard's thoughts wandered for a moment, and she remembered a specific use of time. When she had been a PhD candidate, she had illicitly dated a famous linguist, but then, she regarded American prudishness as a problem for Americans. She recalled the way his hands had lingered on her shoulders or hips, before and after their lovemaking, or as they walked together, for long, languid seconds. These had been the most loving words of time ever spoken to her.

One could say a lot with time. One could speak volumes. A universal grammar of time, Hildegard decided, would be a fitting masterpiece in her graying years. Perhaps she should begin one after this appointment.

A tick of the clock brought her back to the present. It was two minutes after two-thirty, and her appointment was late. She wondered what the police were trying to tell her by being late. But since her life had been uninteresting for fifteen years at least, she was sure their visit couldn't mean *she* was in trouble. She had, she observed, been spending all her years in a prison of her own making long before the police officers inquired with the department secretary.

Twenty minutes after the appointed time, a timid knock came at the door to the outer office which her teaching assistants used. Hildegard walked through the clutter of desks and paper-decorated cubicle partitions quickly, a bit irritated. Shouldn't police be firm and assertive? Didn't they batter down doors with rams if occupants weren't responsive enough? Why should they knock like undergraduate students who fear they've been caught plagiarizing their term papers?

She yanked opened the outer office door abruptly, and was confronted not with a square-jawed, suit-wearing detective, but a large, strong-looking young woman in a blue uniform. She wore no badge or gun. Her bright red cheeks and dry brown hair gave the impression of an active lifestyle and little concern for grooming or grace.

"Dr. Teschke?" the woman asked, respectful, but not timid as the knock had suggested. The professor, taken aback by the difference between her expectations and the person who had appeared, nodded and opened the door further, stepping back.

"Hi, I'm Faith Haversham," the young woman offered her hand as soon as she entered. The professor gave it a perfunctory shake, still not knowing what to make of her visitor. "I'm a fire inspector with Ithaca Fire Department."

Hildegard spotted a metal engraved nameplate reading "Haversham," and the blue and orange patch sewn on the shoulder of her blue shirt which read "Ithaca, New York Fire and Rescue." She marveled that the linguistics department secretary had mistaken the woman for a police officer. To be sure, there was a uniform, but she carried no gun and was clearly not a grim-faced warden of the state.

At this point a girl of ten or eleven years peered out from behind the firefighter. Inspector Haversham brought the young girl forward by the shoulder. "This is Janey." Janey looked the professor up and down, and in a display of bad breeding, gave no greeting of her own.

Dr. Teschke wanted to be curt with the woman. She had expected this visit was official business, and for this reason she had ordered her assistants away for the afternoon so nothing would be overheard. But now she wondered if this firefighter was a part-time student who had failed an exam and if Faith would present the girl as part of a sob story in a plea for a lenient grade. The professor had no patience for women who chose to have children and then use them as shields for their lack of professional performance.

"I was told this was a police matter. I'm not sure what you mean by bringing your daughter," she answered. She decided, whatever "Inspector Haversham's" issue, she would resolve it in her own office, and indicated her door to the other woman.

The firefighter laughed as she walked through the office with Janey in tow. The tinkle of her laugh was small and fine for a woman of her size, and because it sounded forced, it grated against Dr. Teschke's sour mood of suspicion. "Oh, she isn't my daughter, Doctor. We don't know who her parents are. That's why I'm here."

Hildegard frowned. If this was about some issue of paternity involving one of her graduate assistants, she would be sure to make the young man regret it. But she then recalled she had only one male graduate assistant at the moment, and she was sure his grooming and hygiene would prevent his reproduction entirely. And he would have to have been precocious as a youngster to already have a child so old.

At Dr. Teschke's motion, the firefighter took a seat in a stool which was small under her. She waited as the woman used hand motions to coax the girl into sitting as well. After a delay for a puzzled look, Janey sat and surveyed the office, peering at posters and pictures.

"Please explain, Inspector Haversham. I am a busy woman and this is a busy department. How would I know anything about this child's parents? I have no children myself, nor living brothers or sisters."

After a moment of a puzzled look, the woman grasped Dr. Teschke's confusion. "Oh, I'm sorry. I was told the police had explained everything to you already. Officer Noonan was supposed to come with me, but he got held up at the courthouse. Instead of making you wait, I came without him."

This explanation softened the professor's feelings. The firefighter was respecting her time, and their confusion with the situation was mutual. And it seemed the young woman would not be begging for a grade change. "I see. I haven't been told a word about this girl," Hildegard motioned to Janey. Janey took no notice of this. Her eyes were fixed on a poster showing the word "peace" reprinted in one hundred and five languages. "Can you explain how I can help you?"

Faith was now looking at Janey, trying to catch her eye, but gave up. She turned back to the professor and let the girl stare at the poster. "It's an issue of child welfare. We found Janey at the scene of a fire in Tompkins County this past weekend. It was a nasty one that burned an old carriage house out on Triphammer."

"I heard about it," Dr. Teschke recalled, taking her seat. "Didn't one person die?"

"What you didn't hear was about Janey. I knew right away the fire was arson. Since we didn't find any other human remains in the fire, and no other survivors, we had to assume the fire was set to kill her. So we told the reporters we might have found some human remains to protect her."

"I see." Faith's unsophisticated way masked a quick thinker. Hildegard doubted she would have assembled those facts so nimbly. The two women regarded each other until she felt obliged to continue. "But how can I help you? I am a professor of linguistics."

"Doctor, Janey understands some English, but she doesn't speak it at all. None of the schoolteachers in the district have ever seen her in a class. We don't know anything about her, and we can't understand her answers to our questions. When she does say anything, it's in a language no one understands."

At last Hildegard understood how she fit in. "Ah. So you want me to try and talk to her?"

Inspector Haversham nodded.

The professor rubbed her temples and pieced together a polite explanation. "I am a linguist. That means I study the structure of languages and their relationship to one another. I speak only German, English, and Japanese well. You would do better to take her to the Department of Modern Languages. The professors and instructors there can speak many more languages than I."

The firefighter sagged. "But we've been there already. No one understands her there, either. Doctor Kramer sent me to you. He said you were the best thinker about languages, even if you didn't speak many."

Dr. Teschke bristled at Frank Kramer's jibe, come at her through this woman. The man loved to show off his mastery of nine languages. She made a mental note that she would have to scold him later for his joke over their next cup of coffee. "Not one person in all of the Department of Modern Languages knows her language?" She looked to Faith to confirm this, incredulous. If no one at Cornell knew this girl's language, perhaps no one else in the world would.

"No, and they tried all kinds of people, including some exchange students from Africa and some ancient language experts from the classics department. Most said it sounded like a romance language, but they couldn't understand it. They thought maybe you could guess the language family or give them some idea of where to start."

Hildegard now studied the girl over for clues. "Child, aren't you a mystery," she said absently. The girl gazed back at her, dangling her feet beneath the seat of her chair, before turning to face another wall and another poster. Dr. Teschke saw now it had been foolish to assume Janey was Faith's daughter, because the two looked nothing alike. The inspector was tall, muscular, and fair skinned. But the child was short for her apparent age, fine boned and featured,

4

and had darkish skin, black glossy hair, and brown eyes. She could be Italian. Or Greek. Or Filipino.

The girl's skin color didn't mean she was foreign. Could the problem not be linguistic at all, but an organic problem in Janey's hearing or speech? She gave voice to the idea. "Is it possible she's hearing impaired? She responded to you when you spoke, even though she wasn't looking at you, so she isn't deaf. But if she were hearing impaired, her speech might be unintelligible to anyone not used to the way she spoke, even if she was speaking English."

"We had her checked out as well as we could at the hospital, Doc. No sign of anything wrong with her." Janey's eyes were still fixed on Faith, and the girl got down from her chair and stood by the woman, putting out both hands. Inspector Haversham took them and held them, smiling.

"Is it possible she has an organic problem such as brain damage induced by heat or smoke?" Hildegard asked. She regretted it as soon as she said it. She should presume firefighters recognize such symptoms.

"You aren't the first to wonder that. It would be a very atypical problem if it were. None of the doctors could rule it out, but it's hard to get kids with no known health insurance the kind of expensive special tests needed to rule it out completely."

"Maybe something like autism? It could be what she speaks is no language at all." With this, Dr. Teschke was out of organic explanations for the puzzle Janey presented.

The inspector shrugged. "I'm not an expert on autism, but I suppose someone at the hospital would have wondered that, too."

With this exhaustion of alternatives to this girl being her problem, Hildegard focused. For a couple of hours at most her life would be different than she had expected. The prospect should excite her. Had she been queen of this department so long that novelty filled her with dread? It was time to muster those powers which had made her department chair: reason and forthrightness.

The professor reached into her desk drawer and pulled out a cassette recorder, then fished about to find a blank cassette tape. She used these increasingly rare media to record speech for her research, despite her Japanese teaching assistant's many respectful attempts to get her to use a digital recorder to create sound files more easily imported to a computer. She found the digital recorders puzzling, since, because they had no wheels or gears to confirm they were in operation, it was difficult to tell when they were working. Dr. Teschke had tried them, missed recording two or three conversations in rare dialects because she had mis-set the digital gadget, and gone back to working with cassette tapes. If her assistants found tapes inconvenient, they were assistants, after all, so this wasn't her problem.

After setting up the tape recorder and pressing record, the professor then stood and moved around the left end of her desk to face Janey's chair, which had been at the right end of her desk. This left the firefighter between her and Janey, which she hoped would make the girl more comfortable. She puzzled for what to say to prompt body language or speech and provide clues to the child's origins.

Janey's eyes were on her as she moved around her desk, so it took a fraction of a second to catch the girl's gaze. When she had it, Hildegard stepped forward and introduced herself.

"Good day, Janey, my name is Dr. Teschke. I'm pleased to meet you," she offered a handshake.

There was a second of silence as Janey analyzed her actions. Then the girl pushed off the stool, ignored the offered handshake, and spoke in a serious tone.

"Es-TAS pleh-ZUR-o ren-KON-tee veen. Mee no-MEE-jas ro-SET-a."

Having said this, Janey bowed her head, bent at her knees, and brought her hands down to her sides, palms open, before straightening again. Hildegard retracted her hand, and took a step back again from Janey.

"There you go. That's the way she talks," the inspector confirmed.

Janey, looking uncertain, cleaved back to the woman and rested against her. The firefighter gave her a hug while looking expectantly at the professor.

Dr. Teschke replayed the strange words in her head. "It did sound like a romance language," she said. "And unless I'm mistaken, her gesture at the end of it was a curtsy. Both those things would suggest a European heritage, but a curtsy is old-fashioned everywhere. How odd."

Faith nodded from her chair, supplying no more help. This was where the younger woman had decided to leave theorizing to the "expert." That curtsies were old-fashioned was an understatement for her, she doubted most American women had ever executed a curtsy or even seen one outside the odd romance movie.

Hildegard stopped to make a note on the pad on her desk: "Ask Frank: Ruled out Rhaeto-Romanic?" This language was an archaic survival of Latin, spoken in rare places in and around Switzerland and all but dead. It would sound like a romance language because of its roots, but be mysterious to most listeners. "Also Romanian?" she wrote further. She had never been to Romania, but she understood the country had old-fashioned customs and the language was also similar to Latin.

All the scribbling she was doing on the pad gave her a thought. She watched Janey, who was relaxing again. The girl was scanning her bookshelves, eyes resting on each title. This reinforced her idea. "Does she read or write?" she asked.

"No, but she'll draw all day. I have some of the pictures in my clipboard." Inspector Haversham began to rummage through pages stored in a metal clipboard she was carrying. The professor stopped her.

"Another time. But she has not written anything, or read anything?"

Faith paused, and then shook her head. "They offered her a pen and paper in the Department of Modern Languages, but she began to draw, not write."

Dr. Techke concluded that the most likely explanation at this point was a disability or some combination of an unfamiliar language and a disability, rather than a novel language. She appraised the girl again, feeling sympathy rather than resentment. This child might have watched her family burn to death. Why did she feel so cold toward her? *"She did not wake up this morning determined to ruin your day, Frau Doktor,"* Hildegard mocked her own vanities. *"Lighten up!"*

"Did they offer her anything to read?"

"Not that I remember." The firefighter answered, now looking intrigued.

"Asterix," remembered Dr. Teschke aloud. "I have Asterix somewhere." She went to her bookshelves and, sure enough, in a dusty stack atop the furthest shelf, she pulled down some thin and oversized dusty copies of a European comic book, Asterix the Gaul. Asterix had been a cultural fixture in Germany and most of Europe for decades. The original stories of Asterix the Gaul and his village's constant fight against the encroaching Roman legions had been an echo of the Second World War when the first of many volumes was written. But the comic book had met with such universal acclaim that its author, Goscinny, had worked to have each volume translated into every major world language. After his death, more had been written by Goscinny's collaborators, so Asterix lived on into the modern day, even though she felt the later volumes had lost Goscinny's edge and originality.

This stack of Asterix comics she had were all copies of the first volume in German, English, Japanese, Italian, French, and Latin. She had used them when she taught her course "Introduction to Universal Grammar." It occurred to her that she hadn't offered the class in years.

She pulled a wooden desk chair up to her desk with one hand as she plunked the pile of comic books down on the desk. "Janey, I have something for you to read. It may be more fun than sitting there," she said to the girl, motioning to the chair. "Would you like to read Asterix? It was my favorite when I was your age." With that statement she felt a twinge of memory. It was true, more than true: Asterix had been the frosting on a cake of freedom.

Hildegard remembered sitting with her brother on a train car, riding from gray and walled-up West Berlin to their new home in Hamburg, reading Asterix aloud and with flourish. It had been one of the most pleasant and memorable moments of her young life. Her mother bought the comic book for her with their only western marks at a train station kiosk as soon as they had crossed the border from East Germany. Her mother had nothing to read of her own, and so she and her brother had read the Asterix to their mother. They had each voiced different characters and enacted bits of the story. The laughter and encouragement of her mother, an older woman passenger, and the *Bundeswehr* soldier who had joined them in the train compartment had made her flush with pride. It was then Hildegard had decided she liked to speak in front of people, and this was a skill that served her well even in her present job.

Turning to face Janey, she saw the child was staring at her, eyes searching her face, as if looking for some trace of her true intent. As she did so, Janey stepped away from where she had been clutching Faith's hand, followed Dr. Teschke's gesture to the wooden chair, put her hand on the professor's arm and sat down.

Hildegard kept her eyes on the comic books as she moved around her desk to sit in her own chair. Janey picked up the first comic book in the stack with her right hand, sweeping dust off it with her left in a practiced gesture. Once clean, she placed it in front of her , rotated it so the title and picture were up, and opened it. With the first page her round face went from seriousness to delight, and she laughed even as she turned the first few pages.

"Uh, wow," commented Faith. "Your comic books are a hit, Doc. I'll get her some on the way home."

"That will be difficult," Dr. Teschke replied. "They won't have these at the convenience store. Janey is reading Japanese."

The two women watched in silence as Janey's bursts of giggling brightened the room. In about twenty five minutes, Janey had finished the first <u>Asterix</u>, reached eagerly for the second, and then grew disappointed when she saw that, though written in Italian, it was the same story. She pouted at the professor as if she'd been tricked.

"It's too bad I sent away my teaching assistants expecting unrelated business from the police. One of them is from Tokyo and would be able to speak Japanese to her."

"But Doc, the Department of Modern Languages already tried Japanese. Are you sure she wasn't just looking at the pictures and laughing at them?" The woman rose and stretched forward over Janey's shoulder to pick up the Asterix and examine it.

"*She caught you making an assumption. Not so sharp in your old age, are you?*" The professor reproached herself.

"That's an excellent observation. Let's test your hypothesis." Dr. Teschke reached for her stylus, tore a sheet from her note pad, and wrote in her careful beginner's calligraphy in Japanese: "My name is Hildegard. What is your name? And where can we find your mother or father?" When she had checked it, she passed the sheet to Janey with the stylus.

Janey held the page up, and read it. Then she put it down on the desk, examined the stylus, made a trial scribble on the page to test the point, and began to write. At first, Dr. Teschke was delighted, but grew puzzled as she realized the girl was writing her reply left to right and hence not in Japanese.

When finished, Janey put down the pen, picked up the paper, and passed it back. Her reply was three separate lines. The professor studied the neat, girlish print.

"Mi nomidʒas Rozɛta.

"Sertʃadu patron mian kaj patrinon mian en vian keron. Oni lodʒas en tʃiun keron.

"Finos mi malbenon de la turo."

Hildegard sounded out the words as she used them. She assumed the non-Roman letters such as dʒ were pronounced as they were in the International Phonetic Alphabet, which was the alphabet linguists used to write languages which had no known alphabet or a non-standard alphabet that couldn't be typed into a computer. Even with this assumption, the words puzzled her.

"Can you read it, Doc?" asked the woman after the professor had struggled with it a bit.

"I think I can read parts of it. It has a romantic influence."

The inspector pursed her lips in confusion. "Doesn't romantic mean European? I thought you said she was reading in Japanese."

Both of them turned to Janey. Janey's back was to Faith, but Dr. Teschke could see the girl's faint smile. Dr. Teschke watched for a sign of a smirk which would indicate the girl knew she was being clever, but her expression was patient and steady.

"She can read Japanese. But instead of answering my questions in Japanese, she wrote answers to my questions in this romance language."

"So.... she reads Japanese, but doesn't write it? Is her family Japanese, then?"

Hildegard felt a flash of anger. The situation was too preposterous to continue. No twelve-year-old American read but didn't speak Japanese, nor did a normal twelve-year-old use linguists' characters in their writing. This situation was so bizarre as to be a prank. "Ms. Haversham, is this a joke?"

"Excuse me?" The firefighter seemed too surprised to be hurt, at first, but her expression changed to anger and certainty. Her tone became flinty. "The fire was real, Doctor Teschke. And this girl was in it. I helped the nurse at the hospital scrape off her melted clothes. She has burns all up and down her back. The fire might have been set as a prank, but if so, it was plain reckless. I still want to send that prankster to jail. After the boys at the sheriff's department and I horse-whip him."

"You misunderstand me, but even what I meant to say was out of order. Forget I said it. I find Janey puzzling, and for a moment I imagined this situation was a linguist's hoax Dr. Kramer had put you up to. I have become used to thinking I know a great deal, and this girl is proving me wrong." The professor glanced at Janey. Indeed, the child sat with her back stiff and straight.

"Oh." Faith mulled this confession over. "It *is* a weird situation. My dad was fire chief for years and he never encountered anything like it." Her tone softened again, but the hard edge of the woman's anger lingered in Dr. Teschke's ears. She resolved that if she needed to start any fires, she would go to the next county to avoid this woman's wrath.

"Would you like to see this?' Hildegard offered the page to the inspector. She leaned forward and took it over Janey's shoulder. The girl's gaze followed the paper, eyes projecting hope.

"Huh. Looks kind of like Spanish. Or Italian. Isn't 'mia' Italian of for 'my', like 'Mama mia?'"

"Yes, it does look like Italian, but Italian is not written that way. The word order doesn't match, it has letters which are not used in Italian, and it doesn't make sense if read as Italian."

Faith frowned, staring at the page. "But it's related?"

"I think so. I suspect it may be a sister language of Italian, called Rhaeto-Romanic. But that language is moribund, and those that speak it are not only old, but also speak French or German. They would never travel to Japan and also read Japanese."

"What does she say?"

"I believe in the first line she says her name is Rosetta. In the second line I think she is saying her parents live in, or were traveling to, a place called Keron."

"I know every town for three counties in every direction. No place around here called Keron," said the inspector.

"Let me get my atlas," said Hildegard.

"You've got a computer, Doc, why not Google it?" countered the younger woman.

"I don't use the internet as my first resort when looking for information," admitted Dr. Teschke. "Why don't we trade chairs, and I'll use my atlas, and you can use the internet?"

Inspector Haversham was happy to be included. "Sure, no problem." The professor logged the firefighter into her university computer (which she was sure was against some rule or another) and then pulled her atlas from a bookshelf and took the woman's former seat against the wall.

After a moment of searching the index, and not finding a reference to Keron, Dr. Teschke began to page through maps of the Alps, looking for a village or region named Keron. "Sweden," interrupted Faith, after a few minutes of typing and clicking. "There is a city in northern Sweden named Keron. It's the one town I could find with Google." Hildegard turned to Sweden in her atlas. Sure enough, on the mountainous part of northern Sweden, in the Swedish Samiland, was a town named Keron.

"Ithaca, New York is hardly on the way from the Alps to Sweden," commented Dr. Teschke. But she was careful not to simply dismiss the hypothesis and examined Janey again. She *was* dark-skinned and dark-haired. Could she be an ethnic Lap of northern Sweden, speaking some rare Lap dialect written in Roman letters? The professor stood, went to her bookshelf, and pulled out her linguistic atlas. She paged through it while still standing.

"If she is from Keron, she could speak a language called Sami, which is closer to Hungarian and Finnish than Italian, not a romance language at all. The Sami people are darker skinned and darker haired than southern Scandinavians, and so at least that part fits. But there are very few speakers of Sami left. Some dialects of it are dead."

Faith looked up from the computer. "So, she speaks Sami, do you think, Doc?"

"She may, but what she wrote was not anything like Hungarian or Finnish. Let's keep searching for another place named Keron. Look for a place in central or eastern Europe."

After another half-hour of searching, both women came up empty handed. Hildegard felt her confidence in her hunch that Janey was central European fading. But the inspector had latched onto the idea that the girl was from Sweden.

"She's from somewhere, Doc. If that's your best guess, your guess is about the best money can buy."

Dr. Teschke was flattered by the younger woman's deference. "Nonsense. There are many other ethnographers and linguists, more specialized than I, who may have better guesses."

"What did you say her real name was?" the inspector asked.

"I think she wrote it was Rosetta."

"So, I guess I'd better stop calling you Janey, honey," the woman said. She knelt down, pointed her finger at the girl, and said "Rosetta."

"Row-SET-a," said the child, also pointing to herself and beaming.

"Faith," repeated the firefighter, pointing to herself.

"FEY-tha," repeated Rosetta, smiling even wider.

"Rosie," replied the woman, holding open her arms. The girl stood up and hugged her, but the inspector stopped herself before returning the hug and touching her back. "I promise you, honey, I'll do my best. I'll do everything I can to bring you home."

Dr. Teschke, now tired, decided that now was the opportunity to reclaim her seat behind her desk. She hoped she had correctly read the message. If she hadn't, the inspector might be renaming the child after a preposition or a verb. But her doubts went away as she stepped behind the two of them. The girl's face was streaked with tears.

The professor pursed her lips at the sight. *"Thirty years of linguistics, and I finally made a real difference to someone,"* she thought.

As her two guests reintroduced themselves, Hildegard stepped out into the central office to make the inspector a photocopy of the notebook page with her Japanese questions and Rosie's mysterious replies. She wasn't sure where the public servant might take the child next, but was sure that some social service agency or other investigator would want it and pressed it into the woman's hand anyway. Faith left her card and urged the professor to call if she had any questions or ideas.

Hildegard wasn't sure she wanted to be involved in the case day-to-day, but took the card. She then took a half hour of quiet at her desk, poring once again over maps of the Alps, before shutting her atlas in disappointment.

The clock over her desk ticked a minute. By now, it was past five in the afternoon, and she should be on her way home. She'd put this puzzle to her assistants in the morning.

An odd urge struck her. She felt a desire for pastry, and coffee. It was time for *kaffee und kuchen*, like she hadn't enjoyed in a couple of weeks. She knew the bakery downtown she would go to, sit down, and enjoy something sweet. After an afternoon like this one, she deserved it.

As the clock ticked again, she sifted through the pile of comics for the German copy of <u>Asterix</u> and walked out the door. She wanted to read it once more.

David Haversham stood up from his TV chair as Faith pushed open the front door, arms filled with groceries and hands clutching her keychain. Janey at once stepped forward and hugged him, forcing his daughter to sidestep both her and him as she teetered in the door with her double armload of paper bags.

"Why, hello, Janey dear," he said, surprised by the girl's hug.

"Her name isn't Janey," said Faith, trying to grip a runaway grocery bag with her elbow. The bag wriggled and slithered like a snake determined to find its way to the floor. "I know she's a cutie, Pop, but could you give me a hand before I drop this?"

10

He stood up and snatched the wayward bag as it began falling to the floor. The girl reached up without a word and took another bag and then followed them both into the kitchen.

"So what's the dumpling's real name? Can I pronounce it?"

"Rosetta. She speaks a language like Italian, Pop."

"Italians are good Catholics." David pronounced. He put the slippery bag on the counter and reached to take the other bag from the girl. "Why, thank you, Rosie," He then turned to his daughter. "What's with all the groceries? I went shopping two days ago."

Faith was amused to find her father had also shortened the child's name to Rosie. Sometimes it was clear that she and her father had been struck from the same mold.

"The Chief asked me to bring her home with me. The social worker is not sure the firehouse is a 'safe place' for a child. And I'm not feeding a kid those frozen pot pies every night. Fine for a grumpy old man like you and a spinster like me, but not for a blossom like her."

He was aghast. "Not safe in the firehouse? I raised you under those trucks. You spent half your childhood in a firehouse. No safer place than a house full of professional EMTs and rescuers. This girl would be the queen of the place: the boys would spoil her rotten."

"Pop, that social worker is from the city and suspicious as hell. She wasn't worried about the trucks, she was worried about the men. She said a child amongst so many men 'unsupervised' was 'vulnerable' and she wasn't a fire department mascot."

"Vulnerable, my ass," he growled.

Faith sighed. Her father was right, but not for the reasons he thought. It was true, she had grown up in the firehouses, and no fireman had ever laid an unwelcome hand on her as she grew older. But it was as much because she had "property of David Haversham" stamped across her forehead as because of firemen's good character.

The effect of her father's aegis persisted into the present day. Now that she was in her mid-thirties and looking to find someone and settle down, the "property of David Haversham" sign on her head was downright inconvenient. Her father had made more than one firefighter miserable for indiscretions, and even in retirement he was still feared and respected. He'd even shown up at two fires since retiring and the captain had let him direct the action out of fear and deference. So when it came to dating from her social circle, no one wanted the risk of breaking her heart or incurring the wrath of "3rd Degree," as the old man was known.

Faith didn't share these musings. They would lead to an argument where David challenged her to name the fireman who wouldn't treat the girl like a piece of cut crystal. She knew her father would trust her instincts and doubt the firefighter ever afterward and cause problems for the man through the "old boys" network that ran the fire department. So instead, she blamed the social worker.

"The new social worker is from New York City, pop. Things work differently there. Forgive her for being suspicious," she explained. She sometimes wondered if her father had ever left Tompkins County: if it wasn't for his honorable discharge hanging over the mantle she never would have believed her father had traveled at all until 9/11. "In any case, it was either bring Rosie home or down to the shelter."

David grunted at this. "You did the right thing. I hate how they send kids who've lost their family to that miserable place. They're victims, not criminals. They ought to leave them with neighbors till they can contact next of kin."

"Out on Triphammer no one had ever seen her before. We're the closest she has got to family, so I took her. Jenny Santini said she'd sit her for a while if we needed a break or if you needed to go up to Syracuse."

Her father soured at the mention of both the woman and the hospital. Jenny Santini was the widow of one of his firemen, and a hot-tempered Italian to the bone. Faith was privately of the opinion the two should marry: they could both shout stones into dust and both loved to hang around the fire stations. But he grew sullen if she even mentioned him dating. And the hospital in Syracuse was the reminder to him that he was getting old. He carried on as if the pacemaker was a personal humiliation. She could see where his thoughts were headed and changed the subject.

She decided to try something out. "Pop, I bought asparagus and potatoes. Can you do your magic on them, like you used to? I'd love to feed Rosie here a better meal than the hotpockets the boys push on her at the firehouse. I can cook the kielbasa, but I can't do the vegetables like you can."

At this, David froze and she waited for him to respond. This was a moment of truth. As her mother Constance had ailed, her father had taken over cooking, and gone from klutz to a respectable gourmand, his love for her mother driving him to create fresher and better tasting food to match her restricted diet. He had even brought her lunch and dinner in the hospital every day, spurning hospital food as too expensive yet not good enough. As his skill had reached its height, her mother had joked that if she'd known her husband could cook, she would have gotten cancer sooner.

Faith remembered how, on the ride home from that visit, her father had sobbed into his hands, loudly and unabashedly, the one time she'd heard straight emotion from his mouth. Usually he formed his emotions into some stoic catchphrase or an ear-reddening curse to God and the world. Even when her mother died, he had been still as a stone beside her hospital bed. And since she died, he'd never picked up a skillet or a spatula. And so they both ate microwave food off the wrapper. She knew her request that her father cook faced long odds, but it could have a high payoff.

The silver-haired man looked down at Rosie, who was watching them both from the kitchen door as they moved food into the refrigerator. The girl smiled back at him. "I don't suppose your mother would mind," he said.

"Mom would tell you 'stop being sorry for yourself and put your considerable talents to work.'" Her mother had been a school teacher, famous for finding hidden talents in problem children. More than one Ithaca high school student had found their considerable talents welcome at an upstate fire department with a letter from her father and mother.

David made no reply, as if she hadn't spoken. Faith made a mental note under "buttons not to push hard." Instead, he walked up to Rosie and put a hand on her shoulder. "First, let's get this blossom set up watching something at the TV." At his touch, her hand went up and clutched his arm, and he led her away into the living room as if the child was his own.

Faith finished packing the groceries away, feeling guilty. She left the asparagus and potatoes on the counter, and walked into the living room, moving quietly up behind her father, and put her arms around him.

"I love you, Pop. I'm sorry."

"I miss your mother. That's all. Being in the kitchen makes it worse. But you're right." He kept his eyes fixed on the TV program he'd picked for Rosie. She knew he was screening it for things which offended. It was something from Nickelodeon, and it captured the girl's attention.

"I wasn't right to say it that way," Faith struggled to refine her apology until he would take it. The stubborn old bastard always imagined he deserved whatever he got.

"Everyone needs a kick in the pants sometime," he grunted.

She took a deep breath, but said nothing after. Her ideal partner would be a lot like her father, except for this part.

David went into the kitchen. For over a year, he'd eaten pot pies, TV dinners, frozen pizza, anything that meant he didn't have to cook. He'd once had this kitchen in perfect order, and he dreaded opening the first drawer to find his daughter had changed everything and he'd have to spend ten minutes finding each utensil.

When he pulled open the drawer he was relieved to find everything was where he'd left it. Relief changed to sadness. "None of these has moved since she went away. And she hasn't come back." He rested his hand on the bamboo spatula, not wanting to move it. It felt like infidelity, contemplating cooking when Connie couldn't eat. He considered telling Faith he didn't want to cook, but he abandoned the thought. She was right. On thinking of his daughter and her probable reaction to him deciding not to cook, his eyes drifted to the living room doorway.

First a slender olive hand appeared on the doorframe, and then Rosie's face with big brown eyes. She grinned coyly when she saw him looking at her and took a careful step through the door.

"Hello, TV was boring for you?" First he wondered how he would get the child out of the kitchen: he couldn't cook with someone watching.

At the mention of the TV, Rosie glanced over her shoulder into the living room, and then back at David. She then walked decisively through the kitchen and put a hand on the counter in front of him. She stared at him then, brown eyes patient.

"Look at yourself," David scolded himself. "This young thing has got a back full of blistered burns, has probably seen her family burn up in front of her, and has an empty stomach, too, and here you are feeling sorry for yourself." He picked up the spatula from the drawer and looked at his wife's picture over the stove.

He felt Rosie's hand on his arm as he moved away. She was being clingy. His instinct was to push the girl away, but he didn't. "With all this kid has been through," he thought, "How about you don't shrug her off like a stranger?" But another part of him gritted his teeth: he hated to cook with people watching.

After a moment, he set up his kitchen stool to the left of the stove. Then he picked up the unresisting girl and put her on it. This allowed him to get her disconcerting hand off his arm, but still project to her that she was included in the cooking.

"There you go," he said to her. "You can watch me cook." He took a moment to smile at her. She smiled back, but said nothing as he laid out the cooking. He washed, preheated, chopped, and stir fried, yet she didn't say a word. David felt awkward with her so quiet, but recognized that she might feel as awkward talking as he did with the silence. She'd only be here a couple of days anyway. After a while, the silence became comfortable, and he began whistling as he cooked. It was "Wild Irish Rose," he noticed.

A moment later, while tossing the woody asparagus bits into the garbage, he found Faith was watching him, too, from the kitchen door.

"Get on, would you? So many spectators I feel like a circus act. This is a private show for our survivor here."

"Haven't heard you whistle for a while, Pop," she needled him.

"You haven't seen me cook for a while, either. So would you get on before I get uncomfortable?"

Faith ducked back out of the doorway. "Is this a macho thing, Pop? If no one sees you cooking, then you're still a man's man?" she jibed at him from behind the wall. He could tell from her voice she was laughing at him.

David cleared his throat. "I have an answer for you, you ungrateful child, but I won't say it with tender ears present. So why don't you... go soak your head?"

"I *was* thinking of a shower before supper. Do I have time?"

"Go on already. I'll make time if that's what it takes to get rid of you for twenty minutes."

"Alright." He heard her tramp up the stairs to her room, and in a few minutes heard water in the shower pipes. He glanced at Rosie, who was watching the cooking with obvious hunger. With this, he fished out a sautéed potato wedge with spices on it, let it cool, and offered it to her. She ate it greedily, never taking her eyes off him.

After a few more moments he had tipped out the kielbasa, potatoes, and asparagus onto plates and prepared to bring them to the table. Upstairs he heard the squeak of the plumbing as Faith turned off her shower. His timing was perfect. Dinner would hit the table a moment before his daughter came down. His earlier guilt was gone, and with another glance at Connie's picture, he saw no reproach in her eyes.

He felt a light touch on his arm. Rosie had put a hand on him, brown eyes still patient.

"*SHEE estAS tSHAY dee-on,*" she said. Whatever it meant, she meant for him to understand, because she took a firmer hold of his arm and looked him in the eyes. Her expression was serious and sincere. She wouldn't let him pull away.

He pinched her nose. "I don't know what you're saying, honey. But I feel a whole lot better having cooked for you." With that, he put the carton of milk in her hands, picked up the plates of food, and marched to the dining room. He heard Rosie's footsteps follow him.

He felt good. Better than he had in a long while.

Chapter 2

A New Tongue

David awoke to his daughter's voice outside his door the next morning. "Pop? Pop? Time to get up."

"Go away," he said. "I'm retired, damn you." He picked up his head enough to look at his clock. It was late: seven, he noted with mixture of shame at his decadence and sheer glee. He could sleep in for another hour. It was a prerogative of retirement.

His daughter, however, acted unaware of that retirement. "Pop, I need you on your feet this morning. I'm going to the senior staff meeting to do a brief about the fire and I need you to watch Rosie so I can prepare."

The old man groaned. He hadn't realized he'd become a babysitter as well as a cook. "Can't you take her with you?"

"C'mon, Pop, I can't have her in tow. As it is I think they want me to have her because they think I miss having my own babies. I don't want to drag her around in public like a teddy bear and confirm their suspicions. Besides, I need some uninterrupted time to get this done."

"Won't Marcus ask you where she is if you don't have her?" he rolled over to look at his daughter in his bedroom doorway. Marcus Bauer, one of his rivals and old friends, was now the fire chief.

"I'll tell him she's with you. And what an excellent cook you've been, and how good you look in an apron," his daughter threatened.

David stared at the ceiling while his daughter awaited his reply. Here was his daughter, a successful fire inspector, about to brief her chief. It made him so proud to think of it. And all she was asking was for him to take this child who was neither hers, nor her fault, off her hands so she could succeed.

"I'm proud of you, Faith, and the way you're succeeding. I'll sit with Rosie, give me a minute."

"A minute is all you get, because I want to go down and proofread my slides and reports beforehand, so I need to get out of here." With that, he heard her footsteps recede downstairs.

His eyes scanned his ceiling. Yet another demand from his offspring. No good deed went unpunished. He wondered if the bedroom's painted tin ceiling was appreciating the magnitude of his suffering, and then laughed at himself.

"For today, I have another job," he decided. He got up, threw a robe over his pajamas, and went downstairs.

Once downstairs, at the dining table, he found Faith plying Rosie with some shredded wheat. The girl ate it without enthusiasm. She wore only one of his own fire department T-shirts. David flinched to notice that she was sitting with the shirt hiked up, with one bandaged butt cheek raised off the breakfast bench, and her back held stiffly away from bench back.

"Kid doesn't have any pajamas?" He cocked an eyebrow at his daughter.

Faith shrugged. "She has one set of pajamas and one set of day clothes, both from the Goodwill bin down at the station. One of her burns had soaked through the bandages and stained the pajama shirt. So I threw them in the wash last night, put them in the drier when I came down this morning. They'll be done in about twenty minutes."

"I can't have a woman not kin to me walking bare-assed about my house. It's not proper."

"I've seen you cut the clothes off perfect strangers in the middle of the street," she countered.

"Those were emergencies, done for first aid," he said. "This one's emergency is four or five days gone."

His daughter pursed her lips, making the expression which had preceded rejections of his guidance since she was three. It was plain she found his worry silly, as her Scandinavian mother had. Constance would have walked through the town square nude on a lark, he recalled. But instead of some zinger of a reply as he expected, his daughter said something that gave him some relief. "I'll dress her before I go."

"Thank you," he said. He watched Rosie's eyes follow him as he sat down. "Shredded wheat for breakfast. Mmm," he said to her. The child prodded the biscuits with her spoon listlessly.

"They fed her Froot Loops down at the station. I think she's used to the sweet stuff," Faith said as she bustled away.

"This cereal is good for you," the man intoned to the girl as he poured a bowl full from the box. The child went back to eating hers. She'd spilled several biscuits of it on the table. "Guess she doesn't like it," he thought.

David again found the stranger's silence awkward, but after watching her unhurried way and careful glances at everything around her, he fell back into the notion that the silence was companionable. He resisted the temptation to turn on the radio at the table side charging stand and eat listening to firemen's chatter as he had for thirty years. It would be impolite.

In this silence, he saw why Rosie was spilling her shredded wheat biscuits. She was holding her spoon in her fist, like a toddler, rather than across the top of her hand like an American child her age. Without a word, he reached out and took ahold of her hand. She said nothing, but did not resist him as he changed the position of the spoon in her hand, and then raised his own hand to show how he was holding it. She began to clumsily eat the same way, and smiled at him after her first successful bite.

"What sort of a child can't use a spoon? Don't they have spoons in Italy?" he wondered. Then, he remembered that the night before, as they'd sat in front of Nickelodeon eating, she had picked up every piece of food from her plate with her fingers and eaten it. David had assumed it was because she was eating from a plate in her lap, not because she was unfamiliar with the fork and knife on the coffee table. He'd have to watch tonight and see how she ate, if she was still with them for supper.

"Bad news, Pop," warned his daughter warned breathlessly as she hurried back into the dining room.

"What now?" he asked.

"Her clothes are going to be done soon, but I remembered she needs her bandages changed and a shower before I dress her. And I am not going to have time."

It was his own turn to look unhappily at his shredded wheat. This was too much. "Faith, I-" he began, and she cut him off.

"Dad, you checked the water in my shower until I was eight years old. This kid is ten, maybe twelve, has burns on her backside and buttocks she cannot reach or clean. She's somewhere between too young to care about nudity and a first aid case. Can you handle it?"

He would be stubborn about this. There were some lines which shouldn't

16

be crossed. But rather than argue, he decided to invoke outside authority. "What would the social worker say if she found out you'd left this child with an old man and no pants on?"

His daughter paused, but was not yet beaten. "If I told her I left Rosie with a sixty-five year old trained EMT, firefighter, and father to change her bandages and watch her for the day, I'd be telling her the truth. And she'd think it was a better deal than the fire station." With this, Faith snatched up her clipboard. "Going to rise to the challenge, Pop?"

David felt sullen, but a glance at the girl's careful new way of using her spoon changed sullen to workmanlike.

"I'll do it," said he said. "And I appreciate her position. But neither you nor I are social workers or orphanages. I don't have anything against this kid, but how long is she our problem?"

Faith shook her head, tightened her uniform belt, and took her service radio from the charger by the breakfast table.

"Remember, Dad, someone was trying to kill her."

"So you tell me," he said. "But you haven't told me why you think so."

"Trust me on this, Dad. Everything you taught me, and my hunches, tell me this was no accident. The facts are too damn weird."

David didn't know what to say to this. He suspected that soon his daughter would be a better fire inspector than he ever had been. He'd only held the job for seven of his thirty years in the department and she already had five in the job. "Arson doesn't mean murder. The landowner might have wanted to recover insurance money. Jersey lightning."

Faith glared at him. "I'm not dumb, Dad, I checked. The carriage house was not insured for anywhere near what it was worth. Finneas Corning's policy on it hadn't been updated in a decade. It was mostly stone: it shouldn't have burned at all."

"Maybe it was disposal then. Someone didn't like how it looked."

"Again, financial suicide, Pop. The owner had two offers to turn the place into a bed and breakfast. Eighteenth century? Lots of stone? Would have been perfect."

David saw Rosie had stopped eating and was looking at them with a frightened expression.

"Aw, nuts, now I'm upsetting her," the man complained, checking his angry tone. "And I upset you, too. You're right, I wasn't there. I shouldn't argue with you. I'm frustrated."

She was unfazed. "It's alright, Dad, you're playing devil's advocate, making me prove my argument. And unless animal control put a tranquilizer dart in the Chief's ass this morning, the Chief will be as skeptical as you are and have all the same arguments. So in the big picture, you're a warm-up." She patted his shoulder, powered on her radio and pressed transmit: when it squawked, she dropped it back in its carrier and turned to go. "This is Ithaca. Crime could hurt our property values. You think the Chief wants to go to the common council with this?"

David snorted. "This is Ithaca. People don't murder each other, they try to empathize and buy each other lattes, and if they hate someone they buy a fancy imported car to make them jealous."

His daughter laughed. "If only, Pop." She waved to the girl. "Have a good day, Rosie! Take care of my grumpy old dad!"

The child was in the middle of a chewing a spoonful of shredded wheat, but raised her hand anyway in an imitation of the woman's wave. Then Faith put on her uniform cap and walked out. The screen door hissed and banged behind

17

her, accenting the silence which followed.

David and Rosie finished their shredded wheat together wordlessly. When his bowl was done, he poured a cup of coffee from coffee maker and raised his cup.

"Here's looking at you, kid," he said, in his best Humphrey Bogart voice, and winked at her.

The girl gave him a quizzical look while she continued to munch.

"Not a Bogart fan," he decided. What would he do with this kid all day?

David took Rosie upstairs to the master bathroom where there was more room. There, he let her take a shower in lukewarm water until the scabs and crusts on her burns softened, and then guided her out, dripping wet and naked. Seeing the betadyne and bandages, she bent over and offered her back to him, probably used to the drill from the firehouse. He peeled off the old gauze as carefully as he could, collecting the bandages to one side for later examination.

Despite his best efforts, some of her burns bled, and as he led her back to the shower to finish washing her hair, she began to cry in earnest, a stiff-lipped mewling which was troubling to hear. The firefighter in him was inclined to be sympathetic. He'd had his share of bad burns, and hers were the most painful kind: widespread, shallow second-degree burns with lots of broken skin and blistering. They covered a third of her back and a good swath of her right buttock and thigh.

She bounced up and down on her toes, clutched the shower curtain and soap dish handle, and mewled louder as he rinsed the soap from her hair. He'd had her lean forward and rinsed her hair from back to front, but he suspected he'd still gotten soap in her wounds from her reaction. He began to steel his emotions, as he often had to with burn victims, and look at her as a food inspector would meat on a hook: stare at the flesh, and see what he saw.

A look at the old bandages and her back showed little discoloration from infection. She was on antibiotics, but this sterility was nonetheless a blessing: burns were prone to infection and he'd seen them infect even with antibiotics.

Scattered throughout the burn were flecks of melted plastic. He guessed Rosie had been wearing some kind of polyester when she was caught in the fire. Tentatively, he poked at the plastic blobs with tweezers he'd dipped in alcohol, but she flinched at the lightest touch of them, so he decided to leave them. It wasn't as if they would feed bacteria, and they would come off her on their own as her skin sloughed from the burns or naturally shed.

He then scrubbed his hands in the sink for the second time, put on latex gloves, and peeled open a sterile burn kit from the box the hospital had sent with her. "It's a tradeoff, Champ," he told her. "I've done this for worse burns, but I'm old and clumsy now and you'll have to bear with me." With the finger of one glove, he smeared the gauze pads with an antibiotic ointment. "Putting the ointment on it will make them less absorbent, but keep them from sticking so much. This will be easier tomorrow."

She began to sob as he poured betadyne over the burns, and then applied the ointment-smeared bandages. But she held still for him, clenching the sink edge, and he had to turn her around to loop the first aid tape around her thigh to hold the lowest bandage in place.

He couldn't help but notice when he did so something he had never seen before: Rosie had no visible navel. Her stomach was a flat expanse from her ribs to her hips.

"Odd," he wondered, "how is that possible? Doesn't everyone have a

18

navel?"

When he stood up again, she fell against him and began crying.

"Wait, no, let's put something on you, sweetie." But it was no use: she had a firm grip on the back of his shirt and would not be pried away. He remembered Connie admonishing him once when then six-year old Faith had skinned her knee: "Sometimes the only medicine that does any good is a hug."

So he knelt again, on the bathroom floor, and hugged Rosie, careful of how his arms rested on her back. Her sobs quieted to deep gasps, then quieter ones, and then finally she stepped back and gave him a thin smile.

As she did so, David felt a visceral anger. "Whoever did this to you, better hope I never meet him," he said as he handed her one of his clean t-shirts. "Because I'd love to make him understand pain."

With her still sniffling, and blinking on his own tears, he led her out of the bathroom.

When Hildegard returned to her desk the next morning, only Akiko Nakamura, her Japanese assistant, was already in the office. She stood as the professor entered and greeted her.

"Good Morning, Dr. Teschke." Akiko's English was perfect. The younger woman bowed, and the professor bowed in return. They exchanged these when no one was looking: it pleased Akiko, and Hildegard knew for her part that practicing body language kept it natural. She would bow with confidence on her next trip to Japan.

"Good morning! When Selene and Mr. Douglas come in, please bring them both into my office. I have a project I need the three of you to start on right away."

"Yes, Ma'am."

Hildegard unlocked her own office, went in, and sat down. The original note, complete with the girl's test scribble, was still on her desk, front and center, where she'd left it. As she sat down she opened the file drawer in her desk, pulled out a blank hanging folder and file tab, and created a new folder titled "Rosie." She dropped the folder back into the drawer, and in it dropped Ms. Haversham's card for future reference. If her assistants were as good as she suspected, with a few days' work, she might be giving the woman a call back.

The clock ticked. She logged into her computer, opened the campus email program, and started a letter to Dr. Kramer.

> "Frank!
>
> "I saw yesterday the remarkable child the fire department sent over. Not sure I can help them, however. I have some hunches, will have Akiko and the others follow up on them.
>
> "I would enjoy lunch to discuss this riddle later in the week to be sure we haven't overlooked anything. How is Thursday for coffee with Mr. White? I'm inviting you at 1300. I'll bring your usual.
>
> "Yours,
> "Hildegard."

Frank was one of her only confidants, and they met about once a week to discuss linguistics, university politics, and whatever else. Frank was happily married, with grown children, and she found his down-to-earth approaches and native instinct for American culture to be useful. She suspected she brought her intuition and merciless logic to the trade. But whatever the case, she inferred that Frank also valued their meetings. He had yet to turn her down without rescheduling and would suggest a meeting if she skipped a week.

Shortly after she pressed "send" Akiko's crisp rap sounded on her door. Good. Her teaching assistants were ready. She checked the clock. It was eight exactly. Mr. Douglas was punctual for a change.

"Come in," she said. Her assistants filed in.

Akiko was her senior assistant and the apple of her eye. She was precise, well groomed, and more professional than most of Hildegard's professors. The department members were looking forward to her thesis concerning an underlying grammar of indigenous Asian tongues, and she knew that the young woman's thesis defense would be self-assured and clear. Hildegard trusted the younger woman not only to deal with most student issues, but also to teach her own classes on the rare occasions she could not be there.

She also sympathized with Akiko. Like her, the woman was in the United States for its freedoms and unlikely to return to her homeland, where her abilities would be overshadowed by the fact that she was an unmarried woman. The similarity of their situations had not gone unnoticed by others: she had once heard an assistant professor refer to the two of them as "the Axis of Bitch." That professor had not made tenure.

Selene was the middle assistant, and older than Akiko by ten years. She usually, as today, dressed in loafers, jeans, and a clean unmarked t-shirt in a primary color. She had already had a job as a certified speech therapist for the California public school system.

Hildegard thought Selene scatterbrained, impulsive, and soft-hearted. She was the kind of teaching assistant who, left unchecked, would give every complaining momma's boy an "A" after spending an entire afternoon in one–to–one instruction. Every person, to Selene, was a special case, with special needs. She supposed this patience stemmed from the woman's previous work with the developmentally disabled, but she found the attitude inappropriate here. Cornell, after all, was supposed to be producing the crème-de-la-crème, not hand-held linguistic ninnies. And the professor would be damned if she would let Selene's attitude flatten the department's grading curve, which she took pains to keep a bit closer to statistically normal than the Dean of Arts and Sciences liked.

Shawn Douglas was the last in the door. It was his first year in the PhD program. His family was from the Caribbean, but his skin was as black as if he had stepped out of a central African tribal camp. Crowned with a tangle of unwashed dreadlocks and followed everywhere by a powerful herbal smell (today it was cinnamon, she smelled), the young man's casualness, slow imprecise speech, and personal hygiene grated on her.

As an undergraduate, he had been an admired music theory student at Columbia. And Shawn's proposed thesis, which was to study commonalities between music and language, had been promising, but she had found that in person he was not. Hildegard doubted he would finish a PhD program, and hoped in the next two years to get a more useful assistant whom she could put in charge. She wouldn't use Shawn as a senior assistant to manage student affairs as things stood. His demeanor was much too informal.

She motioned to the three chairs across from her desk, and they all sat. Her temptation was to explain things to Akiko and let her run this show, but her favorite assistant would be leaving in the next year or two and she had to cut her dependency on the young woman. So she addressed all three.

"Good morning. Yesterday evening the authorities came to visit our department with a mystery they needed my help on." With this, her eyes flicked to

Shawn, whom she suspected used marijuana. The boy showed no concern at the news the "authorities" had been in the office. So either the department office was marijuana-free, or her junior assistant was cool under pressure. She continued.

"With them they brought a young girl orphaned in a fire who speaks no English. The authorities would like to identify the child's next-of-kin, but since they are unable to communicate with her, they cannot. They had already been to the Department of Modern Languages which, despite a great deal of effort, could not identify the girl's native tongue, except to say it was probably a romance language."

Akiko wore her expressionless face. Selene sat forward, intrigued. "Already she's wondering if her language is a pathological one induced by fire or disability," she concluded. In any case, working with a child would brighten Selene's day. Hildegard suspected Selene found the linguistics department stuffy and theoretical and longed for applied problems.

"I did what investigation I could, and stumbled on an interesting fact. Presented with a stack of comic books," she motioned to the stack of Asterix comics still on her desk, "she selected and read the copy in Japanese."

Selene nodded approval at her handling of a child issue with comic books. Akiko's eyes widened. An American youth who read Japanese was a rare thing indeed, and the young woman knew it.

"Since I suspected Dr. Kramer and the modern languages people had already tried Japanese, I assumed that for some reason of trauma or disability the child was unable to understand Japanese spoken aloud. So, instead, I wrote the three crucial questions down in Japanese and gave them to her to read."

Akiko and Selene both nodded again. Shawn stared at her. She guessed his was a bit above his level at this point.

Hildegard expanded the mystery for them. "To my surprise and confusion, the girl did write replies to my questions, but not in Japanese. She wrote it in the same mysterious romance language which she speaks. If her written statements are replies to my questions, than we have on our hands an unusual child: one found at large in the United States who speaks no English but reads or writes two other languages."

She then picked up three photocopies of the notebook sheet. "I have my hunches as to the origin of this child but I won't taint your thinking with them. I will present you with the bare facts and let you make your own conclusions. I have here a copy for each of you of my written exchange with the subject. The three of you drop whatever else you are doing this morning. I want you to spend the morning analyzing this document in collaboration. Come to me before lunch. Summarize your findings for me then and make recommendations as to how to proceed in clarifying the girl's origin. Any questions?"

Akiko stood, and after a startled moment, Selene did the same. All three assistant each took their copy of the page, and as the closest to the door, Shawn reached for the doorknob.

"Stop," said Hildegard. "I'm not finished." The boy let go of the doorknob, and the three turned back to face her. She lowered her voice, and also injected a tone of non-academic gravity.

"Based on facts found at the scene by the fire inspectors, the child is believed to have been the target of arson. If true, her would-be killer is still at large. This is why I am using you for this project, and not my fellow professors. If word of this girl leaves my department and reaches the press, I will discipline all of you. This is a liberty I do not have with my tenured peers. Do you understand that I have chosen you not just for your ability, but also for your vulnerability?"

Akiko remained expressionless. Selene nodded her understanding. Shawn sat mute.

"I want the three of you back in my office by twenty minutes to noon. We will discuss where we will go from there. Ms. Nakamura, you are in charge." Her assistants filed out.

Once the door closed, she opened her calendar, which she realized she hadn't even checked since the day before. Her heart leaped. "My goodness, with all the excitement, did I miss an appointment?" Luckily, she had not.

"You are not yourself," she commented out loud. Not checking her calendar until 8:15 am was lax indeed.

Faith struggled to align pictures with text in her PowerPoint presentation on the carriage house fire. The laptop computer she used, one of the oldest in the department, got cranky when her files contained too many pictures. And there was enough unusual or downright weird about the carriage house fire that she had plenty of pictures to overcome any doubters.

"As if this wasn't challenging enough, I have to deal with this computer," she sighed, reaching for her enormous "International Association of Firefighters" travel mug. She'd flavored her coffee with vanilla, which she found helped her relax, but as her computer lagged and left her sitting with idle minute after minute, the pressures of the day seeped in.

One of the pressures she faced was that Marcus, the chief, and Pierce, the deputy chief, had been fire inspectors in the past. Back in their day, building and wildfires had been much more common than today, with modern alarms and appliances, so they had each investigated many more fires than she ever would. She would not be able to tap dance past any missed details. And another was that most of her day-to-day work was fire prevention and alarm calls, which most line firefighters tended to regard as busy work or "light duty," and hence Faith as a "paper pusher."

She had time in the line firehouses, and she was also a certified EMT and a hazardous materials responder. She had gotten her associate's degree in fire science from SUNY Cobleskill, and finished her fire science bachelor's online from Colorado Technical University. On paper, she was every bit the firefighter her father was, but with every degree or certification she got, line firefighters resented her more.

She supposed from their perspective it made sense. The former chief's daughter, who had grown up playing hide-and-seek in the firehouses with the men and had all her birthday parties at fire station barbeques, had gone on to get fancy degrees. And now she was getting all the easy work up and full-time pay at the headquarters. She supposed it seemed like nepotism to them.

In any case, this presentation was a chance to prove her stuff to both her bosses and her peers. It had to impress with its professionalism, and it had to make the mysteries surrounding the fire look like actual mysteries, not gaps in her knowledge. And it had to be ready by noon.

Her computer abruptly resumed normal operation. To be sure she didn't lose the pictures she had inserted at great cost of minutes and patience, she saved, and then set about to typing the text bullets which would guide her briefing of each picture. She had hand-written the text out in bed the night before when she couldn't sleep, so she guessed she needed two more hours to assemble the briefing and she had three and a half hours to go.

"You'll be fine," she thought. "Focus."

She was busy putting circles and arrows on a picture showing fire-cracked stones from the carriage house when she heard her the office door open behind her. A glance showed her it was her office mate, Karl. Karl was an older firefighter and was the other fire-prevention officer. He had been given the job as fire-prevention officer to prevent him being discharged for disability for his bad back.

"Morning, Karl!" she said, hoping he wouldn't take too much of her time with his morning complaints about his back. Even with his medication, it bothered him, and she knew that, as each year passed, Karl toed the line between chronic pain and drug addiction more closely. When he was trying to lay off the drugs, he was grouchy and apt to fill a morning complaining.

"Morning," Karl said cheerfully. "Already at work on the briefing?"

Faith felt relief. It was one of Karl's medication mornings.

"Yep."

"Been up all night?" he asked from behind her as he hung up his coat. She grinned. Karl had known her for her whole life, and it showed now.

"Not *all* night," she answered. "But if I'd brought this computer home I would have been. But then, if I had, I might be done already, and I could sleep now." She plucked at one of her bangs as she moved a circle around on the picture.

Karl walked around to his desk, which was pushed up facing hers in the unpartitioned office. "No, you wouldn't be sleeping. You'd be reviewing it to be sure it was perfect."

Faith frowned, but didn't want to spend time bantering with Karl at the moment. "I guess," she demurred, moving on to her next picture. "Back feeling okay?"

"Yup," said Karl. "It's a happy hydrocodone morning. How's Janey Doe?"

"Good news," she answered. "Cornell figured out her name. Her real name is Rosetta."

"Great!" said Karl. "One fewer member of the Doe family, and she even left the clan alive."

"Nope, still a Doe. They couldn't work out her last name."

Karl blinked, but said nothing about that odd shortcoming. "So, it's Rosetta Doe. Any idea where she's from?"

"Maybe northern Sweden? Maybe Switzerland? Maybe Mars? Who knows?" She shrugged. She hoped he wouldn't badger her all morning.

Karl chuckled. "Only in Ithaca...or New York City." Karl's phrase was a common joke in the department. The university brought in strange folk from all over the globe, and many of them trickled down to become the problem of the city government. These visitors gave Ithaca a range of social problems and bizarre culture clashes not shared by any other fifty-thousand strong upstate New York town.

"Yup, only in Ithaca." Faith replied, so as not to prolong the conversation. Karl switched on his computer, checked the radio charger, rotated the batteries between handsets, and turned up the scanner volume from the subdued low she had set it at. The radio squawks and terse exchanges between the dispatcher and the units immediately began grating on her concentration. She tried to focus and soldier on, but soon relented.

"Mind if I put my earplugs in?"

Karl was hurt. "I'll stop blathering if I'm distracting you."

"It's not that, Karl...It's everything. The radio, you, the ventilation, my own breathing. You know how I get with pressure."

"Got it," Karl said. "I'll give you a poke if someone calls for you on the radio."

"Thanks," she said, already beginning to roll her foam earplugs between her fingers.

A moment later she was working in blissful silence with her ears stuffed with foam. Years before, when she had been working on her first high-school report, her mother had showed her the trick of earplugs. Faith had kept a pair ever since, since at times like this, they paid off in spades.

The earplugs worked like fast-forward. Pictures and graphics started flying by and she knew by instinct where to cut, paste, and explain. Karl bustled about the office, answered the phone, and came and left without disturbing her.

As Faith worked against the clock, she found ways to improve the briefing: she added new text, chose different photos, and found supporting references. She was sure to balance her changes against the time remaining, but as the hour of her deadline approached, she realized she had worked all the slack out of her time line. She now had to work flat-out to finish the brief in time to present it.

She took a long swig of her coffee, draining the cup. Chagrined, she saw she'd drunk a liter in two hours. "I'll regret this later." But she rose to pour some more.

Hildegard was partway through correcting her graduate level weekly papers. One of the papers was Shawn's, since the class was mandatory for all first-year PhD students. His work was short and clearly written. He argued that Chomsky's deep grammar, if it existed at all, was related to fundamental rules of music more than any existing conventional rules of grammar. It was an interesting assertion, but his paper lacked proof, or even more than an illustrative example and some suppositions. At the least, he could discuss an experimental test of his theory. Linguistics was, after all, an experimental science.

There was a knock at her door. "Come in," she said, not looking up. She assumed it was one of her fellow professors, since her assistants would all be busy and might not be in the outer room to prevent the professor from coming straight to the door.

Instead, it was Shawn and his wave of cinnamon perfume. She wrinkled her nose.

"Yes, Mr. Douglas?"

"Ma'am, I believe I know what language the girl speaks."

"Wonderful, Mr. Douglas," she bristled, turning back to his paper. His timing was poor, aggravating her while she graded his paper. "Now, why are you in my office?"

This was not the response he had expected. His mouth was open to speak, but whatever he had been going to say had fled from him. He puzzled over her question.

"I thought it was important, Ma'am."

"It is important. I have no doubt," she said. "But even had you solved the whole mystery and had the cell phone number of the child's parents in your hand, I would still ask you, why are you in my office?"

Shawn turned his eyes to the floor. Hildegard decided he was speechless and if the conversation was to proceed apace, she needed to take the initiative.

"Mr. Douglas, I asked the three of you to work together for a reason, and I put Akiko in charge for a reason."

"Yes, Ma'am."

"When working on novel problems, collaboration often produces the best results. Though you may feel you have the whole answer, you may not. Your peers were selected for their ability and perspectives. Respect them, and put your idea to them. At the least they will take nothing away from your discovery, and at the most, they will point out a flaw and prevent you from making a fool of yourself. As I suspect you will, *if* I let you continue. And I am, by instinct, unkind to fools."

Shawn's eyes widened. "Yes, Ma'am."

"Next, I have many things to do this morning. Akiko is a good organizer and communicator, and I can count on her to explain everything you discuss with all my obvious questions already answered in twenty minutes. She will not waste my time, I am sure. Are you as prepared as she could make you? Or are you unprepared?"

Her assistant still kept his eyes on the floor, growing a bit stiff. "No, Ma'am, I'm not that ready."

Hildegard turned her eyes back to the boy's paper and motioned to her door. "Go forth and collaborate. And send in Akiko."

Shawn left, crestfallen. However, he shut the door with only appropriate firmness. Though she could not tell on a man of his skin tone, she was sure his ears were burning.

A moment later came Akiko's distinctive knock.

"Come in!" She found her voice had more color in it than she wanted. Her feelings about the younger woman changed her tone. She couldn't fight her feelings, so she succumbed to them and decided to speak to Ms. Nakamura woman to woman.

Her assistant bowed, and sat in the chair she indicated.

"Shawn was in here, on his own."

"Yes, Dr. Teschke," the woman nodded. "The fault was mine. We had agreed to break, and I think he feels I did not value his discovery enough and decided to bring it to you while I was away."

"So you do believe he has discovered what language the girl wrote in?"

"Yes, Doctor, he has."

Hildegard took note: if Akiko thought so, the boy had. So he had been correct. Still, it didn't change what she had to say. "Let me advise you after years of observation of American men."

"Yes, Ma'am."

"By doing this I do not mean to imply you are a traditional and deferential Japanese woman. If you were, we both know you'd be forgetting your undergraduate degree and squeezing out some businessman's babies in a Tokyo high-rise. What I'm saying I've also had to say to many 'liberated' American women."

For a moment, her assistant smiled at her bluntness before recovering her neutral expression. She took this slip as a sign she had correctly guessed the alternative fate her student had avoided as a female university graduate in Japan.

"I put you in charge of the collaboration and the findings. I expect you to present them, giving credit where credit is due. Mr. Douglas running in here with his discovery is unacceptable."

Akiko's expression chilled. The professor was pleased she had spotted this change. When the young woman had arrived she had seemed inscrutable. Inscrutability was an art Japanese practiced.

"If you let them, American men will steal your thunder every chance they get. Everything you discover for yourself, discern from evidence, or produce by coordinating a group's efforts they will steal. One of them will be swift to jump up and take all the credit and be in charge as soon as they have grasped your idea. For most of them, it isn't even deliberate. They are socialized to 'catch the football and run with it.'"

Her assistant's expression was frosty now.

"You are the most talented young linguist on this campus. You may be a better linguist than I, I suspect you are. But all your talent as a linguist will get you is some publications and maybe tenure. If you want to be in charge, you must take charge and produce coherent plans and teachable summaries that guide other experts. And not permit others to loot your ideas or the products of your collaboration."

"Yes, Doctor."

"I know your summary this afternoon will be good, and will be child's play for you: that's not the issue. The other aspect of taking charge is setting rules. When I put you in charge, I expect you to set rules and boundaries that keep you in charge. And I expect you will be the one reporting to me. A male department head, say, Dr. Kramer, would already be talking to Mr. Douglas and ignoring you, had you let this happen in his office. And whatever you and Selene had to add to the picture would be heard only as an afterthought. If at all."

Akiko nodded. "I understand, Doctor."

"That is all." she said. With a calm nod, her assistant left and closed the office door behind her. Other than a brief impression of the younger woman's raised voice from the office a few moments later, Hildegard worked undisturbed until twenty minutes to noon.

At twenty minutes to noon, Hildegard's assistants filed in. Akiko held some index cards in her left hand, but the other two carried their notebooks and pens. As a draft of cinnamon air from Shawn settled over the room, she stopped typing and looked up at them.

"Go ahead," she prompted. Ms. Nakamura cleared her throat and began.

"Our bottom line up front, Doctor, is that we have identified the language the girl wrote in, but still have no good places to start in identifying her family or country of origin. Shawn will begin by talking about the language, Selene will continue with some suggested hypotheses, and I will outline a plan for a second interview with the subject, if it is possible."

Akiko had a good deal of practice presenting to her, and this preamble was in keeping with her previous work. Only one question nagged the professor: "How can we have identified the language but not be any closer to guessing her nation of origin?" But rather than interrupt, she shifted her eyes to Shawn. He stood up to speak, but began to stammer.

"Sit, Mr. Douglas. Akiko is the main presenter. You should remain sitting unless the situation requires you to move to a speaker's podium or a microphone," she admonished. The criticism rattled him. He sat down again.

"Odd how a person who dresses and grooms to stand out from the crowd is so afraid of the judgment of a small group," wondered Hildegard. Usually she found iconoclasts to be confident speakers, if not good ones.

"Um, Ma'am, the kid wrote her replies in Esperanto," Shawn stammered at first, but picked up speed. She waited for him to start sounding confident before she interrupted. "In response to your question about her name, she replied tha-"

"Wait, Mr. Douglas," she interrupted.

"Yes, Ma'am." Shawn stopped, at first looking uncomfortable, but then relaxed as the pause grew in length. She closed her eyes, put her fingertips to her temples, and drilled back through the years of language history stored between them.

"When you say *Esperanto*, you are talking about the artificial language invented by the optometrist Dr. Zamenhof, in Poland, in the late eighteenth century?"

"Yes, Ma'am."

After a moment, she snapped her eyes open, donned her reading glasses, and held up her copy of the written exchange between her and Rosetta to the optimal reading distance. Indeed, the girl's writing had some of the hallmarks of Esperanto, which had been based in large part on Latin, explaining why both she and Dr. Kramer's people believed they had been dealing with a "romance language."

Hildegard regarded artificial languages as fool's ventures. The fact few of them ever succeeded was validation, to her, of Chomsky's much maligned theory of a "deep grammar," which suggested there might be rules embedded in human neurology that were common to all natural languages. Artificial languages always had simplified rules of grammar to make them easy to learn, but this same simplicity also made them feel "unnatural" to every user as being incompatible with the rules of the "deep grammar."

But her theoretical reservations about Esperanto were the most abstract reason why Rosetta's writing in Esperanto was highly unusual. There were much more practical reasons to be skeptical. She voiced them, keeping her eyes still focused on the page so as to give Shawn a chance to think without reacting to eye contact. "Mr. Douglas, aside from the detail that no child is raised speaking Esperanto as their native tongue, there is also the problem of the alphabet. Esperanto, if I remember correctly, is written in the Czech alphabet, which uses all Roman characters, some of them with circumflexions. Her writing contains some non-Roman characters, and shows no characters whatever with circumflexions." She lowered the paper and gave Shawn her best critical look over the top of her glasses.

Surprising her, he held up to her challenges and looks with minimal stammering. "M-M-Ma'am, I did not say Esperanto was the girl's mother language, I said that was the language she used to write her replies to you. And as for the alphabet, I have an answer. Do you want to hear it?"

"I do want to hear it, Mr. Douglas, before you translate her writing. Hearing you explain it first will lend your translations credibility they might not have if you translated first and explained later."

At this, she saw Selene scribble a note. Somebody was paying attention and learning presentation skills. At this, she looked back to Mr. Douglas.

The boy continued. "The non-Roman characters she uses are all characters from the International Phonetic Alphabet." She recalled noticing this the night before, but had assumed the characters were analogous to the IPA, not a deliberate use of the IPA itself.

The International Phonetic Alphabet, or IPA, was an artificial alphabet used by linguists and speech therapists for precision in transcribing spoken words. Most people encountered it only rarely as the "funny alphabet in the dictionary" used as a pronunciation guide. But she used it more often than daily in describing and analyzing language. Its chief advantage over standard alphabets was that every letter in it had a distinct sound. Whereas in English, the character "i" might be pronounced as "eye", "eee", or "ih" depending on the word, in the IPA "i" represented the sound "eee" and only that sound. The other English sounds for "i" had separate characters in the IPA.

Using the IPA was a basic task of any descriptive linguistic work, and Hildegard was pleased to find Shawn was so familiar with it. She made a note to compliment Dr. Marshall, the associate professor teaching introductory linguistics, since it was unlikely the boy brought his knowledge of IPA forward from his studies of music at Columbia.

Nonetheless, the use of IPA in normal communication was unheard of. And it was not an alphabet used or even seen by children, except those rare children who still went to the trouble to look up unfamiliar words in dictionaries.

"Is there any pattern to the substitutions she makes of the IPA for Roman characters?" she tested to see how far he had taken his reasoning. She was beginning to reconsider her opinion of his talents.

Shawn rose to the question. "Yes, Ma'am. I believe she uses an IPA character whenever Esperanto's standard pronunciation of a letter varies from the IPA's pronunciation of the same letter. For example, since the IPA does not use circumflexion, by default any Roman letter with a circumflexion would need to be substituted with an IPA character. And if you look at her writing, she does exactly this, leaving no circumflexed letters at all, as you already pointed out. In fact, it would be as fair to say she was writing *all* her Esperanto in the IPA as it would be to say she was substituting IPA characters occasionally."

"So, Mr. Douglas, you are asserting that this ten to twelve year-old girl is writing Esperanto, an artificial language, in the IPA, an artificial alphabet?"

"Yes, Ma'am." Shawn sounded more confident as his argument became more absurd. "I believe the translation proves it."

"It had better. Because, to an audience of linguists, a child who writes as you describe is all but impossible. And your translation is about to make you a hero for a day, or a laughingstock." She put her fingertips together under her chin and leaned forward. "Please, translate for me."

"Ma'am, I can't read Japanese, but Akiko tells me that in your first line of Japanese, you introduce yourself and ask the subject for her name."

"Yes."

"She replies: 'My name is Rosetta.'"

"So much I already deduced. A clever name for a child with apparent linguistic gifts."

Shawn continued. "In the second line of Japanese, you ask her who her parents are and where they can be found."

She was pleased her Japanese had been good enough that Ms. Nakamura had translated it thus far. Often, writing it the elaborate pictograms of formal Japanese, she feared she was making grotesque mistakes. "That's right. Go on."

"The girl replies: 'Look for my father and my mother in your heart. They live in every heart.'"

She began to fear her assistant was wrong about the language being Esperanto. This line sounded like a mistranslation, and at worst gibberish. But then, she was assuming Rosetta was, behind her Esperanto, a conventional American child. If Rosetta was from a tribal culture, this reply could be traditional, or an indirect way of saying that her parents were dead and in the spirit world.

Hildegard nodded without comment. "Go on. What was the third line?"

Shawn began to look nervous again. "I had the most trouble with this line. It's not a response to your questions, so your questions could not guide my translation."

She sighed. "Esperanto is designed to be unambiguous in grammar and vocabulary, Mr. Douglas. Whatever you read is what she wrote. Tell me what you think she said."

"She says 'I have come to end the curse of the tower.'"

At this she drew a deep breath. "Mr. Douglas, the second line sounded suspect, but this line sounds like gibberish. Are you certain this is Esperanto?"

"Yes, Ma'am. The prepositions, the word endings, the word order, it's all correct for Esperanto."

28

"If I may ask, how did you come to read Esperanto?" Hildegard braced for some sloppy reasoning, since artificial languages were often the realm of dreamers or ideologues. Dreamers and ideologues ranked right up there with "fools" on her "people to be impatient with" list.

"I read a lot about it when I was growing up. In science fiction books. I never learned to read it, but the grammar is so simple I was able to learn to read it in an hour or so using an internet site. I still have to look up most of the vocabulary words, but the grammar rules and pronunciation are easy."

She put her face in her hands. "Mr. Douglas, if this affair ever becomes a subject of public academic study, under no circumstances admit you thought of Esperanto because you were a fan of science fiction. Find a better excuse before then so you don't look the fool. Make it look like you have an encyclopedic knowledge of languages, but don't say you got your idea from the 'Space Family Robinson.'"

Shawn swallowed. "Yes, Ma'am."

"Excellent work," she nodded at him. "You are making me reassess your potential. But don't let it go to your head. A haircut could have the same effect."

Akiko and Selene both giggled at this jab, but rather than look shamefaced, Mr. Douglas laughed along with them. He then motioned to Selene, and Hildegard attended to her middle assistant.

Selene began without discomfort. Her age and experience in the public schools made her a confident speaker. Put this together with her scatterbrained approach to speaking, and it meant she could ramble on.

"I've never seen a case like this, Doctor, but-"

"I'm certain the case is unique. Spare me discussion of its uniqueness and move on to your theories as to how it came to be."

Selene swallowed, and started over. "I have five theories as to how the subject came to read but not speak Japanese and still respond to you as she did in Esperanto."

"Go on."

"First, she could be mute or have difficulty speaking for developmental or psychiatric reasons."

"The girl did speak once or twice. So she can speak," she noted. "But that wouldn't rule out the psychiatric explanation. She may not want to or feel able to respond in Japanese."

Selene took this as her cue to continue. "Second, this could be an elaborate prank on you, or a fictitious case you created to test us. This could be why you barred us from talking about this with others, and gave us a short deadline, so as to keep other people from giving away your joke." Selene looked at her meaningfully. Selene's "we're both adults here, doctor," manner had grated on Hildegard before, and it did so again now.

She discarded the sarcastic reply that came to her mind first and used the opportunity to praise her assistant instead. "I'm glad to see your thinking cap is on. Any German delights in the occasional practical joke, and especially jokes which illustrate one or another fault line in 'conventional' thinking. But no. If this is a prank, it is not my prank. If it proves to be a prank, then its author has fooled me, too." She waited for Selene to continue.

"Third, she might be a native speaker of Japanese who was taught this version of Esperanto as a way to communicate with foreigners. She might believe you would find Esperanto easier to understand than her Japanese."

Dr. Teschke grunted a disbelieving note here. "Except that she saw me write in Japanese. So what you are saying is that she might have assumed a language she hadn't seen me write was easier for me to read than one which she had seen me write. Your logic here is weak. But go on." Selene made a note in her note pad. Akiko frowned but did nothing.

Selene kept theorizing. "Fourth, she might be a native speaker of a third language, but also speak Esperanto and Japanese."

"Possible. In fact, difficult to disprove, since her failing to speak in a third language is not proof she cannot speak one. But since this hypothesis is not testable, it is not useful." Selene again made a note on her pad.

"Last, she might be a native speaker of Esperanto who also knows Japanese."

"Is there any such thing?" She glanced from Selene to Shawn. The boy cleared his throat, and, at a nod from Akiko, answered the question.

"Two or three websites I have visited mention now that there are some children being raised in households where Esperanto is the only common language of the two parents. In this case, Esperanto is the child's 'household' language. These children would represent Esperanto's first generation of 'native' speakers."

Hildegard drew a deep breath. "My hunch tells me this 'native speaker' hypothesis is the best so far. If her parents shared Esperanto as a common language, this might explain her familiarity with Japanese and her clever name of 'Rosetta.' Her parents might have been aware her linguistic situation would make her a 'bridge' between languages."

At this, all four of them lapsed into a moment of silence. The professor finished her thinking and then turned to Akiko. "Tell me what you would like to do to unravel the mystery of Rosetta."

Ms. Nakamura referred to her index card for a moment, and then began.

"I would like to interview this girl again. We know she can read Japanese, and we know Shawn can translate Esperanto. Put this together with Selene's experience with children, and even if we cannot solve all the mysteries of her languages, we can ask the questions the government needs answered to find her home."

Dr. Teschke was pleased. Her assistants were on track: their first obligation was to the welfare of the girl. Only after her needs were cared for could they ethically study her as a case in linguistics.

"If, beyond this, Rosetta and her guardians will agree to more interviews, I think we should study her and make recordings of her speech and writing before she begins to learn much English by exposure or schooling. If the person who wanted to kill ever succeeds in killing her, we will thus have a record of her case suitable for a study."

"Yes, I agree. This subject could be the start of an article or thesis for someone..." Hildegard eyes rested on Shawn. He said nothing.

Akiko made her last suggestion. "Finally, in addition to interviews, we could do some field observations of Rosetta. Her body language and reactions may tell us things she cannot."

Dr. Teschke folded her hands in satisfaction. "Excellent. You keep our ethical obligations to Rosetta straight, but do not overlook the baseline academic work which could be done even under her present circumstances."

Ms. Nakamura smiled. Shawn and Selene both nodded in agreement, and so the professor felt no reservations about continuing on this line. "This is the kind of rare opportunity for a linguist to both justify his existence to society and do some interesting work at the same time. I will use all my weight to give the three of you this chance: if you make careers of linguistics, you'll still be talking about this case twenty-five years from now." Hildegard fished out Faith's business card. "I will call the child's guardian now. Are the three of you prepared to spend the afternoon with her if I can get her guardian to bring her in?"

All three assistants nodded.

"Wait while I make the phone call before we make more plans for this afternoon," Hildegard said.

She referred to the business card the firefighter had left her the night before, dialed the office number and waited.

"Hello? Ms. Haversham? This is Dr. Teschke from Cornell. I'm fine, thank you. I have some news: one of my assistants has worked out what language it is Rosetta speaks, and while we don't have a native speaker on campus, we do have someone who can read the language. I thought if the authorities had more questions they needed answered, if you bring her up with a list of those questions, we might be able to work out some of the answers. No, it doesn't need to be you who comes with her. Your father? That would be fine, but my assistants would prefer to work directly with Rosetta if he's comfortable with that. No, no. No need to wait: whatever your father decides we'll work around it. I can be convincing if I need to. Yes. It's nothing, but thank you. What was the number again? I'll wait ten minutes to call so you can talk to him first. I hope we can help solve your mystery! Good bye!"

The professor put down the phone. "If all goes according to plan, the guardian's father will bring the girl up here. She forewarned me her father can be particular and stubborn and is suspicious of 'university people.' Do your best to look down-to-earth, please." Her eyes flicked again to Mr. Douglas.

"I'll duck into a closet," he joked.

"I'm about to call this father and arrange a meeting." She tossed Ms. Nakamura her "you know what to do" look.

The younger woman stood up, indicating for the others to do so, already giving instructions. "Selene, do your preparations for your one-forty class now so you can help us later. Shawn, help me prepare the recording equipment. Leave the Doctor alone for now." Once Akiko had pushed them out the door, Dr. Teschke took a deep breath and picked up her office phone again.

"Now for the tough part," she considered. She had to call Inspector Haversham's father, who had been titled by his own daughter as "a grouchy old man."

31

Chapter 3

Ashes

Faith was partway into her third mug of coffee and vibrating with productivity when her own cell phone rang. She was half tempted to pass the phone to Karl and keep going, but it was her personal phone, and the ring tone did not suggest it was anyone from within the department.

She groped for the phone while she tried to fish an earplug out of her ear with the other hand. The test of coordination proved too much, and she first dropped her cell phone, and then, as she managed to flip the phone open with her chin, dropped the earplug while setting the phone to her ear.

"Hello?" she greeted, bending over to feel around under her desk for the earplug.

"Hello? Ms. Haversham?" the caller inquired. The voice was unfamiliar, but accented, and after a moment, she recognized it as the voice of Dr. Teschke.

The professor carried on for a while about how one of her assistants had figured out which language Rosie spoke. Faith was pleased, as this would give her some good news to bring to the briefing. As the only available witness, the girl's story could be central to the investigation. But she hesitated when the professor asked to see her afternoon at two-thirty. That would be in the middle of her briefing.

"Doc, I can't make time. But I might be able to get my father to bring her in for you."

As soon as she suggested this, she wished she hadn't. Her father regarded Cornell as somehow severable from Ithaca itself, and as full of rich, pretentious know-it-alls who demanded everything of the city while requiring that none of the gears, cogs, and tanks of municipal workings be visible from their bedroom windows. He had proclaimed many times that the only two good things Cornell had done in his life were bring his wife Connie in from Syracuse for school and founded its own fire department. This bad relationship with the university was the reason he hadn't run for the common council after retiring.

Nonetheless, the professor had already latched onto the idea of working with her father. "Suit yourself, Lady, you have no idea," she thought. As a kindness, she promised to call her father first, so as to introduce the idea and shorten their conversation.

As she hung up the phone, however, she felt a tap on her shoulder. Another interruption? Interruptions always came in clusters, and she had been making such good progress until the phone call.

"What, Karl?" she said irritably and loudly because of the one earplug still in.

She stiffened as she realized Karl was in front of her, a warning still frozen on his lips. She looked up over her shoulder to see the Deputy Chief, Pierce Tomlan, peering into her computer screen.

"Oh, sir, sorry," she started.

"Earplugs again?" Pierce said. He took no notice of her grumpy tone, for which she was grateful.

"Yes, sir," she said, abashed. It was a running joke around the department that if she were to lose her hearing, she'd never stop working. "I'm working against the clock."

"Is something going on with your Dad?" Her boss scanned the screen, his narrow chin and black-dyed hair framing his serious look. She wondered if the question was a genuine concern for her dad, or the small-talk prelude to a critique of the slide she was editing.

"Less about my Dad, more about our Jane Doe," she replied. "Cornell has got the language she speaks figured out, but since I'll be in the briefing, my Dad has to cart her up the hill."

"Huh," he replied. "Maybe we'll learn something from her." Pierce's face was serious, but interested.

"I hope so, sir. This fire is chock-full of weird. It's like nothing I learned about in school. It will be all I can do to get all the weird into these slides in time for the brief."

"I'm sorry to say, I have to slow you down," Pierce said. "I need you to pre-brief me."

Faith felt exasperation. The last thing she needed was for the Major to demand his own personal version of the briefing. That would kill forty-five minutes, and leave her so strapped for time she would have to go with the briefing as it stood at the moment.

"Sir, I need-,"

"I'd be doing you a disservice if I didn't preview this briefing. And if it's not ready, I'll go to the Chief and get you more time to prepare it. We'd like a prepared brief this evening more than a less-prepared one this afternoon."

"Whew," thought Faith. In that case, she could afford her boss's interruption. "Alright, sir, grab a chair," she motioned. Karl, however, was already bringing him one. When the Major was seated, Karl grabbed another chair and pulled it up to watch the brief as well.

"Great. An audience before I'm ready for one," said her stage-frightened self. Frazzled by the sudden intrusion of her boss, she composed an introduction in her head, snapped her cell phone closed, and left it on the desk.

David contemplated Rosie as she sat on the couch, dressed again in her laundered clothes: his daughter's keepsake scout shorts and a t-shirt reading "Maxie's Supper Club - Ithaca Little League #40." She had pulled up an afghan blanket and was snuggled against it, staring at the television tuned to a weather station.

She was in a lot of pain, and letting her lie there would mean all she could do was dwell on pain. He should keep her busy. But how?

"You've done this before," he recalled. After all, he'd helped to raise a girl, though Connie had been the last word in childrearing issues. What had Faith liked at this age?

"Jigsaw puzzles?" He remembered building a jigsaw puzzle of a French castle, with a moat and swans, which his daughter had kept on her wall for years. He also remembered the burns on Rosie's buttock and thigh, and how his own burns of similar degree had felt to him. A jigsaw puzzle would not be distracting enough, especially if she had to sit on her burns on a breakfast bench to do the puzzle.

"Horseback riding?" he thought. His daughter loved horses, and though they had never owned one, she still went trail riding from time to time when one or another date hadn't worked out. Again, though, the burned buttock would be a problem in a saddle.

"Needlepoint?" Several objects of needlepoint his wife and daughter had made together were still about the house, framed on the walls or covering throw pillows. But, like jigsaw puzzles, this would not be compelling enough, and he didn't know the first thing about needlepoint to show Rosetta how to do it.

"Clothes shopping?" Faith was not much for clothes now, since as a firefighter she was in uniform often for twelve hours a day or more. But in her childhood she had loved new clothes. She would spend the whole summer looking forward to Labor Day when her mother would take her shopping for the next year's school clothes. David had found clothes shopping dull, but it didn't involve much sitting, and if Rosie was to be away from her family much longer, she would need more than one set of clothes. He could take her clothes shopping, and that would mean he wouldn't be doing laundry every day until she left, and she wouldn't be trotting around half naked much of the time.

"Can I safely take her shopping in public?" he wondered. After all, if there was an arsonist, he might be anyone around town. Then he reconsidered. "Go on, if you were an arsonist who believed you'd succeeded, would you be hanging out in JC Penny? No. You'd be off spending your payoff money on whores or drugs or whatever." So shopping it was, he decided. It was sure to be a hit with Rosie, solved some practical problems, and bought him more time to think of what they would do next.

He scooped up her shoes from beside the doorway and put them on the floor in front of the couch. He then sat down next to her and began tying on his own loafers. Shaken out of her staring by David's movement of the couch, the girl sat up and watched him put on his shoes. After a moment, she stood up and put on her own, then looked to him for what to do next.

"To the truck," he said, jangling his keys. She pursed her lips at the word "truck," but stood up to follow him. He led her out the front door, locking it behind her. The house was on a steep hill, as many houses were in Ithaca. So he walked beside Rosie as they descended the steps to his driveway.

His truck was a vintage Ford, fire engine red, with flared wheel wells and a gear box in the bed filled with his first aid supplies and firefighting gear. His truck was the butt of much humor at the fire department, and one of the firemen had even gone so far as to stencil the bumper number "IFD-3927" on his rear bumper, like the fire trucks had. With fuel prices the way they were, it was expensive to drive, and living on a fixed income as he was, he feared that before too long he would have to trade in his truck for something more efficient. But for now, he would drive it proudly. It was made in America, like him.

He spotted a new crack in the retaining walls edging his driveway and sidewalk as they walked. They were the original retaining walls, and his house had been built in the mid-1800s, so he couldn't complain about the craftsmanship. Trying to stop all the earth on the hillside from sliding down Ithaca's steep "Buffalo Hill" might be a task Hercules would fail. Most of the tree cover on the slope had been downed, and half the hillside had been paved to drain into the other half. The erosion got worse every year. David decided that he'd have to get a landscaper out to look at it, and maybe a concrete man. He knew one or two from the city who might give him some advice.

He opened the passenger door for Rosie, and the child stared up at the passenger seat with visible uncertainty. She had ridden in it twice before, once between the hospital and the firehouse, and another time between firehouses. He knew the child found the climb into the seat troublesome. Still, she searched out handholds and climbed in with all the adroitness school children used on jungle-gyms. He closed her door behind her and went to the driver's side.

34

Once at the wheel, he found Rosie had already fastened her seat belt, and was starting a difficult balancing act. She tried to sit with her seat belt on in such a way that her back still did not touch the back of the bench seat. David started the truck, waited until the rumble of the engine had become regular, and backed out as smoothly as he could, trying to avoid sudden stops and starts which would bump her back into the car seat. For the most part, he succeeded, but he checked again at every light to see if she was wincing. At one point she caught him looking, and he felt self-conscious. *"Drive,"* he told himself. *"If you dote any more, you'll cause an accident. She'll live without you checking on her."*

After picking his way through Ithaca's downtown and back up the east hill to the shopping plaza, he took one more glance at his silent passenger. Her head and shoulders were turned so she was looking out her passenger window, with her right forearm against the seat back to steady against the truck's starts and stops. *"See, she takes care of herself."* Nonetheless, he remembered his own burns from this or that time in his career, and wished for her a swift end to the pain, and then the itching which followed.

When he'd parked outside Pyramid Mall, he walked around to open the passenger door for Rosie, but let her jump down, without intervention, since she enjoyed doing this. She beamed and added a skip to her landing beside the truck before she reached for his hand and walked with him across the parking lot.

Once inside the department store, he wanted to let go of the girl's hand, but she did not. So they walked together through the mall halls and kiosks, which were still empty in the mid-morning. The child went wide-eyed at the displays, but did not tug on him to look at this or that item as Faith had when he and Connie had taken her shopping downtown at this age.

Once in JC Penney's, the old man felt lost, and wound up standing in the perfume section inside the doors, staring overhead and looking for a sign that said "girls clothing." Rosie was sniffing at the perfumed air and looking at the glass bottles, and he caught the woman behind the counter smiling at her. He gave a tug to get her attention and move on. He didn't want his charge taking an interest in perfume this young, and as soon as he did so, he spotted the sign for "Young Miss Fashions." He frowned at this label. He guessed "girls" no longer existed to retailers like Penney's: the children had all become miniature super models who needed "fashions."

Once in the section, David found the underwear and pointed Rosie to them. Underwear was the chief deficiency in her wardrobe. He could dress her in his old shirts and a pair of Faith's old shorts, but there hadn't been even one pair of panties her size in the house anywhere. She was currently "going commando" and the bandages on her buttocks were exposed to wear. The girl scanned the racks of underwear as if she had just noticed them, and then looked at David.

"Pick some, Honey. You'll need some. It may be a while before we find your Ma and Pa."

She shrugged indifferently and began looking around at brightly colored socks. He clucked at her and pointed again. "Pick out some underwear. Do you know your size?"

Rosetta ran her eyes over the packages without saying anything.

"The number... around your waist? The number for your underwear?" he said, gesturing to his waist line. Rosie shook her head helplessly. He searched himself for a solution. She wasn't wearing underwear to read a size off of, and the scout shorts were large to use as a guide and hadn't had a size tag on them, anyway.

"She's an eight," came a voice from behind him with the answer to his problem. He wheeled to see a store clerk working behind the rack to their backs, a medium-built and cheerful black woman with a tag reading "Billie." "She looks about the same size as my nine-year-old, and mine wears an eight," the woman explained helpfully.

"Thanks," he smiled back at her, "She's not my kid, and I never did the clothes shopping for my daughter when she was growing up."

"The other clothes she can try on before you buy, but you can't do that with underwear, so you want to take your time guessing," said Billie. "But the underwear is forgiving, you can be a bit off and it'll still fit. Good thing, too, at her age they grow like weeds. Err on the big side. If it's too big, she'll grow into it, like, overnight."

"Heh, yeah, I remember," he said. The eight years between Faith being a charming girl and a teenager full of wrongheaded ideas had gone by in a blink.

"Granddaughter?" Billie asked, breaking his distracted thoughts by nodding to Rosie, who was looking Billie up and down.

"Who?" said David. "Oh, no, she's not kin. She's foster care, until we can find her family. Doesn't speak English, she speaks some kind of Italian."

"Oh, you lucky thing! I'd love to live in Italy," Billie said. "I've seen pictures, and it looks so pretty! I hope you get to go home soon."

The girl blushed at Billie, said something unintelligible, and smiled back at her.

He gestured. "I'm not sure she understood you, but that's about as good as communication gets with her."

Billie grinned back at him. "When you pick out some underwear, what will she need next?"

"I figure she should have a set of clothes that isn't from the Goodwill bin. So I'll let her pick some out."

"Whatever she chooses, her sizes are along the wall, skirts and pants down by the mirror and blouses by the changing room door. But they won't have much in her colors. Not many dark-skinned people around here," Billie added, perhaps recalling her own clothes shopping.

David noted that forewarning. "Thanks, Ma'am."

"No problem. Ask again if you have questions. I'll be around." Billie went back to shelving clothes, and he searched for size eight girls' underwear. It didn't end up being simple. There were different colors, patterns, and shapes to choose from, including thongs, which made David scowl at the indecency. Rosie shrugged at all the other kinds but those with moons and stars on them. Since the moons and stars prompted the least indifference, he picked out four pairs of those and four pairs in a lavender.

They then visited the shoe section to get her feet measured, since her Goodwill sneakers were big for her. He tried to get her to pick out a pair of new sneakers, but she pouted at all the pairs he offered her. In the end, he wound up picking a pair of white ones which would go with anything. But when it came to socks, the girl definitely had opinions. She favored colorful knits with loud patterns. She chose calicos, argyles, paisleys, and rainbow stripes, and no two of the eight pairs ended up alike.

Presented with the pants, skirts, and blouses, though, Rosie became downright stubborn. She shook her head at everything David brought to her attention, and repeated several things he despaired of understanding. He started to feel some impatience with this choosy creature fate had foisted on him and began to wonder if clothes shopping had been the best idea to elevate both their moods. Then his cell phone rang, and tone indicated the call was from a stranger.

"What a time for a business call," he grumbled, looking around to see Billie's eyes still on him from behind the clothes rack. Great, and he was being

36

scoped out, maybe it was true what people said that men with kids were woman magnets.

"Hello?" he said to his phone, feeling the awkwardness he always did while talking to a phone in a public place. Long ago one of his favorite writers had said that "Any sufficiently advanced technology was indistinguishable from insanity," and talking to empty space via a cell phone fit this description to a T.

"Hello, is this Mr. Haversham?" The caller was a woman, with a foreign accent. From this, the man guessed the call would have to do with Rosie.

"This is. Who's calling?"

"This is Dr. Teschke from the College of Arts and Sciences Department of Linguistics. I believe I was working with your daughter yesterday on the mystery of Rosetta."

Rosie chose then to fold her arms and purse her lips into a picture of dissatisfaction with the clothing selection. *"All this stubbornness about clothes from a girl wearing oversized wool shorts and a second-hand little league jersey,"* he marveled. "Yes, I'm working on that mystery right now myself," he confided to the caller.

The professor paused, puzzled by his statement. "Your daughter had said she would call you to tell you I would be calling. Hasn't she?"

"Umm, oh, no, she hasn't, Ms..."

"Dr. Teschke," prompted the caller with a voice which suggested sensitivity on the subject of titles. He stopped short of making one of his stock cracks to university people about how if they were doctors, he needed to ask them what could be wrong with his backside. He decided to stand up for his daughter instead.

"Yes, Faith has an important meeting this morning and she probably got overwhelmed. How can I help you, Ms. Teschke?" he asked. He saw Billie was still keeping her eyes on him, and was close enough to overhear. Maybe it was a bad idea to have Rosie out in public after all. Maybe he should have left this work to Faith.

Dr. Teschke's voice charged through his worries heedlessly, dragging him into the moment. "Mr. Haversham, one of my assistants has made a breakthrough in Rosetta's language, and I also have the services of a certified child speech therapist available today. If you have the time to meet me, in, say, two hours with a list of whatever questions you might have for her, we might be able to work out some of the missing facts in her case."

"Umm, yeah, sure, no problem, where on Arts and Sciences? Are you on the square by the big libraries?"

"The *Arts Quadrangle*, yes," the woman corrected him. "Are you familiar with the coffee bar called the Green Dragon?"

David did remember it. "The lunch bar underneath the art school with all that ancient cloth-wrapped wiring? Yeah, they had an electrical fire there once."

The caller paused at this, and then continued. "If you have no objection, then, we'll meet at the Green Dragon at three o'clock. I'd invite you to my office but it is small and busy with students at this time of day. Not appropriate for the circumstances this case."

"So they understand the need to lay low," he thought. "No problem, Professor. We may be late: finding parking is always a challenge," he answered.

"There is visitor parking behind the building. I'll see you at three o'clock, then?" The professor's tone suggested his confirmation was important.

"Yes, three o'clock is fine," he reassured her.

"Until later, Mr. Haversham. I look forward to helping the city resolve this issue."

"Until later," said David, struck that he was repeating the caller's strange farewell rather than using a more conventional one. He snapped the phone closed, puzzled for a moment. He then admonished Rosie. "Hurry up and choose, Honey, we're on the clock now. Two hours to be up on Ivory Tower hill."

At this warning, the girl began hemming and hawing, showing no sign of making a choice. He couldn't help but roll his eyes to heaven. "Okay, God, help me out, here."

About fifteen minutes later Faith's ringtone played. He flipped open the phone again, biting back on the irritation he felt.

"Let me guess, three o'clock, Arts quad, Professor hoity-toity what's-her-name, bring the state paperwork," he answered.

His daughter paused, then apologized guiltily, "Sorry, Dad, the Deputy walked in after I put the phone down and -"

He cut his daughter off. "You do your job. Rosetta isn't your daughter any more than she is mine. I'll handle this part; you knock Marcus dead with your briefing."

"Thanks, Dad!" said Faith. "It takes a load off. I want to get this firebug, but this will take time and resources and I need the Chief to buy in with this brief."

"Talk to you tonight," he concluded, anxious to get her back to her work.

Faith paused again. "Dad, the professor's nice, she's just foreign and stuff. Go easy on her."

"Don't worry. You forget, I've lived with one or two women who thought a lot of themselves," he replied.

She laughed. "Oh, right, what was I thinking, Pop? I'm sure you meet women like her every day! Good luck!"

"You too!" David snapped closed the phone to see Rosetta had gone from looking stubborn to downright sad for some reason. He guessed this clothing shopping thing wasn't working out as he'd planned. "No need to get upset, honey. We'll take our socks and underwear and go somewhere else, huh?" Rosie made no protest and reached up to take his hand and follow him to the cash registers.

The Major sat through Faith's briefing, making comments as she went. At first, she had resented them, but as she adjusted to Pierce's no-nonsense approach and learned to hear praise in his silences they became less trying, and she began to see some of his suggestions as more useful than critical.

Better still was that, as he left, the Major said he would juggle the briefing order so that the chief would get the briefing from the union representative first. This would buy Faith as much time as she had lost to briefing him, and she was sure she could make the briefing better in the interim. With Karl gone for lunch, she shut and locked the office door, pushed in her earplugs, and typed away. As she worked thoughts about this or that aspect of the mysterious fire tickled her mind, but she focused, scrawled notes on an index card, and continued. She would leave conjecture to her superiors, or do so later if the Chief approved an investigation, but now she had to focus on presenting the available information.

Karl returned from lunch during her reverie, and refilled her coffee cup when he did so. When she was finished, her hands were shaking from the volume of coffee she had drunk, but she had a good twenty minutes to spare. She saved the file and made a last trip to the ladies' room, hoping her caffeine overdose would not make her have to go again *during* the briefing. Then she folded up her laptop and carried it through the headquarters to the conference room.

She slipped quietly into the large room, since she could still hear voices from outside it. Sure enough, the current fire Chief, Marcus Bauer, and the deputy Pierce Tomlan, were at the head of the table. To their right was Marcia Ostrander, the human resources manager, Jorge Saturno, the comptroller, and Vivian Leblanc, the elderly French-Canadian secretary to the chief. Across from them sat the senior fire Captain, Dwight Earling, and Steve McCallister, the union representative for the Department. The union representative was in the middle of a long exposition.

Steve paused and shot her a smile she did her best to politely return. While she found the man funny and energetic, and had since she was a young teenager, she did not find him attractive. This lack of attraction had deepened over the years as the department and community rumor mills brought back to her details of his personal life, including one-night stands and routine marijuana use. In addition, she wanted to remain out of the conversation at hand, and she hoped his smile did not mean he was about to bring her into it.

McCallister resumed speaking, but Pierce looked over his shoulder, saw her, and nodded when she pointed at the image projector. With this permission, she tiptoed in and began hooking her computer up to the projection system. As her shaky hands fumbled to hook up various cables and adjust knobs, she eavesdropped on the going conversation.

Steve was speaking loudly and directly in his "hate to break it to you," tone she was all too familiar with from their lifetime of acquaintance. He had come to the department as a rookie firefighter as Faith had turned sixteen, and she had first heard his swaggering then. At the time, the brashness made him seem bold and independent, but she had begun tuning it out when it became tinged with union slogans.

"Look, this is all finger-pointing," the union foreman was saying. "Ever since the Market Garden bombings, two of our divers have been suffering these symptoms. They've been paying for therapies the department insurance doesn't cover out of pocket, but it can't go on, it's bankrupting their families. You can tell me the feds should be paying, or the state should be paying, but the bottom line is it's the divers who are paying now. Who will fix it? Will we let a good man and a good woman suffer into the poorhouse, or will we help them while politicians blame each other?"

Marcia Ostrander was especially harried, but none of the other people in the room were happy. Marcus was even wearing the oblique smile he had always showed at her father's late-night poker games during her youth, the expression her mother had termed the "Marco-Lisa smile." Jorge Saturno was drumming his fingers and biting his lip. Vivian tapped her pen in boredom. The fact that no one else at the table was happy with him must have dawned on the foreman, but he showed no signs of being discomfited: once he got to arguing, he would take on the world alone.

Faith grinned ruefully. Whatever she didn't like about Steve, she couldn't complain about her union representation. He was relentless.

"Sir," Marcia Ostrander spoke to Marcus as if the union were not at the table. "The department's insurance providers won't reimburse for the condition, claiming it was an injury incurred in the line of duty and hence compensable by workman's compensation. The state compensation board, however, has ruled that respiratory conditions cannot be linked to either 9/11 or to the Market Garden bombings and are hence not compensable. I understand the Union's position, but what do they want the Department to do?"

Steve spoke up. "Now, I've said what I want the Department to do. I want a payment to cover the past costs of these firefighters until some sort of resolution comes down."

Marcia said nothing in reply. Marcus maintained his "Marco-Lisa" smile but sat back, as if to reflect.

"What's our budget? There's not enough slush in there to help out two firefighters who have contracted what we all know to be work-related conditions? Conditions which have affected hundreds of firefighters involved in 9/11 and the Market Garden bombings?"

Pierce was ready to wrangle with Steve. "Look, the 9/11 conditions I can believe. I was there with David and the crew. There was a haze for days, weeks. But these two were divers at Market Garden. A bridge collapsing into the Mississippi does not generate as much dust, plus they were breathing containerized air whenever they were in the water."

Steve was unfazed. "Three major hotels collapsed or were demolished during our Market Garden operation, overlooking the dust and smoke from the pulverized bridges. And the 'containerized' air you are referring to, sir, was from compressors set up along the riverbank, so it was compressed air *from the disaster scene* that the divers were breathing. For all we know, compressing the air and re-using the cylinders concentrated the contaminants. Not to mention what contaminants the water and sludge itself might have had along the river bottom."

At this, Dwight spoke. "It's true. We set up the compressors on the shore at my direction and Chief Haversham's. The air was clearer than it was at ground zero, Chief, but it might have only seemed that way."

Faith remembered her father's description and pictures of the site of the bombed Martin Luther King bridge in St. Louis from the volunteer effort he and Captain Earling and a dozen or so local divers had participated in there. Steve's argument was in line with this and with the captain's own recollection.

Pierce had no immediate rebuttal. Faith took the pause to open her presentation on her computer, flip through it to ensure it was working, and then flip it to her title slide "Carriage House Fire, Village of Cayuga Heights, 4 April." She then clicked on the projector, checked the image, and flipped the "image blank" switch so as to wait for the going meeting to finish.

Jorge took the moment of silence to introduce his concern. "Sir, our budget is approved by the Common Council. If we reallocate funds already designated in our budget, we risk raising questions during the next budgeting cycle in August."

Jorge's comment prompted a long pause from Marcus. He sat forward again. Faith waited. "If anyone would have an answer to this, it would be chief," she thought.

At length, the chief spoke. He had a high voice for a man in charge, and was short and slender of frame. But despite the impression his size and manner gave when he stood next to one of his own firefighters, he was respected because of his thoughtfulness and tact. Marcus had been her father's deputy and friend for many years, and his voice brought back memories of the many poker games for M&Ms Chief Bauer, David, Constance, Dwight, and Faith had played together in her teens.

Since Marcus had known Steve nearly as long as the Havershams, his tone with the younger man was even a bit avuncular. "I appreciate your determination on behalf of our brethren. It's fitting and you remind us of our duties to each other and the reason we all organize under the IAFF. Unfortunately, as Jorge has mentioned, our budget is approved by the Common Council. If we wish to keep their goodwill *and* our jobs, we won't shuffle around large blocks of city money without consulting with them.

"Also we must be careful about the legalities of redirecting funds. We can't redirect money we receive from the state or the federal government for specific purposes. Nor can we redirect money which has already been matched by federal and state funds, is committed to contracts, or is set to be spent on equipment and operations that impact the public's safety. Our budget is an impressive sounding sum, but it's not a big slush fund from which we can underwrite good causes. It's a public trust. The public trusts us to do right by our employees, but it trusts us to handle the money it gives us carefully and transparently. This is Ithaca, not New York City.

"Pierce, please work with Steven and our affected firefighters to get a sense of how much they need and I will take the issue to the Common Council. Be sure whatever costs I present will stand up to skeptics as due. The issue at the council must be about whether or not we help our firefighters, not if this or that expense is a fair one."

"Yes, sir." Pierce said. His expression, as always, was serious. Whatever disagreement he may have had with Steve vanished at Marcus's direction. Faith felt a bit of envy: she wished other people's orders and directions would neutralize her feelings so swiftly.

The chief turned to his human resource manager. "Marcia, could you summarize for me the situation with the insurers, the state, and the federal courts? Something for a layman, so I'm not confusing myself in front of the Common Council?"

Marcia scribbled notes, relieved to have a task so manageable.

"Jorge, I need your recommendations as to which pot of money we could draw these payments from that would minimize concerns about legality and impacts on public safety."

Jorge raised his palms. "I don't need to tell you this budget is already tight, Chief. The Common Council approved seventy percent of our request this year."

Marcus was not put off by this. "I hear you. I trust your judgment. But I believe in this situation, this is an issue the department should be involved in. If we involve the department, we involve the city. When we involve the city, the issue will begin to have more traction with the county and state."

Marcus attended Pierce and Faith, ready to move on. But Steve was not.

"Sir, I have to ask you for your commitment to help these firefighters. Will you personally get behind this?"

The chief was unflappable. "You watched me put my staff to work on it. What more do you want?" Captain Earling, who usually sided with the union, echoed the chief's question with his eyebrows.

"I want to hear you take a stand. I want to hear you say we *will* help our brothers and sisters who fell ill stepping up to help in the hour of America's need."

Marcus demurred. "I know you want me to make some statement which will sound like an unequivocal reassurance to the divers. But I won't lie or say empty words. We have to look at the problem, and see what we can feasibly and legally do."

Steve wasn't finished. "When the 9/11 syndrome cases crept up in our ranks, Chief Haversham didn't study it. He said 'we will help our brothers and sisters. We will carry away these last stones and girders.' Those were his words. As the representative of this bargaining unit, I'd like to hear you match them," he challenged.

Everyone in the room froze at the mention of Chief Haversham's words. Pierce grew angry. Marcia and Jorge glanced at each other and then refocused themselves on their notes. Dwight nodded in approval. And Marcus fell speechless. But not for long.

"You don't need to lecture the people in this room on what David Haversham did. I was his deputy. Pierce was a fire captain. Jorge and Marcia held these same positions. We remember what he did. He was an inspiration to all of us, and a reminder that being true to the public does not mean forgetting to be true to yourself, and your comrades," he said. "And your family," he added with a nod to Faith. At the thought of her father's return from the Market Garden bombing, and his tearful announcement to Constance that he would resign as Chief so they could spend their last months together, her lip trembled.

Pierce was the second to recover. "I think this discussion is over for the time being-" he began. But the chief interrupted him with a raised hand.

"We admire David. And we remember him, and rest assured that when I make my decision, I will have talked to him about it, because he's the wisest firefighter I know. But he made that decision in a different time. The city budget was in surplus. And America was behind the heroes of 9/11, and these facts helped us smooth over the bumps in the road and arrive at his desired goal.

"But those times are gone. Now we face deficits, public war fatigue and tax revolt, and significant changes to the role and degree of workman's compensation and health insurance in our lives. Chief Haversham made the best decision *at that moment in time*. It falls to me and the others in this room to make the decision that is best in this moment."

"Right doesn't change," Steve replied. Again, Dwight's face showed silent approval.

Marcus laughed, betraying only a hint of exasperation. "Right doesn't change. But the best we can do in pursuit of right may change. It's the challenge of the union representative to remind me of what's right. But it's my job to sort out what's best."

The foreman knuckled down. "I hope the big bucks you make can be a salve to your conscience. sir."

Faith grit her teeth in frustration. The foreman had gone too far. There was a line somewhere between being an advocate and being disrespectful, and the man had predictably crossed it. But she said nothing. The chief would defuse the situation himself, she guessed, if Pierce didn't jump up and down on the younger man first.

Marcus gave the remark no notice. "Speaking of the Havershams, I'll move on now to the next briefing. You're free to stay for it if you like, Steven."

"I would," said the union man, turning to face her. And with as little warning as that, Faith changed from a guest in the room to the center of attention.

"Are you all set?" Pierce checked.

"Yes, sir," she said. "I have my earplugs out and everything." At this, most of the people in the room laughed. As she pushed the first control button to present the title slide with theatrical flourish, she felt relief to be starting.

"Gentleman, ladies, this is the report of the initial findings from the Cayuga Heights carriage house fire. Karl and I were called to the scene four days ago after two engines responded to the fire under a mutual assistance request from the village of Cayuga Heights." She flashed by the title slide.

The first picture slide was one of a stately stone carriage house. It had three wide sets of barn style doors, green and white painted trim. The former groom's quarters at one end of the building had normal doors and windows. Adjoining the building were two medium-sized steel storage tanks.

"This was the carriage house prior to the fire, circa 2011. The current owner then and now was Finneas Corning, a descendent through marriage of DeWitt himself. Originally part of the DeWitt estates, it was used as a test garage for some of the agricultural machines and implements developed at Cornell after

42

the land grant. It was more than one hundred and fifty years old. It was listed in the National Register of Historic Places and was the oldest operating agricultural structure in Tompkins County.

"Finneas Corning lives in Ireland, and manages the property through Finger Lakes Property Management as a horse pasture and hayfield. In recent years the building itself had been idle except to house haying equipment and tools. Finger Lakes Property Management reports that their latest visit to the property was ten days prior to the fire to check the condition of the property and test the tractors per their contract with Mr. Corning. "

She flipped to the next slide. It was of the same carriage house, but one could only guess this with reference to the blue-gray gravel drive, the road passing by it, and the same grain silos in the distance. In this picture a flat pile of black and sandstone colored rubble covered about twice the same area as the building had, and a large fragment of one of the carriage house's metal storage tanks lay in the foreground. In the background was the charred form of an overturned pickup truck.

She heard mutters of dismay, and someone said "What a shame."

"This is what remains of the carriage house. Insurers have adjudged the structure a total loss, and Finneas Corning has said finances prohibit him from reconstructing the structure in its original form or materials. A salvager has already been awarded a contract for any recoverable stone or furnishings, pending the closure of this investigation."

Marcus frowned. "It's a real loss. It was a landmark."

Faith flicked to the next slide. It showed the ruins of the carriage house standing in an enormous blackened circle of earth which overlapped the adjoining road. "This is an aerial photo, courtesy of Google Earth and SatStar at my request, of the carriage house site. You can see the blackened area spans two hundred yards, the edge of it abutting Auburn-Triphammer Road on one side. Even living trees within the area caught fire and scorched. County transportation reports that portions of Triphammer road's asphalt caught fire and the road will require emergency resurfacing before the end of the summer."

This picture brought silence. "Two hundred yards?" asked the chief in disbelief.

"See for yourself, sir," Faith replied, motioning to the picture. Marcus looked to Pierce, and then to Dwight.

"Two hundred yards, then." He said. "Suggestions, gentlemen?"

"None, sir." Pierce replied.

The captain told his story. "When we got there, sir, it wasn't that hot. It was raining, and Cayuga Heights's engines were already pulled close to the building to hose it down. It's a good thing it was in the middle of a field. If there had been more fuel around, we would have been hard pressed to put it out with the water in the trucks. There are no hydrants out Triphammer road."

"Two hundred yards across?" Marcus pondered.

"We can be pretty sure it wasn't an oven full of unattended chicken wings," remarked Steve. There were chuckles around the table.

"Now I know why there has been all this hubbub to brief me," Marcus said. "I'll drive out there tonight and take a look at it myself."

Faith sighed. Part of the reason for preparing good briefs was so the Chief didn't have to go driving around looking at fire scenes. But she had to admit this one was remarkable. She might not have believed it if she hadn't been on the scene. She flipped the slide.

"This is our subject, Janey Doe," Faith said, flashing a picture of Rosetta inside a firehouse, wrapped in a Red Cross blanket and flashing a fragile smile.

"She is the only probable direct witness of the fire, and, near as we can tell, the only survivor. She was found at the scene with about five percent third degree and twenty percent second-degree burns, with melted remnants of synthetic clothing stuck to her skin, but her hair intact. She was found unconscious at the edge of the burned area by one of our firefighters.

"Most of the burns were to her back and buttocks, leading to minimal visible disfigurement. She was treated at Cayuga Lake Medical Center and released into the care of the Department. Children's Services then requested she be removed from the fire house and placed in direct emergency foster care. For reasons of discretion and with the advice of Ithaca Police Department, myself and my father are serving as her emergency foster parents while Children's Services attempts to arrange long-term foster care compatible with this investigation."

Marcus nodded, his features softening. "How is she doing?"

"She's on painkillers, and antibiotics to prevent infection, but she's still in a lot of pain."

"Has she been able to tell us anything? I heard she spoke Italian?"

"She's at the university as we speak with my father, sir. We're hoping they can tell us something there. On the phone this morning one of the professors said they had identified her native language."

"That's a start. Maybe she'll have something to say."

"I hope so, sir," said Faith.

"How is your father faring with the temporary addition to the family?" Marcus grinned. The rest of the people in the room attended to the question. Her mind raced for an honest answer that wouldn't share too much of her father's business.

"Umm, he's been great. I guess he doesn't want to do it forever, though. He has reminded me he is retired and wants to sleep in."

Everyone at the table grinned at this. "If anyone deserves to sleep in, it's Chief Haversham," said Captain Earling. "That man was up at the crack of dawn for decades."

The fire captain was more right than he knew. It had been clear when Faith was growing up that for both her parents, Constance the school teacher and David the fireman, work came first because the community came first. From 5th grade on she had woken up in the morning for school in an empty house, with both her mother and father already at work. Her mother came home at four in the afternoon and was home all summer, thanks to the teachers' union, but her father had often been home late, or not at all, year in and year out. When he had been Chief, but before her mother had gotten sick, he had insisted on being at work for all three shift changes five days a week.

She returned her thoughts from her childhood to the briefing at hand and flipped the slide.

"This is a close-up of one of the loose stones from the carriage house walls. All these stones were living stones from local quarries. Note most stones are not blackened, but are cracked in many places. Most of the stones in the structure were cracked like this, but only the ones abutting wooden members were blackened. In addition, faces of the stone exposed by cracking were blackened, suggesting the cracking happened before any blackening."

Her audience was intrigued. Even Jorge and Marcia, who often checked out of discussions of actual firefighting, were paying full attention. Marcus, Pierce, and Dwight all exchanged glances but made no comment. Steve sat with his chin on his hand.

The next picture Faith flipped to she expected to be a jaw dropper. It showed a melted lump of metal hanging by one end from a shovel head held by

44

Karl. The original shape of the metal lump was gone, and the piece itself featured bands of flaky black metal and shiny polished steel.

"This is a piece of high carbon steel recovered from the scene two days after the fire. We guess from its weight and composition that it was a tool of some kind, possibly a high-quality socket wrench near the apparent center of the fire. As you can see, its original form was lost. It was reduced to liquid during the course of the fire. However, this forge-hardened shovel head, found about thirty feet further out from the first piece, shows signs of heat damage but kept its original shape."

"Huh," said Marcus. "So there was a big difference in heat between the two locations?"

"Very," said Faith. "Based on this tool and supported by other signs such as the damage to the concrete floor, we estimate the center of the heat source or fire exceeded forty-eight hundred degrees Fahrenheit and probably much more. In addition, the melted piece of metal is now magnetic."

"It's magnetized? What does that tell us?" The chief asked. "I've never heard of metal being magnetized by a fire."

She had done her homework on the curious piece of metal. "A metallurgist at Cornell explained to me by phone that all steel could be magnetic, since each iron atom has a magnetic charge. In normal steel, though, the iron atoms and crystals all face in random directions. If, however, all or most of the crystals and atoms are aligned the same way, the steel becomes magnetic as it cools down."

"So, all the iron atoms in this wrench, or whatever, are now aligned in the same direction?"

"If I understood the metallurgist correctly, he said a strong magnetic field and vibration or pressure while the iron was melted and cooling could align the crystals in one direction, and that's how some magnets are made." She explained.

"Was the shovel also magnetic?"

"Not so we noticed, sir. We only found the melted wrench because it stuck to the tools we were using to move ashes around."

Marcus paused. "Did they teach you about this as part of your fire science degree?"

Faith laughed. "No sir. I had to take physics, and we talked about different ignition and melting points as clues to the sources and temperatures of a fire, but nothing like this. I'd never heard of a piece of steel magnetized in a fire."

"Neither have I," said Marcus. He looked around the table, but everyone else present shrugged.

She continued. "Finally, a large area of the six-inch concrete floor slab, added over the structure's original stone floor, was turned to glass. This vitrified area was eight feet in diameter, and at its center point the glass was spongy and thin, allowing us to chip it away and see the original stone floor had also been heated and cracked." She flipped through pictures showing the circle of class and the hole down to the original stone in the middle of the glass formation. Her audience remained silent.

"This suggests a heat of much higher than forty-eight hundred degrees over a span of eight feet for a fraction of a second. Likewise, the heat damage to the nearby roadway indicates the heat at the roadway was in excess of four hundred degrees Fahrenheit. With all grass and small plant life blackened or burned to ash, it's clear the event was hot. But other than the destruction of the building itself, there are no signs it was correspondingly forceful."

By now her audience had gotten past their expressions of disbelief. They were not yet to the eyes-glazed-over point, but Faith could see it was time to stop showing pictures of weird stuff and start drawing conclusions. She skipped forward to her interpretive slides. She brought up the first of them, titled "Initial Recommendations."

"Sir, having examined the scene of the fire, I suggest this case be kept open. My working theory is this fire resulted from a massive electrical discharge, along the lines of a dozen lightning strikes. Electrical discharge could explain both the observed intense but instantaneous heat and the low explosive force. Any explosion would have resulted from overheated air and any stored fuels at the scene exploding with much less force than explosives."

Her theory raised eyebrows across the room. Captain Earling spoke up. "I've seen downed power lines light fires, melt asphalt, and even turn concrete to glass. But even a powerful line only burns a small area. I've seen a power line which feeds a city block burn a hole half that size when it was on the ground for fifteen minutes. What kind of electrical machine do you think it was? Because I can't think of even one except for maybe a whole power plant."

Faith stopped before she referred to the fire captain by his first name. When she was a schoolgirl home playing poker for M&Ms with her father and his friends, Dwight was Dwight. When she was picking up her father from a football game at the man's house because David had too many whiskeys, Dwight was Dwight. But here and now, he was Captain Earling.

"I don't know, sir. I'm not an expert on electricity. But if you put together the features of the fire and the other evidence I've found, it looks like this is an electrical event. In order to figure out what caused it, I'll have to spend some more time at the university getting ed-u-ma-cated."

"Convince me," interjected Marcus into the banter between the two. "Make me understand why you think this was electrical."

She had prepared for this question. "Many of the things we observed at the scene would be best explained by an electrical event. First, the event was short and extremely hot, with the main discharge on the order of less than thirty seconds. The intense but shallow melting of the concrete is one sign it was hot but short. The fact that many stones in the walls burst from the heat before they were blackened by fire from wood structural members also speaks to a short, intense heat. And the blackened blades of grass in the affected area but the unburned roots mirror this. Most of the damage wasn't caused by flames, but by raw heat, or radiation. It's like the difference between burning yourself by holding onto a match too long and burning yourself by getting too close to arc welding. Welding burns take a fraction of a second and the burns are uniform over a large area. A match burn you have a second to get away from and there are parts of your skin which are more or less burnt.

"A lightning strike can be hotter than the surface of the sun. At their hottest point, they can get as high as thirty thousand degrees. That's why electricity can be used to cut through metal. It can vaporize metal if you crank it enough. Plus, a lightning strike or something like it can create an explosion by superheating the air until something combustible or even the air itself explodes. But these explosions would have a lower overall power than regular explosives. So these two features fit my theory: the extreme short heat and the relatively low power explosion.

"But that's not all," Faith continued, searching through her slides. "We have evidence from other sources. First, check this video. Cornell shared some of their 'Blue Light' security camera footage with me. This cut is overlooking their North Campus dormitories from the time of the fire." She started the video.

"It was overcast and raining steadily on the day of the fire, if you remember, but it wasn't a thunderstorm. Now watch." The view showed Cornell's Mary Donlon dormitory, its curved, modernist face looming up against a gray sky.

46

A gray digital clock counted up from 13:18 in one corner. And after a moment, there was a series of bright flashes against the clouds across the sky, followed two seconds later by what sounded like a long, rolling thunderclap.

"Seemed like lightning, didn't it?" she asked. The audience nodded. "Within three minutes after this Cayuga Heights will get a call from the county 911 center that motorists have reported the carriage house and parts of the surface of Auburn Road are on fire.

"But in case you think this was a coincidence, check this out." She flipped to a gray map, overlaid with silver angular lines which represented roads. The main silver stripe was labeled "Auburn Road/Tompkins County – 34." Across the map was a large lightning bolt reading "multiple concentrated strikes." Faith explained the photo. "This is a detail of NASA's National Lightning Detection Network map data. They keep a map of the whole country, hour by hour, tracking how many lightning strikes have occurred and where and when, using ground and satellite sensors. Between 1315 and 1320 hours it detected an isolated, but large, cluster of apparent lightning strikes. Now, these sensors only send their data to the network every five minutes. So those strikes could have occurred anywhere within a few miles of the scene, and at any time in the same five-minute window. Still, from this we know that in the area around our fire scene, at the right time, there was a lot of lightning activity. And, according to the sensors, there was no more lightning, before or after the event, for sixteen hours either way anywhere else in the county."

"So, we can see with our own eyes from the university's security cameras there was a visual signature of a lightning strike at the time. And the NLDN map places it in the area of our site. And the heat and shockwave damage we found at the scene suggests an electrical event."

"Aren't most buildings protected against lightning? I mean, wouldn't a lightning rod prevent lightning from destroying the building?" Steve challenged her.

"Both Finneas Corning and Finger Lakes Property Management confirmed that the carriage house had lightning protection both for the structure and for the diesel storage tank there. And if it were normal lightning, or even multiple normal lightning strikes, these lightning rods should have protected the building. Maybe they failed for some reason. Or maybe the lightning was abnormal."

Marcus held up his hands to his shoulder, palms facing her, to gesture as he spoke. "Okay, you've convinced me this could be lightning. You've convinced me so well I'm wondering why you're asking me to keep this case open. You've shown me there was lightning in the area, and you've shown me there are things at the scene which make you think lightning. So why shouldn't I chalk this up to a freak lightning event and/or inadequate lightning projection and close it?"

Here was her boss's boss, asking her the most important question of the briefing, and she was struck instead by how gay some of Marcus's body language was. It was an open secret that Chief Bauer was gay, the first gay fire chief so far as anyone knew, and the man avoided the issue by not asking, not telling, and acting "straight." But there were some mannerisms which gave him away, and this talking with his hands bit was one of them.

Faith recovered when she saw the man put down his hands and look at her expectantly. She cursed the cups of coffee she'd guzzled for making her concentration so brittle and returned to the brief.

"Because, Chief, there's a good chance there were people at the scene. Not only are we duty bound to keep the case open long enough to make a concerted attempt to confirm or deny it, but there's also a chance these people either created this lightning event or were its intended victims."

Faith could see the disbelief in Marcus's expression, and indeed, most people in the room had gone from nodding agreement with the Chief to looking at her funny.

"We've had arsonists with kerosene. And IPD picked up someone last year with some white phosphorous grenades, God help us. But we've never caught a firebug with a lightning bolt in his pocket. So if we decide it's lightning, we have to decide that it's not arson, because arsonists don't control lightning. But tell me about our potential John Does who might have gone along with our Janey Doe."

"We have names for them. Thanks to this." She flashed the display to a picture of the burnt out truck that showed its blackened, but still legible, license plate. "This pick-up found at the scene was registered to a William Kopp of Syracuse, New York. William Kopp is a building contractor and preacher, and was last seen in the company of two other members of the 'Pillar of Flame' church, Mary Joe Rudolph of Manlius and Randy Knight of Owasco. All three had been reported missing by their families and fellow church members. Syracuse police department was very interested when I called to ask if they could tell me anything about him. The last they had found them, they were videotaped the night before our fire buying pizza and gas for this truck at the Hess station at the intersection of Route 34 and US 20 W in Auburn. The videotapes also show a girl Mary Joe escorted to the bathroom, and while you can't make out her face in the video, there's a good bet it is our Janey - our Rosie - Doe."

"The fact that they left the truck at the carriage house doesn't mean they were at the scene," challenged Marcus.

"I think they were," Faith answered. She brought up the next picture, a close up of the pick-up's ignition lock with the keys in it. "You might walk off and leave your truck in a remote place while you caught a ride with someone," she noted, "but you'd take your keys with you."

Marcus leaned back, impressed. Marcia chewed on the end of her pen.

"Ouch," said Steve out loud. "I smell crispy critter."

There were muffled grunts of grim laughter from others in the room. She struggled between her own impulses to share in the humor and continue with the briefing. She began to resent the foreman and his wisecracks that were ruining her focus. She managed to clamp down enough to show the slimmest of smiles, and continued. "When we found those keys, Karl and I spent the rest of the day searching for other human remains like teeth, bones, or metal accessories. We found nothing. If they had been ash, then the hose pressure and the two days of rain would have washed it away. If they had been...destroyed by the explosion, their remains were so dispersed that finding any piece of them might be a lost cause." Faith felt bad saying this. She felt she had failed on this point. Her father had told her they had even been able to find human remains at Ground Zero after that fire and explosion. Still, she recalled, many of the 9/11 victims had been crushed by falling skyscrapers, not blown to bits or vaporized by the plane.

"So from the presence of the truck, and the keys in the ignition, you conclude there were more people present than 'Rosie Doe' at the scene, and those people are unaccounted for."

"That's it in a nutshell."

"But if it was a lightning event as you say, it could be impossible to ever prove they were there."

"Maybe so, sir, but I'd like to give the investigation more time. To do it I'll need two weeks to do a more careful investigation of the scene and send out information to experts and wait for their reply. And it might involve some expensive tests."

Marcus put a hand to his chin. "I'm sold. We'll keep this case open for another two weeks. Do the best you can with available resources. If you need tests which cost more than five hundred dollars, get approval from Major Tomlan. If the total will be more than two thousand, come to me for the thumbs up or thumbs down."

The rest of the audience nodded as though this was reasonable, except Dwight, who frowned. "C'mon, Chief, bump up her budget. Two thousand dollars isn't enough for three DNA samples anymore," he grumbled.

Faith was grateful to the captain for saying this. Her initial elation at having the chief approve her two weeks extension had evaporated when she thought about how little she could do with two thousand dollars. Instead, she felt trapped by Marcus's decision. She now had plenty of time to investigate the fire scene again, but not a lot of resources with which to analyze what she found. She felt sure with such a small budget she'd have nothing to show for her two weeks, because she wouldn't be able to arrive at much more certainty about what had happened with two thousand dollars in lab tests.

Marcus rebutted the man's complaint. "I'm not saying she can't have more, Captain. It's true I'm counting all this department's pennies, but because I'm counting them doesn't mean I won't share them. With luck, in two weeks Jorge can work something out with Cayuga Heights or the county so we can share the costs of this investigation. But think about it from my position. Do you want the Common Council in our business asking why we're spending ten grand on lab tests for Cayuga Heights's fire?"

"I gotcha, Chief, all I'm saying is two grand won't buy her much."

"Do you know anyone in Cayuga Heights you can call?" Marcus shot back at him. "If so, make the call. If they agree to share, her budget will go up."

Captain Earling rubbed his chin. "I do know some people. I'll make some calls, explain the situation, try and nudge people."

Chief Bauer beamed. "There. We succeed when we pull together."

"Amen," added Steve loudly. "Solidarity for everyone!" Marcia and Jorge drew simultaneous sighs at this.

Something in Faith's head clicked, and she felt she had to speak up. "Can you butt out of my briefing? First the jokes, and now you return everyone to the union issue? I'm trying to get a decision here."

The man protested. "What union issue? I'm agreeing with the Chief. Solidarity is what we need in this department."

Marcus raised his hands, palms forward. Both the union representative and Faith froze mid-breath, and she now felt embarrassed that she, too, had spoken out of turn.

"Yes. Solidarity is what we need. Let's remember solidarity does not mean agreement, it means the willingness to care for one another and work together. We will disagree. Is everyone still willing to care and to work together?"

They relented and nodded.

"Okay now, Faith has a point. You wouldn't want her cutting in on your union briefs with fire prevention issues," the chief said.

"But I didn't-" the foreman protested.

Pierce Tomlan cut across him. "McCallister, shut it. We heard your jab and it's out of line. Now respect Haversham's hard work, stay in your lane, and quit editorializing during decision briefs or you'll become unwelcome." Pierce's eyes were ablaze with irritation, and the foreman shrank away in response.

"Got it. Sorry, sir," the foreman said.

Pierce spent another second or two scowling, and then collected his temper. "We have your decision, Chief," he confirmed. "Two weeks, expenses up to two grand with my approval, beyond that with yours. Anything further?"

The chief shook his head. "That's all. Thanks for putting us back on track, Pierce."

"All in a day's work. If you have nothing else-" the deputy replied.

"The meeting is called," answered Chief Bauer. He got up, folded and stowed his eyeglasses, and gathered his notebook and cell phone to leave. Jorge and Marcia crowded to him, stepping in front of Captain Earling. The man rolled his eyes and sighed patiently.

Faith switched off the projector, saved her briefing and closed it, and began packing up her laptop. As she did so and the room emptied, Steve approached her.

"Sorry. The Major was right. I let my own issue get control of me, so I was disrupting your briefing."

She grumbled at her computer rather than at him. "I get it. It sucks what's happening to those divers. And I'm glad someone's looking out for them. But I'm trying to do my own job, too."

"Yeah. Sorry," Steve said. Faith waited for him to say something else or move on, and when he didn't, she took the end of the conversation into her own hands.

"I need to get back to work. I've got a lot to think about. There's a little girl waiting at home praying she'll see her mom and dad again and I've got two grand to get her there."

To her relief, the foreman didn't take this dismissal amiss. "No sweat, I'll get out of your brain. Catch you later."

"Thanks," she said to him, closing her notebook. She wondered what he had been going to ask, but only for a second. She put the thought out of her mind and made a quick scribble on her note pad as a question for her investigation jockeyed for dominance over her packing up her computer. She tried to write it down but lost the thread of it. She hoped that tonight, with a cup of coffee in the quiet of her own house, she would remember it.

Chapter 4

A Meeting of Minds

Dr. Teschke frowned at the Green Dragon. Akiko had suggested the oddly-named student cafe as a nearby place to meet Mr. Haversham which was out of the way and quiet, and it was. Its dark reaches held only a handful of students, who acted surprised and fearful to find a professor and her entourage in their midst. One by one, they left or shifted away so as to become invisible in the corners of this cellar.

Restaurants and cafes in cellars were commonplace in German cities where space was at a premium. But those cellar establishments had atmosphere, décor tested by time, traditional menus updated with nouveau cuisine, and wine and beer. This "Green Dragon," in contrast, struck Hildegard as just a cellar art students had dressed up and supplied with a hot dog grill and microwave. The walls were thick with cracking spackle painted green and scrawled with either dragons or odd Escher-esque geometric shapes. The chairs were old cable spools not at the right height for anyone to sit on, and the tables merely large pieces of lacquered slate balanced on even larger cable spools at a height not right for sitting at. The light was an inadequate, yet harsh, fluorescent, filtered through a screen of various sizes of tin food cans which had been tacked together, wall to wall, to form a kind of drop ceiling.

All in all, the place gave the impression of having been created thirty years before by a class of art students using trash from the university cafeterias and a lot of paint. She wondered if anyone, heaven forbid, had gotten an "A" in a class for creating the space. The food available was as unappealing, which was inexplicable since Cornell had a 'hospitality school' which taught fine cooking. Hildegard made it a point never to eat a "hot dog" or the other sausage-like meat substitutes offered in American fast-food joints, and she wouldn't start at the "Green Dragon." The microwaves in the cafe were overworked, and even the tea she had ordered had been microwaved, rather than properly steeped in boiling water.

Whatever her own misgivings, her assistants were at home in the cafe. Selene and Akiko chatted as they watched people come and go. Shawn sprawled on the other side of the table, somehow managing to take up as much space as three normal people by dangling limbs on or over adjacent furnishings like a dreadlocked climbing ivy.

It occurred to her that she was the only person in the group who knew who they were looking for, and she would recognize only the girl. So she wiped the critique she would write of the cafe for a gourmet magazine from her mind, composed a greeting and some introductions of her staff in her thoughts, and sipped her unappealing black tea.

She recognized Rosie as the girl entered, hand in hand with an older man. The man carried a folder and seemed stern. When Hildegard waved, the girl returned it energetically, tugged the man's hand, and pointed to their table. The pair started toward them.

Dr. Teschke then glowered at Shawn such that he retracted into a seated position on one cable spool, and glanced to the man to motion him to the liberated chairs.

Mr. Haversham was anything but a frail old man. He had broad shoulders, a square jaw, a fine full head of gray hair, and handsome features. She felt her expectations rise as she did.

"Mr. Haversham, I presume?" She asked, and stepped forward to shake his hand.

"That's me," he nodded back, dropping the folder on the tabletop and returning a firm handshake with his huge hand. "Professor Teschke?"

She detected the change from "Ms. Teschke" on the phone to "Professor Teschke" in person. It was progress. If he was educable, maybe he would even leave referring to her as "Dr. Teschke."

She pushed the vanity out of her head. *"Listen to yourself. He's the first piece of like-aged attractive manhood to pass in front of you for some time, and you're standing on your titles with him like he was nineteen years old."*

"Hildegard, please. Call me Hildegard," she demurred.

"David," Mr. Haversham replied with his name and a smile.

She motioned. "These are my assistants, Akiko, Selene, and Shawn."

Akiko and Selene both exchanged handshakes with the older man. Shawn, however, had begun relaxing and sprawling again, and didn't stand, acknowledging Mr. Haversham with a simple "yo," and a wave. Dr. Teschke stared in a way she hoped he would notice, but hesitated to correct him in front of their guests since the boy would be central to the rest of the discussion.

David took his seat, as did Rosie, gingerly as she had the day before in the professor's own office. The man looked amused by the cafe, and Hildegard was not sure he was prepared to take her seriously. "I apologize for the setting," she said, motioning to the basement cafe, "but your daughter mentioned that we should try to be discreet. While there are students here, there would be more in my department offices at the moment."

"I appreciate it," he said. "And any information you could give us about where Rosie came from and what she saw at the fire could be as important as any discretion. So I don't much care how fancy this place is or isn't."

Emboldened by his cooperativeness, she took a sip of her tea and came to her point. "Based on the samples of her writing I was able to gather yesterday, Shawn has determined Rosetta speaks an obscure language called Esperanto, or a dialect of this language. Esperanto is so rare we have not yet found any fluent speakers on this campus. Most of the speakers of Esperanto died in Soviet gulags in the 1950s and 1960s, and those that lived in the United States hid during the McCarthy era and never re-emerged."

The man mused. "Why would the Soviets and Senator McCarthy dislike the same language?"

Hildegard studied David, looking for some sign in his features of how much of a critical thinker he might be. The question itself betrayed some critical thinking, but most Americans, she had discovered, remained ignorant of the history of the Soviet Union and its internal struggles. They acted as though the Soviet Union had been a monolithic and unified enemy of the United States from the moment it was created. If you questioned them, they were usually unaware Stalin had killed nine million of the Soviet Union's own citizens to consolidate power, many of them those who were too "communist" for the communist leader's taste. She decided to present the matter neutrally.

"Esperanto is not a natural language. It was created in the 1800s to serve as an auxiliary or trade language, like Swahili or the native American's sign language. It was popular with fundamental communists who believed in the unity of all mankind. Hence it was disliked both by the Stalinist regimes of Russia and

52

those who feared communism in this country. Its use all but died out in the 1960s.

"How a girl comes to speak this language as her mother tongue is of some interest to us. So is *how* she speaks it, since there are precious few documented examples of children who speak an artificial language as their mother tongue."

David took all this in. He watched the child, who was smiling and watching the people at the table alertly. He evinced no political opinion on communism, and raised no questions about the history of Esperanto. He focused on the practical matter. "So if you can't speak this language, and no one else on this campus can, what can you even do for her?" he challenged.

Dr. Teschke felt as if this man was implying she was out her depth. She schooled her features to eliminate any sign she might have noticed. "Esperanto is a simple language. It was created to be easy to learn and to share root words with many European languages. My assistant Shawn has already begun studying it," she said, nodding to the young man. "Likewise, my assistant Selene is a certified childrens' speech pathologist. By cooperating, I think we can begin to do some basic translation to help your daughter and the city determine this girl's origins and re-unite her with her family."

The man sized up Shawn, as if judging the credibility of Hildegard's claims by the boy's appearance. But rather than lounge there looking indolent and shabby, Mr. Douglas chose then to speak and sound credible. "There's a bunch of Esperanto dictionaries and grammars on the internet. There are also two networks of Esperanto speakers who are willing to answer my questions. I've already started to compose some questions to ask her if I get the chance," he said. "It shouldn't be too hard."

At this, Rosetta smiled ear to ear, clapped her hands together, and beamed at Shawn. Everyone at the table focused on her.

"Did she understand him, or was that a behavioral outburst?" she wondered.

"I guess she voted 'yes' to your plan," explained David.

This turn of phrase puzzled the professor. "The more important question is whether you vote 'yes' to our plan."

"Sure," he said with a shrug. "We have next to no information about her. So it can't hurt."

Hildegard was pleased. "*You see,*" she thought to herself, "*You should have more confidence in your credibility with laypeople.*"

"*Prima!*" she enthused out loud. All of her assistants suppressed grins at this. She felt self-conscious again, *prima* was one of her Germanisms which came back to haunt her English. She wouldn't change it, even if they found it amusing. If she did, they would find something else amusing about her to giggle at, and she would be more self-conscious than before.

Her assistants' amusement had slipped by David unnoticed. He was more concerned with the girl, who was still smiling and looked ready to jump out of her seat. "How will this work?" he asked. "Do you need me present? Or do you need me to drop her off with you for a while?"

Hildegard shrugged "You could stay if you have interest, but I think my assistants could carry on alone. Selene was a special education teacher in California, so while all of them are responsible, she has ample experience with children."

David assented. "I could use some free time. My daughter sort of dropped this girl in my lap yesterday after the childrens' services officer said she couldn't stay at the firehouse any longer."

"Then when would you like to return for her? An hour? And hour and a half?" she prompted the man.

53

"One and a half would be about enough. Where should I meet you to pick her up?"

"Here is as good a place as any. Is this acceptable?"

"Okay, right here," the man confirmed. He then slid the folder he had been carrying across the table toward them. "These are the forms Children and Family Services was hoping we could complete to help them begin a search for her parents and a formal foster care proceeding. If you guys can answer enough questions to fill them out, that would be great."

To Dr. Teschke's great pleasure, Shawn leaned forward, took the folder, and said, "I'll get on it."

The man rose. "So, back here, then, at about five o'clock?"

"Done," Hildegard said, rising and extending her hand again. "I hope we can help."

They shook hands again, and David explained the situation to Rosie, who had stood when he did. "I don't know how much you understand, sweetie, but I'll leave you with these nice people for a while. I'll come back here to meet you in a couple of hours. Try and answer their questions." The girl's expression did not change at all while he spoke, suggesting that she did not understand. The man pointed to Shawn. "He may be able to read your language. Esperanto."

"*Esperanto,*" Rosetta echoed in reply, looking at Shawn.

When the older man took a careful step back, the child evinced no anxiety. When he took a couple of more steps back, Selene stepped forward and offered her hand. "Rosie, would you like to go for a walk with us?"

With no hesitation, the girl took the woman's hand and smiled up at her. She then waved to David.

"I guess I'm free to go," the man decided. "See you in a couple of hours, Doctor."

"Until later," Hildegard replied. David left the way he came, stepping aside to let a gaggle of scruffy students through before exiting.

She smiled contentedly after the man's departure. He had called her "Doctor." Life contained some surprising pleasures.

The professor inspected her assistants. Selene still held the girl's hand, Shawn still held the folder containing the paperwork, and Akiko wore her focused expression. Everything was in order.

She checked her watch. "The office should be empty after the 3:40 class," she reminded her assistants. "As it is, I'm meeting Dr. Kramer in a few minutes. I'll meet you back here in ninety minutes. Be sure you're on time. I don't want to give Mr. Haversham a bad taste."

Ms. Nakamura bowed slightly, and Hildegard returned it. It was all she needed to see to be sure the process was in good hands. With some relief, she walked to the green-painted doors of the cafe and pushed her way out. With luck, her assistants would make something of this opportunity she was cultivating for them. But she would not do their jobs for them. Time swept by.

Shawn was dismayed by how crowded the linguistics department main office was. Professor Vilsap, a visiting scholar whose office also adjoined the graduate assistants' office, was holding office hours, and students of his were waiting in many of the available chairs (including his own) and the office was positively a-chatter. To make matters worse, Rosie grew bewildered by the crowd, staring wide-eyed around the room.

"I don't think this is a good spot now," he said to Akiko. She nodded in agreement and looked to Selene.

"The language lab?" the older woman suggested. The language lab was filled with desks equipped with recorders and microphones, and was often empty.

"I still need a computer to type with and look things up," explained Shawn. "I haven't got the hang of Esperanto yet, and all the vocabulary and grammar stuff I can find is on the internet."

Akiko looked at him crossly. "Download it to a thumb drive tonight. You will need it, and it will be good if it is portable." Her tone suggested this was too elementary for her to need to explain it.

"Dammit, bitch, I'm never good enough for you, am I? I would have to work with no less than two omnipotent perfectionists." Shawn thought. "Great idea, thanks," he answered, "but what about now? I think the student computer labs will be as crazy as working here."

Selene piped up, "Is the professor back yet? We could use her computer."

Shawn glanced toward her office. The door was closed, and the light was off, suggesting she was still away. "Hey, yeah," he said, and started to move in the direction of Dr. Teschke's office, but froze when he got Akiko's frosty look. He grinned and shrugged at her. Her face was placid again, but her voice projected a certain edge as she raised it to the throng of undergraduate students.

"Attention," the senior assistant commanded of the room. The babble of voices subsided. "If you are here to see Professor Vilsap, you will wait in the hallway until the student who was visiting before you has left."

"But there is nowhere to sit in the hallway," someone complained.

"This is unfortunate. You are free to bring your complaints to Dr. Teschke or the ombudsman if you like. However, you will move to the hallway. Now."

With much grumbling and muttering, the sullen knot of students retreated into the hallway. Most of them had encountered Akiko before, and those who hadn't got the message that resistance was useless from the quick obedience of their peers. In a few seconds, the office was quiet and peaceful.

"Thank you," Dr. Vilsap spoke up from his office, "I'm sorry I let it get out of hand."

"My pleasure, Professor," the woman reassured the invisible professor, her face manifesting no pleasure whatsoever. She shut the professor's office door, wheeled to face Shawn, and pointed at his desk with a thrust of the finger.

"Right. I'll, uh, get to work," he said. "Thanks." He gave Rosie a grin and a tug and walked toward his desk. He pulled out an old metal and vinyl stool from a side table and offered it to her, and then sat down. The first document in the folder the foster parent had left with them was titled "Emergency Foster Care Child Information Reference Sheet." "Sheet" was a technical misnomer, he noted, since the "sheet" had three double-sided pages. He scanned the long list of blanks on the form and put a hand to his brow. His hours-old expertise in Esperanto was about to be tested.

He glanced up to see Akiko and Selene step out into the hallway themselves. "Hey!" he protested. "Don't I get any help here?" He guessed not, as the door closed without a reply, and left him and Rosie in the graduate student office. The girl looked up at him expectantly.

After a moment, he pulled out his digital voice recorder and plugged it into his computer. Akiko used one regularly, and he had set up a number of them both for her and for Dr. Teschke, but this was the first time he would use his own for an academic purpose.

"Alright, cutie, you may or may not understand me, but I'm going to record what we say so I can check later to be sure I've understood you. Or maybe if we find a real Esperanto speaker, he or she can check my work." By way of reply,

Rosie tapped her feet on the desk leg, shaking the desktop. He wondered if she would do that all through the interview. *"Boy, I'd forgotten what an imposition it is to expect a kid to sit still."*

"Last name of child" the form demanded. A simple question if this was any normal situation. He hoped this part would be close to normal. A few clicks brought up an Esperanto dictionary he had found on the internet and Google's translating window. He identified what he hoped were the correct question words and vocabulary. Using a word processor, he typed the sentence he would read out first, checked it with Google translate, and then rehearsed it in his head.

He narrated to begin the recording. "Okay, the interview subject is a girl named 'Rosetta,' who speaks Esperanto or a dialect of Esperanto. I'm guessing Rosetta is between eight and twelve years old. The purpose of the interview is to learn enough about Rosetta that I can do her emergency foster care paperwork. My first question, based on the form, is 'What is your last name?'"

He composed his translation of the question, sounded it out in his mind, and then asked Rosie *"What is your family name?"* in what he hoped was intelligible Esperanto. She beamed at the sound the language and said something unintelligible in an excited reply. From the tone, he guessed it was a question. Rather than play back the recording and try to translate it, he decided to practice Esperanto as a living language and tried to repair the conversation. He looked at another file, a page of key Esperanto phrases, and asked:

"Could you please say that again?"

At this, the girl looked less pleased, but repeated her reply. Again, all Shawn could tell was she was asking a question, and which contained the word *"name."* He felt foolish but had to repeat his request. *"Could you please say that again?"*

At this, Rosie looked downcast. After a moment of looking around the room, she walked over to the office printer and took a piece of paper from the paper tray. She then returned to his desk and took a pink highlighter from his pen cup. She wrote a reply in the same strange alphabet Shawn had first seen that morning.

He took the piece of paper and sounded out the individual letters. He then typed out the message as he pieced the sounds together, and looked up words. Rosie sat, doodling with the highlighter, while he cobbled together what she had said.

When Shawn unraveled her reply, he felt his blood pressure go up. *"Must everyone have a family name?"* was her question. It was a good question. Did everyone in the world have a last name? He supposed everyone in the U.S. did. Even immigrants would have to have a family name they gave for a green card.

"Yes," he answered while pointing to her question on the page.

She pursed her lips, took the paper from him, and began writing again.

If they kept talking this way, he fretted that not much of this conversation would be available on the voice recorder. Maybe as he got better at Esperanto, she would speak more and write less. When she was done, she pushed the paper back at him.

He translated. *"What is a good name to have?"* He scratched his head. He was supposed to be the one with the questions. He decided to change tack, and ask the questions a different way.

"What name did your mother and father give you?" he questioned her back. She read this and smiled wide and happily. While Rosie was not a pretty girl, the smile was charming.

She wrote back *"My mother and father are God. They know my name without saying it."*

"Okay, so, not only does this kid have a weird language, she's got too much religion," he said aloud. The girl raised an eyebrow at him. Belatedly Shawn remembered his remark had been recorded. He doubted such a candid remark would be regarded as "scholarly" by future listeners. He contemplated turning the recorder off and pretending he hadn't recorded any part of the conversation, but the scornful look this would get him from Akiko made him decide to lump his mistake and continue. *"Got to get a hang of this recording thing."* He composed his answer.

"What are your parents' names?" he essayed aloud after a moment.

She wrote out a one-word answer: *"Amata."* He did a word-search in the online Esperanto dictionary, and while there were words which began with Amat-, nothing came back for *Amata*. It was a name, then.

"Finally!" he thought. To be sure, he decided to confirm he had understood her. *"Your parents are both called 'Amata?'"*

She nodded and wrote again. Her answer made Shawn sure he finally had his answer. *"Everyone who knows them calls them that."*

"So your name is Rosetta Amata?" he confirmed excitedly.

"You can call me this if you love me," she answered with careful pink highlighter strokes. *"God calls me this, too."*

He walked over and made a quick photocopy of the front page of the "Emergency Foster Care Child Information Reference Sheet." On the copy, in the block beside "Child's Last Name," he wrote "Amata." Next to first name, he wrote "Rosetta."

While he worked, Rosetta doodled a geometric pattern around the edge of her sheet of paper. Occasional breaks in this pattern featured a flower or an animal. Her drawing was good and regular. It was better than Shawn could do, and he'd had many art classes. He turned back to the form copy. The next line was "Address of Parental Home."

To his surprise, Rosetta began writing again. When she finished, she passed him the page, and he translated again.

"I am thirsty for wine."

Shawn laughed and searched through the dictionary. He answered *"I can't give you wine. But we have water in the hallway. We can pretend it is wine if you want."*

"If we pretend it is wine, we will be right." She got down from the stool, and he followed her out of the office and into the hallway.

Outside the door, two or three undergraduate students were sitting on the floor focused on their textbooks. Further down the hall, not far from the water fountain, were Selene and Akiko. They both looked up at the sound of the office door closing.

"Having any luck?" asked Selene as they approached.

"I think I have her last name. That's it so far," he admitted.

Akiko glanced at her watch. "That is not much for twenty-five minutes."

Shawn felt his ears heat up, but decided not to rise to the teasing. He motioned for the two others to step down the hall with him, and then bent his head to speak to them in hushed tones.

"It's somewhere between a question and answer session and a philosophical duel with a Zen master in a language I knew nothing about until this morning. So I feel good about getting a last name in twenty-five minutes." He decided to put some of the responsibility back on the two women. "Do you want to take a turn? I could use the help."

"You're right, we should be helping you," said Selene. Both the women looked down at Rosie, who had walked past the water fountain to study a poster of language family groupings despite her complaint of thirst.

"So, are you taking her out for a walk?" Akiko scolded, with a "stop monkeying and get back to work" tone.

"She said she was thirsty, so I'm taking her for a drink. This isn't like Abu Ghraib here, she's not my prisoner," he said, putting a hand to Rosie's back and guiding her to the water fountain. The girl seem bemused when confronted with the fountain, pushed the button, and began drinking. Shawn stepped away and bent his head again.

"She wanted wine to drink. And she talks about God like every other sentence. Call it a hunch, but I have the feeling her family may have been a bit, you know...religious nutty." The women gaped at his assertion.

"That could explain a lot," said Selene after a moment. "She may be under-socialized."

"Even if she's home-schooled...who gives their kids wine?" Shawn rebutted.

Akiko spoke up. "It's not uncommon in Japan for children to get a taste of rice wine with dinner. Maybe her culture is different than the American mainstream," she observed.

"Yeah, that's for sure. I had to explain what the term 'family name' or 'last name' meant. Her culture is either totally different, or she didn't get out at all."

"I'll come help you," Selene decided, looking at Akiko. The senior assistant made an expression of relenting as well. Rosie finished slurping at the fountain and looked up at Shawn, and the four of them headed back to the office.

"What's the next question?" said Akiko.

"Parental home address. I have the feeling it will be tougher than it sounds," he muttered.

Karl rose as the clock struck five-thirty. He stood and took his uniform jacket from the coat hook, and turned to Faith over his shoulder as he pulled it on.

"Working late again?"

She didn't want to say yes, she discovered, though it was obvious Karl had the situation figured out. "Not too late. I'm checking up on some emails and looking up a couple of things."

"Uh-huh," replied Karl. "Don't work too hard. I don't want the chief asking if he needs two fire prevention officers."

She saw his worry coming. "I'm doing fire inspector stuff. If anything, my work on this project makes it plain to the chief that he needs you so we can keep up with inspections, alarms, and hydrant calls when I do investigations."

Karl was less certain. "Remember, my family eats from this job." But he stopped as the office door opened.

Faith did not turn around, confident Karl could handle a visitor even at closing. But she flinched as Karl said, "Hey, Steve. What brings you to our closet in the HQ?"

"Great," she thought. McCallister was the person most capable of intruding into her thoughts and stopping her work momentum. She tried to focus through the interruption, but the man's presence seemed to freeze her thoughts in their tracks.

"What do you want?" she asked the visitor. "I'm working here."

The foreman showed no discomfort. "Yeah, that's why I'm here. You're both here after hours, and this union rep is curious why. But first I wanted to chat with Mr. Rand. Were you done for the day?"

"Maybe..." said Karl, casting Faith a sidelong glance.

"Yeah, you can go. Don't worry, I can handle him."

"How's the back, by the way?" Steve inquired.

"Cranky. But my supply of happy drugs is steady, so I deal with it," the older man explained doggedly.

The foreman latched on to this. "Don't encounter any miracle cures or re-injure yourself in the next few months. I was reviewing the accreditation standards, and there's a lot of stuff in the personnel standards no external organization has any business dictating to a unionized agency. When the accreditation inspectors come, they're be all over you to determine that you're not underutilized in this position vis a vis your disability. But if you are too disabled, they'll demand that you be severed because your capacity doesn't 'warrant your retention.' You're walking a tight rope now, follow?"

Karl blinked. "Yeah, I follow."

"I'll let you know if I get more details. But I was talking with my buddies in the Binghamton Fire Department and they said two injured guys lost their payroll spots over those standards because management reneged on their labor agreement so as to make accreditation. So you and me, we have to play it tight until accreditation is over. We need to walk that tightrope so our Chief isn't put in the position of having to let you go or put you back on the line and break you for good."

"Okay. Thanks for looking out for me."

"All part of my job as union rep. Don't thank me now, vote for me next time around," Steve smiled. He shook Karl's hand.

"Sure thing." Inspector Rand gave Faith one last glance, as if to be sure he could leave. She nodded to him again.

"Thanks for picking up my slack on the inspections. You're a champ and I'll tell any accreditation inspectors that," she said, trying to soothe some of the worry the foreman had put there.

"Yeah. See you tomorrow."

"See you tomorrow. Say hello to Isabelle for me."

"Right." Karl left with an uncertain look on his face. She guessed his evening would contain some anxiety, thanks to Steve's announcement. There was no help for it. The foreman's bedside manner stunk but he was looking out for Karl.

Faith waited a few moments after the door closed behind her co-worker. "So..." she said, without looking up from her monitor. She could always harbor the hope that if she didn't look at him Steve might disappear.

"I can't help but notice," McCallister said, "every time I've passed the HQ at night since the carriage house fire there are two cars still here. Yours, and the chief's."

"Yep."

"Now, I know enough about our chief and his lifestyle that I can rule out the most obvious explanation. So I guess you're here because you're working too hard. But such dedication is hardly, you know, healthy. It's not as though you're management."

"Spare me the 'you raise management's expectations of everyone when you do unpaid overtime' speech. I'm trying to catch a firebug."

"No speeches. If you want to do every other working firefighter and their families wrong so you can satisfy your conscience over an investigation that's not even in our jurisdiction, suit yourself."

"That sounded like a speech," Faith rebutted.

"It was a sentence. Speeches contain more than one sentence," Steve countered. He crossed over to Karl's desk, pulled out the man's special back-support chair, sat in it backwards, and rolled it to a spot where he could face her. She wished for a moment Karl and she had agreed to have their office cubicled, but working face to face with Karl was so natural that they hadn't. And so now the foreman would roll about in her field of vision until he had her attention. Faith took a cleansing breath and looked up from her monitor.

"So if you're not giving speeches, what will you do? Are you and Rocco from the station house coming to break my legs so I stop working?"

He shook his head. "This isn't the 1920s. I'll save the leg breaking for when they sic the Pinkertons on us. As a modern union rep, I have a more creative and compassionate solution."

"Maybe you will help me with the investigation so I get home on time?" She raised an eyebrow hopefully.

"Nope. I will help you with your down time. Give you some incentive not to work."

She knuckled down to hear the man out. She was sure this would be painful. If he suggested she take up the needlepoint she used to do as a girl or something like that, she would do her own leg breaking.

But instead of making inane or snide suggestions, Steve reached into his jacket pocket and pulled out two emerald green tickets. "I have in my hand two tickets to see 'Wicked' in Syracuse on Friday, acquired today. I was wondering if you had plans and if you'd maybe, you know, like to see a play."

"Well, color me stupid that I didn't see this coming," she thought. "Me?"

"Is there another Faith in this room?" the man fretted, looking around. "If so I'd better break her legs while the rest of us still have jobs. Yes, you. Did I stutter?"

By now she had collected her thoughts. She disliked McCallister's downstate brashness. The man's shit-eating grin and casual lounging in Karl's chair set her teeth on edge. But it had been months, no, more than a year since she'd had a spontaneous offer for a date. She didn't count the online service dates because they had all sucked. And a public date with him could help her establish some useful cover, as well as give her a chance to ensure he never approached her again. She composed her answer.

"Huh. You have a reputation. And I'm not sure I'm a girl who wants to be associated with your reputation. But your offer is tempting."

"It doesn't have to be a date. It could be social," said Steve.

"Do you have a romantic interest in me?" she checked. "I mean, I know you did back in the day, but that was almost twenty years ago."

The man didn't look happy to talk about this, but wasn't afraid either. "Is it a problem if I do?"

Faith considered how to respond. She decided to keep her secrets her own and answer his question.

"I'll tell you now you won't get anywhere with romance. If you're okay with that, then it's not a problem."

His response kept the discussion light. "I don't think any man likes to hear that he's uninteresting, but, I have these tickets, and I'd like your company, so if you can grit your teeth enough to stand me, you're welcome to come along."

Faith thought on it. "I'll be plain. I don't have many prospects. I don't even have much experience in the dating scene, so I could use a practice date. I'll use your generosity and candor as an opportunity to help me learn how to date people I am interested in. Can you live with that?"

"Sure," said Steve. "Sounds good. I'll take the opportunity to practice, too."

"Alright then," she said. "How are we getting there?"

"Let's take my truck. I'll drive. I'll pick you up at seven tomorrow. So be sure to go home on time!" He winked at her. She grimaced.

"I'll rush home!" she said with mock enthusiasm.

"That's all a man can ask for," the man replied with a smile. "And never let it be said this union rep does not do his best to find win-win solutions."

Chapter 5

Missing Persons

David sat down heavily on his breakfast bench. Faith had called to say she was on her way home from work, and he had supper waiting on the table for her. Rosie sat opposite him at the foot of the table, intent on her drawings on sheet after sheet of paper. He watched her for a long moment, his attention drifting as he followed the waggling point of the mechanical pencil she was using.

He was bone tired, he realized. Carting the girl around to shop for clothes had been followed by her visit to Cornell, during which he had gone to the hardware and garden stores and brought home many supplies for the summer. Then he had gone back up to the university, picked her up again, started the laundry to include all her new clothes, and then made dinner. It was more than he had become accustomed to doing in a day, retired as he was, and now he was ready to rest and maybe even watch some TV.

Relief came when he heard Faith's keys in the front door. Rosie looked up from her drawing. "Welcome home," he said when he heard his daughter's own deep breath of relaxation.

"Thanks Pop! Ooh that smells good," she said. "I'll be back in a flash."

The girl's eyes followed her, and he could tell from their angle and the sounds behind him his daughter had hurried upstairs to change.

"Are you ready for supper?" he asked the child so as to keep her from feeling left out. Rosie glanced up at him, but said nothing. So he let silence settle on the room until his daughter came back downstairs in a pair of jeans and, judging by her smell, the same t-shirt she had been wearing under her uniform. He made no comment but closed his eyes, said a silent grace since he knew Faith would not want to share it and the girl wouldn't understand it, and began serving up the farfalle with poppy seeds and broccoli.

He held his questions until his daughter's eating had slowed and she began to relax.

"How did your briefing go, honey?"

She frowned at the question, and David regretted having disrupted her rest. "Mixed. But the chief gave me two weeks and two grand to investigate."

At this, David furrowed his brow. "Two weeks is a fair bit of time. But two thousand dollars isn't a lot to fund an investigation. It's not much at all."

To his surprise, Faith contradicted him. "Money's tight, Dad, like I don't-know-how tight. And this investigation isn't under our jurisdiction. We're only doing it under a mutual assistance agreement which says City of Ithaca will perform complex fire investigations for the Village of Cayuga Heights in return for the Heights performing some pest control duties in Ithaca. Two grand is all Ithaca can spare for a Cayuga Heights problem. If there will be more money for my investigation, it's got to come from Cayuga Heights, and that's that."

"That'll never happen. The Heights has been in the red for over five years," he reflected.

"You're right. So if I break this case in two weeks and find Rosie's family, the break will come from my elbow grease and shoe leather, not from expensive tests, because I can't afford them."

"If you can't do it, it can't be done," said David.

She paused, her hand on her fork. "Thanks for the vote of confidence, Pop."

"Remember you said that the next time I tell you you're screwing up," he chuckled as he raised another forkful of pasta.

Faith shook her head and opened her mouth to reply, but then reached back into her jeans pocket as he heard the buzz of her cell phone. "Oh sh-, I mean, sugar, I forgot-" she began after she checked the screen. Her eyes widened in a plea to her father. "I have to, uh, go back to work."

He saw the quiet, Rosie-free evening he had been looking forward to slipping away.

"What? Why?"

"I forgot I had a meeting."

"A meeting? After seven-thirty at night?"

"It's...it's with one of the night shift guys. Will Lamarsh, the recent hire from Cornell Life Safety. He had some ideas for me. I promised I'd check in with him after his shift started."

David felt his eyebrow go up in skepticism. "Then why not make a phone call?" he began to say, but then he stopped. If his daughter, now in her mid-30's, was making plans to meet eligible university-educated men after hours, did he want to stand in her way? Didn't he want grandchildren? So he banished his skepticism. He gave his daughter support so she would succeed at work, and he had to support her in this way, too, he decided.

"Alright. Go to your 'meeting,'" he said. "I'll keep our young charge busy. And we'll talk about what we learned at the university today after you get back."

His daughter flinched at this. "I hear you. It's been all about me since I got home. Sorry I didn't ask about your day."

"*Damludo!*" piped up Rosetta, pointing across the room. David's eyes followed from the empty plate along the girl's finger and across the room to the checker and chess barrel which stood in the corner.

"Look for me at the checker table when you come back," he instructed. "If I'm not sagging under the weight of my many defeats at Rosie's hands, I may be comatose from fatigue, but we'll see what we can do."

Faith laughed as she stood up. "You sure know how to make me feel good. You had me feeling confident for a minute, but now we're back to normal."

"What the Father giveth, the Father taketh away," David replied.

Faith left Buffalo Street at the bottom of the hill and parked her car on Tioga Street. She checked her watch as she got out, and was relieved to find she still had some time. She could have parked closer to the Unitarian Church, but she didn't want to be seen entering it and then have to answer the probing and disappointed questions she would get from her father.

Her meeting had nothing to do with the church, anyway. She had been to some Universalist services, and while they were less bigoted and orthodox than the Catholic services of her youth, they did nothing for her. In fact, she felt no communion with the divine in any church. But the Unitarians were one of the few churches in town which still gave shelter to her kind, and for this, she was grateful to them. However dull their services, she always left something in the donation box by the door.

She headed to the church's cellar entrance and paused at the door. "Ithaca GLBT Coming-Out Support Group – meeting room 2," read the photocopied sign taped there. She glanced around, saw that no one else was on the street, and darted through the glass door.

Once inside the church her anxieties faded. The gold wall-to-wall carpet had been freshly shampooed, and she could already hear the chatter of her fellow "innies" and "outties" echoing down the hall.

"Faith!" shouted an older, gray-haired woman from down the hall. The woman trotted to her in her heels and gave her a brisk hug, and then walked beside her. "We were hoping you were coming."

"Yeah, Retta, I'm here. I come every month. What's the big deal?"

"There's no big deal..." answered Retta facetiously as they passed through the prayer room doorway.

The crowd of fifteen people or so in the tiny room obscured her view. But as the people recognized her, they stood aside and revealed a large rainbow-frosted sheet cake with five large candles in it, some of them in phallic shapes and others made of a wax filled with metallic sparkles.

"Unless you count your five-years-in-the-closet party!" continued Retta, her voice rising into a shrill squeal of delight. "And other than missing a suntan, you look great!"

"Surprise!" shouted the rest of the people in the room.

Faith put a hand to her face in embarrassment and dismay, but these feelings soon vanished into the good cheer filling the room. She went and examined the cake, and had a moment of anxiety when she saw that the words "Faith Haversham is lesbian and loved!" had been frosted onto it.

For a second she had a horrifying vision of a baker in the local Wegman's grocery, sporting a look of concentration and a tongue clamped between teeth, delicately frosting the words "Faith Haversham...lesbian..."

"Omigod, guys, where did you buy this cake? Tell me you put my name on it."

"No, silly, I made it!" said an extravagantly dressed skirt-wearing older gentleman. "I work in catering! I frost names all the time, but boring stuff like 'best wishes, Joe and Jane Smith. You know, for breeders!" he admonished. "I'm happy to do it for you! I do all the ones for Maxie's Supper Club."

Her anxiety melted away. "Oh, thank you, Elmer. You guys gave me a heart attack for a second."

"We understand your position. Your father is a public figure. It's harder for you than the rest of us. We're not judging you or saying that you should be 'out' already. We're celebrating five years of your courage and trust in us." This last understanding voice came from Margrethe Peletow, an older, compact woman in a heather gray jacket, black slacks, and conservative tie.

Faith gave Margrethe a hug. The older woman had been one of her mother's close friends, and when Faith had first come to her GLBT coming out group and found her leading it, she had wanted to flee in abject embarrassment. But her mother's friend had been patient and non-threatening, and had not even let on that she recognized Faith until after the meeting.

"Thanks, everyone. Sorry I reacted that way. It's been a heck of a week at work, and I'm wound up tight. Let's have some cake," she apologized. "I think this is what I need."

Margrethe took up the cake knife, and the line for cake formed. Elmer was first in line, and held out his hands eagerly for the paper plate of cake, but woman refused him, teasing him with a slice of cake. "What are the magic words? You know the deal, Elmer, you've done a few of these things."

"Oh yes," said Elmer, then cleared his throat. "My name is Elmer Wiggins, and I am *gay* and *proud*!" he proclaimed. "I'm fabulous, too, and I have glitter dust to prove it. May I have my cake now?"

"There you go," said Margrethe, laughing. "Next?"

"My name is Retta Goldstein, and I am bisexual and *fearless!*" Retta roared to the applause of the room.

"My name is Peter Ljumovic, and I'm here to support everyone and remember my son Calvin. My son was a gay soldier, and I am *proud* of him!"

The line of people continued, each making their affirmations as they received their cake. When at last her own turn at the cake came, Faith appreciated the slice. It had orange and red stripes across it since it had been cut from the top of the pride flag, a flag she never saw flown anymore. She looked around before speaking. Butterflies filled her stomach, as they always did every time she said these words, but she clenched the cake knife and said them anyway.

"My name is Faith Haversham, and I am a lesbian, and *loved* by a cool crowd of people!"

After the applause had died, she went and took her seat in the circle of chairs in the center of the room. When the cake plates were all empty, Margrethe went and took the last empty seat.

"Let us pray together. Pray to God, or the green mother, or if you don't pray at all, then envision. Let us dream together, and make together, a world where no one lives in fear because of who they are, or who they love. This world is far from us today, and since the election, it's grown further away. But it will come, and come faster with every act of love we share with each other, our community, and ourselves."

Faith closed her eyes. She didn't believe in prayer, but the imagining of a world like the one Margrethe described made the hair on her arms stand up in happiness. And here, for two hours every month, she needn't feel shame or doubt about her dreams. The only thing that spoiled her happiness was the mental image of her father, sitting awake for her at the checker table, eyes drooping and tired.

Friday morning Faith came back to work early. She saw Karl out the door with the long list of fire and alarm inspections for the day, and then sat down to a couple of uninterrupted hours of work on the carriage house fire. Around 10 am, she heard her office door open. In walked a tall, balding black man, handsome but graying, with a serious look and a brown suit.

"Are you Inspector Haversham or Inspector Rand?"

"I'm Inspector Haversham," she said, glancing at her uniform shirt to be sure she'd worn her metal nameplate that day. She had, but didn't point it out. "Inspector Rand is out doing compliance inspections. Can I help you?"

"Ah, you're the one they wanted me to talk to," the man said. "I'm Detective Cassius McCrae, Syracuse Police. I am on the disappearance case for Mary Joe Rudolph, Randy Knight, and William Kopp. They sent me down to Ithaca Police with some evidence to return so I could drop in and talk to you.

She smiled, standing. "You could always email or call."

"I like to know who I'm working with. The report about the lightning was a little unusual, and before I bought into my boss's conclusions, I thought I'd like to meet you in person."

Faith raised an eyebrow. "So you can tell him whether I'm a crackpot or not?"

The detective grinned. "Remember, we have to live with the public when we close a case. Closing a case on three local people, all churchgoing folk with lots of friends, based on 'hit by lightning or something' could raise some eyebrows if the evidence wasn't rock solid. And your credibility matters in that determination."

"So, in other words, yes, crackpot check," said Faith. "That's fine. You're not the first one. Only, after what I've learned in the last couple of days, I'll sound even more like a crackpot."

Cassius came forward to shake her hand. "That's not how I'd say it. I'd say before we shut the book on William Kopp and consign him to history, I want to be comfortable with the reasoning used to determine he was hit by lightning."

"That makes sense," she said, standing and shaking his hand. "Wasn't my initial report enough? Did you see the picture of Kopp's truck at the fire scene I sent up in return for the missing persons data?"

"I heard you had his truck down here, which is more than we'd seen of him since a security video from a Hess station. What happened to it?"

"Before I start talking details, can I see your badge? You could also be a reporter or a private citizen, for all I know."

"It's a fair request. Here you go." He produced an ID and badge from his breast pocket, and she inspected them before continuing.

"Listen, rather than explain it all to you, do you mind if I set you up with a PowerPoint? It's the same brief I gave my chief, and I'll be right here to answer questions for you. But I've got to get our compliance inspection plan for the next quarter together before the end of the day so I can give all the affected landlords good notice."

Detective McCrae shook his head. "Oh, goodie. PowerPoint."

Faith opened the brief on her laptop. She guessed from his response that Ithaca Fire Department was not the only agency to overuse PowerPoint. "Here you go. Sing out if you have a question."

Cassius began flipping through her slides, and she returned to the draft schedule she'd been scribbling out in her notebook. The low-income housing units were due for a re-inspection, and she liked to knock them out first every time they came up because the buildings were so flimsy yet so packed with people. On the flip side, if she made the Collegetown student apartment landlords wait, they were the first to squawk to the chief, and while she knew Marcus would stand behind her, she didn't want him to have to. But to do both, she'd have to move a school inspection, and school inspections couldn't wait either. And there were the parks and recreation inspections which needed doing before the grilling and swimming seasons started.

She had a tight grip on her bangs with one hand, and the beginning of a breakthrough in her inspection log-jam in the other, when Cassius came up with his first question.

"You found a child at the scene?"

Faith shook her head and glanced at the brief. He had it open to the slide which showed Rosie. "Yeah, I mentioned that to Officer Mayes at your department like how many times hoping for a lead. All he could tell me was Kopp didn't have any children."

"That's not accurate. He had two sons, and three grandchildren so far. What Mayes was trying to say was that he had no daughters or granddaughters in this girl's age range."

"It's nice to have that clarification. How about Mary Joe Rudolph or Randy King?"

"Let me check," said Cassius, producing a small tablet PC and working through some notes.

"I wish my budget included tablet computers," thought Faith. In a moment, the man had her answer.

"No. Mary Joe Rudolph had no children, and Randy King's children live in

66

Wyoming with their mother and are all accounted for."

"That's more information than I've been able to get, thanks. Up until now I've only heard 'No children associated with any of the missing persons.'"

"But there was a girl child in the Hess gas station security videos."

"Yeah. I know. I figure that's her," she said, pointing to the picture. "Any evidence they were involved in, I don't know, child pornography? Maybe they were planning to make a movie with her."

"Nothing like that. No one we talked to had any idea who the girl was, and when we seized his computer, what we found wasn't kiddie porn." Cassius frowned.

Faith heard what he wasn't saying. "What did you find on his computer?"

The detective got a look of resolve. "This is why I need to talk to you about your lightning theory. If you can't prove to me it was lightning, I'll recommend this case be taken to the FBI."

"We're already working Rosie's identity through the FBI's kidnapping records and the Center for Missing and Exploited Children. No hits yet."

"Yeah, not for kidnapping. For domestic terrorism."

"What?"

"William Kopp was a true believer. A member of the Army of God, an emerging network of domestic Christian extremists. His computer had a lot of information on it from a couple of the more extreme websites. They believe, for example, that Satan and his representatives are behind the Democratic Party, the European Union, and stem cell science. He had information on his computer about bomb-making, and about incendiary devices, as well as a whole bunch of anti-gay, anti-Islamic, and anti-abortion materials. I'm glad this guy has met his end. If he hadn't, we might not have noticed him until something went up in smoke."

"He went up in smoke!" she exclaimed.

Cassius nodded. "Couldn't have happened to a nicer guy, too. Better him and this barn than a gay bar or a doctor's office."

"Abortion is illegal now," said Faith.

"Yeah, but that doesn't mean it isn't happening, and it doesn't making killing the doctors who do it okay," said Cassius. "Besides, it's not illegal to be gay, or Muslim. Not yet, anyway, and he had a lot of hate material, and some names and addresses, on those people."

"Woah." She reflected on this. Some of the hate crimes that were going on in southern cities made her shudder. She hated to think of the hate wave coming to New York.

"So you think he might have blown himself up?" she guessed.

"Yep. It fits."

"I don't think so," said Faith. "Not that he *blew* himself up. Evidence at the scene doesn't support explosions. It supports lightning, or something else hotter than the sun. Check it out." She flipped him through the slides to expose the large circle of concrete turned to glass. "That doesn't happen with ammonium nitrate. That's something else. Something a whole lot hotter."

"Thermite?" Cassius countered. "You can make thermite with iron filings and aluminum oxide. It will burn through steel, and we can't control access to the materials to make it."

"Yes, it will. But if it were thermite, parts of the concrete which were in contact with thermite would be wrecked, and parts which were even a short distance away would be unharmed, since concrete conducts heat poorly. But here a large area of concrete was affected. What it looks like is a wide-area flash burn to concrete."

"Maybe it was a lot of thermite," the detective persisted.

"A lot of thermite would have vaporized its way into the ground making a hole. And at the bottom of the hole I'd find residues. There's no hole, and no residue," countered Faith. "Parts of the concrete are more burnt, and parts less burnt, but the difference between them is not that great, and there's no sign that whatever burnt the concrete ever touched it."

Cassius raised an eyebrow at her. "You're passing my crackpot test thus far."

She still felt prickly from being challenged on the thermite. "I'm not saying I know what happened. I'm saying I know what didn't happen. And it wasn't thermite."

"Okay, so sell me on lightning."

"Read the rest of it. And then if you're convinced that it's lightning, I'll convince you that it's not lightning, and we can be confused together."

Detective McCrae shrugged and shook his head. "You university types sure know how to make things complicated."

She bristled again. "I am *not* a university firefighter. I'm not putting Life Safety down, they're a great bunch of guys and they know their hazmat techniques cold, but they don't work for the public or the public interest. They work for the reputation of Cornell and its liability issues. I don't even think private firefighters should be legal."

Cassius sobered. "I'm stepping on your toes all over the place, aren't I, Inspector? Bear with me, we're on the same team."

Faith sighed. "Sorry. I'm tense. I haven't slept a lot, I've drunk too much coffee, I've got a house full of a cranky orphan and a crankier father, and people keep challenging me on this report. I'm wondering why I went to school for fire science if everyone is going to disbelieve me when I do this work. I mean, the concrete is *right there*. Do your own damn site survey or send it away for petrographic analysis if you don't believe me."

"Okay, okay, I got it. I'll read on," said Cassius. He went back to flipping through the briefing, hemming and uh-huhing from moment to moment. Faith went back to her calendar and had her big break. She could justify postponing the school inspections until after the low-income housing since the schools would have fewer people in them over the summer quarter. And the student apartment inspections would have to wait, but she would have two time slots open to hit any landlords who complained early in the quarter.

Her grip on her bangs eased, and she closed her eyes and took deep breaths. When she opened her eyes again, she could see that the detective was on her conclusions slides.

"You sold me on lightning," he admitted. "The clincher was that satellite lightning map."

"It's not a satellite map per se," she said. "It mixes satellite data with ground based sensors. But yeah, it's convincing. Maybe too convincing."

Cassius gave her a quizzical look. "So you thought it was lightning when you wrote this brief, but you don't think so anymore?"

Faith nodded. "Yep. And I'm ashamed I didn't question it earlier. But think about it. If lightning hit a building with poor lightning protection, wood parts might catch fire or even water trapped in it might turn to steam and burst parts of it, like wet masonry or storage tanks. And the tractor fuel tanks attached to the building might explode. But what was left wouldn't look anything like what we found. The walls would still be standing, except maybe where the fuel tanks blowing knocked them over. The main damage would have been from fire and normal heat, and it would have been to the roof and the building's outer shell."

68

"But look at these pictures. Think about what they mean. Whatever happened here happened *inside* the building. The floor of the carriage house was melted to glass, and the *internal* surfaces of the wall stones were cracked from heat damage. The walls fell *outward,* not randomly inward or outward as they would if the wood structural members burned away, and not away from the fuel storage tanks as they would have if the fuel tank explosion had driven the collapse. So whatever happened there happened inside the building. So lightning is less convincing now. And maybe your domestic terrorism should be more so. I don't know."

"But what about the lightning maps?" Cassius said. "Maybe it was an internal explosion somehow set off by lightning. Like they were putting a bomb together when lightning struck."

"Except then you have the problem that the temperatures and damage on the inside of the building could only be caused by lightning or something else which exceeded, oh, maybe 22,000 degrees Fahrenheit for a short period. If lightning had set off the bomb, the damage would look like bomb damage, not like lightning damage."

"Wow! How did you get 22,000 degrees?" Cassius asked.

"It's a guess because that's supposed to be the average temperature lightning can create by turning air into plasma. But think about it. Concrete starts crystallizing at about forty-five hundred degrees. So work inward from the edge of the circle on the floor. If we assume the edge of the glass circle is the edge of the hot space which reached forty-five hundred degrees, then the center of the space had to be a lot, lot hotter. The law of inverse squares says that energy diminishes as the square of distance as it moves through space, so even moving four feet you'd lose a lot of temperature. If you bear that in mind, and accept that it's a flash burn pattern from a short event, then the center of the short event had to be super, super hot."

"What gets that hot besides lightning?"

"There's lightning. Then there's all kinds of science fiction," she said. "Kopp wasn't, by any chance, a closet physicist or anything? Any evil scientist credentials? Failed PhDs?"

"I doubt it. If you read his letters, the guy could barely spell unless they were words you find in the Bible. We're talking about a guy who can't spell 'homosexual' but uses the words 'forsaken' and 'abomination' in every other sentence. So I don't see him doing secret physics."

"Just because he's a Jesus freak doesn't mean he can't do physics."

"He's not a Jesus freak. Jesus never taught this stuff. Kopp was a 'Book of Revelations' freak. But there's no sign he had any education beyond high school, and nothing in his internet browsing about physics."

"Maybe someone else gave him some kind of special device or bomb."

"It's possible. His email records showed he'd volunteered to a number of people as willing to 'kill for God's kingdom.'"

Faith leaned forward to the computer and closed the briefing. "So, I did some brainstorming with Professor Bronner, a university physicist, as to what could flash burn concrete to glass at a distance between four and eight feet. We came up with some ideas. But the math leads you to numbers which are scary."

"Oh?"

"Take this for example. Let's assume concrete turns to glass at something like forty-five hundred degrees Fahrenheit. Nobody I've talked to knows at what exact temperature that happens, but it has been seen before around downed power lines."

"Okay."

"So, the circle of glass is about eight feet across, or four feet or one hundred twenty-five centimeters radius. If that heat source was at the center of the circle and was instantaneous, the energy at one centimeter from point source would have to be about seventy million degrees Fahrenheit."

"That sounds like a lot," said Cassius.

"It's more than a lot. Nuclear weapons top out at like ten million degrees. The hottest point on the surface of the sun is fifteen million degrees. But humans can create a point that hot. By focusing lasers, scientists trying to start a fusion reaction create a point of heat of more than one hundred million degrees. So if it was an instant point source of heat which melted the concrete, we can rule out anything natural. If something a lot cooler was around for a second or two instead of an infinitely short time, maybe like a ball or sphere of plasma which floated, then it could have been some kind of unique natural event."

"What's plasma? You say 'plasma' and I think of EMTs giving transfusions."

"Yeah, so do I. But plasma in this sense is the fourth state of matter, even higher energy than gas. In plasma, the atoms are so high energy that even their electrons fly off. Plasma only occurs on Earth in and around lightning strikes or arc welding or around super-hot events like explosions. So, since we had lightning strikes on the lightning map, we assumed the event was electrical. The maximum measured heat of the plasma in a typical lightning bolt is about 22,000 degrees."

"Okay."

"At that temperature, the ball of lightning would have to have been just one inch smaller than the burned area in order to make the damage we observed. So if it was normal lightning that did this, it involved a ball of lightning plasma eight feet across. Or a smaller one which persisted for a time longer than an instant."

"I think I'm getting it. Because this hypothetical lightning cloud was much cooler than the hypothetical point of light, its surface had to be closer to the concrete, or it had to burn the concrete longer, or both, to do the same amount of damage. But it's much more likely to have happened, because it could be much cooler."

"Right. And although humans could create either condition, the question would be how these three Army of God types pulled it off. And it doesn't help me with my end of the problem, which is what the girl was doing there, how she survived whatever happened, and who her parents are or were."

"So you're saying it's possible Kopp and these other two *did* create the conditions."

"They *probably* did. I'm not sure how they did it, but it is sure they didn't do it with conventional explosives or homemade incendiaries. If they did it, they did it with some kind of fancy technology they shouldn't have their hands on. At least, I *hope* it's not something you could cook up in your garage legally."

"That's...scary. Are you sure about this?"

"Look. I'm not sure about anything but that I've got an eight-foot circle of glass which used to be concrete out on Auburn road. If you take an eight-foot circle of glass and do the math and physics backwards to the event that could have created it, you start to see numbers which make Dr. Bronner go 'hmmm.' And numbers which make physicists go 'hmmm' are numbers that make firefighters wet themselves."

Cassius began. "This is alarming. I mean, domestic terrorist types always give you the chills, but the 'how they did it' part is often clear. Here we have a domestic terrorist and we don't even know how he did what he did."

"Yup."

"Consider what I said about the FBI. I think they ought to know about this. If what you're telling me is true, it's not simple arson, and not haters with ammonium nitrate. This could be a big deal."

"Now that we've talked about it, it seems like a good plan. I'll go to my chief to recommend it, once I've talked over some ideas with Dr. Bronner. Bottom line is, I don't want to go to the FBI and have them tell me I overlooked something obvious which could explain this. Understand my position. This could be a career-bender if I end up with egg on my face. But let's get away from the explosion for a moment. Can you help me explain Rosie?"

"She doesn't match the description of any missing child we're aware of or any child relatives of the three missing adults. But it sounds like you're taking the necessary steps. The Center for Missing and Exploited Children is the best bet if her parents are looking for her. If they're not-"

"Or if they're wisps of greasy smoke-" interjected Faith.

Cassius nodded and continued. "Then she'll end up in the foster care system or a childrens' shelter. It breaks your heart, but it's part of the job. I think it's safe to assume, though, that she wasn't there for an innocent purpose. She was certainly a victim or a planned victim. This guy fantasized about killing any number of people. Homosexuals. 'Surrenderists,' whatever those are. Non-Christians. Doctors. Scientists. He has got a longer hate list than most."

"Have you been doing missing persons long?" she asked him.

"Homicides. Going on eight years," said Cassius. "But missing persons has been a booming side business over the last couple of years."

"Oh, sorry, man."

"Someone has got to do it. I've got the grit for it, and it bothers me less than most. And it's steady work in Syracuse," he said with a gallows grin. "Listen, would you mind showing me out to the fire scene? I'd love to see it if you've got the time."

Faith thought about it. She had a lot to do, but, she noted, she could do some of it at home on her laptop. Right now was she pleased to be talking to another thoughtful person who was taking her seriously.

"Sure. What the hell," she said. "Let me grab my jacket. Did you bring a camera?"

"I did," said Cassius. "It's out in my car."

David waited, irritated. Faith had told him that morning a social worker would be coming to the house to follow-up on Rosie's welfare. There was no discussion about whose responsibility it was to talk to the social worker. She had presumed he would meet the woman because she had to go to work, and this presumption had left him in a shouting mood. He contemplated calling up Marcus and asking when he had become an orphanage. He was tempted to leave the girl at a shelter. He was tired, he was cranky, and he felt mean as hell.

Rosie was quiet on the other side of the breakfast bench. She kept her eyes on her cereal, holding her spoon with care and lifting shredded wheat biscuits to her mouth. He was grateful, in his current mood, that she was being so quiet. He would have snapped at her, he realized, if she had made any trouble or even no trouble at all.

He took three deep breaths. What did he have to do today which made one more day with this child so damned inconvenient he couldn't do this instead? He had planned on restarting his woodworking. He wanted to take a look at one of the senior-oriented dating websites. And, after hours, once Faith was home, he would head to one of Marcus's poker games. None of it was crucial so much as just fun. So he had time today to handle this social worker. Today America was asking him to take care of a child rather than work on his coffee table. He was up to the task.

He relaxed after this reflection. He had known some of the local Child and Family Services social workers in his day. One of them, Margrethe Peletow, had been one of Connie's lifelong friends, though he couldn't say she'd been his. He always had the impression the woman thought Connie had settled for too little when she'd married him. He might be imagining it, but whenever he and Connie had a fight, the woman had shown up to whisk Connie away to a cafe with a hard stare.

The social workers were, on the whole, a good if harried bunch, but they dragged paperwork along with them by the boatload. He'd heard Margrethe complain about it more than once. First there were all the state forms, then all the county forms, then some federal forms, a lot of duplication of medical records, and then all the forms from whatever university studies the county had agreed to participate in. Firefighting had become similarly burdened by paperwork, and David had often joked that he'd love to take all the paperwork out to a Dumpster and burn it, but he couldn't handle the paperwork which would result.

He scanned the house. What would be a problem for a social worker to see? There were last night's dinner dishes on the coffee table where he and Rosie had eaten while watching Nickelodeon. He should clean those up. The floor needed a vacuuming. He supposed he should check the bathrooms to be sure he hadn't left medicines out somewhere.

He checked the clock. To his surprise, he had only an hour or so until Faith had mentioned the social worker might appear. He had gotten up later than he ought to have. He resolved to start setting an alarm clock again. Since the girl could now be affected by his sleeping in, he couldn't write off sleeping late as affecting no one else.

Rosie was finishing off her shredded wheat with intensity. He rose and set up the television, but before he could finish, she had jumped up, left her bowl at the table, and gone to sit at the checker table with a grin. "Sorry, Honey, I can't play now. We'll have company soon, and I want to do some cleaning." In reply, she shrugged at him.

He shrugged back, switched on the TV controller, and channel-hopped until he'd found Nickelodeon again. He indicated she should sit on the couch, put the remote on the coffee table, and began clearing away the night's dishes. She pouted, which he ignored. "You're the third woman in this life to try and control me with pouting. Good luck with that," he replied, and marched off to the kitchen.

He was rinsing the dishes in the sink when Rosetta brought in her own cereal bowl and David's half-empty coffee cup. "Why thank you! It's nice to have help! But you can watch TV if you want."

Rosie shook her head. She did not like TV, he concluded. "It's there if you want it," he offered. She left the kitchen, and David soon had the dishes in the dishwasher and ready to go.

The girl was on the couch when he went upstairs to check the bathroom, and sure enough, he'd left his pill bottles on the back of the sink, where they ought not to be with a child in the house. He took his morning pills, then opened the medicine cabinet and cleared off the top shelf, examining the bottles he found there.

On doing so, he wished he hadn't. The bottles were all labeled for "Constance Haversham," and most of them were the painkillers she had refused to take. He dwelled for a moment on his resentments about this choice. What things

72

might they have been able to do, what last moments might they have been able to enjoy, if she had taken enough of these pain pills so she hadn't been so miserable much of the time? Maybe a cruise, or even more walks out at Taughannock Falls, or even one more night of lovemaking might have been nice. He had understood her aversion to pain medication, and how it might cloud her feelings and thinking or lead to dependence, but she had been a terminal patient. Drug dependence wasn't a hazard for the dead.

He stared at the bottle. The pills were opening old wounds and arguments even after Connie was gone. So he lifted the toilet seat, opened each of Connie's bottles, and tipped in the pills. Then he flushed them, closed the bathroom door, and, for lack of anywhere else to sit, closed the lid and sat on the toilet to have a good cry.

He cried quietly, aware Rosie was in the house. When he had begun to calm down, he had a flash of alarm about how much time had passed. The social worker might be here any minute. He crammed his own pills onto the top shelf, wrapped the empty pill bottles up with a CVS store bag Faith left around her maxi-pads to hide the box, and tossed them into the wastebasket. He thought for a moment about other hazards around the house, and decided to head to the cellar and be sure he hadn't left his carpentry tools in a child-threatening disarray in the cellar.

He stopped as he opened the bathroom door. The girl was outside it, looking concerned.

"What?" he asked in irritation and chagrin. "Look, kid, you can't be following me around the house all the time. A man has got to have his space."

Rosie responded by hugging him.

"Heard me crying, did you? Thank you for the hug. But don't coddle me. I've got to get over it." He returned her hug, noticing when he did so how comforting it felt. He stopped.

She's no kin to you. Why should her empathy matter?" He held on for a second longer, wiped his eyes on his sleeve, and then patted the girl's back. "C'mon," he said. "I've got stuff to do."

Rosie followed around after him as he straightened his basement workshop and vacuumed the living room floor. He had rolled the vacuum cleaner away and begun to wonder if he should change his shirt when he heard the doorbell.

"That would be her," he said out loud. He wondered how he knew the social worker would be a "her" as he walked to the door. Couldn't social workers be both men and women? David strained to remember ever having met a male social worker. He couldn't.

When he opened the door, he saw the caller was not only a "she," but *the* "she" he had dreaded. In front of him stood Margrethe Peletow.

"Good morning!" he greeted.

Her narrow Polish features smiled in return. "Hello, David! I'm here to check on your Jane Doe."

"Oh. Well. Sure," he said in reply. He wished now he'd made time to change his shirt, he'd heard this woman joke with Connie about slouchy men, and he was sure he was being judged harshly for his twenty year old green flannel shirt. Margrethe's professional gray sweater, dark slacks, and dress shoes made him feel at a disadvantage.

"May I come in?" she asked at length.

"Sorry," he stood aside. Then he wondered why he was apologizing. It wasn't her house.

She walked into the living room and looked around. He stood, waiting for her to critique the layout or the furniture. But then he considered: Connie had chosen all the furniture and the layout, so if she would make some comment, she'd be critiquing her own friend.

Margrethe said nothing about the furniture. "Where's Faith?"

"At work," David replied.

"So are you watching the child?"

"Rosie's right here," he indicated to the checker table where the girl sat quietly.

"Rosie? Is that your name?" The social worker stepped forward to offer the child a handshake. After a moment of looking at the woman's hand, she shook it uncertainly.

"She doesn't speak English. They've figured out what language she speaks, and I'm getting translations done up at Cornell. But we know her full name now. 'Rosetta Amata.'"

"Does this mean we're on the way to locating her parents?" the woman queried.

"Couldn't tell you. I know my daughter's working on it sixteen hours a day, and she sent all Rosie's information into the FBI and the Center for Missing and Exploited Children, but we've had no answer yet. She has indicated to me there is a possibility the girl's parents or caregivers died in the fire."

"Hmmm," said Margrethe, staring around the living room. "Do you want to sit? This will take a few minutes." David indicated the couch, and reached for the remote to turn off the television. He then sat in Faith's chair, leaving the couch to his guest.

"You're uncomfortable," she observed.

"We were never friends, you and Constance were."

"True," she agreed. Rosie stood from the checker table and approached them. To keep her busy while they talked, David gathered a fresh stack of printer paper and Constance's old box of colored pencils and put them on the coffee table. The girl inspected the pencils, selected a sheet of paper, and began to draw.

"She looks comfortable," remarked the social worker.

"Sure," he agreed. The woman raised her eyebrows as if she expected him to say more at first, but when he didn't, she resumed command of the conversation.

"How have you been?" Margrethe checked him up and down. The question surprised him.

"Never better. Parties every night, fast women, whiskey by the barrel. What else did you expect from a husband as worthless as I was?" he replied.

The woman did not rise to his tone, but interpreted his message. "You feel I was critical of you as Connie's husband?"

David was irritated by her understatement. "I don't see that there was much 'feeling' about it. You were critical."

"Let me be clear. I never married myself, and I felt Constance abandoned... certain things and dreams to marry you and settle down. But that's me being critical of *her* and her choices, not of you."

"It amounts to the same thing. And how does it feel to be a social worker against marriage?" parried David. "Got to make your job interesting."

Margrethe twisted the bun in her silver hair. His eyes traced the old scar on her neck once again. As the woman aged, it stood out more than it had when she was younger and her low and open collar suggested she made no attempts to hide it. He had always wondered how she got it. "I'm not against marriage. But it's not always a person's best choice."

"You thought that about Connie?" he hazarded.

74

"Sometimes, yes," she answered.

"And yet here you sit in her house, entrusting a child to the remains of her family. So how wrong could her choices have been?"

Margrethe saddened. "Maybe I was the wrong one to come. If you want, I can go and send down someone from my office. I thought that with as odd as this case is and my past connection to you, I would give it a try."

David contemplated her offer. "Now that you're here, let's do what you came to do so I don't have to give up another morning waiting around on someone else."

The woman breathed deeply, closed her eyes for a second, and resumed. "That sounds good. And maybe next time I'll send down one of the other girls if it will make you more comfortable."

"Suit yourself. You're the head of Child and Family Services, not me. But without Constance or Faith around to ride herd on our conversations, don't expect me to mince words," he said. It felt great to speak his mind to this woman after all these years. "If you want to talk business, talk business. But if you ask personal questions, then expect personal answers."

Margrethe blinked, briefly at a loss for how to reply. She then refocused him on her work. "I don't know how much Faith has explained to you, or how much she knows about foster care in New York. But we have two stages in foster care. The first is emergency foster care, when a child is found without shelter or family, or her parents are found to be unable to care for her for a short period. Emergency foster care is temporary, lasting no more than thirty days. If she will stay in the foster care system, though, we will try to place her in long-term foster care which can last until she reaches adulthood. Our goal is to move the child as little as possible so she is not ping-ponged through the system."

"Makes sense," said David. "What do you need from me?" He felt better as they came to the business at hand.

"Two things. First, it's clear to me that Faith, who is the one listed as her emergency foster parent, is not the one providing the majority of her care, so we should redo the paperwork so you're listed as her primary care-giver. Second, we're coming up on the two-week mark in her emergency foster care, and if she'll stay longer, I should do a basic household inspection and ensure this home meets minimum safety standards."

He adjusted the magazines on the coffee table, sliding an issue of "Card Player Magazine" out of the woman's line of sight. "So you came here expecting to give me foster care responsibility?"

"It's more appropriate if you're the one giving the care, yes. Let me put it to you this way. I can't keep listing Faith as the foster parent if she is never home. Either we list you, or the girl comes with me."

"Can't Faith and I both have responsibility like, you know, foster parents?"

"Faith is your daughter, not your wife," Margrethe said in an explanatory tone.

"Yes, thanks, I'm clear on that," said David, deciding to forgo the more colorful response which had come to his mind.

"You'd have to be married or in a domestic partnership with her to hold joint foster care responsibility."

He thought on this. "So, let me get this straight? Gays and lesbians can provide joint foster care, even though their relationships are so...unnatural? But my daughter and I can't, even though we're a natural family?"

"Umm," replied Margrethe. Rosie stirred at her drawing, disturbed. He paused. His tone must be frightening her.

"Never mind," he relented. "You don't make the laws, I know. So go on."

"It's not as...common for a father and grown daughter to live together long-term as it is for a gay or lesbian couple to live together for extended periods. You're kind of in a loophole. I'm not saying the arrangement is wrong, but-"

"Uh huh," he said. "When I die, this will be her house. She works the same place I used to. There are parts of the arrangement which are awkward, believe me, but big parts of it make sense."

"I understand," said the social worker in a tone which suggested she did. "But let's get back to Rosie's foster care. If she'll stay here, and Faith will work long hours, then to be fair to the child, you have to become the foster care-giver. I'm not being critical of her, I'm saying legal responsibility should reside with the person doing the majority of the care-giving, and that is you."

"And you don't have a problem with that?" he said.

"Unless my inspection turns up something which gives me concern, no, I don't," answered Margrethe. "I never questioned your abilities as a parent. You have a well-adjusted and successful professional daughter as a testament to your ability. But we're skipping an important question. Are you willing to be a foster care-giver? For as long as thirty days?"

David looked at the girl. She'd gotten comfortable. While the prospect of putting the pleasures of retirement on hold for thirty days didn't appeal to him, Rosie's need was great, and it would help Faith with the investigation if one of the chief witnesses was readily available. Besides, they'd established this relationship with the university. If he could stick it out, it could be an important thirty days for the foundling.

"Sure. I'm not saying it's not a pain in the neck, but it won't be a less of a pain in the neck for anyone else. Besides, she fits in here so far."

"Great! So, to make it official, I'll have to do some paperwork. And then I'll need to look around your house. I won't go in your safe or your diary or anything, but I'll need to check any parts of your house where a child might go."

"Okay," said David, again surprised by the woman's enthusiasm. This was a part of her he hadn't seen. She'd always acted a dour old biddy, even in her twenties. "Go on."

Margrethe produced a form from the metal clipboard she was carrying and began to fill out blocks. "Could you spell the girl's name for me? Both her first name and last name are unusual."

He did so, and relaxed as the social worker bombarded him with very standard questions. But at length they came to the issue of his medical conditions.

"Do I remember you have a pacemaker?"

"How did you know that? I got it after Connie died."

Margrethe shrugged. "Word of mouth, I suppose. I filed the fact away. I'm in the people business, you know. Elder care is another of my responsibilities."

He bristled at the term "elder care," but chose to remain focused.

"So, do you work or hold any part-time jobs?" she continued.

"No. I'd thought about it, but I don't yet. I'm still a homebody."

"It's good in her case. I don't know how we'll get her into school this late in the semester, especially if she can't speak English."

"That's not all. It's not clear that she is, you know, normal," he recalled, glancing at the girl. Rosie continued to draw.

"What do you mean?" Margrethe asked.

"The people at Cornell who translated for her suggested she may have a disability, or a psychological problem. They say she's overly religious."

The social worker dug into this. "What religion? Clergy can be a great help in finding long-term foster care."

"They didn't say. They said she talked a lot about God."

"Oh. Let me know if you find any specifics. In particular small religious groups will go to great lengths to keep a child in their community, so it could make a difference in a willing long-term placement that suits her needs."

"Okay," said David. "I'll ask them if they can figure it out in their next interviews. They're interested in her. We can make them work for us."

The woman checked her clipboard. After some more questions, and some silence while she filled in blocks he guessed had nothing to do with him, she stood.

"Now I'll need to look around."

"I assume you know your way," David said, hands in his pockets. "Suit yourself."

Margrethe blinked. "Do you want to accompany me?"

"If you want." He was more interested, he found, in whatever Rosie was drawing. She was focused, and her subject was taking colorful shape on her page.

The woman compromised. "I'd do the ground floor myself. But the rest of the house I'd like you to come with me. So there aren't any questions."

"Fair enough," he grunted, still focused on Rosie's picture of a river with does drinking at it.

The social worker headed into the kitchen, clipboard in hand. He had a fleeting anxiety she would move something, but then dismissed it. The woman had better things to do than hide his spatulas or switch his stir-fry spoon with the mixing spoon. He heard her open and close a few drawers and cabinets.

Afterwards, Margrethe checked into the library and the downstairs bathroom, then came out and nodded to him. He rose, tousled Rosie's hair, and followed the woman upstairs. True to her word, the woman stuck her head in every room, and he was soon glad he'd purged medications and moved the remainder to the top shelf of the medicine cabinet, because she inspected it.

The woman flipped a page on her clipboard. "Can you show me where she's sleeping?"

"The guest room next to Faith's room," David answered. He led her down the hall, and the woman opened the door and entered. Once inside she stared around it with a lot of focus. He didn't know why. The room was as it always had been, even when Margrethe had stayed there while Connie was sick and he had been away for his job.

She turned back out of the room and step out into the hall. "Sorry. I was having some memories. The room looks fine for the girl, but you might want to let her add some decorations or change a few things. So it feels like her safe space."

David felt a criticism in her suggestion. "All she had was some Goodwill clothes and a fire blanket when she came from the department, and I sent the fire blanket back with Faith. But yeah, if she wants, I'm fine with her changing things."

"I'm not sure if I told you this, David. I'm sorry. Connie was a good friend, and I know she was grateful to have you with her at the end. It comes to me now being in this room. I slept here a few nights while you were working in St. Louis after Market Garden."

David was taken by surprise that Margrethe would pay him a compliment, and felt tears beginning in his eyes when she mentioned Connie. He blinked them back. He would not make drama in front of this woman.

"I do miss her," he restated his emotions into a safe phrase and faced the stairway. "Do you need to see anything else?"

Margrethe sighed behind him. "No, that's all. I want you to look at keeping your medications and any dangerous household chemicals out of her reach, especially if her mental age is lower than is typical."

He flinched at the suggestion that Rosie was stupid. But he supposed the social worker might be right, he didn't know what Rosie might think to do next.

"Let's go back downstairs. I'll finish the paperwork and you can ask any questions you might think of."

"Sounds good," he said. He could hardly wait for the woman to leave, but he had to focus on doing the job at hand. He might think of some real questions once he'd had a minute to calm back down. They went back downstairs and resumed their seats. Rosie remained where she had been left, still working on the drawing of the riverside. It was much fuller now, and she had begun to fill in color around the shapes.

Margrethe sat, tightening her silver bun behind her and holding the clipboard a careful distance from her face. She began making notes, but in a moment she spoke. "The records show her as having burns. Are these being treated?"

"Typical burn after-care. Regular bandage changes, painkillers, iodine, antibiotics. They were bad, but most of her pain has passed."

"If you have to pay for any medical supplies, save your receipts. There is a modest stipend for foster care, and some of her medical expenses may be reimbursable if you can present good receipts."

David perked up at this. With the dollar's value crashing, his retirement income wasn't anywhere close to what he had planned, so this could make a difference. "Thanks, I'll do that." After a moment he thought of his next question. "What happens if we don't find her parents?"

"If you find her parents' remains, then we begin a search for her next of kin. But once thirty days have passed, she will have to be placed in long-term foster care or moved to a youth shelter."

"Which shelter?"

"Since she's not an offender, I'll have to see if Equinox thinks they'll have any space. Last I checked, they were packed tighter there than the old lady who lived in a shoe, and they're focused on children able to ultimately become independent, and she may not...fit that category. Then I would look in Syracuse for foster care. Failing that, there is the new wing at Austin McCormick."

David shuddered. "That's a youth prison."

"It's got a variety of services, from therapeutic to correctional," responded Margrethe neutrally. "It's better than having her live on the street. With state and national deficits and ongoing wars, we're at the point of last resort with homeless children. There's not a lot of foster parents, and not a lot of public interest, but a bounty of Dickensian attitudes about homeless kids. Texas introduced its 'learning to labor' program, even, heaven help those children. And it will get worse, not better, with abortions now illegal."

He countered. "Outlawing abortion was the right thing to do. The issue is following it up with good youth services, not backpedaling."

The social worker stood her ground. "That's a debate I'm won't enter. I'm saying there's a real lack of resources and public interest, and whatever the morality of abortion, outlawing it means the problems of our youth are bound only to increase, and this has already started. What this means for Rosie is unless I can find a long-term foster parent for her, institutional options, some of them austere, are what I have left. You asked."

David took a deep breath. He had asked where Rosie would go, and while it was plain Margrethe and he did not agree on the abortion issue, that was neither here nor there. "Sorry. You're right."

"If you're so concerned about this, David, consider foster parenting, either for Rosie or someone else. If everyone who opposed abortion would get behind their values by foster parenting or adopting, my problems would be solved."

David blinked at her. "Aren't I old for that?"

She shook her head. "New York State is not in the position to be picky. As long as you're fit enough that it's clear the child will not become a live-in caretaker and your other credentials check out, it's a possibility. Do you have any other medical conditions I should be aware of?"

"That you wouldn't already know about? Mrs. people person?" David needled her. The woman grinned at her clipboard as she began writing again.

"I'll take that as a no. Then think about it, David. If you're against abortion, that's fine, but put your money where your mouth is and you'll make a believer out of me, too."

"I pay taxes," he said, "What further proof do I need to show you?" Margrethe raised an eyebrow at her clipboard but said nothing.

"That's all," she said, checking the form after a moment. "I'll need you to sign at the bottom. My business card is stapled to the bottom of the form for your wallet, and printed again on the form itself if you have any questions. If her family resurfaces, or anything comes up so you can't care for Rosie anymore, let us know immediately. Unless we extend it, her emergency foster care period with you terminates in thirty days, so my girls will be working their tails off trying to find her a more permanent situation."

Margrethe stood, and David admired the leather and malachite lashing which kept her bun in place. She always did dress smartly. When she faced him, a serious look resettled itself over her narrow face. "Anyhow, I have two more homes to visit before noon. I should go. It's good to see you."

He tried to find a comparable but honest reply. "Thanks for the giving the city so much of your life."

"Only a few more years," she said, resolute. "Then all these 'someone else's problem' children are someone else's problem." She headed for the door, and David saw her out with a wave.

Once the door closed, he turned back to Rosie. She was holding up her drawing to examine it, and as he walked around behind her to look at it, the sun from the bay windows made the riverside, the deer, and a picnic scene light up like stained glass.

"Very nice!" he complimented her. It was as good as some of the art which had been for sale at the Farmer's Market. Back when it was still open.

Rosie beamed at the compliment, and said something he couldn't understand. He patted her shoulder in reply.

Cassius and Faith stood outside. In the sunlight, with a week and a few rainstorms past, the ruins of the carriage house were tranquil. The gutted hulk of Kopp's truck was skeleton-like with its glass gone, paint burned off, and frame exposed, but even so, it was a thought-provoking rather than sinister sight. If she stood with her back to the ruined truck and ignored the yellow border of fire scene tape and steel pickets, the silence and the fresh green weeds poking up through the blackened earth were just thought-provoking.

She led the detective straight to the foundation, ducking under the tape while the tall man stepped over it. She had brought the shovel with her in case the ashes and rubble had resettled over the glass, but the burned concrete was still visible. She walked to its edge and followed the detective's gaze down with her own.

Cassius's face was a serious frown. An eight-foot sheet of dark, wavy, blue-green obsidian said a lot for itself.

"So, this is vitrified concrete," she said after he'd soaked the sight in. "Again, this vitrification is estimated to occur somewhere between forty-five hundred and forty-eight hundred degrees Fahrenheit, with the color being determined in part by the composition of the concrete and contaminants such as metal dusts present during heating. I guess it turns different colors if it's steel-reinforced. So, if your superiors in Syracuse think I'm crazy, they're free to come down here, look at this, and come up with better explanations."

She stepped carefully onto the glass. It wasn't that slick; in fact, the surface was rough like an orange peel, and it showed no signs of crumbling or breaking under her feet, but the idea she was walking on glass made her careful. The detective emulated her caution, following her to the center of the glass sheet.

Toward the center she pointed to a circle of glass filled with holes like a sponge. "It was much hotter there. Dr. Bronner said this formation of glass would be consistent with glass or things trapped in it boiling away into gas. So at this point, we're talking about vaporizing concrete, not melting it."

"Yikes," said Cassius. "It's kind of weird to stand here. It's a moment of destruction frozen in time."

"Tell me about it," Faith breathed. She reflected for a moment on the porous glass, and wondered what the two men and one woman who had probably died in the event were trifling with which could have caused such fury.

"Yeah. So. Mr. Kopp was in over his head, I'm thinking," said Detective McCrae.

"Me too. But let's take a look at the truck." They left the floor pad of the carriage house, the detective stumbling on stone rubble, and came to the truck. Rust was already covering bare metal, but the side that faced away from the blast still showed patches of a sky-blue paint. She directed the man's eyes to the charred rear license plate.

"There is your plate. Should be a match."

He pulled out his tablet and poked at it. "Yep, matches his registration. Chevy Tahoe pickup, color blue."

She shrugged. "Okay, so there you go. I'm thinking your man died here. And whoever was with him. Except for the girl."

"Yeah. How did that happen? I mean, this place is rubble. Anyone near this should be..."

"I'd like to think they had sent her outside to play while they did whatever in here. Or maybe she was sitting in the truck and was thrown clear when it rolled. But she had bruises and scrapes appropriate to her being bound. So I don't think it was anything benign. All I can think is they sent her outside to pee, or that she saw the danger and managed to bolt. We found her naked, with some burned clothing stuck to her back."

Cassius was concentrating on the glass. "I wish I had something to add. I don't know what to say. This is out of my league. But what I am sure of is we can't let this happen again. If anyone else in that *cirque du freak* Kopp ran with has this technology, we have a problem."

"Let's try and put it together," said Faith. "Why would a man like Kopp and his two friends come to this spot, this old carriage house, with a child and some kind of destructive device? I mean, my initial impulse when I saw her wrists was child pornography or abuse of some kind. But if you were going to film yourself having sex with a pre-teen, would you bring a bomb with you? It doesn't make sense. So, what I'm thinking is, they brought her and the bomb out here together, because they planned to kill her with it."

"But why?" fretted the detective. "If you want to kill a girl, you can choke her, decapitate her. I've seen it..." he froze up. His expression grew distant.

She reached forward and touched his arms. "Whoa. You with me?"

"Sorry, yeah," the man said with a grimace. "Going places in my mind."

Faith felt both pity and wonder at what the man might encounter in his day-to-day. "No problem. Take your time."

The man was quiet for a long time. "I've got a daughter who's thirteen. Sometimes, talking about this stuff, I imagine her as the victim and I lock up."

"It's okay," she said. She wondered if she would be able to handle his job. She decided she wouldn't.

Cassius spoke up again. "Anyhow, if he planned to kill her, there are easier and cheaper ways to do it. So why would he do it that way? Some ritual significance?"

Inspector Haversham speculated. "Maybe because it would destroy all evidence? Whatever it was Kopp set off, it takes care of the killing and the disposal all in a ball. I mean, we can't even be sure *he* died here. There is no DNA evidence, no body parts, no nothing. Maybe he and his friends had done evil to this girl and wanted to get rid of her, so they planned to have one last fuck fest and then burn her up. Only they mishandled the bomb and burned themselves up."

"Any sign of sexual trauma on the victim?" he wondered.

"None visible to the docs. And she hasn't complained or showed any of the usual symptoms they told us to watch out for. So it either happened before they got to her..."

"Or it wasn't why they brought her here." The detective speculated. "Maybe they wanted to kill her plain and simple. And leave no trace. They might have been looking to make her not just die, but disappear."

"What kind of people did Kopp hate that much?" Faith asked. "You read his email."

Cassius snorted. "It's a long list. Homosexuals. Abortion doctors. Genetic researchers. Muslims. Democrats. Communists. Jews. Heck, even another group of Christians called 'red-letter Christians.' I'm sure 'blacks' fit in there somewhere, but I never saw him say it."

"Yeah, but those don't describe the victim. She's not any of those. She's too young to know if she's a lesbian or political, and if she was Muslim and spoke Arabic or something, we'd already have the story out of her. She's this little disabled thing. Being disabled isn't something people hate you for."

"He was so generous with his hate she may fit one of his categories in some way a normal person couldn't think of," countered Cassius. "Or maybe she was the daughter of someone who did. And he was killing her to get at them."

"I hadn't thought that way. With arson, you're dealing with a rational actor looking for insurance money or something. With murder, you must see a fair share of the irrational."

"Yeah, crimes of passion are often weird. But if it was a crime of passion or a hate crime, it was higher-tech than it usually gets with this seventy-million-degree stuff. Any chance they were out here on a picnic and got hit by lightning?"

"No match. We talked about it. Lightning would burn down the building if it was unprotected, but it wouldn't blow it into pieces and it wouldn't create a glass circle like we see inside the building. Plus, there are the binding bruises on her wrists."

"Yeah, you're right," the detective conceded. "If the victim gets to the point where she's ready to talk and we're ready to translate, I need you to call me. I want to hear her side of it."

"Yeah, no problem. We're working on it."

Cassius shoved both hands in his pockets. "Look, I hope you don't take offense, but some of this is out of our league. I think it's time to involve the feds. You game?"

Faith realized the prospect would daunt her less if Cassius came along. "You want to go together? Sounds like we hold different pieces of the same puzzle. Plus, they might take us more seriously if they saw more than one jurisdiction was knocking on their door."

"They might."

"We've got an FBI Resident Agency office in Ithaca," Faith recalled. "But I've never met them, I just asked them for the kidnapping information center. But I bet you know your Syracuse FBI agents, and it's a bigger outfit."

"Yeah, but that's not an advantage in this case," Detective McCrae noted. "If I take you to Syracuse, you're a country bumpkin with an unlikely story and I'm a cop they're tired of looking at. If we go to your office, you're local and important to them, and you've got back up from, you know, a 'big town' cop like me."

She smiled at him. "Okay, Mr. Salesman. Let me clear it with my chief and we can work through this from my house," she extended her hand for him to shake. "It's nice to have a partner for a bit. So what will you tell your boss when you say this country firefighter wasn't making this weird shit up?"

Cassius shook his head helplessly. "I'll tell him 'the truth is out there!'"

Their laughs vanished into the open space, the crannies of the rubble on the ground, and amongst the bare bones of the truck. But Faith felt good to laugh nonetheless.

Chapter 6

Gambling

Faith pulled up and parked beside the house. Her father's truck was there, and the central air conditioner buzzed in its enclosure under the dining room windows. She sighed and lingered in her seat for a moment. It was Friday, and with all her work this week on the briefing and on the carriage house investigation, she was ready for a break. For a fleeting second, she anticipated her date with Steve before her feelings on it went back to being muddied. McCallister was the biggest sleaze she knew. Why had she agreed to date him? She'd rather sit around with a beer and watch TV, or go out to the Rongovian Embassy for live music. But instead she had to go in, hunt up the right clothes and jewelry, make herself up, and then go out again on an uptight pity experiment. It was pity for him, and self-pity, which had made her say yes. She considered whether it was too late to call it off.

"Grown-ups make choices and live with them," she mumbled. She turned off the engine, got out of her car, and went inside.

Her father was quick to greet her from the checker table. "Hello! Good to have you home."

"Thanks," said Faith. "Long week. And it's not over yet." She rounded the corner to talk to him face to face. The stack of pieces indicated the man was giving the girl more of a run for her money than usual.

"How so? You're not going back to work tomorrow, I hope." David countered.

"No. Marcus told me he expects to have the HQ to himself on Saturday, and if I did go in I was subject to disciplinary action. And he also said something about a poker game Saturday night.

"Yeah. He called about that. He wants you and Rosie to be there. I'll host, so it'll be M&M stakes, like old times. One pound bag each."

"Ooh, a one-pound game. Brutal on the diet."

"Only if you eat them," David said. "Anyway, what else is making your week long?"

"Tonight," said Faith. "I have a date with Steve McCallister."

Her father's eyes narrowed at the name. She was ready for this reaction and counterattacked before it came.

"Dad, we talked about this. If we're going to live together, I have to be able to date who I want when I want. If you make this hard on me, I'm moving out," she said firmly.

"You're too good for him," the old man grumped.

"Yes. Agreed. But that's not the point. The point is he's my first date in a year. The point is living at home with you puts people off. I need a date to make myself believe I can still have one, and to make myself believe you'll be good for your side of the bargain and let me date who I want in the future. And I won't risk a real date trying to figure that out. So I agreed to this date with Steve. If you chew him up, I'll be angry, but I won't feel like I lost out on a real prospect. So, put up and shut up, or help me pack my bags."

David grumbled something.

"Quit your bellyaching, Pop. Jeeze. You and mom were married and I was four when you were my age. Doesn't that worry you? Don't you want grandkids?"

"On the subject of grandkids," he said, turning back to Rosie. "It turns out I'm a father again, thanks to you."

"What?" said Faith.

"Margrethe Peletow was the social worker I met this morning. She decided since I was the primary care-giver, I would have to sign the emergency foster care paperwork. So, thanks to you, I'm now a foster dad."

She took all this in. "Oh, congratulations! There, the pressure is off me. I can go be a lesbian now," she said. "*If he only understood I was only half joking.*"

"Well, don't be too happy about it. I've been taking care of this pumpkin all week. So tomorrow, I want a break. They're having a VFW charity stakes poker game in Syracuse tomorrow to benefit Shriners' hospitals. And I thought after Rosie's close encounter with fire, supporting Shriners' pediatric burn units would be a good way to put my poker talents to use."

"Jeeze, Dad. What's the entry fee?"

"A hundred bucks."

"Plus gas?"

"Okay, I think it's fair to ask that if you don't want me kvetching about your social activities, you don't kvetch about mine. I'm aware that it's steep but I've got the money."

Faith remembered to stay away from the money issue. Her father was not charging her rent, and so if it ended up that she had to step in for this or that household thing, she was still coming out ahead. In fact, between her steady job and her boring lifestyle, she had a good bit of money in the bank. "Alright. Fair enough. I'll sit her tomorrow. But then in the evening we'll go straight to Marcus's poker game? That's two poker games in a day. Do we have a problem here?"

David snorted. "It's not a problem, it's a hobby. If it were a problem I'd be down at Tioga Downs dropping quarters in electronic slots. I haven't had a card game in two weeks, so no, it's not a problem."

Rosie interrupted the conversation by getting up and tugging on the man's sleeve and pointing toward the kitchen. Faith laughed out loud at this. "Hah! She's telling you it's time for supper! Guess I know who's in charge in this house!"

"Yeah, maybe you do," said David bitterly. He got up and started toward the kitchen. "Chicken wings, snow peas, and salad tonight. Go powder your nose or whatever. At least change your clothes. I'm tired of seeing you at the dinner table in uniform."

"So, you've achieved empathy with mom yelling at you for coming to the table in uniform?" she said.

"Yes, I have. Thank you for another small turnabout in my life," he grumbled.

With this she smiled and started up the stairs to her room. She'd take a shower and throw on some sweats for dinner, and then go upstairs to get dressed for her date afterwards so she didn't have to listen to her father comment on her choices. But it was, she reflected, good to be home.

Faith was in her bedroom trying on different earrings when she heard the horn honk outside.

"Sounds like McAllister is outside," her father bellowed from downstairs. "Yep, there's a black truck in the street."

"I'm on my way!" she said. "Don't you say a word to him!" The last thing she needed was her father starting the evening off by upbraiding Steve for his numerous deficiencies. She turned her head one way and then the other, comparing the two different earrings. She chose the pearl stud in her left ear, removed the dangling bangle from her right ear, and put in the matching stud.

"He's not coming to the door, the coward," she heard her father bellow some more. "Can't be that interested in you if he's that scared of me."

Faith rolled her eyes. "Don't start, Dad," she shouted back down the stairs. She gave her head a shake to check her hair and then shot down the stairs as fast as her boots would let her. Her dad was at the bottom of the stairs, standing by the door. Rosie was with him, leaning against him and smiling at her as she descended.

"You look great," her father said. "Any man would be a fool-"

"Shush. You're hardly an impartial vote. With these rosy cheeks and shoulders, I look a cross between an overgrown 'Campbell's Soup' kid and a linebacker." Faith gave him a hug and pinched Rosie's nose, causing her to cover it with a startled expression. "You'll be in bed when I get home," she told the girl. She shot her dad a look. "You can wait up if your dad-instincts compel you, but she'd better be in bed."

"Why? So she can get up early and interrupt my retirement? She can stay up until she's tired," David said. "I'm the foster parent, not you."

"Listen to you, Dad, you've gone soft." She caught the child's gaze. "Don't let him fool you. He's a hard ass." In reply, the girl hugged tighter to the man's waist.

"She has got you wrapped around her finger," she observed.

"Maybe," he said, ignoring her attempt to focus him on Rosie. He stared at her instead. "I won't say what I'm thinking. I guess this living arrangement has made finding men of your own caliber difficult. Anyhow, enjoy yourself."

"Fair enough," she answered. This kind of detente with her father on the first date was a better outcome then she had expected. She opened the door and stepped out into the failing summer sunlight. Sure enough, Steve's locally-famous mag-wheeled black truck, windows tinted and hood painted with silver buck's antlers, waited on DeWitt Terrace in front of their garden steps. Known by some as the "Shag stag mag", rumor had it that under the cap the man had set up a temple of love, including a wet bar. She was curious if it had a 70s décor, or if he had gone for more class.

She walked down the driveway with what she hoped was a casualness which expressed indifference to her neighbors, her father, and Steve himself. She reached up, opened the door to the truck, and clambered into the passenger seat.

The smell of the man's citrus cologne filled her nose as she settled in. He was freshly shaven, and wore his IAFF jacket with a checkered shirt underneath.

"Welcome aboard," he said. "I guess you're used to high seats," he said, motioning to her father's red truck behind her.

"Drive before the neighbors see me," Faith said, arranging her purse between them and yanking the door closed.

"Hello to you, too," he said, sounding not the least bit hurt.

"We talked about this. My point in going out with you was to practice for real dates," she flipped down his sun visor to touch up her lipstick in the mirror.

"Fine by me. I need some practice with real women," Steve replied, looking over his shoulder to back the truck up and turn around. "Where should I start? You could practice being less bitchy."

"I know what you do for a living, and I hear what your personal life is like through the grapevine, so not with those two things," she explained.

"Um, okay," he said, pausing until he reached Buffalo Street and headed downhill. "Read any good books?"

She tossed him a look. "I read all day for work, and you're asking me if I read for leisure?"

Steve frowned. "Throw me a bone, here. It's a long way to Syracuse and we've got the ride back, too. We can enjoy ourselves or you can sit there and put me down until you get bored."

"Bottom line up front again," she acknowledged. "How about music? Does this lorry have music?"

He smirked. "I have an mp4 player, yes. What do you like? I have most of the last three decades in a collection." He pushed a console button, and an LCD screen lit up on the dashboard. "I've also got about twenty-five movies uploaded."

"How many aren't porn?" she asked.

"Seventeen, thank you very much," he replied "I've even got Casablanca." She sucked in her breath as Steve narrowly missed a lamppost on a turn.

"How about music. I don't want you distracted by a movie," she said. McCallister was also famous for his reckless driving, a fact she had failed to consider when she had agreed to let him drive.

"Take your pick. What do you want?"

"How about-" she decided to test his collection and his patience with something she had never heard a man say he liked. "Olivia Newton-John?"

He gave no sign of distaste. Instead he said "Pandora. Olivia Newton-John. Xanadu." In a moment, Olivia's sweet voice poured out of speakers that were everywhere in the cab. Faith could feel the bass beat shaking her boots against her legs.

"Umm, volume," she shouted, palms on her ears. He pointed to the LCD screen, which featured touch buttons for the fade, volume, and balance of the sound. She used one of her fake nails to tap the screen and adjust the volume to her taste, noting the glue was holding as advertised. She'd use that brand again.

Steve turned onto Rte. 13 and headed east out of town. She listened to Olivia in polyphonic sound and enjoyed a view of Cayuga Lake in the setting sun as they rose up and out of the valley which held the City of Ithaca proper. Away from the city and the concerns that people were laughing at her for dating this man, she felt better and more relaxed. When the track ended, she decided to give him a break.

"So, okay, I was being kind of a jerk. I knew who was asking me out when I accepted, so I shouldn't be spending my time putting you down for who you are. I'm sorry."

"Thank you. Apology accepted. Think of me like a fat chick. Now that your friends aren't watching, you can have some fun."

She drew a breath to make a retort, and stopped. "We're supposed to be helping each other out, right? That's the idea of this date. Practice and feedback and stuff." Ahead of them, Rte. 13 narrowed to two lanes and the townhouses gave way to the farmland and hills of the Finger Lakes.

"That was my understanding," said Steve. She saw the lanes were narrowing so his truck filled the space between the lines, and began to worry again about his driving. She focused instead on their conversation.

"So, a tip. Don't make jokes about 'fat chicks' to women who are insecure about their weight. You made negative yardage with that play."

"Are you insecure about your weight?" he hazarded.

"Yes, I am, thanks for asking," Faith said. "Should I be?"

"I'll give a cop-out answer, and say your weight is a matter of your taste, not mine. You look great to me, or I wouldn't have asked you out, because I'm superficial enough that I only date women I find beautiful," Steve countered.

"Fair enough," she dismissed, "You're not enough of a confidant to have to answer that question anyway."

Her date watched the road for a minute. "Can I give you a tip, too?"

"Go ahead," she said. She braced for something crass.

He took a more explanatory tone. "Avoid making references to football, like 'negative yardage on that play.' You're already built like a fullback and you'll make a less secure guy feel intimidated. I'm a secure guy, but the next man might not be."

The similarity of the man's comment to her own conclusions about her looks jolted her. Judging by his comment she wasn't fooling herself. "Thanks, I know I'm tall for a woman, but I wouldn't have thought of the intimidation bit."

"My pleasure," he pointed to the touch screen. "More Olivia? I was kind of enjoying this 80s moment. I've got others. A-Ha? Men at Work? Asia?"

"Maybe later. For now, I'm amused enough by the fact that we're having a conversation," she said, checking her nails.

Steve shook his head, laughing. "Man, you are the stuck up bitch you act, aren't you?"

"Every inch. My dad convinced me I'm solid gold and I've never gotten over it," she answered. "Now I'm thirty-something, a knock off of my Dad, and a marriage prospect is nowhere in sight."

"Mm. Yeah. If it's anything, you are solid gold."

Faith grew irritated. McCallister's smarmy side was coming out. This would be a long ride if it kept happening. She hesitated a moment, but found a way to say what she was feeling. "Okay, so, if football references are intimidating and unfeminine, can I make a field hockey reference?"

"Shoot," he invited.

She struggled for a more delicate way to put it, and gave up. "Keep flattering me like that and I'll lay a field hockey stick upside your head," she said.

"Check," Steve said. "Flattery canceled for duration of date." He glanced at her. "There. Was that so hard?"

Faith breathed out in some relief.

"However," the man added, "since you've vetoed flattery for the rest of the evening, I need a moment to regroup and consider how to carry on this conversation, because by ruling out flattery you've exhausted my arsenal of cheap bachelor tactics. Would you mind if I took a break? Is A-Ha ok?" He gestured at the radio screen.

"Go ahead. But don't touch the volume." She took in the passing landscape, which was now in the darkness of early evening. White wood frame farm houses, Agway stores, and Depression-era cooperative farm silos paraded by to the tune of "*The Sun Always Shines on TV.*"

Faith enjoyed the play. She had loved Frank Baum's "Oz" books growing up, and though she had as an adult never read the book <u>Wicked</u>, she enjoyed the inside story of the Wicked Witch of the West. The darker Oz with its political overtones added something to the story, though she would still prefer the more innocent magical kingdom of the childrens' stories in her memory.

As she and Steve left the theater and walked toward the truck, she was struck again by curiosity about what he had under the truck cap. Since she had no intention of dating him a second time, this was her one chance to discover if there was truth to the rumors she'd heard. The conversation so far had been no-holds-barred, and the man had shown not the least bit of interest in hiding anything about his past or his lifestyle. So she decided to go for broke.

She glanced around, saw they were at the edge of the rapidly emptying parking lot, and that the back of the truck faced a shuttered commercial court. No one would see them if they climbed into the back, and even if they did, better that they did so here in Syracuse than in Ithaca.

"Open the cap, I want to see if the rumors are true."

"Okay," said Steve. "But if the rumors call this thing a fuckwagon, they're true, and you can skip the nickel tour."

She fumbled in her purse for a nickel, which she handed to her date. "They do. And innocent me, I've never been inside a 'fuckwagon' before, so I'm taking the nickel tour." She smiled at him, then walked around the back and motioned for him to open the lift gate for the cap. He did so, cast her a displeased look, and then dropped the tailgate for her to see the whole interior.

Sure enough, the bed of the truck was that, a bed. The décor was black and white, keeping with the color of the truck cap itself. She reached up and felt the mattress, and felt it give way, forming around her hand. The gray satin sheets were also a nice touch.

"Wow," she gaped. "Is that one of those fancy Swedish mattresses?"

Steve's expression went from uncomfortable to pleased. "Yeah, it's a recent addition. The foam is off patent now, so they're less expensive than they used to be. You like it?"

"Don't know. I'll have to try it," she said, and climbed up into the back and lay down on the mattress, facing the front. Out of the corner of her eye, she caught the man's raised eyebrows of surprise. *That's it,* she thought, *Let me defy your expectations.*

The front of the truck bed was a mirror inset with a fair-sized LCD screen. The sides of the bed, she saw, were camper-style chests with lids and/or drawers. She lay down on her chest, put her feet in the air, and explored.

The mattress was indeed pleasing, folding around her but still buoying her up. She began pulling open drawers and flipping lids. She would make sure Steve would never forget this night.

"Drawer one: empty," she observed.

"Yeah, Faith, I haven't used this part in a while," he protested.

"Drawer two: a large variety of condoms," she tossed him a look over her shoulder as she held up a translucent box filled with single condoms of various descriptions.

"Some girls insist," he shrugged. "I've got ribbed, smooth, licorice flavored, all kinds."

"Some insist? You mean *you* don't insist? You like living dangerously, do you?"

"Uh-" Steve stammered.

Faith didn't give him a chance to regroup. "I notice they are all regular size, contrary to rumor."

"It's not the size, it's how you use it," the man clichéd. "With sufficient skill on my part, I suppose a woman might get an exaggerated impression."

She wasn't about to let him get away with it. "Oh, the rumor wasn't that you were *large*." She thumped the drawer shut and watched his disgruntled expression in the mirror. She had the sense she might have crossed the line into hurting his feelings and felt the briefest tinge of regret. She turned over her shoulder to him again. "Are you going to hide out there, or are you coming up?"

Steve stared out into the courtyard, keeping his back to the tailgate. "I was staying out here, where I was less likely to get a field hockey stick upside my head."

"Suit yourself. I never picked you for uptight," she replied. *"That's right, you player, untangle these mixed signals,"* she chuckled to herself.

The other containers were two coolers, both empty, a large bin of sex toys, some of them large enough to make Faith wince, and a box with a collapsible fishing rod, reel, and lures.

"A fishing rod?" She said in disbelief. "Do I want to know?" She tried to picture the obscene uses of a fishing rod. She wondered if he was into some weird pain thing with fishhooks.

"Fucking to fishing in five. It's one of my favorites on a weekend, out at Taughannock Falls," Steve said, back to her.

"Must be a hit with the ladies, left sitting like a used dishrag," Faith envisioned how she would feel.

"I get no complaints. Sometimes they fish with me. Usually they're busy smoking my joints."

"T-M-I," she said, slamming the lid.

He twisted his neck to grin at her. "Let me get this straight, you're tearing uninvited through my temple of shag like a Catholic school girl on a 'sleepover' weekend, and now *you're* saying 'T-M-I?'"

"Hypocrisy is my prerogative," she answered, poking buttons beside the LCD screen. "Besides, weed is a huge turnoff. Heck, *smoke* is a turnoff. Don't you get enough smoke putting out kitchen fires?"

"*I* don't smoke the weed. It's a perk for my guest. Between the smoking and the munchies that follow, it reduces the burden of conversation."

Faith grinned at Steve's shamelessness. "You are the corruption of minors made manifest." One of the buttons she poked switched the screen on.

"I don't corrupt minors. Minimum age is eighteen," he sounded defensive. "I've even carded some. You'd be surprised how young some women go hunting."

"Aren't you the boy scout," she complimented his restraint.

"I *was* a boy scout, as it happens. Eagle scout, even." She felt him sit up on the tailgate. From the sound of his voice, his back was still to her.

"*Eagle* scout. That's *nice*," she sneered.

"I hear you were a girl scout," McCallister rejoined.

"I was. Then I had an accident, got a bad burn on my leg, and never went back."

"Hmm. How bad?"

"3rd degree. Eight inches. I still remember the smell. It's why I always wear slacks. It tore up my leg bad, and the scar is ugly."

"Ouch. That's the suck."

She had been poking the buttons on the LCD screen in between comments, and the screen flashed to life, showing two pornography actors going at it full steam and filling the truck bed with lush, polyphonic sound.

"Oh my!" she said, getting a much closer view of anal sex then she ever cared to. She flushed with embarrassment. She wondered how to turn the volume down and if anyone in the parking lot had heard the sounds from the truck. "It's like you're caught smack between their genitals in here."

"Don't *even* try to blame me for that one," Steve shouted over the sound. "*You* pushed the buttons."

"You watch this stuff?" she said, with fascination. "You get your rocks off with this?"

"I get my rocks off over *doing* it. Don't you?" he shouted again.

She wasn't obliged to answer, she decided. She put her chin on her palm and watched.

Steve grew more uncomfortable as the film played on, leaning over to peer around into the parking lot to see if they had drawn any attention. "Hey, if you don't mind turning it down, that would be nice. The FBI warning reminds you it's not licensed for public performance."

"How?" she said. "I don't see a volume control."

"The knob on the right," he said. She looked around frantically, not seeing a knob anywhere.

"On the *right*," he elaborated only with emphasis. She shook her head at his useless help.

He sighed, climbed into the truck bed, reached across her back, and dialed a knob she hadn't seen. The orgy faded to a whisper. She went back to watching.

"You know," he said into her left ear as she continued watching, "the volume knob trick is a guy thing, not a gal thing." The smell of his cologne was strong now.

"Is that so?" she answered. She wondered if her perfume was reaching him through his own personal cloud of "don't I smell good?" "Look," she pointed at the screen. "You think real women ever walk around with cum on their face?"

"Wouldn't know about women. I've recently discovered I've been dating girls for years," Steve remarked dryly. "And they occasionally do. I've been with one or two who loved to be smeared with it, finger paint style."

"Hmmm. Everyone's got a twist I guess."

"I suppose," the man said. "Maybe I've seen enough 'everyone' that twists aren't unique to me anymore."

She had a flash of sympathy. "Have you wondered if your relationship with sex may be, like, a disease? That you need help?" She'd read a book once by a woman who claimed to be a sex addict.

"Yes, I'm getting help, thanks," Steve muttered.

She laughed out loud. "Is it *working*?"

"Yes," he said. "Which is why even now, as the curve of your neck and back and that sweet ass beckon me, and take me back through years of desire for you, I'm not laying a hand on you." He sat up so his back was against the truck cap and he was further from her.

The sullen man's candor gave her a start. She hadn't realized he was so far along. "If that's so, I guess I've reached my desired effect of teasing the shit out of you, and it's time to get out of this thing," she said.

"Yeah, thanks," her date said. "I was wondering when we would get to that part. I mean, it's not like I go digging through your purse or lying on your bed."

"True enough," she said, sliding backwards with her elbows until she could bend at the waist and put her boots back on the ground. She stood up and pulled her shirt back down as Steve climbed out.

"Thanks for the nickel tour," she smiled her best shit-eating grin. "The mattress *is* nice."

"Next tour will cost you a dime," he remarked with a frown. "No credit given." He lifted the tailgate.

"Do you rent this thing? In case I meet someone?" she said, walking around to the passenger side door and waiting for him to unlock it.

"It's seventy dollars an hour plus mileage if I drive, forty dollars an hour if I don't, and more for me to video record the fun." She heard his boots come up his side of the truck, and the door lock pop open behind her.

"You get that much for it? A motel room would be cheaper," she gawked as she opened the door and climbed up again.

"Yeah, a motel room won't get you to Syracuse airport and back while you screw your brains out and drink, and you can't go from fucking to fishing in five at a motel," said Steve. "That's why this baby becomes a cash cow. Valentine's Day,

90

anniversaries, and graduations are my big business. All those city kids with too much money but too many roommates."

"People let you record them?"

"What do you mean 'let?' They pay extra for it," the man said, climbing in and popping the truck into gear. He slammed the door and started forward. "Everyone wants to be a porn star."

She reflected on what she had seen. Some wells of darkness were better off unplumbed, but she had just plumbed this one. "Thanks for showing me a piece of a sordid and decadent lifestyle I never knew existed in our sheltered town."

"You're welcome," he said with a depressed air. "Now that we're through talking about my life, what did you think of the play?"

When Steve dropped her off, her father was awake, watching television. Rosie was asleep beside him on the couch.

"Hey Pop."

"You smell like cologne," her father observed with distaste.

"Half of Syracuse now smells of the man's cologne. That doesn't tell you anything," she countered. "He must bathe in it."

"Did you have fun?"

"In a slummy kind of way, yeah. He was a fresh look at a person living by the lowest common denominators. Sex, drugs, easy women, and fancy cars."

Her father grunted the "I could have told you that" grunt. She waited for a statement to that effect while she hung up her jacket, but it didn't come. "How was the play?" he asked at length.

"It was good," she said, relieved to have a different topic on the table. "Remember the Oz books you read me when I was little?"

On his way back from the charity poker game Saturday afternoon, David pulled up to Clever Hans bakery and parked in the fifteen-minute spot. He was feeling good from having come in fifth overall out of two hundred players. Since his daughter had been with Rosie all day, he planned to use the winnings to pick up some of the bread Faith liked and cookies the girl might enjoy.

He pushed through the glass door and breathed in the sweet smells of the bakery. Pumpernickel was in the ovens and the macaroons had finished, he guessed. The woman behind the counter spoke with one of the customers in the cafe section of the restaurant in an on-and-off monologue in German, with only occasional replies from the customer. As she bagged his purchases in wax paper, the customer gave a longer reply, and he recognized the voice even if he didn't understand what was said. Without thinking, he turned around.

There, in a white blouse with green pants and an artfully folded scarf, sat Dr. Teschke, a coffee in one hand and a book in the other, reading. He chuckled to himself. *"She can find her way down from ivory tower hill."*

After a moment of confusion about what he should do, he decided to greet her, in case she had seen him. "Hello Professor," he said, "I didn't think you ever made it down into our town."

The academic looked up and recognized him. "Ah, Mr. Haversham, you have good taste in bakeries." She nodded to the cashier behind him. He swiveled, realizing to his embarrassment the baker had been holding the bags while he stared at the professor but had been too polite to interrupt him.

"Oh, thanks," he said, taking the bags hastily before turning to the professor. "It's not for me. My daughter likes the bread from here," he admitted. "And the pastries are for Rosie."

"You make the picture of the grandfather, spoiling the younger generations," she said, putting down her coffee to pick up a ribbon which she closed into her book. She motioned to the chair beside her. "Do you have a moment to sit?" She beckoned to him, much more relaxed and much less formal than she had been on campus.

"Uh, sure, I guess." He went over and took the seat, sitting at right angles to her so as not to act familiar by sitting beside her or challenging by sitting across from her. She offered him a piece of chocolate. He noticed the book she was reading, a gray book called <u>Collapse</u>.

"I've had time to think after our meeting the other day," she said, "and it occurred to me I had two things I left unsaid."

"Go ahead," he prompted, curious.

"The first is thank you for your public service. Public service is a long tradition in Germany, since the Renaissance, and it is much better respected there than here. So, since I suspect your fellow Americans rarely say it, I want to thank you for protecting me, indeed everyone, even if I never had need of your protection myself."

"Don't thank me, thank the men who do it today. I got good pay, and I have a good retirement if I'm careful with my money," David disclaimed.

"Is it one of your characteristics that you never take a compliment?" she tested pointedly, eyebrow raised. "I won't waste more time complimenting you if that's so." She made a motion as if she would pick up her book again.

He remembered Faith making this complaint. "Yeah, my daughter makes the same observation. I guess I am bad at compliments."

"In that case, you need practice. Take another compliment then. You're a handsome man," she said, smiling over her coffee cup before taking a sip.

With this, he felt his face flush. "I... I haven't heard that for many years," he stammered.

"Mm-hmm. Now you have. On to business?" she asked.

"I guess I should say you're well dressed," David replied, scrambling to catch up on the compliments. "Scarves are something I don't see much of around here."

"Why, thank you for the compliment," she accepted it. "I'm afraid I will never adapt to the American notion that scarves are only for winter and should only be made of wool. They also serve to hide my long neck."

"Nothing wrong with a long neck," he shrugged. She smiled at him, but he wasn't sure she'd taken the statement the way he intended.

"Necks like mine are better on swans than people. Anyway, to business," she redirected the conversation. He saw that Hildegard was not as good at taking compliments as she supposed. "My assistant, as you know, worked out what we think is Rosie's last name, and got some descriptions of the place she used to live, which we emailed to your daughter."

"Yes, she mentioned."

"There are some other observations my assistants had after speaking to her in Esperanto which you should know, but we wanted more time to figure out how to describe them delicately." The professor took another sip of her coffee. "The first is the girl is very religious. So religious, in fact, that the one assistant of mine who has worked in, how do you call it here, 'special education,' thinks she may have emotional or mental problems."

"Selene mentioned this in her email, too. But I can't say I've noticed," David replied. "Maybe I should take the girl to church with me tomorrow."

"If you think encouraging that sort of thing is a good idea," she said coolly. "At any rate, if she does anything which manifests a religion, you may get more of a clue as to her identity. Does she pray at certain times, or do rituals you don't recognize?"

"No. But she's quiet when we say grace, like she understands what we are doing."

"But nothing you would recognize as being, say, Jewish, or Catholic, or Muslim?"

"I wouldn't know about Jewish or Muslim. We had a Jewish firefighter, and he went to church on Saturday, and that's about as much as I know about being Jewish."

"Ironic, that the nation which spared Judaism from the blade of fascism knows so little about it," the professor observed.

"You don't have to know much about a religion to know people shouldn't be killed for practicing it." He wondered what sort of German Hildegard was.

"I don't question freedom of religion. I note the irony," she replied.

"Until my father's time, there were scarcely any black people in Ithaca. But my great-grandfather went south in the Civil War to free black people he'd never met," said David. "I guess we're like that."

"Though it's part of how this government manipulates you, I wouldn't change it. It's done much for the world, not in the least for my own homeland. But anyway, I talk of politics, which is bad manners amongst acquaintances," she took another sip of her coffee, nodding at him. "Forgive me."

"Nothing to forgive," he waved. Nonetheless, he was glad to move on to other topics.

"My assistants' second observation was that she was starved for attention, and showed behaviors which suggest she has spent little time with children her own age. Letting her play with other children her own age could be both good for her and revealing."

"She won't be with me much longer, just another few weeks, but I can see what I can do," he replied to the suggestion.

"I was under the impression you were the planned foster parent."

"Not so far as I know." He wondered where she had gotten that idea.

"Will she go to an orphanage, then?" Hildegard asked. David guessed, by dint of his having been a fireman, she considered him an expert on orphanages too.

"Maybe. In New York, though, the government tries to put children in foster care instead of orphanages. But with her not speaking English, they might have a hard time finding volunteers to take her," he realized as he said it to her.

"A shame," she said, uncrossing her legs and leaning forward to look at him. Her green eyes seemed to draw his. "She is a fascinating case. I'd love to follow her, and to learn the answer to her mystery when she tells her story. It would be terrible if she went somewhere where they made her feel bad, or stupid, because she spoke no English."

He envisioned this version of the girl's future. "It would. But the important thing to me is that we catch the person who set the fire. Especially since he tried to burn the kid alive."

"Naturally, this should be your first priority," she agreed and drained her coffee cup. "But if you decide to foster her, or if she continues to live in the area, I would love to follow her case. In fact, my office might be able to help with more translations from time to time if no Esperanto speakers can be found. She charmed my assistants."

David clasped his hands together to conclude the conversation. "I'll pass that on to Child and Family Services. They may take you up on it. They are short staffed and so far as I know only have Spanish and French speaking social workers, because New York City and Quebec are so nearby." He stood to go, sensing she had reached her point.

"I'd appreciate that. In the meantime, would you mind if my assistants had another go at her? On Monday?"

"Ah, the plot thickens," he thought. He wondered what the basis for their interest in her was. At the same time, he had no plans for Monday.

"Sure," he said. "Why not? What time?"

At this she smiled with satisfaction. They agreed on one in the afternoon, and David left with his purchases.

"You've got an eye on that one, Hildegard, you rascal," observed the baker in German with a grin.

"It's mostly business. But he is handsome, not true?" she replied. *"And smart also."*

It was Saturday night and Marcus's "Fire Chief Invitational Poker Pit" was in full swing in Faith's living room. She checked her new hand of cards, and compared them to the faces around the table. She had a pair of tens, which was not enough to bet against Dwight, Marcus, or her father, all of whom were able to produce fancy combinations like full houses and straight flushes out of thin air. So this was another round where she was giving up her ante without a fight. She crunched a yellow peanut M&M and leaned over Rosie. The girl was drawing, as she did almost without a break if allowed. When she leaned over to look at the picture, she saw it was an enlargement of the queen of hearts card from their deck. It was a special deck which did not show the classic pictures of abstract kings and queens but Dalmatian dogs in fire helmets doing various firefighting things.

Faith looked from the drawing to her hand. She was holding the queen of hearts card, which featured a Dalmatian dog carrying a medical bag. She wanted to scold Rosie not to draw her hand, but reconsidered. The girl had to have started the drawing long before she herself had been dealt the queen for the picture to be this complete. Besides, scolding her would give away that she had the queen. Not that it would make a difference unless she got lucky on her draw cards.

She took her cards from Marcus and worked them into her hand. She still had only a pair, and no flashy combos to pull out and surprise people. So she folded when her turn came.

"Folding again?" asked the captain.

"I haven't got squat," she rebutted. Dwight and David rolled their eyes to each other.

"The stakes are M&Ms. Be bold! Take some chances! Have some fun! There's a strategy in poker called 'bluffing,' you know," the fire chief reminded her. "It's daring! Show some panache!"

"He totally just did that gay hand thing with 'panache.' Do I do giveaway stuff like that?" she wondered. "No sense in betting if I can't win," she said, fitfully sorting her M&Ms.

"Whiny chicken-shit penalty. Five M&Ms," Marcus ordered.

"Woah, chief! Tender ears present! What if her first word of English turns out to be her mimicking your bad language? How will you feel then?" Faith protested. A glance at Rosie suggested the girl had given the vulgarity no notice.

94

She knew, however, from the long tradition of her father hosting these games during her childhood that when the current fire chief called a penalty for violating the spirit of the game, it got paid. She forked over another five M&Ms. This time, a green M&M met its end consoling her about the loss of its five comrades.

"There. You see? Being a wet blanket spoilsport will cost you M&Ms too! So you may as well bluff," said David with a wink. She punched his shoulder and then rested her chin on her palms.

"Wait? Whose house did this woman grow up in? The 'great poker master' David Haversham? You taught her to play like this?" Captain Earling said mockingly.

"You all taught me to play like this," said Faith. "By always beating me at poker when I was a girl and crushing all my dreams and confidence..." she sniffled. Instead of laughing, though, the men seemed hurt, so she gave up her joke. "I'm sorry guys. Don't get me wrong. I'm glad to be included in the game. It's nice to see you guys together. I guess...I guess my head is still at work."

"What about it?" asked Dwight with interest.

"It's the carriage house fire. The burn pattern on the concrete. It doesn't make sense, and it makes less sense the more I-"

"Shop talk, five M&M penalty." Marcus interrupted. Then he rounded on the captain. "Ten M&M penalty to you for encouraging her. You should know better!"

"Drat! Busted!" The man complained. "You have to admit it was a good set-up. She walked into it." He paid his ten M&Ms into the pot.

Marcus smiled at her. "I'll be happy to discuss it in a break in the game. Between the four of us we've got a hundred years of firefighting experience in this room. We can put our noggins together for ten minutes. If you want us to. But while the cards are out, we don't talk shop."

"Sure, sounds good. I'm not too proud to ask for help. Since I'm folded, I'll go start some coffee for that break." She got up and went to the kitchen. When she returned, Rosie was coloring in her queen of hearts and David and Captain Earling were facing off. She had caught a glimpse of both sets of cards, and so she suspected her father was about to get more M&Ms than a man with his heart condition needed. Sure enough, a moment later he was doubling his pool of M&Ms.

"You're not going to eat those. The ones Uncle Dwight has had his icky hands all over."

"You have a point," her father conceded.

"Yeah, you don't want to know where I had those hands," said the captain, bending forward to scratch his behind exaggeratedly.

"Here, give them to me instead!" she said, grabbing one of her father's red winnings and eating it. Her father was offended, though, so she replaced it with one of hers. Her father took poker etiquette seriously, even when the stakes were M&Ms.

Soon the game was under way again. Rosie had finished her picture and was admiring it when Faith got a break. She had a pair of queens, and put down three cards for draw. Marcus dealt her a three, a nine, and the queen of hearts.

She glanced at the girl's drawing of this same card and grinned. When her turn came, she raised her father's ten M&Ms to twenty.

"Twenty. Wow! Now we're talking real calories!" said the chief. He saw her. Dwight folded.

"Screw it. If she's putting down that means she's got something."

"Go on, she's decided to bluff now. She's getting bored of sitting there like a bump on a log," swaggered her father, seeing her and raising her another ten.

Faith raised him another ten. Marcus and her father called her with gleams in their eyes. "Let's see what my daughter has got this round."

Everyone laid down their cards. The chief had a pair of aces, and David had three jacks.

"Hah!" she cackled triumphantly, raking in what must have been a quarter pound of M&Ms.

"I spit on some of mine," said Dwight. "But I forget what colors they were." She stuck out her tongue at him, and everyone laughed.

Rosie reached over and took an M&M from her winnings.

"Hey!" protested Faith. "No stealing, you!" she said, forgetting she'd stolen one of her father's. "You've got your own, anyway," she reminded her, pointing to the coffee cup full of M&Ms beside the pencil box in case she didn't understand they were for her.

Rosie grinned and tapped her drawing of the queen of hearts by way of reply.

"Okay, that's a good drawing of a lucky card. I guess it deserves an M&M. But if I'm paying an M&M for it, I get to keep it."

With this, Rosie thrust the drawing at her as if this was fine, and then leaned over to give her a hug.

"Aw," said the chief. "Looks like she's settling in with you guys."

"Shop talk," Faith warned, waggling her finger.

"Okay, it can wait till a break."

"Which, in the time-honored tradition of the lady of the house calling the breaks in the game, I decree is now," she said. "Move your butts to the couch and I'll go get the coffee."

Dwight, Marcus, and David nodded in smiling agreement, and she heard the men discussing her mother as she got the coffee pot and a collection of mismatched cups and placed them on a tray.

"Yeah, Connie used to call breaks after she won, too," Captain Earling remembered.

"She explained it to me. She did it so she had time to savor her victory before Marcus or Marten kicked her ass the next hand," her father explained.

"Language!" Faith shouted her reminder at hearing the word "ass."

"Right, right," conceded David. "But we're not at the table, so no penalty."

"I think I can assign penalties at any point until the last hand is down," said the chief. "I'm feeling a five M&M penalty coming on per cuss word. To keep us honest around the ladies."

Faith emerged with the coffee, which the men accepted gratefully. Rosie came to the coffee table too, as if to be near them, but showed no interest in coffee and sat down and began to draw again. Faith sat beside her in turn.

Her father was the first to speak. "Hey, while I have you gentlemen here, I wanted to say something. I feel lucky that my daughter, who saw the misery and long hours of our profession her whole life growing up, decided to put on the uniform and wears it so well! I am proud of you, Faith, and I want to say it where my friends can hear it."

"Hear, hear!" said Dwight, raising his coffee cup. Marcus did the same.

Faith felt her ears turn bright red, but she was pleased and surprised by her father's praise and the support of the other two men who had known her all her life. She couldn't let it go by, though, without making light of it.

"Don't get too excited. I don't need to stay a firefighter. I could still change careers. For example, I could become, I don't know...a super model, for instance!"

"Oh yeah!" cheered Dwight. "Let me be your photographer! I'll do all your nude pictures! Trust your Uncle D with your negatives, baby!" This netted another roomful of laughs, but a worried glance showed that, once again, Rosie tuned out of the bawdy conversation. On seeing her glance at the girl, the captain sobered.

Marcus was quick to lay out the invite for her to speak her doubts. "So, tell us what has got you puzzled. Something about the burn pattern?"

She had a moment of appreciation for her chief. He was not timid, nor indecisive, but he had a gay man's way of making people comfortable.

"Okay, you remember how I showed you guys a photo of that circle on the floor of the carriage house where the concrete had turned to glass?"

"Sure. One of the most striking photos in your briefing," said Marcus. But David just stroked his chin.

"I didn't see it, but I guess there was a big circle of vitrified concrete," said her father.

"You didn't show your old man the briefing?" Captain Earling raised his eyebrows at her. "And here he was heaping praise on you?"

"Hey, he's retired," she pointed out.

"She's right. You guys are lucky I'm indulging this shop talk," he said. "So, for concrete to turn to glass, it has to get very hot. Go on."

"Yes, but you said the only thing on Earth which got so hot was lightning, and then you showed us the lightning map and the footage from Cornell security cameras," resumed Marcus. "It was conclusive, if weird."

"Yeah, I know," said Faith. "Lightning is one of the only things that gets hot enough to turn concrete to glass. But think about it. If lightning struck the carriage house, even multiple times, what would it do?"

"Catch the roof on fire, and any wooden members in contact with a lot of metal might ignite," offered Dwight.

Faith looked around significantly. "See, that's it! It wouldn't create an eight-foot circle of glass on the floor! It also wouldn't blow the building apart from within."

"Maybe it was the diesel fuel storage tank for the tractors which blew up," countered the fire chief. David said nothing, but showed careful attention.

"Nope. That was attached to the side of the house, and the burn marks suggested that it didn't explode, but that it was thrown outward with the walls and sprayed burning diesel fuel over about twenty yards. And diesel doesn't explode like gasoline anyway," she explained.

"So, you're saying whatever got that hot had to be *inside* the building," her father remarked.

Faith pointed at him. "That's it. I think whatever it was, it was inside the building."

"Could it have been, I don't know, some kind of electrical device which shot lightning or blew up?" proposed Marcus.

"Who knows? I don't think so, based on the burn pattern, which I'll get to, but it's a point I want you guys to remember. If it happened inside the building, what the fu-, er, heck was it?"

The three men nodded to themselves.

"Yeah, there you go, old guys. Think for a minute and see if you can get me off the hook with this one. And while we're at it, let's talk about the burn pattern."

"What about it?" asked Dwight.

"You said you'd seen down power lines turn concrete to glass. How did it look when you saw that? Was it a big area, or a small one?"

Captain Earling squinted in recollection. "It was a stripe shaped like the down end of the power line. It was a just a bit wider than the power line itself."

"Was it a big power line?"

"Yeah. One of the trunks for the city," he recalled.

"But, see, it only vitrified a little concrete, for all that power."

"Sure."

"So if it was a man-made electrical device of some kind which destroyed the carriage house and burned the floor, where did it get the wattage to do it without popping a fuse or transformer somewhere or causing a blackout? A 110 or 220 volt outlet? I think not."

"Ah, good point," Marcus said. Even her father seemed intrigued.

"You didn't tell me it was this interesting, Faith," he complained when she raised her eyebrows at him.

"Oh, you're retired. Anyhow, I have to be desperate before I ask you for help. I feel like I'm letting you down when I do."

Marcus raised his palm to reassure her. "We like to pretend fire investigations all have knowable answers, and we find or manufacture knowable answers to give homeowners or insurance companies closure or to make the Common Council happy. But one thing you'll learn about fire investigations is the answers aren't always knowable, or knowable on our budget."

"Got it, Chief. But if someone was trucking around this county and our sister jurisdictions with some kind of device which could turn fifty square feet of concrete into glass, wouldn't that be an issue which commanded some budget? Or some help?"

"Yes. If you think this a man-made device which did this damage, we do have a problem. "

Faith brightened. Marcus had struck her lure, now she had to reel him in. "Okay, hold that thought. Now get this. I talked to a materials science professor, Dr. Bronner. He said the pattern I observed, where the surface of most of the area was turned to glass, but only in the center was the concrete glass all the way through, suggested a flash burn. In other words, he thinks the heat was so intense as to vitrify concrete, but so short that except close to the center it had only time to vitrify the surface. But it gets better. The shorter the event is, the hotter it would have to be. And he did some physics backwards and forwards, lots of numbers. The results suggested that to do so much damage to concrete over such a radius in an instant, the center of the event had to reach - hold on to your pants - seventy five million degrees."

There was a long silence. It was broken by Dwight whistling in amazement.

"Which is hot like what?" wondered Marcus. "Give me a comparable heat event."

"Nothing. Not the sun, not a nuclear weapon, and sure as hell not lightning. So there are two explanations. The doc was wrong about the flash burn pattern, and whatever was hot was cooler and hung around longer, or we have a huge fu-, er, fracking problem. So now you know why I'm preoccupied. Every time I think I'm crazy and it was lightning or the fuel storage going up or both, I go look at that eight-foot circle of glass and get all confused again."

"Didn't you take the police officer from Syracuse out there? McCrae?" Chief Bauer asked.

"Cassius McCrae?" Dwight whistled again. "He's famous. Black guy? Straight talker?"

"That's him," Faith confirmed. "Down-to-earth. He read my whole briefing and listened to me. It was great working with him."

The captain waved a hand at Marcus. "Yeah, Chief, if Syracuse sent McCrae, they care about this too. Get on the horn with the chief of police in Syracuse. McCrae could be working anywhere. He's solved three cases from the 'Cold Case' TV show. He's a celebrity."

"I had no idea," Faith said. "He didn't act important."

"I had no idea either," said the fire chief. "If it's true I will call up to Syracuse and talk to them. Was Detective McCrae helpful?"

"He couldn't help me with the fire part of it. He was as confused by the facts as I am. But he did make a good suggestion about how to react. After thinking about it, I agree with him and I'm about to propose it to you."

"Which is?" Marcus prompted.

"That we go to the feds. He suggested we take the issue to the FBI guys downtown, and get their ideas. If there are people running around with a device which can create that kind of heat and doesn't even need power from the power grid to do it, it needs to come off the street."

Marcus rubbed his chin, and donned his Marco-Lisa smile. After a moment, he said, "Get a pen and paper."

She grabbed a blank sheet of paper from Rosie's supply and one of the colored pens the girl wasn't using. "Shoot, Chief."

"Write this down. 'Based on the totality of technical circumstances of this case, recommend referral of case file to federal authorities for consultation.' Put those words in a memo to me on Monday, and I'll approve it. The line should still be vague enough that if someone sticks their nose into the file before we're finished, they won't get hysterical about why we sought federal assistance. But if there's some kind of terrorist stalking our county, we need to act, and the feds are the best guys to help. You and Detective McCrae were on target. We don't need another 9/11 or Market Garden attack. Good job with the recommendation."

"Whew," said Faith.

"Whew? You've told us there's something out there hotter than a nuke and you're saying 'whew'?" Her father squinted at her.

"No, I mean, 'whew,' you guys didn't look at me and say 'Duh, everyone knows a whoozie-whatsamajigger gets that hot. You call yourself a fire investigator, Inspector Haversham? Why, I've got a two-month rookie who knows that.'"

The three older men all gave various versions of a grin. "Nope. Can't say I've run across anything which gets to seventy five million degrees, or a fireman who's dealt with it," the fire chief conceded.

"There might be a fireman from Nagasaki who has," Dwight pointed out.

"Yeah, but dead people don't count," Marcus replied.

"Now that I have your agreement, I wonder again if I've overlooked something," she fretted. "I don't want to make us all look foolish."

"Would standing on fifty square feet of concrete-turned-glass again help?" the fire chief tested.

"No," Faith admitted.

The man continued. "Then this is how I see things. You have solid physical evidence of something weird and there's no need to second guess it more than a couple of times. The worst that can happen, after all, is the feds come around and say 'silly locals, everyone knows a whoozie-whatsamajigger gets that hot.' And the only consequences would be that we would be smarter and the feds would feel good because they got to put down a local."

At this, everyone laughed, and Rosie smiled at her picture to hear it.

"What could that girl tell us?" Dwight wondered.

"It so happens I might have us some help with that," David said proudly.

"Oh yeah?" the other men raised eyebrows at his tone.

"I ran into the professor who figured out what language she speaks. And, after some sweet-talking, she's agreed to keep working with us longer term," he swaggered.

Faith felt amazed. Her father sweet-talked a woman into something? She wished she'd been there to see it. She would have sooner envisioned a bear figure skating.

"Oh ho, secret agent Haversham laying on the rakish charm?!" Marcus said.

The retired fire chief flexed facetiously. "Yeah, it's my rugged good looks. Plus, chicks dig a pacemaker when you explain to them the benefits of extra, you know, voltage."

The men laughed uproariously at this, but Faith shook her head and started gathering coffee cups. It pained her to hear her father boast about his way with women. He was a great many things, but until her mother's last few months of life Faith had never seen her father do much she would consider charming or sweet. She decided to break up the discussion before she dwelled on this much.

"Alright, now that you guys have smothered me with praise and agreed to all my wonderful ideas, back to the card game!" she ordered. "You guys have made a good start at pleasing the queen of this house! Now feed me M&Ms!" The men got up and assumed their places at the table and Rosie, without looking up from her drawing, gathered her pens and paper and followed. When Faith returned from the kitchen to take her seat, the girl tapped her arm and handed her a picture.

The drawing impressed her. It was a good rendering of a firefighter's helmet, not a Merryweather American-style helmet with the broad brim, but a rounded, more enclosing style she remembered from a safety class as being more common in Europe. "Hey, guys, check out our artist's work." She passed the picture around.

Dwight admired it. "Hey, chief, that's an F-1 style helmet. I know I've talked to you about getting those."'

"Oh, are you *still* going on about the F-1s?" groaned David. "Don't you ever quit?"

"I'm telling you, Chief, they're great. They protect your face, too, and they're much less apt to come off your head if something falls on them. You can walk into a structural fire and go home with lily-white cheeks. You save a bundle on foundation and cosmetics," Captain Earling patted his cheeks jocularly.

"He's been babbling about those F-1s since he did the exchange firefighter thing to Belgium as a rookie," David explained.

"Huh. She drew a Quebec flag on the helmet," said Marcus, holding up the drawing. "Isn't a white cross on a blue field with those french flower things Quebec?"

"I think so," said Dwight.

"We should know. We border on Quebec," said Faith, abashed.

"Oh, come on. How many Quebecois can recognize the New York State flag?" David countered.

"That's not fair. Two-thirds of American state flags are dudes in togas standing next to a random object on a blue field," the captain rebutted her father.

"It's not a dude on our flag. It's a dude-*ette*. And an Indian," Faith corrected.

"Well, our motto is easy to remember. '*Excelsior*,'" her father said.

She shook her head at the consternation the drawing had created. "The motto of Quebec is '*Je me souviens*,' which is like 'I remember' or something. You guys are overlooking this could be a clue. She might be from Quebec. Take that in with you to the professor, Dad." She handed her father the picture.

"Okay, okay, back to the game," Marcus reminded everyone as he dealt cards. But he had a serious look on his face as he did so. Faith guessed the older

100

man was now sharing her 'preoccupied by work' problem. She felt bad that she'd spoiled his game.

Chapter 7

Baptisms

As mass concluded on Sunday, David searched the crowd for the youth minister and catechist, Marten Jostens, who usually sat across the nave from him. He was frustrated in his search by the greetings and well wishes of his fellow parishioners. But as he weaved through the crowds of people rising to go, he caught sight of Mr. Jostens standing in front of the nave of the church, chatting with a young Hispanic couple carrying a babe-in-arms. He stood back until they finished talking, and waved to catch the catechist's attention.

"Got a minute, Mart?" he asked. The catechist's eyes brightened.

"Of course! Retirement suiting you?"

He smiled. "It's growing on me. I guess all stones stop rolling eventually."

"That they do," said the youth minister. "Even Mick Jagger's will someday, rest his soul. But let's hope it takes you and him a while yet. What can I do for you?" He tossed David a smirk, a smirk the firefighter had grown familiar with at more than one poker game. Since gambling was poor form for church staff, the stakes Constance, Marten, and the others had always insisted on were M&M candies rather than actual money. The catechist, rakish and endearing, had always won all the M&Ms while flashing the same friendly smirk.

"I have a favor to ask," he said.

"Oh, is this about the foster child you brought to youth group? Michelle mentioned you had called ahead to ask if you could leave her with the group, thanks for that courtesy by the way, I gather she had special needs."

He paused at this, displeased to hear Rosie described thus, but knowing his friend meant no harm by it, he continued without comment.

"She doesn't speak any English, that's part of the challenge. Not so needy otherwise. If Faith had been so little trouble, I'd have many fewer gray hairs."

At this they both enjoyed a long laugh. Constance had still been a Sunday school teacher, and Marten brand new as the childrens' minister, when Faith had scandalized the parish with her rebellion against her mother and a penchant for older men and public nudity. Her refusal of her confirmation and departure from the Church had hurt Constance a great deal, but she had decided arguing with her daughter would drive her further away. As a veteran of those times, and an old friend of Connie's, the catechist was one of the few who could appreciate the number and origins of David's gray hairs.

Marten thumped him on the back and threw a lanky arm over his shoulder. "Bless your good wife. I think of her every class I teach."

The two of them teared up together in silence, and, with some surreptitious blinking to avoid getting the attention of the other parishioners, got to business. Marten stood back a moment to wave at a departing family before turning back to him.

"So what's the favor?"

"It is about Rosie, you guessed right. I wanted to know if she could be baptized. I don't think she ever has been."

"Is she raised in the church?" his friend asked. His tone suggested this favor could be simple. David hoped he kept that opinion.

"Don't know. I haven't seen her pray at all, though she becomes quiet and bows her head when Faith and I say grace for supper or if someone gets angry at her."

"So you don't know if her family was Roman Catholic?"

He paused again here, unsure of how much he wanted to say. Churches were not great places to keep secrets.

"We're not sure. We don't know a lot about her parents," he admitted.

"Hmm. How old is she? Twelve? Thirteen?"

"She doesn't know how old she is, believe it or not. I'd guess ten to twelve, since I've had to shower her. You know, not yet *that* old."

"Ah. Say no more," Marten said. "Twelve is a lucky number anyway, you know, so let's use that." He gave David another smirk and chuckle. "I can ask the Pastor. But he may say no."

David felt surprised. "Why?"

"Baptism at birth is to wipe away her original sin, but she's old enough to have willfully sinned. So before she can be baptized, she has to repent of her sins, understand she is joining the community of the Father, Son, and Holy Spirit and understand the significance of Jesus's sacrifice. The usual limit these days for child baptisms is seven years. If they are older, children have to undergo an adapted form of the Rite of Christian Initiation for Adults."

David felt some anger at this obstacle, but knew Marten would not lightly refuse him, and was only warning him so he was not let down, so he said nothing in reply while he managed his feelings.

But the catechist could read his face. "It's a new Vatican. Things aren't...open like they used to be."

David struggled to compose his answer. He found it ironic that while he argued with Faith about the authority of the Pope, here he was arguing against it with the catechist. "It's the same old church, Mart. The same church where for centuries good people have sheltered each other from tyrants, war, and sin. It doesn't belong to one old man whatever rules he may make. Children are as innocent now as when the Lord suffered them to come unto." He expected this to hit home. Connie and Marten had worked together for years on the underground railroad, smuggling political and economic refugees through Ithaca to other northern states or to Canada. The man's sister had even adopted a Salvadoran orphan with great expense and shuffling of paperwork. The reference to this secret, he was sure, would not be lost on his friend.

Marten turned his eyes to the floor, and then back up. "I'll ask the Pastor, brother. Stay here." Seeing David's surprise that he wasn't being invited along, his friend paused. "Don't think I'll take you to see him. Both of you are so hardheaded you'd argue so long we could use you for church pillars and hang censers from your noses. You can go see him on your own if you want, but I don't want to be there."

The firefighter sighed and shrugged. He hoped he didn't have to go outside the Catholic Church to get Rosie baptized. He was sure a Protestant sect would do it, but he didn't want to admit they might do something his church would not. "Go ahead, Mart, I'll take whatever answer he gives you."

David sat in a pew and prayed. He asked for help with Connie, with Faith, for his own good health, and with a baptism for this stranger. After a long while, he felt his friend take a seat beside him on the pew.

"No, huh?" he guessed at the answer from the respectful silence.

"No, he won't. Baptism for someone this girl's age is supposed to be an act of faith, not the cleansing of original sin."

"Well, I tried. I had to try, since the darling is in my care. Couldn't not try,

103

anyhow."

Again, Marten threw an arm over David's shoulder, and they sat regarding the crucifix behind the altar. Eventually he drew a long breath, and then spoke.

"Would it be okay if I did it?" he asked. "I wouldn't be able to get you a certificate, but if what you're after is the removal of original sin, I suppose you won't care."

"What?" Mr. Haversham was startled by the suggestion.

The catechist kept his eyes on the crucifix. "I'd do it. I've had the sacraments training. All that says I can't do it, after all, is some funny old man in Rome, represented by the Pastor," he swaggered. "Since the Pastor has told me I can't, I can't promise my baptism have any weight with God. But I'm not afraid to try. I suspect if St. Peter stops me at the pearly gates because I baptized a child in a way that contradicts church rules, since that's a sin he'll sympathize with, we can work out some kind of deal. Besides, you could go down the street to the Episcopal church and get a baptism Rome would recognize, so what sense does it make not to let you get one here?"

Marten's compassion, bravado, and friendship struck David full on at this moment. Faith and Constance had more than once remarked that he was better at fighting than mending fences. The man's offer was a prime example of what Constance would have called a "constructive middle ground," a thing which he himself was always unable to find.

"You're on, you rascal," he said, standing. "Let's go save a soul."

His friend rose beside him. "Technically, I'm washing out her original sin. Only the Lord and genuine contrition saves souls. So long as we're clear."

"Limitations and reservations accepted," said David. The two men grinned at each other. At Marten's gesture, he led the way to the Sunday school classrooms.

They found Rosie waiting with Michelle and three other girls in the youth group classroom, which was nothing more than a regular weekday classroom in the attached School of the Immaculate Conception. Michelle had a stack of hymnals she had gathered up from the students, and Rosie and the other girls were sketching on the classroom whiteboard with colored markers. Already he could see that his foster child had finished the black and white outline of her sketches and was beginning to fill in different panels with solid colors.

David and Michelle nodded greetings to each other. Michelle had already been a Sunday school teacher when Constance had given up the job.

"Was she any trouble?" he asked.

"Umm.... not in a bad way," she said doggedly. "She likes to dance, I guess."

"She's nice," said one of the students. "And she dances great! She danced while we were singing hymns." They went back to sketching on the whiteboard, asking Rosie what color to use to fill in the next frames.

Michelle turned back from the whiteboard to face the two men. "Her parents aren't in the church, I guess," said Michelle. "Will she be coming next week?"

The two friends exchanged glances. It wasn't like Michelle to express any apprehension at all about a student, but the tone of her voice did suggest she would like more warning if Rosie were to come again.

"Probably not. But if she is still with me, I can keep her at home with Faith during mass next week. I brought her with me to see if the Church got any reactions from her. I take it she was disruptive, then?"

Michelle sighed. "She had things to say, but no one understood them. And every time we sang, she wanted to dance, which I suppose isn't a bad thing, but it distracted the class a lot."

Another girl's voice piped up from the blackboard. "If we're going to sing anyway, why don't we dance too? It makes sense to me!"

Marten laughed. "Another few weeks of this and our younger sisters may nail a petition to your door."

"We could change the lesson plans, I suppose. Are there any Vatican-approved dances, Mart?"

At this the catechist found his smirk again. "I doubt it. But I'll look, since it's so popular with your audience."

Michelle caught David's gaze. "I don't mean to sound unwilling. She was a test, but I could cope again. She wasn't rude, or mean, but once we started singing, it was like she was in her own world, you know?"

"The Office of Children and Family Services is looking for a permanent foster care arrangement for her, so she may not be with me next Sunday. But thanks for being patient with her. If nothing else, I enjoyed mass, and you helped me be there," he explained. Michelle turned back to her class.

He put a hand on his charge's shoulder and, with a wave to the other children, led her and Marten from the room. A chorus of "Bye Rosie!" followed them out the door and his foster daughter resisted his tugging so as to have time to wave back.

"So, follow me. I have a plan," suggested the catechist in a low voice. David assented under his breath, but to his surprise, Marten did not lead him to the sanctuary with the new immersion font, but to a door off the narthex. "If I close the door, this will only take a minute." When the entry hall was empty, Marten unlocked the door, and then stepped through, tugging Rosie quickly behind them.

Marten closed the door gently. David let go of the girl's hand and looked around. Two walls of the room were the inside of the outer walls, and the other two were also made of stone. The traditional metal and wood font with a crucifix behind it stood opposite the door and an ornamental metal grate around its base let the water drain away. On the left edge of the font stood a brass bowl.

The door clicked shut behind him. He had a moment of recollection of standing in his firefighter's dress uniform, still a Sergeant, as the pastor had baptized Faith in this same old font, with the same bowl. He let the memory go. His daughter's leaving the Church was water down the ornamental floor drain. There was nothing to be done for it. "I didn't know we kept this font," he said.

"Not many people do. But enough of the old guard insisted," explained Martin. "Immersion is too evangelical for some. Okay, so, how much English does she understand?" Marten inquired as he inspected the font.

"She understands it better and better, but she doesn't speak a word," said David.

"So, should I try to interact with her, or do you want me to treat her like a babe-in-arms?" the man mused.

"Satisfy yourself," Mr. Haversham suggested. "You're the one doing the baptism."

The catechist gave a jagged frown of concentration for a second. "Since we're winging this, there are no rules. And since she'll be leaving you soon, we won't even need godparents."

The youth minister paused to fill the baptismal bowl, and then gestured to Rosie. "Come join me, miss."

The girl turned from where she was examining the crucifix. The two men gestured and she came over and stood in front of them. The youth minister took one knee so he was her height, and offered her his hand. He looked into her eyes.

105

Rosie returned his look placidly.

"In case you understand, I'll explain what I'm about to do. When we are born, each of us carries some of the sin that was involved in the act of our parents conceiving us, and from some of the sins of the first man and woman, Adam and Eve. What we will do is wash that sin off you by pouring some water over your head and praying. But you will still have all the other sins you have committed in your life on you. Do you understand me?"

The girl looked at him, cocked her head, and then nodded.

"Now, I am not a pastor of this church, and neither is Mr. Haversham. By the rules of this Church, you cannot become a member of this church until you have accepted Jesus Christ as your savior and gone through a baptism as an adult. Do you understand that I am not making you a Roman Catholic with this baptism?"

Rosie was silent for a while, and then shrugged, saying nothing.

"How do I interpret a shrug? Is she saying she's indifferent? Or is she saying she doesn't understand?" Mr. Jostens asked.

David consulted his growing lexicon of her gestures. "I think she's saying she's indifferent. When she's saying she doesn't understand, she raises her arms and holds her palms..." He stopped in mid-sentence.

Rosie had picked up the baptismal bowl and poured the entire contents over the catechist's head. The water flowed over his forehead and ran down into the man's pale blue shirt and tie, creating a darkening wave which rolled down his back and front.

Marten spluttered in surprise, but laughed thereafter. "Well, I'll be..." he said. David cringed in embarrassment. It was a "Rosie moment."

The girl beamed and replaced the bowl on the edge of the font. "*Pura.*"

Mr. Haversham felt his ears burning. "I'm sorry, I had-"

His friend was unflappable. He raised his hand to stop the apology, and grinning ear to ear, stood and dipped the bowl in the font a second time, blinking away the water still running into his own eyes.

"For as long as this child is in your care, will you raise her as a Christian, to reject Satan and accept the Holy Trinity?"

David knew his part here. "I will."

"What is this girl's full name? Do we know it?"

"Rosetta Amata," he said.

"Then Rosetta Amata, I baptize you without authority or certification, but as layman with the fervent hope that, given your circumstances as a ward of the state without church or home, and the particular challenges the Lord has given you, He will absolve you of all original sins and you will embrace the Holy Trinity your whole life long." Marten said. He raised the bowl toward her.

Rosie dipped her head before the catechist, and he poured the bowl of the water on her head. Her black neck-length hair flattened against her head in the water and the water coursed over her brow. David saw, as he did each time the girl left the shower, that with her hair flat she was less than pretty, but her smile was as large and warm. As he watched her playfully blow some of the dripping water off her top lip, he felt a weight of worry lift off his shoulders. Whatever her origins, her original sin was now lifted. He stepped forward, and using the thumb of his right hand, drew a cross on her forehead, as he and Connie had drawn on Faith's forehead so long ago.

When he was done, Marten spoke. "I had been going to do the full liturgical piece, but you'll forgive me, it struck me as out of place. And since I'm not a pastor, it's kind of meaningless for me to recite the whole Roman manual anyway."

It was David's turn to reassure. "Don't worry. You did great." He clapped his friend on the back of his wet shirt. "Sure you don't do this more often?"

"Umm....Never.... The love and forgiveness of God is only for the ordained clergy to share." The catechist looked down, and Mr. Haversham followed the turn of his friend's eyes with his own.

Rosie was reaching over the edge of the font and refilling the baptismal bowl. Her expression was intent. When she was done, she raised the bowl toward David.

"Your turn, I guess. You're the only one in the room not wet already," his friend observed.

Mr. Haversham looked down at Rosetta. He had thought she poured the water over Marten as a mistake or a misinterpretation of his intent. But here she was, intent on doing it to him, too.

"Honey, I've already been baptized. Many, many years ago. So was Mr. Jostens."

Rosie either did not understand or was not moved by his claim. She cocked her head again and raised the bowl a bit higher.

He wondered if by giving into her he was satisfying some imperative she felt or encouraging her to be charming but lawless. He decided he wouldn't figure out which on the spot, however, and knelt, wetting his knees on the edge of the wrought metal drain grate.

Without word or ceremony, she poured the water over him. He gasped. The water was cold and his thin dress shirt absorbed little of the water, so it flowed down to his waistline.

"*Pura,*" Rosie pronounced again, and replaced the bowl on the font. She then stood and waited while he rose and collected his wits.

"You happy now?" David grumbled. She nodded. He turned back to the catechist.

"This takes a load off, Mart."

"All in a day's work," said his friend. "Now let's skedaddle. If the Pastor finds us using the baptistery font for Marco Polo he'll be obliged to, um, 'reproach' me." David took the girl by the hand and followed him out the door. Some of the parishioners were already in the narthex gathering for the next mass. The three of them walking by with soaking wet heads drew some stares, but he pretended not to notice, the catechist made no excuse, and Rosie was as unconcerned as ever.

They stopped on the steps, since he knew Marten would have to return to his office. Sunday would be his busy day.

"Thanks again," David said.

"Stop thanking me already. You're welcome. If we've done anything wrong, I'm sure the Lord will see his way clear. But because of where I work, it will take a trip to Rochester to confess this."

"I'm sure," he agreed.

"If you get any good card games going, let me know. M&Ms are getting so expensive I might as well play for real money," Marten winked.

David tapped the man's shoulder. "Marcus has started running those card games again. I'll drop your name the next time he sets one up. I'd love to have you. And don't worry, Faith is still lousy at cards, you'll clean her out. It'll be like old times."

"Peace to you both," Marten farewelled them. The girl waved as he did. David led her by the hand back to his truck, which was the only large pickup at all on the half-empty floor of the parking garage.

He had Rosie climb in the driver's side door and scramble across to the passenger's seat. He was hungry. He should think about lunch for the two of them.

The State Street Diner should be open, so he would give it a pass by on the way home.

The girl laughed at something apparent only to her as he backed out of his space and began driving away. David didn't worry over what it was. Much of her internal life was unknowable anyway. He wondered if it was more or less unknowable than those of other people, or if it just seemed that way because she couldn't talk to him. But now he could be sure that, even if he couldn't take care of her forever, he had done his best to take care of her spirit. For all he knew, she'd already been baptized, but he'd have been remiss if he let Rosie go on into the world of foster and institutional care without being sure she was free of original sin.

Sunday traffic in Ithaca was light. It often was.

Chapter 8

Zurich

Dr. Vincent Foster looked out his second floor office bay window onto the street outside. Pear trees shaded the avenue, and to his left, he could see Zurich's Hallwylplatz beckoning him to take an afternoon walk. He'd taken the walk many times since setting up this Zurich office in the 1960s. While at his age a trip to the square wasn't the five-minute stroll it used to be, it was still near enough for days he felt pent up or he needed a change in perspective to help him with a sticky problem. And today was such a day, for at the moment both things were true.

"Your noon tea, sir," said his assistant, Sharrah Bassi, behind him. Vincent swiveled in his leather office chair, which was the only concession to western décor in his office. The rest of the office his assistant had decorated with furniture and art from her native Pakistan. The doctor had at first been overwhelmed by the ornateness and color of the office: it had previously been beige and conservative. He had felt chagrined at having authorized the young woman to redecorate the office however she saw fit while he traveled. But he had grown used to its color and welcoming warmth in the two years since. The one thing he had changed was his chair.

The desk chair she had originally chosen neither suited his aging back nor swiveled to the window, and the view of the avenue was one of the reasons he had chosen this office so long ago. So that gilded chair now stood in front and to the left of his desk, and was set aside not for guests, but for Sharrah herself. And it was that seat she took as she smiled at him, lowered the lunch tray to the desk top, and poured his tea. "Cucumber sandwiches with lemon, butter, parsley, and cumin, sir," she announced. She presented him with his lunch and a small plastic cup of his daily medications, and then slid his tea beside the small plate.

Dr. Foster returned the smile. The woman was always glad to see him, which was not something he experienced at all of his many offices around the world. As the president and CEO of Vincent Foster Associates, most of his other offices were at research laboratories or industrial centers. When he arrived at them he was normally greeted by an anxious department or section head eager to show the company president what was being done with his considerable wealth. So he grew tired of these travels, the simpering of his employees, and the exaggerated and paper-thin cheer of ninety percent of the flight attendants and hotel clerks he met along the way.

"Thank you," he said, and meant it. She packed his daily pill boxes for him, took his clothes to the cleaners, and had even once or twice packed his suitcases. He had on those occasions gone without things a woman could not be expected to think of and no gentlemen would ask her to remember, so he had established the boundary that he would pack his own suitcase. But her care and patience were welcome.

He took his sandwich. It was, he considered, not his wealth about which he was so particular to his own detriment. His wealth was not his own, or it hadn't been until he had begun to turn a massive profit. It had been wealth taken from innocent people, from victims, and it had come to him by foul means. And it was on him to redeem it, and the sacrifices of these innocents, by making the money serve mankind. This was why he demanded results, and made no mistake about demanding them. And that, he supposed, might be why Sharrah was the only one who made him feel unconditionally welcome. She was the only one of his employees of whom he made no demands. He made requests from time to time, and she received them with an enthusiasm which suggested she lived to serve him. Vincent was now careful to avoid any but the most delicate criticism of her work, since criticism left her crestfallen and bereft.

He bit into the sandwich. It was marvelous. The woman had a gift for turning something bland and western, like his office or the cucumber had been, into something flavorful and memorable. "Mm, oh, you outdo yourself. I wish my mother were alive for these sandwiches."

Sharrah beamed. "It's inspired by my mother, sir. On hot days she would serve cucumber with lemon juice and cumin and parsley for lunch. I'm glad you like it."

"Please, take lunch with me."

With a nod, she took her own sandwich, which she had prepared and left on the tray, doubtless hoping for an invitation.

"How was Hong Kong, sir?"

"Excellent. New progress and three new clients. The new rich of China are willing to spend money on fertility medicine, and they are more willing to accept risk than American clients, who are always on about 'results contracts' and 'malpractice.' So I think we'll be seeing more business through Hong Kong."

"Should I expect or require anything new of the Hong Kong office then while you stay in Zurich?"

Vincent tapped his forefingers together. "No. Dr. Ling has things under control. I'm sure he'd forward anything I needed to see. I have so many offices crying out for my attention I shan't trouble the ones which run without it."

His assistant nodded while she chewed her sandwich. "Yes, sir. What are your plans for the rest of the day? Will you need a cab this evening?"

"No, I'll have supper at my usual spot, I think. But I will be taking a walk this afternoon. I have a sticky problem I need to think over. And I wonder if you might come with me."

The woman raised her eyebrows at this new request, but had no objection. "I'll leave the answering machine on. You have no appointments, so I don't foresee a problem."

"Wonderful. And now I'll stop talking and savor your tea."

"Very well, sir," she answered. She reached for her cup as he did, and they raised their cups to each other before they sipped.

Sharrah, Dr. Foster noted, was a happy outcome of one of his few acts of direct philanthropy. She had been one of his patients. He had, following an earthquake in Pakistan, taken up with an international charity to do surgery and emergency medicine. He did this for four weeks a year, both to keep his skills sharp and to stay in touch with the world, as he found it was easy to lose touch with the wants and pains of the world in Zurich. On one such stint after an earthquake in Pakistan, she had been brought to him, not because of an injury, but because she had been diagnosed with ovarian cancer the week before the quake.

From time to time these cases came up, and Vincent was always on the lookout for genetic material for his laboratories. Having set the ovaries he would remove as the price of the surgery, he removed them, and she went on living her life. When he had spoken with her after the surgery, he had learned she was not a peasant farmer's wife whom he could never speak with or understand, but the English-speaking daughter of secular Pakistan's education minister. It turned out

110

she worked for a NGO too, teaching women's health and doing reproductive counseling. The doctor knew a good connection when he saw one. He set aside some money to underwrite her projects and told her that if any more women came to her with problems similar to hers he would arrange for their surgery if they agreed to the same terms.

The arrangement hadn't worked out as he'd hoped. Shortly after the earthquake, some group of fanatical religious barbarians called the "Taliban" had emerged from the western part of Pakistan and expelled the civilian government. And the Taliban frowned on such things as teaching women's health and providing reproductive counseling, but Sharrah was far too willful to stop doing it. As her situation became more precarious through the years, Vincent had arranged to smuggle her out of the country. After all, it made no sense to save someone's life and support her work just to let some lout hang her from a goal frame in a stadium. When the woman had arrived in Zurich, she had been so profusely and tearfully grateful for her rescue that the doctor had felt embarrassed. He hadn't planned on her becoming his executive assistant, but when his current assistant had quit to start a family, he'd offered the job to Sharrah, and she had jumped at the chance. It had worked out for both of them, since her asylum application had gone on so long that she faced interim deportation by the Swiss. And he knew for certain there was no risk she would be quitting this job to start a family. She would be his executive assistant for a good long time.

The tea was not exotic at all; it was a good and unspiced India tea with honey. He enjoyed it and its smell.

Over her second sip of tea, Ms. Bassi reached for a second small plastic cup on the tray and took her synthetic hormone replacement pills. She hadn't had any hormone replacement after the fall of Pakistan's secular government. But since arriving in his care and enduring some trial and error with the dosages, the woman had shed a great deal of the weight she had gained and was less emotionally variable. Part of the change doubtless stemmed from having the time to process the things the Taliban had done to her. Those things were, Vincent conceded, so horrific in her recounting he had gone from disdainful of the Taliban to hating them. He had seen their kind before. He had worked for them before he'd gotten better sense, and he wouldn't make the mistake of tolerating them now that he knew better. He was no ally of the Americans and their web of global greed, conceit, and callousness, but he was sure the Taliban were worse.

Thus, despite his many sins and omissions in his life, he had been rewarded for his volunteer work with a welcoming, earnest, and thoughtful assistant who attended to him with great care and real affection. He had, she pointed out, saved her life twice. And while the doctor knew it was not so much he as the silent millions of innocents who had given him his resources who had saved her, he was nonetheless grateful and gratified by her day to day. And his stays in Zurich became longer each time.

He was, he had to admit, getting old despite his best medicines. Someday, he would have to retire, but until that day came he would let Sharrah's ministrations husband the last few good years out of him.

Vincent finished his lunch with a pinch of the sugar-coated fennel seeds his assistant had left on his saucer for him and, when she herself had finished eating and drinking, he stood.

"Let's go for that walk after we've had a moment to digest. I'm sure there's pleasant sun and shade both on the Hallwylplatz."

Sharrah walked down the stairs from the office beside Dr. Foster. Vincent owned the narrow beige building tucked in between two apartment houses. The first floor was her own apartment, and the second floor was the office. On the third floor was what the doctor referred to as the "old lab," a dusty space full of computers, filing cabinets, and other things she didn't know the use of, and the top floor was the doctor's own residence. He seldom stayed there for longer than a couple of weeks, and she had a key but rarely used it. The man did most of his own housekeeping, and while he never said as much, Sharrah had come to understand that he preferred his privacy and that her job was restricted to the office. But as she watched him descend the stairs carefully, she wondered if he wouldn't benefit from some domestic help, or if they ought to trade apartments so he didn't have to manage the stairs.

She wasn't sure how old Dr. Foster was. His wit was sharp, and he did not have a stoop nor was his face very wrinkled. He looked like a man in his early sixties but moved and spoke like a man in his early nineties. His medicines, most of which she did not recognize beyond what their daily dosages should be and when and how they should be taken, did not include any familiar painkillers, though from time to time he moved stiffly.

She was happy to go with her employer to the park, but he usually made this walk alone. She wondered why he wanted her along. Did he not feel well? Did he want her nearby in case he was ill?

She waited at the bottom of the stairwell beside her apartment door for the doctor to open the outside door, as he preferred to do. She had gathered it was polite in the west to let men open doors for you and then walk through them first. Vincent opened the door, and she stepped out and waited for him at the bottom of the landing, taking his offered arm once they were both on the same level. The pear trees whispered in the breeze, and the rows of rounded smooth cars on either side of the street reflected bright sunlight into their faces whenever it broke through the leafy canopy.

They walked a moment, and then Sharrah felt it was the time to ask. "It's nice to walk with you, sir, but you often make this walk alone. Was there a reason you asked me along?"

"Yes, and it's selfish. I felt I wanted to have you along. It's as simple as that."

"Yes, sir. It's nice to get out of the office."

"I chose this building when I bought it because of this walk. There were many open houses in Zurich at the time, all expensive. This one was less expensive, since this part of the city was regarded as boring and middle class, and it had this wonderful walk and view from the windows. The area has become more expensive since then, but I wouldn't dream of selling this office. It's the closest thing I have left to a home.

Sharrah walked along with him, marveling once again at how green everything was. It wasn't that Pakistan didn't have trees, but the impression the countryside left one with was dun-colored and hazy. In Zurich, if it wasn't painted dun-colored, it was green all summer long, and there were places where the ground was green, the trees and shrubs and hedges were green, and the leaves overhead were green. The lushness of it struck her still, even though she'd already lived in Zurich for more than two years.

"This is an amazing place. I saw London on a trip from my prep school in Karachi, but it was winter and it was nothing like this."

"I'll never put old London town down. I'm English by birth, after all," said Vincent. "But Zurich has a special charm. You can travel many places in Europe, but you won't find anyplace as peaceful, orderly, and humane."

They continued the stroll, and Sharrah again appreciated the small details of the street. Not a cobblestone or a brick lay out of place along the avenue. If something was supposed to be straight, plumb, level, clean, or shiny, it was. She hadn't ever imagined a place like this until she had come here.

"How go your affairs?" her employer asked. "Do you fit in?"

"I wouldn't say I fit in. But I feel safe, and everyone I meet is friendly. The teachers in the German and French classes are patient with me, and I've met other immigrants in those classes. People from Brazil, Iran, South Africa, China-"

"Oh? You're not taking any Italian?" He grinned at her. She smiled back.

"Please! Even learning two new languages at once is bad enough. Besides, if I took Italian at the same time I took French I'd always be confusing words with the same roots. It's bad enough with German and all the loan words from French. And from English, for that matter."

"What they speak here is hardly German anyway."

"The German you speak on the phone is different from what I hear in the street."

"Yes. I learned my German in Germany. That's high German I'm speaking." She detected a note of pride in the man's voice. "What they speak here is a different dialect. Almost a different language. It's like the difference between received pronunciation and...I don't know...bayou English. History and circumstance has made different what used to be the same language."

Sharrah took this in. She had begun reading about the history of Switzerland in her language classes, and she tried to piece Dr. Foster's statements together with what she knew. It didn't fit yet.

"And what else do you do for fun? Still taking Kung Fu classes?"

"Yes. I'm studying for my green belt now."

"Bravo!" Vincent enthused. "Get your black belt and I can add 'bodyguard' to your duties."

The two of them laughed at his joke. "On that note," his assistant explained, "the new security devices are ready in your office. I've hidden them in those new vases I bought. There's a remote for them in your desk drawer, and I have one, too. They should prevent any microphones in the room from working. That also means you won't be able to use your telephone or the intercom while they're switched on."

"Splendid! Thank you for researching and installing them for me. All the most important conversations I have with my clients are face to face, and I'm sure they'll feel much safer knowing they can't be overheard. Discretion matters to my clients."

"Yes, I gathered. If I may say so, some of the women are nervous when they see me."

"It's not you. They're nervous about bigger things. Many of them feel that asking for my help means they are failures as women."

Sharrah reflected on this. She could understand it. From time to time she would meet a golden- or brown-haired Swiss child or see a Swiss family together and feel a void. She could never have children. But she had her life. And that was thanks to Vincent. She pulled closer to the man as they walked.

"Are they all like me? Can they not have children?"

"Some of them," nodded the doctor. "Some of them can't have children, some of them are afraid to have children because of a genetic disease which runs in their family. Some of them don't want to experience the pain and disfigurement of pregnancy but feel ashamed of this. All of those things, I suppose, might make them nervous around a woman who is both young and fertile."

"But I'm not."

113

"Yes, that's the irony," he said. "In any case, carry on as you do. I get many positive comments about how polite and thoughtful you are."

"Thank you, sir."

They walked on. Ahead of them was Hallwylplatz, a tree-covered triangle to one side of an intersection of many Zurich streets. A pleasant smell of roasting meat filled the air, and smoke could be seen rising from Hallwylplatz.

"Ah, they are barbecuing. It's too bad you fed me lunch, or I'd love to have some."

"What's barbecuing?" asked Sharrah. It smelled wonderful.

"It's an American thing. It's roasted meat that has been soaked in various sauces, and sometimes smoked with specific varieties of wood to give it a pleasant flavor."

"Ooh, that does sound good," she said. But then she remembered her diet. She'd been losing weight steadily once she had been able to resume her hormone replacement regimen, but she still had to watch what she ate.

"Let's investigate," her boss said. Sure enough, they were barbecuing. As they got closer Sharrah decided, diet or no, she must try something. The smell was mouth-watering, and Dr. Foster made the decision she wanted to. He exchanged words and francs with some cheerful young men and bought a chicken wrapped in aluminum foil. He then led her to a bench, and put the chicken down between them.

She didn't know how to begin. The doctor was particular about how he ate, using different forks and knives for different things in unduly complicated ways which were wasteful of wash water and soap. In this context, though, the man pulled a piece of chicken off the bone with his fingers.

"Go ahead. You can eat with your fingers."

Sharrah was willing to eat with her fingers, as many things in Pakistan were eaten with one's hands, often with a banana leaf between fingers and food, but she had never imagined Dr. Foster eating with *his* fingers. He even picked up the sandwiches she made him for lunch with a napkin or on a toothpick. The sight was comical until she saw the man reach down with his left hand and pull off a chicken wing, and then she felt nauseated. This surprised her as she had watched classmates eat with their left hand often and thought she had gotten used to the practice, but she supposed that it was different now that she was being bidden to eat from the same piece of food. She picked up a napkin, took a deep breath, and pulled off a chunk of the chicken. The taste of it soon dispelled her misgivings, and soon there was nothing left but bones, aluminum foil, and smiles between her and her boss. Still licking her fingers, she said, "I'd like to have lamb prepared this way."

"Barbecuing is for beef, pork, or chicken. Americans don't eat much lamb or goat. If you went to America and asked for 'BBQ lamb' they would think you odd."

"Oh, that's a shame. I'm sure it would be good." She wondered if she might make barbecue at home. After a glance at the hulking metal ovens with their enormous steel chambers and thickly smoking spouts, she decided barbecuing was not something she would be able to do in her apartment kitchen.

Her employer sat back and turned his face to the sun as a cloud passed and brightened the day. His end of the bench was in the new sunshine, and he was savoring it. As she watched this, she remembered one of his medications had a warning label that said he should avoid sun.

"Will you trade places with me, sir? You shouldn't be in the sunlight."

"You're too right, too right. And I'll trade with you in a moment. But for a minute, I want to feel the light." She waited, and after a few moments Dr. Foster

114

stood and walked around her to the shady end of the bench. She slid into the sun and they sat together again, watching people following the smoke with their noses into the circle of trees and walking away happy with chickens or hunks of pork on bread.

As she watched a young family come through and saw the parents offer the smoked meat to their son and daughter, who regarded the strange meat with suspicion, something occurred to her.

"Sir, you said you help some women avoid the pain and disfigurement of childbirth. I always thought you helped people who couldn't or shouldn't conceive. You know, by implanting eggs and things."

"Yes, that's a good deal of what we do," Vincent confirmed.

"But how do you help women have children without getting pregnant? Do you...find other women willing to get pregnant for them?"

"That's one way. My clients have a lot of money. Some of the women make so much money they would regard six or nine months of not working a great financial loss. Or some of them make their living with their bodies as models, actresses, or sex partners to wealthy men. They may want children but don't feel they can take the risk to their livelihood of becoming pregnant. And they are willing to be generous if we can find a woman to bear a child for them so they can keep working. In those cases, the role of my offices is to find a healthy woman with the desired characteristics willing to bear the child and then handle the legal and medical work all the parties need to have the child. The legal piece is Jean-Paul's watch. I'm sure you've spoken to him on the phone."

Sharrah puzzled over this. She had read about it, but paying other women to bear your children still was a foreign idea to her. She supposed, though, if she ever made enough money, she might do it. And then she could have the family she always wanted. Thinking of it this way, the concept wasn't so impersonal sounding. In fact, she would be downright grateful to the woman willing to get pregnant for her.

"You said that was one way. Is there another way?"

Dr. Foster's smile vanished and was replaced with a grave expression. "Yes, there is."

"How does it work?" Ms. Bassi asked, curious.

"It's risky, and complicated. We only do it for couples who need or a want a significant amount of genetic manipulation of their child, such that the survival rate of the fertilized embryos is low. It's expensive, too, much more expensive than finding a surrogate mother, but we're working to make it less so. We steer clients toward surrogacy, but there are those who have such particular requirements that surrogacy is inadequate."

"But how does it work?" Sharrah persisted. "Are you making children in machines?"

Dr. Foster laughed. "Goodness no. That is a foolish approach. It would take an enormously complicated machine to do that."

"Then how?"

The doctor did not reply to her persistence for a moment. "I forget sometimes you were a family planning counselor in Pakistan," he said at length.

"Yes. And in that job, one learns to talk about what people feel and mean and want. And what I'm hearing from you, sir, is that you don't want to talk about this." She crossed her arms, irritated, but stopped, scolded herself for being angry with her savior, and uncrossed them.

Her employer turned to watch a dog chase a Frisbee. She felt let down that he looked away with no elaboration. The man could trust her. She hoped he knew it.

A moment later the doctor spoke. "There are parts of my work which, if you knew them, would distress you. And there are others which, if you knew them, would put you in grave danger. Eventually what I do will become more widely known, and then all kinds of people, both good and bad, would want to know how I do it. It would break my heart if you came all this way, learned two languages, learned to love and laugh and enjoy the freedoms men and women deserve, just to be cut down by a spy or other villain. So I'd prefer not to tell you. It would involve swearing you to secrecy, putting you in danger and, worse still, having to punish you if you told anyone else. Let me run the risks of my choices, don't you run them for me, and let me never have to think of being angry with you. I'm old, I have no family, and nearly all of my colleagues and friends have passed away. Not to sound dramatic, but your smile and this office are all I have of peace in this life."

Ms. Bassi listened. She heard the man's fears and concern for her, and it eased her fears that he did not trust her. Still, the answer left her curious about how the process worked.

He drew a long breath. "Would it bother you to call me Vincent? Everyone I know calls me Dr. Foster. I've come to the uncomfortable position of talking to myself in the shower or while dressing, and calling *myself* 'doctor.' I don't want my real name to be forgotten."

Sharrah swallowed. On the one hand, she did consider Dr. Foster her friend. He was kind, patient, concerned, and helpful without being nosy. And he had never presumed or even hinted any romantic or sexual interest in her, which was one of the only things about working for him as intimately as she did which made the relationship tolerable. But he was also her employer, and if things went sour in their relationship, she could be out of her job and apartment and even her visa in Switzerland in a minute. She was only allowed to reside in Switzerland as she did on a visa as the doctor's personal servant.

Both her employer and her one true friend in the world outside Pakistan was asking her for a favor. Could she do it?"

Dr. Foster reacted to the discomfort in her pause. "If it crosses a boundary, then don't trouble yourself-"

"No, Vincent. It's fine." She liked the feel of his name. It was unlike Pakistani men's names, though under the Taliban she had rarely used men's first names either. She had even had to refer to her brothers as 'brother.' And using his name made her feel, somehow, more equal. "What does your name mean?"

"Mean? I don't know. I've never thought about it," said the man. "Isn't that odd? After all this long life I've had? It has kind of a Roman feel to it, though my Latin classes were too long ago for me to guess. I'm not sure it means anything, though. Some names are only names."

Sharrah boggled. "You speak Latin, too?"

"Oh no. One never learns to speak Latin so much as read it. I had six years of it but I never ran into a Roman to speak it with. It faded away long ago. I'm afraid I'm stuck with English, French, German, and Italian. I think my German is best. What languages can you speak?"

"English. Then there's Urdu, but I'm afraid it will be a dead language in a generation, the Taliban have half-forbidden it. And some Hindi. And now I'm learning French and German."

"Soon you'll be as accomplished as I. And so young, too."

Ms. Bassi put her hand behind her neck and flipped her hair over the bench, letting the air cool her. The coolness of the city in summer was another thing about Zurich she liked. She had not once been soaked in sweat as she had been under her burqa in Pakistan. The winters could be harsh, but the Swiss had adapted to it, and there was no shortage of cozy places to go in winter.

116

"Do you want me to use your name in front of others? Or only when we're alone?"

"When we're with customers or doing business, please call me 'Doctor' or 'sir.' The rest of the time, Vincent."

"I'll do it," Sharrah said. And she closed her eyes for a moment, listening to the bustle of traffic, the chatter of customers at the barbecue grill, and the sound of a passing bus. After her long journey, her life was becoming good. And she owed a great deal of this improvement to this man who only wanted in return that she use his name.

Sharrah checked her office clock. After their walk down to Hallwylplatz, Vincent (she still felt odd thinking of him by his name) had wanted to be left alone in his office. So she had started work on his patient correspondence, most of which she wrote. She did her best to match the doctor's gentle tones and British diction, and he was pleased with her work and only made occasional corrections. The trick, now that she was mastering how Dr. Foster would write, was to understand enough of his business to know *what* he should write. When she was doing this she could be sure she was saving his time and earning her keep.

She also took a moment to search for the meaning of Vincent's name on the internet. She found he was correct about its Latin origin. His name derived from a Latin word meaning "to conquer" or "to prevail." She decided to go with "prevail." The man didn't act like a "conqueror."

She reread her notes from the phone messages which had been left while they were out walking. The Hong Kong office had called to say they'd received payment from the "Yao" family (the real family names were never used in correspondence). The Rio de Janeiro office had a message stating they had gotten the cattle blight under control (why the doctor was involved in cattle ranching she had no idea). And last, the Russian office had sent word of a new client who wanted to meet with him the next time he was in St. Petersburg. She hoped the messages did not mean the doctor would be traveling again soon. He seemed tired.

When at last the elder man opened his door again, she went in with these notes and briefed him on the messages. None of them, not even the one from the new client in St. Petersburg, prompted a remark.

"Thank you, Sharrah, for taking those calls. Now, I'll need some privacy for a bit longer. Interrupt me only for an emergency, I need to think."

"Of course, S- I mean, Vincent."

The doctor smiled at her slip and swiveled his chair about so he was facing the window. He often faced the window when he was thinking deeply. She left and closed his door. She cleaned the kitchenette she used to make lunch, checked the refrigerator, and made notes on her shopping list. She was part way through vacuuming the floor in the hallway when he emerged from his office.

"I think I'll need a nap before supper. You're free to go for the day, but I was wondering if you'd like to join me for dinner."

Sharrah thought about it. She didn't have anything planned, and neither did she have her German or French classes this evening. Still, dinner together was new. While they'd had lunch out any number of times, they had never spent time together after work hours. She hoped this wasn't a sign he was growing amorous, but she didn't see her way clear to say no.

"Vincent, I...sure. What kind of place is it?"

"Let it be a surprise."

117

"I do need to know how to dress." The doctor had gone to lunch at some fancy places, and while Sharrah wore skirt suits to work, she changed as soon as she returned home.

"It's street dress, I expect. Don't worry. It's not one of those expensive places I've dragged you to. It's a place I think you'll like.

"Alright. That makes it simple. When should I expect you?"

"I'll knock at your door around six-thirty."

"Very well!" she chirped, noticing her voice was high and squeaky. She must be nervous. She had no reason to be, she decided.

She waited until Dr. Foster was through the door into the stairwell, activated the alarm system, and exited into the stairwell behind him in order to close and lock the door within the fifteen-second window. She'd once taken too long to get out, and had been stuck trying to field a call from the security firm that served them. The guards had responded and not been very friendly. It had taken the doctor coming down from his apartment to get her out of trouble, else they would have carted her off to jail or wherever the Swiss sent foreigners found robbing offices.

As Vincent started upstairs to his apartment, Sharrah went down to hers. She pushed through the door and breathed in the comforting smell of green tea warming in her tea maker, poured a cup, and looked at her wall clock. She had about ninety minutes to get ready. If she dressed quickly, she could even take a crack at her French homework before the doctor knocked.

In fact she got through one French exercise and part way through her second when Vincent's knock at the door came. She left her schoolbook open, wrapped on her head scarf and went to the door.

The doctor was dressed in gray slacks, loafers, a black cardigan sweater, a colorful red tie, and a gray felt cap. In her black jeans, turquoise and black shirt, and turquoise earrings, she felt under-dressed compared to him, but he made no comment, so they walked out the door together.

"So, a headscarf. I understand there was some to-do in France about those," said the doctor.

"Was there?" Sharrah hadn't heard. She paid no attention to any news but cricket and field hockey scores. World events were always bad news, and some of the worst news was from Talibani Pakistan.

"Yes, I guess the French parliament re-affirmed the ban on them for women. They thought they were a symbol of the oppression of women in Islamic countries, which runs counter to both the libertine and revolutionary streaks in French society."

"Ah," said Sharrah. She'd have to look up the word 'libertine' when she came back to her apartment, but she was reluctant to ask Vincent for an explanation of the word for fear of disappointing him. She often wondered if her British accent was one of the reasons the man was so comfortable around her, so she didn't want to betray ignorance of English words. "I wear it sometimes and not others. I guess...I guess it makes me feel more-what is a good word? Shielded? Modest? I don't feel as if men are looking at me so closely," she explained as they started down the street.

"It has the opposite effect, I expect. The men here will notice you more when you wear a headscarf. Islamic women are a rarity here." The doctor's gait was faster than it had been in the afternoon, but he was headed to the same place, Hallwylplatz. This made sense. It was a good place to find a taxi cab.

"That may be true, but if they stare they can't see my hair or face. I often wear it with sunglasses."

"You're free to wear one to work if they make you more comfortable,"

Vincent noted. "If anyone chooses to take exception to it, I can afford to do without their business."

"I do keep one in my desk in case you have Islamic clients. But when I'm working for you, I like to dress as western as I can. It's professional and I should look professional. And I don't want to make your clients uncomfortable. Sometimes people I meet are uncertain of how they should react to me and I don't need that at work."

They found a cab at Hallwylplatz, a beige Mercedes with a Swiss driver. She recognized the street names Dr. Foster gave the driver as being in the old city, not far from the main train station. Her eyes were drawn to the window and the many sights of Zurich which paraded by. The river, the churches, the banks, the museums, and the whole bewildering array of it bore examination and re-examination.

"There's a lot to see," the doctor said. Sharrah realized she was being rudely inattentive to her boss and came back to the present.

"I know. When you're away, I go out often, sometimes catching a street car to somewhere I've never been, and I still haven't seen all of it," Sharrah said. "When I get my motorcycle license, I'll see even more."

"How is your licensing going, by the way?"

"My final test is next week. You'll be here when I take it," she said, smiling with anticipation. "And if you're lucky I'll give you a ride."

"Ah, no need," grinned Vincent ruefully. "I'm afraid motorcycles make me ill. All the rocking back and forth, and the pavement speeding by your knees, I'm not made for it. But no doubt the license will give you great freedom."

"My first day off after getting my license, I will drive up into those mountains. Do you know I've been here two years and never been in them?"

The man's eyes followed her finger point up into the Alps before returning to hers. "Then you're in for a treat. While I understand the snow cover is a fraction of what it was when I was young enough to go wandering in them, I suspect their beauty is still unmatched anywhere but the Himalayas."

Sharrah peered out the window at the Alps. The sun was setting behind their peaks. She could see nothing but their silhouettes, but she had daydreams of snow and streams you could drink from and spectacular views for miles and miles. She began daydreaming, but a bump in the road brought her back to the moment. She didn't want to be rude to Vincent.

"I'll bring pictures," she promised. "I have my own camera now."

"Please do. This old man used to wander in those mountains often, and I'd be delighted to see some familiar sights again."

At this point the cab stopped in the old town. Dr. Foster paid the cabbie, and as was his custom, got out of the cab first and helped Sharrah to her feet.

The smell of cooked lamb reached her nose before she even found her bearings on the street. Her jaw hung open. The smell wasn't just lamb, it was bhugal teewarn, a spiced mutton dish she had loved in Pakistan. Her mouth watered.

"Oh! Oh!" She exclaimed. "You found a Pakistani restaurant. I can smell it from here!"

"Not only Pakistani. Sindhi. If I remember correctly, wasn't your family Sindhi?"

"My father was, yes. It smells wonderful! Where is this restaurant?" She turned in circles until she saw it on the other side of the street. It was set in the ground floor of an unremarkable four-story building, with a white sign reading "Lazeez" and sporting the green and white Sindh and Pakistani flags. Some tables were set up on the sidewalk, and she could see more diners, some of the women even wearing headscarves, through the plate glass.

Her excitement and anticipation grew as Vincent stopped her from jaywalking with a scolding look and lead her to the crosswalk to cross the street in the proper way. Sharrah imagined what she would have to eat as they waited and walked. She would start with some kuini kichani, her favorite rice dish. Then she would have some of that bhugal teewarn, and some khirni to drink with extra cardamom, and then-

A loud man speaking in Urdu from the sidewalk table caught her up short. *"The Taliban is the greatest blessing to Pakistan since the revolution itself. We are now rid of the westerners and their lackeys and can run our own affairs in our own way. And now the Chinese will not dare meddle with us in the eastern provinces. With America off our back we can make far too much trouble for them."*

His companion agreed. *"With nuclear weapons in our hands, the nations of Islam now need fear nothing. We are on an equal footing with the west, with India, and with China and they will have to treat us with respect."*

Sharrah froze in her tracks, her heart in her mouth. The wonderful smells still played in her nose, breaking her heart. She was so close to this piece of home, but she didn't dare go a step further. She had been so entranced by the smells she had forgotten. The chalkboard out front teased her with the German words *"Special Today! Bhugal Teewarn made with locally raised lamb!"* Vincent had stopped in front of her, and the look of concern on his face showed he had seen her expression. She faced the street and motioned for the doctor to come closer.

"What's wrong?"

"I can't go in," she said, her eyes watering. "I...can't. There are men, at a sidewalk table, they are Taliban supporters. What if they see me? What if they recognize me? Then the Taliban would know where I am. They would find me. They would... I can't go in!" Her back tingled and itched in alarm, and her palms were sweaty.

Dr. Foster extended a solicitous arm to her shoulders. "Is it a concern? Are you so infamous there?"

"I don't know. I can't take that chance. I know they printed posters which said I could be brought to the mullahs dead or alive. I don't know if they sent any to the diaspora." She cast a furtive look over her shoulder. All of the men at the cafe tables now looked sinister and threatening. She shivered.

She had to walk away from this restaurant now. Walk away, like she had walked away from Karachi, and from what remained of her friends, her family, and her country. She took a step down the street. She didn't know where she was going, except away, reluctantly. Memories of the hangings, the whippings, the shouted passages from the Koran, the canings by the purity police, all came crowding into her head, and she drove them out by focusing on signs in German and French. "Bakery. Brew house and restaurant. Imported tobacco. Coffee, absinthe, and books. No parking Tuesdays 22 hour to 4 hour," she read.

There were tears on her cheeks before she had gone ten steps. The daydream of a cup of khirni faded from her mind and nose, and she willed the tears to fade with it.

"I'm sorry! This was so thoughtful of you. Am I making too much of this? Maybe I'd be safe. Maybe I should go back."

Vincent walked beside her at full speed toward the nowhere else she was headed. "Nonsense. There's no sense in taking you to dinner if you won't be comfortable. Lazeez's delivers, and I'll have them bring lunch tomorrow, and we'll eat it together in safety, even down on Hallwylplatz if you like. We can go anywhere else for supper. Anywhere. Tell me your heart's desire and I'll find it for

120

you."

Sharrah smiled through her tears and extended her arm to doctor, who took it gently. The feel of their arms locked together was comforting.

"You're so good to me. And you have no reason."

"I have reason enough," replied the old man. "Now, name your heart's desire."

She thought about it. "Some more of that-how do you say it-barbecue? That would be nice."

"Done!" Dr. Foster replied, raising his hand to hail a cab. "I know the place."

Vincent pulled out Sharrah's chair. He had never been to a Dickey's BBQ Pit on his trips to the United States. But this location the not-quite-fast food chain had opened in Zurich was popular with American expatriates, so he had reason to expect it was good. It was not at all his style, with vinyl seats and an institutional-tile atmosphere, but it was a sit-down restaurant rather than those obnoxious order-at-the-counter chains like McDonald's or Wendy's. And the smell of BBQ filled the air. It was a step down or two for him, but it was what the lady wanted, and she was content with it as she sniffed the air.

They picked up the menus and began looking.

"Thank you for being so patient with me."

"Think nothing of it," he dismissed. He hoped the subject of her fears would fall out of the discussion of the evening, but was prepared to listen for the evening if it was what Sharrah needed.

"What do you recommend?" she said, paging through the menu.

"I've never eaten here. But in my adventures in barbecue in the United States, I'd say 'pulled pork' is the tastiest of the lot. But it's all good."

The woman shifted queasily. "Oh. Yes. Umm, I don't eat pork."

Vincent felt silly. Being Muslim, she wouldn't. "Ah. Sorry. It's a food taboo, isn't it? Then don't eat the 'ribs' either. They are also from pigs."

"So that leaves beef and chicken." Sharrah said. "And I've never quite gotten comfortable with beef either. My father was Punjabi and wouldn't eat beef, so my mother never cooked it. I suppose it's not a taboo per se, since I'm not Hindu, but it's a habit."

"So chicken it is!" said Vincent, opening his menu to search alongside her and make his recommendation. "I stand corrected. They have turkey besides."

"What is turkey like?" asked Sharrah. "It's a bird, isn't it?"

"Oh, yes, sorry. They are larger than chickens. They have a richer taste and a chemical in them which can make you drowsy. Americans eat them on holidays and other special occasions. It's more akin to goose or duck than chicken."

"That sounds interesting. I think I'll try...." she scrutinized the menu. "BBQ Turkey Breast."

"It's decided then. Will it bother you if I eat pork?"

She wrinkled her nose. "A little, but go ahead and do it anyway. If people respect my customs I have to respect theirs in turn."

"Then I'll test your fortitude with the pulled pork platter," Vincent said. His stomach grumbled. Despite the atmosphere of the restaurant, he was looking forward to supper, no matter how humble it might turn out to be.

He looked over Ms. Bassi. Her turquoise head scarf matched her earrings and shirt, and though she was not a striking or a slender woman, she was garnering plenty of curious interest from the young Swiss men present. He wondered if she noticed. He suspected she did, but that she chose not to give any indication of it. Soon, a busty young waitress arrived in a cowboy outfit which accented her ampleness nicely, and with a passable imitation of a Texan accent, took their orders.

When the waitress was gone, his assistant had a question for him. "On the subject of beef, I didn't know you were involved in cattle ranching. That's an interesting side business for a doctor. Does it make much money?"

Dr. Foster felt his ears heat up. Sharrah had innocently stumbled across another aspect of his work he was not eager to explain.

"It's not strictly 'ranching.' We use the cattle for, um, experiments too risky to try on humans," he said in a low voice.

The waitress returned for a moment to bring them a tub of herb butter and bleached white rolls. Sharrah squeezed them with curiosity.

Vincent answered the question his assistant was doubtless thinking. "Yes. Americans like their bread soft and always bleached as white as snow. For as humble a place as this is, they have the high points of American cuisine down to a science."

The woman took a bite of the roll. "Hmm. It's like naan. Only bigger. And fluffier. And sweet. So I guess it's not much like naan after all." She watched him as he prepared one, and tore the roll open and began spreading butter on it as he did so. His hope the rolls had distracted her from the question of his "ranching," however, proved to be for naught.

"So, you do experiments on live animals?" Sharrah continued.

"Yes. Some aspects of gene modification as we do it are still so unproven we don't dare involve humans with it yet. Cattle are large and easy to come by and maintain, and because they are also livestock animals which are routinely slaughtered, there are few restrictions on what can be done with them. We have four large cattle operations, one in Brazil, one in Chile, and two in Nigeria. The cattle are well kept and humanely cared for, better cared for by far than cattle used for food."

"Wouldn't it make more sense to use smaller and more manageable animals for experimentation? Like rats? Or rabbits?"

"We do use other animals at some labs. But cattle have...desirable characteristics small animals do not. Still, the reasons we use them are complicated and not particularly appetizing."

"Oh. Sorry. I guess parts of your work aren't dinner conversation," apologized Sharrah. "I'm curious, you know, I'm trying to understand your business so I can serve you better."

"You do a fine job," Vincent reassured her. "But to be frank, one of the refreshing aspects of being in Zurich is getting away from all that for a bit. Tell me about this motorcycle you've picked out."

The young woman brightened. "Oh, it's a used BMW motorcycle. It's a touring model with carrying cases already on it so I can take clothes and my camera and things."

"BMW. First rate if it's engineered like their cars were in my day," said Dr. Foster, thankful she had taken to the change of conversation. He'd have to remember to talk to the heads of the birthing labs about being discreet in any messages they passed through his assistant.

"It's white. It's got some scratches on it. I guess the last owner fell over on it. But it runs perfectly, and the BMW dealer has inspected it and is offering me a warranty."

"Are you sure a small car wouldn't suit your needs better?"

She shook her head. "Where would we park it? Besides, for riding around in the mountains when it's warm and maybe carrying some groceries, a motorcycle will do and be cheaper. And I can park on the street outside our building."

"That can't be the only reason," Dr. Foster probed. "There are small and inexpensive cars. The SMART, for instance. I've seen them parked in motorcycle spaces. They would keep you dry in the rain and be much less risky to drive."

Sharrah reflected. "Not long before I met you, I dated a British exchange student on the university in Karachi. He took me for a motorcycle ride. It was...it made me feel free. It was before the Taliban, and I didn't even have to wear a head scarf, much less a helmet. I never forgot it, though it took me two days to get the knots out of my hair afterwards. In comparison, riding in a car is boring, and I can hire a cab or take a streetcar if it's raining. But when I want to have fun, I think a motorcycle will be much better."

"I do hope you wear a helmet, my dear."

"Sure I will," she said. "Most of the time. Who wants all those knots in their hair?"

Vincent chuckled at this. It was the familiar dilemma doctors faced. You put your heart and soul into making someone healthy and they thanked you by doing things which were reckless or self-destructive by way of "living."

Sharrah began to describe the places she had heard about or seen pictures of in the Alps. When their supper came in plastic baskets on wax paper, she could scarcely stop talking excitedly long enough to eat it. The doctor felt relief and wonder to see her this way. She was much different now than the scarred, frightened, and quiet burqa-clad woman who had first gotten off the train at Zurich's main train station, the woman whom he'd again seen a glimpse of outside the Pakistani restaurant. Who would this young woman be, he wondered, if so many evil and thoughtless people had not gone to such great lengths to keep her down throughout her life? The same question could be asked of the millions who had given him his wealth, but in that form, it was an abstract. It could be asked more meaningfully of this one woman.

He couldn't answer the question. But he could still appreciate that the conversation had drifted away from his 'cattle ranches.'

That night Vincent sat awake with his tablet computer. He'd seen Sharrah to her ground floor apartment when, as they talked after supper over slices of pecan pie, she'd begun to fret about her French assignments. And now he had on his pajamas, had brushed his teeth, had set his alarm clock, and had time for more work before bed.

He fired off a brief note to his laboratory heads about discussing the technical details of goings-on in phone messages. He reminded them to encrypt technical messages and email them instead, and that his assistant, though capable, was not read on to many sensitive matters they handled. Afterwards, he looked through some test results, trying to take his mind off the sticky problem of the day.

But he couldn't. His mind inevitably returned to case #490, the girl so aptly named "Rosetta" by the Kano laboratory staff for the extraordinary language learning abilities she had demonstrated before she fell prey to her seizures. She had vanished while traveling in the United States for tests with her handler, Elphabia Wasilatu. It concerned him a great deal, since Elphabia was his most experienced and trusted caretaker of the children, and Rosetta was one of the jewels of his experimental method. In fact, she was the first to turn out without significant disability or illness, at least until her eleventh year. And while her seizures and delusions were worrisome, she would still be a scientific treasure for many more years, if not the rest of her life.

Rosetta's value, and Elphabia's centrality to his organization, created many possible reasons for their disappearance. They might have been kidnapped by his competitors, whoever such mysterious competitors might be. While he had many scientific rivals, so far as he knew he had no industrial rivals. He'd been the only one engineering children for the rich and famous for three decades, and no one else was yet offering this service, or even doing more than thinking about it. His scientific rivals, while all capable men and women, many of whom smarter than he, mostly worked for him or worked for universities and didn't have the inclination or resources to kidnap people. And all but a handful were, or should be, unaware that Vincent's experimental children even existed.

More likely, Elphabia had decided to go into hiding with Rosetta. Perhaps she wanted to remain in the United States rather than return to Nigeria. It would be understandable given the widespread violence and poverty in Nigeria, he had the United States and oil interests to thank for that. Or it could be a competitor he was unaware of had made Elphabia an offer she couldn't refuse. This wouldn't avail the competitor much, since experimental children arrived at the child labs fresh born, with no indication or explanation of where they came from. So far as Elphabia should know, her job was caring for disabled and special needs children of wealthy means and unknown parentage. She should have no idea at all that Rosetta, or any other child at the Kano laboratory, was genetically engineered, and certainly no way of sharing his industrial secrets.

There was another possibility, and this one troubled Vincent the most. It might be, he supposed, that Elphabia had found the treatment of Rosetta too inhumane or inadequate in some way and had gone into hiding to prevent the child from being returned to the Kano lab. While there were parts of his science which were inhumane by most people's standards, once a child was born the doctor spared no expense to care for them until the natural end of their lives. It was no small part of the expense of his business, and it grew with every experimental child born viable, yet he had never flinched at paying it. And he routinely toured the childrens' facilities to satisfy himself this work was done well by the best staff.

He remembered Elphabia clearly. She was the first child handler employed by his enterprise, an earthy, educated, and world-traveled daughter of a Nigerian merchant family who had been a governess to one of Nigeria's presidential families. She couldn't come with better credentials, had never hesitated to speak her mind or write Vincent directly with her dissatisfactions, had gone so far as to breast feed her first charges, and had long been a prized team member. The pay she had received should have left her comfortable in retirement in Nigeria. Dr. Foster remembered her curious half-British, half something-else accent: "Now, good Doctor, I would like to bring your attention to this matter…"

No, he decided, pulling up his modal sheets and light cotton summer blanket, it was unlikely Elphabia would have left for ethical reasons. If she had been dissatisfied with something, he was sure he'd have heard about it ten times over and gotten a few emails with different heartbreaking photos about how whatever inadequacy she found affected the children. If Elphabia was gone, it was for another reason. Nonetheless, to be certain this was so, there would be a shakedown of the Kano laboratory. If there were pedophiles or people without the temper for rearing children, he'd have them gone. He had enough going on with his enterprise that he didn't need those kinds of people making it more difficult.

124

Still, he had to prepare for the worst outcome, not the most unsettling. And the worst he could imagine was that Elphabia had gone over to some competitor. It matched the trail. Elphabia and Rosetta had gone through customs in the United States under assumed names, and their assumed names had even been recorded as having spent one night at the hotel reserved for them near Syracuse airport. Somewhere between Syracuse and Dr. Jacob's lab, Elphabia and Rosetta had vanished.

But so what if this was the case? What would it net his hypothetical competitor to have kidnapped them or bought Elphabia out? They could clone Rosetta, he supposed, but it wasn't like they could deduce how he had assembled her genome. They would learn little or nothing about his transgenic, epigenetic, and exogenic methods. And while no access to Rosetta would certainly be a setback for him, he had other children to observe to deduce how well or poorly his methods worked and how they could be improved.

Vincent meditated long on his next move. In the end, he decided the matter might end up being one of those senseless losses whose cause could never be explained or which no one could reasonably have foreseen. He'd sent his finest creation with his most experienced handler to one of the most advanced MRI labs in the world, so from his end, he'd done his best. Fate and chance both had votes in whatever he did. If no other lesson in his life had taught him this already, the Second World War should have.

He made some notes in his tablet, then set it aside and switched off his reading lamp. He took deep breaths, and focused on nothing, like the monks had taught him to do the year before at the meditation seminar he'd attended.

Clarity came, and then slumber. It was odd, he mused as he drifted off, that what troubled him now was not Rosetta's fate, but what Sharrah might think of him if she knew the truth.

Chapter 9

Interviews with a Child

Shawn clicked the recorder again. Rosie was in her seat, the small metal and vinyl stool to one side of his desk. His computer had the Esperanto dictionary and grammar sites open. He felt confident this interview would run smoothly and more could be recorded. The girl spun on the stool, enjoying the freedom of motion. She sat more comfortably than at her last visit, resting on both buttocks.

"The following is a recording of my conversation with Rosetta Amata. If it runs as last time, she may not speak much, but may spend much of the time writing so her replies are not recorded." Rosie looked back and forth between him and the digital voice recorder. He took his prepared page in hand and sounded out his first question.

"*Are you comfortable?*" he asked.

She nodded, and spoke her reply to the recorder. It was more Esperanto than Shawn could absorb at once, he had hoped to start with simple yes-or-no type questions. Fortunately, Dr. Teschke had been kind enough to share with him a list of "repair phrases" she used when interviewing speakers of rare languages and he had spent a portion of the evening before translating them into Esperanto. As a result, he was quickly able to ask her "*Could you repeat that?*" by running his thumb down this list until he found the correct phrase.

Rosetta repeated it. He made out more of it as "*Yes, I am comfortable, thank you.*" After saying this, she spun the stool around, turning around a few times before facing him again. Shawn was reminded that asking a child to sit still for long was a big request. He had limited time before she lost interest in the interview. He had made some adaptations, he knew, picking up some fruit-scented marker pens and a sheaf of printer paper at the campus store for her to draw and write on. He hoped these added to the appeal of her visits.

"*I am will ask questions about where you lived before we found you. I will ask short questions. Please give me short answers so I can understand them.*"

The girl nodded her understanding. Mindful of the recorder, Shawn gestured to it, and Rosie, with a puzzled expression, answered aloud, "*I understand, yes.*"

"*What was the name of the place where you lived before now?*"

"*I live wherever I am. I live now.*"

This simple answer was nonetheless not the kind Shawn had anticipated. So he had to take a minute to compose the next question in Esperanto.

"*What place do you call home?*"

Her reply was gibberish to him. He shrugged. She tried it again, and then wrote her reply down on the notepad with a grape-scented marker.

"*In the arms of my beloved,*" she replied. At first the reply gave him a start. A girl as young as Rosie was talking about her lover? Then, with a flash of understanding, he saw the word for "beloved" was also the word the child had listed offered as her last name: *Amata.*

This was puzzling. Did she mean to say that home was where her mother or father could hold her? He decided to focus his next question on a literal or

126

physical object to make her replies more concrete.

"*Did your family have a house?*"

"*More than can be counted.*" Shawn translated the girl's reply. "*Yours is one of them.*"

He grumbled at this. He was making no headway. He pictured the looks of disdain his interview results would get from Akiko and Dr. Teschke. No doubt both would regret wasting these valuable interviews with Rosie on him.

"*Maybe I should take a clue from this,*" he considered. "*Maybe I should have stuck with music theory.*" He abandoned his list of prepared questions and let his frustration help him choose and write a new one.

"*Why do you answer my questions with riddles?*" he stammered after double-checking his word choice with the dictionary. At this, Rosie paused her grape and cherry-scented doodling on her notepaper, and gave him a bemused smile. It was a smile like his grandfather had made when he'd won a duel of words with a young rowdy or drug pusher on a street corner.

"*Because you ask only riddles.*" Once she had both spoken this with exaggerated deliberateness into the recorder and written it down, she went back to her drawings, making large arcs with a yellow lemon-scented marker. She even spun around one more time in her stool, as if to emphasize her lack of concern.

Shawn's ears burned. This kid was playing with him. He envisioned explaining this to Dr. Teschke and Akiko, and the incredulity it would net him. He could hear Dr. Teschke now. "The interview is a fundamental technique of linguistics. You must master it if you wish to progress, even if the interviews involve *children*."

As Rosie's marker squeaked away on the paper, Shawn brainstormed for alternatives. He had two goals: to get the subject to answer questions about her past, and to get her to speak into the recorder or write. If asking her questions about her past was only going to dead-end in riddles and disagreement, then he should ask about something else, questions that encouraged her to speak so the academic goals of the interview could be reached.

He composed a new question. "*Who is your best friend?*"

"*God.*" The girl answered without even looking up from her page. "*He's your best friend, too.*"

At this, he tugged on a dreadlock in irritation. He took three deep breaths, reminded himself not to pre-judge the answer, and followed up. "*Do you often talk to God?*"

"*Yes.*" She made more arcs on the paper.

"*And does God listen?*" He tried to scrub any sarcasm or disbelief from his voice.

At this, Rosie laughed out loud, and the laughter was replaced with an ironic smirk as she scribbled small figures on the paper with a licorice marker.

"*Not as much as he should.*"

Shawn decided to try to get away from the whole God theme. "*Do you have any other friends than God?*"

"*Yes. David is my friend,*" she said.

"*What does he look like?*"

"*He is the man who brought me here,*" she said, puzzled.

"*Of course. And finally, a real person,*" he thought.

"*What do you do together?*"

"*We play a game, and he makes dinner, and he changes my bandages.*"

"*What game do you play together?*"

"*Checkers,*" answered Rosie. Shawn checked the time. With all the time he had to spend translating more complicated questions and answers, he had fifteen minutes left of the hour to interview. He sensed that maybe she wasn't having much fun with these interviews, and if he wanted to see her again, he should focus on them having fun for the next few minutes.

He referred once more to the Esperanto dictionary, and then asked, *"What is your favorite thing to do?"*

"I like most to dance."

He paused. Without referring to the dictionary, and using his memory of his words and the rules of verb conjugation, he experimented. *"Will you dance for me?"*

"Yes!" the girl replied with enthusiasm. In a moment, she hopped off her stool, slipped off her plastic clogs, and stood on the office tiles in bare feet. She looked to him. *"Music?"*

"Please wait a moment," Shawn was able to answer her quickly with reference to his list of "repair phrases." He opened the media player on his computer and searched his library of more-or-less legal MP3 files. He settled on an Arabesque dance tune, pressed play, and sat back.

He watched Rosie as the music unfolded. At first, she danced slowly, and as the beat of the music quickened, she began to turn around, smiling as she had while twirling on the stool. Then, with one hand raised toward the ceiling and another lowered toward the floor, she began to whirl around in earnest, first one way, and then another, her loose-fitting t-shirt lifting off her hips like a skirt. She bowed low, stretched high, and then began to leap, all the while twirling. Between leaps she would pirouette on one foot and then another, jumping high enough that he was sure the orphan could have landed back on her stool had she chosen to. After a moment of this the girl began to laugh at the top of her voice, and her laughter, though natural sounding, kept time with the music like one of the musicians' instruments.

Whereas during the first part of the dance, Shawn had watched Rosie in amazement, her raised laughter made him self-conscious. He was sure all this could be heard in the hallway, and while the department of linguistics was more liberal than most, this kind of ebullience would disturb the scholarship of Dr. Teschke's peers. He reached to turn the music down, but stopped, reluctant to disturb her reverie. He elected instead to grit his teeth and hope the other professors would not complain to Dr. Teschke and get him a dressing down.

When the music wound down, so did Rosie's dance. Shawn marveled at how her movements matched the music, as though they had been choreographed and practiced many times. Her placid expression remained past her last step and bow.

He applauded, and the girl drank from the bottle of water he offered her from the department fridge. He searched through the Esperanto dictionary to look up the compliment which had formed in his mind.

"Your dance was beautiful."

"Thank you. Someday you should dance with me," she said in clear English. He froze in surprise, mouth agape.

At that moment, the door cracked open, and then opened wide. In walked Akiko, followed by Mr. Haversham.

"Were you finished? Mr. Haversham needs to take her home," the senior assistant said, motioning to the man behind her, who was watching the girl putting her shoes back on.

Shawn closed his open mouth at the woman's stare. "Yeah, we'd finished. She said she wanted to dance, and I played some music for her. That's what all the noise was if you heard it in the hall."

"Didn't hear a thing," said Akiko, looking curious at his defensiveness.

"Ready to go, honey?" asked David. Rosie said nothing in reply, but replaced the caps onto the scented markers and straightened up her papers on the desk.

"*Goodbye! See you later!*" Shawn read from his "repair phrase" list.

She smiled mischievously over her shoulder as she stuffed the last marker back in the box. "*See you later.*" She left the box of markers and stacks of drawings neat and straight on the desk, and took Mr. Haversham's hand while waving goodbye.

"We'll have our results for you soon, Mr. Haversham. Can we see her again?"

"That will depend on whether Childrens' Services has found long-term foster care for her," said the burly man. He sounded indifferent to the prospect. "But as far as I'm concerned, she can come back so long as she wants to and I'm free to drive her."

"That's great!" enthused Akiko, evincing a charm and emotion so clear Shawn knew it could not be genuine. Rosie sipped from her water bottle, and Mr. Haversham nodded at them both.

"Take it easy, then. Call when you want to see her, but try and give me enough notice to plan ahead."

"We'll email tomorrow to describe this session's results and plan the next one. Thank you again, Mr. Haversham." The woman followed David and Rosie to the door, smiling all the while.

Given a second to himself, Shawn glanced at the digital recorder. The blinking green light indicated it was still recording. Thus, when Akiko closed the door, he was able to meet her angry and suspicious gaze with a confident one.

"I heard that racket outside the building as Mr. Haversham and I walked back here. You'd better have a good explanation! This is linguistic interview, not a discotheque. And what was she doing with her shoes off?"

"I've got better than an explanation," he said, hefting the digital recorder and making a show of clicking it off. "I've got a recording of the whole damn thing."

The woman walked over and took the recorder from him without a moment's hesitation. Her eyes narrowed in deeper suspicion. "We'll let the Doctor decide. Be here at nine tomorrow." Shawn saw that as she spoke the recorder's green light winked off. Her outburst would be part of the recording.

Something in his coworker's expression, in her exaggerated anger and certainty, and in an echo in the air of a dancing girl's laughter, made him grin ear to ear.

"Sure," he said. "I'll bring the donuts. Do you still like vanilla glazed?"

Shawn returned to the linguistics department the next morning and placed his box of donuts beside the coffee maker in the assistants' room. A glance at the clock showed he had a good twenty-five minutes until Akiko's directed time of nine o'clock. The lights were already on behind Dr. Teschke's frosted glass office door. If he listened, he could make out occasional tones of the professor's exchanges with her senior assistant.

At the sound of their voices, Shawn felt anxiety and anger at the two women. They had given him this complex task to study Rosetta's speech without much guidance, he had done his best, but there they were behind that door doubtless passing judgment on his progress so far. Soon he would be invited in to face their judgment after they had already drawn their conclusions without talking to him. It was well into the 21st century, and here he was working for "the man." Or more accurately, "the *wo*man." He wondered if there were any R+B songs about the particular dilemma of working for the white woman.

Shawn employed the anger management training they had given every student at his high school in Detroit. He took three deep breaths, leaned back in his chair, and began to analyze his feelings. "Be honest," he reflected. "Do you know what they are going to say, or are you getting spun up by what you imagine they'll say?" He knew the answer. He was getting spun up. Even if he was right, it did no good for him to get spun up.

After another set of deep breaths, he took a big bite of the jelly donut he'd cherry-picked from the box before he'd sat down. Then, letting the flavor float around his mouth in a smooth wave, he decided to prepare for the coming discussion by reviewing his earlier interviews and notes from talking with Rosetta.

In a moment, though, he was no longer reading. "*What's the point?*" he wondered, "*If this subject* does *speak English, doesn't this make the whole experiment irrelevant?*" After reflection, he decided against this, reasoning that even if she spoke English, what was of experimental value was that she was a native, or all-but-exclusive, speaker of Esperanto.

He drummed his fingers on the desktop. For a while he'd thought he might make his PhD thesis out of this, as Professor Teschke had indicated might be possible. With the way things were going, though, he wasn't even sure he could make a good article out of it. With this thought, he was able to focus on his interview transcripts, and time began to slip by.

At about ten minutes to nine, Shawn heard Dr. Teschke's office door open and looked up to see Akiko standing in her doorway. The woman beckoned to him silently. He stood, took a deep breath, and followed.

He was surprised to see Dr. Teschke did not look stern or angry. His boss motioned that he sit in his accustomed seat, with Selene's usual chair left vacant between him and Akiko.

"Good morning, Shawn," she after he had sat down.

"*Shawn?*" he wondered. "*What happened to 'Mr. Douglas?' I must be in deep doo-doo.*"

"Good morning," he answered, he hoped without too much anxiety. One good thing about Dr. Teschke was she was sure to come to her point swiftly, so even if the news he was about to face was bad, his period of suspense would be brief.

"I notice that your progress, and the volume of recorded and spoken Esperanto you've gleaned from your interviews with Rosetta, is smaller than I might have hoped," she added, still betraying no emotion with this critique.

"Yeah, um, yeah," Shawn replied, feeling his heart sink even as he was grateful the professor was sparing him her sharp tongue.

"I've reviewed the transcripts of your interviews, and listened to the recordings Akiko brought me. It's clear there are more obstacles than we foresaw to getting Rosetta to produce more Esperanto for our study."

"Yes'M." He wondered if he sounded like a sharecropper now. Dr. Teschke paid this new obeisance no notice.

"Chief among them is the matter that you don't speak Esperanto yourself, so it's difficult for you to involve her in a natural or free-flowing conversation."

"Yes'M."

"This fact has lead you to attempt some unconventional tactics to establish a rapport with Rosetta, including an invitation yesterday for her to dance in our office."

Shawn opened his mouth to explain, but the professor continued on. "I applaud your innovation, and have no problem with whatever rapport-building you see most useful, provided it remains reasonable, safe, and ethical."

He closed his mouth and stole a glance Akiko. The woman was reddening and fidgeting with the digital voice recorder she had taken yesterday. The doctor carried on with her monologue and Shawn focused on her.

"Then there is the matter of our limited time with Rosetta. An hour or so at a time isn't enough time for you to prompt her to speak, given the lack of a translator, her age and short attention span, and the normal interruptions of our office space. But we are fortunate to have a unique team in this office with diverse skills," she said. "Involving them will not only help you, but earn the rest of the team some of the credit for whatever it is you *collectively* produce."

"I've no problem with sharing this study, Ma'am," he answered.

It was Dr. Teschke's turn to nod now. "I have decided Selene will help you by taking over the analysis of the transcripts. She has a great deal of experience with this from her studies of childrens' pathological languages and she can also help you with her practical experience in engaging children with special needs. She needn't be present during your interviews. I want you to keep doing these, as interview skills are key to capturing both emerging and vanishing languages. You will need the practice if you are to excel as I hope you will."

At this, Shawn felt great relief. This could have been a lot worse. Instead of yanking him off the project or scolding him, she was leaving him on the project and spreading the workload around. But the doctor continued after a quick frown at Akiko.

"Rosetta's case may require a multidisciplinary approach, and much could be gained by gathering the opinions and recommendations of my fellow professors on this campus. Likewise, I'm sure there is technology available that could be of some use to us in capturing Rosetta's speech and writing while she is not in our office. So Ms. Nakamura will have the job of arranging appointments with these different specialists and helping you select and acquire new technology."

This unexpected chain of events was so surprising and relieving to Shawn that he felt his poker face melt away. Akiko, on the other hand, still kept her eyes on the professor's desk. The professor referred to some notes on her computer, one finger touching the screen. He decided the moment of her silence was a good opportunity to ask his question.

"Ma'am, does Rosetta's use of English yesterday pose a problem to this study over the long term?"

The professor looked puzzled. "I'm sorry? Did she speak English yesterday? Was it after you stopped the recorder?"

He shook his head. "No Ma'am. She spoke English to me after she finished dancing. You didn't hear it on the recording?"

The doctor shook her head, but nodded to Akiko, who handed him the voice recorder. "Play it back if you would."

Shawn switched on the recorder and slid the playback bar on the LCD screen to about the point where he guessed Rosetta's use of English should be heard. His guess was good. When he pressed playback, he heard the music beginning to wind down and his own hands typing notes on the keyboard.

Then, he heard Rosie's voice. But she wasn't speaking English, asking him to dance with her in the future as he remembered. In fact, he couldn't make out what she was saying at all. Not only was it not English she was speaking, but also not Esperanto.

He blushed under Professor Teschke's patient gaze and the other assistant's accusing stare. He snapped the recorder off when Akiko's voice became audible in the recording. Rosetta had been done speaking before she had entered the room.

Dr. Teschke broke the uncomfortable silence with amusement. "I didn't hear her speak English. Is it possible your translation of Esperanto has become natural enough that you understood her for a moment and thought she was speaking English? That's not unheard of. I have had similar experiences before when I was studying the language in which I was also conducting an interview."

Shawn decided not to mention that Rosetta's speech was not Esperanto, either. He didn't want to ruin the gains he had made in Dr. Teschke's esteem and so played dumb. "Yes, Ma'am, I guess my mind was playing tricks on me."

His boss seemed pleased by this fib. "It's one of the pitfalls of interviewing they don't teach you about in class. If you have nothing else, I need to speak with Akiko some more."

He accepted his dismissal, rose, left the office, and closed the professor's door behind him. As he crossed the office, he examined the digital recorder, running it backward as he walked, and playing it forward again as he sat down. Again, he heard the music end. Again, he heard Rosetta's gibberish speech. On this second listening, he noticed that whatever she was saying, it rhymed and was in a singsong voice, as if it were a limerick or a music lyric. And again, he heard the office door open in the recording and his hurried exchange with Mr. Haversham. He snapped the recorder back off.

Shawn bowed his head forward and, using his pointer and middle finger, massaged either side of the point where his nose met his eyebrow. It felt good, and he relaxed, but it didn't change his certainty that he had heard Rosetta speak to him in English.

He checked the office calendar. His next interview Rosetta had been slated for tomorrow. And he was already thinking of one or two new questions for the girl.

Rosie began climbing the stairs of the stone building behind David. She knew she was on her way to another interview, and she could already feel God's increasing presence with each step. She had read about Moses climbing the mountain in a jewish Bible, and wondered if this is how he felt when every step he took brought him one step closer to God. She carried her new backpack in one hand and slid her hand up the polished brass stair banister beside. She enjoyed being able to see the tops of people's heads through the stairwell, where she could see an occasional glimpse of a student or two walking beneath her.

She sometimes felt alarmed by heights, but the man's heavier breathing on the steps ahead of her was reassuring. So she kept climbing, as she had many times before, and when they reached the top level, she took her foster father's hand and led him to Shawn's office.

She turned the brass doorknob and entered, and the dark-skinned man with the fabulous hair was at his desk, waiting for her uneasily. She didn't let this bother her, she was sure she could make him comfortable again by answering his questions, he was a good man, after all. She made a bee line for her stool beside his computer, and grinned when she found the scented markers were once more available beside her sheets of paper.

She smiled at Shawn but did not say anything until David had left with the gray-haired Dr. Teschke. Dr. Teschke's voice became different, became sweeter, somehow, when she spoke to her foster father. The observation made her grin. Love sprang up in God's presence.

When the door closed, Shawn spoke immediately. "*Good day!*" he said in

Esperanto. He was not looking at a list of questions this time. That was different. She wondered if he would be able to talk the whole time without one.

"Hello!"

"Your clothes are pretty today," he said. She didn't agree. The skirt she had on was wool and itched terribly, and it was in a strange rectangular red and orange and black pattern her foster father called "plaid." Likewise, she didn't like the buttons on her white shirt, and the straps on her new brown shoes were too tight. Nonetheless, she had sensed pride in the man when she had worn them at his behest, so she wore them anyway.

By way of an answer, she shrugged at him. *"These are David's clothes,"* she said. *"I am only borrowing them."*

For some reason, this explanation struck her interviewer as funny. Rosie found the sense of humor of the people in this kingdom was hard to fathom at times. She considered which marker to uncap, but in a moment Shawn spoke to her again.

"What language you were speaking to me at the end of our last session?"

At this, Rosie began to feel a faint tingling in her toes and fingers. She could tell God was listening. She knew if he kept asking, God would soon come. This was a good thing.

"It was not me speaking." She decided to uncap the black marker. It was the best one for the drawing she had in mind. She pulled the piece of paper closer.

"Who else was speaking?" he asked.

"Gabriel." She wondered if he would believe her. Faith did not believe in God, she knew. She felt the backside of her knees and inside of her elbows now begin to tingle, and the sensation was making her restless, as if she should stand, or writhe, or dance. *"I think Gabriel likes you."*

The man paused at this, but showed no surprise at the answer. Maybe he was beginning to believe more. He must believe. After all, he had heard Gabriel's voice last time.

"Can I talk to Gabriel again?" Shawn said.

Rosie laughed now. Good feelings crowded out her desire to cooperate with the interview, and she put the cap back on the magic marker, her drawing only begun. If the man kept this up, she wouldn't be able to finish the drawing anytime soon, and she didn't want the marker to dry out.

"He is close. Close enough to touch," she told him.

He looked around the office a bit nervously. *"Will he come here?"* he boggled.

"Only in a tavern. Where we can share wine." Rosie felt like her tongue was thickening as God took hold of it. She could only speak the riddle words now. The other ones he would not let go of. She dropped the marker on the table and turned to him. *"Talk to me more. He is so close."*

She began to resent her interviewer's slow typing as well as the attention he was paying to the recorder, and to the page on the computer. Couldn't he see? Couldn't he feel it? God's vibrations were in everything that touched her. She got up, began to wander around to ease her agitation and fight the stiffening. The stiffening felt good, what was unpleasant was it kept coming, threatening to grow greater, and the wanting for it to be greater was the part that hurt.

Shawn kept typing. *"What do you mean by tavern?"* he rejoined after a moment.

"A place where only believers can hear," she said. *"God will sing."* She studied him as he typed. She couldn't believe he was still sitting there. Couldn't he feel it? Couldn't he hear and smell it? Her own nose was tingling, creating a strange burning sensation which raced from her nostrils through the back of her

head. God was imminent. She had only minutes, and few of them.

"*Come,*" she told him, grabbing Shawn's hand off the keyboard. She was done with his typing. She would make him come with her. He could not miss this. She saw he was uncertain, and maybe afraid. That was okay. She had felt that way her first time. She pulled on his hand, but he resisted.

"*I need the computer,*" he said, pointing. "*Without it I can't understand.*"

For a second, Rosie felt God sliding away now, and thought she should begin to dance to keep and use what was left of him. The possibility upset her, that any bit of Him should be wasted. Her tongue loosened as this happened, and she was able to string words together again.

"*You will understand. Come now, find a tavern, where thieves cannot find us.*" She grabbed his other hand, too, and pulled, and the man came reluctantly out of his chair.

Mr. Douglas fumbled for the voice recorder device, and what she recognized as a set of keys from his desk. As she led him through the main office door, he stopped to lock it. The delay agitated her. It felt like he was doing it to prolong her suffering.

When he was done locking the office, she took him by the hand and all but raced down the stairwell she had climbed with David. Movement slowed God's onset. So it was with some reluctance she stopped when they had both burst out the door of the building.

"*Find. Tavern. Alone. No thieves.*" She hoped her short sentences helped him understand without the computer.

"Okay, let's go," she heard him say in English. He seemed puzzled, but soon he was off. He drifted to the right and led her toward a large stone building, with a tower on it, and another white building next to it. She skipped after him, laughing, enjoying the sights, sounds, and smells God's presence made so much brighter.

She followed him between the two buildings, and to her delight, the tower of the stone building began to ring with bells. She listened to them, listened to birds, and listened to the babble of student voices around her, talking about love, about struggle, about knowledge, friends, and many holy things. She loved this about being with God. When he was nearby, she could see many things which were holy she hadn't seen before.

Shawn led her a bit further, to a smaller but pretty building with red bricks. He pointed to a sign in front of it. "*Here?*" he asked in Esperanto.

She read the sign. "Sage Chapel," it read. "*A house of thieves. A fine place for a tavern,*" she laughed. Shawn merely shook his head at this long sentence. With his Esperanto as it was and God clouding her into riddle-speak, he didn't have a chance of understanding her. So rather than wait for him to sort out the sentence, she charged the chapel doors.

She pushed through one, and then another set of heavy wooden doors, of types she hadn't seen on any other building in her life. They were undecorated, but had the feel of having been pushed by many hands: eager hands, sorrowful hands, and joyous hands. She let these feelings carry into her and through her palms as the weight of the doors resisted her entry to no avail.

Once inside the chapel, all her misgivings left her. It was empty. There were no priests to steal God's meaning, and not even any other students. The interior was dim, and to her left she could see up the hall to the chapel's altar, which was lit with spot lamps. The floor was stone, and would carry voices far, and the low vaults of the ceilings were painted with symbols, all kinds of symbols of things, many of which she had drawn in other places with markers or crayons.

When her eye traced down the curved vault of the ceiling to symbols on

134

the wall, and then to the edge of a corner pew, she knew she had found the place where God would come. In fact, she felt as if she had already seen the spot in a daydream or a movie. Behind her Shawn began to speak to the recording device. "We are now inside Sage Chapel."

"*Such a waste,*" she thought to God. "*You bless them with speech for each other, yet they talk only to machines.*" Gabriel was close now, so imminent he might as well be standing on her head. She wanted to breathe less, to feel the glorious presence and let him inhabit her, but she knew she was not yet at the right place. She had to go a few more steps. To the opposite corner of the chapel. To the far end of the last pew.

She darted for it. She heard Shawn muttering behind her but she didn't dare turn around, or breathe, until she had first tagged the pew with her hands, and then again, when she had run around its end and sat in it.

She faced the man, who had walked to the far end of the pew and was now sidestepping along the front of it to sit beside her. Mr. Douglas was near. Gabriel was near. She felt relief. This might work out after all.

As he sat beside her, she took his hand. "*Ready yourself. He comes,*" she said. The tingling was so strong it felt as if ants were moving under her skin.

"*Who comes?*" said Shawn. The question disappointed her. Didn't he get it? She supposed it didn't matter. If he didn't get it, he was about to. She looked up at the ceiling. Painted above her was the cross she had glimpsed. She closed her eyes and let it transform.

"*I am ready,*" she said to God as the cross began to dance. Before her eyes it changed into a bird, a bird made of triangles with thunderbolts in its heart.

"*I am ready,*" she said again, breaking the shape before her eyes loose from the bird. It shifted again, becoming instead a pair of antlers, then the horns of a crescent moon embracing a star, then a burning spear, and then...

She felt Gabriel touch her. He was here. She sighed at his touch, reached up to the shoulder she had felt his hand upon, and then floated away.

"*I am beloved,*" she knew. She knew it for a long time.

Shawn watched in puzzlement. As he had taken the seat beside Rosie in the pew, she had grabbed his hand, said what he thought amounted to "he is coming," and then started babbling in Esperanto. It was too fast for him, and too garbled, but he knew this didn't matter. The voice recorder was running in his pocket, and he would be able to play back whatever it was she was rambling and translate it. He wasn't sure letting her religiosity run amok would be productive in terms of Esperanto texts, but it could yield some clues as to what her religion was, and that could provide a clue as to her origin.

"*Bad linguistics, but maybe good detective work,*" he told himself. He attended to the girl, who was staring at the ceiling. After a moment, she closed her eyes, and began breathing in short shallow breaths.

"Rosie?" He asked, half out of concern and half out of impatience. He hoped that, having dragged him from the office and then dashed to this chapel pew, she would say something after all.

Slowly, with a long exhalation, Rosie lowered her face and nose to the horizontal and, with eyes still closed, turned her head toward him and tucked her legs up under her. Then she opened her eyes and fixed them on his.

Her expression was unfamiliar and serious. Her voice was slightly lower when she spoke, saying one word, in English.

"Recite," she said, and then nothing more. It had the tone of an order.

135

"Recite what?" He sought clarification in English. Rosie said nothing, still waiting. He tried one of his repair phrases from Esperanto. *"I don't understand."*

"RECITE." Rosie commanded, again with her deeper voice. Shawn glanced around, but the chapel was otherwise empty. No one would hear them. He stared at her, and then began trying to piece together a new sentence in Esperanto from his memory.

"What...do you want... that I say?" he asked her.

"RECITE!" she bellowed. Her voice was bass now, with an odd whispering overtone. He was amazed her small chest and throat could produce it. For some reason, her tone, or her command, or the fact that they were in a chapel, brought to mind things he had said in a mosque. He began as he had when he still attended Salat on Fridays with his father. He was amazed how smoothly the words came back to him. "Oh, Allah! All glory is due you, I praise you, your name is the most blessed, your majesty is highly exalted, there is none-" he began.

The deep bass voice interrupted him. "SON OF CAIN, FOLLOWER OF ISHMAEL, LOST LAMB OF MOHAMMED, HEAR ME."

"Wow, son of Cain? Follower of Ishmael? Now that's way too much home-schooling for a kid." He looked at her again, concerned. "Are you okay, honey?"

The girl's face betrayed no expression other than a faint blissful smile. Her eyes glistened, as if she were crying before a candle. But the voice which answered him had lost all trace of a child's natural tone. "HAVE NO FEAR FOR THIS BELOVED TERPSICHORE, THIS MOST PROFANE CREATION OF MAN THE LORD NOW CLAIMS TO HIS OWN BOSOM AS THE MOST SACRED. SHE IS HIS, AND NO HARM WILL YET COME TO HER, AND ON HER PASSING SHE WILL REST EASILY IN HEAVEN. FOR SHE IS HIS SERVANT, AS I AM."

"You're kind of scaring me," Shawn admitted to the voice.

"FEAR NOT. YOU DO NOT SPEAK TO THIS CHILD, SHAWN SON OF FRANCIS, FATHER OF THEODOSIUS. YOU SPEAK TO GABRIEL, AND THROUGH ME TO GOD."

"Father of 'Theodosius'?" he pondered. If he ever had a son, why would he name him "Theodosius?" "Umm, okay. Hi, Gabriel," he answered. He suppressed a wave at Rosie/Gabriel. That would be flippant. He didn't want to put the girl off her channeling groove.

With this, the chapel lights flickered and then dimmed out. Either lightning had struck or yet another failed experiment on the Engineering quad had drained the campus power supply. With the lights out, the stain glass windows of the chapel went from dim walls of glass to bright panels showing symbols of faith and scholarship. In this light, her eyes glinted, showing orange from somewhere behind her irises as he had seen raccoons' eyes do at night beside the gorges on campus. Combined with the darkness, he found their light disturbing, like a B horror movie.

Her body remained motionless, but her head and eyes moved to follow him as he drew back from her on the bench.

After a moment Rosie spoke again. "SHAWN, SON OF FRANCIS, FATHER OF THEODOSIUS, DO NOT PRESS ME FOR MORE SIGNS OR MIRACLES TO PROVE TO YOU THAT YOU SPEAK TO MORE THAN A MORTAL. I HAVE FOR YOU A REVELATION FROM GOD. ABANDON YOUR SKEPTICISM AND PAY HEED. MY TIME IS SHORT AND SUCH DEMONSTRATIONS EXHAUST MY ENERGY."

Shawn nodded obediently, reaching into his pants cargo pocket for a notebook and pen. He should write all this down, he decided, in case the voice recorder picked it all up as gibberish again.

Rosie/Gabriel waved dismissively. "FORGET THE PEN AND INK. LISTEN, AND OPEN YOUR HEART, AND I SHALL ENGRAVE THESE WORDS ON THE GOLDEN TABLET OF

YOUR MIND, SUCH THAT YOU COULD NOT FORGET THEM IN A LIFETIME OF LIFETIMES."

He let go of his pen, closed his eyes, tried to relax, and listened.

Gabriel's voice began beside and all around him, quiet, yet still loud, like a stage whisper amplified by speakers. "THE REVELATION IS THUS: NO ARMY SERVES GOD, BUT EACH SOLDIER MAY SERVE GOD BY HIS CHOICES. NOW RECITE."

"No army serves God, but each soldier may serve God by his choices," he recited, then listened for more. When he realized no more was forthcoming, he opened his eyes. Hers were still fixed upon him, still orange with reflected light.

"THUS SAYETH THE LORD," completed Gabriel.

"Thus sayeth the Lord," echoed Shawn.

"YOU NOW HAVE THE REVELATION," the voice answered. Without warning, or preamble, or farewell, the light went out of Rosie's eyes and she slumped on the bench. The chapel lights flickered back on as the weight of her legs began to pull her limp form out of the pew. Shawn reached forward and caught her, easing her to the floor.

"Rosie?" he asked. He could hear her breathing, but she didn't answer him. "Nuts," he said, reaching into his other cargo pocket for his cell phone.

Chapter 10

Around the Bedside

Shawn was dozing off in Rosie's hospital room. He was tired, though it was only five in the afternoon. He stood beside the girl's bed so he would not be sleeping when Dr. Teschke and Mr. Haversham arrived. He had called Dr. Teschke and Mr. Haversham immediately after he had dialed 911 from the chapel, and he had not reached them. As the ambulance had carried him and his charge to the Cayuga Medical Center on the other side of the lake, he had, in desperation, called Akiko. The senior assistant had taken the call calmly without scolding him, and, even though she had been teaching a class, had run to find the professor and Mr. Haversham at the coffee bar.

Rosie had been motionless since she had been admitted, and he had endured a brief and terse discussion with an admissions officer who was frustrated that he did not have any of her insurance information. In any case, there was nothing to do but wait. Akiko had called back to say the two were on their way. Since they were not in an ambulance, they would take longer to travel to the hospital than he had, and that and the delay in reaching them meant he would be here for a while before they appeared.

A tone sounded in a breast pocket of his shirt. He snapped his hand to the pocket and looked down. The tone and light indicated the audio recorder's memory had just run out. *"I have the whole damn thing, ambulance ride and all, on record. There won't be much argument about what I did or didn't do,"* he told himself.

It was then he heard another tone, first steady, then repeating, then steady, from the televisions in the waiting area outside the emergency ward. Then came a calm, steady voice Shawn recognized as being that of CNN's main anchorman, mentioning something about "invasion" and "divisions on the ready line."

"Invasion?" he thought. *"Where?"* He wondered who was invading whom and flipped in his mind through the various world hotspots: India/Pakistan, North Korea/South Korea, Lebanon/Israel/Syria, and he did not recall having heard of military buildups in these areas.

He refocused. He had bigger fish to fry than some white man's invasion of yet another brown man's country. All pretenses of "declarations of war" or "mandates of the people" aside, those invasions were among life's uncontrollable inevitabilities. They were like weather or earthquakes. He waited beside Rosie's bed, and within a few moments, he heard Dr. Teschke's voice in the waiting area. This simultaneously brought him a deep sense of relief and one of dread. What would she say?

Dr. Teschke glanced up from her conversation with Mr. Haversham in surprise as she saw Akiko push through the door of Zeus's coffee bar. A reprimand formed in her mind as she remembered her senior assistant was supposed to be teaching an undergraduate session and not out drinking coffee. But those words died on her tongue as she saw her assistant scan the room and then head directly for her table. Mr. Haversham turned over his shoulder, presumably alerted by her own facial expression that someone was coming up behind him.

"Professor, sir," Ms. Nakamura addressed them. "There's been an emergency. Shawn was trying to call you on your cell phone but couldn't reach you."

Hildegard recalled, with a feeling of guilt, that she had switched off her cell phone so as to talk to Mr. Haversham uninterrupted.

"Go ahead, what is it?"

"The girl Rosie. He said something about a seizure. He was about to get into the ambulance with her when he called. He said they were on their way to Cayuga Medical Center and he would stay with her until someone else came for her."

At this, Dr. Teschke and David exchanged glances, rose, and left their cups on the tabletop.

"Thank you for being so quick to find us," she said, feeling badly for having suspected her assistant of shirking.

Akiko gave her suggestion of a bow. "I must get back to my class." The young woman walked quickly back to the door.

"What next?" Hildegard asked, both sad to have their visit cut short but aware he could not stay.

"I have my truck," he said.

"May I come with you? I could get a taxi ride home if I needed it, you could stay at the hospital."

"Sure, I guess," said David, with a grim but resigned look on his face. They walked out of the coffee house, and Dr. Teschke followed him quickly down an asphalt sidewalk on the quadrangle toward where he had parked his truck.

She felt the impulse to run, or jog, but her companion gave no sign of the same.

"Should we hurry?" she prompted, trying to remove any accusatory or scolding tones from her voice.

"If she's already in an ambulance, I can't do anything more for her," David replied. "Best we can do is not make ourselves casualties, too, by rushing to the hospital and getting in an accident."

"Oh." On reflection, she saw his point. He had more experience at controlling himself in an emergency than she.

"But I am grateful for your company. I am feeling upset by this," he admitted. Hildegard caught up to him and walked beside him at this, throwing a hand up onto his shoulder.

"It's nothing. Besides, I suspect Shawn will be upset. He's sensitive."

The two of them rounded the corner of the architecture school. Ahead of them, in a visitor parking spot, Dr. Teschke saw a large red truck, its cab lifted high off the ground by its wheels and suspension. When she stood at the passenger door, it wasn't clear how she was supposed to get in. Then she spotted a flattened area on the chrome tube that ran under the passenger door which might serve as a step, but trying to step into it in her high heels would be foolish. She gestured to David for help. He shook his head, opened the truck's passenger door and gave her a hand up. After a precarious moment on the foothold, she grabbed some handholds and shifted her hips into the passenger seat. She looked down the long distance to the pavement and felt a tremor of vertigo before she leaned back and faced the windshield.

"What an absurdly large vehicle," she said. "Did your wife ever ride in this?" She wondered how tall Mrs. Haversham had been.

"Yes, but my wife wore sensible shoes." He walked around behind the truck and climbed into the driver's seat. Hildegard fastened her shoulder harness before leaning out to grab the passenger door, so as to prevent falling to her death. Then, using both hands, she wrenched the door closed.

In contrast to her, he closed his door as easily as she did the door of her own Citroen. The truck idled in a way which reminded her of a locomotive and then began to back up.

She waited until he had backed out and was moving forward down the hill toward the west campus before commenting.

"Didn't you tell me you were living on a fixed income?" she asked.

"Yup," said David. It took a while for the professor to translate this half spoken, half-grunted answer into an affirmative. Accents made English more challenging.

"So, wouldn't something more fuel efficient be sensible? Like, say, a Prius?"

He didn't take her joke. She concluded humor would not snap him out of whatever funk he was feeling.

"Okay, I'm sorry. I shouldn't make fun of the size of your truck. If nothing else, the Freudian connection should have been obvious to me," she said, crossing her legs and leaning on the door to get a better angle to scan his impassive face.

"No, you're right," said David, his eyes on the road. "I'm being quiet because I can't think of a good answer to the question. All I can say is, I love my truck, and that's all there is to it."

"Hmm. An irrational attachment to a machine?" she pondered. "Is that masculine?"

"People who don't understand that love deserve to be pancaked in tiny Volkswagens," the firefighter replied.

"Ah. So it's Darwinism, not Freud," Dr. Teschke deduced. "This truck is the top predator of the roadway food chain, is it?"

"No, that title belongs to semis, fire trucks or, at the railway crossings, to freight trains. But I'm close to top of the food chain," he retorted.

"Ah. I'll count myself lucky then," Hildegard grinned, rubbing her palms together in excitement. "What shall we have for supper then? A Honda? A small school bus?"

The man smirked. "How about a skinny German lady I made get out and walk?"

"Sounds tasty," she grinned at him. "Anyway, I am only making fun of you to keep you from being upset. Is it bothering you?"

"Yes," he admitted."But it is keeping me from being upset."

"In this case, it's mission accomplished! Shall I make more jokes?"

"No. But I could worry out loud if it makes for better conversation," he answered.

"If it makes you feel better."

David sighed, and began. "I knew when I agreed to foster care that, sooner or later, Rosie would encounter a medical problem. She's so unusual, so smart, I figured there had to be some kind of problem hidden somewhere. A downside."

"Ah. The cancer in the rosebud," she said, remembering her poetry and punning. But this jest fell flat with him, too. She guessed it had been unwise to raise the specter of cancer. "I'm sorry. I guess I'm out of step with your mood, aren't I?"

"Totally," the man observed. "Why?"

Hildegard pondered this, staring out the windshield at the gray sky, the wet streets, and passing rows of fraternity and apartment houses.

140

"It's my turn to worry out loud then," she replied. "I worry I will miss my chance with a most interesting research subject. I worry my assistant may have made some mistake, or done something inappropriate which endangered your foster daughter. And I worry if this is so, we will no longer be friends."

"I can't promise it won't happen. Promises mean little," the man said, turning downhill. "But on the other side, I can't see how it could happen."

"That's good to hear," she said.

What followed was not an uncomfortable silence, but a contemplative one. Dr. Teschke felt her own reflections had now drained her sense of humor out of her. After a moment, David switched on the radio.

The voice on the radio was Australian, though with a glance at the radio dial, Hildegard could see he had the radio tuned to the local National Public Radio channel.

"If you could see where I'm standing now, you would see a long line of Bradley fighting vehicles, strykers, and humvees behind me parked or refueling along what the 3rd Cavalry Regiment is calling phase line Chicago. About 10km to our front, I am told, the lead elements of the 3rd CR have established a screening line. They are already within Iranian territory and engaging Iranian forces just an hour after the American president, less than a year in office, announced the invasion of Iran."

"Richard, you're an ex-military man with prior service with the Australian army. Could this invasion have been prepared in five months' time?"

"I was a sergeant when I mustered out, Farriah, so I'm not an expert on logistics at this scale. But I'd have a hard time imagining a mobilization of this scale conducted so quietly in just a few months, even if the president began issuing his orders on the first day of his term. So much depends on permanent infrastructure built in Iraq and Syria over the last decade, including bases, depots, fuel storage, and port facilities which were ostensibly constructed for, and turned over to, the Iraqi military."

Hildegard couldn't believe what she was hearing. *"It's the American blitz,"* she thought. To break the obvious tension at the announcement, she made another joke. "Oh, look, they've gone to war to fuel your truck."

David said nothing, but rounded another corner in tight traffic. The radio reporters carried on their discussion of the invasion.

"So, in other words, Richard, the preparations for this invasion were made while even the Democrats were still in power?"

"My guess is yes! The scale of the operation suggests it."

"God keep you, Richard. Stay safe and give us a call when you can."

"Thank you, Farriah."

"So, for our listeners who just tuned in, this is NPR, and we're tracking the progress of the invasion of Iran. Forty minutes ago, the president announced to Congress he had initiated the invasion to halt Iran's construction of nuclear weapons. Here to help us understand that decision is Stanford University's nuclear physicist Dr. Morgan Castleton, and..."

David punched the radio off again. "Fuck," he said.

Hildegard was amused by his one word. "It's strange how Americans always claim it's the British with the gift for understatement."

They drove on in more silence. Once they had reached the low part of town, rain began to fall in heavy flat drops on the windshield. The truck's wipers began beating them away. They crossed through the snarled intersection at the southern tip of the lake, which was aptly named "the octopus" for its many branches. It had been "re-engineered" twice since she came to Ithaca and was not noticeably easier to navigate for all that effort. They began traveling uphill before turning right into the medical center's parking lot and approach drive.

"Can you call your assistant and find out where he's at?" Mr. Haversham asked. Dr. Teschke took out her phone, searched through her directory (Akiko was on her speed dial, but Shawn was not, she noted) and rang. She was transferred to his voicemail.

"It's off," she said.

"It means she's already inside being treated. They don't allow cell phones inside the ER or in exam rooms." He stopped the truck in a parking space, got out, and began walking at a fast clip toward the ER.

The professor had opened her door, but was stymied in jumping down by the fact that she was wearing heels. Either her shoes would break, or she would stumble, or both. So she kicked off her shoes to the ground below the truck, jumped down, then picked the shoes back up. Closing the door required all her back and arm strength, but she managed it on the second attempt and jogged to catch up.

"Shoes again," she explained, pausing to pull her shoes onto one foot, than the other. David grunted something else inarticulate, but waited for her. In a few moments they both pushed through the doors into the emergency room waiting area.

They both stopped and looked around for a moment, but continued when they saw no sign of either Shawn or Rosie in the waiting room. Then he led the way straight to a reception and triage desk. From there a nurse led them to a triage exam room.

When they entered, Hildegard saw Rosetta lying flat in a gurney bed, asleep with an IV tube in her arm. On the far side of the room, Shawn stood beside a chair, and roused from his daze as they came in.

"Mr. Haversham, I'm so sorry," he apologized. Dr. Teschke wondered if her assistant was apologizing for the circumstance, or for some act or omission on his part. But she didn't interrupt him. She decided to let the two men talk and ask any questions she might have for him in private.

"What happened?" the older man asked. Hildegard was impressed by his calm.

"After you left her with me, she became agitated, and told me to follow her. She took me to Sage Chapel, began to babble, and collapsed after she was finished," the boy reported.

David was steady at this news. "Did she faint away? Or was it a seizure of some sort?"

Mr. Douglas furrowed his brow in recollection. "More like a seizure, or a possession. She started babbling religion, acting as though she were the angel Gabriel before she passed out."

Mr. Haversham glanced at her. She shrugged back at him. *"Yet again the American obsession for religion reveals itself as a disease,"* she thought.

David said nothing in answer. Shawn wordlessly offered the older man the one chair in the exam room, and he in turn offered it to Hildegard. Sensing that they could be here for a while, she decided to take the chair. Besides, the chair would allow her to get a closer look at the girl.

Her assistant turned to face her as she sat. "Ma'am, if it's all the same, I'd like to head home now. I'm tired, and I'm kind of rattled by all this."

"I can't make you stay, but I'd rather you waited for the doctor's visit. You're the one eyewitness to her seizure and they may have questions for you. Plus, you are the only one who can translate for Rosie."

The young man reached into his pocket and took out the small black voice recorder he used for his interviews. "It's all recorded here, even the ambulance trip. Take it, Ma'am, in case there are any questions back on campus."

She reached for the player and stashed it in her jacket pocket. "Do you have whatever dictionaries you might need to translate if she wakes up?"

He pointed to his courier bag, which still lay next to the chair in a rain-sodden lump. "I have most of my Esperanto notes in there."

"*Prima,*" Hildegard said.

Shawn moved around the bed, leaned on the wall opposite her, rubbed his eyes, and resumed his description of the events. "I caught her before she fell. I think I kept her from hurting anything."

"Did the seizure come all at once, or did she go down slowly?" asked Mr. Haversham.

Shawn paused to recall again. "The passing out happened quickly, but she was acting weird for about ten minutes before it. She kept saying God was close and Gabriel was coming."

Dr. Teschke decided not to venture any opinions. If David had to hear the child was mentally unwell, he should hear it from doctors, not from her bottomless supply of unqualified opinions. But insanity could explain the girl's compulsion to speak Esperanto rather than any of the languages she could read.

Silence resumed, and she searched for something to say, though neither of the men gave talking any effort. Finally she hit on something she was genuinely curious about.

"Did you hear anything about the invasion?"

He shook his head. "I only heard snatches from the waiting room television. Who was invading whom?"

She sighed. "The United States is invading Iran."

The young man showed no surprise. "They've been drooling over that oil for years. All that stood in their way were 'little brown people.' We should fuel our cars with blood. It would be more honest."

She challenged Shawn's opinion. "Who is this 'they'? Aren't the invaders Americans like yourself?"

"No more so than they are Americans like you," he answered. "They don't represent me. They never have."

Hildegard looked at David, expecting a more conservative opinion from him. But the older man made no response. His eyes were focused on the wall behind the girl. "*He's too preoccupied with Rosetta to have an opinion,*" she reflected.

Everyone was quiet until the doctor arrived. He was a late middle-aged man with north Indian features. His nameplate read "Dr. Taneja."

"Sanjay," Mr. Haversham nodded at him with familiarity.

Dr. Taneja nodded back. His expression was calm and thoughtful. "Good to see you. Am I being rude? Should I know your companion?"

She flushed with embarrassment, and saw David do the same. "Oh no. This is Dr. Teschke, head of Cornell's linguistics department. She and her graduate assistant Shawn are helping us translate for the girl, since we can't find her family."

"Nice to meet you, Professor Teschke." The stranger's use of her title put a smile on her face. Dr. Taneja shook her hand, but then clasped it so lightly Hildegard wondered if the man thought she was made of glass.

"So, what happened?" he asked.

David pointed to Shawn. "He saw the whole thing. I wasn't there."

The young man scooped a dreadlock out of his face and took his cue to speak. "Mr. Haversham and Dr. Teschke left Rosetta with me to conduct some linguistic interviews, as I have done a couple of times before. After they left, the

143

girl became agitated. She said she felt God was near and led me to a campus chapel. There she spoke as if she were the angel Gabriel and then collapsed."

Dr. Taneja listened but gave no sign of surprise or concern at this story. He stepped up beside the bed and read a colored plastic clipboard that was hanging next to it. He then reached down and put a hand to her forehead, and then held his hand near her nose and mouth to confirm her breathing.

"Was she conscious when she collapsed? Or did she go unconscious before she fell?" the doctor checked.

"She was unconscious as she fell. She was sitting, and her eyes rolled back, and she started sliding off the bench. I caught her before she hit the floor, and her eyes were already closed."

Dr. Taneja kept his eyes fixed on the girl. "You said she was agitated. Was she angry, or sad, or uncomfortable?"

Shawn shrugged. "She was restless and impatient. She spoke only in short sentences."

The doctor read over the clipboard again. "Her blood sugar and insulin are normal. Her blood pressure is low, and her heart rate is slow," he observed. "Did she urinate or lose bowel control that you saw?"

Shawn shook his head. The doctor leaned over and pushed open Rosetta's mouth with a hand on her chin. He searched the inside of her mouth with an exam light. After a moment he let go, and her mouth stayed open as she dozed.

"No sign she bit her tongue," he said. "Probably not a *grand mal* seizure." The doctor turned then to David. "You are her guardian?"

"Yes."

"And this is the same child the fire department and your daughter brought here after the Cayuga Heights fire?"

"Yes."

Dr. Taneja pursed his lips. "She was in a similar state then."

David showed surprise. "I had no idea."

The doctor continued. "We assumed at the time her condition was the result of smoke inhalation or psychogenic fainting. Based on this man's description, however, she may have been experiencing an aura or a hallucination of some kind. Has she acted unusual in your home?"

The foster father puzzled at this question. "Almost everything about her is unusual. She is calm and happy despite her circumstances. But she often dances or laughs at odd times. She likes to draw. She would do it nonstop if I let her. And no one can beat her at checkers."

"She talks about God all the time," Shawn added. "Every interview I translate relates back to God, or a lover, or about wine."

Dr. Taneja frowned at this. "Has she had access to alcohol?"

"Not in my house," said David. "Maybe her actual parents gave it to her."

Dr. Taneja gave the younger man a hard look. "Did you give her anything but water?"

Hildegard saw the graduate student stiffen and take his eyes off the doctor, staring instead at the ground. "Whatever, doc, whatever. If you think I pushed a ruphie on this girl, Dr. Teschke has a digital recording of the whole event from the time she arrived to when the ambulance got here."

The doctor's eyes stayed fixed on the younger man for a long minute. Without clarifying his first question, he continued. "Did you give her anything which might induce an allergy or an insulin reaction? Fruit juice? Candy? Nuts of any kind?"

Hildegard realized what she was observing. Despite there being no sign of misconduct at hand, Shawn's initial story was being questioned. Maybe it was

144

because of his skin color and hair. She made a mental note to have Akiko make her a copy of what the recorder had captured. Not only might it shed some light on what happened for the doctors, but it could also serve to protect her assistant and her department.

Dr. Taneja continued despite the young man's silence. "I'll take that as a no. Do you have this recording now? Could you play it back? I would like to hear it."

Dr. Teschke fumbled in her jacket pocket for the recorder. She glanced at its controls, but the smooth black plastic device featured one button surrounded by symbols and a view screen with cyan blue numbers and menus. So as to avoid demonstrating her technical incompetence to an audience, she handed the recorder back her assistant. It occurred to her that with so many older people in the room, the boy might be the only one who could make it work in any case.

Shawn took the recorder from her, clicked the central button a couple of times, and held the device up. A recording of the conversation of his interview began, complete with the bumps and rustles which suggested the recorder was being handled throughout.

"What language is that?" Dr. Taneja had put a finger on his cheekbone in concentration.

"Esperanto," answered Shawn with a touch of pride. The three men harkened to the recorder again.

"Now she's saying that I can talk to God if I follow her to a tavern," he narrated. "Now she's getting restless and leading me out of Roberts Hall. I'm not sure she knew where she was going. Now we're entering Sage Chapel."

In another few moments, Hildegard was surprised to hear a third voice in the recording speaking the inscrutable language, and her assistant answering the third voice, not in Esperanto but in English. The young man looked surprised on hearing the recording, as if he was hearing something he'd forgotten.

"Who else was present?" Dr. Teschke interrupted him. He hadn't mentioned anyone else, and while it wasn't a problem if someone had been with him during the interviews, she did expect to be informed of this.

"That's not someone else. That's her. Talking like Gabriel, the angel," replied Shawn. "We're getting close to the end."

"It couldn't be her," she said. "That is an adult's voice."

"C'mon, doc, we're to the point where she collapses," the student said, hushing her with a gesture. Hildegard snapped her mouth shut, feeling sudden resentment at being shushed in public by her junior-most assistant, but aware of the doctor's need to hear the events. In a moment, the recording became a mishmash of bumps, rustles, and Mr. Douglas's voice as he caught the girl, lowered her to the ground, and began calling 9-1-1.

At this point, her assistant stopped the playback, and Dr. Taneja paused in concentration. "Forgive me, but I'm not a Christian, I am Hindi. I have heard the name of the angel Gabriel before. Is he important in Christianity?"

"Very," said David. "He announces to the Virgin Mary that she will give birth to Jesus Christ, and later announces Christ's birth to the shepherds of Bethlehem."

Shawn had more to add. "In Islam, Gabriel reveals the verses of the Koran to Mohammed, and in some stories is the angel who accompanies him to the temple mount of Jerusalem in his night journey."

Dr. Taneja bobbed his head strangely, in a way that seemed both a nod and a shake. "I see." He stared with a hand on his temple. "I must go and consult some of my colleagues with more expertise in this field, yes? Have the nurse send for me if she wakes up. Otherwise I will return and discuss our treatment options."

"Sure, Sanjay. Thanks for looking in on us, I know you're not the usual ER doctor."

"It's my pleasure," said the doctor. "I am on my ER rotation and am curious about this girl. Some of my colleagues and nurses told odd stories about her last visit, and if you don't object, I might ask her some questions or do some simple exams not related to this event to follow up on some hunches."

"No problem," said the older man. Dr. Taneja gave Shawn one last measured look and left.

The student stepped back, and began leaning against the wall again opposite David. The earlier silence resumed, but Hildegard resolved not to chatter and folded her hands to watch how the men would react to one another. Mr. Haversham was of a different stock of American than she met at Cornell, and Mr. Douglas was too, so their interactions could be informative.

The two men regarded each other. After a moment, Mr. Haversham gave a grin that put the younger man at ease.

"You have somewhere you need to be?" he asked.

The younger man nodded. "Yeah, I have a stack of quizzes to grade for Akiko by tomorrow afternoon. I could stand to go, if it's okay with you, Doc." Her assistant looked to her for approval.

"The recorder," Hildegard stood up to reach for it.

"Oh yeah." Shawn handed it to her.

"I'll have Akiko save the recording," she reassured him. "If you need some rest, you don't have to come in until noon tomorrow."

"Uh, thanks, Doc, I'm beat," he said, looking as though fatigue had caught up to him as his anxiety left. "I'll take you up on that."

"Until tomorrow," she affirmed, tucking the recorder into one of her pockets. "Good work today!"

"Thanks," he replied cheerlessly. He waved to Mr. Haversham and then left.

They watched the young man leave, carrying his rain sodden satchel bag with him. They turned to each other after he left. She thought about taking Mr. Haversham's hand, but remembered his sudden discomfort when Dr. Taneja had misidentified her as his partner. So she restrained her impulse to touch him, and spent the moment in contemplation.

The mysterious child's features created for Hildegard an awareness of the passage of time in her own life. They made her feel old, and pressed on her the realization that, as this girl's life was beginning, her own was winding down.

She hoped some of the wisdom her life had brought her would be useful enough to help Rosie.

David sat in the exam room. About two hours had passed since Dr. Taneja and Shawn had left. Nurses stopped in every ten to fifteen minutes, checking monitors and IV fluids and asking if the girl had moved or spoken. She had not. Rosie dozed, not a sign of discomfort anywhere on her features. Hildegard sat next to him, close and more familiar than before, and he was grateful for her company. Nonetheless, he was not sure the situation warranted her staying. He was about to formulate the suggestion that she go and get on with her professor life when Sanjay walked back in.

Sanjay's expression gave him a start. The doctor's face and voice reminded him of long, terrible, nights at Constance's bedside, and the fact that this doctor was one of the few other men in this world ever to see his tears made him feel transparent to the man. And regardless of the professor's chaste positioning, he was sure Sanjay had already guessed she was not exclusively a professional interest.

It was a small town. He and Connie had learned this fact the hard way when news of their shouting arguments had come back to them through the rumor mill. If he ever dated Dr. Teschke, she wouldn't stay a secret for long. He followed the white-coated man with his eyes as the doctor crossed the room to the side of Rosie's bed. After checking the girl, he seemed mystified. "I'm at a loss. All her signs are normal, and she looks perfectly healthy except for the fact that she won't awaken. I'm going to suggest an MRI, but it's an expensive process, as you remember. Would you like me to order one?"

David raised his palms. "It's the state's medical bill, not mine. If you think it's warranted, go for it, Sanjay."

Sanjay pursed his lips and stuffed his hands in his pockets. "Okay. I do think it's warranted. I'll order them. We'll call in the tech and start them as soon as we can."

"Okay," he deferred to the doctor.

Sanjay paused, looking at him with a stern pair of black eyes and bushy eyebrows.

"You've spent enough time in this hospital. I suggest you go home. The girl is not in any danger. We'll call you if something changes. Visiting hours start at eight tomorrow."

David felt stubborn for a moment at the suggestion, like he had every time he'd heard Sanjay make it before. But a look at Hildegard's sympathetic smile and a moment's reflection on his own feelings at being in the hospital changed his mind. He longed to be somewhere more private, and to take the woman up on some of the solace she offered. And he had to talk to Faith. He was surprised his daughter hadn't joined them already. She ought to have overheard the ambulance call on her department radio.

In any case, he knew Sanjay's look, and to be fair, Sanjay had never been afraid to tell him when it was a good idea to stay the night. In fact, thanks to Sanjay's recommendations, he had been there at the moment Constance passed.

He picked up his jacket and cap. "I'll go. Thanks." Beside him, he heard the professor's heels click to the floor and her jacket rustle as she donned it.

"Thank you, Doctor," she said.

Sanjay nodded. "Professor."

David walked out. He stopped in the waiting room, looking around in case Faith was in a seat. But he did not see her.

What he did see was Hildegard at his side. She was here, they were together, and there were no rules against enjoying it. He was grateful, though, that she did not ask him to speak.

Hildegard rode beside David in silence. They rode down the western edge of Cayuga Lake and back into Ithaca. It was late enough that it was now dark. As the man began to drive through the city, she considered that if he returned to his home, she'd have to take a cab.

"Can I trouble you to drop me off near my apartment?" she asked, reluctant to break the silence.

"Sure," he said. "Where should I take you?"

"I have a loft down by the Commons. By the creek and the old student enterprises building."

"One of those new fancy condos, huh? What's the best place to park?"

"There's parking in the central courtyard, but you could drop me off in front. Or even anywhere on the Commons, it's a short walk."

"I could drop you at Seneca and Tioga at the edge of the Commons. Is that good?"

"Certainly!" she said.

David pulled around the western edge of the Commons. "Thanks for coming with me. It was good to have someone with me. It helped to keep me from getting excited."

"My office had a hand in this, and if we're serious about studying her, we have to take responsibility for her welfare while she's with us. I hope today's events haven't put you off to the idea of letting us work with her?" the professor fretted.

The man's answer came quickly. "I will lay it on you straight. My primary reason for taking care of Rosie is my daughter is looking for answers in the carriage house fire. If there are any more answers to be had, they're going to come from the girl, and your office is the key to getting them. It's frustrating that it goes so slowly, but she's a frustrating child. So I've got no hard feelings to you or to Shawn, provided you don't find anything out of order in the recording."

"I understand your frustrations at how slowly it goes. Please try to remember Shawn is working not just through her strange language, but also through whatever...disabilities...Rosie has. I sometimes wonder if we shouldn't have her tested for autism, to tell the truth." Then a thought struck Hildegard. "You know, I should cast a wider net. With your permission, I could search among the other departments for people who could help us. I haven't done much up until now because your daughter expressed the need for discretion."

David pulled to a stop at the Tioga street entrance to the Commons. "Honestly, I think she's stumped. So from my perspective, as long as you're careful, feel free to ask around for help. I'll take anything I can get."

She saw her opening in this remark. "If I can get appointments with various specialists, do I have your permission to take her writings and drawings to them, or even Rosie herself?"

"Sure. For what it's worth," the man gestured, palms up. "Try and give me a day's notice if you need me to bring her up. I do have things I'm trying to do. But I do pay tax dollars for the all those smart people up on the hill. Let's put them to work."

"You only pay for the state school's smart people. But those of us from the private side are happy to help, too."

"You'll have to explain to me sometime how the whole state-private campus thing works," David said.

"I'm not sure even we know. But somehow the university keeps from going broke and stays satisfied the money is being spent correctly," Dr. Teschke admitted. "Anyway, we keep graduating students, so something is being done right."

He grinned to himself. "I'm familiar with the different kinds of money which can only be spent certain ways. I managed a fire service."

Hildegard blushed. "Sorry if I treated you as though you were simple. I'll get started looking for help with Rosie tomorrow," she said. She felt for David, whose expression was empty and distant as he stared out the window. Hildegard then followed her intuition. She reached out and covered one of his hands, tight on his steering wheel, for a moment.

"Take care."

His face reanimated and refocused. "Sorry. Tired I guess. Thanks. For everything."

"Until later," said Hildegard, twisting off her high-heeled shoes with a grin, opening the passenger door, and jumping down to the sidewalk in her bare feet. She shut the door behind her, and with a last wave, saw David off on his way.

Though damp, the concrete was warm and grainy under her feet. She hadn't walked barefoot outdoors in many years. Since she was a short stretch across a pedestrian zone from her apartment, she didn't see the need to put her shoes back on. She grinned as she set out. The texture beneath her changed as she moved from the broomed concrete sidewalk onto the worn cobbles of the Commons and crossed the smooth cool surface of the steel streetcar rails still set in the street.

She laughed aloud. If it weren't for Rosie, she wouldn't be a fifty-eight year old woman walking barefoot in a public space with a silly smile on her face. It was strange what turns the girl was creating in her life.

Chapter 11

Art History

Shawn kept the cardboard lid of the printer paper box across his knees. In the box top was a collection of Rosetta's drawings he had found around the office. A faint bouquet of the many flavors of the magic markers floated up from the box top, and he amused himself trying to distinguish one or another flavor. Rosie was still in the hospital after her seizure the night before, and Dr. Teschke had sent him out with a list of professors to visit with the girl's drawings while Akiko analyzed the audio recording.

The fine arts building he sat in was one of the oldest buildings on the campus. It sprawled across the northern edge of the arts quadrangle, and the careful maintenance Cornell apportioned it was always was one step behind the crumbling which was overtaking it. From time to time there were rumors some "university planning board" was discussing removing the building, but these rumors were always met with protest by students and alumni, so for now the building and its grand dome were locked into a process of stately decay.

Dr. Mayfield's office was on the top floor in the Art History section. He admired the view of the arts quadrangle from the hallway window while he waited outside the professor's office, watching students on foot, bicycle, skateboard, and in-line skates crisscross the Arts Quadrangle. Soon the knob beside him turned, and a smiling gray-haired man poked his head out into the hallway.

"Ah...Are you Dr. Teschke's assistant?"

"That's me," Shawn answered, glad his wait might finally be over.

"Come in. Sorry to keep you waiting. Phone calls. Always more phone calls." The professor withdrew his head back into his office. Shawn stood with his box and pushed through the now open office door. "I'm helping the Met search its prospective acquisitions for frauds, but there's only so much you can tell from a digital image, you know. Everything plays in. The context, the age of the canvas, and even the smell of the paint matter in my determination. So I spend a lot of time on the phone asking questions."

Shawn ignored the professor's rambling. He was used to old white men who either were too out of touch to make much sense or felt that everything they had to say was a pearl of wisdom. He watched the man cross the room.

Dr. Mayfield was skinny and tall, wore shorts which exposed shockingly white legs, and let hair from the crown around his balding head grow to his neck. He gave Shawn the impression of a stork, an impression reinforced when Dr. Mayfield folded his lanky frame behind a paint-stained wooden desk. On it was a stack of copies of a textbook. "Mayfield – Identifying and Dating Paintings and Art – A Field Guide."

"So, Dr. Teschke has said you had some pictures for me? Something a child had drawn?" Dr. Mayfield's tone was amused. No doubt he found examining a child's art a trivial use of his time and talents.

"That's right, Professor. We're trying to help the county identify an orphan. We were hoping you might be able to identify the style of her artwork and give us some clues.

"The orphan can't tell you?" The professor raised an eyebrow as he sat.

"She doesn't speak languages anyone is familiar with, Professor. She has...special needs and can't articulate much to us even when we are able make out what she says. We're hoping her drawings will tell you something." Shawn offered the box top full of drawings to the professor and took the seat the man indicated as he received them.

Dr. Mayfield put the box down on his desk, rotated it side to side until he found an angle which satisfied him, and strapped an odd device to his head. The device had colored LED lamps and interchangeable lenses on telescoping arms. It reminded Shawn of a gadget from a Spielberg childrens' movie.

The professor snapped on a white light on the device which was so bright it made Shawn shield his eyes.

"Here we are," the professor said, twisting a lens on the contraption into place. "The Dean did say it was important and to offer Dr. Teschke my best assistance." He donned some white gloves and picked up the first piece of printer paper from the box top.

With obvious concentration but no other expression, the professor studied the drawing. He ran his palm over it slowly, then flipped it over and studied the back. He sniffed at the page. After a moment, he spoke.

"What's the medium?" he asked.

"The what?" Shawn was taken by surprise by the question.

"The medium? What was this drawn on? What was this drawn with?" The professor rephrased the question.

"Oh, um, scented magic markers. On printer paper. Whatever kind of paper the university usually supplies, I guess." Shawn had thought the medium obvious. "She drew them in our office. I got the markers from the campus store."

The professor rolled his eyes, grinned, snapped off the LED light, and removed the device from his head. "I won't need this, then. No clues in the medium." He kept his white gloves on, however, and leaned back to look at the drawing.

Without expression or remark the professor then placed the first drawing on the desktop and began examining the others. He created a second pile, then a third.

"How old did you say this orphan was?" the professor checked.

"It's unclear. Elevenish, I'd guess," Shawn replied.

The professor's eyes widened, but he was soon lost in his examinations again.

After twenty minutes had passed, the professor set down the last drawing, rose, went to a battered electric teakettle, and began boiling water. "Tea?" he offered.

"No thanks, Doc." He decided to try out the familiar form of "professor" on Dr. Mayfield. The man gave the change no notice.

The professor waited for the kettle to boil, filled one cup with a powerful mint tea, and returned to his seat, once again making his long limbs fold and vanish behind the desk like magic.

"First let me say-" the professor began. But Shawn raised his hand, reached into his pocket, and pulled out the digital recorder.

"Let me record this so Dr. Teschke and whoever doesn't have to call you and make you repeat yourself a million times. I know you're busy."

The professor pursed his lips at the sight of the device, but became pleased with the explanation that it was intended to save his time. The balding man straightened and spoke more deliberately.

"Plainly the artist is gifted for someone her age and the medium in question. Beautiful use of lines, expressive arcs, telling composition in many of the pieces. I'd be pleased to receive these drawings from many of my students.

"Her artistic style and subjects are a mix. However, there are certain underlying rules and practices she always follows that allow me to classify her work as Islamic art."

The professor's observation clicked in Shawn's head. Now that the man mentioned it, he could see the drawings did echo the art from the Mosque in Detroit he had attended as a boy with his father.

"Observe the key elements of Islamic art," the professor continued, choosing a paper from the pile. "For one, while there are pictures of household objects, or tools, or toys, there are no actual pictures of people. The traditions of Islamic art forbid pictures or icons of people as idolatry, similar to the Protestant prohibition on graven images of Jesus." He handed the chosen picture to Shawn. It was a drawing of a picnic setting by a riverbank. The drawing was lush with animals and birds bejeweled or embroidered in their beauty, but there were no people in the drawing. It showed a parasol, a blanket, and picnic items on the blanket, suggesting the people were nearby, but no longer in the picture.

The professor passed him another picture. "Also note some pieces are repetitions and rotations of myriad forms in geometric or other repeating patterns. This is rare in modern Islamic drawing and painting, but ubiquitous in Islamic tile work, ceramics, and textiles. In fact, the English word for this type of rotation and repetition of disparate objects is 'Arabesque'."

Shawn marveled at hearing an actual person use the words "myriad," "ubiquitous," and "Arabesque" in actual sentences. If these words hadn't been covered in his SAT prep course, he wouldn't have even known they existed, but they rolled off this man's tongue like he was born speaking them, and they made perfect sense, too.

"But in case that wasn't enough, here's the final clue," said the professor. "A calligraphic pictogram."

"Huh?" said Shawn. "A Californian what?" he stumbled on the word.

"There," said the professor, pointing to a specific spot on the page. "That's one, right there." He put his fingertip on a curious squiggle.

The drawing was of an empty courtyard garden with a fountain. Most of the flowers were roses, but one of the flowers, he noted, was not a rose, but letters drawn and bent so the word they formed was also shaped like a rose. Shawn stared at the word. He didn't recognize the word itself, but the characters included an "l" and an "o", as well as an international phonetic alphabet character. It was a word in Rosetta's peculiar version of Esperanto.

"What did you call this thing, doc? This word drawn as a picture?" He asked as he fumbled in his bag for his printout of the Esperanto dictionary and began to flip through it, looking for the word.

"A calligraphic pictogram. They are everywhere in Islamic art, and they are considered one of the most unique and clever forms of art in Islamic culture," the professor beamed, pleased with his discovery. But then he took back the picture, and held it up to his face. "However, it is a bit atypical. Muslim calligraphic pictograms are always drawn with letters in the Arabic alphabet. Arabic is the language of the Koran, and held to be the language of the divine. But this pictogram has Roman letters in it, I think."

"Already on it, doc." Shawn said. "I think it's a word in the language she speaks."

"What language is that?" The professor inquired.

He almost blurted out "Esperanto," but remembered at the last moment Dr. Teschke's admonition that Esperanto was not taken seriously in academic circles. "It's obscure. It's a romance language with central European influences."

152

"Ah," said the professor. His tone suggested he was unsatisfied. "Romanian?"

"Err, no, doc, but along those lines. I shouldn't talk about it," hedged Shawn, hoping he didn't press the issue. "Okay, here it is, I think."

"Here's what?" The professor asked, leaning over to peer into the pages of the dictionary.

"The word. In the calli-californian-picto-thing."

"Calli-GRAPHIC picto-GRAM," the professor corrected with a sip from his cup. "Give some attention to detail. Dr. Teschke would be disappointed if she heard you barbarizing a straightforward term like that. I'm sure a young linguist should be able to use both words with facility. If you're the lazy sort who doesn't want to be taken seriously, you can call it a 'calligram,' I suppose."

The student ignored the professor as he tried to sound out the calligraphic pictogram and match it to the words in the dictionary. "L....L-ing-vo. Lingvo. Language."

"Hmm," the professor's enthusiasm fell a bit. "In most cases, calligraphic pictograms are drawn so the word spelled is also the shape formed. In one famous example, the word for 'ship' in Arabic is rendered in a pictogram which looks like a sailing ship. In this case, though, she has drawn the word 'language' into a rose in Roman letters. Not a match."

Shawn had to agree. The professor sighed. "I stand by my assessment. Your orphan may or may not be Arabic, or from an eastern European country influenced by Islam, but her drawings show many of the signs of being Islamic art. That's my best guess I can give you without more samples." The professor then spoke directly to the recorder on the desk. "If you need any more assistance beyond this recording, Hildegard, give a shout. Ciao! We must go see the Klimt collection while it's still in America!"

With this finish, Shawn assumed the professor was done, and clicked off the recorder. "Thanks a lot for your time, doc. This gives us someplace to start."

"Refreshing!" The professor enthused. "It's like a puzzle! On most days if I have a challenge it's helping to determine if a piece of work is a fake. People are never happy if I succeed because it means a museum or collector paid millions too much for something. It's nice to be the bearer of happy news for a change."

"Umm, yeah." He supposed if he were making a tenured professor's salary at Cornell he wouldn't care if he was useful or not. Ivory towers might become gilded cages after a time, though. He slapped his loose-leaf dictionary closed, and he and the professor began stacking the pictures back into the box top.

The professor stopped Shawn before he picked up the last stack of drawings. "I kept these out because these are not - strictly speaking - 'art.' They are reproductions. She's copying or repeating something from memory, not creating these. I've seen these pieces before."

This seemed promising. For Rosetta to draw something from memory, she must be familiar with it. Something she was familiar with could be a real clue to her origins.

"What are they?" Shawn asked, glancing at the first one. He hadn't seen all the pictures when loading them into the box, and he saw the professor's point. This one was not a drawing at all. It resembled the periodic table, but with strange squiggles or letters in each cell.

The professor threw up his hands. "I don't remember," he apologized. "I remember that they were scientific or pseudo-scientific. Please understand that in my line of work I see thousands upon thousands of images a year. But I know I've seen these before. This one," he said, pointing to the table of squiggles, "is Renaissance. And these two are Judaic. I'd say you should take them over to the history department, or maybe the theology department. For the Judaic ones, I'd say your best bet would be Professor Zuckermann. I know she has a formidable reputation, but she's approachable as long as you're polite."

Shawn nodded. He'd never even heard of Professor Zuckermann, as Judaic studies was last on his list of subjects he'd ever take an elective from. The Jews he had encountered in Detroit were not unfriendly, but they had always kept their distance from him, so he had learned to be uncomfortable around them. Then again, it was possible Zuckermann was not Jewish, but only learned in things Judaic. Not everyone who studied Egyptian or Roman art or history was Egyptian or Roman, after all.

"Thanks again, this helps," he said, stuffing the diagrams in his bag rather than putting them back on the box top.

"Don't mention it," the professor dismissed. "For my part I had a pleasant puzzle and it'll make the dean happy, to boot. He's always on my back about some deadlines for reports or summaries so it will be nice to be able to tell him I helped with something for a change," he glanced at his watch. "But I should go. I'm giving the campus art tour for special applicants and alumnae in a few minutes."

"See you around, Doc," said Shawn, slipping out the professor's door and back into the hallway. He reviewed the map of the campus in his head, trying to remember where he could find the theology department. If he had time, he'd make it his next stop so he'd have even more for Dr. Teschke in the afternoon.

David puzzled over the checkerboard with a cup of coffee in his hand. He and Rosie had left the game unfinished, and with the girl still in the hospital, he had a chance to look at the game and figure out how the child was beating him each time they played. He leaned back in the chair, and felt he was getting a sense of her strategy from the pieces when the phone rang. He was tempted to let the answering machine take the call, but rose to get it when he recalled it could be the hospital.

"Hello?" he greeted.

"Hello David? It's Margrethe."

David grimaced into the phone. He supposed he should have expected the social worker to call.

"I got word today that Rosetta is in the hospital, but the hospital won't tell me anything. Can you fill me in?"

"I left her at an appointment with the linguists up on Cornell. While they were doing their thing with her, she had a seizure or something."

"A seizure?" Margrethe sounded dismayed. He understood why instantly. Finding Rosie a home would be a step harder if she was prone to seizures.

"Yep. That's what they said. She started babbling, fell down, fell asleep, and wouldn't wake up. Dr. Taneja said she was fine, except she wouldn't wake up, and they were going to keep her overnight for observation.

"Oh. Have you heard anything?"

"I called this morning and they said she had awoken and was eating. They were going to run some more tests and call me if they were ready to discharge her. If I hadn't heard anything by two o'clock I planned to drive out and visit her."

"Thank you. Be sure you save the bills from this. Between Medicare and Medicaid and the state's portion, I want to be sure you pay nothing."

David grinned to himself. "Yeah, I'd like that, too. No worries, I'll save all the paperwork."

Margrethe barraged him some more questions, and sounded much more

154

satisfied when he hung up the phone. It felt strange to have a simple and civil discussion with the woman.

He was back across the room to his checkerboard and coffee cup when the phone rang again. He rolled his eyes to no one and returned to the phone.

"Hello?" he greeted again. *"David's Taxi and Babysitting Service,"* he felt like adding.

"Hello, is this...Mr. Haversham?"

"Yes."

"Hi, this is Moira Fairchild. I'm a social worker with Cayuga Medical Center Psychiatry and Behavioral Medicine. I'm calling because you're listed as the foster parent for Rosetta Amata."

"I am," he said. He wondered why the psych ward was calling about Rosie.

"The doctors have had a look at her and she's ready for discharge. Can you come to pick her up or do we need to arrange transportation?"

David surveyed the checkerboard. He had better think fast, because the girl would want to finish this game when she came home, and he was losing as always.

"Yeah, I can pick her up. No problem. Where can I meet her?"

"Come to the admissions section. She's in the general pediatrics ward. They'll show you in."

"Okay. Thanks." He hung up as soon as the woman let him, and went to find his outdoor shoes. Another perfectly good day he could have spent entirely in slippers was spoiled. Nonetheless, he was looking forward to picking Rosie up. Even if it meant he would be drubbed in checkers a few times to make up for her lost night.

Shawn found Dr. Zuckermann's door cracked open to the hallway on the north side of the third floor of Annabel Taylor Hall. Given Dr. Mayfield's reassurances that this professor was not as formidable as she was reputed to be, and therefore was reputed to be formidable, he stopped before knocking to prepare for the encounter.

Dr. Zuckermann's door was plastered with taped articles, journal covers and book jackets, all of them featuring her name prominently. From this he guessed she was widely published and loved to share it. In the center of the frosted window glass of her door was a poster featuring a six pointed star overlapping the zodiac symbol of Venus. It read "Through the woman only is the true blood passed. The Jewish woman always has been and remains the gateway of Zion."

Zion was a word which bothered him. Shawn explored this feeling. He knew it was the word some people used to describe a fortress or land where the Jews of the world would take refuge. Islamic newspapers he'd read as boy used "Zion" as a code word for "Israel" and all the land it could claim at gunpoint. When he thought about the word, he recalled "Zion" was a term he had first heard in his father's mosque, and the tone used was always resentful or fearful. The rest of it he wasn't sure he understood, but the terms "Zion" and "true blood" served as warning enough. In his experience the term "true blood" never included black people.

He pushed open the door and stepped in.

"Can I help you?" He heard a brusque and accented voice inquire. Behind the door, to his right, he saw a woman seated at a corner desk and computer. Her large glasses, heavy frames and steep twist of her neck away from her computer screen created the impression of a large, and irritated, owl.

"Ma'am, I'm looking for Professor Zuckermann."

The woman's expression became more quizzical, and her accent was thick and unfamiliar when she answered him. "You've found Professor Zuckermann, *boychik*. What do you want from her?"

Shawn did not understand the word "*boychik*," but he bristled. It sounded dangerously like the term "boy." He decided that since he didn't understand the word, and he was on a mission, he would not get upset about it. He also was put off by this woman talking in the third person.

"Umm, yes, Ma'am, I don't know if you got an email from the dean about helping Dr. Teschke, but I'm here following up.'

Dr. Zuckermann shook her head. "I don't read emails from the dean. He wastes so much of my time with emails for this and emails for that. But Hildegard I know well, the dear. She is good German. We will help you."

Shawn looked around and didn't see anyone else. He guessed the batty old lady was now using the royal we. *"Wow, they sure get crazy in the Ivy Leagues. Maybe it's inbreeding."*

The old woman turned her chair until the back was against the V of the corner desk. Shawn had dropped off the box top full of drawings back at his office, so he pulled the diagrams professor Mayfield had selected from his messenger bag and presented them to her.

"Doc, can you tell me what these are? Doc Mayfield said you might know."

"Doctor Mayfield admitted he did not know something?" she raised an eyebrow at him. "Ah, people change, they do change, sometimes in unlikely ways." She took the diagrams from him, and despite her bulk, leaned forward to place her elbows on her knees while she studied them.

In a moment she began to chuckle. "Yes, I know these...pictures. Where did a *goy* like you find these?" She looked at him again, impressed.

"A girl drew them. An orphan. She does not speak a language anyone understands, but she draws a lot, and these are some of the drawings."

"Ah, yes, yes. This girl. Black hair? Skin like an olive? Burns? Poor *meydele,* this world makes so many orphans." The woman clucked in dismay.

"You've met her?"

"Yes, yes, they brought her here to ask me if she spoke Yiddish. She did not. I understood some of her words, but I told them I thought she speaks Italian. Not so?"

"No," Shawn shook his head.

"These diagrams, very Jewish. Almost no Jewish person would know them, so Jewish."

He shook his head in incomprehension. "If they were Jewish, why would no Jewish person know them?"

Dr. Zuckermann raised one eyebrow. "What faith do you have? Are you a Baptist?"

"No ma'am, my father was Muslim. I...I don't keep any religion."

The doctor slid her chair over to him, eyes wide. She plucked his sleeve as if to check that he was real. "You are...Muslim? And you are here talking to an old Jew?"

"My father was a Muslim. I'm not anything," Shawn shrugged. "I didn't see a reason to be rude."

"I am flattered. The world changes. Blacks, Muslims, not always so polite over the years. It's a shame. America was not kind to your people. Europe was not kind to mine. We have much in common. More and more as America changes."

He didn't know what to say to this, so he said nothing. The professor smiled. "Come to my table. I teach you a piece of Judaism many Jews do not even

156

know. Yes, a prize for being so polite, polite young man." She rolled her chair across her office to a small round table, and patted a stool there. He walked over and took a seat.

She held up a diagram which showed ten circles arranged in three chevrons, one pointing up and two pointing down, with the tenth circle beneath the lowest chevron.

"This picture, yes? Ancient. Many copies over many years. To understand, you must know some history of Jews. Jews lived in the beginning in Israel. But many times over thousands of years, other people conquer the Jews, and forced many Jews to live in other places. Like the black people, yes? Like your people. Taken from their home and forced to live many places. We have much in common."

Shawn nodded at this.

"This time is a sad time, because many Jews believe Israel is the Zion, the fortress and the place given by God to the Jewish people, and to live in another place is unholy and separates them from God. And the elders of the Jewish tribes, they are worried Jews forced to live other places forget the teachings of the Torah. Do you know what the Torah is?"

"Umm, the Jewish Bible?" Shawn tried to recall from his western civilization class.

"Yes, this it is those books, but not only those books. The Torah is also all the customs and rituals and traditions and studying, the rules about how to treat each other and pray correctly. The Torah is important to the Jewish elders, because they believe if a Jew prays incorrectly, he becomes lost to God, becomes no better than a gentile, a non-Jew.

"All this is racist. I do not think God created all people and then chose one kind of them to be special. God made his covenant with the Jewish people, but I do not think he forgot all his other children. Nor do I believe in this Zion-kingdom. Zion is not a place, and it is not a race. But the old men in this time think it is important, and they invent a system of interpretation of the words of Jewish Bible books, and of the rituals of Judaism. They keep this system secret, and teach it only by word of mouth for many generations. This way the teaching stays pure, because without the system, no non-Jew can grasp the inner meanings of the Torah, they think. They call these secrets 'Kabbalah.' You hear this word before?"

"Isn't a cabal like a gathering of witches or conspirators?" Shawn asked.

"Yes, the Christians make a bad word out of 'Kabbalah.' And I don't like it much either. It makes simple things complicated sometimes. But I make it sound only evil. Kabbalah can be a good thing because it makes Jews think about the Torah. It teaches four different ways to think about the Torah: a literal way, an allegorical way, a comparing way with other faiths, and a spiritual way. In this way, Kabbalah is maybe good, as well as bad. Anyway, Kabbalah helps Judaism survive many wars, many centuries.

"It is not so different from Islam. Muslims use many parts of Kabbalah to interpret the Koran. And Muslim scholars also read the Torah. It is similar.

"And maybe it is not so different from, how do you say it, voodoo? Rituals and prayers from Africa taught by only words from person to person so they stay secret but are not forgotten. Forgive me if I offend! I do not know much about voodoo. I only imagine this may be similar."

"Huh," said Shawn. He did not remember being exposed to any tools for interpreting the Koran other than two years of dull Arabic classes on Friday. "So how does this connect to the diagram?"

The professor smiled at the question. "*Bubele*, this is a picture of the

157

sephirot, the ten ways of thinking about God, or arriving at God, or ten faces of God. It depends who you ask. But it is an important picture whomever you ask. An important part of Kabbalah. Some call this picture the 'tree of life.' It does not look much like a tree to me. Maybe the similarity is an allegory," she smiled.

"Hmmm," mused Shawn.

"You said that girl drew this?"

"Yeah," he answered.

"Did she copy it from a book? Or did she draw it with no book?" the professor interrogated.

"She drew it from memory."

"Hmmm. Very...unusual," Dr. Zuckermann. She stood up, walked to a bookshelf, and removed a wooden box from the highest shelf she could reach. Afterwards she walked back to the table, breathing heavily, and opened an ornate catch. She took out two rolls of paper, each around a stick, and pulled the sticks apart, then rolled them from right to left, pausing intermittently. Between the rolls different pages of text appeared. Shawn realized with some amazement the professor, in this day of computers and the internet, was reading from a scroll.

The professor twisted the scroll's rods until she found a portion of the scroll with a diagram just like the one Rosetta had drawn. The professor pushed her glasses up on her nose, and then held the scroll at arm's length, at the distance which allowed her eyes to focus on the fine figures of the text. She glanced back and forth from the scroll to Rosetta's drawing. "She got all the sephirot right, each in its place, even the symbols for each one. She knows the picture well. Even I could not draw this from memory easily, and I study Judaism my whole life."

He twisted a dreadlock in thought. "What does it tell us about her that she knows this picture?"

Dr. Zuckermann twisted a hinge on her glasses. "It could be her family is orthodox, very religious, and teaches this early. Most Jews are not taught this until they are thirty, and today not many adult Jews even know it," she hypothesized. "But if they were orthodox, they would not teach this to a girl. For many orthodox, such things are only for men, not for women or even boys. So maybe not orthodox.

"Maybe her father is a rabbi. A progressive rabbi. Or maybe she steals his books and reads them. Who knows?" Dr. Zuckermann speculated. "It would be rare for a gentile to know such a thing, but nothing is certain. Children can read. There is internet now." She sat back and fixed her owl's gaze on him. "Do you have more?"

Shawn handed her the next of Rosetta's drawings and retrieved the first as Dr. Zuckermann looked it over. He had already puzzled over the drawing. The picture was of five concentric circles with a dot in the center, like a black and white bull's-eye, but with a voided white line running from the center dot to the top of the picture.

"Hmm-hmm," she said. She wiggled her glasses again. "Difficult, so difficult to say in English. This is the ein-sof. It is a drawing of, how do you say it, the infinity of God, God's infiniteness. But not just this. It is a symbol of things which are opposite each other, but also part of God."

"Contradictions?" asked Shawn.

"Yes! Yes! That is the word! Smart boy! This symbol is also of Kabbalah, but not only of Kabbalah, some Christians use this too. They call it, how would you say it...the mark of Gabriel?" She traced the voided line which passed through all the concentric circles to the center. "The path of Gabriel? If you follow this path, the Christians think, you do God's work in the world."

At this, he felt goosebumps stand up all over his arms.

"This picture is easier for a child to copy," the professor noted, handing it back to him. "No symbols, no order of the circles to memorize. But still unusual for a child to see or remember."

Shawn was still recovering from the electric feeling which had gripped him at the mention of Gabriel's name. Unbidden, the passage came into his mind, booming as it had from Rosetta's own mouth. *"No army serves God, but each soldier may serve God with his choices."*

"Thank you, professor."

The professor sat back. "Even more questions?"

"No...Well, yes," he stopped himself. "Maybe one question. If it's not too rude."

The professor relaxed. "Yes, *bubele*. Ask me. At my age, I have only answers, questions are the interesting things."

"If you don't believe Zion is in Israel, where is Zion? Where is the home of the Jews?"

At this, the old woman seemed impressed. "Such good questions." She closed her eyes. "Zion is not a place where you kill. And it is not a place you can go. It is only a place you can carry with you, a fortress only inside you, a fortress of faith."

She leaned forward, and surprised Shawn by putting a wrinkled and spotted finger in his solar plexus. "Here is Zion. Here Zion begins. Who knows where it ends?" She withdrew her finger and shrugged. "All this about staying in Zion, or keeping people out of Zion, it is nonsense, so much *mishegas*. You can't keep a soul which is ready for Zion out. And if you could keep people out of Zion, you wouldn't belong in Zion if you tried. Zion is a gift to the Jewish people, but not a gift only to the Jewish people. Anyway, I talk too much. Go, come back if you have more questions. I am professor...emeritus. I have nothing but time for students. It is a good life."

"Thank you, Professor," he said, picking up his things. He felt much more comfortable now than when he had entered. *"Assalamu alaikum,"* he added.

The professor grinned back at him, ear to ear, showing her crow's feet and gold tooth. *"Aleichem shalom,"* she answered, and plucked at his sleeve one more time.

Shawn left her office lost in thought. He wasn't sure what he'd learned about Rosetta, but he had learned something. And learning, after all, was what he was paying the big bucks for.

David angled his kitchen scissors under Rosetta's plastic hospital wrist band. Rosie wriggled and pulled on her wrist in discomfort, but he kept his grip firm.

"Hold still," he commanded. He wasn't sure she understood his words, but maybe she would understand his tone. "Hold still. I don't want to cut you."

At this explanation, the girl let her arm go limp, and he could at last shear the vinyl band from her wrist and toss it into the trash. She chafed her released wrist, and he smiled at her. "There. That wasn't so bad, was it? Welcome home!"

Rosie shook her head, gave him a hug around his waist, and then darted out of the kitchen into the living room. He listened and, sure enough, he heard the breakfast table bench being pulled back and the pop of the plastic pencil box lid. This was fine by him. If she started drawing, it would give him more time to analyze the checkerboard. But first, he had to make a phone call.

He opened his wallet and took out the slip of paper on which he'd written the professor's home phone number. He hesitated for a moment, feeling reluctant to call the woman outside of business hours. He felt shy. He liked Hildegard, and now he *knew* he liked her. Being aware of this made a simple phone call awkward.

"She told you to call her if Rosie got out before tomorrow. Focus on the mission," muttered David. He squinted at the tiny numbers on his cell phone keypad and dialed the new number. The phone prompted him for a name to assign to the number before dialing it. He hated this part, because inputting letters into the phone required pressing a number key multiple times until the correct letter appeared. He contemplated hunting around for his glasses so he could enter "Hildegart" or "Hildegarde" or however her name was spelled, but then he couldn't be bothered. He was trying to make a simple phone call. Trust technology to make this hard. To satisfy the phone that it had a name for the number, he stabbed in the letters "Dr. T" and pressed "dial" again.

He searched for the skillet he wanted while he put the phone to his ear, and had his head in the fridge when his call was answered.

"Teschke," a woman's voice said. At first he didn't understand the word and experienced a moment of uncertainty. Had he dialed the wrong number?

"Uh, Hildegard?"

"Yes, this is she. David?" The woman replied. He felt some relief she had recognized his voice. Answering with your last name is an odd way to answer a phone! He wondered how many other people it confused. But it was becoming clear she was the sort of woman who expected you to get used to her and like it.

"Yeah, hi. Umm, you wanted me to call if Rosie got out of the hospital tonight."

"Yes. I take it she's out then. Is she well?"

He paused again. The professor sounded abrupt. He hoped he wasn't interrupting anything important. He didn't hear any company in the background, so he continued.

"She's fine. Already at her markers and paper, drawing away."

"All is good then. I have a lead on someone who might speak her language. Could you bring her in at three tomorrow? Is this enough notice?"

David reflected. He didn't recall having any plans. "Sure. Three o'clock at your office? How long will you need her for?"

"If I am able to find this translator, we would need a longer session. Two hours would be ideal. Could you leave her that long?

He thought about the things he might do with those two hours. Grocery shopping, housecleaning, maybe find some peace and quiet. "I could do two hours. Hell, I could do a bit longer if you think you need it."

Dr. Teschke laughed. "I don't want to work my assistants so hard the graduate student union hangs a 'bourgeoisie' sign on my office door. So let's plan on three until five."

"Done," he said. "Anything else?"

"No, but thank you for calling."

"No problem."

"Until tomorrow!" she chimed.

"See you tomorrow!" David replied. He hung up and pulled his head out of his refrigerator. He had stood the whole time with his head in the fridge, he grimaced. He looked around in embarrassment, but no one was around to have noticed.

"Senility is coming for you," he sighed, slapping the phone down on the counter and reaching for the ground beef from the meats drawer. He then searched around until he found some frozen broccoli and mixed vegetables, and a box of hamburger helper when he caught some motion out of the corner of his eye. When he turned, he saw Rosie was now sitting at the checkerboard.

160

She smiled at him, and then, with flourish, pointed to the checkerboard. His time had run out, and she now demanded he come be defeated. "Not now, honey, I'm cooking," he excused himself. Maybe he'd think of a good move to make over supper.

Hildegard stood as Mr. Haversham entered her office. "David, good to see you!"

His acknowledgment was quick but sincere. "You, too!"

Dr. Teschke walked around her desk to shake hands with Rosetta. As she caught the girl's eyes and hands, she tried out the Esperanto greeting Shawn had taught her.

"How do you do, Miss Rosetta?" she asked.

"I feel great! And you?" Rosetta returned brightly.

"I am well, thank you!" the professor replied. She then switched to English because her supply of Esperanto was exhausted, and if her professional credibility would remain intact, she had decided, she should never learn much more. "I have a surprise for you," she winked. "Something I'm sure you'll like. As a thank you for being so patient with Shawn and the rest of us." She went to shelf and pulled out a new copy of *"Asterix and the Golden Sickle."*

Rosie clapped her hands and took the volume. She then bowed her head and bent her knees in her strange curtsy, saying in Esperanto what sounded like profuse thanks, and then made a beeline to the nearest chair to read the comic.

The woman turned David. "I have only a few minutes until I have to go meet the translator."

"Oh. Nuts. I was hoping we might go out for coffee," he mentioned.

Hildegard was pleased the man was thinking of coffee, too. She guessed if she wanted she could make it a regular habit with him. "I'm sorry, but I want to stay and supervise. There's the potential to get a lot more translated with a fluent speaker, and I want to be sure it gets done so we can get some answers for your daughter. But next time I'd be more than happy to!"

David seemed only mostly satisfied at this, and the professor suppressed a thrill. She had someone who was interested in spending time with her who was not a colleague and not a student! *"Let's not make mountains out of molehills,"* she cautioned herself. "You're welcome to stay for this session, if you like," she offered.

"I guess I'd rather not," David decided. "There's a lot of errands I can get done more efficiently while she's with you. So, I should come back around five?"

"Yes please!" she said. "Have a good afternoon!"

"Likewise."

Chapter 12

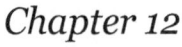

The Rose Knight

Bertolt Kay sat in Zeus's Cafe. He didn't often come over to this part of campus. His office was in Collegetown, in the performing arts building across the Cascadilla gorge from the main campus. He appreciated the cafe's dark corners which gave him places to be invisible, as well as the classical sculptures which filled the cafe and caused him to reflect on the Greek comedies and tragedies he'd either performed in or directed. But on the whole the crowd of busy undergraduates and the concentrated smell of coffee made the nook of a room less pleasant than if they had met at his usual haunt, *Cafe Pretentious* in Collegetown.

It was before the appointed meeting time of three-fifteen in the afternoon. His department chair had told him the head of the linguistics department wanted to meet him here and to be punctual or, if he couldn't manage it, early. He wondered for a moment as to who the woman was. He had identified the linguistic department head in his university directory, and knew her name to be "Hildegard Teschke", a Prussian sort of name. But he had no idea what she looked like. He'd only thought of doing a Google image search after arriving at the cafe.

He wondered what the department chair of the linguistics department would want with him. The only way he could think of in which the orbits of their studies would cross was on the issue of thespian skills. He could produce a wide range of accents. But if it was something so trivial and harmless, why had his department chair suggested he might want to keep a low profile and not discuss this appointment with anyone?

The students began to filter out of Zeus's, and those that remained settled into chairs with laptops and earbuds in place. He was catching sight of the coffee grounds toward the bottom of his cup when an older woman walked into the cafe from Goldwin Smith Hall's foyer.

Bertolt recognized her as a woman who had come and sat in the front row of many of his class performances of Brecht and Schiller. He had heard the woman use German and always assumed she was a German expatriate living in the mélange of diaspora which made up the City of Ithaca. He hadn't guessed she was a professor, however, to say nothing of an important one like a department head.

"*Good day,*" he said in German, coming to his feet.

Her face lit up at his German, and she offered him a handshake. "*To you also, Doctor Kay. I'm Doctor Teschke.*"

"*I should correct you,*" he said. "*I have no PhD. I'm afraid I serve the university based on my critical acclaim alone. And nowadays it's as much due to his bad habits and laziness that my department chair hasn't replaced me with someone more credentialed. One doesn't earn fresh acclaim teaching students.*"

"*You are too modest. I've taken friends visiting from Germany to see your shows, and they appreciate the care with which you translate works from German. I think you would do as well in Berlin as here. Please, call me Hildegard.*"

Bertolt laughed. "*I am Bertolt. Maybe I would thrive in Berlin. But I am superstitious about walking under cranes. So I should not live in Berlin for maybe another ten years or so with the EU military headquarters moving there.*"

At this the woman laughed with him, an honest belly laugh. He was gratified to have his jokes understood. She motioned for him sit back down. He did so after she sat.

"*I must ask for what you need to see me? Not that I'm unhappy to get to know someone so often in my audience. But my department chair was mum about why I should meet you.*"

"*Ah, that is as it should be. He was discreet. This matter is sensitive. Both for the other people involved, and for you.*"

Bertolt blinked. Was he in some kind of trouble? He couldn't be. He hadn't slept with one of his students since that small indiscretion...more than ten years ago now. And he kept his marijuana use off campus and limited to his circle of friends, with whom he had smoked for years without incident.

"*Please explain,*" he said. He hoped he didn't project his nagging guilt.

Hildegard spent a moment in uncertainty, and tugged on one of her earlobes. Then she was out with the matter.

"*I'm told you're an Esperantist.*"

Bertolt frowned. He was glad they were still speaking in German. The chance of anyone understanding them should they be overheard was much smaller. "*I'd hoped that wasn't common knowledge.*"

"*It isn't. I had to do a bit of checking around. I had no idea you were. Then your department head indicated I should talk to you.*"

"*He must have an old copy of my resume. Back when I was hired, it was another oddball credential. Since Market Garden, being a known Esperantist gets you on lists. More than one prominent Esperantist has gone missing since this presidency began.*" Bertolt felt cornered now. "*I cannot bring myself to join internet Esperanto chat anymore. I'm never sure who I might be talking to, or who might be listening.*"

"*Ah, history repeats itself,*" mused Dr. Teschke.

"*Quite,*" said Bertolt.

"*You said you do Esperanto chat. Do you speak Esperanto?*"

Bertolt shrugged. "*As much as anyone does, I suppose. When I travel, particularly in China, my guest family sometimes uses it. It's an exercise for them, too, but much easier than learning German or English, I'm sure. I feel much more natural writing Esperanto. I suppose most of us do. Or did. Before the lists.*"

"*We have an unusual case we need your help with. A girl has been brought to our department for help. She was found orphaned. And she speaks only Esperanto.*"

"*Speaks only Esperanto,*" Bertolt laughed. "*You're joking.*"

"*I had a similar response to the idea. Nonetheless, it is the fact of the matter,*" the professor said. "*I have an assistant hard at work learning Esperanto so he can make a linguistic study of her, the county would love to be able to ask her some questions as soon as possible. They need the information so they can begin a search for her family.*"

Bertolt shifted. "*I can't turn away from a noble cause like that. Who would know?*"

"*No one outside my office. I can tell the state one of my assistants did the translating, or we had a visiting scholar translate for us, or something else plausible. No need for your name to come into it if you don't want it to.*"

"*Please, no mention. You have tenure. But if I came to the attention and displeasure of the government, and they leaned on the university, I'd be on the street in no time.*"

"*I think you might be surprised at the degree to which Cornell would* stand up for you." Dr. Teschke challenged. *"We still teach Darwin's theories, after all, at the cost of a great deal of federal funding."*

"I think you have lived in this ivory tower too long to know. No offense, but it's not my impression that unions please the university's administration, and Esperantists are often involved in unionization. Some might sympathize, but on the whole... I think if a government agency fingered me management here would find it a convenient excuse to get rid of a troublemaker."

"Are you involved in unionization?" Hildegard asked.

"Do I need to answer that question for some reason?" Bertolt raised an eyebrow at her.

"No, I suppose not. But you would be willing to translate, then?"

"Yes. Only keep my name out of it."

"I will," Dr. Teschke asserted.

"Again, I want to emphasize Esperanto is more often read than spoken. So I will want a dictionary on hand to look up words I may not remember."

"My assistant has such a dictionary. It should not be a problem."

Bertolt felt a moment of fear and unease. Why should he stick his neck out to translate for this tenured expat with the U.S. government taking an interest in every use of Esperanto? After all, the Esperantist who'd been the treasurer of the now failed Wal-Mart unionization effort had vanished last week. But he stopped. *"What was the point of learning Esperanto if I lacked the courage to help my fellow man? That's the whole point. Solidarity,"* he rebuked himself.

"When and where would you like to meet to do this?" he acquiesced.

The older woman smiled. *"Follow me to my office. The girl is there now."*

"Clever woman," thought Bertolt. She'd set him up. With luck, he'd leave the office in a few minutes and no one outside the campus would ever know he'd been involved. They rose. Bertolt recycled his coffee cup, and they passed the time walking around the arts quadrangle talking. Their topics ranged from their latest trips to Berlin, the next play he had in mind to do, and the best places in town to find chocolates, nutella, and good bread. Although Dr. Teschke was ten years his senior, he found her charming. His experience with European women, though, was that they signaled their interest, and he got no such signal, so he curbed his impulse to ask her for a social date. Besides, a romantic connection could link him to this case.

Dr. Teschke's office was on the arts quadrangle itself, a prestigious and historic address. He admired the building's tall Victorian windows, stonework, green copper roof, and shiny brass interior trim as they made their way into the building and up some spiral stairs. At length they came to Dr. Teschke's department, and she opened the door to what was the common office. There were already people there waiting.

"These are my assistants, Akiko, Selene, and Shawn." Akiko was an attractive but serious looking Oriental woman. Selene was about his age, and approachable in jeans and a t-shirt. The boy dressed like a reggae artist with his mop of dreadlocks jammed through a tam. The fourth person was a gangly, homely, dark haired girl, whom he guessed was the mysterious Esperanto-speaking orphan.

"What a mix you have," he said in German, prompting puzzled looks from the three assistants but earning a grin from Dr. Teschke. "Hello, I'm Bertolt Kay," he gave his own introduction all around.

"Herr Kay, errm, Mister Kay, is here to help us with the translation so we can satisfy the needs of both the fire department and the child welfare services."

"Wow! Do you speak Esperanto?" Shawn asked.

"Yes. Or I speak it rarely, but I used to chat with it in the internet a lot,"

Bertolt answered, taken aback by the student's enthusiasm. Rather than belabor the point, he extended the orphan his hand.

"*Pleased to meet you. I am Bertolt Kay,*" he said in Esperanto.

The girl lit up. "*It is wonderful to hear someone speak Esperanto! I have been lonesome. I am called Rosetta.*" She bobbed her head, leaned forward from the stool she was sitting on and touched his sleeve. Bertolt felt odd at this, but seeing conversations were already underway, Dr. Teschke motioned everyone into chairs.

Bertolt was curious about the choice of words. "*Is Rosetta your name, or what you are called?*"

She shrugged as the assistants scrambled around the room, gathered up a recording device and a stack of forms, and set them on an empty desk beside him. Shawn, the black assistant, took a position at his elbow and began selecting forms. Bertolt guessed he had a few minutes to chat with this curious creature.

"*It is one of the things I am called. I am also called a number.*"

"*Really?*" asked Bertolt.

"*Yes. I am also called case #490,*" she answered.

"*Ah. What do your mother and father call you? That's what counts.*"

She answered slowly, as though she thought him thickheaded. "*My mother and father do not call me by name. They speak to me.*"

"*So who calls you Rosetta?*"

"*The people who cared for me. They named me after a stone. It is good to be named for a piece of the Earth. To Earth we all return.*" Rosetta fidgeted distractedly as she answered.

Bertolt decided to ask for elaboration. "*These people were not your mother and father?*"

"*No.*"

"*Where did you live before now?*"

"*A place. It was warmer than here. There were many rooms, and many other children. Many of them sick.*"

"*Did you have brothers and sisters there?*"

The girl was nonchalant. "*I have brothers and sisters everywhere.*"

"*How did you learn Esperanto? Did your parents teach it to you?*"

"*No, I learned it from a book,*" she said.

"*What language did you speak before?*"

"*Any language I heard. It was nice.*"

"*Why do you speak only Esperanto now?*"

The girl stopped swinging her feet under the stool. With a serious expression, she said "*God commanded me to speak only Esperanto. He said I was the unmaking of the curse of the tower. And now when I try to speak other languages, I cannot. God ties my tongue in knots. If I try to write them or type them, only nonsense comes out.*"

"*The tower?*" Bertolt reflected. "*Do you mean, the 'Tower of Babel?' The one in the Bible?*"

Rosetta nodded.

Bertolt sucked in a deep breath. This child either had psychological issues or had been raised in some sort of religious institutional setting. He wanted to speak aside to Dr. Teschke to see if she was aware of this, but didn't want to do so in front of the girl. If, as she said, she could speak many languages, she would understand his comments and might think them rude. So he decided to check this theory before doing so.

"*Do you understand the language these people speak to each other?*"

Rosetta blinked. "*They're speaking English.*"

"Do you understand questions if they ask them to you, or do you need me to translate their questions into Esperanto?"

"I understand their words. But I often don't understand what their words mean. They ask questions that make no sense."

"Do you hear God speak?"

"Of course," Rosetta said.

"God talks to you?"

"Sometimes. Other times he sends meanings, and I understand them." She pointed to a bookshelf. *"Those books. In their color and in their order is meaning God has put there."*

"How strange," said Bertolt under his breath in German.

Rosetta squinted at him, as if scanning his face for a freckle. *"It's not strange. But you can't hear God, either?"*

Bertolt blinked. Rosetta understood some German. He had grown used to using German as a secret language for him and a select few others. The child's unhesitating translation of it startled him. He put aside his startle response and answered the question. *"I'm afraid not."*

"He didn't tell you to speak Esperanto, too?" She seemed let down, but not angry.

Bertolt shook his head in wonder at the question. *"No, he didn't. I taught it to myself. So I could speak to people from other countries."*

"That is a good reason to learn it," Rosetta approved, but still seemed unhappy.

"Thank you!" Bertolt nodded to the others in the room, whom Rosetta was all but ignoring. *"These people may have some questions for you soon. But before they ask them, I have some questions for them. I'll be back."*

"Okay, I can wait."

Bertolt whispered in Dr. Teschke's ear. She tilted her head to her private office, and he followed her in.

"I'm not convinced that child is all there," he said in German once her office door was shut.

"It's a distinct possibility. You're not the first to conclude this. Do your best."

"She...thinks she talks to God. She says God commanded her to speak Esperanto so she could end the curse of Babel."

Hildegard was unsurprised. *"Yes."*

Bertolt was surprised the academic wasn't more concerned. "This might be a fool's errand," he said, back in English.

"It might be. Do what you can. You're the best we have, and given the current political climate, we won't find better anytime soon."

Bertolt felt relief that the woman's expectations were realistic. "Who will ask the questions?"

"Let Shawn choose the questions. If you need to develop them or ask more to get the answers, go ahead, don't wait for him. He's new at interviewing."

"Alright," he said. "Let's get started." They re-entered the main office. Dr. Teschke sat between her two female assistants, and Bertolt found his original chair beside Shawn. The younger man handed him a printed list of questions and a pencil, and the Japanese woman started a digital recorder and put it down beside them.

Bertolt scanned the list and formulated a translation of the first question. When he felt he had it, he examined the girl, who was sitting smiling with her eyes closed.

"Rosetta, you were found at the scene of a fire. How did you come to be

at that fire?"

"Two men and a woman took me there."

"What were you doing there?"

"They had tied me up. They wanted to kill me in a special way," she said.

"They wanted to kill you?" Bertolt asked. *"How do you know?"*

"They talked about it. They had the tools to do so and said that this city was the perfect place to do it, because finding my body would teach the people who live here, who love only the devil, to fear God. They said I was an abomination and not part of God's plan. Then Gabriel came and burned them."

"So, this person Gabriel started the fire?"

"Yes."

"But Gabriel is not one of the people who wanted to kill you."

"Gabriel is the messenger of God. He acts for God in this world. He protected me."

"So you mean, Gabriel the high angel?" Bertolt was not sure there was a word for Archangel in Esperanto. The people he spoke Esperanto with were rarely religious.

"I mean Gabriel, the messenger of God." Rosetta answered. *"I do not know how important he is to other angels. He is the one who comes to me. He is my lover."*

Bertolt took care to write this all down. He wasn't sure what use it would be, but who knows what facts the police or fire department had that might make some sense of this. But even if they had nothing, the existence of a man who took a girl this young as a lover would be of interest to the police. *"Where did you live in before you were taken to the place of the fire?"*

"A place across the sea."

"You said this place had many other children at it, and some were sick. Was it a kind of hospital? Or a school?" Bertolt wondered if it might not have been an insane asylum.

"It was called the laboratory."

"What country was it in?"

"I do not know. It was where it was. It was not important to know where it was. I was never anywhere else until I came here. It's not important where anyplace is. It only matters who I find here."

Bertolt scribbled notes. *"Where are your parents?"*

Rosetta raised her arms, palms up. *"They are all around us."*

"What do you mean?"

"The father is all around you. The mother is all around you. They cannot be anywhere else, but everywhere, all the time."

"How can they be all around me? Can they be all around me because they are dead?"

Rosetta rolled her eyes in exasperation.

It was all Bertolt could do not to meet this with exasperation of his own. *"You had to have a mother, you had to be born, or you could not be alive now,"* said Bertolt.

"God has been my mother and father since the day I came to be."

"Then who took care of you at this laboratory?"

"Nanny Wasilatu. I miss her."

"Where is Nanny Wasilatu now? Do you know?"

"She is gone to God." Rosetta squirmed with distress in her chair. *"She came here with me on the airplane. The people who took me killed her with a gun."*

"Can you spell Wasilatu for me?"

167

Rosetta paused and spelled it out for him. Her pronunciation of the letters was precise and sing-song, as if she'd memorized them as a song, even though they were out of order to have been part of an alphabet song.

"Is Wasilatu her family name or her first name?"

"It is her name," Rosetta reiterated.

"What is your family name?"

Curiousity perked her features. *"This question makes no sense. What is a family name? Shawn asked me this before."*

Bertolt cast an aside glance at the boy, wondering how he coped with the girl's cryptic answers in a strange language. He guessed not well, since Dr. Teschke had summoned him here. *"The family name is the same for every member of your family, so you know you are related,"* explained Bertolt.

"Then my family name is beloved. Everyone in the world is my family, and God loves everyone. So our family name is beloved. So my family name must be 'Amata.' I already told Shawn this."

"'Beloved' is not a family name," corrected Bertolt. *"It's an adjective."*

Rosetta twisted restlessly in her chair. *"Maybe my family name is case, then. I was case #490. My brother Lionel was case #511. Both of us had the name 'case.' What case are you?"*

"No, that doesn't sound like a family name either," Bertolt prompted. *"Those sound like numbers someone gave you."*

"Then my family name is Amata. As is yours," she answered. *"Bertolt Kay Amata, part of the family of God."*

"Do you know the names of the people who wanted to kill you?"

"William Amata. Randy Amata. Mary Joe Amata," Rosetta listed.

"How did Gabriel kill them?"

"He came. There was white fire. It burned them up, and burned the building, and the things in the building, and the trees and the animals," she began to sniffle. *"I didn't want him to hurt anyone. I didn't understand."*

Selene stepped forward to put her arms on Rosetta as she began to cry. Hildegard indicated to Bertolt that he should stop. Selene muttered some comforting things and exhorted the girl to be brave. Shawn and Akiko both watched in silence.

When the child had stopped crying and wiped her eyes on her sleeve, the professor gave him a nod. Selene pulled up a chair alongside Rosie and sat with her.

"Are you ready to talk some more?" Bertolt prompted the girl before continuing. She nodded, eyes reddened.

"How did Gabriel make the fire? Did he use matches? Torches? Gasoline?"

Rosetta gave Bertolt a long stare, as if he were mad.

"He was the fire. They died. I remember them screaming. They covered their eyes. They only screamed for a second. Then they were gone, and their souls went to God. One of them touched me while he was burning, and where he touched me, I was burned too."

Bertolt paused to review his notes. *"If we showed you pictures of William, Randy, and Mary Joe, could you identify them?"*

"Maybe. What does it matter? They are with God."

"Yes, but if we knew who they were, we might be able to find out if others like them helped them, or wanted to kill you. And we could tell their families what happened to them."

Rosetta made a thoughtful frown. *"I don't understand, but I want to help, so I will try. But if anyone else tried to kill me Gabriel would stop them, too, so it is not necessary to do this for me."*

"*Does Gabriel know where you are now?*" Bertolt asked.

"*Yes.*"

"*Where is he now?*"

"*Here,*" she answered with certainty.

Bertolt's check of the room showed no sign of a sinister arsonist, or a man with a flamethrower, or a glowing angel of God.

"*Can you describe Gabriel?*"

"*He is light. He is fire. He is holy words and holy voice.*"

"*Okay, but what color is his hair? Gold? Brown? Is he a man like me or a woman like Akiko?*"

Rosetta looked askance at him. "*Bertolt Kay Amata, you are a strange man.*"

Bertolt put down his pencil and massaged his temples. "*Let's go back to your Nanny. What did she look like?*"

"*She had brown skin like Shawn. And gray hair like Doctor Teschke, but it was short and curly. She had a big smile, and white teeth, and she wore dresses with flowers.*"

Bertolt continued. "*What language did she speak?*"

"*She spoke English, and Hausa, and Swahili.*"

These were concrete clues. He had no idea what Hausa was. But Swahili suggested Africa.

"*What sort of English did she speak? English like Shawn?*"

"*No. Different.*" Bertolt guessed from this that Wasilatu was not African-American.

"*English like Selene?*"

Rosetta shook her head. So Wasilatu was not from southern California, either. Bertolt was proud of his array of English accents and dialect, and now he had a chance to put them to good use.

He moved on to his second page of notes, handing the first to Shawn for everyone else to mull over. As he did so, he tried out accents.

"Did she sound like this?" He tried again, adopting an Oxford accent.

"*More like that than like Shawn.*"

He adopted an eastern Australian accent. "How about like this?" She shook her head.

"Did she sound like this?" He tried a Caribbean accent. Rosetta grinned.

"*She sounded much like that. But not the same.*"

He didn't know any other creole accents to try on her, but he made a note this nanny probably spoke an English creole.

"*Describe the place where you lived?*"

Rosetta reflected. "*It was white and green. It was large. It had metal roof and concrete walls, and thick glass windows. It had a tall wall around gardens and men with guns to protect it. Everyone there was nice to me, but Nanny Wasilatu was in charge of my room.*"

"*Who else lived with you in the room?*"

"*My brother Lionel. My sister Suliya. And Devon. But Devon died.*"

"*They were all your brothers and sisters?*"

"*That goes without saying,*" answered Rosetta.

"*Were they your real brothers and sisters, or were they your brothers and sisters in God's family?*"

Rosetta scowled. "*Both kinds are the same.*"

"*How did Devon die?*"

"*Sugar in his blood, Nanny Wasilatu said.*"

169

"Diabetes," recognized Bertolt. So if it was a hospital, it not was not strictly a mental hospital. He decided to follow up on this idea.

"*Did your brothers and sisters talk to God?*"

"*Yes. Every night before they went to bed, like Nanny Wasilatu taught them.*"

"*Did God talk to them?*"

"*Yes, he speaks to you. He is speaking to everyone, all the time. You need to listen.*"

"*What is he saying to me, then?*"

"*You want me to listen to God for you?*" Rosetta rolled her eyes, as if it was something she was tired of doing. Before Bertolt could answer, she exhaled sharply, closed her eyes, and became still.

The pause this created made the assistants restless. He turned to talk to them.

"Okay so far?" he asked.

"I don't know. I guess I'd envisioned doing this more line-by-line," Shawn said. Akiko agreed.

"Look, she's not answering me line by line," he said. "It's like everything she says needs clarification."

Hildegard intervened. "It's fine, Bertolt. Keep going as you are. We might wish for a more ideal academic method, but at the root, you'll get to the information the authorities need faster than we will, and this information is needed to ensure this girl's welfare. Plus, we have a recording we can study later, and she's saying much more to you than she ever said to us." With this, she shot Shawn a meaningful look, and younger man relented.

"*Do not fear. The bold and the righteous have seats in heaven,*" interrupted Rosetta.

Bertolt refocused. "*Please repeat that?*"

"*This is what God is trying to tell you. Do the good you fear to do.*"

"*That's what God is saying?*"

Rosetta tilted her head. "*Kind of. I'm translating. He speaks in riddles.*"

"*Rather like you do,*" Bertolt thought. "*Don't translate, then. What is he literally saying?*" he prompted.

"*He's asking a question. But he doesn't want the answer. He wants you to remember you know the answer.*"

"*Ask it.*"

She focused her eyes on his face, and then on some point past him. Her expression was innocent and blank. "*Mr. Kay, if sharks were people, would they be nicer to the little fishes?*"

Bertolt's jaw went slack. The question was the opening line from one of Brecht's most famous short stories. Then he laughed a long laugh which faded from nervous to appreciative. This girl was clever. He wondered how she knew he taught postwar European theater.

"*God asks this?*" he sought confirmation. He wondered at this. "*Do I really think the girl is asking this, instead? How could she? And if she isn't, does it mean I believe in God?*"

"*Yes,*" Rosie answered. "*He also says he enjoys your plays. He also thinks you should go ahead and try the 'Rosenkavalier' in the spring semester. Your students are ready.*"

Bertolt put his fingers to his temples and rubbed them. Learning Esperanto had been one of those interesting choices that had complicated the rest of his life.

170

Chapter 13

Meeting the Friend

That night Rosie felt lonesome. She didn't understand why. David was nice to her and had lost many games of checkers to her with no sign of getting tired of it. But as she kicked down the blankets which made the bed too hot in summer, she examined the feeling. Why was she discontent?

After a moment, she figured it out. Her encounter with Bertolt Kay made her feel lonely. For the hour or so of the interview, she had been able to speak and be understood. She had felt like a real person, not like a baby. If the man had stayed, she might have even tried long sentences on him.

She turned these thoughts over in her head. Nanny had taught her to explore her feelings, to listen to them, so she could find out what they told her about what she wanted. "Your feelings keep the secret to your strength," she had said. "Listen to them to become stronger."

When she felt she understood what she wanted, she resolved to put her request to God. She got back out of bed and knelt beside it, bending her head to the floorboards. She focused her eyes on the only thing she could make out, the grain of the wood floor. She tried to make her mind empty, but began thinking about the blonde rivers of the wood grain. Her mind followed how they flowed, and how their flow had once represented the growth and life of a tree, which represented the growth and life of the land, and of the world....

She felt him. He was silent, but his presence alone was pervasive. Not in the way of Gabriel, whose own senses entangled her, but in a way that enclosed her yet left her herself. The patterns of the wallpaper told her exactly where he was. He was sitting two feet behind her shoulder, but she didn't dare turn to look. It was futile, after all. One couldn't look anywhere without seeing God.

"Hello!" Rosie said inside her head when he had been there for a while without speaking. Her knees hurt from being folded under her on the wooden floor for so long, but she felt she had to have arrived at the right feeling of calm and patience before daring to ask.

"I was waiting for you to finish your thinking and be ready," answered God.

Rosetta felt relief flood her and calm her stomach. She'd been good, and she'd prayed enough, and God was hearing her. "God, I'm lonesome with this job you gave me. Everyone can talk to me, but I can't talk back, because none of them understand this language. I feel silly a lot, and people treat me like I'm stupid, even the ones who are nice."

"I understand," God replied. "But your job is important. And you're doing it excellently."

"But why can't I talk to them in their languages? I understand all of them. They are so easy to learn."

"It's hard to explain in a way you would understand. But it is important."

"Please try to explain it. Don't talk to me like I'm stupid, too." Rosetta answered. She wondered if she had offended God by being upset, but she showed no sign of having noticed when she spoke to her again.

"You're not stupid, Rosetta, but your job is hard to understand, and, if you understood it, you couldn't do it as well. When it is done, you will understand what it was, and you will be satisfied because you will be part of a great change. And I will welcome you home, and all will be clear to you."

Rosie puzzled over this, opening her eyes as she did so and seeing only a blurred double image of the wood grain and their rivers of life.

"That's stupid," she said. "How can knowing what I'm supposed to do make me not do it as well?" She was nervous God would be offended by her frustration and not want to talk anymore.

"It's that way," said God. "You'll have to trust me."

The girl sighed, feeling her breath and some dust reflect against her head from the floorboard. "If I decide to trust you, will you help me be not so lonely?"

There was a pause. "I can do that. I will send you a friend who will understand you perfectly."

"Who? When can I meet them?"

"You will meet them tomorrow," said God.

"What is his name? What does he look like?"

"You will know him when you see him," said God. "Learn what he teaches you and you will never be lonely again."

"Promise?" Rosetta asked. But God was already gone, and silence was her only answer. Rosetta guessed God didn't like to make promises.

Still, she was excited. Tomorrow she would have a new friend, who would understand her perfectly. She felt bad for a moment, wondering if David would be upset if she had a new friend. But she could see the man sometimes wanted time away from her, and maybe a friend of her own would make the situation easier for him.

David could see Rosie's bare feet on the stairs first as she stepped down them one at a time. Her skinny ankles and then her narrow shins followed with each careful step onto the carpeted stairs. At length, the whole girl was down the stairs and in his living room. With a quiet wave she turned into the kitchen, and a few moments later he heard those cabinets and drawers open which corresponded to the kid getting her own breakfast.

He felt his first sweat of the day. His house was shaded by both the steep relief of the East Hill and the century-old trees that surrounded it, but even so summer heat still radiated from his windows and walls. It would be another smoking-hot day. He didn't remember summers being this hot when he was younger. Maybe it was his age making him sensitive. Maybe it was his pacemaker. Whatever the explanation, the day looked to be oppressive. He hated running the air conditioner all day. It was expensive, and it made a man soft to sit around in air conditioning.

Rosie emerged with her bowl, took her seat, and began to eat. David exchanged smiles with her and reflected while he sipped his coffee from the bench. With the investigation over, he supposed the time for keeping her indoors was past. They would escape the house today. He could take her anywhere. He considered taking her to Taughannock Falls. The great falls were a thing of beauty. But he thought better of it. The walk into the falls would be long and hot, and the views afforded by the trails would show only green leaves. He would save Taughannock Falls for the fall, when it was cooler and when the leaves had changed color. What the girl needed was a place she could blow off steam and play without overheating.

He heard his daughter's voice over the radio for the first time that morning. "Ithaca, Spot," called Faith. She had gotten the nickname "Spot" after dressing as a Dalmatian dog for a firehouse Halloween party as a girl. She had crawled around on her hands and knees and barked so much the name had stuck hard. Twenty-two years later it was still her call sign in the department.

"Spot, Ithaca. Go ahead," the dispatcher answered.

"Found a hydrant leak corner of Plain and Center Streets. Stopped to investigate."

"Roger, Spot. Showing you 10-61."

Rosie perked up at the sound of Faith's voice and exchanged another glance with him. David grinned, both at Rosie and his memories of that street corner. His childhood home had been his mother's shaded and broken-down bungalow on Plain Street. It was two blocks away from Dwight's fire station and the old fire headquarters building. He remembered standing at that corner in winter, shivering while he waited for his school bus, and looking up and envying the grand houses on the east hill while he froze. Through a trick of marriage, he now lived in one of those houses. And he remembered standing on the same corner, cheering as the firetrucks rolled by, hoping he would someday become a firefighter. This, too, had happened. It was a lucky street corner for dreams, he guessed.

Hydrant leaks, however, were becoming common problems. The first problem was the water pipe network of the city was old, one of the oldest in the state. It was overdue for both replacement and upgrade, especially given the task it had of moving ever larger volumes of water up and down the East Hill. But overhauling the system would be a slow and expensive process, involving closing and repaving every street at some point. It could be done with a municipal bond offering and a water tax, but no one in the city council had the stomach to undertake the unpopular task. So the system was getting patched as it broke or as old structures were torn down and replaced.

To make matters worse, the water table under the city had risen as the regional climate had gotten warmer and wetter. As it did so the roadways softened and more and more water pipes were damaged by heavy traffic. To slow the damage, David had sought to get the common council to restrict heavy vehicles in the downtown, and they had agreed to this in part. Heavy vehicles were now restricted to the most improved roads like route 96.

Now the irony was the biggest pipe-busters in the downtown area were the fire trucks themselves, since on all but a few of the streets they were the only heavy vehicles allowed. And all the leaks in the downtown had lowered the water system's pressure to the point where the fire department had trouble getting the necessary pressure to put out fires on the East Hill. He had proposed building a high-volume emergency cistern on the hill to compensate for this lack of pressure. In the event of a fire on the hill, the system could be pressurized from water stored in the cistern which had already been pumped uphill to the tank. That plan was much cheaper than a citywide water system upgrade, but his rich and powerful neighbors had still rejected it. They claimed in more or less coded language that the system would be ugly and they didn't want large water tanks cluttering their rarefied addresses.

All of these factors contributed to an irony. Though they were firefighters, David and Faith lived in one of the houses in Ithaca in which it would be most difficult to fight a fire. They lived on the slope of East Hill at the longest distance from a fire hydrant of any house on their street. It could be worse, though. Their house could be subdivided and full of college students smoking cigarettes, doing pot, and burning up TV dinners in their ovens. If only because of their jobs, he and his daughter were both careful with fire.

He should stop caring about the city's infrastructure, he supposed. No one

173

had listened to him about it much when he was fire chief, and they wouldn't start now.

Faith's voice came back on the radio, returning him to the present. "Ithaca, Spot."

"Spot, Ithaca. Go ahead."

"10-8. Not a hydrant leak at all. Someone had opened the hydrant. Though all the kids on the street were playing in the water, none of the adults had *any* idea who had opened it. I closed it back up and told the kids to go to Buttermilk Falls if they needed to cool off. If anyone else finds a hydrant open today, tell the kids Buttermilk Falls is free during the summer and the route 68 bus will take them there."

"Roger, Spot, will pass that on. The weather report is calling for another hot one today. Showing you 10-8."

David nodded at his daughter's handling of the issue. She was good at dealing with the public. It was Connie's influence. And not only had she handled the public, she had given him an idea for what to do with Rosie on what promised to be one of the hottest days of the year.

"Feel like going for a swim?" he asked the girl. She gave a helpless shrug. He supposed she hadn't understood the question. But he hadn't met a kid yet who didn't like to play in the water, so he was sure once she'd arrived at Buttermilk Falls, kid instincts would take over no matter what language she spoke or didn't. She needed a bathing suit, but the Salvation Army store was on the way to the Falls, and he was sure they could find something there.

"There will be lots of other kids there. Maybe you'll make some friends."

Rosie's eyes brightened at the word 'friend.' At least she understood that much. David stood with his empty coffee cup and headed to the kitchen.

Rosie stood and marveled at the Buttermilk Falls. Not only did she feel pretty in the purple and red bathing suit David had found for her, but God's work was evident in the falls themselves. Layer upon layer of stone God had spread upon one another like a cake emerged from the ground. A thin but wide trickle of water ran over the whole steep face of the outcropping, foamed and created a wall of whispering silver water which gathered in an emerald green pool at the bottom. Into and out of the pool danced children her age and younger, splashing, screaming and playing. The infinite majesty and variety of God's art was on glorious display. It was a paradise. She wished Nanny Wasilatu was with her to see it. The more children she had around her, the happier her nanny had become.

She glanced at David. Her foster father had spread out a blanket on the ground and had pulled both a book and a bottle of sunscreen from the bag he had brought from their truck. He wore no bathing suit and was unaffected by the obvious allure of the place. When at last he took a seat on the ground and opened the book, it was clear he was not going to join her in the water. She wondered why not.

He noticed her looking at him. "It's okay, honey. Go on and enjoy the water. I'll be here if you need me. Do whatever the lifeguard tells you do to," David said, pointing to a strong young man perched on a tall chair. Whenever the man blew a whistle, all the kids stopped what they were doing. That could be a fun game, too. She wondered what poses she'd have to freeze in when the whistle blew. She went down to the water's edge.

She was a few steps into the water, appreciating its welcoming coolness, when a green felt ball splashed down in front of her, showering her with water.

She picked it up and searched for who had thrown it to throw it back, but the whole of her vision was soon taken up by a large brown dog. The dog bounded into the water after the ball and then pranced from left to right, trying to snatch it from her grip, water sluicing from his glossy brown hair. She giggled, and then spluttered as the dog shook itself, splattering water into her face and eyes.

"Throw it! Throw it for him!" shouted other children. It sounded less like encouragement and more like an order, and she felt afraid for a moment. She threw the ball out over the water, and the dog dashed after it, even to the point of having to swim to take it in his mouth. While the dog did so, Rosie retreated to the beach, uncertain of how she felt about the other children shouting at her.

She turned to face the falls again, heart pounding. The jumble of voices came at her. She could make out English in all accents, some Spanish, and even one voice in Tagalog. All of them spoke about non-threatening things like games, friends, ice cream, and how to hold one's breath underwater. She relaxed again.

The dog walked up to her out of the water. Out of the whole crowd of children, he picked her out. From this she knew he liked her even if she couldn't talk. He walked up to her, dropped the ball at her feet, and shook, giving her another shower of water.

"*Good day, pleased to meet you!*" she said. The dog's tail wagged faster in anticipation, and she reached to pick up the ball.

David looked up from time to time, and saw Rosie at uninhibited play, dancing with other children, paddling in the water, and tossing a tennis ball with someone's unleashed brown Labrador. The open back and narrow cut of her swimsuit showed the pink burn scars on her skin, but because of their positioning, he had been loathe to be seen putting suntan lotion on some of them and had done a rush job of it. He hoped the scars wouldn't burn again. He spent a long time watching the girl to be sure she was getting along with the other children. She was fearful of them at first and limited in the interactions she could have because they couldn't understand her speech. But after a while she fell in with a crowd of like-aged children led by a teenager to play "Marco Polo."

He went back to the book. It was one Hildegard had recommended to him, a fiction story about the Second World War called "The Tin Drum." He enjoyed it, trying to envision the professor in the scenes and cities it described. He gave it his best effort, but reading at length gave him a headache, so he switched between reading, people watching, and checking on Rosie.

Soon it was noontime, and many of the young mothers, some of them tanned and easy on the eyes, called their children back to have lunch. He supposed it would be a good time to do the same, and when he next caught her eye, he waved her over. Through their ongoing practice of communicating with signs the girl recognized the gesture. She gave the Labrador one last toss of the tennis ball which sent the animal splashing out into the water.

He took out the sandwiches he had prepared, and then showed his foster daughter how to apply hand sanitizer before handling her sandwich. She did so, and began to eat standing up. David began to eat his lunch, but stopped in dismay when the Labrador bounded back up with the ball and dropped it for another toss. She put one hand on the spittle-coated ball, threw it, and put the hand back on her sandwich.

"No, come on, you just cleaned your hands. Here," he said, offering her the hand sanitizer bottle. "Now don't touch the ball again until you're done eating. You'll get dog germs on your sandwich. It's not good for you." Satisfied he had made his point, David went back to eating and looking around.

A moment later he turned to find Rosie with one hand on the tennis ball again. She threw it hard, the dog tore after it, and before he could stop her, she had put the hand back on her sandwich.

"Now what did I tell you?" he reproached her before he caught ahold of his frustration. He shouldn't shout. There was no telling how much of his English she understood, or even if she understood what a "germ" was. But it was too late. Her eyes widened at his tone, and she began to look tearful.

"Oh, never mind," he reassured her. "I'm trying to keep you from getting sick, that's all. You should only eat with clean hands." She went from looking tearful back to upset, but sat down to eat her sandwich.

They shared lunch in careful silence. The dog did not return, and after a few minutes David felt the girl had relaxed again. He took a few moments to spread a fresh layer of sunscreen on her shoulders and nose like other parents were doing, and then sent her off to play. After a few casual looks at some young mothers or nannies, he went back to reading.

One of his intermittent checks showed him Rosie's knee had blood on it. He summoned her again, and found she had scuffed a knee and had a cut on her shin. He applied the hand sanitizer to these scratches and she hissed and complained about it. As he did so, he found her shoulders and cheeks were taking on a pinkish tinge. He guessed the sunscreen was not as waterproof as advertised.

"Hey, honey, you're starting to sunburn. I think it's time to go home," he said. "You've had a good long day of it. When your skin is rested, we can come back later in the week."

David braced for her to resist, but instead she started putting things back in the basket and taking their trash to the trash can. He felt relief at this. He remembered a much younger Faith making a real fuss when he or Constance had told her it was time to leave Buttermilk Falls. He watched Rosie as she stood on a drinking fountain made of blocks of stone cut from the layers of the falls themselves. As she stepped down, the Labrador returned with the ball and dropped it by the fountain. The dog then followed her back to him. When he rolled up the blanket they had been sitting on and hoisted the bag, the girl followed him, and the dog began to follow her in turn.

He stopped, hoping the dog's owner would appear and intervene. But no one came forward to claim it. It wore no collar or tags, but judging from its behavior, it was a pet dog, and it looked mature. Mr. Haversham questioned the lifeguard.

"Do you know whose dog this is?"

"No idea, man," said the boy. "Wait, I think it belongs to a Latina girl in a red and purple bathing suit."

David glanced at Rosie. From behind his shades, and without looking back, the lifeguard had described his foster daughter reasonably well.

"That's my kid. And the dog isn't hers."

"Then I couldn't tell you, man. He's been here all morning. Must belong to somebody."

David gave up his interrogation and faced Rosie. He guessed the dog would find its owner or own way home. Or maybe it was stray and lived in the park, playing with kids and scavenging dropped food all summer.

"Okay, honey, say goodbye to the dog."

His foster daughter pursed her lips and put her hand on her hips. He saw in this gesture storm clouds similar to the dark gray anvilhead clouds which had appeared over the west edge of the lake to deliver the daily afternoon thunderstorm.

"*Neh,*" she said with emphasis, and then broke out into a string of her spoken language. He didn't understand the words, but her tone and posture was negative enough.

"Honey, he's not our dog. He has to stay here so he can go home with whoever brought him here. Maybe he'll be here when you come back."

Rosie shook her head and stamped her foot. The gesture brought Mr. Haversham to the end of his patience.

"Okay, come on," he snapped, taking her hand. "The dog's not yours. You can't take him. He belongs to someone else who will miss him if he comes with us."

She sagged and clawed the hand he had clamped around her wrist. Then she sat down on the ground and wailed. He stopped. He didn't want to drag her. Already the spectacle of her resistance was drawing stares from the rest of the assembled families. Her behavior was out of step with her apparent age.

"Listen, you need to chin up. You're acting like a baby."

The child cried and clung to the dog with her free arm.

If the girl wouldn't leave the dog, he might get the dog to leave the girl. He rounded on the dog. "Go on!" he shouted. "Go!" He pushed the dog away and waved his free arm at it.

The dog's only reaction to his shouts was to wag his tail more slowly. David's memory of other encounters with this breed told him Labradors were so friendly that, short of getting a kick, they didn't understand when someone else being *unfriendly*. But Rosie wailed at his actions, and he felt his ears go red.

His frustration then got the better of him. Without thinking, he reached down and hoisted his wriggling and kicking charge onto his shoulder like he had used to carry panicky children from burning buildings during his prime. A moment later, he wobbled, lightheaded, as his pacemaker and heart struggled to keep up with the demand. Fueled by his frustration, he walked across the parking lot, pulled open the passenger door of the truck, and tossed the howling child in. The truck bounced on its suspension as the child landed on the seat, and he passed her the beach bag. She continued to scream as if he was torturing her. Closing the door provided him with a welcome moment of silence, and he slumped against the truck to rest. When his heartbeat had slowed back down, he scanned the lawn before the falls to be sure he had left nothing behind. The dog caught up to him there, still wagging his tail.

"Sorry fella," David said to him as he opened the driver's door. The interior of the truck cab concentrated Rosie's sobs into his ears. He ignored them and kept talking to the dog. Why was he talking to a dog? He supposed it made as much sense as talking to this girl who barely understood him. "I've got to take this bundle of joy home now. You should head home, too."

Faith stood up out of her Toyota and walked around to the front of the house. The wind rattled the summer leaves overhead, and the faint shushing sound of water in the gorge complimented the calls of birds. All her life she had heard these sounds yet somehow, after a day's work filled with squawking radios, roaring diesel engines, and many types of alarms, the whispers of the gorge never failed to enchant again with their calmness.

She leaned on the post of the wraparound porch and listened, soaking the sound in, until some music started blaring from the window of the next house downhill. She savored the stillness of the moment as it fled from the harsh music. Beauty and stillness, and the lack of appreciation college students had for them, were part of life on Ithaca's East Hill. She'd had her moment of peace, in any case. She considered coming back out with a cup of tea or coffee to appreciate the summer day again once she'd been in to say her hellos to Rosie and David.

She turned to go indoors. She stopped in front of the door, her eyes drawn down and to the left by a thumping on the porch deck.

She stepped back when she saw the dog. It was a brown Labrador retriever. It lay flat on the porch, with even its head pressed to the ground. It did not move, but its tail beat a rhythm on the porch floor in friendly enthusiasm.

"Oh, hello, you," she said. She often encountered dogs in her work while doing alarm calls and inspecting fire escapes and extinguishers in the apartment houses and subdivided Victorian homes throughout Ithaca. She took a knee to the dog's level and, keeping her hand in the dog's view, reached out to pet it.

The dog stood, shook itself amiably, sniffed her hand, and then waited by the door to be let in. She noted the dog had no collar, but it didn't act or look like a stray. Maybe it had been tied up at one of the nearby college houses and slipped its collar, then come to their porch for shade. She'd ask her father if he knew anything.

She stood again, cracked open the door, and slid into it so as to block the dog. The dog seemed put out at this, but its tail still wagged. She closed the door behind her and made for the dining area to drop her radio into its charger by the breakfast table. She could already smell supper cooking, and heard a pot clatter in the kitchen. She poked her head into the kitchen.

"Hey, Pop." Faith said. "What's for supper?"

"Lamb, potatoes, and fried tomatoes. I got the tomatoes at farmers' market today."

She sniffed the air. "Smells good! Thanks, Dad." She saw Rosie's kitchen stool was empty, and she hadn't seen the girl in the living room on the way through it.

"Where's our dumpling?"

"Upstairs. Sulking," David reported as he cooked.

She blinked. In the weeks Rosetta had been with them, she had shown cheer, good manners, sensitivity, confusion, and sometimes even frustration, but not sulking or anger. This was a new one. She guessed the honeymoon phase of foster parenting was now over. "What happened?" Faith wondered aloud.

The old man shrugged. "We went to Buttermilk Falls. She went swimming and had a good time, but she got attached to a dog running around loose there. She didn't want to leave the dog when it was time to go. Acted like quite the harpy, stomping her foot and screaming. Finally I had enough and had to carry her back to my truck. As soon as we got back, she ran upstairs to be angry at me."

Her father's tone struck her as familiar. It was the tone he had used to describe his decisions to others when her mother had been angry at him, or to explain things to her mother when Faith had been angry. It smacked of both firmness and resignation. It was his "I made a good decision for good reasons and I'm not going to budge" voice. She also wondered how his heart had taken carrying the girl, but she thought better of asking the question.

She recalled the strange dog on the porch as she pinched a slice of tomato from the bowl before frying nullified its farmers'-market goodness. "This dog...it wasn't by any chance a brown Labrador, was it?"

David stopped and stared at her. "Yes. Why? Did you get a call on it? Did it bite someone?" His voice grew testy, and she could hear him ranting as he had done when he was fire chief and city hall had called to ask for a firefighter for a not-firefighting-related call. *"What job are will they dump on the fire department next? Snot wiping in the nursery? Mopping the floors at the courthouse?"* she

178

could hear him thinking.

Faith laughed. "No, Dad, they haven't dumped the dog catcher duties on me...yet. I'm asking because there's a chocolate lab with no collar on our porch."

"What?" Her father frowned. He put down his spatula, marched out to the living room bay window that overlooked the porch, and peered out. She followed behind him and hung up her coat by the door.

"Looks like him," he confirmed.

"You didn't bring him here?" She raised an eyebrow.

"Nope. Left him in the park."

"So he covered the four miles or so between here and there quickly. And he knew the house to come to," she said. "One of you must smell strong for him to follow you all that way. Maybe one of you needs to shower more often."

He marveled out the window. "Never put anything past a dog's sense of smell. They can smell things you can't imagine." David retreated to the kitchen, a thoughtful look on his face. She watched him go, then decided to go upstairs and check on the girl.

Sure enough, Rosie was on her bed, face on her pillow, and shoes still on her feet. Red eyes betrayed that she'd been crying, but she wasn't crying now. Faith sat at the foot of the bed.

"Hey, honey, I'm home."

The girl said nothing, and didn't even look at her, but sat up and rubbed her eyes. After a few moments, she slid down the bed to a companionable distance, still saying nothing, but warming to Faith's presence.

"My dad can be a real pisser, huh?" she volunteered. Rosie nodded agreement.

"It's not you," she sighed. "I wanted a dog all the time when I was a kid, and we never had one then, either. He always said we couldn't have a dog because we didn't have the time to treat one right. I was at school, and both of them were at work all day, and the dog would be lonesome, he said."

Rosie was unimpressed by this story of the elder Haversham's life of consistency. Faith reflected before offering more words of comfort.

Her father's excuse no longer held any water, she concluded. He was home all day most of the time He could have a dog and it would get plenty of companionship and maybe be a friend to Rosie. So why not have a dog?

Then she remembered something her mother had mentioned once. But now was not the time to bring it up. She would wait until the man was relaxed. In the meantime, she would be careful not to undermine her father.

"Sweetie, I'm sorry you're upset. But when you're ready to come down, we'll both be downstairs. Dinner will be ready soon." She gave Rosie a squeeze and got up. The girl gave a wan acknowledgment as she left.

Faith went to her bedroom, changed out of her uniform into some shorts and a t-shirt, opened her bedroom window to start letting in the cooler evening air, and then went back downstairs. She helped her father set the table, told stories about her day at work, and was as cheerful as she could be. Sometimes you had to paint a smile on a day which didn't rate it. This was one of those days.

Rosie sat alone in her room on the edge of her bed, resenting God. The room was stifling with the heat the day had brought to the upstairs of the old house, and the air-conditioning reached her room last in its long journey up the many stairs. The sunburn on her shoulders made her feel even hotter and more sullen. God sucked, she concluded. She'd heard other kids use the word today to describe things which displeased or disappointed them, so now she would use it (if only in her own mind because it was an English word) with abandon. God *sucked* today.

She couldn't speak any regular-person language because God had told her not to. Then, when she had asked for a friend because she was lonesome, God had promised her a friend who would understand her perfectly. She had even met the friend, played ball with her friend, and then God had let David carry her away and leave the friend behind. She had half a mind to start praying so she could maybe talk to God and tell him he sucked. It would feel good.

At first, she had been angry with her foster father, not God. But she had to let go of this anger. The man had feared for good reason someone else might miss the dog, and she hadn't been able to explain to him the dog was supposed to come home with him because of the stupid rule God made up about her not being able to speak English. So it wasn't her foster father's fault, it was God's fault. After all, if he had wanted to stop the man he could have. God could have made him love the dog as she did, or made the dog look special, or even put a collar around the dog's neck with a tag which read "Dear David, this dog is for Rosie. Sincerely, God." But no, God had done nothing.

She considered the meaning of this. Maybe God had only meant for her to play with the dog for one day. Maybe that was all he had intended. But she remembered him saying she wouldn't be lonely again. Well, she was lonely now.

She sulked. She could feel God in the room, but she ignored him. She wasn't in the mood for him, and she stared at shoes, the pattern of the tin ceiling, and even her hands in a bid to focus him out. But eventually a voice came to her, unbidden.

"Whose fault is it that you're sitting in a room all alone?"

Rosie reflected on this. David hadn't *told* her to go to her room; she had fled here in anger when they'd gotten back from the trip to Buttermilk Falls and the farmer's market. Likewise, Faith hadn't told her she had to stay in the room. And if God had told her to go to her room, she was angry enough to ignore him anyway. The truth of it was she was sitting in this room, feeling lonesome, because she was choosing to sit there. It didn't make sense. She didn't want to be lonely, so she should go downstairs. If God wouldn't help her not be lonely, she would do the best she could.

"I want my tongue back. Give me my tongue, stupid old God," she lamented.

She breathed in deeply through her nose and out through her mouth, as Nanny Wasilatu had taught her to do to let go of anger. After her third breath, it was already helping, but she gave the process a few minutes. When it was done, and she was sure she wouldn't be pushing on anyone else the resentment she felt toward God, she went downstairs.

Rosie came down before she was called for supper. The girl hung around the dinner table, sometimes sitting, sometimes standing, but not reaching for her drawing pens and paper as she usually did when idle. Faith talked with her father about her workday and about the travails of the investigation, and he related to her something of the C-SPAN he had watched in the afternoon. Faith tuned out at this part. Politics bored her, and the endless recriminations which flew between both the American parties made her disgusted with the senseless and gridlocked system.

When supper was over, Faith searched for a way into the conversation she wanted to have with her father. She was anxious, she found, which was silly for the most part. But David had always been mum about his past, in particular the war in Vietnam. She had learned from her mother's example not to pry, and on the rare occasions he mentioned the war, to listen with supporting interest.

When the dishes were off the table and her father was sitting down to coffee, she felt ready to ask the question.

"Dad, tell me about Smoke."

He grimaced into his coffee as if it had gone sour. "Who told you about Smoke?" He put down the cup and looked at her. "Your mother?"

Faith explained. "When she was in the hospital, near the end, I mentioned it might be a good idea to get a dog, you know, to keep you company." Remembering her mother in the hospital bed, and how she was always composed and calm even as her condition worsened, her eyes began to water. "She told me not to be in a rush, and before I did it, to ask you about Smoke."

David sighed. "You can ask me if we can have a dog. I'll answer no."

She felt irritated by the man's attempt to shut down a conversation she'd had to work so hard to begin. Rosie's face betrayed no feelings, but she was listening, so she wanted to hear the story, too.

Faith decided not to be deterred. "Whether or not we get a dog, I want to know about Smoke."

Her father massaged his forehead with his fingers. "It isn't a thing I'm proud of. It isn't a time I'm proud of. If it's your curiosity at work, let's watch some Discovery channel instead."

She raised an eyebrow. "How about you share your wisdom with the younger generations, your wisdom that says we can't have a dog like any normal family. Maybe then you won't sound like a crazy old man."

David's face was sullen. He took a drink of his coffee. "If you insist."

"Mom wanted me to know," she shrugged, giving her father the option of second guessing her mother. She felt a vague twinge of shame at playing the "mom card," but it worked, as his resigned expression told her.

"Suit yourself," he said. "You want the short version or the long version?"

"Whichever version you want to tell," she said. "I'll ask questions if I'm not satisfied."

Her old man grinned at her. "Oh, I know you will." Then he sat back, and let his eyes settle on something behind her. Following his gaze over her shoulder to the mantelpiece, she decided he was looking at the bronze framed honorable discharge there. It had been there ever since she could remember, but despite its prominent place in the house, it had never been discussed.

David stood up and crossed the room to the mantle and took down the frame. He brought it back to the dinner table, pushed aside the thumb levers, which were stiff with disuse, and lifted off the black cardboard backing. There, from the space between the Army discharge in the frame and the cardboard back, he removed a picture, handling it by the edges. He offered it to Faith.

She wiped her hands on her napkin and reached for it. It was a black and white picture, old but still glossy from the care with which it had been handled. It was a picture of her father, in a drab Army uniform and canvas boots, standing at attention beside a shepherd dog. It looked like a German shepherd but with lighter colors and shorter snout and ears. It sat to her father's left, ears raised in a dog's version of the position of attention.

To the front and right of her father in the picture there was a black felt placard with white letters on it. "SSgt Haversham and Smoke. Mine/Tunnel Scout Dog Training Class 68-02. 10 December 1968. 60th Infantry Platoon / Mine Tunnel Scout Dog Detachment."

181

"Oh, wow, Dad." Faith stared at the picture. "You sure were a hottie."

"There were many soldiers, many better than I was," David said. "But there were few soldiers better than Smoke."

"He looks impressive. Like he was born for the Army."

Her father picked up his coffee, his expression an unreadable mix. "No, he wasn't. He was born to have friends, to have pups, to do good work, to grow old and die with family, with me and your mother if he'd made it the whole war and the Army had let me bring him home. But he didn't. One day I asked him to do something he wasn't trained for, he made a mistake, and he didn't make it."

She reflected on the picture. "I'm sorry."

"It's all water under the bridge. I gave up my tears years ago for Smoke. I have to live with my choices. It's no one else's job."

She studied her father's detached look. The corners of his eyes betrayed that not all his tears were, in fact, already shed. "What did he do? Did he track Viet Cong?" she asked. She was beginning to regret now that all she'd seen about Viet Nam had been war movies when she was a teenager.

David shook his head. "He was an explosives detection dog. They use them in the Middle East now, too. He would detect explosives and even trip wires. He did a damn good job. He never missed a trap, he even found pungi stakes and other non-explosive traps he wasn't trained to find. He never ran when the shooting started like some others. He'd bark his head off and hold his ground. He found over thirty-five hazards of different kinds. There's no telling how many lives he saved." He drained his cup, put it down, and stared out the window. "Too bad for him I couldn't save his."

"What happened?" Faith asked.

"He was an explosives dog, not a tunnel dog. I let a platoon leader I was attached to talk me into checking a tunnel with him. Some dogs had been able to do both jobs. As it turned out, the tunnel *was* booby-trapped. I guess Smoke was confused enough by all the smells of the hole that he didn't detect the trap.

"We ripped open the tunnel with shovels and rushed him out, which was damn stupid because there might have been a second trap, but no one cared. Another wounded soldier even gave up his stretcher and walked to the LZ so we could carry Smoke to the medevac. The doc did everything he could. He had all the medicine he needed, all the supplies, the Army hadn't skimped. But Smoke had lost too much blood. You can't use human blood. They sent for another dog from the next brigade area for a transfusion. It didn't arrive in time. Smoke died."

David said nothing further. Rosetta got up and walked around the table corner to give him a hug, leaning over his knees to wrap her arms around him. The man gave no indication of having noticed, at first, but a moment later Faith could see he was crying and tousling Rosetta's hair.

She didn't know what to do. Her father so rarely cried. "Dad, talk to me. Share what you're feeling. Mom wanted you to talk to me."

David's voice was more like a sob. "We made our choices. We all made our choices to volunteer, to answer the draft, to flee to Canada or go to jail. We knew the risks. We could tell our leaders when a plan was stupid or fucked up and if they made us do it they should watch their backs. But Smoke didn't know the risks. To him it was a game all his friends were playing, and he played it as best he could, too. In the end, we let him down. I let him down. I lost the game, and he died for it. He couldn't look at me and say 'this is dumb, Sarge.'

"I've never been able to look a dog in the face since. Not a search and rescue dog, not a Dalmatian, not even your aunt Chastity's nasty little *shit*...Shit dog." He waved his hand dismissively.

"*Shitzu*," she reminded. "Chloe is a *shitzu*."

182

"Whatever," David snapped. "Anyway, there's my story. Like every other old man, I've got more than my share. Why your mother felt you needed to know that one, I wonder?" His face pinched with bitterness.

Her father's story made sense to Faith, however, as her mother's insistence that she ask before bringing home a dog now did. It explained his refusal to have a dog during her childhood unless the home conditions for a dog would be perfect, and no matter how many conditions changed or what she had promised to do for the dog, the conditions were never perfect enough. It explained his refusal to dog-sit for the neighbors, but the way he had become unhinged as a fireman when he learned about abuse of dogs. It even explained why while he was fire chief the department mascots had been cats, *Soot, Ash,* and *Galoshes,* rather than the traditional Dalmatian dog.

At this point even Rosetta was crying, a pathetic sob which touched her heartstrings. She wondered what to say to the girl, and how the child was able to understand her father's feelings. She was envious of how transparent emotions were to Rosetta.

She shook her head to clear out the jealousy. Since she was the only one at the table not in tears, she would have to be the grown up. She let her father and Rosetta cry themselves quiet while she pondered different choices.

When her father had recovered enough to pick up his coffee mug and look displeased it was empty, she proposed her compromise.

"Did you take good care of Smoke, Dad?"

"The best I could," David answered with confidence. "Until I fucked it up."

"The dog on the porch didn't come here for you. He came here for Rosie. So if you know how to take care of dogs, why don't you show her how to take care of *her* dog? Or even show me, for that matter. Maybe then she'll get it right, if it's even possible to do it better than you."

He said nothing in response at first, except to pat the girl's back and cast a glance at the picture Faith had left lying face up in the table in front of her.

"You always know how to split a difference. You got it from your mother."

"I'm not splitting anything. It's not your dog, Dad, it didn't come here for your sunny personality," she sighed. "And besides, we may not be Rosie's foster parents forever. If she has to go, maybe the dog could go with her."

"That's unlikely, a family willing to take a foster dog and a foster child," David rejected this.

"There's a better chance of them taking a happy kid who's good with pets. She needs to socialize, some kids start with animals."

Her father rolled his eyes. "You win, we'll take in the dog. But before we make it too permanent, we should put up posters in case his owners are looking for him, and take him to a vet to see if they can find a microchip or whatever."

"Makes sense to me," she said. She turned to the girl. "Does it make sense to you? Will you take care of that dog if he's lost his home? You know what that's like, right?"

Rosie nodded, wiping her eyes and clinging to the David's arm with one hand.

"Sounds like a deal, then," said Faith. She picked up the picture to lay it face down back in the brass discharge frame when she saw the writing on the back in faded felt-tip pen.

"SSgt. Haversham,

Thanks for two good tours and for your help during our evaluation phase in-country. Found this when we were cleaning out the files for the platoon. You know he'll be waiting for you in heaven, standing tall, with Moran and the

183

others.

Consider this a toast. Raise a beer at your end to absent friends, and fallen comrades. I'll do the same at the O-club tonight.

Capt. Sypniewska."

Faith wondered at the rest of the untold stories her father had as she replaced the backing and closed the frame again, and how she could ask him for them without causing him pain. She wanted to know. She knew everything about his career as a firefighter. Between everything he had told her, everything she had overheard in their home, and stories told her by other old salts at Ithaca Fire Department about the virtues and vices of "3rd Degree" David Haversham, she was the expert on her father's life. But his military service was an empty space in this life story. She wanted to know more.

She stood up. "Let's let in our stranger, if he's still there after listening to this crazy family." She went to the front door, and the man and the girl filed after her. She pulled open the door. The summer sun was getting low and working on sunset. On the porch, in the ruddy light, the brown Labrador stood up, shook himself as he had before, and wagged his tail.

"Come in!" She motioned into the house with her free arm.

The Labrador walked through the door, unhurried, but paused to look up at David. Her father said nothing. The dog's tail-wagging increased in speed and emphasis when, with a squeal of joy, Rosie fell on her knees and gave the dog a double armed hug. She paused in her delight only to splutter at the face-licking she received in response. In a moment, she pulled off one of her shoes and threw it into living room. The dog retrieved it for her. The girl clapped her hands in delight and threw her shoe again.

Instead of running after it, the dog simply watched it fly, as if to say "but I already got that for you!" As an alternative to retrieving the shoe, he licked her, and the squealing and spluttering began again.

Faith looked down at the two. She was grateful again for both her father's public service and his willingness to change, because the girl and the dog matched, somehow, like they clicked. She wondered if the dog was housebroken. She guessed they'd find out.

She stuck her hands in her pockets. "Any more walk-ins, Dad, and I will put a 'homeless shelter' sign on the door."

David threw an arm over her shoulder. "I think 'loony bin' is more accurate," he grumbled.

Chapter 14

Best Judgment of Experts

Faith was puzzling over the transcript of Rosie's exchanges with the Esperanto translator when Cassius entered her office. They had planned to meet, but he was close to an hour early, she noted.

"Hard at work I see," he said.

"You have no idea," she answered. She was getting sick of the carriage house fire and its aftermath. She needed a break and the transcript was not helping.

"Is it the transcript you mentioned?" The detective asked, looking around before pulling out Karl's chair.

"Yeah. It's clear as mud, too. This girl is straightforward and easygoing at home. I guess my Dad and I are lucky we can't talk to her, though, because this transcript is like gibberish and make-believe."

"Maybe it's the translation."

"Maybe. But I doubt it. They found someone who speaks her language, so this should be as clear as it can get. But it doesn't tell me much."

"Summarize for me."

She shook her head. "I can't summarize this." She passed him the transcript. "Read. I've already been through it a couple of times."

Detective McCrae took the printout and began to read. At times he frowned, and at times he chuckled. Midway through it his expression became grave.

"She names them. William, Randy, Mary Joe," he said. "I guess this clears up what was going on at the carriage house. They were going to kill her. Her story puts them on the scene, explains what they were doing, and even confirms your theory they were burned up in the fire event. It even gives us another lead. We should be looking for a late middle aged african woman who died by gunshot somewhere not too far from Syracuse airport and another male suspect named Gabriel. I'm finding plenty of good stuff here. Why don't you like it?'

"But why? Why do they want to kill her?"

"She says they called her an abomination."

Faith saw Cassius was missing the point. "But *why* do they consider her an abomination?"

The man shrugged. "Maybe it's because of her...you know, special needs. Or maybe because she speaks Esperanto. Or maybe because she dresses funny. You don't understand. This guy Kopp and his friends can justify killing anyone using Revelations or the Old Testament. Anyone who's not a white, straight, churchgoing evangelical who has never taken a government dollar in his life is an 'abomination.' There might be no good reason we'd ever understand. I suppose we should be thankful this fellow Gabriel put an end to it."

"Yeah, and who is this Gabriel? And how the hell did he turn fifty square feet of concrete to glass yet not harm Rosie?"

Cassius shook his head. "One step at a time. That's how investigations go. We didn't get all the answers, but we got some. Any chance you could set us up an appointment with this translator?"

Faith shook her head. "I guess the translator guy was passing through. A visiting scholar or something. The professor said she'd try and find someone else, but for the moment, this is the best we've got."

"We can't use this transcript as evidence, because the girl wasn't sworn and wasn't informed of her rights and there's no information here about the translator. Plus there's got to be extra procedural steps because of her disability and her foreign language before any DA would try to use it as evidence. But we can still use it for clues in our investigation. And I'd say it answers a lot of questions."

All she saw were the gaps in the information. "So now we need to know why they wanted to kill her, and how to find this Gabriel."

"Yeah. She didn't give us a lot to go on. I'd love to ask her more questions about this guy."

"I'll tell the professor to try and find another translator, then. But maybe she made him up. Maybe she actually means the Archangel Gabriel."

"Even normal kids will believe a lot of funny stuff. That doesn't make it true. Gabriel is probably another religious nutjob."

"Maybe he doesn't exist at all."

Detective McCrae stared at her. "And then what? If he doesn't exist, how did our three would-be murderers go up in smoke?"

"Maybe she did it. She said she didn't mean to hurt them."

"Kids blame themselves for all kinds of things which happen around them. And if she made Gabriel up, do you have an explanation for how this kid vitrified fifty square feet of concrete...and walked away?"

Faith shook her head.

Cassius continued. "So I think it's more likely this was an accident of some kind. Or maybe there was some fourth guy named Gabriel, possibly a leader in this cult, who decided to cover his tracks by using a device to burn up the girl and his co-conspirators. When she survived she interpreted Gabriel's actions as intended to save her. It would also explain the lack of any sign that Kopp was using high technology as well as the girl's survival. How's that for a scenario?"

She chewed her lower lip in concentration. "It fits the facts okay, I guess. As well as anything. I could go with it. As a working theory."

"It's all working theories until the jailor throws away the key. And even now, with DNA evidence, sometimes it doesn't stop there."

Faith drew in a big breath. "I'm glad you're here with the perspective. I'm up to my neck in this stuff and I feel like I'm flailing."

"You're doing great. Don't get down on yourself," Cassius said. "If you weren't nailed down here, I'd take you back to Syracuse and get my boss to pin a badge on you."

"For real?" she boggled.

"Sure thing," said the detective. "Let me know if you want an endorsement for the police academy."

She studied the man's face. There was not a hint that he was exaggerating.

"Some days I feel trapped in my father's footsteps. A change of job, a change of venue, it might be what I need," Faith pondered aloud.

"Let me know," said Cassius. "But let's get back to the concrete-turned-glass. Ready to visit our local feds?"

"Sure. We're on in fifty minutes, and I've got my briefing on this USB," she said, waggling the thumb drive on her keychain. "If we hurry we can grab some chow on the way."

"You're reading my mind. Burger King?" he suggested.

"Burger King," she snorted. "Please, this is *Ithaca*. We have both a food science school and hotel school at Cornell and half the graduates hang around.

186

You can get take-out anything. Take-out Indian, take-out Argentinian, take out ancient Roman and Sumerian. Heck, there's even take-out French if you're feeling fancy. How do you feel about Thai food? There's a nice place off Route 19, I can phone it in and we can eat as soon as we arrive."

"Mm. Thai. I could go for some pad thai. It's been a while."

"You'll love this place. Their chili peanut sauce is to die for. I'll call ahead," she said, reaching for the phone.

Cassius went back to reading the briefing while she dialed. His intense expression made her feel lazy watching him. *"Man, any day I feel like I work too hard, I need to hang around this guy,"* she thought.

Faith put down the wireless gyroscopic mouse the FBI used to control their briefing projector. She had presented her revised fifty-two slide briefing in twenty minutes. The FBI agents had showed no sign of impatience, however, and showed no relief that it was over. They glanced at each other before turning back to her.

Agent Ingle was fair haired, graying, and in charge. Agent Foxworth had dark curly hair and was more animated. Contrary to Faith's expectations, they did not wear black suits. Ingle wore faded brown with a blue shirt, and Foxworth had a gray pinstripe with a vest. Both of them sported expressions of earnest concern at her briefing. They both sat up straight in overstuffed leather executive chairs. Cassius was leaning back in his, and looking like he was enjoying it. She wished she could have an overstuffed chair. But she had been trained to brief while standing up.

"Alarming, Inspector," said Foxworth. "Thanks for bringing this case to our attention. You said you'd already had a search done in our database to see if the girl matched any known kidnapping victims?"

"Yes, it came back with no hits."

Foxworth seemed unconcerned. "It's not uncommon. I hate to say it, but there are many more kidnappings and instances of human trafficking than we're aware of. In fact, there's a human trafficking network which passes through Ithaca bringing slave labor to the socialist governments of Canada. We're doing our best to crack down on it. Free Americans should never be condemned to socialism."

Agent Ingle joined in. "I'd like to point out that as a matter of procedure, having the victim and sole witness live in your home will give the defense attorney a field day. If you ever catch this Gabriel and the survivor's testimony is used against him, the defense will be able to argue you influenced her testimony while she was living in your home."

Faith bristled. "What was the alternative? Turn her over to an institution and try to get the facts from her while she was living on the other side of the state with no translator?"

Ingle raised his hands soothingly. "The child's welfare and accessibility for your investigation are both important. With so many people dead and the girl without a family, in the grand scheme of things you may have done the greatest good which could have been done. I'm pointing out that, from a legal and procedural point of view, the caretaking arrangement is...irregular and may complicate prosecution if there is anyone left alive to prosecute. But I'm not New York State bar certified."

Foxworth elaborated on Ingle's approach. "We're not criticizing you. We're trying to help you anticipate a problem. So let's refocus. What you need from us is some expertise on...bombs and incendiaries, rather than prosecution?"

"Yes. Officer McCrae and I feel the physical evidence at the scene suggests a weapon of mass destruction or something which could be used that way. We're wondering if you've seen anything like it."

Ingle and Foxworth glanced at each other, and Ingle spoke. "Understand, we're field agents. We'd be happy to look at your site, but we have no specific expertise in this area. I'm an anti-corruption agent. Foxworth is a human trafficking specialist. Our experts on these weapons would be down in Washington."

"We figured," Faith said. Cassius nodded his agreement with her.

"The time of these experts is valuable, given the current national security situation," said Ingle. "But you've made a clear case this is worthy of examination. I'll file a request for an expert this evening. If the request is approved at the state level office, it will be sent on to Washington. If it is approved there, we'll let you know. It sometimes takes up to fourteen days to get a reply. Please bear with us during the review of your request."

Foxworth followed up. "We thank you for your clear and professional briefing, Inspector Haversham. It's rare to find someone at the local level who can cover complex subjects so concisely."

She flushed. "I've heard that, but it's nice to hear it from people who don't know me."

Agent Ingle pursed his lips. "We're all on the same team. When you see someone on your team doing something well, you need to tell them so they keep doing it." He swiveled toward Cassius. "Do you have anything to add, Detective McCrae?"

Her companion spoke up. "Syracuse is interested in this case and would be grateful for the bureau's assistance. It involves three area residents going up in smoke. We haven't shared what we've learned with next of kin yet, but if we do, there will be some public interest. Credible closure could reduce the degree of interest."

"Good point," said Ingle. "And that brings me to my final item. Please, neither of you share what you've learned further than is institutionally necessary to pursue your investigation. If this turns out to be a matter of terrorism, public discussion of the events needs to be...managed. So as not to strengthen or embolden future terrorism by rewarding it with media coverage or public concern."

The detective spoke up. "Yeah, we don't need reporters crawling all over this, either. We've already got some attention from the *Post-Standard*."

"It's natural and proper for the media to ask questions. But if any media should show undue interest, bring it to our attention. We'll take care of it," said Ingle through his steepled fingers. After a short pause, the two agents used some invisible rapport to agree with one another that the briefing was over.

Even once the doors to the Center Ithaca building closed behind them, Faith still felt the need to speak in a hushed tone. "That was-" she began.

"Short and sweet," Cassius finished her sentence. "Your briefing hooked them. I'll be surprised if we don't get an expert."

"I was going to say 'weird.' Those guys were strange. Listening to them talk is like hearing only two-thirds of a conversation."

The man seemed unconcerned. "You get used to it. The FBI guys are stiff, and they play their cards close to the vest, but I haven't met one who's a fool. Get one of them on your team and the bad guys are in deep trouble."

"Yeah. I don't know. They gave me the willies."

He clapped her on the back. "I didn't know girls could get the willies. Is it anatomically possible?"

She shook her head to stop the thoughts on this. "Okay, don't explain that. It's just an expression."

Cassius laughed again. "It's good working with you. The next lunch is on me."

Marcus looked up from his office as Faith Haversham came in. It was after normal office hours. He had called down to her office on the sneaking suspicion the fire inspector was still in it, and found his suspicions confirmed. So he had invited her up to his office, both to get an update on how the carriage house fire investigation was continuing and to admonish her for working too late.

As the woman came into his office, he felt the march of time. He remembered when he'd first seen her. She'd been a dimpled imp of a girl peering out from under the checkered tablecloth of David and Connie's breakfast table on his first visit to their house. Later there was "big hair" teenage Faith who'd gotten in trouble going topless at a rock concert. And then there was "I have more tattoos than all the men in your firehouse and I hate God" rebellious Faith who had so exasperated her mother. Next had been the college-aged version of Faith who had visited him at his home on the lake to confess, tearfully, she thought she was a lesbian. He supposed he'd been a "safe" one to tell as it was an open secret that he was gay. He'd made her some coffee and popped the flip question: "So, you're a lesbian. What did you say you wanted to do with your life?" Maybe this ploy had been a bit trite, but it had snapped her out of her self-pity and gotten her through college, and even to her current job as one of his firefighters.

But his pep talk in the previous decade hadn't worked well enough, he knew, because now he was dealing with the "I'm in denial so I have no life and I work late" Faith. Marcus hoped, for a moment, she'd be able to put aside her image of him as her fire chief and see her as "Uncle Marcus." But he'd play the fire chief card as he had to.

"Hey Chief!" the woman chirped, and he motioned her to one of his guest chairs. She sat, leaning back and running her palms over the leather. "Ahhh, these are comfy; I need one in my office."

He smiled. "That's a twelve-hour chair. They're designed for salaried management who stay at work until all hours. Your office chair is a nine-hour chair. When your chair becomes uncomfortable, it's trying to tell your ass to go home. Maybe you should listen to it."

She rolled her eyes. "Oh, don't you start, too-"

"Stop sitting on me, and go home," Marcus did an impression of the muffled voice of her chair. "They don't pay me overtime to hold your butt up, you know..."

The younger firefighter laughed at this. "Okay, got it, Chief. But cut me some slack. My dad worked late and-"

"And what did it get him? A marriage with some serious voids in it, and a daughter he barely knew and still doesn't know is a lesbian. Do you want to follow his model?"

"You're still here, and it's eight."

"It's different. I've chosen this lifestyle. I have no family. And I'm paid correspondingly. When we last talked on these matters, you still wanted children and a family."

"Yeah," she said. "But the 'Defense of Wholesome Parenting Act' and 'Defense of Marriage Act' makes it kind of a like a pipe dream now, doesn't it?"

"Those laws haven't made a dent except in states that wanted an excuse to oppress gays. Gays and lesbians are still adopting here in New York." Marcus countered. "You could start the process any time you were willing to come out to the world and to your father."

"That's kind of the sticking point, isn't it?"

He shook his head. "Look, if you want me to be your personal Harvey Milk and starting handing out invites to an 'Isn't It Wonderful Faith's a Lesbian?' party you let me know. But as it stands I'll let you tell your father the truth on your own time. Your father didn't even blink when I told him I was gay, so I don't know what you're waiting for. He's deeper than you give him credit for."

A frown made the woman's dimples vanish. Her sad face pulled at Marcus's avuncular heart strings, but he was prepared to press on.

"Yeah, but you aren't his only child," she replied.

"True," he said. "But I suppose being his best friend counts for nothing, does it?"

The two sat in silence.

"I love you, Uncle Marcus," she said. "Does it do me any good to say?"

"Oh, there you go, playing the family card on this kindly old man. Connie taught you all her heart-softening skills, didn't she?"

"She didn't teach me, I watched her use them on Dad," Faith replied with a grin.

He leaned back and put his redwings on his desk. "Your defense is you came by your manipulation skills honestly?"

At this both of them laughed. When enough time had passed that Marcus felt he could change the subject without blunting the point he had made, he continued.

"So, having put in those long hours, I expect you've solved the carriage house fire case?"

Faith shook her head. "I was staying late checking the inspection schedules to include solar system inspections on city buildings. The proposed changes to the electrical code for decentralized solar electricity generation could be an inspection nightmare for the city."

"That's a problem for the code inspectors, not the fire inspectors. I appreciate your expertise with the building code, but if you get too far into that line of work the city will turn around and make it our job, so I can't say I approve. Now, back to the carriage house fire, which is the only conceivable - though still inadequate- reason for you to be working this late?"

"The meeting with the FBI went okay. They agreed to put up their request for a weapons-of-mass-destruction expert. And Cornell managed to give us a translation of Rosie's account of what happened."

"So what's her story?" Marcus asked, now curious.

"She claims to have been living at some overseas hospital with other children before coming to Ithaca. She says her nanny was bringing her to the area to visit a doctor, but the missing Syracuse trio killed her nanny and planned to kill her. She then claimed the fire was started by someone named 'Gabriel' who came to save her and killed our three missing persons. If she has a family, or a family who's aware of her or wants her, it's not clear."

He squeezed his chin. "Any leads on this 'Gabriel'?"

"Cassius is looking. He figured it would make more sense to start looking back in Syracuse than here."

"How is it working with him?"

"He's such a down-to-earth guy, but so smart. If he wasn't down-to-earth, I'd feel inferior all the time working with him."

"Nothing you need me to lean on the Syracuse police chief for, as if a mouse could lean on a cat?"

"Nope, nothing. Unless it's to clone Cassius and send us two or three for our police department."

He contemplated all Faith had told him. "Okay, so, I didn't hear anything in all that which sounded like a reason for you to still be here. So you'll be leaving directly from my office?"

"My uniform jacket is still back in my office-" she began.

"Where it will be when you come back in the morning," Marcus said. "Inspector Haversham, don't make me escort you to your car. As fire chief, I still have important matters to attend to here..." he winked at her. "Besides, somewhere in this city is a woman looking for a strong, hardworking, cheerful, and big-hearted girl like you to brighten her life. You won't find her working late here. Get yourself out to a singles bar tonight, though, and you might."

She put her hands to her ears, as if walling out his voice. "Okay, Chief, I get it. Like monopoly. 'Go directly to car. Do not pass office.'"

"Because you sure aren't collecting any $200 in overtime from me," he called to the departing woman. If his office had a window, he would have opened it to be sure she was good to her promise to leave. But he didn't have such a luxury, buried deep in his headquarters as he was, so he had to take her at her word. He suspected she'd be good for it.

Faith sat in the disco. Her reception at the Haunt, the disco club she had frequented her whole life, had been warm by those few who remembered her, a group which had included only the bartender. And the younger man only remembered her from her recent occupancy inspection of the club. It was ironic to her. She had been one of a gaggle of early teens who had beaten down the doors of the place when it had opened its first location in the 80s. She had met her first boyfriend at the Haunt, and even taken her first girlfriend here to dance on a break from SUNY Cobleskill. She could remember the disco at all its locations and stages of evolution, but barely a soul in it could remember her.

She chased off the depressing thought. *"The whole disco-aged population of this town changes every four years. And the last you spent any time dancing here was four years ago. So who did you expect to remember you?"*

Faith saw that in the four years or so since she had last come dancing at the club, the décor had changed little. Every surface was still spray-painted black, the elevated dance cages and poles were worn down to their brass, and the disco ball still hung front and center. But the style of music had changed. Gone were the trance, industrial, and gothic tunes, and Latino hip hop and disco were the predominant themes. The change didn't bother her much, she would try to dance to anything, but the unfamiliar music with its abrupt halts and jagged beats meant she was often out of step.

The dance floor was crowded. Students who through luck or design had no classes on Friday often went dancing Thursday night, and the crowd of younger and svelter people enclosed her in her own self-doubts. But after some dancing, she noticed a brown-haired woman who kept looking at her. Though she was much smaller and fine boned, she was Faith's age and dressed with deliberate care in a smooth green art-deco style dress. Something about her face was familiar. She wondered if she had seen the woman at a fire drill or inspection. A couple of long up -and -down looks from the stylish woman made her feel awkward in her jeans and large hoop earrings. At the next break in the music, she bought a drink and went to sit down. She hoped to either drink away her self-consciousness or convince herself to leave.

Contrary to her expectation, sitting didn't make her feel any less self-conscious. She was the only woman so seated, and the men from the bar cast her glances she did her best to ignore. She lifted her drink for more courage. When she was only half done with it, the same woman who had scared her off the floor sidled up to her table.

"Not the sort of place I would've expected to see you," she said over the music. She took the seat opposite. "I had planned to call you, but here you are."

Faith struggled to remember where she had seen the woman before. "Yeah, it's not where I expected to find myself tonight. But I thought I'd give it a try. On a lark. I guess, though, that I'm getting too old for this crowd. It sucks living in a town where half the population is eighteen to twenty-two years old."

The woman did not agree. "You're only too old if you tell yourself that. I'm older than most of these kids but I seldom go home alone."

"Another few years and I'd be cougaring in here. I should-you know-move on," she replied. She gave up trying to remember the woman's name. "Should I recognize you from somewhere?"

"Oof," said the woman. "So much for my local celebrity status," she replied. "I'm Taryn Thomas. I write for the Ithaca Journal and I do local spots in Tompkins County for YNN."

She smirked as she balanced the woman's identity with her suggestive looks on the dance floor. "Oh, okay. I know we've talked on the phone, and I know I've seen you at fire scenes. But have we met before?"

"Not formally. I know you as the old fire chief's daughter."

She felt her ears burning. It was comments like that which made her want to run screaming out of Ithaca. She was just a few lines into a conversation with an attractive woman and she had already been pegged as the "old fire chief's daughter."

"I prefer to think of myself as a firefighter," she replied, knowing she was sounding brusque but feeling too irritated to put a smile on it.

The reporter grinned. "Wow. I guess that came out wrong. Let me start again. Taryn Thomas, for the Ithaca Journal and YNN. Pleased to meet you in person, Inspector Haversham."

Faith flinched again at this. "I liked it better when you were flashing the black triangle at me. I come here so I don't have to be Inspector Haversham for a bit."

The woman tilted her head. "Would it help if I bought you a drink? I do have some questions I'd like to ask you, and I'm not above bribery."

She hesitated a moment before deciding to take a chance on the reporter. "Sure. What the hell," she said. "As long as we're off the record. I like margaritas."

"Maybe it's not about work. Maybe I'm buttering you up, making you feel good," Taryn turned with a wink and a grin, and walked over to the bar.

"*Definitely out of my league,*" she decided. "*Need to keep my eyes on this one.*" And keep her "eyes on" she did. The reporter's hips shook as she swayed from one foot to another, and she barely swerved for the dancers in her way, walking between them with no effort. Faith tried to look at someone else, but found her eyes drawn back to the woman over and over. She gave up, and beamed in spite of herself when the woman headed back with her margarita in one hand and her own drink in the other.

"Love the mai-tais here," she said, pushing the margarita across the tabletop as she sat.

"Maybe I'll try one," Faith replied, lifting the margarita straw to her lips, taking a sip, and hitting a lick of salt. The smoke machines began droning, pouring a cloud onto the dance floor from the DJ's second-floor crow's nest. The smoke lit up with the lasers from different angles made her think of Dr. Bronner's explanation that scientists could focus many lasers on a point to reach a hundred million degrees. She pictured all the disco lasers focusing through the smoke and evaporating one of the slutty Ivy League wisps who had hogged the dance floor for her entire adult life. This fantasy gave some satisfaction until it occurred to her she was thinking about the carriage house fire again.

"Here I scolded you for calling me 'Inspector Haversham' and now I'm thinking about work," she said.

Taryn was watching her with amusement. "My fault. I used your title."

"Yeah, so I can blame you," she chuckled back, warming to the woman. "So, what's your question?"

"I understand you're the lead investigator for the multi-agency investigation of the Triphammer carriage house fire."

She groaned. "Oh man. You have no idea. The thing is eating my life. Wait, this is off the record, right?"

The reporter nodded. "Sure."

"Yeah. I'm the lead investigator."

"Isn't it unusual for three agencies, including the Syracuse police, the Cayuga Heights Fire Department, and Ithaca fire department, to work on a fire together? Especially considering the remote location?"

Faith looked at Taryn. She supposed the fact she was cooperating with Syracuse Police was a matter of public record, but she wouldn't chance confirming or denying it. "Without saying who is or isn't involved in the investigation, I'd like to point out that inter-agency cooperation is the norm in cases where human remains are found," she parried.

The reporter took a sip of her mai-tai and leaned back. She guessed the other woman was now catching on that though Faith was chunky and insecure, she wasn't stupid.

"A polished answer," Ms. Thomas replied.

"Daughter of a fire chief," Faith grinned over her drink.

"So, when people talk *off* the record, they're more...forthcoming," the woman complained.

"Mm. I have my reasons."

"So what's it like working as a lead investigator with a celebrity like Cassius McCrae? Is he all he's cracked up to be?" Taryn raised an eyebrow and tilted her head. Faith guessed the gesture was supposed to make her more "forthcoming."

Faith began to feel impatient with the game, but she was still drinking the margarita so she had to concede the reporter still had cash on her meter. "Who?" she feigned ignorance.

The woman took it in stride. "Any truth to the rumor federal experts are being called in from DC to examine the site?"

Her own eyes narrowed. She wished they hadn't, she suspected her response had given away the answer. She wondered where the journalist got her information. It was awfully good and fresh. "Without confirming or denying what you've said, I will say that if it was appropriate, the department wouldn't hesitate to ask for federal assistance."

Taryn cruised by this non-response too. "So, were the human remains found those of a resident of Syracuse?"

Faith had expected this question, and had the answer. "I refuse to speculate on the identity of human remains until we have conclusive lab results. Mis-identification of remains can cause needless distress and confusion to all parties."

"Even off the record? So I can have somewhere else to pick up the story? Throw me a bone here. If I can find another lead to start with no one would have to know we ever talked. There's a story here waiting to be told!"

The woman's curiousity, looks, and the drink worked together, and Faith opened her mouth to relent and give some answers. But as she began, she thought of Rosie at home in bed, healing from her burns and feeling safe. She was tempted to give this reporter something, if only to keep the game and her own romantic fantasies going, but she wasn't about to trade a girl's safety for a kiss-and-tell.

"Yes. There is a story here somewhere. And it's waiting to be told," Faith confirmed.

Taryn sighed in exasperation. "That was plainly a wasted margarita," she smiled ruefully. "I'd hate to see what you're like *on* the record."

"I'll buy the next round to make it up to you, if you promise not to ask me any more questions," Faith made her counter offer. "I'd like to stop thinking about work at some point." She leaned forward and stared the woman in her eyes. She resolved to test the woman's 'black triangle' credentials with this stare.

Taryn welcomed the suggestion, and the stare, without a blink. "Deal. Work sucks anyway. You feel like... dancing?"

Rosetta recalled the old building in her dream. It was cool, and the stone walls and sheet metal doors which enclosed the space let in little light. Most of the light came from a pair of amber bulbs which were nailed to the rafters of the building and draped with dust and cobwebs. A thrumming on the sheet metal roof told her it had begun to rain outside. The boards behind her pressed against her back and shoulder, and splinters from them worried her skin. As she moved away from one splinter, however, another caught her, and she had given up moving. She had also given up asking what they were doing to her. They could not understand her, and they did not try.

"In order to have a soul, a person must be born of God," she heard William explain. "God creates the soul through the act of love, when two people meet and choose each other. It's God's gift. This doctor in Switzerland, he creates children without love, and he creates soulless slaves of a New World Order. You can see it in this one what he is making. She doesn't show fear. She doesn't even speak a language, just the socialist made-up language."

The woman, who was out of line of sight from Rosie, was now arguing. It was the first time she had heard them argue.

"Then what about rape? Pregnancy doesn't only happen because of love."

"A woman's body will reject a child if it's really rape. Any woman who gets pregnant from rape wanted to be raped. So children of 'rape' have souls and must be preserved. But this child is dangerous. Not only does she have no soul, she's part an animal. And not only is she part an animal, she's been programmed into socialism, because only animals could live like that. She's been programmed by those damn Europeans."

Rosie twisted her head. "*God loves you,*" she said. No one listened. She frowned, and began to struggle again. If she didn't break free, they would soon find out the truth of God's love. Splinters at her back began tearing at her skin, but she didn't stop. She could feel what was coming, and smell the anger and the murder on William and Randy, and the cool subordination from Mary Joe.

"We'll nail her here. Then we'll drive her to the edge of Cornell, raise up the cross, and burn her like the witch she is. Let all those godless socialists see

194

what happens to their kind. We stand for America, the seat of God's kingdom."

"*Each of your hearts is the seat of God's kingdom. They are the Friend's fortress, the rose which unfolds into the beauty and completeness of his love,*" Rosie said. Her back felt wet, and her wrists and ankles burned where they were bound. She supposed she was starting to bleed. But if she did not get away, their fate was certain.

Randy came toward her with a wicked looking tool. It had a bright orange plastic body with a pistol grip and metal spines protruding from its front. "BOSTITCH-Pneumatic Framing Nailer" she read on its side.

She struggled more.

"If we nail her to it now, the blood may lead the police back here," said Mary Joe.

"We want that. We want them to come. We kill the first one of them who comes, and then, when they hold the funeral, we go to it and kill a bunch more," said Randy.

William entered from the side of Rosie's vision, nodding and pulling his gray beard. "And then we surrender," said William. "Either they'll kill us and cover it up, in which case we'll be martyrs, or they'll put us on trial. When we speak in the trials, the whole world will hear us. They won't be able to control it like they controlled it after Michigan. You see how it is. The greedy and gossipy can't stand not to have their news. The devil in them will make them hang on every word we say. We will be replayed over and over on the networks. And Christian warriors all over the world will know that the time is now. The socialist president has been overthrown. The antichrist will follow when the hutarees of the world join together."

"Death to Javier Solana," said William. She wondered who Javier Solana was, and what he had done to these people to make them so angry.

Mary Joe walked up beside Rosie. The woman's graying red hair and wrinkled face were less wild than those of the men.

"This isn't about you. You can't help the way you were made. You're a symbol. It will all be over soon."

"Yes," said Gabriel in her mind. "Their suffering will end soon."

Gabriel's words made her feel even colder. "*Gabriel, don't hurt them!*"

"From ashes they came. To ashes they will return. No harm can be done to the part of them which matters, the part God created," answered Gabriel. "I cannot harm their souls any more than they can harm yours. But God commands you live so you may do your work in this world. Unless they repent soon, they must die."

"*But will they suffer?*"

Gabriel paused. "Are they not suffering now? What suffering leads one spirit to torment another, or to turn the bodies of their young into signposts of their cruelty? Their suffering, their loneliness, and their fear are incomprehensible, and every second they live brings them further from grace. Better they are stopped now. You and I will begin their journey to peace. One day they too will rest beside the Lord. All come to grace, regardless."

Rosie contemplated this. It was true William and Randy and Mary Joe did suffer. The miracles of God's world flowered around them every day in infinite diversity and variation, but all they could do was reject it and deny it. It was as though they hated it. She tried to imagine hating life so much you needed to kill someone to make it better. She couldn't. But on reflection, she had to concede Gabriel's chief point. There was no question these people were suffering.

She stopped struggling to get free. She was not in the position to quibble.

Gabriel had always helped her before and she had to trust him. She would work with Gabriel, and help these people find eternal peace.

"Dear God, heal their souls and bring them to your bosom. Let them know the joy you have shown me, be their friend as you are mine," she said.

"Please, oh please, she's a child," said Mary Joe abruptly and loudly. "Don't let her suffer. Kill her now so she doesn't have to feel the fire."

"Not even a child," said William, pointing to her belly. "Look at that. No belly button. She's not even a human, you know she's part animal. You ate a hot dog on the way down here. Abraham burned sacrifices to the Lord. But you're squeamish about this?"

"Yes, but the pig wasn't alive when they cooked the hot dog," said Mary Joe. "It was killed quickly. Humanely."

Mary Joe had a point, Rosie had to concede. *"Make it quick for them, Gabriel. As quick as you can."*

"I<small>F YOU WISH IT, I WILL ACT WITH AS MUCH SPEED AND INTENSITY AS THE FABRIC OF THIS WORLD ALLOWS. I WILL CREATE THE HOTTEST POSSIBLE FIRE FOR THE SHORTEST QUANTA OF TIME. PREPARE YOURSELF,"</small> answered Gabriel. She nodded, looking into Mary Joe's eyes.

"R<small>EJOICE. PEACE COMES,"</small> she felt Gabriel say to the woman with her tongue. The woman's eyes went wide with comprehension.

"Don't worry. I'll use a lot of nails. She'll bleed to death before we even put the gasoline on her. Besides, we don't want her to fall off the cross while we're driving." said Randy. He gave the tool a test squeeze. There was a loud "pop!" sound and a large metal spike clattered to the floor. Randy leaned toward Rosie on her cross, and spoke to Mary Joe. "Satan is weakening you at this moment of truth, Mary Joe. He's got a strong hand with women. And she's going to cry a lot. So get your war face on." He raised the tool to the Rosie's hand, pressing it against her wrist.

"N<small>OW,"</small> said Gabriel calmly. She let him all the way in, feeling his power flow into her, warming her, and heard the harmonic roar of his voice fill her with a thrilling vibration. She imagined him holding her fears for these people and cradling it, and treasuring it. Blessed was Gabriel. He was God's greatest gift to her.

Randy and Mary Joe both shrieked. There was another "pop!" from the tool. Rosie could hear in their cries pain, confusion, and fading hopes.

And then there was light.

She awoke with the sounds of Mary Joe's cries still in her ears. She knew Mary Joe was beginning her journey to a place of indescribable joy, but something in the woman's cry still haunted her. The woman had suffered, she knew. And she was still suffering, somehow, on her way to God, and Rosie didn't understand that part. God was so near to her that sometimes she could speak to him. But in her dying moment, Mary Joe had understood how far away she was from God, and had felt alone. The thought was terrifying.

She cried into her hands. *"Bring them close, God. Bring them to you."*

God did not answer her. But in a moment, the door of the room she was sleeping in creaked open, and she sat up to see the shadows of Faith and David in the hallway light. When she rubbed her eyes, the woman rushed in and sat on her bed. She stank of unfamiliar smells, including a smoky smell of burned leaves, the sweet reek of alcohol vapor, a great deal of her own sweat, and the smell of another woman. But she didn't let the smells spoil the hug.

196

"What's wrong, honey?"

"*They're far. They're so far,*" said Rosie. She knew the woman wouldn't understand her words, and indeed, didn't even understand what had happened. But her embrace was a comfort, and she clung to Faith and her strange smells as she once had to Nanny Wasilatu and her familiar ones.

"Shhhh...It's okay, honey, we're here for you. It's over," the woman said, holding tightly but avoiding her remaining bandages.

"*It's not over,*" she sobbed. "*It's beginning for them. They have such a long way to God.*" She understood now she had made the wrong choice by letting Gabriel save her at the stone house. In fear she had let him do the unspeakable. Gabriel had never been alone, since he was always a part of something. And he didn't experience time the same way, since for him it flowed in all directions and at many speeds. But Rosie understood now, from her own experience at feeling alone and isolated, that loneliness was a terrible feeling. It made time slow down horribly, dragging seconds out into hours. And with the way she had died, snuffed out before she could become her full understanding self, Mary Joe had such a long time until her reunion with God.

It would have been better to die than inflict that torment on another. If she had died, the weight of their actions would have weighed on the souls of Randy, William, and Mary Joe. Over the course of their lives, they would have re-evaluated themselves and changed for the better and even found the joy of God within their lifetimes. And why had she clung to life, and called out to Gabriel, when she had already experienced the joy of union with God in her own life? She felt selfish. She hadn't even earned her link to God the way that Mary Joe would have had to earn it. God had created her to be his servant. But in her fear, she had let Gabriel kill those more worthy than herself. And now Mary Joe faced an eternity of loss and isolation.

When David came in and put a hand on her head, her visceral comprehension of the void Mary Joe had to travel vanished, and her cries became ragged breaths. She could feel her foster father was a man who had lived well, and he would be beside God very soon. He would never know the void Randy, William, and Mary Joe faced. The feeling was a great comfort, and after a few moments her sides stopped heaving and she felt much better.

"*Thank you,*" she said to them. "*Thank you.*" Her sides ached, but Faith lowered her toward the bed. When she was swaddled in her sheets again, Rosie was surprised to see the woman turn and put her arms around her father.

"How could anyone do this to a kid?"

David shook his head. "I don't know, honey."

Rosie closed her eyes, and began to pray for Mary Joe.

The Friday morning after being remonstrated by Marcus for working too late, Faith overslept. She guessed she had come home too late and too tipsy from Taryn's apartment to remember to set her alarm clock, and getting up in the middle of the night at Rosie's cries hadn't helped her sleep thereafter. So she was still smelling Taryn's Chanel No.5 on her skin while she cursed at the downtown traffic, already ninety minutes late for work. While stopped at the stoplight, she tried to yank a comb through her hair. It caught in some knots, and as she tugged on it, she got a cell phone call from Cassius. She cursed more loudly, left the comb dangling in her hair, and groped for her "hands-free" headset. After fumbling with it so long she was sure the detective would hang up on her before she could answer him, she at last heard his voice.

"You there, Inspector?"

"Yeah, sorry, I'm caught in traffic. I'm late. Tell me you're not in my office waiting." The light changed and she traveled a whole three car lengths before she had to stop again.

"Nope, I'm still in Syracuse. I wanted to relay some good news. The weapons of mass destruction expert we requested from the FBI will land in Syracuse with some kit this morning. Are you available to meet us at the carriage house?"

"Holy shit! I didn't even know our request had been approved! And he's landing today?"

"Think about it. You don't go around announcing to the world 'We've got a WMD expert coming to town!' People ask questions. I'm sure they held off telling us to keep things on the down-low. Anyhow, are you free to meet us?"

"No problem. What time?"

"He's coming in around eleven. So I'm thinking three-thirty-ish. That will build in some slack in case his kit takes some time to claim from baggage or whatever."

A car honked behind Faith. "Crap!" She had gotten so distracted by the call she was stopped at a green light. She darted through the intersection. "Yeah, sure, three-thirty's fine. Should I bring any special gear?"

"He said he's seen your briefing already, but you might want to bring your laptop in case he wants to review it."

"Check. Laptop. Anything else?"

"Not that I can think of. I'll let you get back to your commute."

"Yeah, what a thrill. But thanks for the good news! I need a break in this case."

"You and me both," replied Cassius. "See you at three-thirty."

She hung up in time to notice her next light turn green. She would now have some news to share with Marcus or Karl if either of them bugged her for coming in late. In fact, it was the perfect excuse. She could pretend she'd known the expert was coming and she would have to work late. She could say she'd slept in so as to follow Marcus's guidance not to do overtime. Heck, armed with this rationalization, she could even take some time to comb her hair properly once she got to the HQ parking lot. She reached up and removed the stalled comb as she at last passed under the next traffic light.

She congratulated herself on the happy coincidence that was saving her bacon. She hoped it stayed happy.

That afternoon Faith arrived early at the carriage house site with her site kit. Once again she swept the glass clean of cinders, and when Cassius did not appear, she took the time to widen the cleaned area of the carriage house's floor pad. Around the outside of the glass area the pink concrete was cracked and flaked away in places, exposing reinforcing mesh which was beginning to rust. Likewise, crabgrass, dandelions, and clover were springing green and fresh in patches from the burned soil surrounding the carriage house, but only at the outer edge of the burned area.

Eventually the detective arrived in his usual maroon unmarked sedan, and she could see the silhouette of a second person through the tinted glass. She set aside her broom and walked over to greet them. The FBI's expert was a skinny, silver haired, balding man with a large nose and a nervous smile.

"Faith? This is Special Agent Coleman."

198

"Pleased to meet you. Thanks for coming up our way." She shook hands with the man.

"The pleasure is mine," said the agent, his voice high and thin. "Anything that gets me out of meetings where I have to listen to politicos 'what if' and try to find ways to protect against all threats with no money. It'll be great to get my hands dirty." He released her hand and peered at the ruins of the carriage house. "So, this is the site?"

Detective McCrae swept his arm through an arc that included the ruins. "This is it."

"Not much of a target," said the agent, looking around at the quiet orchards, pastureland, and remote farmhouses. "Why blow this up?"

"One possibility is that whatever blew up, blew up by accident. They might have planned to take it somewhere else, somewhere with a higher...payoff." Cassius explained.

Coleman pursed his lips. "It's been known to happen. You'd be surprised how often we stumble on organized crime or some whacko militia building weapons when they blow up their garage or their hideout by mistake." The man stared at the area for a bit, then turned back to the detective's car and hoisted out some black plastic cases.

"Can I get one of you to help me carry this?"

"Sure." Faith took the larger case. The FBI agent was shorter than she was, she suspected she weighed half again what he did. The case was heavy, but she lifted it up onto her shoulders like a roll of fire hose and carried it out to the damaged floor slab.

The agent began unlimbering the cases on the slab and, without stopping to take pictures or ask questions, began setting up various devices on tripods. One device she recognized as an IMAX type three hundred and sixty degree camera, and another looked like a surveyor's theodolite, but the other devices she didn't recognize.

"Wow, what is all this?" she asked, when Coleman paused.

"Many things, many things. A camera complex. It will take pictures in visible light and other wavelengths. It's also a geodata sensor. It's a fancy GPS this will give me exact height and elevation and position on the ground to the nearest centimeter. If I combine the camera image and the geodata sensor, I'll be able to recreate the entire scene in my computer, including the positions of every piece of rubble larger than about four inches."

Cassius nodded appreciatively. "Slick."

The agent agreed. "Yeah, it's sure nice. When I started in this business we did scene maps by hand. A site like this would have taken a crew a better part of two days. Now I set things up and it's done in a couple of minutes. Technology has come a long way, what with government emphasis. Now this is a variable spectrometer, called the sniffer. It's sniffing for trace residues from most common explosives. How old is this site?"

"Three weeks," Faith supplied.

"Hmmm. That's old." The agent frowned. "We'll see if it finds anything. I'll have to let it sample for an hour or so instead of ten minutes. Now for the hand tools." He went to his second case, opened it, and hung four devices around his neck on straps. The small man was comical with so many devices slung over his neck and shoulder, but he showed no sign of discomfort.

"That's a lot of tech," Cassius noted.

"Yeah. We haven't invented a tricorder yet like they use on 'Star Trek.' So I'm still stuck lugging this crap around." He held up a cylinder with a readout on it. He walked away from the slab, and stood at the edge of the burned area. When he switched the device on, it made a familiar "tick-tick-tick" sound.

"A Geiger counter?" The detective observed.

"Yep. Getting a background reading. Once I know what normal is for this area, I'll walk back to the center and see if we get more REMs." When the ticking had gone on for a minute or so, Coleman faced about and walked straight toward the slab. The ticking increased as they approached it.

"Hmmm," said the agent, stopping about two thirds of the way to the slab. "It's not high, but it is elevated. And I'm not even at the slab yet." He stopped and scribbled some notes on a green notepad, which Faith recognized as made of the kind of waxed paper which could be written on in the rain. He turned his back on the slab, checked his Geiger reading, and then continued to the slab. The ticking increased, coming to a peak as he pointed it at the sponge-like glass in the center of the green glass circle.

"Jeeze, Special Agent, do you think it was a nuke? Like a mini-nuke?"

Coleman chuckled. "There's no such a thing as a mini-nuke. Below a critical mass of initiating explosive to create the pressure necessary to begin the fission reaction, the fission reaction won't occur. So there are no marble-sized nukes or something. Not that we've been able to figure out how to make, anyway."

"We?" Cassius asked.

"Oh, I used to work at some national laboratories. Back in the cold war. I worked on 'tactical' back-packable nuclear weapons. Back-packable for some real ox, I guess, I never could have carried them far. The smallest of those babies would have leveled an area a hundred times this size. But after the cold war I had to find a new job. Mini-nukes are only cool when you can blow them up in someone else's country, and Europe stopped volunteering for the job. Wusses. Anyway, I don't think this was caused by a mini-nuke."

"Then what?" Faith prompted.

Coleman pinched his lower lip in reflection. "Search me. The radiation level is elevated, and linked to the center of the blast marking we see here. But it's not at a level, nor is the damage such, that a nuclear weapon is possible. It could have been a dirty weapon, I suppose."

The detective understood this term better than she. "Dirty weapons aren't nuclear weapons, but they're weapons designed to scatter radioactive dust, right?"

"Yep. Much, much easier to make than a nuke. And much less dangerous in the short term. But if it was a dirty weapon, it wasn't a very dirty weapon. The radiation level is only high enough that you'd even have to wear an OSHA film badge standing in the center here. There are probably cellars full of radon around here which are as radioactive. So we might be better off calling it a 'not-quite-clean weapon.'"

At the mention an OSHA film badge might be required in the center, Cassius and Faith stepped away from the glass circle and stood together at a comfortable distance. The FBI agent, unfazed by his own discovery of radioactivity, stood where he was and made notes on his pad.

Coleman then slung his Geiger counter and took out another device. He approached them while he fidgeted with it, and then held it to his eyes like a pair of binoculars. He scanned the area through them.

"What are you looking for?"

"Snowflakes," said the agent. "These are magnetic resonance scopes. They were developed to help soldiers on the battlefield see mines and improvised explosive devices through the ground. They're useful in my business for finding small fragments of metal lying on the ground or buried just below the surface. They twinkle like snowflakes through these scopes, and are easy to find." Coleman began wandering around, scanning this way and that and bending down to examine pieces of metal. Each time he did it, he consulted a third device, a GPS, and wrote down the coordinates, and then bagged each piece in a Ziploc baggie.

"You're writing down where you find things so you can recreate the scene," observed Cassius.

"Yes. Most of these fragments are far too small to be tracked by the geodata device, so I write down the coordinates for my reference."

"I wish I had all this high-speed gear," she said.

"This suite cost the taxpayer close to twenty million dollars, and most of it is handy widget size, perfect for walking away. You wouldn't believe what a nightmare it's been to track the items in this kit and be sure field agents bring all the pieces back. So don't be so sure you want one in your department. If a piece goes missing or gets 'borrowed,' it can take a four-and-a-half million dollar chunk out of your take-home pay."

"Yeah, I bet," the detective laughed. Coleman continued scanning for maybe another ten minutes, and Faith and Cassius stopped following him. They let the older man wander while they talked about the scene.

"Dammit. I wonder how much radiation I've gotten coming out here to look at the site. And then there's Karl. And you."

"It's spilled milk now. Don't sweat it. Besides, he said it wasn't dangerous. It's not like you've been tenting on the hot spot for days at a time or something."

"Yeah, I guess," she admitted. "Still, kind of freaky. I never thought to wonder if the place might be radioactive."

Coleman rejoined them. "So, you guys want to take a look through these before I pack them up? It's kind of cool. Get some thrill for your tax dollars. Maybe you'll spot something I missed." Seeing her eyes light up at the suggestion, the agent hung the strap around her neck and showed her how to adjust the focus. "You look around some while I go tweak the geodata device."

Through the goggles, the mid-day was night. Faith could only faintly make out the outlines of solid objects. But the visitor's description of "snowflakes" was fitting. The ground was spotted with points which twinkled like the first layer of snowflakes fallen on grass or a sidewalk. She followed them around, looking for something interesting, but the items she found proved to be boring fragments of metal like nails, chunks of barbed wire, and an occasional coin. Her hopes of finding some clue, like a key ring or a locket, soon vanished, and she gave the detective a turn with the goggles. He wandered around with them in fascination.

"These would be awesome on a crime scene. They could help you find bullets stuck in walls, knives, guns, all kinds of stuff," he said.

"Yeah, that device is four-and-a-half million dollars of the twenty million dollar kit. It's not in a local agency's equipment budget," Coleman commented from the tripod he was standing at. "Besides, indoor spaces are usually crammed with so much metal junk you can't see the interesting metal bits for all the crap in your way. Nails, electrical cable and conduit, and even drywall screws show up. And heaven help you if you get one of these new homes built with steel two-by-fours," he griped. "But the gadget is good for field use, out in the open."

"Yeah, I didn't think of the limitations. You would see everything metal in the house."

"Plus, anything that's carrying a live electrical current glows like a light bulb. I have to cut the power to the room to use that scanner indoors," Coleman added. He came and reclaimed the device from the detective. "Alright, now it's picture time. Then I sit and think while the chemical sniffer sniffs."

The agent pulled out a normal looking digital camera and began shooting pictures. Faith and Cassius followed along a distance behind, in case he had any questions. He photographed the approach, the rubble, the remains of the diesel fuel storage tank, and herself and Detective McCrae besides. After this he returned, as everyone who came to the site did, to the circle of glass.

"Let me test your knowledge, young inspector. At what heat does concrete turn to glass?"

"About forty-five hundred degrees, I'm told," Faith replied.

Coleman continued his test. "Good! And why is the concrete around the glass area pink?"

"It's heat damaged concrete. I've seen it before in structural fires."

"And what determines what color the glass is?"

"Lots of stuff. The metal used to reinforce it, any contaminants present when the concrete is heated, and any chemicals used to help it cure faster or slower or keep it air-entrained."

"Excellent!" said the FBI agent. "Someone taught you well!"

"The university is full of eggheads."

"I'd forgotten Cornell was right here. Did you attend?"

"No, I went to a state school for my fire science degree. But the university is helpful. It pains me to admit it, because they can be jerks about a lot of things, but if you come to them with a question, they'll get you an answer. That's their latest jingle. 'Cornell: New York's Answer People.'"

"It's a great resource to have. Make use of it," he said. "If I had more time on the ground here, I'd love to ask some questions."

"Where are you off to next?" asked Faith.

"Missouri. Some meth lab blew up. Or they think it was a meth lab. Anyhow, they want me and miss sniffer to check it out, and be sure it was meth and not bombs they were making," the FBI agent explained. "I swear, half my calls are for Missouri and Arkansas. It's either meth labs or whiskey stills or leaking eighty-year-old in-ground petroleum tanks going up. The initial reports don't look like it was a bomb, but the next one could be the big surprise, so off I go."

"How soon do you leave?" She hoped she could pick his brain for a few hours, anyway.

"I have to take him back to the airport tonight," the detective interjected.

Coleman elaborated. "I'll have about two hours slack once the sniffer is done. Is there a restaurant in this town called the Moosewood?"

She nodded. "Yeah, it's a too-rich-for-its-britches vegetarian place down near the Commons."

"I'd like to eat there if there's time. But no rush," said the agent. "Got to let miss sniffer sniff."

She and Cassius glanced at each other. The Moosewood was the last place she expected an FBI agent to want to eat. Raiding it and testing all the deserts for pot, she could understand.

"Sure, I suppose if there's time. It's an expensive place, though."

"My treat," said the FBI agent.

"Huh?" she said.

"Most days of travel I don't come close to using up my *per diem*. So tonight I'll splurge, and we can talk about bombs!" Coleman said. "You're both such a good audience. A fellow gets lonesome hip hopping from one place to another, and never learning much about the stories surrounding the investigation site. I sometimes wonder if I ever make a difference." The older man prepared to carry on with his explanation, but then the sniffer device began squawking with an urgent tone. "Oops, filter is full. Coming, darling, coming!" said the agent to his machine as he scampered away.

Cassius waited until the agent was a good distance away to mutter under his breath. "He's unusual."

202

"Yeah, you said it," said Faith. "But he's not as creepy as Ingles and Foxworth." She grew resigned to a long Friday evening while the sniffing device sniffed away.

"Now this is the life," Special Agent Coleman said from his corner seat at a corner table in the Moosewood. The low pile carpeting, sculpted pinewood trim, dividers, and souvenir shelf sections swallowed and scattered sound, so though the restaurant was crowded, they still enjoyed a sense of quiet and privacy.

"If only every scene investigation ended with a glass of spiced carrot juice at a nationally-known restaurant." He sipped from his glass and sank into his chair. "Most times all I get is coffee from whatever agency I'm supporting, or, if I'm lucky, dinner somewhere classy like a 'waffle house.' I'm lucky I don't have an ulcer or heart disease. I will give you guys my card. If you need me back here for anything, drop a line and I'll make something up to come out here. My friends in the gourmand club will be so jealous! I ate at the *Moosewood!*"

Faith drank her ice water. The list of exotic fruit juices hadn't appealed to her, and even though the money wasn't hers, she didn't feel right spending two hours pay on a glass of juice anyway. She wondered what she would say next. Fortunately, Coleman had questions in mind.

"So, tell me about the child's injuries," the FBI agent asked.

"Child?" she asked.

"The one found at the scene. Your briefing said she had minor injuries. What kind?"

"Yeah, sorry, she lives at home with me at the moment. Her name is Rosie."

"Rosie, then. How was she hurt?"

"Cuts and bruises suggesting she was restrained for extended periods, which matches her later testimony," said the detective.

"And about five percent third degree burns, with second-degree burns covering her backside and part of her buttocks," she added.

"Had any unusual symptoms? Hair falling out? Diarrhea?"

"Nope," said Faith. "Hair wasn't even singed. Had her eyebrows, head of hair, body hair, everything."

"Hair falling out? Are you thinking of radiation poisoning?" Cassius mused.

"Yeah, I'm wondering if there was more radiation at the time of the incident. But she must have been far from the blast to keep all her hair. Maybe the burns were caused by splattered diesel fuel."

"Maybe," she conceded. "But she says the burns came from the people present, that they touched her while they were burning."

"What *did* she say started the fire? This wasn't in the briefing."

"Yeah. I didn't have her statement at the time I wrote the briefing. And that part is...garbled in the transcript we got of her interview," she explained.

"Garbled?" Coleman asked, scratching his head while he took another long, slow sip of his carrot juice. Bliss mingled with the curiosity on his features. She wondered what the Moosewood put in the carrot juice that made the man so crazy about it.

"The girl has special needs, maybe a developmental disability," she explained. "Sweet kid, harmless, but not all there."

"She claims another party came and set the fire to save her from her captors," Cassius clarified. Faith appreciated how well the man could make Rosie's claim of having been saved by the archangel Gabriel sound both plausible and sane. "We're looking for the third party now, but her explanation does not match all the facts at the scene."

"Oh yeah?" asked Coleman. "Tell me, then, what does match the facts? Because I'm stumped. I won't admit defeat until I get home, plug everything into the computer, and puzzle till my puzzler is sore. But as of this moment, I haven't a clue what could have done the kind of damage we observed."

Faith felt her heart sink at the man's candor. She'd been counting on him and the FBI for a breakthrough on the case.

Cassius was less dismayed, so he was quicker to follow up. "It's that unusual?"

"Sure. The damage doesn't match the signature of any device I'm familiar with. There was elevated radiation, but not high enough to come from a dirty bomb, and certainly not high enough or big enough to come from a nuke. There were signs of intense heat, heat like I'd expect from a nuke, but not even an infinitesimal fraction of enough corresponding blast or fire damage for the device to have been a nuke. Finally, there are metal fragments from the diesel storage tank melted on one side and with writing visible on the warning labels on the other. Whatever did the damage caused an insane amount of heat in an instant, and then vanished. And there are no sign of chemicals. No trace of explosives, accelerants, or thickeners from napalm."

"The sniffer didn't sniff anything?"

"Oh, sure. It smelled residual diesel fuel, two cycle engine oil, vehicle exhaust from the roadway, methane which was probably from some nearby cows, an insecticide used on fruit trees, and something that matched the 2007 formula for Chanel No. 5. But all those things were likely present in the carriage house prior to the fire. Except the perfume."

She started. "Oh. Um, that'd be...me. The Chanel No. 5."

"Yeah, I figured," said Coleman. "If it wasn't, Detective McCrae here has unusual tastes in cologne," he chuckled.

"Well, you're corroborating my stumpedness-confusion-whatever," she explained. "I'd hoped for answers from you, because I couldn't figure out what would leave such a heat signature, and neither could the university eggheads. But if the experts are stumped I don't have to feel stupid."

"Consider this national expert stumped, but not quitting. You're a smart young lady, it's a puzzling case, is all," he said. "If you find an answer, call me straight away, and I'll do the same. But, in the meantime, to the menu!" Coleman picked up the full menu and began to look through it. The oohs and ahs he made, and the finger he stuck behind his tie, told Faith the agent would enjoy this meal a lot more than she would. But what the hell. The price was right. She supposed she couldn't go too far wrong with five-cheese macaroni and cheese. Even if the vegetable sides were fresh, local, and organic, and hence probably covered in dirt.

"Here's to solving mysteries," said Cassius. He raised his glass in a toast, which she acknowledged and Coleman greeted with a grin and another sip of carrot juice.

"To solved mysteries! Past and future!"

David regarded the partially finished table leg on the lathe. It had been pinned in the lathe since Connie's passing a year before: he had started the coffee table project so as to not feel lonesome while she was in the hospital. The wood looked none the worse for wear and, once dusted, still had some of the red-blonde color of fresh cedar. He hoped it wouldn't stain a different color than the other three coffee table legs which he had shaped and stained long ago.

He flicked the lathe on and off and it spun up and down in response. He checked the cardboard shaping guide from the pattern kit, blowing the dust off of it and sliding it onto the lathe rail. Its markings told him where to put each tool to make this leg match the others. He felt around for his ear muffs and safety glasses, and after wiping the glasses on his shirt, put them on.

He worried for a second. Once he started this tool, he wouldn't be able to hear a thing, so if Rosie were to get into something, he wouldn't know it. But he'd left her drawing, with a plate full of Oreos, a glass of milk and a fresh stack of paper, which should hold her for a while. "She's twelve years old. Not that she's all there, but she hasn't shown any tendency to mix household chemicals." He resolved to check on her in ten minutes, and, so fortified, started the lathe.

In a few minutes David was cussing into the buzz of the lathe. He was sure he was making mistakes. It had been foolish to try and pick up where he'd left off. He was out of practice. He slowed down his work, using the tools less aggressively, and glanced at one of the finished legs to compare. It didn't match. If it got bad enough, he could always go to the lumberyard and get some fresh two-by-twos to shape until he got it right. So he had no reason to get down on the project.

These thoughts relaxed him, and after a while he forgot his misgivings about the table leg. When he thought he had gotten it as close to the others in shape as he was able, he dismounted it from the lathe and held it beside the other three. It was, he decided, different in several ways, but maybe not so much that you'd notice if you weren't holding them side by side. Maybe he'd keep it after all.

Guilt jolted him when he remembered he hadn't checked on Rosie as he'd planned. David put down the leg and started up the cellar stairs. He was surprised on the way up to find he heard music. Then he recalled Faith had shown the girl how to use the CD player. He guessed the sound of the lathe had disturbed her and she was playing music to cover it up.

Instead, he found the colored pencils and paper were lying idle on the table beside an empty milk glass, and Rosie was dancing in the middle of the living room. He didn't recognize the music, so it was probably one of his daughter's pop albums. He went and picked up the CD case and examined it. It was titled *Achtung Baby* by a band called U2.

David stopped and watched the girl. He knew from her other outbursts of dance she didn't mind an audience. She would start dancing when the mood took her, regardless who was present. But this was the first time he'd seen her dance to music she had chosen.

He wondered where she had learned to dance as she did. Perhaps the institution she had come from had dance classes. He supposed if you had a lot of energetic kids on your hands, dance classes could be one way to keep them busy without a lot of expensive equipment. And she was good at it, although some of her dance moves were adult for her age. Or adult for her mental age anyway. He supposed these days kids as young as Rosie hung around in dance clubs and did far naughtier things. He wondered if anyone had ever explained the birds and the bees to her, but backed away from this responsibility. This wasn't his problem. Given her disability and the fact she wouldn't be staying long, this was better handled by someone else.

"It's alright, it's alright, it's all right, she moves in mysterious ways," chanted the singer. David grinned at this. He did not know how Rosie moved her body some of the ways she was doing it, so the lyric was appropriate. He couldn't say he liked the music, but her dancing was graceful.

He started when, during one move, she opened her closed eyelids and showed just solid whites: her eyes were rolled back into her head. Frightened, without understanding why, he snapped off the CD player.

The music stopped, but the girl took a moment to finish her last move, eyes again closed. When she opened them, they were normal, and she flashed a nervous smile, as though she didn't know what to expect but feared she might be in trouble.

"Are you okay, honey?" David checked when they had eye contact. Rosie nodded emphatically. He relaxed at her earnest expression. He guessed he'd overreacted.

"Do you want me to put the music back on?"

She outstretched her arms to a dancing pose as her answer. He pressed play, and after a whine of the disc spinning back up, U2 resumed, though not on the same song. She didn't mind, however, and was back in motion. There was no harm in her dancing, however startling the strange roll of her eyes was, so he went back to his lathe.

"If only Faith had been this easygoing," he mumbled on the way down the steps to the cellar. He recalled then his daughter had not come home until after midnight the night before, and hoped that she wasn't slipping back into her old habits of drinking late and running with sleazy men. She was old for that.

As David restarted his lathe and picked up his tools, he avoided thinking about the grandchildren he hoped to have one day. He could share his paternal impulses with Rosie, who needed some caring for, and leave his daughter to find her own way, whatever way that might be.

That night, after Rosie was in bed, Faith left her father in front of the television and went to her closet to get dressed for the Haunt. She sorted through some of the flashier shirts she had, but by now, she was sure, they were all five years out of fashion. Besides, she was bound to sweat while dancing, and they were synthetics which didn't breathe.

Rejection tainted her consideration of her wardrobe. Taryn had not returned her texts about meeting. Faith didn't know how to feel about this. On the one hand, she felt used, since as the night of their first tryst had worn on, the reporter *had* asked her more questions about the carriage house fire, which Faith had laughed off and not allowed to spoil their fun. But that fact, in conjunction with the woman's terseness since, made her wonder if Taryn hadn't been taking things a step further sexually to see what information she could get, rather than because she felt chemistry. For a couple of days Faith had actually felt attractive, but the woman's now apparent insincerity left her to crash back down to ground level.

She stared into her mirror. She was too tall, too busty, too hippy, too big around in the arms and legs, and yes, she had to admit, too old. What was she thinking going to a nightclub? Most of the women were younger and looking for something more like a barbie doll anyway, even on a 90s dance party night. She held up different shirts in the mirror as she wondered where else she might go.

She supposed she could go to the two or three gay bars in town, but it was a small town, and people talked. She'd end up having to make excuses to her father if she did, she was sure. She could go to some singles-oriented gay, lesbian, and bisexual support group meetings, but again, this would lead to her father learning of it. She could try the Syracuse scene out, but that would involve long drives to and fro. No, the Haunt was the only club with a busy enough dance floor and a general enough clientele for her to prowl and not have anyone remark on her presence except to note she was old for the place.

"This is a problem you made," the self in her mirror said. *"Tell him. End this charade so you can have a life. He might not react like mom did."*

She ignored the image in the mirror and continued to swap shirts in and out. She settled on a white cotton blouse with a flat V-neck. It showed off her bust. "What the heck," she thought. "If you have more of it than you can hope to hide, you may as well flaunt it."

She felt her cell phone buzz with a text. She picked it up, and to her delight, saw Taryn's reply to her latest text. But then she sighed at the message.

"Can't visit tonight, in Syracuse."

She absorbed the disappointment. But a moment later she began texting back, trying to hit the tiny phone keys with her oversized fingers. *"Need to be in Syracuse tomorrow AM for work. Could meet you there tonight, stay over."* She sent it but did not wait for a reply. She should count on 'no', she decided, and continued her preparations for whatever Ithaca night life she could find. She went back to examining her shirt in the mirror, resolved not to be disappointed when Taryn refused the proposal. She had grown comfortable again with her V-neck when she got the text back.

"Sounds good. Meet me outside Alibi's at 10."

"Yes!" Faith cheered with a fistpump to her naysayer twin in the mirror. She began throwing together an overnight bag. She carried it down the stairs, and, seeing her father at the television, she tried to slip out with it. But he called after her as she darted for the door. "Bye honey. I'll cross my fingers for Mr. Right tonight."

"Why not Ms. Right?" Faith wanted to ask. But she didn't.

"Thanks, Dad," she answered instead. "I may stay out late, and I have to meet Detective McCrae in the morning, so I may stay in Syracuse."

"Remember your aunt while you're out there," said David. She muttered her agreement and stepped out the door.

She paused on the porch, and listened to the rushing of the falls in the gorge for a moment. The water rushed past her family's house as it had all the days of her life. Time was passing her by at a rate of one day per day. She had to start living, and to do that, she needed to move out, or tell her father the truth.

Faith fingered her keychain for her car. There was no point in telling him anything, she supposed, until she found someone worth coming out for. Which was the point of tonight. She had to do the first things first.

Chapter 15

Explorations

Faith opened the door to Alibi's, letting Taryn enter before her. She supposed she was the "butch" of the two of them, since she was larger and less feminine, but she felt no obligation to fill any role, and neither did the other woman expect it. Rather than waiting for her to be chivalrous, the reporter held open the bar's inner door in turn, and Faith was the first to enter.

The pub felt run down. A laminate dance floor, while new, covered what she could feel through her shoes was a softening and uneven subfloor, and the low pile carpet in the seating area had a griminess which permeated the space above it. Walking across it made her ankles itch as if bits of grit were jumping up and sticking to her skin. Faded photos of demonstrations in New York City and Syracuse, and a smiling portrait of Harvey Milk and a grimacing photo of Brenda Howard, both without captions, decorated the walls. The "members pay less" sign over the register was scrawled with "but still pay too much!" But the bartops, tables, and glasses hung over the counter were clean, as were the walls, although she could still see in one wall the outline of a rainbow flag through the white paint. And once inside, there was no mistaking the signs. The short hair of many of the women at the bar, and the closeness of many of the men, told her all she needed to know.

"It could be cleaner," she said to Taryn under her breath.

The woman smiled. "I don't know. I like it gritty. I have to apply makeup for an hour before I go on TV, so I like a space with a bare face." She then waved to two women who were looking at her from the bar. "Hey ladies, how *are* you!"

"Oh look, it's the movie star!" One of them, a heavier woman with dark curls hanging in her eyes answered. And indeed, Taryn's dress was more feminine and glamorous than any other in the room. As if playing up to the woman's comment, the reporter sashayed across the room to her and her companion, a serious-looking older woman all in silver.

"Don't hate on me because I'm the prettiest," she retorted. Despite the woman's snarky greeting, Ms. Thomas's tone was soft as she closed on the woman. "I heard about Robin and the boys. I'm so sorry." Faith admired how smoothly the journalist's voice slid from scolding to empathic.

Mel shrugged her shoulders. "I told her not to move to Pennsylvania, that they wouldn't be safe there. It's one thing to divorce me and take my boys from me, it's another to move to a bigot state and then get the boys taken away even from her. Now they're 'wards of the state,' because Pennsylvania won't even consider giving me custody. So Lilly's buying me drinks till I'm too stupid to think about it."

"Did they say why they took them?" Taryn asked as Faith closed in behind her. She tried to look present in the conversation.

"Do they need to? She passed all the home inspections, so they invoked the 'Wholesome Parenting for America' Act. I suppose they think they saved some straight marriage somewhere else by taking my kids. And who are you?"

Taryn remembered she was there. "This is Faith, my new find in Ithaca. Be nice. She's been hiding in a closet for a couple of decades."

"Oh," said Mel. "Welcome to the wider reality. You picked a hell of a time to figure out you were a lesbian."

"Yeah," she agreed. "But I'm ready to stop fooling myself. I guess I'll have to deal with the mess which follows."

Mel's companion spoke up. "I'm Lilly. Pleased to meet you. I'm sorry we're grouchy. You found us at a rough time."

Faith envied how Lilly said "we" and "us." The woman was part of a couple, with Mel, like it was nothing, but for all of her own wanting and daydreams, she hadn't been able to keep a steady relationship with a woman. She felt like the freshman in this class. Everyone else here was "real" already. But she resolved not to be daunted and let her real dismay at Mel's story give her something to say. "It sounds like it. I'd heard Florida and North Carolina were taking kids from couples, but I didn't know PA was doing it."

Mel spoke up again, eyes blurry and her beer bottle loose in her grip. "They just started. My kids will be one of their 'test cases' for the 'Wholesome Parenting' act. That is, a test case *if* I can even afford to hire a lawyer. Otherwise they belong to someone else now." At this, she took a long pull from her beer bottle, and she followed it with bleary eyed contemplation of something distant behind them.

Taryn grasped, as Faith had, that Mel had checked out. She turned to Lilly. "If there's anything I can do, Lilly, call me. For real."

"Thanks. It wouldn't do any good to run a story on it. But if we think of something, we will."

There was Lilly's "we" again, she noted. Even with her kids taken from her, Mel still had something to be happy for. She hoped the woman remembered in time.

"Let's find a table and let people come meet you. They'll come around. You're fresh meat." Taryn led her to a corner table under a tattered banner reading "We will not hide! We have pride!" Ironic, that the gay community of Syracuse would hang a banner about coming out in the dark corner on the inside of their hardest-to-find bar. But if the Syracuse crowd was now shy, they didn't show it inside these walls. People filed past their table to introduced themselves and chat with the reporter as though she held some special rank in the community. Those who came by did talk to Faith and showed some curiosity, but none stayed.

When the stream of visitors had ended, her companion flashed a sign at the immaculately dressed hulk of a bartender. After a moment, the man brought over a pair of Singapore Slings, and Ms. Thomas took her first sip as she slid the second glass over to Faith.

"You need to loosen up. I got you in the door, and I'm here to introduce you. But I can't do it all. You've got to get off your duff and talk a lady up."

Faith started. She had seen this trip as a date, but maybe this was not how Taryn was seeing it. She decided not to let the woman slip away from her without making her position clear.

"Hey pretty lady, what's your sign?" she replied, pulling her chair closer with flourish and turning it to watch whatever her companion was watching.

The journalist chuckled and drummed her fingers on the tabletop before she answered: "Bridge freezes before roadway."

Faith crossed her arms. She would not be cowed by Taryn's tone or social standing amongst the other guests. "Wow, that's kind of cold and prickly after you went to the trouble to bring me here. Want to explain?"

Her date drew a long breath and her eyes wandered around the room. "I remember this place at a different time. Cuomo had legalized gay marriage, club membership here was at an all-time high, and we even talked about closing the bar and making this place a LBGT family center. Hell, even this carpet was clean. For once, the center of our life was not about getting drunk enough to forget the lashes of the day and see who we could find to sleep with among those who dared to self-identify. I was going to announce my wedding to my fiancée on the air on YNN! I had a plan to do it after the election. But that time is gone."

"What happened to your fiancée?"

"She got cold feet. She was Christian, hard core, and was even working at a church. When our guys lost the election, her superiors grew bold and threatened to fire her when they found out she was lesbian. So she let them choose her life for her and dumped me."

"Ouch," sympathized Faith.

"Learning point for me. Don't get serious with women who hate themselves, and don't date Christians.

"But Mel had to learn her own way. Mel was the one of us who embraced 'family values' and went 'all in' on her family as soon as they made us legal. She did everything right. She got a domestic partnership before the law was passed, a real marriage afterwards, even adopted the kids as a step parent to be extra sure. Then she changed diapers and drove a minivan for five years, and look what happened to her. You sound like you want someone, for real and for good, like she did. That's not me. My family is my cats. Everyone else is visiting." She slugged half of her drink. "People who aren't mine cannot be taken from me."

Taryn gave a lopsided grin. "But anytime you need an itch scratched, go ahead and make a phone call. You're smart, and sincere, and you have the best intentions, so for a moment at a time, I can rise to your occasion. The problem with us isn't you. It's me."

Faith blinked. "Do you always follow cold and prickly with bitter and despairing?"

The woman smiled broadly. "I like a girl who gives no quarter. So let's talk about who we're looking at here. That one, the blonde on the end, is Ashley. Bat shit crazy, not even good in bed, but loaded. Her daddy coaches Orangemen basketball. That one that just came in is Jessica. I think she's your best bet in here, she works like a dog and doesn't know how to stop hoping-"

Faith reached out and put an arm over Taryn's shoulders. The woman didn't shrink away, but didn't stop her monologue until Faith interrupted her. "This one is Taryn," she said. "She's smart, but she drank the cynicism Kool-Aid and is bad at changing subjects. Still, *she* is the one I want tonight."

Her date fell silent, picked up her drink, and leaned into her, her bony shoulder compressing Faith's breast so hard she had to flinch. But after a second the reporter took a more comfortable position, took a long swallow of her drink, and smirked. "If you're into lost causes, who am I to tell you different? Throw your pearls before me, baby."

Faith grinned at this. "Let me throw them now, while it's still early. I've got to work tomorrow."

Taryn was already on her cell phone. "I'll get us a room at my favorite pig wallow. We can head there after these drinks."

When Faith awoke in the Jefferson-Clinton Hotel in downtown Syracuse, Taryn was already up and getting dressed, sliding into her dress of the night before. She admired the woman's figure, and the grace which allowed her to easily close the dress's back while it was on her.

"Got to go," Taryn explained, massaging her face in a mirror. "I've got a stack of copy to read and a make-up call back in Ithaca before I go on TV today, and I don't dare show up in yesterday's clothes. And didn't you have somewhere you had to be?"

Faith glanced at the alarm clock. "Yeah, you're right. I'd better get up and at them." She wanted to say how she was meeting Cassius to see the home of the principal suspect in the carriage house fire. But on the other hand, she didn't want to raise the issue and invite the woman's renewed questioning. The reporter hadn't said a word about the investigation this time, and it would be easier if it stayed that way.

She rose and stepped through a misty halo of the other woman's perfume and walked into the bathroom. While she washed her face, Taryn came to plant a kiss on her cheek. "Be safe, love."

"You too! Think of me while you're being all famous and stuff on TV."

"I always think of my public. Mwah! Mwah!" she blew kisses from her palm as she backed toward the door.

Faith laughed and shook her head in the mirror as the hotel room door closed behind her. She contrasted it to how the woman had clung to her before during and after. It was as though when the lights went out, she took off a mask.

In thirty minutes she was enjoying the hotel's free breakfast, and the faintest waft of perfume when she arrived told her Taryn had done the same. Then she plugged the address of William Kopp's home into her cell phone, texted Cassius "twenty minutes away!" and left.

She followed the GPS directions, and for once it took her where she needed to go. Kopp's home was on the edge of a long residential through-street, and she pulled up and parked behind the detective's car. Not clear on where he was, she gave a quick honk with her horn and scanned the houses beside the road, but to her surprise the man stood up out of his car.

She got out and shook his hand. "I'm on time for once."

"Did you get lost?" he asked.

"Nah, I followed the GPS."

"It took you a roundabout way then. You should come up the street from the opposite direction if you come from Ithaca."

"Oh." She was about to explain she had been in Syracuse all night, but reconsidered. Detective McCrae was a great guy, but there were certain things he didn't need to know.

"Anyway, here's the old homestead," he said, motioning to one of the homes. It was an old single-story ranch, painted goldenrod yellow. Contrary to how she had envisioned the home or hideout of an apparent Christian terrorist would look, it was not run down and sinister-looking with cracked smoked glass and heaps of scrap machinery in the yard. Other than the long grass and stack of accumulated pizza and car wash flyers on its porch, it seemed like a home where one might find a sweet old couple doting on their soldier son overseas. It had new aluminum siding, a carefully patched concrete walk, and a U.S. flag, and the shingles and glass were all in apple-pie order.

"What did you say Kopp did for a living?"

"When he wasn't a doomsday preacher, he was a general contractor and carpenter."

Faith contemplated the trim house. Would someone who was building mystery weapons give such time and effort to keep their home perfect? That was incongruous.

"And you said there was nothing here?"

"No bomb making materials. Only his computer, filled with his hate mail, and boxes of vintage white supremacist propaganda. I mean, I should donate it to

211

the Southern Poverty Law Center for their archives, the stuff could make a historical exhibit. Judging by the dates on the material, this guy was a full-fledged Christian apocalyptic believer by the time he was ten. He's taken part in three 'end times' prophecy communities. He even gave up some family property in one of them back in 2011. You'd think a man would get happier after the world didn't end so many times in his life, but he got angrier."

"Huh. You'd think if he'd made a bomb of some kind, there'd be signs of that kind of work. You'd need materials, instructions, places to test things."

"Not a hint. There were plenty of reference works for electrical work and code, plumbing, and fire safety. The guy could have figured out how to burn down a building from those. But we found nothing which would explain the kind of heat we saw at your end."

"Can we go in?"

Cassius shrugged. "Sure. I didn't come here to show you the neighborhood." They walked up the cracked but neatly patched concrete walk and ducked under the tape, and he took a moment to gather up the accumulated flyers.

The house's interior was in gold and brown. Like the rest of the property, it was neat, but it had a spare feel to it, as if things were missing. After a moment, Faith had worked out what struck her as odd. First, everything in the place dated to the early nineties, but a new and large LCD TV took up a good portion of a wall. Over it hung an awkwardly high portrait of someone who, based on his wavy brown hair and beard, antique dress, and sad eyes, could only be Jesus. The picture was framed in knurled oak with gilt edges, whereas everything else in the place was in synthetics or vinyl. And there were no family pictures anywhere, and no other sign that Kopp had a wife, girlfriend, or child.

"Didn't you say Kopp had family?"

"Divorced over twenty years ago. I've talked to his wife. She's very Christian too, but she said he was too much for her.'"

"Huh. No sign of that family here."

"Nope. But he's not a loner. Has plenty of friends at his church, did charitable work for Habitat for Humanity, and I was even told he hosts a mean Super Bowl party. He told his friends this year's Super Bowl would be the last ever."

"If the rednecks are all going to heaven, there would have to be Super Bowl parties in the afterlife."

Cassius shook his head. "I hear you. The house is freaky. But let's not take cheap shots at a dead man. We're here on business on my weekend. So look around. Tell me what your fire and building inspection eyes see."

"A well-maintained, but not updated, home. This is a guy who knows everything about carpentry and nothing about color palettes."

"Alright. I'm with you so far."

She scanned the room. "He burned a lot of food, used to smoke, or doesn't change his smoke alarm batteries. I can see three smoke alarms from here and all their monitor lights are out."

"There's a wood stove in the kitchen."

"That explains this, then." She stood on the couch and popped the cover off one of the smoke alarms. It was a cheapie battery-driven "First Alert" stick-on, and it didn't even have a battery in it. "Wood stoves are a major cause of smoke alarm malfunction...and smoke alarm tampering."

"If that's true then we can't assume he disabled his alarms because he was playing with pyrotechnics," the detective observed. Faith replaced the cover and stepped down again, noticing as she did so another framed picture beside the couch. It was a print of a painting showing Jesus walking on the water toward a boat full of apostles.

"Even in your moments of doubt, the Lord will come for his sheep," read the brass plate.

She pointed. "Heavy on the Jesus art, huh?"

"It's the only image in this place. No pictures of family or friends. I had to get file photos from his wife."

She headed into the kitchen. Solid maple furniture which showed a lot of wear and care filled the open space, and a large rectangular wood stove filled one corner. She inspected it.

"Installed to code. Insulating rings, flexible metal ductwork, leading to a type two up-and-out chimney. I'm guessing it was a recent addition. Compared to the rest of the house."

"Alright. Nothing unusual, then?"

"Nope." She opened the stove and peered in. "He burns lumber scraps. There are a bunch of bent nailgun nails in the ashes."

"Not surprising for a contractor. He's also got a woodshop in his garage."

Faith perked up at this. "Let's have a look."

"Okay, but there was nothing much there. Just carpentry tools."

"If he was going to build bombs that's where he would do it. Lead on, Holmes," she replied. She followed him out the door at the far end of the kitchen into the garage.

The woodshop was as neat as the rest of the house. All-wood benches, clean tools, and a well-swept floor with no accumulation of sawdust put her at ease. Sawdust and metal dusts alike were common fire hazards in workshop spaces. But the back quarter of the workshop drew her attention. It was filled with three large wooden crosses laid on their sides and propped against the wall. These were sturdily made from pressure-treated four-by-fours, with scab plates nailed over the joints.

"Huh, guess he had a project underway."

"Probably a contract. I have no idea who all these trusses were for, and no one's come forward to claim them. I'll have to put a message into Habitat for Humanity and see if it was something he was working on for them."

"Maybe they are planter trees for a garden. They're pressure treated like they're meant to go outside, and I've seen people put those hanging tomato planters on wooden hangers."

"Yeah," said Cassius. "Maybe."

She wet the tip of one of her fingers on her tongue, ran it across the floor, and put it back in her mouth. She tasted grit from the concrete, bitterness from softwood and hardwood dusts, but not the metallic tangs of iron or aluminum dust for thermite, or even the eggy taste of sulphur for gunpowder. "Tastes like a straight woodshop. No sign of metalworking, and there are no tools for it."

"Let me give you a few minutes," he said. "We've been up and down this place, and I need a break on this guy. Maybe your fresh eyes will see something.

Faith stood, leaned back against the stack of wooden crosses, and scanned the room from her new vantage. "Maybe they built whatever it was at one of his accomplices' places."

"Both of them lived in apartments. They're small and if they'd been doing any machine work or construction, their neighbors would have noticed. We could tear them apart but I'm not going to until I'm sure what I need isn't here."

"How about another place? A storage area somewhere?"

Cassius shook his head. "Can't rule it out. But find me a storage area key or a bill and we can make a start."

"Maybe...Maybe their church?"

"We've been over their regular church. I'm looking for a way to get access to a Christian retreat center the three of them frequented, but I've got to establish a reasonable suspicion to convince a magistrate to give me a warrant. And that's not happening. I've been turned down once, and I want to build a strong case before I go back, because once a magistrate says 'no' to a warrant twice, don't bother to ask a third time."

"Huh. I guess we have to assume for a moment any clues we're going to find are right here." She shifted her seat on the stack of lumber trusses, surrendered her other thoughts, and tried to let the room speak to her.

David paged through the enrollment application to place Rosie in the coming fall's class in the Ithaca public schools. The packet Margrethe had sent him had a bewildering number of pamphlets from the state and county and a stack of forms from the local public schools.

It hadn't been this hard to send his own daughter to school. All he remembered about the process was immunizing Faith and walking her to the bus stop. If there had been anything else to the process, Constance had handled it, and since Constance had been a public school teacher, enrollment had probably been straightforward to her.

But now he was faced with this paperwork. He wondered why Child and Family Services couldn't handle this school enrollment process for him. He was, after all, a foster parent, not Rosie's actual parent, and they had done most of the work for her health care bills. But Margrethe's handwritten note to him was short and not helpful, and the forms were not much help either. For example, the "Special Education Application" had a block for a "diagnosis" for his foster daughter so the city could select appropriate services. David wondered how he should answer this. "Talks to God? Refuses to speak English?" Likewise under "special talents," should he list "eyes glow orange in low light" and "keen sense of smell?" alongside "learns languages fast?" And another form asked if she had an existing IHIP? What the heck was an IHIP?

In addition, the prospect of enrolling Rosie in school raised the question of how long she would stay with them. Under the current plan, as he understood it, Faith's investigation had to end, one way or another, in a few weeks. And Rosie's emergency foster care arrangement with him would run out before school began again in the fall. If he enrolled her, was he committing to be her foster parent through the school year?

He decided he was in over his head with this paperwork, and would call Child and Family services to ask these questions on Monday. He began to gather the documents back together when, at length, he heard the screen door piston hiss. He looked up to the door to see the blurred silhouette of his daughter through the chiseled window glass.

Faith had been out all night. It shouldn't bother him, he considered, he should be happy she was out and about. So he prepared a warm greeting for her as she came through the doorway.

"Welcome back! A good time was had by all, I hope!"

"Yeah, it was fun! I guess nineties music is kind of 'in' again, the Haunt was packed!"

David remembered the Haunt. It was a low single-story concrete masonry block building tucked away on the edge of a residential area in central Ithaca. When his daughter had first started going there, it had been painted in a woodland camouflage pattern. He had ordered a fire inspection of it when he'd learned it was where Faith went dancing, and would have closed it for safety reasons if she hadn't pleaded with him to block pyrotechnics but give them sixty days to fix the deficiencies. Since then, he hadn't heard of any problems with the place, and his daughter had been there on-again, off-again, ever since.

She walked past him, and he averted his eyes from a purple smear he spotted on her neck. It puzzled him. His initial impression was it was lipstick, but he decided it had to be a hickey instead. He changed the line of conversation to his present problem.

"I have a stack of papers to do if we're going to send Rosie to school."

Faith returned from the kitchen with a glass of water in her hand. Her squinty eyes and pained look told him volumes about her night. But she sat down next to him.

"That'll be challenging. Special education, do you think?" she speculated.

He nodded.

"Look at it this way. It'll give you your days back. You'll be able to go back to what you want to do."

David cracked his knuckles. "I guess I feel too involved. Someone who knows her better should be making these decisions."

She put one hand to her forehead and opened her eyes wider to give him a stare. He recognized it as his daughter's version of his wife's "get real" stare. "Dad, at this point, you know her better than anyone else on the planet that we know about. I'm sure you'll make the right decision. And you can't go wrong with Ithaca's schools."

David felt better. Faith was making good points. Sending Rosie to school would make his situation easier in the long run. And, while the paperwork might be a pain in the butt, it was true he knew the girl better than anyone else he could think of.

"Thanks. I'll stop whining now," he said.

She tipped back her glass of water and drank. "Another family service brought to you by your heathen offspring," she joked. "I'm going for a shower. Afterwards I might take Rosie horseback riding."

He glanced at his daughter. "Riding, huh?"

She shrugged. "I used to like it. We'll see if she does. No big deal if she doesn't."

Rosetta was less excited about the idea of going horseback riding than Faith had expected. When she was a girl, it had been her favorite thing, but Rosie just looked puzzled at the explanations of what was involved. Still, she got into her jeans and sneakers willingly and followed out to the car.

The route to the stables took Triphammer Road toward Aurora. To the left green fields turning blond at the coming of harvest sloped downward to the lake, and hand-painted signs were going up to advertise "fresh sweet corn" and "pick your own apples starting Aug. 15." She remembered how her father loved sweet corn.

She pulled over at the next roadside stand, and was pleased to recognize Imelda Fargo, a woman she had interviewed following the carriage house fire. It was unusual to have someone from Central America settle in the area. But her husband, Nahlem, had boasted during the interview about the woman's skill growing corn, and since corn was Nahlem's primary crop, she supposed the woman had come down in the right place in the United States.

Her English was less than perfect, but during the carriage house investigation the farmer's wife had been able to describe vividly enough the power brownout and sound of the explosion from the carriage house.

"Hey, remember me?" Faith chimed.

The older woman squinted at her. "Ah, yes. You are the *bombera.*"

"That's me! I'm here for a sack of your sweet corn," she said, reaching for her wallet. "My dad loves this stuff. Can you pick me your best?"

Imelda reached down behind the counter and began filling a sack. "I picked these this morning. *'Muy dulce.'* But it cost you extra." The woman's merry eyes twinkled at her as she pushed the sack across the table. "Sometimes I think my husband puts *asucar* on the ground to make it so sweet. It's not like we had in El Salvador."

Faith motioned to Rosie to take the sack of corn, and was about to formulate a pleasant goodbye when the farmer continued. "So, they not fix the stone house?"

She guessed the woman meant the carriage house. "Nope. Too expensive. When we're done investigating the fire, the owner will tear it all up."

"Ah," she said. "It was pretty. Too bad."

"Yes, I agree." She put her hand behind Rosie's back to guide the girl back to the car and signal an end to the conversation.

"Where they take the stone?" Imelda asked.

Faith ignored the error in tense. "The owner sold the salvage rights. That's all I know. They'll come for the stone when I'm done investigating it."

The woman smiled as if she only partly understood her. "*Buenos Dias.*"

"You too!" she replied. A moment later she and Rosie were back on the road. The girl peered into the sack of corn, and then peeled back the husks from one ear to examine the corn silk threads.

When they came up on the carriage house site, Faith gaped. The yellow "fire investigation-do not cross" tape she had set up was in tatters. As she pulled over and got out, open-mouthed, she saw the site was crisscrossed with truck and caterpillar tracks. The stone rubble, and the entire floor slab, glass, concrete, and all, was gone.

"What the fuck?" she exclaimed, remembering too late she was not alone. She wanted to jump back in the car and hop on the radio, but her personal car didn't have a radio in it. Instead, she reached for her cell phone and called Cassius.

Her foster daughter came and stood beside her, wide-eyed at the scene, and still holding the sack of corn. In a moment, the detective answered the phone.

"Hey Faith, what's up?" he answered.

"I'm at the carriage house scene. Someone's been here with heavy equipment. It looks like they ignored the fucking tape and dug everything up!"

The man sounded concerned, but his reply was the calm, thoughtful, sort she expected. "Huh. Guess the owner or the salvage company decided they wanted the stone *now,*" he answered.

"When I get in tomorrow, I'm calling up Finger Lakes Property Management and making a stink."

"Relax. You've already spent plenty of time on the site, and even the feds had been there to take their pictures and measurements. What more did you need from the site? We had to give the owner his access back sometime."

Faith considered this. "Okay, but we still can't have people trampling across fire investigation tape."

"I'm with you there. It's something we need to talk to the property managers about, but it's not an emergency in my mind. And I've got to get the family to church. Can we talk about this tomorrow?"

She concluded she had indeed overreacted. She was grateful Cassius was so patient with her. "I guess you're right. Talk to you tomorrow when I've chewed some ears off."

He laughed at this. "Take care."

"See you, Cash."

She glanced at Rosie, who was still standing beside her. She wondered if being at the scene of the fire would make the child anxious. But there was no sign of this: the girl stared up at the white fluffy clouds overhead, smiling at the sun. Faith followed her gaze to the blue sky. It was a beautiful day. She shouldn't let a greedy or stupid property manager ruin Rosie's fun. Or her own, for that matter.

"C'mon," she said, squeezing the girl's shoulder. "Let's go ride horses." They clasped hands and walked back to her car.

Rosie gaped at the animal Faith and her friend Whitney, a tall, elegant woman with gray hair, pulled up to her in an elaborate harness. The harness was ornamental, with shiny chrome disks and studs scattered through the leather pieces, and elaborate relief stamped into its leather strips. Large metal hoops hung from the side of the harness like enormous earrings. The harness was a strange piece of native art, she decided, unlike anything she had seen in the villages surrounding her laboratory or on any of her field trips.

In contrast, the animal strapped into the harness was familiar. After a moment of concentration and frowning, Rosie remembered that she had seen one of these creatures before, though the ones she had seen had been different colors. Back in her laboratory home, Nanny Wasilatu and other grown-ups taken her and the other older children on a bus ride through a wide grassy space called a "savannah." It had been filled with all sorts of wonderful animals, herds of small ones called gazelles, big ones with long necks called giraffes, and white and black ones called...

"*Zebro*," she said out loud. She knew it was a waste of breath, since no one would understand her Esperanto, but the word had come to her lips unbidden. The two women laughed, and their laughter felt a bit cruel to her in a special moment like this. But Faith's tone soon made it clear they weren't making fun of her.

"No, it's not a zebra! It's a horse! Zebra have black and white stripes, and I think they're smaller," her foster mother corrected.

"This horse is named Habakkuk," said the strange woman. "He's my oldest. He doesn't like to run anymore, so he gives people trail rides."

"*Chevalo*," Rosie corrected, recognizing the word as one which had come up in passages she had read about wars and soldiers. She hadn't known "horse" was a kind of zebra. This animal wasn't ready to kill anyone, though, and she wondered what people did to zebras like these to make them ready for war.

Rosetta's understanding of the situation gelled. As Faith had driven her car toward the sprawling white house and large red building which stood beside it, she had seen a wooden sign reading "Aurora Heights Farm - Riding Lessons - Trail Rides - Animal Therapy." The sign hadn't made much sense at the time, but now it did. Probably this horse had been used in a war, and now it was getting "animal therapy." Rosie had been sent to "therapy" once God had commanded her to speak only Esperanto. The therapist, she recalled, had tried to convince her God was not speaking to her, and had encouraged her to draw to express her feelings. Then the woman had given her pills she claimed would make the voice of God go away. She had obliged the woman by taking them, though they made her drowsy. When they hadn't worked (as she had suspected they wouldn't) it was the therapist who had suggested she needed to see an "expert" in the United States.

This meant that Whitney was the expert who did therapy for animals. Perhaps Habakkuk had been sent from far away, like she herself had. She took a step toward the zebra, and reached up to try and touch its snout, which was wrapped in a painful-looking leather muzzle.

"Here," Faith said, reaching into a pocket and producing a small rectangle wrapped in paper. "Horses like these, so you can feed him this. Hold it up to his nose." She unwrapped it, revealing a white cube of sugar.

"Faith Haversham," scolded the other woman, "I taught you to ride horses. I know you know better than to feed my horses sugar cubes."

The zebra responded to Whitney's tone with concern, turning away from Rosie and lifting his ears. Whitney stepped forward and reached into her own pocket, producing a chunk of a white carrot. "He likes parsnips, and they're better for him. Go ahead and feed him this."

Rosie took the carrot piece from the woman, and then offered it to Habakkuk. The zebra plucked it from her hand and gave a snort she interpreted as approval.

"They get along." Whitney concluded. While Habakkuk chewed up the carrot, she caught a glimpse of the zebra's tail flicking back and forth. She walked around the side to get a closer look at the tail, but the two women grabbed her.

"This is important. You can never walk behind a horse. He might kick you. And it would hurt a lot."

Whitney added an explanation. "Horses get frightened if there is something behind them they cannot see. So they kick to protect themselves. The best thing to do is never get close to a horse's rear. Do you understand?"

She nodded to the old woman, but she didn't think Habakkuk looked nervous. "Stand where I am, or closer to his nose," Whitney demonstrated, standing to one side of Habakkuk's right leg. She gave up on watching Habakkuk's tail and went back to stroking his nose.

"Okay, we'll show you how to get up on his back. Watch Faith."

At Whitney's prompting, her foster mother put a foot in one of the funny metal rings hanging from the harness, put a hand on the top of the harness and, to Rosie's horror, threw her other leg over the zebra's back and sat on him.

The girl didn't know what to say. She loved her foster mother, but this was a mean and senseless thing to do to a zebra. She thought of a scolding, and began to say it, but the blank expressions the women gave her showed her it was pointless. She tugged at Faith's leg and boot, and when the woman did not climb down off Habakkuk, put her face into the zebra's side and began to cry in frustration. She was angry with Faith for sitting on the zebra, angry with God for not letting her talk, and angry with Whitney for letting people sit on Habakkuk.

Whitney consoled her. "Oh, sweetheart, she's safe up there. She knows how to ride, and Habakkuk hass given hundreds of rides to people." The woman, who had been nice enough at the start, now seemed menacing. Whitney made zebras into slaves and let people sit on them for money. She was horrible.

Rosetta shrugged the woman off and continued to hug Habakkuk, until after a moment she felt a shift and heard a thump, and then Faith was standing beside her.

"Hey, honey, what's wrong? I'm okay. I did this a lot when I was your age. My mother and I did it together, like my mother and her mother did."

Rosie felt her anger and frustration with the situation abate. She wiped her eyes on her shirt sleeve and glared. But her anger subsided further when she realized something. Habakkuk didn't *smell* angry or afraid. His smell hadn't changed much at all when Faith had jumped up on him, or when she had jumped back down.

She dismissed this observation. Because Habakkuk didn't object to exploitation didn't make the situation any better. If Habakkuk was used to his lot of being sat on, or didn't feel he could object, she would stand up for him. She had seen how zebras were supposed to live. They were not supposed to be sat on. They didn't even like people. They ran away when people and cars got too close.

"Look, here, you try it. I'll show you how." Faith grabbed ahold of the metal loop twisted it around and pulled it toward her. "The first thing you need to do is put your right foot through this."

Rosie shook her head and laid her ear against Habakkuk's side, listening to his heartbeat. The women withdrew and began whispering to each other, but she tuned them out to listen to Habakkuk instead. Metal bits on the harness jingled, the leather squeaked as it stretched or rubbed on itself, and Habakkuk's heart thundered in her ears.

The two women stayed locked in intense conversation. "I've seen autistic children react like this on their visits, Faith."

"She's not autistic, they've tested her."

"Autism is a spectrum. Maybe she's mildly autistic. What do they call it? Some syndrome?"

"Aspergers."

Rosie objected to this discussion of illness. Why did everyone always think every way she was not like them made her sick? And why was it her fault God had told her to speak Esperanto? That wasn't an illness, that was doing what God told her to do. As if she had a choice, anyway. Even in her moments when she despaired, disobeyed, and tried to speak English, all she could do was gurgle.

At any rate, Habakkuk the zebra stood still and didn't mind her. So she stood with him, ready to confront the two women if they approached to try and sit on him again. She didn't know what she could do, but she would try to stop it.

After a moment, Whitney came forward again.

"Okay, you're upset, honey. That's fine. You don't have to ride Habakkuk if you don't want to."

Rosie turned her face into the zebra's flank. The evil woman's friendliness made her feel warier.

"Listen, we can take the horse for a walk. You won't have to ride him, but the rule is you have to hold this rope, this 'lead.' The reason we have this rule is because horses are bigger than people, so we don't let them run around free. If we did, the horse might hurt someone by mistake, or they might run in front of a car and get hurt themselves. So you need to hold onto this lead to keep him safe. You won't even have to pull on him, he'll follow you because you're holding it. Do you want to hold it?"

Rosie regarded the end of the rope. She wasn't sure she believed the stories about the zebra getting hurt or hurting someone else if it ran away. But holding the rope was less obnoxious than sitting on the zebra, and it gave her an idea. At the woman's gentle insistence, she took the rope, and when the woman stepped back, she dropped it and looked to Habakkuk.

"*Run!*" she said in Esperanto. The zebra stood there, watching the rope swing from its nose.

Whitney stepped forward, grabbed the end of the rope, and handed it back to her. "You have to hold onto it. I'm sure Habakkuk would like to go for a walk in those fields," she pointed to the grasslands which ran down to the lake, "but he won't get the chance if you don't hold his lead."

Rosie took hold of the rope again, trying to puzzle out Habakkuk's reaction. Why hadn't he fled?

"Come on," said Whitney. "Follow me around, sweetheart, and he'll follow you." Whitney began to walk backwards toward the fence, and Rosie took a few steps after her. Sure enough, Habakkuk followed her, and soon Whitney was leading them both in a big circle around the inside of the fenced-in area."

"There you go. He needs his exercise, and you're helping him get it. Without people to visit him, he'd sit in his stable all day, eat hay, and get fat."

Rosie doubted that story. Without people, zebras walked all day, ate grass, played with other zebras, and stayed muscular. She had seen it with her own eyes.

On their second lap around, Whitney motioned to Faith, and then opened a gate in the fence. Beyond the gate lay a dirt path which passed through a thin line of trees and into wide open grassland dotted with flowers and crisscrossed by birds and insects. "Okay, now, keep doing what you're doing, and we'll take Habakkuk for a walk on this trail. He walks this trail all the time, and he likes it. But because of the rules about horses, you have to keep holding his rope. Can you do this for me?"

Rosetta looked up at Habakkuk. Even though the fence was now wide open, the zebra showed no sign, and gave no smell, which suggested he would run away and be free. So she supposed she would hold the rope and pretend to go along, and if he gave her a sign she he wanted to run, she could drop it. They could be conspirators.

She nodded to Whitney, and Whitney stood aside and motioned for her to pass through the gate. She led Habakkuk through the brief shade of the trees, and out into the bright sunlight again. She was grateful, given the intensity of the sun in the still air, that Faith had insisted she wear her blue baseball hat with gold stars and EU on it.

As Rosie walked down the path, Habakkuk followed her, leaving plenty of slack in the lead, and the women walked on either side of the zebra. She faced front to avoid stumbling, and marveled at the colors of the flowers and the birds. There were even some butterflies, but they were different, and much smaller, than those which had visited the laboratory gardens where she had lived before. She became distracted, as she always did, by the reflection of God's love and design in this amazing world.

It took her by surprise, then, when her lead went taut. Habakkuk was ready to make his run for it! She dropped the rope, turned around, and clapped her hands in delight to celebrate Habakkuk's escape, but stopped a second later. Habakkuk was not running, but bending his head to the ground to eat a strange, round, purple flower growing there.

"Oops! Here you go," said Whitney, catching the rope and returning it to her to hold again. "He stopped for some clover. It's his favorite thing. If you want him to keep following you, tug on the lead and he'll come. He's not missing anything. The clover will be here all summer."

Rosie would do no such thing, she resolved. If Habakkuk wanted to eat clover, she would let the zebra have it. She let the lead hang slack, and after locating some more clover nearby, plucked the flower out of the ground and carried it to Habakkuk. Habakkuk took it from her hands, and there the two of them stood, the girl plucking whatever clover she could reach, and the zebra eating it as fast as she could find it.

Whitney stood back and watched. Faith ducked under Habakkuk's lead to avoid going behind the zebra, and stood beside her. She shook her head and mumbled. Rosetta felt no sympathy. If the woman was disappointed she couldn't ride Habakkuk, she'd have to live with it. No one would ride this zebra as long as Rosie held the rope.

"Some things don't turn out like you plan, do they?" sympathized

Whitney.

"Nope. I don't even know why I make plans anymore. They never survive the first minute of reality," answered Faith. "Especially when they involve this kid."

"Let the moment be. What you're seeing is all that needs to happen today. You can come on back and there will be a next time. The farm's not going anywhere. If she wants to feed the horses bring her back and I'll teach her to brush them, too. No charge."

Rosie smiled at this remark. Despite Whitney's evil trade, the woman understood the value of one of God's moments. Habakkuk tickled her hand with his lips as he pulled her most recent handful of clover from her grasp. She laughed out loud at the bright sun, and enjoyed the moment with the butterflies and zebras which made her think of her faraway home and her friends.

Chapter 16

Case Closed

Faith made a point of driving in early the next morning. She wanted to get a few things done before calling Finger Lakes Property management, but she planned to start the fall school fire inspections at noon. The only way to squeeze in enough time to do a proper "don't tamper with fire scenes under penalty of law" speech to the property managers would be if she started before she clocked in. So she walked by the timecard machine and went right to her office. When she rounded the corner from the main hall to the fire prevention office, she was surprised to see Agents Foxworth and Ingle waiting there. She froze with her office key in her hand.

"Hey guys," she said. "You looking for me?"

Both the men straightened themselves. "Good morning, Inspector," said Ingle.

"Yes, we were looking for you," added Foxworth.

"You guys need to talk to me about the carriage house fire? Have I got a story for you. I passed by the site yesterday and someone had-"

"We should talk in your office," said Ingle in a low voice.

"Okay," Faith agreed. She opened the office, went to hang up her uniform jacket, and motioned to some chairs. Foxworth closed the office door behind them and turned the lock. Something about his expression raised some apprehension. Karl knew all about the carriage house fire, in fact, most people in the headquarters knew about it. So why lock the door?

She regarded the two men. "Alright, so, what's up guys? You're acting kinda secret-squirrely."

Foxworth took a seat. "Inspector, have you spoken to any media about the carriage house fire?"

"Umm, sure. But not a lot. The Ithaca Times ran a story on it after the fire. I talked to their gal then."

Foxworth seemed relieved. "Any interest since then?"

Faith pursed her lips and recalled. "She called a couple of times to see how the investigation was coming along. I said we had no resolution and I'd let her know when I was ready to talk about it. She'll hold me to that, I'm sure, since it's not often someone dies around here, so it sells papers."

"What's the reporter's name?" asked Ingle.

They were talking an awful lot about the media and not at all about the fire. But whatever hesitation she felt about sharing her media contacts with the agents was overwhelmed by her anxiousness to keep her lesbian identity hidden. "Taryn Thompson or something. Brunette. Kind of hyper. This tall," she indicated. "Why?"

"Okay, so it is her who contacted you," said Ingle with concern. "You're not the only lead she's been following up on this case. She's getting in over her head, and, as I'm sure you know, some of the parties involved in this case are dangerous people. If she contacts you again, please refer her to us. If she continues down the road she's headed on she'll end up in big trouble."

She nodded. When she reflected on Taryn, the woman was someone

222

whose attitudes and methods could get her into trouble in a hurry. When Ingle and Foxworth relaxed, she returned to the statement she'd been trying to make. "Hey, about the case," she began, "I should tell you guys something. The owners have salvaged the fire site. Everything is gone. The stone rubble, the slab-"

"Yeah, it wasn't the owners, that was us," said Foxworth.

"Oh," said Faith. She sat down and swiveled her chair to face them. "Nice of you guys to tell me, I was about to rip Finger Lakes Property Management a new asshole."

Ingle reassured her. "It's alright. It's a good thing. The Department of Homeland Security has taken your case. They made the call Friday evening. Since all they have in Ithaca is a recruiter, we're handling the investigation for them until they can get someone up here."

She blinked in confusion. "And they tore up the scene as part of the investigation?"

"They wanted the salvage for petrographic analysis and further tests. The results their investigator brought back were so...unique they were concerned there might be a novel type of technology involved. So they wanted the rubble."

"They needed all of it? They couldn't take just part of it? How am I supposed to finish this investigation with the scene gone?"

"You don't need to worry. We and Homeland Security will take it from here. Your investigation was excellent, and, in fact, we've put you in for a commendation for it."

"A commendation?"

"Homeland Security Commendation Medals for you and Detective McCrae. Not promising they will go through, but your work was excellent."

"And timely," added Ingle.

"Okay, so what about the girl?" Faith continued.

The two agents blinked at each other. "Oh, you mean the potential witness found at the scene,"

"Yeah. Rosie."

"We have the transcript of her account you got from Cornell. Has she said anything else of interest since?"

"No," she said.

"And she's in local foster care with your father, correct?"

"That's right."

"I'm sure Homeland Security will contact you if they have any further questions for her. But given her disability, they may not consider her an important source of information."

"But what about sending her home? I'm still trying to find her parents. Will they keep looking for her family?"

Foxworth turned to Ingle, and Ingle leaned back. She recalled that Foxworth was the expert on human trafficking. Ingle, however, cleared his throat and spoke for the two of them. "Child welfare is a state issue. If the state has awarded foster care to your father, then we don't have a thing to say about it at the federal level. I'm sure if they stumble across the information, they'll forward it to you or to us, but the principal concern of DHS is whatever weapon was used here, not the origins of the girl."

Faith sighed. "Great," she said.

"Sorry," Ingle apologized. "Final disposition of children belongs to state authorities."

"Alright. So what now? If the investigation is over, do I need to do anything else?"

Foxworth shook his head. "We'll need your computer and whatever cameras or other digital devices you used during the investigation."

"What?" she gaped.

"We need to secure any records relating to this. We're authorized to provide comparable replacements from nearby commercial sources. Staples has a good supply of cameras and computers which might suit your needs. We can go there today to minimize your inconvenience, or if you prefer, we could reimburse your department."

"But all my work is on the computer!" She clutched her laptop defensively. "All my fire inspection schedules, inspection records, deficiencies. I need the data from the computer!"

Foxworth's face softened. "Alright, one public servant to another, would you say the other data you have there is irreplaceable and essential to the provision of municipal services or governance?"

"Yeah," said Faith. "Without it, I lose track of who I'd agreed to inspect when and who still has fire safety violations still outstanding. It's not a matter of convenience, it's a matter of public safety."

"Then we'll make an exception," said Foxworth, producing a USB drive from his pocket. "You can move the data onto this drive before we take your computer. We can make an argument that letting you keep the data is justified for reasons of municipal governance. You show me what files to copy, and I'll inspect them and move them to the drive. I have to do all the moving so I can be sure you're not keeping any files related to this investigation."

Faith stared at the drive in disbelief. Could they take her computer from her? She sat down in Karl's chair, and Foxworth and Ingle took this as a signal. Foxworth opened his steel clipboard, fixed a piece of paper under the clip, and handed it to her.

"Read this," he said. "Let me know if you have any questions." She began to read.

"To whom it may concern,

"The United States Secretary of Homeland Security issues this National Security Letter pursuant the USA Patriot Act, title V. Disclosure of the existence and contents of this National Security Letter is grounds for arrest and imprisonment under the USA Patriot Act, title V.

"The State of New York and its agencies and executors will surrender any records concerning the fire and explosion on Aurora Road in or near the village of Cayuga Heights, New York. After transfer, the State of New York and its agencies and executors will destroy any duplicates. Any records discovered after initial transfer and purge are to be considered TOP SECRET and surrendered to responsible federal authorities as a matter of national security.

"The Secretary of Homeland Security, after consultation with the Secretary of Defense, has determined the preponderance of the evidence suggests that the aforementioned fire and explosion were consequent to an act or conspiracy of foreign or domestic terrorism. New York State and its agents and executors will immediately suspend and close local investigations of these events and forward inquiries from the media or the next of kin of any deceased to the Department of Homeland Security. The State of New York and its agencies and executors will not discuss this case further than institutionally necessary to suspend and close investigations with anyone but a duly authorized agent of the Department of Homeland Security or the Department of Defense.

"Public knowledge of the details of this event(s) could cause alarm and upheaval and undermine national resolve. Agents of the Executive and the States

224

are directed to proceed with discretion. Knowingly releasing or distributing details of this case to the media or unconcerned public may be punishable as fearmongering under the USA Patriot Act, Title V, as amended.

> *"By order of the President,*
> *Bailey Harbour,*
> *Secretary of Homeland Security"*

The office emptied around four in the afternoon. Shawn waited alongside Dr. Teschke, who, rather than waiting in her office, was sitting on Rosetta's stool, smiling and humming to herself. He wondered what was making the older woman so cheerful, but didn't feel it was his place to ask. He decided to pump the professor for some guidance and reassurance instead.

"What if she has another seizure?" he worried to the professor.

"Then do what you did last time. Mr. Haversham and I will be across the arts quadrangle at Zeus's Cafe, and my phone will be on this time. Ring if there's a problem and we'll come back."

"Why don't you stay for the interview, Doc?" he persisted.

The professor frowned. "When the situation requires I will stay. As I did when Mr. Kay was translating for us. But with me unable to even understand her speech, there is no reason for me to remain. You must develop interviewing skills and technique on your own."

"I'd feel better if there was someone else here," Shawn replied, remembering the suspicion the emergency room doctor had radiated when he had been dissatisfied with the description of Rosetta's seizures. The word of a black man didn't go far against the word of a white woman, or in particular a white girl, and the arrangement made him feel vulnerable.

"As an academic linguist, there will be times when you must work one on one, either with students of the opposite sex or with interviewees. Insisting on a second person present will make your research more costly and complicate forming a rapport with some subjects who hesitate to speak in front of a group," the professor replied. "If you're concerned about protecting yourself from suspicion, be sure your recording device is working."

The professor's matter-of-fact replies indicated the conversation was now closed as far as she was concerned. And Shawn knew better than to tangle with the woman when her mind was made up. But he knew Dr. Teschke was not the only one with a vote in the situation.

Soon enough, Mr. Haversham came through the office door along with Rosie. The girl bounced over to the stool and took it while the professor rose, and Shawn exchanged a wave with Mr. Haversham before he became distracted by the professor. He popped his question, confident the doctor would not dress him down for it in public. "Sir, you aren't staying for the interview?"

Mr. Haversham looked confused. "Should I?"

He shrugged to the older man. "I thought you might. I mean, after what happened before," he pointed out. Dr. Teschke arched her eyebrows at him, but said nothing. David pondered the question.

"I guess I see your point. Do you feel as though you need me here?" the man asked.

Shawn mulled the question and his feeling of vulnerability. His answer surprised him. "Not if I have your confidence, sir."

The older man nodded. "I think I understand where you're coming from.

From time to time I wonder what might be said or suspected about my relationship with Rosetta if something went wrong."

"Yes, that's it," he confirmed. "Since I'm black-"

David raised his hands. "You handled the situation last time." The man's remark and tone reassured him. "Do the same thing if something happens, and we'll try to react better." He then turned to the professor. "Would it be better if I stayed, Hildegard? We could always get coffee another time."

Mr. Haversham's use of Dr. Teschke's first name made Shawn's ears prick up. Were the professor and this man forming a personal relationship outside of the interviews? It could be another, and less professional, explanation for the professor's flat reluctance to stay for this interview. It would mean he was not only interviewing the girl, but kind of...babysitting her for a bit. A more coherent explanation for what was going on gelled in his mind.

Dr. Teschke's answer was quick and displeased. "There's no need. I think Mr. Douglas is feeling anxious is all. It's understandable but it's something he *needs to overcome.*"

If his misgivings were understandable, he heard no hint in the professor's voice that they were understood. His gambit had failed, but he had learned a tasty morsel about the professor in the process. "We could go out for coffee another time..." he recalled Mr. Haversham's words and grinned.

"Thanks, sir, I'm glad you feel that way. I wanted to be sure you were comfortable leaving her with me."

"No problem," Mr. Haversham answered. "We'll be over at...at the place with all the statues. Pagan's Cafe."

"Zeus's Cafe," the professor corrected with a visible flinch at the error.

"Okay, see you in an hour," Shawn waved. The doctor left without saying another word to him, and Mr. Haversham followed her out. The door closed with a bang, leaving him alone with Rosie.

He straightened his papers, started the voice recorder, and then gave his mouse a quick shake to wake up his computer before he began with Rosie. To his surprise, the markers and paper he had left out for her were as yet untouched. The child's eyes were instead focused on him, with the same passive, heavy stare he had seen before in Sage Chapel.

"*Uh oh.*" His dread had not even faded before Rosetta began to speak, her voice again that odd combination of whisper, childlike, and basso profundo.

"No church serves God, but a priest may serve God through his choices."

"Gabriel?" Shawn greeted.

"Recite," said the girl and her voices.

He looked to the door, hoping something would draw Dr. Teschke and Mr. Haversham, or even a random other person, to the office in time to see this for themselves. Something told him, however, that the chance of this was zero.

"Recite!" repeated the voice. The change in tone rattled him a bit. But her eyes weren't glowing this time. The light was different. He supposed this explained it.

Shawn tried to marshal a manlier voice and more confidence in his wording than he had the last time. "Oh, Allah! All glory is due you, I praise you-"

Rosie shook her head. "Recite what I have revealed to you."

"Oh," he corrected himself. "No church serves God, but a priest may serve God through his choices," he repeated. For some reason, the words came to his tongue as if he had been born saying them.

"Thus sayeth the Lord," she concluded.

"Thus sayeth the Lord," he answered.

"You now have the revelation," said the girl, her eyes still unblinking. Shawn stood and moved toward her, ready to catch her if she fainted away again. But she simply watched him as he moved. When they had stared at each other for a moment, the girl and her whispering, booming voice spoke again.

"I have a limited amount of energy and time I can use to inhabit this form. Ask questions but choose them well. The harder the questions, the fewer I may answer before I depart."

"What makes a question hard or easy to answer?" he asked. He was curious how a servant of an omnipotent God could strain himself answering spoken questions, but he would take Gabriel's statement at face value. For the time being, anyway.

"The more...probabilities or outcomes my answers affect...the more energy I must consume to give the answer. The less energy I have, the shorter the time I can remain." Rosetta's brow was furrowed as if Gabriel was straining to put this reply into words.

Shawn drew a breath. Like the poor soul in the desert who rubbed a lamp and could ask three wishes of a genie, he had to be careful what he asked. He had to make the questions good, but perhaps not too good.

"Gabriel, is there a God?"

Rosetta was expressionless. "To transmit a nuanced answer to that question would take exactly one iota more energy than exists in your universe. The only way that answer can exist in your creation is if it emerges from within it."

He twisted one of his locks in concentration. If he was indeed speaking to Gabriel, Herald of Allah, shouldn't the angel answer "yes," and eliminate any uncertainty? He considered what his next question would be.

"Why do you possess this girl? I mean, this girl, specifically?"

Rosetta's eyes showed no mirth, but the corners of her lips did turn up in a faint smile. "She is the creation of a creation. She is the corner of the world the doubters and the heedless believe furthest removed from the Lord, yet she knows Him every moment. She is the contradiction which shows the divine ubiquitousness. She is so open to Him that through her We may speak."

Shawn absorbed this. "I don't understand." But Rosetta supplied no more help from Gabriel. Her answer, however, had helped him formulate another question. "What language do you speak to me?"

"The true name of the tongue does not exist within the tongue. It is a tongue of tongues," Gabriel replied. "It is known by all creation."

He thought about this. "If it's known to all creation, why does it sound like gibberish to everyone else who hears my recordings of you speaking?"

Gabriel was nonplussed by the question. "Because I was not speaking to them. Had I spoken to anyone else, you would not have understood me."

Shawn made a mental note to look up the term "tongue of tongues," but felt frustrated Gabriel's answers were not bringing any immediate enlightenment. Instead, the angel was just giving him "spooky answers at a distance." He wondered why it was. Maybe that was a good question to ask.

"Why do you answer my questions in riddles?" he challenged the angel.

At this, Rosetta smiled, a warm, fraternal smile.

"This is a wise question. There is a limit to the amount of understanding that may flow through this gateway and this mortal frame. To give you even a fraction of a complete answer to many mysteries would take so much energy and probability that my gateway to this person would close for a long time, for longer than your lifetime. It is more efficient and

227

HELPFUL TO MANKIND TO ANSWER YOU WITH CLUES AND LET YOU GROW TO FULL UNDERSTANDING THROUGH YOUR OWN EXPERIENCE OF CREATION. THUS I CAN TRANSMIT A LITTLE, SPEAK LONGER, AND YOU WILL COME TO UNDERSTAND MUCH." Rosetta spread her hands, palm upward, in a gesture of patience which echoed Gabriel's tone. "EVENTUALLY."

Shawn paused. "Eventually," he repeated in dismay. He had heard the word his whole life. Eventually he would be a grown up. Eventually black men and women would be equal to white men and women. Eventually his brothers and friends would stop killing each other before their lives had even begun. Eventually a million things would be better. He was tired of eventually. He was tired of "God," "the Man," and "eventually."

"Fuck eventually. What the hell," he figured. *"If I've got God on the line, why not go for broke?"*

He felt an urge to challenge Gabriel and his pat but cryptic answers to simple questions. "Okay. So what is the most important riddle, then?" he challenged.

Rosetta's expression grew serious. "IF I ANSWER THIS QUESTION, I WILL HAVE TO GO FOR NOW. I HAVE TO BE CONSERVATIVE, EVEN A SMALL OVEREXPENDITURE OF ENERGY CAN LEAVE THIS CHILD UNCONSCIOUS FOR SOME TIME. ARE YOU SURE YOU WISH ME TO ANSWER IT? I WILL NOT ANSWER MORE QUESTIONS AT THIS MEETING."

Shawn weighed his choices. The biggest riddle seemed worth a pause in these interviews. "Yes. Please give me the biggest clue."

Rosetta sighed. "THIS ANSWER WILL CONSUME THE ENERGY I HAVE LEFT, AND I WAS ENJOYING TALKING TO YOU. BUT THE GREATEST RIDDLE IS THE EXISTENCE OF LOVE. LOVE ELUDES THE SEARCHER AND STALKS THE UNWARY, REDEEMS THE UNWORTHY, HUMBLES THE MIGHTY, IS BOTH THE LAW AND THE LAW-BREAKER, AND IS FOREVER UNCOUNTED IN SATAN'S ABACUS OF GOLD. THE CHANCE TO GRASP THE MEREST FRACTION OF LOVE WHILE LIVING SUFFICES TO INSPIRE MANY TO SUICIDAL FOLLY, YET THE TOTALITY OF LOVE AWAITS YOU ONLY AT YOUR DEATH. THE EXISTENCE OF LOVE IS THE RIDDLE. THINK ON THIS."

He blinked. "Love is the answer? That cheesy old chestnut?" he said out loud, but then wished he hadn't. He watched Rosetta to see any signs he had offended Gabriel.

Rosetta blinked, and Gabriel corrected him. "I DID NOT SAY 'LOVE IS THE ANSWER.' I SAID THE *EXISTENCE* OF LOVE IS THE *RIDDLE*. I SPENT MUCH ENERGY TO TELL YOU. SO REMEMBER MY REPLY."

"Love is not the answer, but love is the riddle." Shawn repeated.

"THE *EXISTENCE* OF LOVE IS THE RIDDLE," corrected Gabriel. "GOODBYE. WE WILL SPEAK AGAIN." Rosetta looked sad. She slipped off her stool, took two steps away from the chair, and lay down on the vinyl office floor.

"I WILL LIE THIS BLESSED CREATURE DOWN SO SHE IS NOT HARMED WHEN I GO," said Gabriel. "I REGRET THAT I WAS NOT SO AWARE LAST TIME OF MY IMPACT UPON HER, AND I AM THANKFUL YOU WERE THERE. CARE FOR HER, SHAWN SON OF FRANCIS, FATHER OF THEODOSIUS. SHE IS BELOVED OF US." "Beloved of us," came through in Rosetta's normal voice, even the whispers had faded.

"I will," Shawn said. Gabriel made no reply, and Rosetta closed her eyes. In a moment, she was sleeping.

He bent down. "Rosie." He whispered. She did not respond, but her eyes opened. He shook her shoulder gently. "Rosie?"

She lay there, peacefully sleeping.

He growled in frustration. He felt in his pocket for his cell phone. As he searched for Dr. Teschke's contact in his contact list, however, the girl sat up.

"Hello," she said in Esperanto, rubbing one eye with the back of her hand.

"Was that enough wine for you?"

Relief overtook him, and he snapped his phone shut. To be sure, she had been channeling Gabriel and doing her weird voice thing again, and she had been unconscious for a minute. But now she was awake, speaking Esperanto. If he pretended it never happened, it would avoid a lot of questions.

Rosetta stood, dusted off her clothes, sat at the stool, and turned to the marker and paper.

"Clouds. Arms like six hundred clouds," Shawn thought she said. He let the phrase pass. Without the context of a question he had phrased, he must be mistranslating whatever she was saying. He watched her for signs of unsteadiness or discomfort. But, for all his caution, all he heard was the "pop" of a magic marker cap coming off and then the squeak of a felt tip on paper.

Shawn glimpsed the time. He still had forty-five minutes left. If he worked at it and Rosie cooperated, he could ask enough questions and get enough answers that no one would suspect a thing had happened.

Shawn relaxed as the office door opened. He and Rosetta were nearing the end of their interview, and he was tired. He hoped it might be Mr. Haversham and Dr. Teschke at the door returning a bit early. Instead, the caller was a dark-haired man he recognized as one of the instructors of Farsi.

"Mr. Yedida?" he asked. The man turned from where he had been frowning at Dr. Teschke's closed and dark office door.

"Yes? How are you? The professor wanted to see me."

"She did. About Rosie." Shawn motioned to Rosetta, who stood up and did her curious bow.

"Ah, about a girl?" said Mr. Yedida, growing closer. "I'm not sure why. Should I know her? Does she want to learn Farsi?"

"Actually, no. We had heard you were Baha'i."

Mr. Yedida walked up to Rosetta. He was a tall man, a head taller than Shawn himself, and the vertical stripes in his dark wool suit pants and vest accented his height. The hand he held out was smudged with whiteboard ink, but Rosetta took no notice as she clasped it.

Mr. Yedida showed no surprise at either Rosetta's adult-like handshake or the discussion of his religion.

"I am a Baha'i, as it happens. In fact, I just came back from pilgrimage at the start the summer semester."

Shawn nodded as if he understood what the pilgrimage implied. He had no idea but didn't want to offend. "We were wondering if you spoke Esperanto."

This remark drew Mr. Yedida's attention back to him. He shook the man's offered hand. "Yes, I do. An interesting question. Not many people know some Baha'is study international auxiliary languages."

"Thanks to her, we've had to do our homework. Many people who might have studied Esperanto in the past are less forthcoming about it now. It took us a long time to find you."

"And yet I work downstairs from you," said the man. "Strange how little we know about each other. Let's correct this over lunch someday. So, does the young lady speak Esperanto, too?"

At this question, Rosetta began babbling away. Mr. Yedida's eyes widened in surprise, and he answered. Soon the older man and the child were carrying on animated conversation.

"She tells me she meets with you twice a week, or more, and God told her to speak Esperanto," he repeated. He gave no sign he thought this odd.

"Yes, it's true. And I've been studying Esperanto since she was brought to us so we can interview her. She's an orphan, and we're trying to find her parents."

"It might be simpler to find someone who speaks her native language," Mr. Yedida suggested.

"Umm...Esperanto is her primary language," Shawn explained. Mr. Yedida went from wide-eyed to bug-eyed, and resumed the conversation. After a few minutes of back and forth, Rosetta sat back down at her markers and began tapping one on her paper, and Mr. Yedida faced him.

"Remarkable. She speaks like a poet." He pulled up a chair sat to watch the girl.

"I have some phrases and passages in her speech which are giving me trouble. And our last Esperantist was reluctant to help me more than once, since he's afraid he'll end up on a list."

"He's correct. He would end up on a list. The reasons I'm not hiding my knowledge of Esperanto are that I'm a Baha'i and an Iranian. Those two facts put me on a number of lists which are a great deal shorter and more dangerous," Mr. Yedida grinned and stuck his hands in his pockets. "But I've lived a Baha'i, and I'll die a Baha'i. Whoever wants to come for me can come.

"In any case, show me your passages and I'll help you," he said. Shawn began to shuffle through his collection of transcripts to the places he had marked, and then Professor Teschke and Mr. Haversham pushed in through the door.

"Ah, Mr. Yedida, thanks for coming!" the doctor said, crossing the room to shake his hand. "I see Mr. Douglas has already explained to you our predicament with the young lady."

"Yes," the man replied. He offered his handshake then to Mr. Haversham.

"Have we met, sir?"

"I'm David Haversham, her foster father."

"Ah. That must be challenging, unless you also speak Esperanto."

"Just a few words from the internet. Not a lot. I'm too old a dog for new tricks."

Mr. Yedida sat again, and picked up the texts. He retraced his finger over some lines. "Remind me to discuss with you your use of prepositions." He read further, and then stopped and leaned over the text. A moment later, he laughed and laughed.

Everyone except Rosie watched him, all faces waiting for an explanation. But then he kept reading. After finishing a good half of Shawn's collected and transcribed texts, he asked a question.

"Let me guess. You are having trouble translating because of words like this. 'Friend, beloved, thief, inn, wine, flower?"

"No, I know what those words mean," said Shawn.

"You do? As in, you can look them up in a dictionary and translate them?" Shawn nodded.

"That's your problem. She is not literally talking about those things. They are metaphors, or code words, for other things. She is a Sufi, unless I'm mistaken, or in any case, she's using these words as a Sufi would use them."

He looked up to blank stares all around. "Do you know what I mean by 'Sufi?" The professor and David shook their heads. But Shawn remembered what he had learned about them.

"The Sufi are Muslims. Pacifist Muslims, not accepted by militant strains of Islam. They are famous for their poetry."

Mr. Yedida was surprised at his knowledge. "Not exactly, but that's a good start. Sufis are Muslims who believe union with the divine, with Allah, can be achieved in life by those who abandon their will to the divine and live in perfect consonance with his plan. They often spend much of their life in service to the poor or studying with a Sufi master. Sufis lace their writing with symbols and metaphors which reflect their appreciation for the mystical side of religion. As a result, some Muslims regard Sufi poetry, writing and song as the most beautiful and inspired in all Islam, and others regard it as contrary to the Qur'an or traditional Islamic law. In Talibani Pakistan and Afghanistan, for example, books of Sufi poetry are burned when they are found and their owners are killed. In Saudi Arabia, however, these books are the best-sellers outside the Qur'an itself.

"Similar metaphors and symbols are used in Baha'i writing, so I can help you understand them. If you give these words which are giving you trouble their symbolic meanings, what she is saying becomes more understandable. For example, she talks here about this person 'Gabriel' who is her beloved. 'The beloved' or 'the friend' are words the Sufi often use to describe God. In fact, that's one of the reasons some Muslims consider their poetry blasphemous, because some of their poetry can sound like erotic or romantic personal poems to God. If you believe this Gabriel is not a person, but an angel, then what she is saying is not that Gabriel is her lover, but that Gabriel is her link to God, or the emanation of God in her life. The Esperanto word for 'beloved' is what she even gave you for her last name.

"Wine is another such word. A devout Muslim, and this would include Sufis, would not drink wine or other alcohol. It is forbidden, just as it is for Baha'is. Instead, they use wine as a word to mean 'divinely given ecstasy' or 'wisdom revealed by God.' A 'drunk' Sufi is one who has become overwhelmed by his personal relationship with God and is thus joyful, not one who is drunk from alcohol. If you follow."

Shawn took back some of the texts from Mr. Yedida, who leaned over to hand them back to him. "I have to say, it's what makes these transcripts so amusing. You are studying Esperanto and using it to ask sensible questions. And she is too 'drunk,' in the Sufi sense, to answer you.

"So, there is your mystery. Study some Sufi poetry, and I expect you'll find her a lot more understandable. If you cannot read Arabic, allow me to suggest the collection of Hafiz's poems called <u>The Gift</u>."

Shawn paged through his transcripts. Seen in this light, many of the things Rosie said were no less odd, but less disturbing and more appropriate to the context they occurred in.

"So it's safe to say she's not sleeping with this person Gabriel?"

Mr. Yedida shook his head. "I think you should view that statement as metaphorical unless you have evidence to the contrary."

Mr. Haversham interrupted. "Do you think this person Gabriel is a real person or the angel of the Bible? Because there are policemen searching for Gabriel."

The Iranian retrieved the papers from Shawn's hand and paged through them again with a serious expression. "I think she is speaking of the angel, not a person named Gabriel. Whether or not you think Gabriel the angel is real is a question of your faith, I suppose." He returned the papers. "If the policemen should apprehend the herald of God, please let me know. I'd be fascinated to meet him," he said with a wink.

Mr. Yedida then checked his watch. "I have to go. We have a large group of Army officers here for the summer to learn Farsi. I have many papers to grade and I was not expecting to stay this long. But please, feel free to come visit me if you have more questions."

Dr. Teschke nodded in return. "We'll talk about this later, Ibrahim. But it's good to know you're close at hand. It simplifies a great many things."

Rosetta handed Mr. Yedida her drawing. Shawn sidled up beside him and examined it. It was a simple drawing of a flower, a lotus, made up of hundreds of tiny dots instead of lines.

Mr. Yedida took it in, and then once again laughed, his expression charmed. "Clever girl. I will put this up in my office," he said. Catching Dr. Teschke's and Mr. Haversham's stares, he showed them the picture.

"The largest Baha'i house of worship in India is called the 'Lotus Temple' because its design makes the building look like that flower. The last Baha'i socioeconomic forum took place there, rather than in its usual place in Haifa because Haifa was under continuous rocket attacks at the time. There were one thousand one hundred and eight participants from around the world at the forum, of which I was one," he explained. "I think if I went back to my office and counted these dots, I would see there are one thousand one hundred and eight dots."

Rosetta said something in response to this. Mr. Yedida corrected his guess. "One thousand one hundred and *eleven* dots, she tells me. Two more dots for the Báb and the Bahá'u'lláh, our prophets, and one more for a united world." He looked back at Rosetta. "Thank you! I will treasure this."

"That's specific knowledge about that gathering. Is she Baha'i? Like you?" Mr. Haversham asked. "If so, where is your church? Someone there might recognize her if I brought her by on Sunday."

Mr. Yedida smiled. "The Baha'i religious calendar is not a seven day calendar, so our meetings happen on a different day of the week each time, and are held in private in any case. But the local Baha'i do hold public meetings in Annabel Taylor Hall here on campus. If you stop in there you should see our meetings for the next few months posted on the bulletin board. I think the next one is next Tuesday. You're free to bring her there if you think one of us might recognize her, but I've never seen her before today."

Mr. Yedida gave Rosetta and Dr. Teschke a last wave. "Interesting case you have here, professor."

Shawn groaned, staring at the translations in his hands. "Man, this stuff is harder than I thought, Doc. I'm not sure I'm cut out for this. It's not hard enough that she's speaking this weird language, but she's also speaking in metaphors?"

"Look at it this way. If you finish your study, it is certain to be memorable," Dr. Teschke quipped.

"Yeah, thanks," he said. He waved as Mr. Haversham stood again and guided the girl to the door. "See you next week, Rosie."

His subject waved back at him as the door closed behind her. Once silence had returned to the room, Dr. Teschke raised an eyebrow at him, an eyebrow which reminded him he had a new load of practical work to do. Shawn sat down to review the translations. He began by circling the word "wine" wherever he found it.

Shawn unlocked his bicycle, tossed his satchel strap over one shoulder, and began his slow ride back to his Collegetown apartment. Before leaving the office, he had taken a moment to explain in low tones that Rosie had once again been speaking as Gabriel the Archangel. Dr. Teschke had listened, but after she heard the girl had not had any seizures or prolonged loss of consciousness, she was less concerned. The girl's odd delusions were a result of whatever psychological or neurological problems she suffered from, the professor had reassured him. Nonetheless, he had given up the recording of the session to Dr.

232

Teschke or Akiko to archive in case questions arose later.

Overall he had left the office with mixed feelings. He felt good that Dr. Teschke and Mr. Haversham trusted him enough not to worry about his handling of Rosie's outbursts. But the problem remained of how to explain to the professor the girl was making divine "revelations" to him in a language only he understood. If the recording sounded like gibberish to everyone else, how could he prove to anyone else what he was hearing? How could he prove she was doing anything but babbling? How crazy would he sound trying to explain the problem?

"I live my life in fear of Dr. Teschke's skepticism," he realized. But his meditations were interrupted by a pickup truck which stopped in front of him. He cursed at the driver as he skidded to a stop behind the truck's bumper, but his shout did not interrupt the conversation the driver began with two pretty young women standing in the middle of the street. He walked his bike up onto the sidewalk, prepared to go around the obstacle. But as he did so, an oversized LCD television pushed up to the window of an electronics store caught his eye.

"Pope Endorses Invasion of Iran?" topped the screen in white letters. His spine tingled with dread as he drew close to the glass so he could hear the commentators.

"...The papal spokesperson clarified the pontiff's comments, saying that while nothing justified violence on the part of Iran or the United States, if the invasion prevented the spread of nuclear weapons it could nonetheless have benefits for mankind. However, both Sunni and Shia denounced the Pope's speech as an implicit endorsement of the U.S.-led-"

"Sounds like backpedaling to me," interrupted the other commentator. "But let's face it, Muslims aren't stupid because I get the same message. America's right and the Pope knows it. He can wring his hands about the means, but we're acting for the benefit of all mankind. And you heard it first on Patriot News!"

David brought the lamb chops to Faith at the table, still sizzling on the skillet. She hadn't gotten home until after eight-thirty and now drooped with fatigue. He suspected his daughter would not be going out to the disco tonight. He overlooked the fact she was at the table in her uniform and served her up the lamb, dumplings, and string beans he had saved for her.

He had a lot he wanted to talk about with her, but her demeanor suggested she might listen better if he let her eat first.

"Burning the candle at both ends, are we?" he said as he sat down. His daughter ignored the question and began eating.

"Thanks Dad. You have no idea how good this tastes to me," she explained between bites. When she had torn through her first serving of lamb chops and dumplings and begun picking at the string beans (like she had even when she was a tiny girl) David saw his opportunity to start the conversation.

"So, long day, huh?"

She began drinking her beer. "Oh my God let me tell you. First, I was out late last night, and that's my own damn fault. But then I get to work and the FBI agents Cash and I talked to last week are there. They told me *they* were the ones who had torn up the carriage house fire site to collect samples for testing, and then they make me swear myself to secrecy and give up my computer. I mean, they let me save my other files and everything. And the new computer they bought is much faster and better than my old one. But still, it was like 'boom, you're done, investigation's over, give us your computer.'"

David considered this. If it was supposed to be a secret, he wondered if his daughter should even be telling him about it. But he decided not to raise this point. More information was better than less when it came to understanding Faith's job. "They couldn't copy the files they needed from you?"

"It's not about them *having* the information, it was about us *not having* the information. They showed me this letter from the Department of Homeland Security about how New York was supposed to turn over all the documents and not investigate or discuss the case anymore. I guess they're afraid the case will frighten the public."

"They're telling you not to investigate it anymore?" He felt skeptical. He'd been a firefighter his whole life, and never encountered any federal interest or interference in a fire investigation.

"Case closed. We're supposed to tell people that lightning set off the diesel storage tank, that the identity of the casualties is known, and that they should refer any questions to the Department of Homeland Security."

David thought about this. "That's...stupid. Diesel wouldn't explode from a lightning strike, it would burn. Besides, what sense does it make to refer questions about a lightning fire to Homeland Security?"

Faith shrugged. "It sounded stupid to me, too, but that's the way they wanted it."

The firefighter in him felt indignant. "Fire investigations are a local issue. The federal government has no jurisdiction."

"Then write your congressman, Pop," she suggested. "Truth be told, I was stumped anyhow. Maybe they'll be able to figure out what happened and tell us the real story someday. In the meantime, I can get back to my other job. Fall semester is about to start, and there's no way Karl will get through all the student apartment, public accommodation, and public school inspections. The investigation has gone on for weeks and other than Syracuse sending us Cash, no other jurisdiction wants to ante up any more help. Not Cayuga Heights, not the county, and not the state. I've done what I can."

She took another slug of her beer. Drinking beer from the bottle was not his daughter's most ladylike habit, but then, it was he who had taught it to her. He supposed his irritation with it had more to do with feeling like his daughter was giving up and being mistreated. *"Nothing could be further from the case,"* he reflected. *"She has worked like a dog, helped me take care of Rosie, and scarcely taken any time off. Sometimes things are just beyond her level."* He felt bad he and Connie had been unable to provide for more than an associate's degree for her.

He sat and pushed his hand across the table. She took it, her hand now big enough to fill his own. He remembered when her hand had been small enough to hold just his finger. "If you think it's true, if you've done all you can, then I'll stand by you. I think this federal stuff is bullshit, but maybe they'll crack the nut for you, and maybe that's the most important thing for the city."

Faith stared into the open neck of her beer bottle. "Yeah. It's a lot of maybes," she said. "But on the bright side, the federal agents said they'd put me in for a medal."

"A medal?"

"Yup. A 'homeland commendation medal' or some shit."

The name rang a bell with David. "I got one of those. For my work at the MLK bridge in St. Louis after the Market Garden attacks. That's a real honor."

She did not seem encouraged. "Is that so? I guess the standards have come down since then, Pop. They're handing them out to anybody now."

Faith's words saddened David. He stood up, walked around behind his daughter, and massaged her shoulders.

"You're not 'anybody.' You're a dedicated public servant who spent weeks of her life conscientiously following up on a real stumper of a case most others would have contrived a way to close. And while I may not agree with how the case is being handled, the feds and I agree you found something important. If you'd called it a lightning strike and moved on, our country might be much less prepared for what's coming at it."

To his surprise, his daughter hugged him. "Oh, Pop, you're...you're like...I don't know. But what would I do without you?"

He returned the embrace. The generations marched on. "That day will come. And you'll know what to do, like you knew with that fire." When she released him, he took her shoulders and looked into her eyes. "Now, though, I need to know what you think of my new plan for sending the girl to school."

She sat down again. "Yeah. Yeah, there's still the problem of Rosie."

David walked with Hildegard between the statues on the Arts Quad of Ezra Cornell and A.D. White. The woman acted brighter and more cheerful than usual, and he anticipated the coffee they were about to share. The professor was something else, and snooty about some things, but he guessed she must enjoy his company, too, since an important woman could always have a reason to be busy.

"I've got some ideas I want you to hear," she said. "I think we can offer you some tools that will help you with Rosie and help us study her."

He was intrigued. He hadn't heard her sound this excited before. "Sure. Let's hear them."

"When we have a seat we'll talk about it. In the meantime, I should ask if there have been any more discoveries in the carriage house fire."

David was about to launch into the story of how the Department of Homeland Security had snatched the case and all the records away from Faith, but hesitated as they walked into Zeus's. The cafe was small and crowded. It would be easy to be overheard. And after all, his daughter hadn't been supposed to tell him most of what he knew, so he shouldn't repeat it.

"Case closed. It was ruled a lightning fire," he said as they got in line for their coffee.

Dr. Teschke gaped. "What? What about the person Gabriel who Rosie said started the fire?"

He played dumb. "I wasn't party to the decision. I can't say. Perhaps they think she made him up. You can't blame them. After all, didn't Shawn say she dreamed and spoke of Gabriel the Archangel when she was having her seizure? If you were investigating it, how seriously would you look for Gabriel the Archangel? Even if you thought he was real, how would you question him? Go to the pearly gates and knock? 'Heavenly father, we have here a warrant for a search of the premises for one Archangel, Gabriel...'"

Hildegard grinned at this. "I suppose I can see that. I was surprised the case was closed is all."

"Houses burn. Plus Faith has a lot of fire inspections to do before the fall semester starts in earnest. It had to happen sometime."

They bought their drinks, and Dr. Teschke went to sit at her favorite spot, a chair at the foot of a statue of a regal woman with a wreath on her head and a spear in her hand. "Minerva," read the plaque. David took what he guessed would become his customary seat across from her. He fidgeted with the insulating cardboard sleeve on his coffee cup before asking.

"So what's your big plan for Rosie?" he said.

The professor sipped her coffee. He wondered how the woman could drink it so hot without it scalding, but she showed no sign of discomfort.

"Ah, yes, so exciting. My assistants came to me with this proposal when after last week I decided Rosetta was too big a project for Shawn and put all three of them on the job. Akiko had read up on some translation applications which allow a smartphone to translate speech in one language into another."

"Sounds nifty," said David. He could see where Hildegard was going with this. Such a device would be handy. But when the professor wrinkled her forehead at the word "nifty." He guessed he was using too much slang. "Sounds useful. I'm interested," he explained.

Dr. Teschke went back to looking pleased with herself. "We looked into getting one of the applications for our own purposes, but some of the software is proprietary and, in any case, no one makes one yet which can translate to and from spoken Esperanto. Still it at the least gave us the idea. What if we were to make a program which Rosie can use to translate her Esperanto into spoken English? This would allow her to speak to those around her, and since she understands much of what is said in English, the program wouldn't even need to translate back for her. We could get away with making a simpler program and still have it be useful."

"I follow. It would only have to be a one-way translator."

"So, we did some checking with other departments. The computer science department and the university's information technology division would be willing to help us. Since the device would also help us study her, they can justify their work as helping to build a research tool. And, if we succeed, the university will apply for a copyright to the program, and everyone will be happy. You will have a translator, we will have our data, and possibly even Cornell will have its patents."

David shook his head. "I can see how this would help Rosie, and how it might help Shawn interview her. But you could keep doing interviews like you're doing now and save yourself a lot of trouble. Why bother with it?"

"Here's the tricky part, and here's why we would need your permission to do it," said Hildegard. "We could set the program so it stores whatever phrases it translates, and that in and of itself would help us study her use of Esperanto. But, if you agree, we could also set it to record what you say to her in reply, so we can get a better sense of how her Esperanto works in conversation."

He frowned. "So it would be like she was running around my house with a tape recorder in her hand as well as a translator?"

"Yes. Only it wouldn't even use tapes, it would store the sounds digitally. And this would eliminate the need for us to have so many of these interview appointments, and would also make sure we were recording the girl's use of Esperanto in a natural setting instead of in the awkward artificial setting of our office. All you would need to do is stop by the office once in a while and let us download the recorded data."

David saw a catch in this plan. "But it would also mean anything we said around Rosie could be recorded."

Hildegard nodded. "Yes. There is a great issue of privacy there. That's why we need to ask you. It is illegal to record someone without their consent in New York. So not only would we need to have your consent, and Faith's, but you would have to turn off the recording function when she went out into public or you might be violating other people's rights."

David was surprised by his resistance to the idea. He didn't like possibility that, if he stubbed his toe and cursed, or if he and Faith got into an argument, it would be recorded and Dr. Teschke and her students would spend time in their office chuckling over it. On the other hand, he was sending Rosie to school in a few weeks, and a translation device could make a real difference in her chances to learn, make friends, and have something like a normal life. Though, given the kinds of things the girl said when people spoke to her in Esperanto, it might keep her from making friends, too.

He supposed if the whole plan relied on his consent, he could stop it at any time if it was causing problems. Besides, if suspicions arose as to why an old man was foster parenting a preteen, the recordings could help eliminate them. He was an honest man, and while he might do things which were embarrassing, he supposed he had nothing to be afraid of if his life was recorded.

"What I hadn't told you yet is I'm about to send Rosie to the Ithaca schools in the fall. So I'm interested," he said. "Tell me more."

Hildegard leaned back in her chair. "To school! Oh, how exciting! If we got the consent of her schoolteachers, we could even see how she learns and speaks in class!" The professor reflected a moment before continuing. "Okay, we don't have this technology right now, so Akiko and my other students made a plan. In phase one, what we'll try to do is create a program for a laptop computer which translates Rosie's typed Esperanto into English. This laptop will have to have a non-standard keyboard because the alphabet she uses for her Esperanto is non-standard. But then she could even use this laptop for her homework or for her iTunes or whatever."

"Ok," he said. He was trying to listen, but the animation on the woman's face was striking. *"I guess she does love languages,"* he thought. He wasn't even sure Rosie would be as enthusiastic about the idea as Hildegard was.

"In phase two, we'd try to make a more portable version of the device she could carry around in a pocket. Then, in phase three, we'd install voice recognition software on both machines, so she wouldn't need to type anymore. All she'd need to do is speak. And there you have it," she said. "I can't promise yet all of this will work. It's just a plan, and we can only afford to put together something from available technology and use all the smart people we have here on campus. I confess the technology is totally beyond me, but Akiko is smart with that sort of thing, and if there's one thing I can still do, it's write a research proposal."

David raised his hand. "One question. What would it cost me?"

"Nothing. I'm sure I can get enough money if I write a good proposal to provide both the laptop and the portable device. If I can't get that much I should quit as department head," Hildegard said. "But I suppose 'nothing' isn't accurate. We'd like eight hours of recording time a week."

He mused over this. "Sounds like a lot. And that's the part I'm most uncomfortable with. How about four hours?"

"Too few. You can do better. How about six? And you come with me to the opera coming up."

"The opera? Are you asking me on a date in return for your professional services?"

"Kind of," she admitted with just the barest trace of guilt. "I'd be happy if you gave me six hours a week. You don't have to come to the opera if you don't like that sort of thing."

"Where's the opera?" He could already imagine his friends Dwight and Marcus making fun of him for doing something as blue-blooded as visiting an opera down in New York City. "I'm not a big fan of traveling. Especially New York City. It brings back bad memories."

"Oh, it's here in Ithaca," The professor explained. "At the performing arts center. My friend Mr. Kay is directing it. It's not a big deal."

David smiled. Not only was the performing arts center in Ithaca, it was about three or four blocks from his house. They were uphill blocks, but still, the nearness of the performing arts center made this request trivial.

"Do I have to wear a tie? I hate ties," said David.

Hildegard waved her hand dismissively. "Oh, please. The audience will be full of undergraduates wearing those shameful corporate-logo marked rags they call clothes. Dress nicely. No buffalo capes, spiked helmets, garters, or other rude surprises, if you please."

David laughed. "Done. For six hours and an opera, provided Rosie agrees and I have the option to back out if I don't like where it's going,"

Hildegard shook her head. "An option to back out after seventy-two hours of recording. Otherwise, it won't be worth the proposal I'm writing and the technology we're developing. It's an investment. We only have so many dollars to spend in a year and we need something for it."

David reconsidered his position. The date at the opera, he concluded, might be the sweetest part of this deal. "Done. Pending Rosie and Faith's consent. And I now insist on the opera," he said.

"Insist, do you? Maybe I should make the requirement eight hours of recording a week!" Dr. Teschke said coyly. Then she laughed, reached across the table, and squeezed his hand. "Oh, thank you! I was so proud of them when my assistants came to me with this proposal. You're giving them a chance to do serious linguistic work."

"The machines you're proposing could make a big difference. It's a win-win from my point of view. But will we keep having coffee if Rosie doesn't have to come to appointments anymore?"

At this, the woman grinned. "I'll make the time."

Faith wore her dress uniform. Her father stood to one side of her in the department conference room at the Syracuse police headquarters. Cassius stood beside her, also in his dress uniform, looking dashing but serious, his brand new "National Security Commendation Medal" hanging on the breast of his jacket. His remarks on being awarded the medal had been humble, and he had thanked her, Cornell (who had no representatives present), and Tompkins County generally for their hospitality and assistance.

In front of her now stood Marcus and the Chief of the Syracuse Police, also dressed in their finest. The faces of Syracuse police officers who had given their lives in the line of duty stared over their brass bio plaques at her and the detective from their frames on the walls. The police chief's breath was a bit sour, she noted, but Marcus's was minty fresh.

"Trust a gay guy for good hygiene," she mused, holding her lips tight to avoid smiling at the dichotomy between the men.

"Attention to Orders," bellowed Chief Wells. Behind and around her, Faith heard their families stand up from their chairs. She wondered if they felt like jack-in-the-boxes. They'd had to stand for the reading of Detective McCrae's award moments before.

Marcus began to read from the award plaque he carried. "To all those who see these presents:

"The Secretary of Homeland Security, on reliable report of the patriotism and vigilance of Inspector Faith Haversham and her instrumental work in identifying and uncovering a conspiracy of terror against the United States, hereby awards her the Homeland Security Commendation Medal. Her vigilance and service to the United States is in keeping with highest traditions of patriotism as exemplified by the volunteer militias and individual patriots of the revolutionary era. Through efforts like those of Inspector Haversham, the United States shall remain free, under God, and indivisible."

After finishing this, Marcus and Chief Wells stood aside. Surprised, she glanced to one side and saw her father drawing close to one side. Chief Wells handed him the plastic medal case, and her father stepped forward. He lifted the medal up to her chest.

"I won't put this on you like we did in the old days," he said. "It'd be weird."

She recalled how Chief Wells had pounded the metal points of the medal into Cassius's uniform. The man hadn't flinched, but she suspected having two metal needles driven into her breast would make *her* flinch.

"Thanks, Dad," she said as he clipped the medal to her left breast pocket.

"Your mother would be proud," he said. "I know you didn't always see eye to eye, but she did respect your choice of career." As he spoke, she recognized the tie around his neck as one she had gotten him for Father's Day decades before.

Faith didn't know what to say. But as her father's eyes began to water, she felt hers doing the same. She would not cry in uniform, she resolved. When her father stood back, she was sure her eyes were dry.

Marcus looked at her. "It's a small crowd, what with the investigation now being a secret and all. But do you have anything to say to those assembled, Inspector?"

She turned around. Cassius's wife Nidya and his two children stood by their chairs. Hand in hand with their older daughter Mira stood Rosie. Despite having thought about what she would say in advance, being in front of so many people made her feel awkward. She choked and forgot everything she had planned to say. But when she remembered the groggy, frightened girl who'd awoken in the hospital, what she would to say came again in a flash. She reached up to her chest and unclipped the medal.

"There are so many people here who have taught me so much. Cash," she said, with a glance at the detective. "You've been a champ. So patient, so willing to listen, and so good at keeping me from getting ahead of myself. Marcus, thanks for putting a hand to my back and pushing me when my confidence faltered, and then reminding me to go home, or go dancing. And thanks to my Dad, for showing me what it means to serve a community, every day, all the time. I'm so honored." Again, tears came to her eyes. She hated her sentimental streak.

"But there's one more person in this room to thank. She's taught me a lot about what it means to be brave, and gentle, and patient, and reminded me every night of why we do what we do. Even as we give awards to each other, the hard truth is kids like Rosie are the real heroes every day. They confront so much evil in the world we can't undo, and then they bounce back, and somewhere along the way they learn to forgive us. I'm sorry I couldn't find your mom and dad for you like I promised, honey. And I don't know what your future holds, but I'm sure without a family it's going to be hard going. So I want you to have this," she said. She took some steps forward, and knelt down. Mira stepped back, and her foster daughter stared at Faith with incomprehension as she clipped the medal to her shirt.

"Be brave, sweetie," she said. Rosie tilted the medal up to her face, fingered it, and then smiled.

It was hard for the applause of a dozen people to be loud in a carpeted room, but it was nonetheless. "Thanks for listening. And I've got fire inspections to do in the morning back in Ithaca, so I'd better get going," she finished. The audience laughed, and Chief Wells came by to shake her hand once more before leaving.

Cassius came up next. "Nice speech. You shamed me," he laughed. "Have you thought about politics?"

She snorted. "Oh yeah. My Hollywood figure is custom made for an election. I'll stick to public service. *You* should run for something. You've got it all, celebrity status, good looks, a beautiful family. You could be the Obama of Syracuse."

He laughed. "Not me. I want to be out chasing the bad guys."

Faith put her hands on her hips. "See, you don't want leadership. That's why you should have it."

The detective shook his head at her. "Alright, alright, enough. You still coming to dinner? I need to go take this crap off," he indicated his dress uniform.

"You bet," she said. "Thanks for everything, Cash."

"No sweat. Let's work together again. And even if we don't, I'm down in Ithaca from time to time."

When the FBI agents, Marcus, and Cassius's family had all shaken her hand, she turned to her father, who was still staring at her.

She tried to guess what her father was thinking. "It's me," she said. "The same kid you had to paddle for stealing cookies."

"Yeah, that's what I'm marveling at," he said, putting an arm over her shoulder.

Chapter 17

Peccadilloes

Faith rode alongside Karl, feeling relaxed for the first time in many weeks. The inspection schedule she had unfolded in her lap was busy from open to close each day. She and her partner had a lot of work to do in the next three weeks before the fall semester started. But the last few days had been gone so well she was sure she could see the light at the end of the tunnel. Karl was reliable and knowledgeable, and their combined careful inspections over the previous years meant most problems had already been fixed, so few major items were arising during their inspections. If other buildings could avoid burning down in mysterious ways for another six working days, she and Karl could work through their backlogs.

For this reason she felt a mixture of delight and dismay when her cell phone rang with the "Law and Order" theme music she had chosen for Cassius's ringtone. Karl glanced at the phone before turning back to the road.

"Detective McCrae?" he hazarded. She nodded before flipping open her phone.

"Cash? What's up?"

"Hey, how are you, hero?"

"Oh man, going back to my real job feels like a vacation. I don't think I've ever been so excited to spend a day checking fire extinguishers and alarm panels."

The detective laughed. "Yeah, it does sound like a vacation. You deserve it."

"So what can I do for you? Are you coming down to Ithaca?"

"No, I'm calling on business," he said. "Can you talk?"

"Sure," she said, wondering what else might be going on in Ithaca which would interest the man.

"Listen, umm, do you remember by any chance an Ithaca Times reporter named Taryn Thomas?"

Faith felt a twinge of alarm. A couple of nights with that woman were putting her on the awkward end of a lot of questions. She hoped the woman hadn't started blabbing about their "night lives."

"Yeah," she conceded. "She's the reporter that was all over the carriage house fire."

"You weren't the only person she'd been following up with. She'd drummed up some kind of lead on the Army of God. We've intercepted her name in a couple of their communications. And it didn't sound like they planned to throw her a party."

Faith's worries about Taryn returned. With as persistent and convincing as Taryn had been with her, she could see the woman not knowing when to stop in other contexts.

"What do you need to know about her?"

"When did you last see her?" Cassius asked. She recognized the tone of his voice. This wasn't a chat between friends anymore. He was in policeman mode. If this was so, her wiggle room on the subject of her lover had gotten very narrow. It would only be a matter of time before the detective was reading some of their racier text messages. She might as well come...cleaner.

"I ran into her at the Haunt a while ago. She tried to soften me up with a drink and asked me a whole bunch of questions about the case. Then we, well, y'know. Then we met at a club in Syracuse. We, umm, hung out. Pretty casual, actually." She fretted over how to tailor the response to Cash so as not to tell her life story to Karl.

There was a pause. "I don't remember you mentioning that," the detective said in his "I'm not making any judgments" voice. "But you haven't had any contact with her since?"

"Not since that night at that club. We were supposed to meet again, and I left her some phone messages, but she replied with texts. Then the feds took the case over. Why?"

"Taryn Thomas has been reported missing by her friends in Syracuse," he answered grimly.

"Omigod," she said.

"As near as anyone can tell, she was last seen at an alternative lifestyles bar in Syracuse called Alibi's. She was described as a regular there. Did she mention to you anything about anyone she might be meeting there?"

"No, she didn't."

"She left in the company of a brunette no one recognized with a Midwestern accent. Ring any bells?"

"Nothing, Cash. Sorry I can't be more helpful, but I didn't know her well." She supposed it was true she hadn't. Still, this half-truth begged the question of why she had been doing with Taryn what she had been doing. But she now felt remorse. She had been angry at the woman before, but now she was worried for her.

The man sighed. "I'm trying to do what I can from my end. I'm working with Detective Ramin at Ithaca Police Department if you learn anything."

"Wow, I saw her a few days ago," she said. "And she's gone?"

"Disbelief is one of the phases. Remember we don't have a body, so there's still hope. I'm sorry to be the bearer of bad news. Next time I'm in town I'd like to stop in and talk."

"Yeah. Yeah, let's do that, Cash."

"Okay, got to get back to work. Call me if you think of anything. Keep fighting the good fight," he said. "And thanks for leveling with me."

"I will." She closed her phone and looked out the window. They were at the base of Buffalo Street. Karl's route to Collegetown would take her past her house. She worried about who else her work might be leading past her house.

"That sounded grim," Karl said.

"Taryn Thomas, you know, the reporter from the Ithaca Times and YNN? She's gone missing," she explained.

David checked his shave in the mirror. It was something which, now that he didn't have to go into work every day, he often neglected, figuring his aging skin could use a rest from the razor burn and Aqua Velva. It didn't need any more nicks or scars to heal. But for some reason the prospect of a date with Hildegard made him feel he ought to shave. So out came his razor and the increasingly difficult squinting in the mirror which accompanied it. He'd tried shaving with his glasses on, but it was awkward and he was forever getting shaving gel on the lenses. So he settled for squinting a lot and leaning over the sink to reach the best focal distance from his mirror.

The fancy razor itself had been a Christmas gift from Marcus and Dwight, given amidst jokes about his occasional unshaven shadow and him getting soft. It had seven blades and flowed over his face. When he had been in his twenties and shaving to impress Connie on leave from Vietnam, he would have given his eye teeth for such a razor and the certain kinds of intimacy such a clean shave could invite. But now he doubted the audience for his shave would care about these virtues. She simply wouldn't want to be seen with someone scruffy.

He finished his shave, slapped on aftershave, and went to his closet to pick out his clothes. He had gained weight in retirement, but had done no clothes shopping without Connie to pester him about it. So he had few shirts which fit and were appropriate to date in, and they had to go with his one pair of unstained and unworn khakis. He fretted and scowled and settled on a green collar shirt with silver vertical stripes. The choice of shoes was a no-brainer. He had three pairs of black redwing uniform shoes in various states of wear, and he picked the newest of these.

He examined his choices in the hallway mirror and was feeling his confidence in his appearance slip away when Faith peeked up from the stairwell.

"You look great, Pop!" she said. For some reason his residual confidence in his looks evaporated with her enthusiasm. She would only be this enthusiastic, he was sure, to encourage him, and this meant her enthusiasm had little to do with, or was even felt in spite of, how he looked. He grunted something he hoped would satisfy her and stepped away from the mirror so as not to diminish his confidence further with more self-examination.

"She's a nice lady...but I'm telling you, she's not the one I would have picked to ask my dad on a date. She's a bit younger than you, isn't she? And kind of - I don't know - stuck up," she observed.

David felt a surge of devilishness, and repressed the question as to whether or not his daughter thought he was up to a younger woman or to a higher-born one. "Yep. She's a bit younger," he agreed. He started down the stairs, and she gave him a punch on the shoulder as she passed him going up. He grinned. A cup of coffee, maybe, to put a spring in his step and keep him warm up the hill to the performing arts center would be all he needed.

A cup of coffee, however, was not satisfactory preparation for Rosie's taste. She hovered around him as he sat at the breakfast table. She brushed dander from his shoulder, combed his hair over his ear with her fingers, and, in a surprising gesture, buttoned a button he had either missed or his new beer belly had pulled out. In order to re-establish his personal space, David pulled out the girl's chair and motioned for her to sit, and she sat watching him.

"It's my date. I'm supposed to be the one who is anxious."

Rosetta said something unintelligible in reply. She then took a sheet of paper and drew something with deft lines, and after a few minutes of sketching, folded it and handed it to him. When he went to fold it open and look at it over the last of his coffee, she shot him an indignant look.

"Oh, I see. This is for Hildegard?"

Rosetta nodded. He tucked it into a breast pocket. "I'll give it to her."

Rosie smiled and turned back to draw more. David took this as the end of her fussing over him and the end of the conversation, and pushed back the breakfast bench as Faith came down the stairs.

"I made a peanut sauce and tofu stir fry for her. There is extra in the fridge if dinner wasn't enough for her," he mentioned.

His daughter gave him a mischievous grin. "Oh, I've got that covered. I picked up a new fifteen hundred piece jigsaw puzzle and a gallon of Purity ice cream. We'll have ourselves a party while you go get bored by the opera or whatever." Rosie clapped her hands and sprang from the breakfast bench at the mention of ice cream, and was off like a shot to the kitchen.

"Hey, not now, honey, we have to save it for when we finish the puzzle!" Faith called after her.

"Should have kept your trap shut," David said. "She'll either wheedle some out of you now or she's going to do the puzzle in thirty minutes so she can have her ice cream."

"New rule, Pop. She can only place a piece when I do. That will slow her down."

"Good luck," David foresaw that rule running aground. Rosie's skill with jigsaw puzzles was uncanny, and while she was a patient child with most things, she couldn't control herself around jigsaw puzzles. He also remembered the lengths Faith herself would go to as a girl to get ice cream. For a few semesters the promise of a gallon of ice cream she could eat whenever she wanted had sufficed to improve her report card. It might have kept working but Constance cut the practice off when Faith began to get chubby.

"Have fun, Pop," she said. David grinned at her, appreciating how this time the role reversal was working to her discomfort. "Don't, umm, do anything I wouldn't do."

"I'll do whatever I feel like. Your limitations are your problem." He winked at her, and she smirked back and walked him to the door. He slid on his fleece-lined IAFF jacket and walked out the door.

A late summer night, one so cold it carried early dew and the sting of fall in it, greeted him with twinkling stars over the trees and streetlights of Ithaca. Through gaps in the leaf cover, his view from DeWitt Terrace carried out to the far side of the lake. He pulled out his truck keys and checked his watch. Then he considered it was only half the distance to the performing arts center it was to Hildegard's office. So he could walk and enjoy the night without the bother or expense of his truck.

He headed down DeWitt Terrace and walked uphill on Buffalo Street. Without Rosie's dawdling to slow him, though, he tired out quickly on Buffalo Street's steep slope. He began to pace himself so as not to get ahead of his pacemaker. He didn't want to arrive at the theater flushed and hypoxemic. He suspected that while Hildegard might cheerfully call him an ambulance, she might then get in it with him and needle him about his foolishness the whole way to the hospital. For a proud man, it could be a fate worse than death.

He recalled the changes in Buffalo Street as he walked up. His house on DeWitt Terrace had been in Connie's family for generations, and the other houses on the street had long been subdivided into multiple dwellings to make student apartments. But the concrete block sprawl of "Collegetown" was, lot by lot, spreading out into the rows of Victorian homes which made up his neighborhood. As a firefighter, he was relieved to see students living in modern buildings with adequate alarm systems and structures they couldn't set fire to with a careless cigarette or a candle upended by lovemaking. But as a resident, it made him sad. The neighborhood had a unique character which was changing. He guessed when Faith inherited the house, she would at some point have to decide whether to keep it or sell it out to a developer looking to build high-rent gorge-side apartments.

Once in Collegetown he tuned out. The same signs were there which had been there his whole life: Books. Records. Bars. Cafes. Restaurants. Bike shops. Greek food, all you can eat lunches, semester meal plans available, latest fashion boots.... How a district could remain the same while tearing down anything which might be a landmark and rebuilding every structure into bland concrete modernity escaped him. But this was not his lane, it was the zoning board's, he recalled. And then, he was retired, he remembered further, so none of it was his lane. It was Marcus's.

He came to the marble-faced Performing Arts Center at the edge of Cascadilla Gorge. If David had trusted his footing in the dark, he could have taken a student footpath up the gorge from his house to the center and skipped Collegetown. His thumping heart assured him this would have been pushing his luck, however. He checked his watch and took a seat on a chilled marble bench.

People milled about the center's entrance, but after scanning them for signs of Hildegard, he went back to watching the street. Pompadours and knee boots were back in style, he deduced. Two or three hookers, or college girls, he couldn't tell which, walked by, their cold-reddened flesh straining fishnet leggings and recoiling from the many bits of metal driven through various body parts. A car shaped like a 1950s Chevy drove by, sporting a chrome 'hybrid' label on its rear panel. He marveled to consider the legions of creative minds America employed in its constant cycle of recreating and re-destroying form and style. His life had been full of function. The idea of changing form for the sake of it, rather than to further adapt it to function, was both spurious and fascinating to him at the same time.

David heard Hildegard's approach long before he saw her. Something in the loud, purposeful and uniform timing of clicking heels told him it was she who was wearing the shoes, but he did not see her as he glanced around. At length she appeared beside him and put an arm across his back in greeting. "David! Good to see you!" He was surprised by the touching, but she withdrew the arm and sat down on his bench. Whatever she was wearing smelled of juniper and laurel.

"Thank you for agreeing to come with me," she told him, "when Bertolt sent me the tickets I thought of you. It would be a shame to waste a ticket to this show. One doesn't see Brecht often in this country."

"I've heard the name," confessed David. "But that's all. My knowledge of culture extends to visiting the Viet Nam memorial and traveling to New York City to see boring museums with my wife."

"Have no fear," the professor said, patting his arm. "Brecht chose his material to suit sensible working people. Besides, *The Caucasian Chalk Circle* is similar to a story of King Solomon from the Bible. I'm sure you'll find it accessible."

He smirked at the woman's condescension. He wondered if Hildegard struck this tone with all her dates. If so it could explain why she was still single. He feasted his eyes on her. She was far too pretty to be single, and she knew it. She wore a broomstick skirt and leggings over her slender legs, high heeled boots, and a sweater, and accented it all with one of her ever-present scarves in green. It made her quite the picture, and her scarf matched his shirt perfectly. Coincidence was an odd thing. In any case, if she would keep wearing those legs around him, he could tolerate her condescending to him.

David had learned banter was what his companion favored. She was uncomfortable without it. So he came back at her. "I didn't know you consider me sensible. I'm flattered."

"That remains to be seen, doesn't it? We'll see how you like Brecht, and then we'll see how sensible you are for the rest of the evening." She said "sensible" in a funny way, more like "zen-see-bel." Usually her accent wasn't so strong. He wondered if she was nervous too.

"Anyway, I have our tickets. I'm happy to sit here in the cold if it's what sensible working men favor, but we could go in and take our seats where it's warm, too," she said, fanning the two tickets to him to pick one.

He drew a ticket from between her fingers. "Lead on."

"If you like this one, Bertolt wants to do scenes from the *Rosenkavalier* next season," she said, her anticipation obvious as she rose. He said nothing to this. He wanted to be sure he liked the first play before he committed to another, or he wanted to be sure Hildegard was enough fun to make it worth sitting through a second if this one was a bore.

Hildegard watched David throughout the play. He came across like a man who subdued his emotions, and while the student who played Grusha did it movingly, true to form he betrayed only interest, not emotion. She wondered in her less confident moments if her tastes made her too inaccessible to men, and she was hoping to hit it off with this one.

As the play wound down and the final scenes began, she worried about what to do or say next. *"Relax, you cannot plan these things,"* she cautioned herself, *"Just enjoy the play."* Nonetheless, she became stuck in her own play for the last few minutes, a play in which she tried to improvise lines to the different dashing or disappointing things her companion might say. She turned a sad grin as she caught herself doing this. In some ways, she was still twenty.

When the play ended, David said nothing. Instead, he rose and lifted Hildegard's sweater off her seatback so she could slide into it without contorting. She appreciated the gesture, but when she went to take his jacket and do the same for him, he had put it on already. He nodded at the door, and as their aisle emptied, she led him out.

"I liked it," he said at length, to her relief.

"I'm glad!" she replied. "See, there's nothing mysterious about the theater. Indeed, many of your movies are adapted from our theater."

The firefighter shrugged. "I see so few movies anyway. I can't say I'm crazy about Hollywood's movies. Nothing I've lived has had a Hollywood beginning or ending. Most of our movies are dumb for that reason."

Dr. Teschke saw her opening in this as they walked out of the theater. "What movies *do* you like?" she investigated.

"Twelve Angry Men is my favorite. Fonda...I don't know. I hope in the same situation, I'd be as good a man as he was."

"Ah, I think I have seen this movie. This is the movie where one juror asks questions, and the questions make all the other jurors change their minds, and they save a man's life."

Mr. Haversham pointed at her. "That's the one. It's the most American movie ever made, to my mind."

She smiled at this. He was making conversation easy. And here she had been wasting her time rehearsing what to say to him. Through the glass front wall of the performing arts center she could see Collegetown Bagels. She wondered how many of the departing audience would go there for coffee, and if he too could be convinced to stop there.

"What makes it American?"

David thought before answering this. "There's the issue of fair trials by juries. Then there's one man asking questions. It's what we're all supposed to do, ask questions."

"Fair trials. This is American?"

"Yep," he answered. He was so sure of himself. Hildegard couldn't resist the opening.

"Like the Guantanamo trials?" she needled.

"Those are different."

"Yes, I should say so," she replied. "But what else makes the movie

American to you?" She pushed between the glass double doors beside him and felt the cold air embrace her. She was at once glad for the tights she'd worn under her flimsy but favorite skirt.

"The jury. It was all, you know, average guys. Everyday guys. Like me. Like guys I know. It's like they made my poker club into a jury."

"The jury *was* all men," she remarked dryly. David took no notice.

"So I guess that's the other thing. In the end, the trial wasn't in the hands of the judge or the lawyers. It was in our hands."

Hildegard started out for Collegetown Bagels. He followed her without questioning, and so encouraged, she led on. "And this makes you feel, how?"

"It's a reminder that this is our government. A government of the people."

"It hardly seems that way to me. It seems to me your government doesn't trust its own people enough to make the Guantanamo trials jury trials?"

David shook his head at her. "I see where you're going, I get it. You could write for CNN if it still covered news. It must be easy to be critical of our handling of those trials when you haven't had to pick scraps of two week old human flesh out of concrete rubble. But I was there, doing that work. I led details from Ithaca's fire department both to ground zero and the MLK Bridge in St. Louis. If you put me on those juries I'd hang every one of those camel riders for spite. Make no mistake. If they don't get juries, they should count themselves lucky. Maybe our government is doing the best thing. Lord knows none of them have been executed, which is what I and any other eleven men you could find around here might have done."

Hildegard was taken aback by the ferocity of his reply. In all her time at Cornell, she never heard an adult (undergraduates didn't count) voice support for the death penalty. Her date's assertion that any twelve men picked at random might bring the death penalty on the accused at Guantanamo brought into clear focus how he socialized in different circles. She was now on thin ice, where a second before she had felt confident and on the moral high ground. She swallowed, floundered a moment, but then recovered. "I didn't know you had been there. It sounds like terrible work, and you're right, I couldn't understand. It's easy for me to be cynical. I'm sorry. But maybe this is why we should talk about it some more."

David frowned. "I need a break. So let's take turns. Why not tell me what you thought of *Twelve Angry Men*?"

"Hmmm," said Hildegard when they pushed open the door of the Collegetown Bagels. Condensed steam from the hot beverages and many crowded tables had so fogged the windows they hadn't been able to see in from the outside. But once inside, she was afraid they wouldn't be able to get seats for some time.

"It's too crowded, I think," she said.

"Yeah, looks that way," said David, sounding disappointed. She wondered what to do next. There was Cafe Pretentious a block away, and a Starbucks at the end of the street, but neither of those was a venue he would like.

"Do you have any suggestions?"

The man shook his head. "We could call it a night, I suppose," he said. She resolved not to let that happen. She wouldn't want to end the evening on such a sour note.

It was then she had an idea. She'd gone down to Clever Hans bakery in the afternoon to get a dozen pastries for her breakfasts and for some company she would have over Sunday. She could offer some to David now and replace them before her gathering Sunday. It was a big gamble. It would be forward to ask him to come to her place. But then, they were adults and understood both what followed what, and how to say no. She would roll the dice.

247

"I have some Clever Hans cakes at my apartment, and plenty of coffee and tea. We could go there. It would be quiet enough to talk. We could even look for that movie on pay-per-view."

The man blinked, but then brightened. "All right. That's fair. It'd be a shame to end the night like this. I did shout you down."

Hildegard relaxed when David shared his desire to repair the evening. "Okay, let's go. How do you say it? 'To the batmobile?'" she joked.

He chuckled. "My 'batmobile' is back at my house. We'd have to walk back. Maybe stop in and check on Rosie."

Dr. Teschke wasn't sure how she felt about checking, she feared walking into his own house might create inertia or lead to a situation where they ended up staying at his place. She wasn't sure she could relax like she wanted around his daughter. But if it came to it, she decided, she would do it.

With her nod, the firefighter began leading her downhill out of Collegetown. The steep sidewalks were difficult in her high heeled boots, and her toes and balls of her feet soon began burning from sliding downhill into the points of her boots, and her balance was unsteady. She compensated by putting a hand up to the man's shoulder after her second stumble.

"I'll tell you what strikes me as American about that film," she said. "It's the first juror. The one who doesn't let the others influence him. Who asks his own questions, and does his own thinking."

"Yeah?" replied David with interest.

"Yes. *That* is the thing which is most American about it to me. Your country doesn't have fair trials anymore, if it ever did. There are trials for rich people and trials for poor people. But this thing where you stand up and do what you want to do, and to hell with what other people think, that's what America does all the time," she laughed. "The one juror, it's like he's a miniature America being a unilateralist. And sometimes the unilateralist is right. And sometimes he's an ass. Sometimes the American is right, sometimes he's wrong, but most times he stands alone and doesn't mind."

"Ah," he reflected. "I guess I can see the analogy."

"So, what was it like? Ground Zero?" she asked him. "I am sorry if this is too curious a question, but I have never met anyone who was there, except for some students who were children in New York City at the time."

David sighed. He was silent for a while. "If it's all the same, I don't want to think about it. It's too pretty a night," he excused himself. "And you're too pretty a woman."

Hildegard flushed at the compliment, noticing how it offset her disappointed curiosity. "It's okay," she said. Then she stumbled again with an embarrassing shriek, but he caught her before she dropped butt-first on the pavement. If they had another date, she resolved to wear flat shoes. With him, she always ended up in places where heeled shoes were awkward. She hoped no one else had seen her stumble. Heaven forbid one of her students should be walking by and see Professor Teschke tripping up and hanging on a man like a tipsy sorority pledge. But there were no other pedestrians on Buffalo Street. She guessed it was a rare breed of person who walked up and down it. Dates with interesting men never left her with as much dignity as she hoped, no matter how carefully she planned them or how safe what she chose to do was.

"Look. This is one of my favorite views," Mr. Haversham said. "It's a small town, and it isn't much, but it's mine. And I'm proud to have lived here. Even with you university people fucking everything up," he said with a laugh, pointing down Buffalo Street. "All my life it has welcomed me."

Once she had recovered her footing, Hildegard could take in the view.

From their spot on the sidewalk, she could see the lit street grid Ithaca spread out before them. While the view was hardly breathtaking, it was clean, energetic, and enough to take her mind off the pain in her feet. The moment made her feel they were sharing something of his, rather than of hers. She watched him admire it, and envied him. David's home wasn't an abstract or an indifferent cosmopolis thousands of miles away which hadn't noticed his departure and did not await his return. He was standing in his home, and had done so all his life.

Faith closed the door behind her father and Dr. Teschke. They had come to the door long enough for her dad to say he was taking his truck to drive the professor home and wasn't sure when he'd be back. She scowled at his back, but she was unclear why this information made her upset when a few moments before she and Rosie had been content putting together a jigsaw puzzle and listening to music. She should, she reminded herself, be happy her father was socializing. She feigned a smile and sat back down to the puzzle, masking her irritation in a look of concentration as she searched for a new piece.

She wasn't unhappy for her departed mother that her father was out late with another woman, she decided. It's that he was out late with another woman and *she herself* wasn't. Her efforts at the local club had yielded a few encounters with women who wanted to "hook up" for a one-night stand, and some longer conversations with women who had more baggage than she wanted to deal with. But other than her two dates with Taryn, they had not been fruitful. And here her father was, jumping into the sack with the first woman he'd had any regular dealings with since her mother died. And this was ironic given the damping affect her father's attitudes had on her own romantic life and sexual identity.

"How does he do it?" she mused over the puzzle. *"Or what's wrong with me?"* Rosie began to scribble on the paper, bored enough with her delay in placing a puzzle piece that drawing was more interesting.

"Sorry, honey, I'm distracted," she told the girl, whose only response was a silent nod as she drew. Faith picked up a puzzle piece to place it. The puzzle featured anthropomorphized penguins in all sort of costumes holding a large party, in the midst of which was one polar bear. This particular piece featured part of a pair of antlers one penguin was wearing as a part of a reindeer costume.

The sight of the antlers gave her a mischievous thought as she snapped them into place. She didn't *exactly* have to be alone while her father was out on his date, she had only to adapt her standards to the circumstances. Her father had agreed she could bring home whomever she chose, and this would be the ideal test of his claim. So as Rosie took the moment to put down her pencil and scan for a new piece to place, she reached for her cell phone. Sure enough, she still had his number. She dialed it, clearing her throat and humming as it rang so her voice was not nervous and squeaky when he answered.

"Hey hey, what's going on?" Steve answered. She guessed from this he still had her number on his cell phone from their date weeks ago. That was a positive sign.

Faith had worked out a way to phrase her request, but she forgot it as soon as she heard the sound of his voice. She began second guessing her idea. Before doubt could seize control of her, she blurted out the cleverest thing she could think of.

"Not much. Kind of a slow night. You?" she trailed her lure with her voice. A booty call could be the thing she needed to get over Taryn. And Steve was the right man for something with no questions asked.

249

Hildegard threw open her door and welcomed the smells of her apartment. Her juniper potpourri, the smell of her spice collection, and the faint hint of the celeriac root and kohlrabis she'd cooked earlier for supper greeted her like anxious cats. She waved David in, took his coat, and hung it along with her own behind the door. The apartment wasn't as tidy as she might have liked. There was dust on things and a handful of dishes in her sink, since in her pre-date pessimism she had decided she would return home alone and had not been too strict about cleaning. She'd keep him out of the kitchen and he probably wouldn't notice the dust.

She motioned for him to sit on the couch, and went to start her coffee machine and pick some pastries from her box. In a moment she had fresh coffee in front of him, and sat down beside him.

"So, shall we look for your movie? *Twelve Angry Men*?"

David shrugged. "I've seen it enough. But if you want to watch it, we can."

Hildegard thought about it. "I could see it. But I have another movie I like. Hollywood made it into a stupid American movie, *City of Angels*. But the original is excellent, it's called *Wings of Desire* in English or *Skies over Berlin* in German. And it even has an American in it. Peter Falk. Have you seen it?"

"Peter Falk? No way! Colombo?"

She nodded. "The same."

"Huh," her companion pondered. "So it's a mystery?"

"Umm, no," she chuckled. "It's hard to explain. You have to see it. It's about West Berlin while the wall was still up. That's why it fascinates me so much, I grew up in East Berlin, and I always wondered what went on in the magic world over the wall. Imagine if you had spent your whole life in East Ithaca, and could never see West Ithaca, even though you were only a kilometer away. How you might feel sentimental about a place that was part of Ithaca but you never saw. How you might envy and dislike but also feel friendly toward those from West Ithaca."

"Okay. I don't get that part," he said. "But I like Colombo, so I'm game."

"If you don't like it, tell me. We can stop it and do something else." David picked up a pastry, ignored the small plate she brought him, and as he began eating, she searched through her digital movie collection. Soon she heard the comforting opening phrase *"When the child was a child, it didn't know it was a child, and everything was soulful, and all souls were one..."* Before focusing on the movie, though, she put a plate in his lap and waggled a finger at him. He took her point and held it under the pastry he was eating. She took her plate and slid closer to him, and began watching the movie in earnest.

Soon, however, she was scarcely watching the movie. It was more like she was watching him watch the movie. Or noticing how comfortable she felt when her arm ended up in front of his, or his hand ended up on her leg. For all the language and culture barriers, she and David understood each other on one level. Lust was distracting but welcome. This coarser man was fanning flames long stifled by the pretentious and smooth veneer of her peers.

By the time the movie was ending and Solveig Dommartin was midway through her romantic monologue to Bruno Ganz, they were kissing. She felt more than two lonely years coming to an end and desire ran through her like fire, and by the time the movie title screen was playing over and over, she was sitting across the man, kissing with abandon. As his hands moved up into her skirt, she was appreciating his muscles, his strength, and how well he had shaved. As she leaned against him, she heard a paper crinkle in his breast pocket.

The firefighter withdrew his hands.

"What?" she grumbled, miffed.

David pulled a paper from his pocket. "Rosie wanted you to have this."

She shook her head, took the paper from him, and keeping one hand on his shoulder, leaned back with her other arm to place it beside her empty plate and coffee cup.

"I will happily look at it," she said, "at a more appropriate time." She replaced his hand on her buttocks and began kissing him again, and as he squeezed her, passion took firm control of her choices. She put her hand inside his shirt, and things ran their course.

After some time they were both sitting naked on her couch, and she was refilling his cup of coffee. He was admiring her figure, naked in her own living room, and the image of his belt lying across her broomstick skirt stuck in her head as an image to savor. She might not be twenty anymore, but she still had it. She'd marked this man out and gotten him.

"That was nice. It has been some time for me," she stood in front of him while she poured his coffee.

"Me too," admitted David. "I'm glad everything, you know, worked. To your satisfaction."

"Quite," she smiled pouring her own coffee now and snuggling beside him. She enjoyed the feel of his thigh against hers and his arm over her bare shoulder. The main menu *Wings of Desire* was still looping on her screen.. As she sipped her coffee, her eyes fell on the note Rosie had sent for her, and she leaned forward to pick it up. With her one hand, she folded it open, while drinking with the other.

"*Ach, du liebe Guete,*" she said, putting her coffee cup back down and taking the picture in both hands. "*Soll das die Goldelse sein?*" she stared at the drawing.

"What is it?" David contemplated it alongside her.

"It's 'Golden Lizzie,'" Hildegard replied, her voice hoarse. She cleared her throat. "It's the Angel of Victory. It's a statue that stands on top of the Victory Column in Berlin." She showed him the sketched figure of the woman holding up the spear and the laurel wreath. Then she pointed to the looping introduction screen to the movie. "It's that statue," she said, pointing out the similar figure which formed the background image of the menu. "The same statue you see so many times in the movie."

"No kidding," he said, taking the drawing from her and holding it up to the screen. The drawing was of a different angle than the image shown on the screen, but with both images side by side in her vision now, there was no mistaking it. The girl had drawn Golden Lizzie.

"What does she say down here? Is that German?" he pointed to a line of text. The professor brought the picture closer, and then cast about for her reading glasses. She extricated them from her blouse pocket on the floor, put them on, and squinted. It felt strange but pleasurable to be naked but for her glasses.

As she suspected, the line was not German, but had the special IPA characters which were the signature of Rosie's own special Esperanto. She frowned that David mistook it for German: he must not even know English and German shared the same alphabet. She shook her head. "I'll take it in and have it translated."

"Wow. That's....weird," said David.

"Very," said Hildegard. She noted with disappointment how the picture had popped their bubble of intimacy. How had the child chosen this image? Had she had some prescient knowledge of what movie they would watch? And of the love they would make? The girl's dreaminess transformed in her mind from harmless to unnatural. She picked up her skirt, draped it across her lap, and shivered.

"*Unheimlich,*" she said. "Eerie," she translated for him.

Her lover reacted as though he also felt exposed. Even as she hoped to snuggle up to him, he got up to pick up his clothes. And she knew then she didn't want him to go.

"Stay," she said.

"I shouldn't. I should go home and check on Rosie. I didn't tell Faith I'd be staying with you overnight."

"Your daughter can take care of things. I think I deserve it. And you're the one who made me feel – spooky? - with this picture."

The man paused with his belt in one hand and pants in another. She pleaded with her eyes, but began to feel self-conscious doing so. What was she doing asking him for protection? She didn't need it. She needed to get a grip instead. The picture was a weird coincidence.

But her request had moved David. He put his pants down and sat beside her.

"She's an unusual kid," he said. "She does weird things all the time. Relax."

"Thank you," she said. "I know it's a coincidence. But I'm glad you're staying. I'll make it worth your while," she promised, blowing in his ear.

He grimaced. "I'm not so young," he said. "I need time to recharge." He patted her thigh. His large hand was reassuring.

"There's always the morning," she said, leaning into him.

Rosetta resisted impatience. The universe unfolded at precisely the pace God intended, and seen in this light, impatience was silly. But Faith and Steve, the black-haired man she had invited over to "help" with the jigsaw puzzle, were both slow about finding and placing puzzle pieces. By being just as slow as the woman in picking puzzle pieces, the man was not helping complete the puzzle much faster.

At first, she had passed the time examining this guest and his unfamiliar smell of "wanting" while waiting for her turn to place a puzzle piece. But even the novelty of his presence and features had not been enough to fill the long pauses both adults needed to find a puzzle piece to place. Rosie could see a dozen pieces in front of each of the adults they both could place, but they looked past them. So, when she had become sure that neither would find it rude, she had returned to the drawing she was working on, and glanced up from it long enough to snap her selected pieces into place.

After another thirty minutes of silent passages of turns, they had reduced the puzzle to its last few pieces or so. The end was so close Rosie could taste her promised bowl of ice cream already. But Steve broke the rhythm of puzzle completion by snatching the puzzle piece Rosetta had already selected and placing it.

She raised her eyebrow at the man. A number of his actions, including the way he made fun of Faith and the way he had playfully slapped her behind when she had once stood to get coffee, suggested this man enjoyed ignoring various rules and limits. The rule he was now flouting was the rule that you didn't snatch a puzzle piece someone else had picked up to place. So rather than encourage this strange man by complaining about his rule-breaking, she picked up and placed the next most obvious piece and went back to her drawing.

"Will you look at that?" The man marveled.

"I'm telling you, if I had left this puzzle to her she would finished in thirty minutes. She can do forty pieces a minute."

"She has got to be some kind of genius," Steve remarked.

"Yep," she answered. "But this time, I get the credit." And with that, the woman placed the last three puzzle pieces one after the other, also breaking the "taking turns" rule Rosie had understood to be the order of the evening. But she let her elation at the prospect of a bowl of ice cream overpower her dismay.

"*Glaciadʒo!*" she said, pushed up her chair, and went to the kitchen. The adults did not follow her, but she didn't need either their help or the moderation they might impose on her serving size. She had retrieved the round tub of "Purity Cherry Chip" from the freezer and found the bowl and scoop, she was surprised to hear the sound of a slap, and some giggling, from the room. But moments later, both Faith and Steve entered the kitchen, smelling very much of wanting. The smell was so powerful it was unpleasant.

"*Wow, and I thought I wanted some ice cream,*" Rosie thought. "*These two can barely control themselves.*" When she had made her bowl, she passed the carton and the scoop to Faith, who began scooping out her own.

When at last all three of them were at the table, the smells of the adults subsided, and she enjoyed the dark chocolate chips and sweet cherries, savoring every bite. She had eaten ice cream from time to time at the laboratory, but nothing like this. It was richer and more flavorful, like a dream made real. She could imagine God made it from snow (which she had never seen) in some magical kitchen. This was an absurd fantasy, she knew, God didn't make ice cream, he made people to make ice cream for other people. But she was sure ice cream was part of the purpose of existence, and a sign of God's love. People who made ice cream *this good* did more for happiness than any king or queen.

She added it to the list of wonderful things which were indisputable proof of God's love. Esperanto, dogs, checkers, and ice cream: the list got longer every day. She swung her feet in delight under the table, and suppressed the sigh that came when the bowl was empty.

The other two, however, were as slow about the ice cream as they had been about the puzzle. They poked each other, laughed, dawdled, and let an awful lot of wasteful melting happen. This struck Rosie as odd, given how keen they had smelled to have the ice cream to begin with. But when they were done, she didn't feel tired, as she should at this hour of the night, but energetic. She might start vibrating if she had to sit still any longer. Perhaps she *had* taken too much ice cream, she considered.

Faith, however, had it in mind that Rosie should go to bed. "Okay, go find some pajamas, and brush that ice cream off your teeth."

She felt her hand rest impolitely on her hips. She wouldn't accept it! This was unfair because she'd had to spend the whole night sitting watching the two of them think about puzzle pieces, even though she would rather have been drawing or teaching the woman to play chess. She let her disappointment coalesce into a demand. "*Danci!*" she insisted, and pointed at the CD player.

Faith rolled her eyes to Steve. "She wants to dance before bed."

The man stroked his chin in curiosity. "It's up to you."

"Okay," the woman said to her, "but we'll dance together this time. Let's do a dance we both can handle, and you'll help make me less fat as you go." She got up and walked to the CD rack, and then picked out a record.

"Here, I'll teach you a new dance, if you don't already know it. Can you do the 'Electric Slide?'"

Rosie shook her head. She felt intrigued though, since her foster mother had never asked to dance with her before.

"Okay, so, I will put a song on repeat. Watch me, and we'll dance to it. It's the only dance I know, and I've never taught it to anyone before."

The stereo began playing a song with a heavy bass beat, a story about a man and his lover "Billie Jean." Faith demonstrated some simple backward and forward steps and twists which repeated over and over, and before too long Rosie felt she was able to join in with her. It was fun to dance with someone else. When the song started over, she was pleased to find the woman was ready to dance it again, and again, and again. She began to lose herself to the simple dance. Soon they began inventing ways to clasp hands while dancing, or bumping their hips, and she forgot all about the tiresome waiting which had filled her evening.

The excitement was too much for Steve, and he got up and tried to join in. At first, this was frustrating, since he insisted on standing between her and Faith and even clumsily stepped on Rosie's bare toes, but with a couple of repetitions, he had the steps. Soon he too was sharing in the hip bumps and laughing along with them.

"This song is such a flashback," he said over the music.

"Yeah?" prodded Faith.

"Yeah, this played like fifty-five times at my prom."

"It's a good message for a prom. It's all about keeping your pants on," the woman replied. "Heck, that makes it a good message for *you*."

"Keeping my pants on was why you called me over?" he rebutted.

The adults stopped dancing, but Rosie kept it up, so they could jump back in easily.

"Maybe. Maybe I like your company. Maybe you don't make me feel like I have to be someone else to be good enough for you. Maybe that's slumming, or maybe I'm deciding I like you."

"That's a whole lot of maybes," Steve shrugged. He adjusted his belt buckle. "You sure it's not the Italian stallion you're after?"

At this, her foster mother took a step closer to the stranger, and the two adults stared into each other's eyes, both showing a strange expression which mixed anger and challenge.

The smell of wanting had returned, and the air in their carpeted corner of the living room was thick with it. The smell had a shrill, metallic edge to it. It made the girl blush at her own foolishness. It had not been the ice cream the two had been wanting. She stopped dancing and plotted her next move. She could see that dancing was no longer the focus, and she was beginning to feel tired anyway.

"Time for bed, honey," said Faith, settling the issue. Her foster mother waited for the singer to finish his verse and pressed stop. "Thank you for dancing with me. We should do it some more. Maybe I'll start learning something from you!"

Rosie nodded. That would be fun, as even simple dances were more meaningful when danced with someone else. She put a hand to her mouth to stifle a yawn as she waved goodnight to Steve, and headed up the stairs. The singer's last lyric played through her head as she did so, begging her to unravel the pithy mystery of the words *"be careful who you love, be careful what you do, because a lie becomes the truth..."* The contradictions in those words would be good to send to God in her sleep. After all, shouldn't one love everyone?

Faith had a flash of cold feet once she got Steve into her bedroom. He was a fantastic kisser, so good she had to dismiss the idea of getting funky on the living room couch so as to shorten any delay and stay farther from Rosie's bedroom. But upstairs she felt obliged to speak with more of a hush, and the hushing cooled her lust.

The man, however, showed no signs of slowing down. Ina flash his clothes other than his shirt were in a pile on the floor. The reason for his enduring popularity with the ladies was now apparent.

"Wait," she said as he moved to rejoin their earlier embrace.

"What?"

"I want to be sure you understand what this is, and what it isn't," she said. To show him she wasn't breaking the action, and commit in her own mind to the notion she wasn't stopping, she kicked off her shoes and leaned into him.

"This is sizing up to be one of my daydreams," he answered.

"Yeah...That's the thing. I don't want this to mean too much to you."

"Okay," said Steve. "Tell me what this is and isn't."

"This isn't love. It's a hookup."

At this, her co-worker did look a touch crestfallen, but not so much that his apparent "enthusiasm" diminished in any way. "Okay. So it's a hookup. Hookups can be the start of something, though, if everyone agrees," he rebutted.

Faith chewed her lip in a moment of indecision. And if she planned to keep the man as a friend and an emergency booty caller, he needed to know the truth. And he was getting the hang of discretion. She hadn't heard as much about him through the rumor mill over the last few years as she had years before. And if he couldn't keep his mouth shut, well, maybe he would babble enough to solve the problem she couldn't. It would be a humiliating favor, but there it was.

"This hookup won't be anything else," she said. "You need to understand...I'm a lesbian. I can get it on with men, I've done it plenty, and I like it fine, but I only fall for women."

She watched his face for his reaction. She was on her guard for disgust, rejection, or anger. To her surprise, Steve merely blinked.

"Wow. That's hot!" he said after a moment.

Faith sighed. She wasn't sure what response she had expected, but on some level, she felt rejection would have better than the reduction of her entire sexual identity to a porn fantasy, as this fellow had so deftly done. But here she was, all fired up and her clothes half off. It wasn't the time for a discussion of the subtler forms of homophobia.

She put a finger to his lips. "Let's put that tongue of yours to another use before you ruin my mood."

A smirk turned the corner of Steve's mouth. "Say no more."

Chapter 18

Letters from the Past

David awoke in the morning to regret. The first thing on his mind when he opened his bleary eyes was Connie, and the bitter yet familiar smell of the chemotherapy on her skin in the morning she so quickly showered off. Still, here he was in bed with a woman who smelled far better, but he still missed Connie. The nagging sense of betrayal became a keen blade through his enjoyment.

The feeling was nonsense, he decided. He didn't let emotions run his life. So he focused instead on his feelings from the night before. But despite being recent, his feelings of desire and gratitude he'd held for Hildegard somehow felt small and far away. So he pushed the thoughts of Connie from his head and focused on his surroundings. The woman's bedroom had been invisible in the dark, with stray streetlights revealing only the outlines of different furnishings. Now he could see it.

The room had a gold and brown theme, with two large freestanding wardrobes, a vanity, and china cabinet-like glass wardrobe filled with knick-knacks of different kinds. Pictures of places David didn't recognize hung on the walls, most of them cities, and many of them featuring the professor and one or another companion beaming back at him. One wall of the room featured a few paintings or art collection posters. One depicted a golden-haired woman curled on a couch which he recognized as a Gustav Klimt painting, and another print of a lord embracing his lady bore the unpronounceable words *"Kuenstlerhaueser Worpswede."*

He ran his eyes over his companion, who still slept. In her unguarded sleep, with her hair in disarray and her scarf gone, her weak chin and crow's feet were more than evident, but still, it was clear she was a beautiful woman. And a smart one, he recalled from their banter the night before. And this amongst other things is what had made her so attractive to him. Like it had been Connie, interacting with Dr. Teschke was an uphill battle of answering intellect with passion, body language, and action. He remembered from one of his management seminars a discussion of different types of intelligence, and supposed at some level he was, perhaps, as smart as these women. But for the most part, he recalled enjoying the challenge which came with loving them.

He stopped at the word love. Did he love Hildegard? He doubted it. He had been fascinated with her, attracted to her, and horny after more than eighteen months of solitude and a long time before when Constance had been too ill to make love. He had also enjoyed the conquest, too, of this woman who was so cold and aloof at first but was now willing to take him to bed. And he liked her better now than he had a few weeks ago, or even the night before. The recollections of her laughter and her passionate cries had softened her otherwise hard facade. But love was a long way off.

"Have I loved anyone?" David wondered. The fact of his casual tryst with this new woman raised this doubt in his mind. Was she taking Connie's place? And if she was, and if she could, did he love either woman?

He pushed these thoughts out of his mind, sat up, and gathered his clothes and shoes. His Catholic side pricked his conscience, reminding him he had

256

fornicated. But the manager in him rationalized against this idea. The idea of the sin of fornication, he was sure, was meant to prevent young people from bearing unwanted children or to avoid jealousy-induced domestic violence, and neither complication was likely between two single people their age. Distracted by his ruminations over the severity of his most recent sin, he reached for his boxer shorts.

Despite his care, the motion of the bed nonetheless awakened Hildegard. It was only a double. He guessed from her choice of mattress she did not often have company to bed.

"Good morning," she said, sitting up and running a hand down his back. He turned to look at her over his shoulder while he pulled up his boxers.

"Morning."

She squinted at him, and then sat up to reach for her bathrobe. He enjoyed another glimpse of her naked form before she covered it up. "You have a long face," she asked him. "Up so soon? I could cheer you up, I think."

"Yes, I bet you could," answered David. "But I should be home."

She glanced at her clock. "It's five-thirty early. I'm sure you don't need to go home yet."

He didn't know how to reply to this. He began to formulate an excuse about how he'd left his blood pressure and heart pills at home, but Hildegard let him off the hook. "Suit yourself," she continued. "But since you've gotten me up so early, I will make myself breakfast, and tea." She tied the robe's belt around her waist and sauntered out, giving him simultaneous twinges of guilt and desire. "Would you like some?"

"Sure," he relented as his stomach growled at the mention of food. He started dressing the rest of the way, wincing as his back complained at all the bending over. It didn't usually hurt like this in the morning. But then, he didn't usually spend his Friday nights with a seductive woman and then sleep on a strange mattress, either.

"The wages of sin are death, or at least, back pain," David considered. The woman soon re-entered the room, swaying beautifully, and the sight made him want to say her name aloud. But the impulse brought a question to mind.

"Your name is kind of long. Do you have a nickname? Something shorter?"

"A pet name? For me?" Hildegard scoffed at him. "You think you know me that well, do you? I sleep with you once and you want my pet name?"

He stammered. She sat beside him and poked his ribs. "How about 'Professor'? That sounds like a fine pet name," she said.

"It's three syllables. That's as long as 'hil-deh-gart,'" David rebutted.

"How's this one? 'Doctor? It has two syllables,'" she continued, still grinning.

"Yeah, okay, doc. While I've got you here, I'd like to talk to you about my blood pressure. And for some reason I can't figure out, my back is *killing* me," he answered. After a delay, she took his joke. She slapped his shoulder and sighed.

"I think you will know my pet name when it is time for you to know it. Visit some more and it will occur to you sooner," answered the woman with a tilt of her head.

"How about 'Gardie?' No, never mind, it sounds funny," he said, ignoring the pretend pistols she formed with her hands and fired at him. "Maybe Hilly?"

Hildegard plumped her small breasts with her hands to no avail. "Only in Hamburg - or maybe Kansas - would anyone call these hilly," she said, and leaned forward for a kiss. When she'd had it from him, and more besides, she stood and walked out to the now whistling teakettle.

David stood and followed her after he'd tied on his redwings. The breakfast she had set for him at the table consisted of a white ceramic cup, a white ceramic bowl, and a roll on a saucer. He sat down to it, picked up the spoon, and examined what was in the bowl.

"What's this?" he asked of the strange mush.

"It's muesli. You must be careful of your heart, yes?" she cocked an eyebrow at him.

"Yeah," he admitted. But what he saw in the bowl didn't look so much medicinal as bland and unappealing.

"It is good for your heart. Oats, and flax seeds, and hazelnuts, and other things, soaked in skim milk. Eat it before it gets too soft and you will enjoy it more," she said. She sat down across the table from him and pushed him a box of tea bags. He picked an earl grey, which experience told him was one of the few teas he could enjoy, and started on his muesli.

It was, at first, bland. But a few seconds after the first bite, different flavors reached his nose. Nutty flavors, oats, and hazelnuts combined in an earthy bouquet. It wasn't bland, he decided, just subtle. A few moments later he was outright enjoying it, and when he was done, he found he could eat more.

He finished much sooner than Hildegard, so he picked up his tea. His eyes traveled the table and fetched on a stack of printouts beside the woman.

"I read the newspaper in the morning," she explained, seeing his gaze and patting the print-outs. "But I won't be rude."

"What paper?"

"*Die Zeit*. It's a weekly paper, and that's a good thing. It takes you all week to read it."

"Never heard of it," he said.

"No surprise," said Dr. Teschke. "The website is blocked and the physical paper is not sold in this country."

David started when he heard this. "What?"

"Yes, you heard me, it's blocked. I have a friend encrypt each issue and email it to me so I can print it out. I use samples from it in my classes on linguistic timing, so it's essential that I get it. But it's blocked here in America. And it's only in German anyway."

"That can't be true. Why would they block it?"

"It printed some material from Wikileaks back before all the activists were arrested. Now it's blocked. Like *der Spiegel, the Guardian,* and other European news sites."

David wrapped his mind around the claim. It couldn't be true, but yet, he would not believe she would make something like that up. She seemed too well researched for conspiracy theory.

"It's funny," she continued. "Your press is not so free as it used to be, but Americans have so many channels competing for their attention you never notice. If you have five hundred channels of *kramm* filled with corporate-sponsored lies, your press must be free, yes? And since blocking *die Zeit* and *der Spiegel* only inconveniences people who read foreign languages, and your schools carefully teach nothing but English, it only inconveniences us foreigners when something is blocked," she noted.

"Our schools teach foreign languages," he complained.

Hildegard's eyebrow spiked in an acute arch. "Starting to teach a foreign language only once children have grown too old to learn a language easily is not teaching foreign language. It's willfully failing to do so, or choosing to torment children. Proper language education begins with entry into school. If not sooner."

"Huh," said David, hoping to close the conversation. He hoped she wouldn't carry on about American politics like she had the night before. He didn't agree with a lot of it, to be sure, but he didn't like to think about it either. It was a vast, corrupt, and pointless subject he'd given up understanding, and he'd been happier since he'd done so.

"Anyway, eat your roll. It's whole grain. Good for your cholesterol," she said pointedly. He looked around for butter or jelly, but there wasn't any. As if to model her expectations, she took a bite of her roll and set it down for her tea. He did the same.

"So, I'm sorry if this is a bit awkward," said David. "I've got my own issues, you know. I still think about my wife."

Hildegard was unconcerned. "Whatever your issues, you please me. So you get breakfast, and a return invitation. And if you always leave this early I won't ever need to kick you out," she smiled. "And that, too, is something."

He laughed. "You know, for a woman who was begging me to stay last night, you have a hard edge in the morning."

The professor's expression froze for a second. "Oh, yes! The weird picture!" She left the table and then returned with the drawing, taking a seat beside him this time. They both stared at it.

"So, how important is this statue? It must be like the Statue of Liberty for Germans," he speculated. Last night her reactions to it had been strange, but he'd been too preoccupied to ask his questions. But now they had time for questions.

"No, it's nothing like that. She's much more warlike," she explained. "She was built in the 1800s after Germany won many victories at war. And her image was used by the Nazis, too, to drive up war fever. Since Germany was reunified, though, it's more been a symbol not of triumph over our neighbors, but of triumph over our own division and our own tyrants. President Obama, when he visited, gave his speech there. Some people criticized this, because the Nazis had made a big deal about *Goldelse*. But I think it was clever. A black man speaking at an idol of racism. It's like he understood its old meaning, and its new meaning, and wanted to help change it from one to the other."

"Hmm. But why would Rosie draw it for you?"

"I don't know," said Hildegard. "Last night it gave me a fright, like she could see the future or something. You know, I was self-conscious, like she might have seen us lovemaking," she laughed at the idea. "Now, I guess maybe she understood I am originally from Berlin and thought I might like the picture."

"What do you think she wrote there?" David said. The woman frowned again at the writing.

"I have no idea," she said. "Shawn will translate it for me, I'm sure." Then she faced him. "Thank you for putting up with my anxieties last night without mocking me."

"It was nothing. Part of me wanted to stay anyway," he admitted, finishing his tea. "You are excellent in bed, you know."

"I'm excellent on the couch. You haven't tried me in bed," she laughed. "But thank you. I suppose infrequency gives me a certain enthusiasm."

"Me too," said David.

"So," Hildegard said. "Apropos that, I would like it if you gave no sign of our relationship to anyone outside your family. I am studying your foster daughter, and while there are no rules against what we're doing, some people might, you know, raise eyebrows if I was found to be involved with the guardian of a research subject."

"Suits me fine. I'm not sure I want listen to my friends tease me about it yet. I need time, so I don't get angry and feel like they're making fun of Connie."

She squeezed his shoulder and stood again. "I'll change and walk you to your car. Since we've started this early I think I will drive out to my CSA and get more vegetables for the week."

Once down in the parking lot, Hildegard gave David a last hug and kiss and went to her car. She pulled the rain cover off of it and packed it away. A second later she found that her lover, rather than walking to his huge truck, was still standing over her shoulder.

"What's that?" he boggled, jaw hanging slack.

"It's my *Ente,*" she said proudly. "It's a classic." She admired the car. She'd spent tens of thousands on it over the years. In fact, its convertible leather roof had been hand-made for her in Korea when the original one had gotten too brittle to patch again. Its yellow glossy paint and shiny chrome gleamed in light reflected from the courtyard windows. On its bumper was the sticker she had custom reprinted every few years: "*I fly bleifrei.*"

"A what?" he asked.

"An *Ente.* It means 'duck'."

"A duck?" said David. "What kind of a name is that for a car? It looks like a toy to me. It doesn't help that it's rubber-ducky yellow. I thought Germans had cool cars."

Hildegard scowled, a bit tweaked by his dismissal of her gorgeous vintage car. "Go drive your monster truck then. I like my duck." She shooed him away. He went to his truck, and she continued packing the rain cover into the duck's trunk. But a moment later, her lover once again stood at her shoulder.

"Yes? What do you need, duck-hater?" she smiled at him.

"I left my lights on, I guess," he admitted. "Or at any rate, my battery is dead."

"Ah, so your big truck needs electricity from my toy duck, does it?" She was amused by David's awkward position. The opportunity for teasing was ripe, and the good part was, she would be able to tease him again and again about this.

"If your battery is powerful enough to turn my starter."

"Oh, it'd better be. It's new, and I told them to install a powerful one because sometimes this car doesn't move for weeks." She got in, cranked up the duck, and drove it over to the truck. The truck's hood was already raised.

Her jumper cables were a few feet too short to reach the truck's battery. She had to take his word for this fact, since she couldn't see into his engine compartment because it was so high off the ground. The firefighter got out his jumper cables and clamped them to hers, and then connected them in turn to her battery.

Hildegard got in the duck and stepped on her gas, and after a few attempts, the man was able to start his truck. He hopped out, blushing and still sheepish.

"Thanks."

She looked around the parking lot to see if there was anyone obvious there, and then kissed him. "You're welcome. Now don't make fun of my duck."

"Yeah, I guess I paid for that," he said.

"No, not yet," she winked. He shook his head and got back in his truck.

David followed her out of the enclosed parking court and went his own way. Dr. Teschke kept the duck's top down and headed out route 96 to her CSA, enjoying the cold morning air until her ears were numb. She was making the drive strictly for the fun of it. But her CSA farm still had a good selection of many fruits, roots, and squash, and it made sense to keep getting fresh vegetables as long as she could. Winters in Ithaca were cold and bleak, and cheerful root soup recipes from her childhood were one of the best remedies on a quiet night alone in her apartment.

"Maybe not so many will be alone this year," she sighed.

Rosie stretched to reach the box of shredded wheat. Faith was still asleep, and she did not want to wake her foster mother. But David had left the cereal on a high shelf and, as she had foreseen, not yet returned from his date with Dr. Teschke. She could climb onto the counter, but was sure her foster father would be unhappy if he knew she'd put the soles of her shoes on the counter top he cooked on. So she contemplated her alternatives.

The solution came by dragging one of the breakfast benches into the kitchen, standing on it, and taking down the cereal. While she was so high up, she peeked in the high pantry shelves to see what David might have hidden away. She found only dusty kitchen utensils and cookbooks, and not the secret bag of M&Ms she had hoped she could wheedle him into opening. She replaced the bench, placed her bowl and spoon, then came back to the kitchen and fetched the shredded wheat and the milk.

Before starting her breakfast, she went to the door and picked up the newspaper the old man often read, the "Ithaca Journal." She began reading through discussions of local crimes, and the school budget.

Rosie had her concerns about these newspapers. They focused, she noticed, on news which was bad. She scanned in vain for good news. She was sure sometime in the last twenty-four hours, someone in Ithaca had been nice to someone else in some way worth writing about and reading about.

But there were no such stories. It struck Rosetta as inadequate, and unfair to God's work in creating good people, that there was such scant discussion of the good things people did. To be sure, there was great evil in the world, evil which emerged from indifference and unintended consequences and evil which came from malice, but that wasn't the issue. There was good in it, too, and more of the good needed to be retold.

She folded the paper closed and focused instead on her shredded wheat. She wondered if Hildegard had liked her picture, and if she had understood it. Then her eyes fell on the jigsaw which filled a portion of the breakfast table. It pleased her. The picture on it did not matter. Like a giant puzzle, creation itself was made of small interconnected pieces. This made the jigsaw a reality in microcosm. The interconnectedness of puzzles made them a model of an economy, of a church, or a farm, or the world.

She heard the screen door, and then the main house door, open. She saw David returning from the cold morning. She smiled and waved at him, and he waved back, but he was troubled. He hung up his coat and came to sit at the table with her.

"Are you done with the paper?" he asked. She pushed it to him. He didn't read it long, though, and by the time she was done with her breakfast, he had begun reading it and stopped twice.

"He is distracted by something," she observed. Sure enough, his eyes wandered, first to her, then around the room, and he gave a heavy sigh a number of times. His eyes lingered on a portrait of his departed wife.

"He feels guilty," said Constance. Rosie drank the milk from her bowl with loud slurps and watched her foster father over the bowl. She had learned to like the nutty flavor the shredded wheat gave the milk.

"I'm still kind of tired, Sweetie," David excused himself. "Will you be okay drawing by yourself for a while?"

She nodded.

"He always goes to the bedroom to be upset," Constance told her. "He'll cry himself to sleep."

Rosie watched the man go upstairs. She felt sorry that he would be spending time alone, needlessly being sad. Constance was in God's hands, and still loved him.

She picked up her empty bowl and spoon, carried them to the kitchen, and stood on her tiptoes to rinse the bowl in the sink. She then returned to the table, wiped down her place so spilled milk or crumbs would not interfere with her drawing, and then let the cleaning solution dry. When all that was done, she took her seat, reached for the first sheet of paper, and began to draw. She closed her eyes and thought of a subject. She at once began sketching a pattern of brick arches she remembered somewhere, a place where she rose early in the morning, earlier than the dawn, to sing.

She could feel Constance in the room. She was in the pictures, in the bookshelves of dusty books which seldom moved, and in the curious collection of vinyl "records" which sat in a corner but were never played. Constance was restless, she knew. Once the woman's racket had grown so loud she could no longer focus on her drawing, she relented and invited the spirit in.

"Would you like to draw or write him something?" she thought.

"Yes. I think a word to him could end this foolishness," Constance said.

Rosie prepared. She put down her marker, cleared her concerns from her head, and began taking deep breaths. When she had reached a state of quiet, she invited Constance into her. *"Then take my hands. Speak through me as Gabriel does."*

In a moment she could smell Constance, a smell of warm, dry wool, oiled leather shoes, and cinnamon tea. And it was all she remembered until Faith woke her up.

Steve was already gone when Faith awoke. She was glad for this. For as much fun as their tryst had been, she hadn't relished any "morning after" conversations with him. She suspected he would have made lighter of their time than she would have liked, or instead taken it too seriously. Any conversation could only have been awkward. She stood and gathered her clothes, some of which were trapped between her sheets, and as she put them on, she peeked out of her window. Steve's truck was gone, and her father's was back in its place. She smirked. Her father had gone out on the date, but even the babysitter had ended up getting some.

She slid on her long sleeve tee shirt and sandals, and tromped downstairs to think about breakfast. There she found Rosetta slumped over her drawings, snoring with her head and shoulders on the breakfast table. She shook the girl to awaken her.

"Hey, sweetie," she said "I think someone had too much ice cream and stayed up too late last night, huh?"

Rosie grunted and shook her head in denial. Then she rubbed her eyes with fatigue.

"Back to bed, you. You need more sleep by the look of it."

The girl shook her head again, but Faith would not be moved. She then decided to use one of the tricks her mother had used on her when she didn't want to admit she was tired.

"If you don't want to sleep, you can go lie on your bed and think about it. If in half an hour you still aren't sleepy, come back down and we'll look for something on TV."

Rosie gave an exaggerated sigh, examined and picked up a couple of things she had drawn and a pair of folded pages, and stomped up the stairs. Every stomp impressed on her audience how unnecessary the child felt this whole 'bed' thing was. Faith watched her foster daughter go without reacting to the stomping, and then went to the kitchen. The shredded wheat box was standing on the counter top and there was a rinsed bowl in the sink, so she guessed the girl had already made breakfast. And since her father was not downstairs, he was up sleeping off his date with Dr. Teschke. So she took a box of Wheaties, her own bowl, and the carton of milk, and went and sat in Rosie's already warm spot on the bench.

"Good for my dad. It was about time he got out of the house for something other than those poker games with the good ole boys." She wondered if Dr. Teschke's attentions would make him any less grouchy. She was feeling less grouchy. Steve's skills had been, to her surprise, on par with his boasting.

"Blush now, get it out of your system. You'll see him at work on Monday," she reminded herself, eating another bite of Wheaties. Then she winced at the thought, and put her free hand to her forehead. A second flush of blood rushed to her ears, and she felt hot. She fanned her face.

"You have a way of making your life difficult, don't you, dumb ass?" she muttered.

Rosie sat on her bed, arms crossed, and for a moment dwelled on her annoyance. She didn't want to go back to bed. She was sure if Faith had given her a few minutes, she could have explained she hadn't been sleepy, but had let Constance take possession of her for purposes of writing David a note. A few drawn pictures could have explained the situation. But what was done was done.

Chocolate stirred in his bed in the corner as she entered her room, grunting and murmuring at something in his sleep. She was surprised to find him back in bed. He had been energetic on his first-thing-in-the-morning romp in the back yard. Perhaps all the excitement about the puzzle and ice cream had kept him up late, too.

She then remembered Constance's note. And now that she was abed, she did feel sleepy, so the sensible thing to do was deliver it before she went to sleep. She took the first folded sheet Constance had left, peeked enough to see that David was the addressee, and then took it and went to the man's room.

She cracked open the door and peeped in. Her foster father was sleeping with his face buried in a pillow, his shoes beside the bed.

"In his shoes," said Constance. "He'll find it there." So Rosie tiptoed in and left the note in his right shoe. She then went back to bed, picked up the other note and opened it.

On the page, Constance had drawn a climbing rose wrapped around a wrought iron lamp post, a lamp post she recognized as the one outside Faith had left on for her father the night before.

"Pretty," she thought. *"Thank you!"*

"I hope you grow up into the prettiest rose," Constance replied. And then she was gone, and Rosie yawned and put her head down. People tramping through her body did make her tired.

Chapter 19

Bridges

After crying until he slept, David dreamed in crystal clarity of the day he decided to retire. This decision had first come to him while he was racing down the east bank of the Mississippi river, trying to bring his van full of sleeping divers to the scene of a terrorist attack. The attacks had focused on major bridges nationwide, prompting the media to title them the "Market Garden bombings." Once enough information had come in, the Ithaca Common Council had agreed to let him organize this relief expedition to St. Louis. And now, ahead of him, to the right and across the Mississippi, he could catch glimpses of the Gateway Arch, slender and gleaming in the sun. From beneath it still rose smoke, or dust, or some combination of the two.

"Hey Chief," said the younger firefighter beside him, "is that the arch?"

"Looks like it," said another firefighter.

"That's it," David said. "I came through here on my way back from Viet Nam. There's an elevator train in it and an observation room on the top. I bet it's packed with camera crews."

The roadside to their right was an open grassy prairie which ended at the banks of the Mississippi River. The river itself, however, was less a scenic waterway than a parking lot. A Coast Guard cutter was visible further downstream, and it marked the beginning of a line of river barges which had extended for two miles behind them. Beyond this were the buildings and warehouses which lined the western bank in northern St. Louis. On the left they could already see some of the lower buildings and smokestacks of East St. Louis. The opposite lane of their road was all but empty, with only the occasional fire, police, or ambulance vehicle driving by. None of them had been running their sirens. He guessed it was too late for that.

After a few moments, David spotted a sign, black vinyl letters on an orange-painted plywood panel leaning up against a speed limit sign which was hooded with a black trash bag. "Emergency Staging Area- 1 mile. Speed Limit: 35," it read.

"We're getting close," said the first firefighter.

"Wake up!" He shouted to the back of the bus. "It's show time." At this he heard rustling and groaning of his passengers awaking to their various cramps and aches, followed by a babble of conversation he tuned out to focus on the road.

In a half mile there was another series of orange-painted plywood signs. "Family members- follow red stripe to Red Cross Registration Station." Then "Media - follow yellow stripe to Media Support Station." Then, at last , "Emergency Services – Follow Blue Stripe to Command Center Checkpoint."

"They're organized," the firefighter in the passenger seat commented.

"They've had forty-eight hours. Besides, the Falls Church guys probably got here after eight hours and made everything high-speed," another rebutted.

"Yeah, that'd be like Falls Church," someone sniggered. "Got to be on national TV every month or they're not doing their job."

David followed the blue stripe on the pavement which began at the sign. They passed some tan and olive drab National Guard tents beside the road, surrounded by a jumble of civilian vehicles. He guessed the vehicles parked there were whatever local family members had *not* been driving in St. Louis two days before.

The yellow stripe stopped at another cluster of military-style tents which was surrounded by a forest of antennae and satellite dishes. Two reporters were standing in front of cameras beside the road, babbling inaudible sound bites to an anxious nation.

The blue stripe stopped at a large cluster of fire trucks, ambulance and mortuary vehicles, and construction equipment. An Illinois State Trooper flagged them down as they approached, and the fire chief stopped and rolled down the windows.

"Sir, it's emergency personnel only past this point. I'm going to have to ask you to turn arou-"

"We're all firefighters," said David. "We borrowed the van from the church," he said, nodding to the side of the van, which read "Immaculate Conception Church – Ithaca, NY - Diocese of Rochester."

The trooper changed his instructions. "Keep going, then. Go around the hydraulic excavators and park, send your leader and only your leader to the command tent, the one with the big satellite dish."

"Thanks," he said. The trooper nodded in reply and moved to stop the next vehicle. He followed the trooper's directions, pulling into a much more compact lot filled with large trucks, Illinois and Indiana State and GSA vans, and a smattering of construction contractor equipment. On the edge of the parking lot were a line of portable toilets and some trash cans overflowing with an enormous number of take-out pizza boxes.

David stopped the van, and as soon as he did so, his eager firefighters slid open both side doors and jumped out. "Okay," he heard Dwight, his fire captain, say. "Loosen up, go take your pisses, then start inspecting your tanks and regulators for pressure and seal. I don't want anyone suiting up until the Chief has talked to whoever is in charge and found out the deal."

David walked up to the captain and spoke quietly, trying to let the commotion mask what he had to say. "Go easy on them. Chances are they won't have seen anything like this," he said, dodging between the firefighters yanking out equipment and covering one ear as someone started the thundering portable air compressor.

"If 'going easy on them' doesn't make them better prepared, I ain't doing it," the man answered, looking him in the eye. "But if you mean don't put them down, I won't. There'll be enough misery to go around without the extra my bitter-old-man glands can add."

Dwight understood, the chief realized. The fire captain was the only other one of them who had been in New York after 9/11.

"Go," said the captain. "Sniff butts with the big dogs. Tell us what's next."

"Use my cell phone if you need me," he said.

"I won't need you. That's what you pay me for. Come back when you need us."

David shook his head at Dwight's swagger. The man was the biggest hard-ass in the department, which is why he had assigned him to the full-time station house with his worst roughnecks. Since he'd done so, that station house had become his best, hands down.

He picked up his fire jacket and helmet so as to avoid being stopped every few feet by a state trooper or sheriff, and was thus able to walk without delay into the command center.

He blinked when he entered. The black vinyl interior of the complex of linked tents was in strange contrast to the intense halogen field lights which shone from every corner. The drone of diesel generators filled the tents, so everyone speaking inside it was doing so at a near shout.

"Hold it, sir," said another Illinois State Trooper, this one a woman who stood not so high as his shoulder. She showed no sign of discomfort at their size difference as she put a palm in his chest. "What's your business?"

"I'm a fire chief from Ithaca, New York. I'm here with twelve firefighters. I want to know where I'm needed."

"Got some ID to prove it?" she asked. David was surprised by the question, but produced his department ID and national ID. The State Trooper scrutinized them for a moment, flipped them over and scrutinized the back, and then handed them back to him without comment.

"Wait here," she said, nodding to some folding chairs beside the door. "I'll get the operations officer."

David stood there and took the opportunity to look around. Two large monitor televisions dominated the back side of the complex of tents. One showed an aerial view of an area he guessed was downtown St. Louis, the other showed CNN. Behind the reporter was black smoke and fire was blowing across open water, and he squinted to read the screen caption "thousands drowned in San Francisco." America had its hands full.

In a moment the scroll bar announced two survivors had been pulled from the rubble of a Seattle highway tunnel, the fifth and sixth to be pulled out in the last two days. He'd heard on the radio others had been found but not freed and were being pumped air and water.

The camera flashed to a picture of the president standing beside the Brooklyn Bridge, where the bombings had been foiled by motorists. "This bridge stands as a symbol to terrorists everywhere that they have overreached themselves. Some in the press have begun calling this attack 'Market Garden.' If so, then this bridge was a bridge too far for our enemies. But in truth they have gone many bridges too far. They have crossed the Rubicon, and their reckoning will come."

David shook his head. It was the sort of empty-headed rhetoric he expected politicians to use. He focused his mind on the bridge which was close, not the words which were so far away.

The trooper returned with the operations officer behind her. "Sir, this is the newest arrival," she said, and resumed her post.

The operations officer proved to be a skinny gray-haired black man, about Chief Haversham's own age, with a dour expression and a harried look.

"Ken Aubrey," he greeted him.

"David Haversham," he replied.

"How many did you bring, and what training and equipment?" the emergency manager droned, visibly fatigued.

"Counting myself, twelve rescue or recovery divers and their dive kits, submersible lighting, and a portable air compressor for tank refills, plus basic trauma and medical supplies."

At this, the tired man brightened. "Divers? Twelve? *And* submersible lighting?"

He shrugged. "My department is on the south end of a big lake. We're always doing rescue and recovery dives."

The man smiled back at him, clasping him hand. "Holy crap, am I glad to see you! I've got every big truck company in Illinois banging down my doors to help, but I only need so many big trucks! Divers are scarce. You're the first guy to show up with what I needed and only what I needed."

"Glad I guessed right," said David. "I couldn't get the States of Illinois or Missouri to tell me anything useful, so we read the news reports, drew straws, and borrowed a church van."

Ken tipped his head toward the front of the tent and the banks of computers. "Hey c'mon, follow me, I'll give you the briefing. The commander is busy, but he'll wet his socks when he hears we got a truckload of divers." The man led him to a bank of tall LCD monitors surrounded by radios and paper maps stuck with pins.

"Okay," Ken said. "As you no doubt heard, they blew up the Martin Luther King Bridge at morning rush hour on Tuesday. The MLK carried all the cross-river traffic from I-70, I-270, I-64, I-55, and I-44 plus local traffic. In addition, they blew up two more liquid natural gas tank trailers on the vehicle ramps and overpasses leading to the bridge."

"How many vehicles hit the river?"

"We don't have information that specific. But we estimate nine hundred vehicles blew up, burned up, got crushed by collapsing overpasses or buildings, or ended up in the river. Estimating two passengers or more per vehicle based on St. Louis's and East St. Louis's successful carpool program, and adding in bystanders, it looks like about twenty-two hundred casualties, just from vehicle drivers. I'm betting it's more."

David shook his head.

"That's not all of my problem. I've still got live people trying to be dead. The bridge didn't fully collapse, so not only do I have a river full of bodies I have to recover, but I've got river barge traffic stacked up northbound and southbound, with the Coast Guard holding them off. We've already had two barges try to end run the cutters while we had divers in the water. Both captains were arrested and the barges grounded away from the bridge site."

"It's nice when people cooperate," Chief Haversham muttered.

Ken shrugged helplessly. "People get stupid sometimes. I mean, even if I didn't have divers in the water for those barges to hit and drown, I still have a dangerous bridge site. The rubble from the MLK makes the draft too shallow for barges to pass most places. And the spans of the bridge which still stand over those areas where the draft is deep enough could fall into the water at any time. Add to that fast water from the rains upstream-"

"And anything could happen, anytime," David completed. "More collapses, shifting rubble catching divers, vehicles and bodies carried further downstream..."

"It's a perfect storm, without the river traffic helping by trying to become part of this infernal equation," the other man acknowledged.

"So what's the plan?" he asked.

The emergency manager pointed to a chart on the wall, showing a list of phases. "Phase 1. Stabilize the bridge and get human remains out of the water. We're in phase 1 now. It will last another two-hundred and forty hours. This is when I'll need you the most. Can you stay ten days?"

David explained the deal he'd struck before running off with a fourth of his city's firefighters. "I can stay until the Ithaca Common Council tells me to come home or FEMA runs out of money."

"Blank check, but not an unlimited account. I get it," Ken confirmed, then continued. "Phase 2. Demolish and remove the remains of MLK bridge and clear river traffic lanes enough for one barge northbound and one southbound. If we don't have enough contract salvage divers by then, I may ask you guys to hang around for that part."

Chief Haversham nodded without making a promise.

"Phase 3. Regulate river traffic during further clearing operations at MLK.

"Phase 4. Safeguard Ronald Wilson Reagan bridge site until a national guard or homeland security unit gets that permanent assignment."

"Where's that bridge site?" David wondered. He didn't recall seeing another bridge for a few miles on his way down the river.

"We're at Reagan bridge site," the man answered. "Illinois and Missouri had finished leveling this ground to begin work on the Reagan bridge, so it was the perfect place to set up this command center. Construction has been years delayed already, and now we'll wish we had started earlier. The MLK's been overloaded for decades, but the feds weren't interested every time we raised the issue that it wasn't just overloaded, but a sitting duck."

"A perfect target, for a long time," he agreed.

"Yep," said Ken. "But look at it this way. Our airplanes are safe from shampoo bottles and nail scissors. So all that homeland security money was money well spent."

The two men shared a moment of silence as they gazed down on a computer-generated mockup of the bridge site.

"Okay, so, how soon do you need my boys and girls in the water?"

"Seventy-two hours ago. How quickly can you get me how many?"

"Do you want twenty-four hour ops?" David checked.

"Yes," said Ken. "You said you had submersible lights?"

"Two banks of submersible floodlights. But we'll need generators and cables for continuous ops, they run about five hours on a battery pack. Plus, depending on how deep they are swimming for how long, my divers can go maybe four to five hours in a day. We have both cold water and the bends to watch out for. My people are also used to lakes, not rivers with a current."

"Then scratch twenty four hour ops," the officer changed his mind. "You guys get night shift since you brought your lights. There's a Coast Guard lieutenant by the name of Rice down at the near command post by MLK. Drive down the river, you'll see it. Have your divers report to him, I'll tell him you're on your way. He'll give you an orientation while it's daylight, and then you guys should try and get some rack. It's going to be a long, cold night in the big muddy."

David offered his hand. "Thanks. I'll get out of your hair now."

The other man smiled. "Shoot, you're the cavalry in this situation. I now have fifty percent more divers than I did ten minutes ago. If I had a gold star I'd stick it to your chest. You're small-town fire chief with big-town brain. Are they hiding more like you up in the sticks in New York? Send out the call, come one, come all, if they've got divers. The more bodies we can get out before they're silted over or eaten by catfish, the more families we can bring closure to."

"We're the largest outfit in the Finger Lakes. But you might try Buffalo. They have a lot of water, so they've got to have divers."

"Buffalo," said Ken. "Maybe Cleveland and Erie then, too?"

"Wouldn't know," said David with a grin. "Further than I travel on a weekend."

"Welcome to the Big Muddy," said Ken. "Or the Big Bloody, as the Coast Guard boys have been calling it. Come back here when you get a chance, I want to introduce you to the commander."

Chief Haversham left, formulating his briefing to his firefighters in his head. He decided he wouldn't brief them, but take them to the Coast Guard and see they got a proper briefing there. He had no specific information about dive conditions, which is what they would need most in any case. The rest he had heard was not much more specific than what had been on every radio, TV, and computer in America for two days.

268

He passed his orders to Dwight, and in a few minutes everything and everyone had been packed into the van. David had been expecting a lot of questions from his divers, but the captain must have told them to be patient, because he got no questions and overheard only muted, pensive conversations. Despite the humble surroundings of tents, gravel, and mud, he guessed his divers understood they were about to become a part of history.

They left the parking lot and drove down the riverside. Soon they came up beside the Coast Guard cutter which was holding back the southbound river traffic. It was anchored midway in the river, its guns bared and pointing upstream. Motor launches moored on its downstream side. On the opposite side bank was St. Louis arch. And downstream of them were the ruins of the MLK Bridge. Its piers and spans leaned in disarray, and portions of its bridge deck hung over the river by threads of rebar. Multiple portions of its span were gone. Rope foot bridges spanned the gaps from the western shore to the stranded portions of the span where empty cars were still parked. He wondered how the owners would ever get the cars back. Or if they would want them back.

"Jesus," said one of the firefighters.

"Yeah. Looks worse than on TV," said another.

David passed another sign. "Recovery Operations. Authorized personnel only. Follow red line to diver's shore command. Follow blue line to engineering and salvage operations. Follow yellow line to joint state morgues." He drove on, following the red line.

The red and blue lines split from each other after they emerged from the service road which went under the ramps and abutments of the ruined bridges. The blue line turned left off the road and ended in a set of refrigerated container trailers and a construction office trailer. Even inside his van, Chief Haversham could hear the diesel generators running to keep these trailers cold. The red line ended in another set of olive drab and desert sand colored tents, beside which were generators and three refrigerated trailers. He followed it and parked the van beside a collection of other vans and trucks. Coast Guard, Illinois Department of Environmental Conservation, Department of the Navy, Department of the Army, law enforcement, and several commercial companies were all represented.

David parked, got out, and approached the shore command tent. It was much smaller, and did not feature the large plastic boards, TV screens, and antennae of the first. One medium-sized communications dish was all he had seen outside, and two computer workstations were in the tent. A hand painted sign behind his desk read "Valkyrie Joint Service Diving Detachment – bringing home the brave fallen."

A young Coast Guard ensign was seated at one desk. The officer stood as he entered. "Can I help you?"

"Ken Aubrey sent me down here to see Lieutenant Rice. I've got twelve firefighters, all divers, with either PADI or professional certifications."

The ensign grinned. "Oh, man, sir, am I glad to hear it. I'll tell the lieutenant right away." He picked up a radio. David marveled to see someone so young in a uniform. *"Was I ever so young?"*

"Valkyrie Six, Valkyrie Five," called the ensign.

"Six, go ahead, Five."

"I've got someone Ken Aubrey sent down. He says he has twelve divers ready to work."

"What? Twelve?" asked the voice in disbelief. "Is he from the Navy?"

The ensign's eyes followed David's finger to his helmet and coat badge. "City of Ithaca, New York, Fire Department. We have compressors, gear, and submersible lights."

269

The ensign keyed his radio. "Six, he says he's civilian, a firefighter, someplace in New York. He has all his own gear, too."

"Five, I'm coming ashore with bells on. Anything further?"

"Negative, Six. Five out."

The ensign put down the microphone. "Sir, the lieutenant will come ashore outside."

"Check," said David. "I'll wait for him there." He left the tent with its vinyl smell and harried-looking ensign. Outside he saw his divers once again getting ready. Two firefighters were draping gray vinyl tarps over the church van. He guessed the lady divers were inside getting ready to wiggle into their wetsuits.

Chief Haversham walked over to where Dwight was grousing at the diesel generator kit and the fireman working on it.

"McCallister, didn't you inspect this before we left?" the captain demanded.

"Yes, Cap'n, I did."

"If you all weren't taking department equipment camping with you at Taughannock Falls on weekends it'd be more serviceable when we needed it."

"Cap'n, if I never took it camping I wouldn't even know how to use it or trouble-shoot. It'd sit around in storage until it leaked. Anyhow I think the compression is bad. Give me a minute to check the hose seals."

"Give him a moment to check the hose seals." David said, clapping a hand on the fire captain's shoulder.

Dwight turned and frowned at him, his "asschewus interruptus" frown he always gave when his chief thwarted a good asschewing. What would follow this look from Captain Earling was a reminder that when the chief had given him the problem firehouse to straighten up he had also given him permission to use "robust language" and "traditional techniques." To the captain's thinking, if his boss didn't like the application of these things he should leave the area for a spell.

He short circuited this reaction by putting an arm around the younger man and leading him away from the problem. "I need you for a minute. Let the men handle the equipment. I'm sure they want that generator to run as much as you do."

The captain's expression softened. "What's up, Chief?"

"The Coast Guard LT is coming ashore," David said, motioning to the diving boat parked in the river. "I need you to go with them to the briefing and be sure he's straight on our capabilities and limitations. Our divers are used to still water," he reminded, pointing to the white foaming crests the Mississippi's current made at the ruined abutments of the bridge. "And clear water. While I wouldn't call Cayuga Lake crystal clear, it's clearer than the nation's largest river filled with flood silts and pollutants."

Dwight nodded. "I'm with you so far."

"I need to bring every one of these men and women home. Not that the Coast Guard doesn't care and doesn't know their business, but they have a lot on their plate at the moment. They don't know these divers and their strengths and limitations. You do. I need you to work with the Coast Guard and represent them, the Department, and the City."

The captain raised an eyebrow. "Isn't that your job?"

David leveled with the younger man. "Yes, it is. But I won't be the Chief much longer. And if recent history is foretelling, this kind of terrorism will happen again after I'm gone. When it happens, the department will need a fire captain, or a chief, who knows the whole job of out-of-jurisdiction support, not one who knows how to get generators fixed and get slowpokes on their feet." Chief Haversham took a deep breath before he continued. He wondered how Dwight

270

would take what he was saying. "So pick one of our best to get the generators running and the people moving. We know you're an 'A' at motivation, let someone else learn the job while you learn mine."

The captain shifted and stared at the ground. David gave the man a moment of silence. He was, after all, changing the man's job without any notice. After a moment, the other man looked up. "I got it, Chief. I can do it."

"I know you can. But in case I'm wrong, I'll be here to come paddle your ass or fire you," he grinned. "We both know, however, I'm seldom wrong."

Dwight sniffed in mock derision. "You might know that, Chief....I can think of plenty of-"

"-But not about this," he cut the younger man off.

"Not about this," he repeated, sounding more affirmative.

"Now, while you're getting the dive briefing I will call the Department and the Mayor and let them know we're on the ground here. Then I'll find someplace for our firefighters to sleep and somewhere we can stand out equipment and tents."

"I can do that-"Captain Earling began.

"Yes, you can. But I gave you two other jobs. Pick a diver to learn your job and get down the water and meet the Coast Guard lieutenant. Remember those?"

"Oh yeah. Sorry, Chief."

"Be sorry later," said David, motioning to the water, "Be the best now."

The captain gave him a long look he couldn't fathom, and then left. The chief mused at the strange look. Dwight was one of the few men he counted as a genuine friend, and he couldn't recall ever seeing an expression on him he couldn't interpret. But then, these were trying times.

David sighed. It had needed to be done. He needed to step back. He'd been the go-to guy for so long that good men, like Dwight, had learned to come to him and rely on him and, by doing so, sell themselves a bit short in their own minds. But he couldn't stay Chief forever. He was getting older. And Connie needed him. Both things were affecting his focus.

He surveyed the beach. Divers were still swarming about the tarp-covered van, now in wetsuits, running compressors and scanning equipment for leaks. Downstream, he saw a rubber zodiac boat with three men on its way from the Coast Guard cutter. One was probably the dive lieutenant. He wondered if there was a computer up at the main command center where he could try to find hotel accommodations for his divers. Maybe there was even someone there charged with solving the billeting problem for the whole operation who could make it easy for him.

"Chief?" he heard the question behind him. Chief Haversham turned around. One of the divers was there.

"What's up, Falver?"

"Your phone, sir. The girls heard it ringing while they were changing in the van. We found it on the dash. They said it rang a Frank Sinatra tune."

"Thanks," he said, accepting the offered cell phone. He hid his concern. "Under My Skin" was Connie's ring tone. "Are you ready?"

The young man was pleased to be asked. "Yes, sir. I'll get in that water and bring those people home."

"Do good things for Dwight. I've given him a lot of responsibility and he needs your best."

"Yes, sir! The captain will get it!" Falver enthused. Falver was a third-generation firefighter, and David was sure his whole family was behind him. It was good, in a way. Firefighting families knew the kinds of things which happened and a lifetime of stories from one's father or uncle helped prepare a man. In this

271

way, firefighting was unlike soldiering. His own father's stories of World War II had borne no resemblance to what he had encountered in Vietnam.

"Your dad must be proud, Falver," he remarked.

"He doesn't need to be proud of me. We're proud of him," the young man answered, turning to go. "He's the best. And I'll be that good."

David nodded at the young man's assertion. "He was the best. I was glad to have him with me on 9/11." He watched the young man go, hoping the next ten days left the boy as vibrant and dedicated as he was now.

With the young man gone, the chief had what would amount to the most privacy he would have for the next couple of weeks. And while there was much he needed to do, he couldn't pass up a phone call from Connie. He walked down to the water, noting as he did so the zodiac was ashore. Dwight was face to face with a younger man in a white uniform, standing with his hands on his hips and his feet shoulder width apart. Captain Earling had never been in the military, and David bet this Coast Guard lieutenant was about to find the man strong willed and informal. He refrained from intervening. If the lieutenant wanted the divers, and the captain wanted to help, they'd work it out. This would be a good time for him to stand back and let people learn.

He walked south along the river bank, brushing through the tall grass along the stone embanked shoreline. About two hundred yards further on, he saw the parking lot and loading dock for one of the gambling river boats which moored along the Illinois side of the Mississippi. The boat was gone, and the parking lot was empty. The chief expected it would not return soon, but nonetheless a parking lot felt less private than tall grass brushed by the wind. He stopped where he was, searched out a random square of broken concrete above the river's edge, and sat, hanging his legs off the edge.

He dialed Connie back. In a moment, she answered.

"There you are!" she said, laughter still in her failing voice. "How's the drive?"

"It's over," said David, looking across the river into the plumes of smoke, the haze of dust, and the spires of glass and concrete that made up downtown St. Louis. The archway glinted in the cloud-dimmed sun, clean and polished amidst the grayness and ruin. "I'm across the river from the arch now. We're on the ground."

"Is it bad?" Connie worried. "It looks bad on CNN. They keep flashing to it on the TV here, but newscasts spend most of their time on San Francisco and the Golden Gate Bridge."

What did "bad" mean in this context? His mind flashed to what he had seen of the ruins of the Golden Gate Bridge on the news. He could be glad he wasn't there, but the death toll in San Francisco didn't make the problem in St. Louis any less tragic. "It's bad," he decided. "They estimate twenty-two hundred missing just from the explosions. And this isn't like Manhattan. A good slice of those missing are in the river, and have been there for forty-eight hours. There will be no miracles two days from now to raise spirits. Our boys will have to pull out corpses. Hundreds of corpses."

Connie sucked in her breath in response and dismay. "I'm sorry."

"Don't be sorry for me. I still have you," he answered.

"Yes. Yes you do have me," she answered. There wasn't a trace of fear in her voice. He wondered how she could do it. In the background of her call, he could hear an IV pump beeping. He knew the sound too well.

"How was the chemo?" the husband in him asked, trying not to betray the concern, the fear, and the loneliness which flooded through him at the word "chemo."

272

"It's bad," she said. "But don't be sorry for me. I still have you."

David felt his heart skip a beat as she repeated his words to him. Across the river, an ambulance moved along one of the intact roads, lights flashing, but no sirens audible. He choked up, unable to find anything to say.

"Now, how can that be true? How can I be enough?" He rejected the words, hoping she could not hear the tears on his cheeks. How could it be true, with the pain she had to feel and the suffering she went through to buy a few more months of pain? What did he offer her which could be worth it? Especially since he wasn't with her, but was instead on this riverbank a thousand miles away, in the middle of the ruins of thousands of other lives. As if they were a more important problem.

She ignored his question. "I'm proud of you," she said. "For the third time in our lives, our nation has called you, and you have answered, doing difficult things and helping others do them, too. It's an honor."

"I should be there!" David blurted out, longing to hold her hand. "I've been there every time! I promised I would be."

"The strong and capable daughter you helped me raise has me in hand. Besides, we'll have time," she said. "You can come to other chemo sessions and watch me throw up. I promise." She laughed into the phone. "Then you can make me a dinner so good I can't feel queasy anymore and have to eat."

David resented her making light of it. And in a flash, he resented his choice to be gone, resented the "public," and resented this "nation" which always needed him and had interrupted his life and marriage for decades but rarely came forward to say "thank you." Every time some dipshit left his TV dinners in the oven and fell asleep watching football, he would have to leave his family, get a company of other men to do the same, and go clean up the mess, and every time one of his men got injured, he'd have to stomach talk from some state or federal austerity puppet about "curbs on local government *entitlements*." And now, in the middle of his wife's cancer, some Arabs or other lunatics had decided Americans weren't dying fast or painfully enough for their taste and had come and blown up some more. He resented it all.

The flashing of another set of emergency lights across the river caught his eyes. It was a second ambulance following the same path as the first. Chief Haversham guessed the authorities on the far shore had cleared an evacuation lane for the vehicles, and he wondered how they were moving the rubble, too. From 9/11, he knew disentangling people and body parts from the rubble was a slow business. It depended in equal measure on the ability to move rubble and get it out of the way so you could search, and the speed of the average trip to the morgue or the rubble dump.

He was thinking about work, he scolded himself. Even now. Even on the phone with his cancer-stricken wife.

"Connie, I'm a piece of work, aren't I?"

"Absolutely," she laughed. "You come down somewhere between Michelangelo's *David* and a real pain in my ass. God spent overtime making you such a byzantine work it's taken me a lifetime to appreciate you."

That was Connie, using words like "byzantine" in a sentence which he'd be obliged to look up if he wanted to understand her. She had gone to Cornell. She was an Ivy League girl, and while she never rubbed his nose in it, part of living with her was never forgetting it.

He gave voice to the strange answer which came to mind. "You have always been my angel."

"You say that now," she challenged. As she did so, memories of some of their arguments and disputes where he had said things he was not proud of flashed through his mind.

"No," David asserted. "Believe me, no matter where I have gone in this world, no matter what God-forsaken thing I've had to do, you have always been my angel."

For whatever reason, Connie did not have an answer to his outburst. In the river, one of the barges hoisted its anchor and began drifting downstream. He guessed the reality that the Mississippi would be closed for a long time was finally dawning on barge captains and river transport executives.

At length Connie answered, her voice tremulous. "I miss you so much. Do what needs doing. But come home as soon as you can. It's easier to feel like hell when you're around."

"I will," he promised. "I've got a job to do here, but I've got one to do at home. I'll be there soon."

"Goodbye! Call me when you get another chance," Connie finished, sounding so much brighter than he imagined she could possibly feel.

When the line went dead, he closed the phone, following the newly aweigh barge with his eyes as it began its own journey home from the ruins of Martin Luther King Bridge.

David lay awake for some time after he awoke. His mind was a chaos of feelings. Part of him wanted to get up and find out what Hildegard was doing with the rest of her day. But the other part of him was grieving Constance, a feeling made worse by his memory of her courage and selflessness in her final years. And his bedroom didn't help his nostalgia. Everything about it reminded him of Constance. He recalled how good she had looked in her painting jeans and bandanna when she had helped him repaint the walls blue, refinish the floorboards, and pick the wool Persian rug under the bed. He cried more than once as he tossed and turned. This room was the only place he felt comfortable doing it anymore, and at least there was no chance Connie would walk in on him and accuse him of wallowing or offer him undeserved comfort.

He could hear someone downstairs. He guessed it was Faith. Rosie would not make much noise. He imagined for a moment the things she would have to say after he spent the night out. He wondered how she would react to him. It was no use putting it off, he considered, he should go down and face the music.

He sat up and reached for his shoes. In one of them was a note. He opened it, expecting a message from Faith.

"Do not be ashamed to accept the joy God sends to your life," it read. "He will also send hardship, in balance to your soul and his plan. Now stop feeling sorry for yourself and put your considerable talents to work. I love you, Constance."

David froze. His felt his heart jump into his throat. He went to the closet, and pulled out a bundle of letters from the locked receipts box in which he had left them. Most of them were on brittle air mail paper addressed to "SSgt David Haversham" at different posts in Viet Nam.

It was indeed her handwriting. Even the "C" and "e" in her signature were right. His mind raced. How had this happened? What should he do? He stood, with an old letter in one hand and the new one in the other. And, he noted, it was in green ink. Green was the color Constance had always used as a school teacher to write notes and corrections. She had always imagined it less threatening to students than the red ink other teachers used. There was no question the note had come from her. But how?

He went to the edge of his bed, put down the letters, and knelt. He had done this so often as a child, and during the months of Constance's illness when he had the bedroom alone and no longer felt self-conscious.

"Heavenly Father," he began.

Faith came back to the present when she heard her father on the stairs. She had her laptop open. She was reviewing her holiday fire prevention and inspection plan for the local shopping complexes so that, before they filled with customers, she could be sure they were safe and the alarms and extinguishers were all in top shape. Her dad's expression was unexpected, however. He had a tranquil smile.

"Someone was out past his curfew last night. What does he have to say for himself?" she scolded in her best impression of her mother's voice.

David said nothing at first, but ducked into the kitchen. He reappeared a moment later with a cup of the coffee she had brewed and a new shit-eating grin.

"Wham-bam-thank-you-Ma'am," he answered her, taking a seat.

Faith smirked. She suspected a new age in her relationship with her father was dawning. "It's nice you're vivacious into your old age. And I'm betting you'll make all of Rosie's appointments at the university on time now!"

Her father grinned. "I think so. How was your night?"

"Not bad," she said. She decided to immunize herself against anything the old man might hear by volunteering half the truth. "Steve McCallister dropped in and helped us finish the puzzle."

David scowled. "Had I known you would have that rascal over I'd have canceled my date and sat all night on the porch with a shotgun."

"I know," she countered. "But it was a spontaneous thing. I was spurred on by your apparent success and decided I deserved some overnight company, too. Besides, we've had this conversation. You've agreed I should feel comfortable bringing my dates home."

"As long as you don't mind me shooting at the ones who don't suit me, sure," he grumped. But he changed his tone when she pouted at him. "So, umm, a good time was had by all, anyway."

"Yes," answered Faith. "And with Steve around, Rosie had twice as many chances to place puzzle pieces than if pokey old me had been here. It was a good thing, too, because that rule was getting hard to enforce."

"She was awake when I came in this morning, drawing. She'd already taken Chocolate for his walk," he recalled. Her father's eyes fetched on the green marker and stack of paper Rosie had been using, and his expression grew puzzled.

Faith tried to resolve his confusion. "She was head-down on her drawings when I came down. I sent her back to bed. I guess I kept her up too late," she said. "Anyhow, now that you're up, I'll go into the office. I need to take a look at last year's fire inspection records for the Commons so I can make up a plan for this year without re-inventing the wheel."

David frowned at this. "I've raised a workaholic through my bad example," he said.

"Yup," she answered him, pleased that he recognized it. "Live with it." She stood and kissed him on his forehead. When she returned with her radio and jacket he was twirling the green marker in his fingers, lost in thought. She packed her laptop in silence and went to the door.

"I'm happy you got out, Dad," she said. "I think you needed it. I think we both did."

"Thanks, I did need it. Your mother often remarked if I wasn't working, I was a homebody."

"Yeah. So listen to your wife," she advised, and headed to the station.

When Rosie came back downstairs, David was at her seat, spinning the green marker in between his fingers. She waved at him, unsure where to go for a second because he was in the seat she used.

"Good morning again, sleepyhead!" her foster father chimed. She nodded her acknowledgment of this truth. Faith had been right, she had to admit, she had gone back to sleep with no trouble.

"I need to ask you a question," the man said, putting down the marker. The girl nodded again and drew closer, running her hands along the table edge. He held up Constance's note. "Did you write this?"

The question struck her as willfully obtuse. Constance had *signed* the note with her *name*. Of course Constance had written it. She rolled her eyes, which she knew she oughtn't to do, since Nanny had taught her this was rude. So, for clarity, she shook her head, and, after looking around the room for some object which could be linked to Constance, pointed at the portrait picture of the woman beside the window.

David looked where she was pointing. "Yes, that's my wife's picture. But she's gone. There was no one in the house but you, and me, and Faith."

Rosie shook her head. Constance was often around the house. From time to time she was standing over his shoulder.

"And this note was written on the same kind of paper you are drawing on."

She had to concede that.

"And it was written with the same marker you left lying on the table," he continued, holding it up.

She shrugged. If Constance had left the green marker on the table, she couldn't be blamed.

David gave her a long hard stare, trying to fix her eyes with his. "And the note was written in English."

A sigh escaped her, despite all of Nanny's lessons in being polite. Rosie sat down on the bench opposite her foster father and drummed her fingers. If he chose to think *she* had written it, despite all the evidence to the contrary, there was nothing she could do about this. The letter, after all, was written in English, in different handwriting than her own, and signed by another person. It couldn't be clearer.

A glimpse of the penguin and polar bear puzzle made her think of the night before. She wondered if there was any ice cream left. David, however, was continuing to stare at her. She felt awkward about it. An awkward moment of misunderstanding was as fine a time as any to pray. This would be an opportunity for God to send some understanding of one sort or another to either her or Mr. Haversham. Or both, if he was feeling generous.

She folded her hands on the table, reached out and gave the man's hand a squeeze, and began to meditate. Prayer was much better than arguing for producing understanding.

David left the note open on the kitchen counter as he cleaned the counters and stove top. He felt angry and confused. On the one hand, everything in the note sounded like Connie would have said it, the handwriting was Constance's, and it was written in English, which Rosie couldn't or wouldn't write. Yet Constance was dead and gone, and there was no chance she could have written it. He worked the bar mop furiously across the counter.

He would have punished the girl for lying, except he had never seen her lie, not even about the smallest thing. He felt angry at her for pretending she couldn't write in English when she could. Everything about her circumstances had suggested she ought to be able to anyhow, he didn't know why he hadn't known it already. "I've been played for a fool."

"But why?" answered the other voice in his head. "Why would a girl do such a thing? And how? How would she have found enough samples of Constance's handwriting to forge it? And even if she could forge it, how would she know the sorts of things Constance would say?"

He paused to look at Constance's picture over the sink. Her smile, never an innocent one, had always been approachable nonetheless. He remembered something she had often said. "Children are sensible. It's teenagers and politicians we have to keep an eye on."

Rosie was nearly a teenager, if she wasn't already. But mentally she was not so old. Sometimes she struck David as though she were six or seven. What should he do? Did he become angry? Did he scold her? Or did he accept this note at face value, as a miracle supplied by God, by Constance, by Rosie, or some inexplicable combination of the three?

After many long minutes of scrubbing that stripped a few weeks of accumulated grease from his stove top and overhead vent hood, he was feeling calmer. He peeked out to see how Rosie was doing.

She was still sitting at the breakfast table, hands folded in prayer or meditation or whatever special world she retreated to when people confronted her. It was a frustrating pattern, less dramatic than denials or defensiveness or crying, but troubling in its own way. He could make no headway toward truth or an explanation when she checked out like this.

"Only a few more weeks," he recalled, "and she's someone else's enigma."

Hildegard returned to her office from her Monday afternoon class to find Rosie's curious drawing from the weekend paper-clipped to a translation in Shawn's lazy looping script.

"Doc,

"Near as I can tell, the text at the bottom reads something like:

"'When the child was still a child, it didn't know it was a child, and all things had spirits, and all things were united.'

"Weird stuff, huh? She's like a poet or something. Now you see what I'm up against during my interview sessions with her. I'm helping Akiko with her sections this afternoon. Let me know if you want me to work more on this.

"Shawn"

Chapter 20

The Daughters of David

The next Saturday morning when David awoke, Hildegard was already at her breakfast table, reading from the printout of *die Zeit* which permanently occupied one corner of the tabletop. She glanced up at him as he approached, but said nothing until he went to take a seat.

"Good morning!" she chimed. "You slept in later than last week so I started reading. Let me finish this article and I'll be polite company again in a moment."

David glanced down into his bowl. She had once again prepared him a bowl of muesli, although this one had dried currants or some other berry in it. The electric teakettle still emitted wisps of steam, and the box of teas for him to pick from was on the table. The professor was drinking her tea, but her own bowl of Muesli was untouched. Perhaps she was waiting for him to eat.

He sat, contemplating how with his lover the biggest competitor for a hard penis was a newspaper. With Constance it had been books. One might take a break from lovemaking to rest one's neck or use the bathroom and return to find Constance still naked but reading a book.

He guessed from his experience with Constance that, unless he engaged and understood the interest the newspaper held for Hildegard, he would end up in perpetual competition with it. He would strive to understand, rather than resent, this thing which attracted her attention.

He poured hot water for his tea, pawed through the vast selection of teas until he once again settled on Earl Grey, and then interrupted her. He wondered how she would react.

"What are you reading about?"

She didn't answer for a moment. "An opinion piece. One of my favorite editors has come out against the relocation of the EU military command and security apparatus to Berlin and Potsdam. I disagree with him, so I am reading carefully."

David puzzled. "If you disagree with him, why is he your favorite?"

Dr. Teschke didn't answer, but instead raised her hand for silence. David could have been offended, he supposed, but instead he shook the teabag in his cup and took a bite of the whole grain roll she had once again supplied without butter or jam. After a moment she put her page aside and looked at him.

"I disagree with him because I think the change will be good for Berlin, and as far as I'm concerned, anything which brings jobs and prestige to the city is a good thing. But my favorite editor thinks it is problematic in a number of ways. His first fear is it will lead to a remilitarization of Germany. Our constitution, which was written in part by American occupiers and then imposed without the consent of us former Easterners after reunification, says our military cannot deploy outside of Germany except as part of a multilateral force. He is of the opinion this rule has contributed to Germany's prosperity by taking the option of expensive military adventurism off the table. He worries a centralized and German-dominated EU military might prompt us to try and lead multinational efforts and circumvent this constitutional requirement by ordering French and

Italian troops deployed in support of a German-led military operation. I see his point, but I'm not concerned. I haven't seen the day when the French timidly went along with what someone else proposed! And I don't think many countries will go along with any future German military adventurism for the sake of satisfying our constitutional limitations on things. Certainly not Poland, Belgium, the Netherlands, or the Czech Republic," Hildegard asserted.

David reflected on what she had said. It was rare to meet a woman with a developed opinion on international security issues. But it was obvious to him from her explanation that, as Ithaca had been central to his life and thoughts, Berlin was central to hers. Even though, as near as he could tell, she hadn't done more than visit Berlin since her late teens.

He wouldn't venture onto the thin ice of commenting on EU military policy. The notion of a European in arms sounded to him like a farce anyway, unless it was a Brit. But he was sure anything he would say on the subject would lead to a precise analysis of his ignorance. So instead, he came back to what he was sure was near and dear to her.

"It sounds like you care a lot about Berlin."

Her eyebrow pricked up at this. "Why, yes I do," she said. "When I retire, which won't be long, I'll buy an apartment not far from the *Kurfurstendamm* with my savings, find a younger man with ample appetites, and live well! Then I'll die, either at a sidewalk cafe with a copy of *die Zeit* in my hand or in bed in the throes of passion. It's that kind of place, a place for life and death."

David couldn't imagine such a place. He didn't think he'd ever been to one. Saigon had its colonial charms, but even before its fall he'd never been as enamored of it as Dr. Teschke was of Berlin. Despite the mounting evidence he would die of heart trouble one day, when he thought on death, he still imagined he would die in action. He could only envision burning up or suffocating in a fire rather than expiring as Constance had done so gracefully and courageously.

"Ah. Sounds...interesting."

"No. It's a mundane fantasy. I'm ashamed to admit I have an ambition so banal," she said, taking her first spoonful of muesli. David did the same.

Banal. There was a word he had last heard pass from Constance's lips, decades before, until her teaching job and the necessities of raising Faith had made both of them boring and hence "banal" themselves. He grinned.

"Honestly, I doubt you could be banal if you tried, Hilda."

Hildegard swallowed her muesli and pointed at him for emphasis. "I veto that pet name. Further use will result in a whimsically devised torment of my choice. You have been warned."

He finished a spoonful of his muesli to give him time to respond. "Okay. How about 'honeybunches'?"

She smiled. "What is a honey bunch? I'm unaware that honey was handled in bunches. In Germany it was sold by weight. Here I see it sold by volume. Never have I seen a 'bunch' of honey, and I use honey a great deal in tea and baking. Is there such a thing as a honeybunch?"

David reflected on this. "Sure there is. You're one of them."

"Humph," the woman grumped. "Don't expect me to come running when you use it, shedding clothes and calling your name, but it's not as bad as 'Hilda.'"

"Ah...the search goes on," he said.

"I'm glad it goes on. Because the first two stops on this *U-Bahn* were not anywhere I wanted to get off," said the professor, returning to her tea. "Take this train somewhere exotic, somewhere I can feel like a rare jewel."

"How about...how did you say it? *Goldelse?* Golden Lizzie?"

The professor's expression was pained, and she put down her teacup.

"That's crass. The only reason I'm not offended is I know you don't understand what *Goldelse* symbolizes. Millions have killed or been killed because a certain portion of each generation of young men and women were so seduced by *Goldelse* that they were willing to kill to earn her favor. It's unflattering. It's like being compared to Marie Antoinette or Imelda Marcos or some other woman indifferent to the suffering her demands bring to others."

"You have golden hair. You stand on a pillar looking down on everyone around you. It's a fit. I'll get you a wreath and, you know, a 'spear.' Maybe something in hypoallergenic gel, flesh pink."

David realized after he said it there was an even chance she'd be offended. But the similarity had struck him so spontaneously he hadn't even thought about it, or listened to what she was saying, until it was too late. But instead of getting upset, Hildegard searched his face with her eyes.

"Do I strike you this way?" she asked. "Do I look down on you?"

David reflected on his feelings of her condescension. "Not just me. That's what makes it tolerable. You look down on everything. You're an equal-opportunity snob," he said. "But don't change. It's part of your appeal to me. You know, nothing in this world is good enough for you. Except me, on Friday nights. It's kind of flattering when you look at it that way."

The professor was quiet for a long moment. "Let me be clear. I'm not looking for a husband. And I'm not looking for another person who 'completes me.' I value you and do not need you to be anyone else. Nothing in my experience entitles me to demand change of a man who survived a war, raised a family, and went to aid other people in the worst of disasters. Your life has touched thousands, mine a few. If this little girl looks down on you, ignore her, or go ahead and call her '*Goldelse*,' and chase her off so the woman can return."

She extended her hand across the table to him. He took it, grateful he hadn't caused a train wreck. He savored holding her hand. He could feel in it the beating of the heart of a woman who, for no good reason at all, had chosen to show him patience, passion and care in his graying years.

"Wow, I was talking out my ass, wasn't I? That was rude of me. I'm sorry I said those things."

"Maybe," she said, "Yes. It was rude. But it might also be a bit true." After a moment she winked at him. "But I agree to the use of the pet name '*Goldelse*' provided its use is judicious, instructional...and private."

"Thanks...Lizzie."

They finished their breakfast in relative silence. When it was over, Hildegard raised a question about the thing which was weighing most on David's mind. "So, how much longer will you foster Rosie?"

It was the first hand of the night at the Fire Chief's Invitational Poker Pit. They were meeting at Marcus's home at a poker table beside the plate glass windows which overlooked the western edge of Cayuga Lake. Navigation lights from a motor yacht blinked a southward path, and despite the lights in the room's interior, the starry night still shone through the darker corners of the plate glass.

David fanned the cards Marten had dealt him. Marcus, Pierce, and Dwight wore their usual disinterested poker faces. The captain was so detached David sometimes had the impression his friend was surprised to find cards in his hand. Steve McCallister, on the other hand, wore a bright smile. He supposed the younger man was pleased to be at this game. His position as union representative put him at odds with Chief Bauer, something which the Chief was trying to remedy by inviting the younger man to poker.

"So, the big poker game! This is where department policy gets decided by the gray old men who make things go."

"Talking department business. Five dollar penalty," said Captain Earling, pointing to shallow stack of bills growing on the table.

"I warned you," said Marcus. "We don't talk shop while the cards are out."

The young man groaned and tossed in another five dollar bill.

"We're not here for your five dollar opinion," said Pierce. "We're here to relax. Start relaxing, or start paying the kitty. Putting five dollars in the kitty is like paying me to listen to you, which is an acceptable second to relaxing because I can tune you out and collect cash for it."

"Heh. You need a job as a psychiatrist if you like ignoring people and getting paid for it," Dwight remarked to Pierce.

"Licenses sound like stress to me. So does med school," grunted Pierce. "I'll settle for chatty union punks with deep pockets. That's the easy money."

"I will talk shop and win it all back," rebutted McCallister while he arranged his cards. "Then what are all you old guys going to do?"

"Be surprised," replied David, sorting through his own hand. Everyone chuckled.

"So, I notice there are no women here," the union rep added.

"From time to time there are," Marcus explained. "The department secretary Vivian plays occasionally. Constance used to play with us, and Faith, as long as we played for M&Ms instead of cash. Even Rosie has played a couple of hands of M&M poker."

"Wins far too often," Dwight grunted.

"You don't need those M&Ms anyway," said Marten. "And think of the joy you bring to children by losing. Why, you're a regular Santa Claus when it's M&M ante."

The room filled with laughter. David took a sip of his whiskey and glanced at Steve. The young man was relaxing. This was good too. David decided to remind the younger man of the rules.

"So, no, this is the Chief's game. The active Chief makes the rules. The only rule he can't change is that any former fire chiefs have to be invited and we can't talk shop. And the chief hasn't made any rules about women, either to keep them out or bring them in. Funny that."

"This isn't a meat market, it's a poker game," replied Marcus. "I've no objection to women, but it's not my focus." He pushed one card to Marten for a draw.

"Yeah, we know about your focus," said the captain.

Steve adroitly changed the subject. "So, how about those Mets? Trade or hold with their relief pitcher?"

Chief Bauer grinned, David noticed. He wasn't sure if it was at this subject-changing interjection or at his cards, but he didn't see it as a good sign.

Dwight grunted. "Baseball is for rednecks."

"But you're a redneck, Cap'n!" The younger man replied. "You always say so."

"Damn right. But I'm the only one in the room, so sports talk doesn't go far."

"Now there are two rednecks in the room, then. I think they should trade for Ameson."

Marten interjected as he dealt out the replacement cards. "Two rednecks in the room. Anyone want to bet they're related by blood or marriage, or both?"

There was another laugh around the table. David appreciated the man's quickness with a joke.

"So what do you do, if you don't mind me asking. You're the only one here who is not a firefighter," McCallister observed.

"I'm the catechist for Immaculate Conception. If you took your heathen ass to church like any self-respecting Irish/Italian mutt, you'd know."

Steve scratched his head. Mr. Haversham couldn't tell if it was at his cards or at the term "catechist."

"What's a catechist?" the younger man asked a moment later. Based on this, it seemed likely the union man's cards were good.

"Like a junior volunteer priest," Mr. Jostens explained.

"Only they can gamble," noted Marcus.

"And drink," added David, pointing to the full rocks glass at the man's elbow.

"And get busy with the ladies," added Dwight. "Are boys okay if you're a catechist, or do you have to save them for the priests?"

Marten frowned at this one. He opened his mouth to deliver what was certain to be a rebuke, but Chief Bauer cut him off. "Religion foul, yellow card, five dollar penalty," Marcus decreed. The captain snorted and threw in another five.

Mr. Haversham put in another five. "That's for Mart. So he can say what he was going to say when you cut him off, Chief."

"Pay another five for instigating and you have yourself a deal," said Marcus. Once the second five had dropped into the kitty, the chief grinned and nodded his permission to Mr. Jostens.

"I meant to ask Santa Claus over there if he had run out of kiddie porn and was fishing for his new supply," he explained.

Dwight roared out laughing, and the mood relaxed again. "If I ever do run out, I'll give you a call, then, Monsignor."

"Alright, alright, please remember we occasionally have a child at these games," interrupted the chief. "Like Rosie. Or young Steven here, for instance. And children should feel safe amongst firefighters."

The union representative cracked a smile. "Wow, my cards are good. They are so good, I'm going in with ten, and I'll even mention I think the 4-10 shift plan sucks for morale and that station two needs a new basketball hoop." He tossed in a twenty.

"The union rep is spendy," The captain observed. "You might have to raise the shop talk penalty, Chief."

"No, let him talk. I'll take his money but not his advice," said Marcus.

"Hey, since I'm not a firefighter, if I volunteer random opinions about department business, is it talking shop for me? I'm sure I could think of some opinions as loud as this young turk, here, but they'd be worth even less to you," said Marten.

"They might even be worth more," said Pierce with a scowl. David liked Pierce, but did wish he would lighten up. Still, he took it as a sign. Pierce was only 'chatty' like those six words if he had a bad hand. Sure enough, Pierce went out.

The turn came to back to him. He went out, too. So unless Mr. Jostens was holding a bomb, he was sure the hand would go to the chief or Steve.

When the hand was settled, the men still in laid down their cards. Marcus won with four queens. Marten whistled, chagrined, while the chief scooped up the money with a grin.

"So the queens like you, do they, chief?" asked the fire captain.

"All of them do. See for yourself," he said. "You know how it is with girls and gay men."

"Oh, no one said these queens were girls," the captain rebutted.

"And even if they were, does it say much if one-eyed chicks dig you?" Steve said.

"Don't be bitter. Sexual orientation foul, five dollar penalty." The young man opened his mouth to protest, but the older man elaborated. "To Dwight."

"Five dollars well spent. Let's start the next kitty right," said the fire captain as he slapped down a five.

David started laughing at this. It was a long, uncontrolled, belly laugh, a deep and full one like he hadn't had in a while. Marten chuckled at this while he dealt the next hand, and the rest of the card players seemed bemused.

"I like you guys. Even our young union punk here is speaking his mind and parting with his cash like a man."

"Group hug!" suggested Steve.

"Man love penalty. Five dollars," said Marcus with a straight face. There was another set of laughs all around, and this time, even Pierce broke out in snickers.

"Yeah, we miss you too," said Pierce after a while. "It's quiet around the station house. Don't get me wrong, I like my boss, but we haven't had a good top-down asschewing since you left."

"Five dollars, shop talk," said Chief Bauer, casting Pierce a glance. "And an ass chewing could be arranged."

"He doesn't mean *that* kind of ass chewing," Dwight said. The chief ignored this, turning instead to David.

"But you've got bigger fish to fry. Taking care of Rosie." Marcus said.

"Yep, but not for much longer," said the former fire chief, picking up his cards. "I signed up for three months, the maximum length of emergency foster care. This runs out in about ten days. Then I'm a free man." He sorted out the cards he didn't want, and he didn't realize until he'd put them down that the rest of the card players were looking at him. "What?" he asked.

"You're thinking about giving her back to the state?"

"The investigation is over," he reminded his friends. "Over weeks ago. Don't get me wrong, she's a lovely child. But I'm retired. And I've got my own health and life to think of."

"And the university prof you're banging," added Captain Earling. David was glad he had his poker face on, so he didn't betray any surprise anyone knew about Hildegard.

Marcus laid down his cards. "I have to say, I think that girl has been the best thing to happen to you since Constance left us."

"I agree," said Pierce. "For example, I haven't seen you take a second glass of whiskey since she showed up. And you used to drink three, or four, a game."

Mr. Haversham reflected on this.

"And you've been easier to live with," said Steve.

He gave the foreman a curious look. "Like you would know," he challenged.

"I don't," he answered. "But Faith does. And she's kind of, you know, chatty...after action."

The silence which hung in the air was palpable. David had a brief vision of flipping the table like he had done with one of Constance's bridge games. He took deep breaths.

"Wow, okay, that's... ten dollars for a grotesque excess of information," said Marcus.

Pierce piled on. "Faith is like a daughter to every man in this room. Except for you."

"Yeah, and she sure ain't like a sister to me," Steve countered, steady in the face of the indignation around him. He looked at David as he paid his ten dollars. "Okay, I'll overlook the inconsistency that we can joke about the woman you're banging but we can't joke about the one I'm banging. Take what I say right, or take it wrong, old man, but ask your daughter. She said you're about five hundred percent happier and easier to live with. My guess is if you send Rosie away, you'll be living alone before too long. I think you don't want that, and I know Faith doesn't either. It's not my fault if you've got her so intimidated she doesn't talk to you."

David recovered his poise. "I'll take it under advisement. But I'd appreciate it if you didn't boast about sleeping with my daughter."

"We all would," said Marten. Marcus added nothing, but his eyes said plenty.

"Got it. Won't happen again," said Steve. "Well, the boasting part won't happen again anyway."

"Thank you," he said. The silence around the room pained him. The game had been going so well up until a few moments before. "So, you guys think I should hang in there, huh?"

"I do," said Pierce brightly to everyone's surprise. "You are a world different. I mean, no one can judge your circumstances but you, but from where we sit, Rosie has been good for you, and we love her for it."

"And you for it," added the catechist. "It works out your best side. We get to see more of the guy who will go a mile for anyone and less of the guy who shouts at people. You had a lot of resentment and anger built up from Constance's passing."

David took in the advice his friends had all offered. "Thanks guys. It's like the first positive thing anyone has said to me about it. Faith is always complaining I spoil this girl, and Margrethe Peletow says I'm good with her, but that woman has an agenda and a child to keep off her books. Sometimes it feels so frustrating, because the girl's differences make me feel stupid...or powerless."

Marten began dealing out people's replacement cards. "What are friends for if not for the occasional good news?"

"I smell a man love penalty," said Dwight.

"Now how would *you* know what man love smelled like?" Marcus feigned astonishment. "Is there something you're not telling us?"

"Are you asking?" asked the captain in reply. "Isn't that, like, against department policy or presidential order to ask me? I need to file an equal opportunity complaint, I think."

"Shop talk. Five dollar penalty."

Retired chief Haversham smiled again. He was glad for his friends. Plus, smiling kept them wondering.

David opened the door. He didn't like the couple he saw there. He couldn't put his finger on why, but he didn't like them. The dark-haired woman was too skinny, vulture-like somehow, and the bald man was pudgy and bored.

Margrethe was beside them, dressed in a gray high-collared jacket. "Hello! These are Paul and Nanette Ambrose, the couple we discussed on the phone."

Mr. Haversham put away his first judgment. First instincts about people were often more about superstition and baggage than reality. "Nice to meet you! Come on in." He opened his door wide and motioned them in.

Ms. Ambrose stopped to shake his hand on the way through. Despite her distinctly Quebecois name, her English was perfect and had a local accent. "Call me Netty. Thank you! Fostering is an important contribution, emergency fostering even more so." Her handshake was firm and sincere. Ms. Ambrose was not a pretty woman at all, but she moved with energy.

"Yeah, it's been, um, an experience." David felt good to be appreciated.

"Big house!" grunted Paul.

"It's from my wife's family. They were old money," he explained.

"If we lived somewhere like this, each child could have their own room," commented Netty.

"More likely we'd just end up with three times as many children," replied her husband. David raised his eyebrows at this answer, and a flicker of what he recognized as disdain passed over Margrethe's own face.

"Anyhow, this is Rosie," he said, motioning to the living room coffee table where the girl was standing up.

Netty approached her. "Nice to meet you."

Rosie made her curtsy.

"So, she doesn't speak?" asked Paul, looking puzzled at the girl's silence.

"She does. But not English, as we discussed," answered Margrethe. "We're not sure yet where she's from exactly. There's not much information about her family. She's spent a good part of her life in institutional settings abroad before becoming a ward of the state here."

"Oh, right, right. This kid. Yeah," answered Paul. "The mystery foreigner."

"But does she understand English?" Netty asked while Paul got comfortable on the love seat. David sat down too, and motioned to the two women they could do the same. But the woman remained standing across from Rosie.

"She seems to," he contributed to let Margrethe off the hook. "But she doesn't always react as you expect. But she's harmless. Wouldn't hurt a fly," he said. "And if you tell her not to do something, she normally won't."

"How does she communicate with you?" Mrs. Ambrose asked, looking at him with concern. "If she's feeling sick, or lonesome, or angry? Does she sign?"

Without waiting for an answer, the woman made a few hand gestures he recognized as ASL. Rosie slowly formed some hand signs.

"Huh. She says she speaks British Sign Language."

David brightened. Maybe Netty would be a better caretaker for the girl after all. "So you can talk to her?"

"Not really," the woman shook her head. "I sign in American Sign Language. From time to time Paul and I have deaf or communication-impaired children, so I got interpreter training."

He paused. "You can't understand her?" He could understand Britons when they spoke slowly and clearly.

"Nope," Ms. Ambrose shook her head. "They are different sign languages. Less than half the signs are the same between ASL and BSL, and grammar is different."

"Ah." David frowned at this. Why would two countries which shared a spoken language have different sign languages? This was another of the world's contradictions. And was the kind of mystery Hildegard could explain later so he filed the fact away as a conversation starter. But his assessment of Netty changed with the new information. She seemed less vulture-like. And he guessed the fact that Rosie spoke a sign language was information they hadn't had before. "We communicate with pointing, or drawing, or models. Sometimes she starts doing what she wants until I figure it out," he laughed at the memory. "And sometimes I return the favor."

Netty sat, and the girl sat comfortably alongside her, making more signs. The woman shook her head a few times, and turned back to Mr. Haversham.

"She's religious, isn't she?"

"Yes, as a matter of fact," he answered.

Paul found this disagreeable, and fretted with a button on his oxford shirt. "I'm not getting into the religious thing, darling. We've got five kids with us already. I'm not taking them all to a different church every Sunday. I've got things to do between my job and five kids tearing up the house."

Margrethe said nothing, but Netty reassured him. "I understand. We've got a lot on our plate." The woman faced David again. "We don't discourage our children from praying, or going to a church if they want when they are old enough to take the bus or bicycle themselves, but we're not a religious household. We have too many children from too many different backgrounds. We live out in Homer, so we're not a convenient commute other than by bus. Does she go to church with you now?"

He wished he could give a better answer. "A couple of times. I go to Immaculate Conception. But she doesn't show an interest in church so much as pray wherever she is. I guess 'spiritual' would be a better description than 'religious.'"

"That's easier," mumbled Paul. David tried to imagine being in the younger man's shoes, with a job and five foster children to boot. He forgave the man's impatience and distraction after a moment. To Paul, Rosie was another candidate to compete for every free moment of his time, whereas he himself was living with plenty of it.

Netty continued. "So, you communicate through gestures, and body language, and your speech?"

He nodded. "That about sums it up."

She checked her husbands face. "She's got to have a home where she can communicate. She can't do it here. If she's learned one sign language she can learn another."

"It's true, but it sounds like she needs a lot of attention. And what do we tell the other kids? They're in our house so they can have a safe place to learn to make their own way in the world. I'm not sure I have the energy she would need from us if she can't communicate."

"We did it with Ernest," she recalled.

"We had two kids then. And we were fifteen years younger."

Ms. Ambrose faced to David again. "Does she get along with other children?"

He considered this. "She hasn't been around a lot of kids. But the ones at the Immaculate Conception Sunday school liked her. She doesn't seek them out but she'll play with them if they initiate it."

"No fighting? No crying?"

"Nope. If I had a worry about her interactions with other children, it would be that they might push her around or put her up to things. She's easygoing."

Paul gave his wife the smallest of shrugs, suggesting the woman made the ultimate decisions. She faced Margrethe. "You know we're full to the gills. But if you can't find anywhere else..."

The social worker reassured her. "You guys have already done your share. I don't blame you. How many kids has it been?"

"Twenty-six out of the coop so far," said Netty. "Remember Sidney Willsby? She graduated SUNY Brockport last spring."

"Oh, wow. Time marches on," the other woman recalled. Mr. Haversham recognized the name 'Willsby' as an old Ithaca name but didn't know the girl. He mused about what it was like for the Ambroses to look back on years and patience

286

spent on kids they might never see again.

Netty stood again. "Paul and I will need to agree on the decision. But don't send her to Phoenix House without talking to us."

Margrethe gave no sign of having heard the scorn in the woman's voice when speaking of Phoenix House. "Couldn't send her there in any case. The only choice would be to institutionalize her," she answered.

"Goodbye Rosie. It was nice to meet you. Maybe you'll stay with us for a while. Who knows?" Paul got back to his feet and offered the girl his hand. She shook it as David had shown her, and then waved to Netty as the Ambroses headed for the door.

The social worker hung behind as he watched the couple descend from his porch and head to their station wagon. When they were in their car and on their way, Mrs. Peletow turned to him.

"They're the best in the county. And I say this even though I don't even like them particularly. But they take on a lot of kids, and the money they get helps them and the kids get by. Their house is packed and everyone sleeps like sailors. There's scarcely anything but a dining room table, study tables for the kids, and a TV I've never seen on. It's clean, bare, and run like clockwork."

David reflected on the woman's story of the Ambrose home. Her severe gray clothing, severe gray hair, and severe gray manner were starting to make sense to him. Every day the woman had to usher people into and out of harsh circumstances and then paint a pretty picture on it when she spoke to her supervisors. Margrethe's life was a blur of "best which can be done." Unlike in firefighting, there were no heroic triumphs, and no recognition day-to-day.

"Thanks for your hard work," he said. He had said this before, he recalled, but not sincerely.

"It's good to hear that every once in a while," she smiled at him. "And thanks for your work with Rosie." She left, stepping down the porch steps with a slow hand on the wrought iron rail and favoring a knee.

He shut the front door and stood regarding Rosie. The foundling sat again at the coffee table. Without a moment's pause, she was back at drawing, quiet and focused. David went and sat behind her and brooded. He was retired, but was he doing his share? Compared to people like the Ambroses? Some days he wasn't sure.

Wednesday had gone by quietly at work. But on returning home, Faith had the impression her father wanted a serious talk. It wasn't anything he said. They had all eaten supper together with the usual small talk about work and plans for the weekend. At first she had thought her father's laconic mood was rooted in the awkwardness he might feel about asking for another Friday night with Dr. Teschke. Still, even when she had agreed to sit Rosie through Saturday morning again and made reassuring noises she was fine with it, David remained withdrawn.

She finally turned to her laptop. Her father would get around to talking when he was ready, she was sure of it. In the meantime she could study up on the new electrostatic testing requirements for compressed hydrogen containers some of the new fuel-cell equipped houses in the city were using. Hydrogen chemically weakened metal containers in ways which were difficult to detect. So the testing was all high-tech, which was ironic since the chemistry and physics behind fuel cells themselves was simple.

She had a good half hour to focus while her father put Rosie to bed. The two of them had begun praying together at night, and it made her feel awkward to be there, so having her nose on her LCD screen also gave her an excuse not to notice. But when he came back downstairs, his withdrawal become thunderous and filled the quiet space of the living room until Faith could scarcely think.

"Out with it, Pop," she said when she could take it no longer.

"I was getting to it," her father said. He sat down across from her in his lazyboy. She flinched. She knew what that meant. All through her youth, when her father had said they needed to talk and then sat in the easy chair, it had always been a long, serious talk.

"If you're sitting in that chair, I'm getting coffee first," she grumped back. She fetched a mug of steaming coffee and sat where she could lean on one arm of the sofa. "I'm fine with you visiting Dr. Teschke, Dad. Even I find it pathetic my father has a more active love life than I do."

"That's not it," said David. "I'm thinking about whether we could adopt Rosie."

"What?" she froze. "Adopt?"

"Or volunteer for long-term foster care. The system is overburdened, and meanwhile I sit in this big empty house high on the hill and live off the past. What am I doing for my community? For you? For anyone? Who am I?"

Faith was taken off-guard by these thoughts. While it was clear her father liked Rosie a great deal, he'd spoken often enough about how he looked forward to his retirement that the question of her staying had been decided in her mind long ago.

"Are you sure, Dad?"

"I don't know how long I've got. But I think I've got a few years in me yet. I can spend them winning poker, or I can spend them making a difference...*and* winning poker. I can make them good years for me, and good years for Rosie."

Faith didn't know what to say. But her father was not one of those people who demanded people speak to understand they were listening. Her eyes roamed about the house, drifting over bookshelves and paintings and even a Persian rug which hadn't changed since her youth.

After a long stretch, she understood what her father was saying and feeling. It made sense. It matched what he had told her as a little girl, and how he had lived his life. "Get up every morning and make a difference," he had told her. "That's all you need to do to earn your keep."

"Are you prepared to do it yourself?" she challenged. "On your fixed income? Because if you adopt her we'll lose the fostering stipend from the state. And I'm not becoming my mother. I aim to marry, Pop, and maybe not live here. What could be more intimidating to a suitor than a houseful of Dad and an adopted retarded kid? It could end up being you, her, and your retirement check."

"I am."

"You're that serious?" she said.

"Yep," he answered.

"Then I'll see you and raise you a whole bag of M&Ms," she said. "Let's do it. I think we can."

Her father's expression was startled. "We?"

"I was just testing to see if you were taking me for granted, Pop. You weren't. And let's face it, the way things are running I might never have a kid the, you know, natural way. So I think it's a good idea. I want in. Family is what we make. And I'll know the right person for me when they walk in this door and see you and Rosie and say 'I'm home,' not, 'what a freak show.'"

Her father stood up from his easy-chair-of-paternal-power. He spat on his palm and offered his hand to her.

"Shake on it."

Faith knew this ritual. It had been used throughout her childhood for the solemnest of promises between them. Even when she had welched or backed out of the agreements, her father had always kept his end of these bargains. They hadn't done a shake in about fifteen years, and it struck her as childish to do it at her age. But it was crystal clear what her father wanted from the gesture was a promise she meant to keep. This was the time to get from him the promise she needed him to keep in return.

"If you shake on it that I can bring home whomever I want as a date, and I do mean 'whomever.'"

"I already put up with McCallister, didn't I?"

She ignored his diversion. Before all was said and done, her father might daydream about her marrying McCallister. "Shake on it, Dad. Whomever I want," she insisted.

David paused for a long moment. "Alright," he relented with a puzzled look. "Whomever."

Without saying another word she spat on her own palm and shook his hand. They shook, and then they embraced. Faith was careful not to wipe her slimy palm on her father, but a damp spot on her shoulder told him he had not been so considerate. But she had planned to wash the shirt anyway.

Her father laughed. "Thank you," he said after another pause.

"So, on that note, I have laundry which needs doing," she shot back. "Mr. Mom."

People's irresponsible attitudes and inability to cope with their own lives and choices were part and parcel of Margrethe Peletow's job. So it was always a pleasant surprise when someone came forward to take responsibility for something that wasn't their own problem.

"Adoption? Are you sure?" she asked. "We could arrange for a permanent foster care situation. It might make more sense given your financial situation, since the state would continue to chip in for her health care, food, and clothing."

"My daughter wants to be a party to the adoption," said David Haversham. "If she is, then Rosie will get health care through her workplace. Unless you think it's a bad idea."

"No, no, Mr. Haversham. Don't get me wrong, I'm thrilled! An adoption is the ideal solution. I'm laying the other option out there. Foster care could be long-term. In general, unless there's a problem, these days a foster care arrangement can run for as long as the child and the parents want it to."

"No, she has become family. We can't imagine living without her. We want to go with an adoption."

"Okay. I'm sure there will be a lot of work at the courthouse, what with the lack of clarity about whether her birth parents are alive or even her citizenship. But if that's the road you want to take, I'll walk it with you. I'll be interested to see how it works out."

"Thank you," said David.

"Since this will take a few months, we should start another foster care extension so you keep getting reimbursed and retain guardianship while we see this through the courts. And I'll have to do another home inspection and such."

"That's not a problem."

"I'll tell you what. I'll come by. This case should be complicated, so I'll make it mine to shepherd through the courts. Give me a couple of days to find all the paperwork and I'll drop by and we can do a big sign-a-thon."

"Let me know early so Faith can get time off of work."

"I will," she said. "And thank you. Rosie's fate would be an institution. Given her special needs, and the economy, I can't see placing her, so you will make a big difference in her life."

"Thanks for saying so," said David. "I'll wait for your call back."

When Margrethe lowered the phone, her head was already spinning with all the work the adoption implied. She had to resolve the issue of Rosie's dead or missing family, plus work the special consent issue because she was disabled, plus the foster care extension, plus the adoption. She had a full plate with this one. But it was full for the right reason.

"God bless you," she thought to the man. "You make a believer out of this tired old woman."

Akiko felt pride. She disguised it. Many others had made contributions to the translating computer for Rosie, and her upbringing had taught her personal pride in a collective achievement was unseemly. Dr. Teschke had found the money for the project and gotten the help of other university department heads. Shawn had worked tirelessly for weeks interviewing her, and this had gathered the essential linguistic base data and earned the goodwill of the subject's caretakers. Selene had contributed behind the scenes, steering Shawn off of dead ends and handling the student issues Akiko had no time to deal with. And even Google, a faraway group of mysterious software people, had licensed her some of their translation code for Esperanto for this special use.

But now here they were, ready to deliver phase one of the project, a translating laptop computer. The girl's eyes grew wide as Akiko presented it to her and her father.

"Meet LIDIA - *Language-Interpreting Dialog and Interaction Aid*. A lot of people have worked on this for a long time." Akiko placed the computer in front of the girl. The translation program was already open. She had written the program to be simple and she hoped it struck Rosie as intuitive. On the left of the window, presented as buttons she could click, was a special keyboard which included the International Phonetic Alphabet characters they had seen her write. She could use it to enter text in her Esperanto. When she was ready, the computer would then translate her text into English text in a box to the right. When Rosie had reviewed the English to be sure it was correct, she could click the button "speak" and the computer would read the text aloud in English.

The girl stared at the interface. Her father knelt beside her and removed his glasses to watch over her shoulder. She felt someone stand beside her, looked up to see Dr. Teschke. Beside the professor, Shawn and Selene waited and watched. Akiko scanned Rosie's face, prepared to launch into an explanation of how the program worked if she showed uncertainty.

An explanation didn't prove necessary. Soon the child put her hands to the keyboard. She typed, frowned, retyped, pursed her lips, continued at it for some two minutes.

"Lidia is the name of the daughter of Dr. Zamenhof. She was killed for teaching Esperanto," announced the computer's robotic text-to-speech voice.

Akiko and Hildegard exchanged glances and smiled. Their reference had been understood. It had been Dr. Teschke's idea, but it was Ms. Nakamura herself who had spent a whole afternoon thinking of a name for the program which would form the acronym LIDIA. "Yes, we know."

The girl began typing. `"Can I have a woman's voice? This voice sounds funny,"` asked the computer.

Akiko walked around behind the desk so she could point to the laptop's screen. "Sure. Click on the 'text to speech' menu," she said. Rosetta did so. "Then you can pick from any of the different voices that are there. We could even make a custom voice for you some day, if you wanted."

Rosie clicked through the voices on the list. As she clicked, the computer began to read off the sample sentence `"The quick brown fox jumped over the lazy dog,"` over and over. After some more clicking, Rosetta chose "Mary," an older, maternal-sounding voice with an American accent. Great pains had been taken to include some childrens' voices in the list, but Akiko had thought them all squeaky or synthetic sounding, and it seemed Rosetta had, too. The "Mary" voice was the most natural sounding.

`"This is better,"` said LIDIA in the new voice. The girl began typing again. The typing took a long time, and Akiko watched as Rosie compared what she had typed with the text which emerged in the English window, and then retyped her Esperanto until the English was syntactically and grammatically correct. It was at once clear from watching this process that Rosetta's grasp of English was perfect. She was backwards-engineering her Esperanto to produce the English phrase she wanted.

Akiko boggled at this. Whatever problem or psychological issue caused Rosetta not to speak English directly was a complete mystery to her. If her grasp of English was good enough she was changing her Esperanto text to get the correct English sentence, then for the love of her ancestors why didn't she write or speak in English? She made a mental note to point out this process to her peers when Shawn downloaded the text of this conversation. To her mind, it called into question studying the way Rosetta wrote Esperanto if she was altering her Esperanto word choice and syntax to induce the computer to present correct English sentences.

LIDIA's voice kicked on. `"I know you have worked hard to make this computer. I am glad to have it. Sometimes I feel lonesome because I cannot say what I want to. If you are patient with me, now I can speak to you all like this. It is slow, but it works.`

`"God would like it better if you all learned Esperanto, though."`

The comment made Ms. Nakamura grin in spite of herself. To her relief, she saw she was not the only one to do so.

"Even if we did learn it," explained Dr. Teschke, "You would still meet people who had not learned it and want to talk to them, wouldn't you?"

Rosie hesitated, and then began typing. `"Everyone in the world should learn Esperanto! Then we could all speak to each other."`

Her elaboration made everyone in the room laugh. At this response, the girl folded her arms and sulked.

"You're right, honey, it would be the best answer. But it's not likely to happen," Mr. Haversham said, rubbing the girl's back comfortingly. He turned to Akiko.

"Sorry she's being crabby. Thanks for all your hard work. This will be useful for her in school and in making friends, even if she doesn't know it yet."

David held open the front door for Rosie. The small girl moved deliberately under the weight of her backpack and computer bag. The clothes she had picked out included her "European Union" baseball cap with stars, her sunflower shirt, mismatched green argyle and gray socks, and her cork sandals with the crescent moon treads. The entire ensemble had come from the Salvation Army store and was so bizarre as to shame him as her parent, and it contrasted starkly with the plain black of her bags. The prospect of her first day of school had not made Rosie any more receptive to his recommendation that she choose clothes which went together. Instead, she had insisted on wearing clothes which were her "favorites," whether they matched or not. He had been much more persistent with his clothing recommendations, not wanting her first day of school to be one where she was teased because she was dressed funny, but he had decided not to argue with her so much she became either frustrated or late for her bus. If she was teased, and the teasing bothered her, he supposed she'd listen to him next time. But there was always a chance she would be as indifferent to the opinions of her peers as she was to his own.

The girl picked her way down the stairs, wobbling dangerously at one point. David marveled at the sheer weight of the books, clothes, and equipment she had to carry. He recalled going to school with his notebooks, a protractor, a compass, and a lunch bag. *"Guess those days are gone,"* he thought. He hoped that, once she was assigned a wall locker, she wouldn't have to carry all the stuff every day. If she could just remember how to use the padlock, she'd be all set.

He put a hand to the girl's backpack and walked with her down DeWitt Terrace. The late August morning was a bit cooler than he was dressed for, but he knew he would warm up when he had to start walking up Buffalo Street. The school district did not place bus stops on Buffalo Street proper, since stopping a bus laden with children would wear the brakes and engine prematurely. So Rosie's stop was on Stewart Avenue, the first major cross street uphill from DeWitt Terrace.

When they started their walk uphill, David glanced at his watch and saw that, with as slowly as they were walking, they were running behind. He took hold of the backpack, which she gave up with a thankful smile, and they made better time. Once at Stewart Avenue, he smelled the baked goods, eggs, and coffee wafting toward him from the Carriage House Cafe across the street. *"Carriage house,"* he noticed the irony. With luck *this* carriage house wouldn't burn down around his foster daughter. She sniffed at the air as they waited, and then, drawn by the smell, stepped out into the street toward the cafe.

A Volvo going one way and a pickup going the other stopped quickly, and David snatched the girl back from the road and took a firm grip of her hand. He waved to the startled drivers, who waved back in a friendly way. He then spoke to Rosie without looking at her.

"Honestly, you *have* to look where you are going. I know we've practiced looking both ways before crossing the street. Why don't you do it?" he scolded.

Rosie shrugged. She had different flavors of shrug, and this shrug meant "sorry," rather than "whatever!" David scowled. He guessed he would walk to the bus stop with her for a long time until he had confidence she wouldn't die in traffic. He held out her backpack again, and she wiggled into its straps.

He could clearly envision where the girl was headed. They had gone together to the special education orientation at her school. The classroom was modern with "whiteboards" instead of blackboards, a computer projector, and a spiffy multimedia system. She would start out in the "slow" class for regular students and he and the teachers would take it from there. Since she had convinced the language teachers she understood Spanish and Chinese, she was exempted from the foreign language classes and would ironically spend the same period in "speech therapy." Mr. Haversham had protested that the teachers were wasting their time, and Rosie would never speak anything but Esperanto, but the school had insisted, with the principal explaining they were obliged to try. To balance out her "slow" classes, she would do an advanced art class and was already signed up for after-school dance, which would start the next week.

The bus eventually came, rolling down Stewart Avenue from Cornell's campus where it picked up from the married student housing. Even the slope of Stewart Avenue was enough to strain the bus's brakes, and the complaints and hisses of the huge yellow machine were still in David's ears when the bus door opened.

Rosie waved at the driver cheerfully and stood on the curb.

"You getting on, missy?" The driver asked. The girl turned to her father.

"I'm not riding with you," David explained. "You have to get on by yourself. Don't worry, you'll get there. Get off the bus when everyone else does and find your way back to the same classroom we visited last Thursday. Remember you ride route number seven," he said, pointing to the vinyl "7" decal in the window. "Get on this same route to come home. I'll be here waiting for you." He gave her a nudge toward the bus door and leaned in to talk to the driver. "She doesn't speak English, but she understands it. Keep your sentences short and don't let her fool you. If she gives you trouble, let me know."

The bus driver, a short-haired fellow with a weak chin, a patient look and "Operation Enduring Freedom" baseball cap, nodded. "Yup. The school left me a note about her," the man replied. "Welcome aboard the magic bus, stranger," he said. "Come on and join our party!"

The girl looked bewildered. Mr. Haversham knew the look. He braced for her quivering chin and sniffling. "Don't you start with me. I haven't adopted you yet, and I can still throw you back. So chin up and get on the bus. It's not so bad. You'll have fun and make friends."

Rosie gave David a hug which was so fast it was a blur, and then, as if suddenly stuck in glue, climbed aboard in slow motion. He caught a glimpse of her standing in the aisle way, but she disappeared as she took a seat. He stayed where he was while the bus rolled away and watched it continue downhill on Seneca Street.

When it was gone he started a slow walk home. The Ithaca public schools were now his partners in the grand adventure of trying to educate this pensive and spiritual girl. Together, he and his city could do it. They'd done so much together through the years. Together they had raised a daughter, burned and rebuilt some buildings, and even muddled through a socialist Mayor or two, and what could be harder than that? Ithaca was up to this new job, and so was he.

He took a deep breath. The breath brought him the scent of coffee and a more expensive breakfast than he could afford, but the smells still reminded him of the possibilities of the day. He could go home and cook. Or finish building the coffee table. Or go for a walk with Chocolate. The day was all his until he had to come back here to pick Rosie up. Whatever he did, he should keep his phone close at hand. He had the feeling phone calls from the school would be the order of the next few days.

He started back downhill, moving briskly with the push the steep slope gave him. He cleared his cluttered mind and enjoyed the morning sun on the back of his neck and the view of the city. He didn't let it bother him that he felt lonely.

Chapter 21

The Break

Cassius's eyes wandered his desk, set loose by the fatigue his early start had brought with it. He had the best desk in the central homicide office. Yes, it was still a cubicle, but his back was to the window and one side to a wall so there was no through traffic. The coffee maker and water cooler were on the far side of the office so he wasn't burdened by chit-chat unless he made an effort to be so. But he could still see the processing desk and keep an eye on his boss's door. This early in the morning, the office was quiet. The detective knew he had only an hour before his peers began crowding in, so he wanted to use this time as best he could.

He entered his password and waited for his email download while he got up again to pour his cup of coffee. When he returned, he took his first sip before setting it down, and his eyes came to rest on the family photos to one side. Among them was a sepia-toned picture of a black man hung in a noose from a tree. A cherry tree, the detective had long ago noticed from the leaves in the photo. He guessed, despite the photo's muted tones, that the hanging had taken place on a clear summer day.

"Julius McCrae. 1862 to 1921. May his spirit rest anew with his remains, recovered and reburied by his loving family living in the blessings of freedom he sought for us. We went back for our kin. 2008," it read. Under it was a passage from Martin Luther King, Jr. "It may be true that the law cannot make a man love me, but it can keep him from lynching me, and I think that's pretty important."

Cassius put down his cup. It was the dregs from the night shift and tasted burnt. He took another glance at Julius McCrae's limp, stretched form while he waited for his login to complete.

As a black homicide detective, he had a special relationship with lynching. Though racism persisted in the United States, and in particular through the legal system he was a part of, the lynching of old had, for the most part, stopped. Black Americans killed black Americans, now, the whites didn't need to be involved and mostly weren't. And his black brothers killed each other for the same petty fears and suspicions for which whites had killed them before. Though the notion of lynching appalled him, in the end a corpse was a corpse and murder was murder, and the colors of the participants didn't make either case more or less so, to his mind.

He backtracked on this thought. There was a difference. His black brothers of Syracuse didn't kill each other for trying to vote. Few of them did vote, and most of their peers wouldn't know or care who among them did or didn't. But trying too hard to vote had been the crime of Julius McCrae, for which he had been lynched. So there remained an important distinction between what had gone before and the murders which had filled his career up until now.

So now lynching was back. The Army of God outfit *was* espousing murder for ideological or political differences. Far from being gone, lynching was becoming colorblind. It was this conclusion which had drawn him to work this early, this struggle which kept his back straight even while he and Nidya struggled to feed the girls on his paycheck. Horror and unreason were coming full circle back to America, but he was standing in the way of it.

He worked through the overnight emails until he came to one titled "Archival Search Results from the Southern Poverty Law Center."

"Officer McCrae,

"Reference your search on the Army of God. The Army of God has been around for decades, but up until the millennium it was just a name taken by a series of lone-wolf anti-abortion terrorists, each one passing the title to the next as he was arrested. Eric Rudolph of the Atlanta Olympic bombing fame was a member of this 'army,' for example.

Cassius nodded to the computer. This much he knew already. The message continued.

"Federal authorities have been slow and unhelpful to our inquiries about the organization. They will only confirm what we already know but supply little of use. However, individual state public prosecution records show sixty attacks in twenty-two states in the past five years can be attributed to the Army of God. It would take a lot of research to determine if this number is an over- or underestimate. Some reports may attach this name to the case without evidence, others may not list the organization if reasonable suspicion does not exist to link it to the crime. I have attached a list with the points of contact for each case we had on record. The majority of attacks focused on abortion clinics up until the reversal of Roe vs. Wade. Since then, the attacks have centered on churches deemed theologically 'apostate'. 'Apostate' is a flexible description which means anything from accepting of gays and lesbians to advocating harmonious relations with Islam.

"Given the number and breadth of the attacks in a few short years, it's clear that the Army of God is now an organization and no longer a name passed between lone wolves. The lack of federal interest or response is worrisome. And you would think someone in the media should show some interest.

"Another note: despite the sheer number of cases, so far as we know, no member of the Army of God has been prosecuted since the 2010 trial of Scott Roeder for the murder of Dr. George Tiller. Several suspects, however, have been shot dead. Two died after exchanging fire with police, and the others were killed by unknown parties. Please be careful.

"If this information proves useful to you please consider a donation to the SPLC. We are on hard times and justice for the poor hangs in the balance.

Deirdre Tulame
Research Specialist"

Cassius sat back, trying to take in the enormity of what he had read. His own research had shown the Army of God was becoming known to state and local authorities nationwide, and he had put together that they were responsible for a number of attacks. But across twenty-two states? With no successful prosecutions? The scale of power these facts implied gave him pause. Who was he taking on?

He opened the case list to see what the SPLC had learned. Each case had attached to it the name and number of a principle investigator, a list which now included his own. He read all sixty case summaries and, to his relief, most involved conventional, albeit highly effective, arson. No bombs or unexplained technology were mentioned.

Despite the daunting prosecution record and the long list of burned

295

churches, mosques, and clinics, however, Cassius found the list comforting. The detail of the case summaries suggested the officers who wrote them had given their best. So he wasn't alone. Somewhere out there in the sea of three hundred million Americans, there were fifty-nine officers who also cared. They were his brothers and sisters in a thin blue line.

He punched a few names and numbers from cases which were interesting or relevant into his iPad. As he did so his fellows on the day shift filed through the office doors, boisterous as they always were despite the grimness of their work.

"Morning Cash!" one shouted to him.

"Morning!" he called back, picking up his cup of burnt coffee. He resolved to toss it and start a fresh pot. He had, after all, been the first into the office.

"I'll start today with questions," he resolved as he carefully tapped the fresh coffee filter down into the cone. "And I won't stop." The resolution made him feel confident. When he'd had this sensation before, he'd always broken the case.

Cassius clicked "send" before 1900. Unlike TV detectives, who wandered up to houses and workplaces and went in if they found an unlocked door, he had to ask for warrants to search premises. When those premises lay in other jurisdictions, he had to convince other agencies and their magistrates to help him obtain and execute the warrants. While Syracuse PD was a big police department for upstate New York, in the grand scheme of things it was not a multi-jurisdictional powerhouse with a long reach, so this process sometimes took time. But the Kopp case had some attention locally, and with Taryn Thomas also on the trail of the Army of God when she went missing, Cassius felt support from other jurisdictions was likely when he made the facts known.

He hoped the message he was sending would convince a magistrate in neighboring Oswego County to allow him to search the premises of the Pillar of Flame Christian Library near Palermo. This was a church at which, according to interviewees, Mary Joe Rudolph, Randy King, and William Kopp had met and spent weekends together in retreat. It was, to all reports, not an "open" church one could walk into and pray. Its website even stated it was a "closed sanctuary of worship and reflection for select Christian activists and organizers."

This meant Kopp, King, and Rudolph must have all been "select activists." In turn this meant they had been selected by someone. He was certain whoever served as the gatekeeper for the Pillar of Flame Christian Library would know who had selected them, if he or she hadn't selected them personally. All he needed was a magistrate in Oswego County to write him a warrant and a state police, sheriff, or local police officer willing to accompany him. A search of the library could be a break in both cases. Even though the Kopp case was officially closed, he was sure the FBI would be interested if he learned something.

A moment later a receipt message from Oswego County sheriff's office told him his application had been received. The date/time stamp told him it was now 1900, and per his understanding with Nidya, she and the kids would eat at 1930 no matter what, so he was on his own for supper. His stomach grumbled at the image of a Fishamajig sandwich from the Friendly's on the way home. He patted his stomach. "Easy old boy. Help is on the way."

After that, he planned, he could go to the gym and still be home around 2130 to kiss the girls goodnight and have some private time with Nidya.

"Detective McCrae?" a woman's voice asked. He wiped away some tartar sauce the last bite of his Fishamajig had left on his lip and swallowed before answering.

"Yes?" he said, trying not to betray any alarm that an unknown person was identifying him in his plainclothes out of the clear blue. The stranger was slender, had bleached blonde hair with mousy roots, had a graceful if top-heavy figure, and was over thirty years old, if he didn't miss his guess. And he didn't have the faintest sense of having seen her before. But he'd had a long career full of meeting people, so he remained open to the possibility. "I'm sorry, you are?"

"I need your help," said the woman not quite calmly. "I don't dare call the police, but I was told to look for you here on weeknights." Without invitation she sat down in the booth across from him.

Cassius felt interest take over from surprise. "How can I help you, Ms..."

"Emily Isenberger," she said. Her calm pronunciation and intonation reminded him of someone's voice. Someone famous. "I know you're looking for Taryn Thomas. And I want to help you, but I need protection."

The detective paused here. Protection decisions were made by his boss, and ultimately by the Chief of Police. And he didn't know where the woman lived, and if that jurisdiction would cooperate in a protection operation.

"What sort of protection are you looking for?" Cassius tested her warily. "If you're looking for immunity from prosecution, that's a decision that a DA needs to make, not me. If you're looking for physical protection, that's a decision my chief has to make, and you'll have to supply some kind of evidence you're in immediate danger."

The woman didn't hesitate at this. "I'm not in much of a position to bargain. I need to leave here with you or start running." Her matter-of-fact tone suggested Ms. Isenberger, if this was her real name, was no stranger to trouble.

"Alright. Let's talk. If after discussing your options you still want to leave with me, I can take you to back to the station and let you work it out with the shift chief."

"Okay," said the woman.

"Now, what about Taryn Thomas?"

"I know what happened to her. She was shot."

"Go on," Cassius prompted. He reached into his breast pocket for his tablet computer, ready to take notes.

"She....she was investigating a church I used to be a part of. And she was killed for it."

His previously satisfied stomach churned around the Fishamajig. "Let me guess," he began.

"The Pillar of Flame Christian Library," she nodded. "I have friends who tell me you're investigating it."

"What did you do at the library?" he pressed her.

"I was an anti-abortion activist back in Fargo, where I grew up. I came to the Pillar of Flame after college. My professor at Liberty University recommended me," she explained.

He clicked away at the keyboard. "Go on. You haven't answered my question, Miss."

"I was a planner. I helped plan training and local demonstrations against Planned Parenthood and gay marriage rallies. The groups of organizers who visited would think of ideas, and I would flesh them out, make the phone calls, contact churches... you know, make things happen."

"Uh huh. I know about things and happening," grunted Cassius. The demonstrations implied security details, and that implied overtime for police. He had spent many hours he should have been at home or at his office at these details instead over the last few years. And now he was sitting across from the lady responsible.

Emily gave no sign she heard his grumpy tone. "After the last election, a new mandate came down from the central church. At first I didn't know much about it. My boss called it 'the Charge of Joshua.' We started to get money for it, though, and the operations got bigger. Eventually I was asked to help, and I got to see some of the communications."

Sunday school lessons triggered a passage in Detective McCrae's head. "And the Angel of the Lord, being Gabriel, protested unto Joshua: 'If you will walk in my ways and keep my requirements, then you will govern my house and have charge of my courts, and I will give you a place among these standing here.'"

Emily sat back, surprised. "Zechariah...You've read the Bible, then, Detective?"

"Closely," replied Cassius. "In particular, the New Testament and the path to peace and grace."

This reply fetched a brief scowl from Emily. He decided that whatever her discontents with the Pillar of Flame, Ms. Isenberger was still an Old Testament-thumping bigot. Well, he didn't have to like her to need her information. And he didn't have to like her to have a duty to protect her if she was in danger.

"Then you may remember Joshua's acts," she prompted him.

"Joshua destroys Jericho during the Exodus. He orders every man, woman, and child in the city slain except for the one family who betrayed their neighbors by harboring his spies. He's a church father I am grateful Jesus has exempted me from emulating."

"Then you'll understand. The name given to the city of Ithaca in the 'Charge of Joshua' documents was 'Jericho.'"

Cassius took this in. Was he to believe this church, or the larger organization which backed it, had on its agenda the complete destruction of a city of sixty thousand? He searched the woman for signs she was contriving her story. She looked calm and serious. "Seriously? That's a civil-war scale operation. It would take more than a handful of militiamen with guns. They might be hippie freaks, but I'm sure someone in Ithaca would shoot back. They did used to make guns there, after all."

"Leveling a city doesn't take men with guns any more. It takes one man, and one bomb, if it comes to it," said Emily flatly. Her tone, and a memory of the mysterious circle of green glass on the floor of the devastated carriage house, reminded him not to decide anything was beyond the Army of God's capabilities. "But I don't think the plan was literally the destruction of the city. The papers I read stated a number of places the goal was to restore a fear of God in the city's culture and science through a series of symbolic, but not necessarily bloodless, acts."

Cassius reflected on this. "Why Ithaca? Why not Berkeley, or Madison, Chapel Hill, or New York? So Ithaca is a liberal city. Big deal. There are bigger liberal cities."

Emily had a clear answer for this. Her matter-of-factness and composure when giving it was disturbing. "Bigger cities have significant national infrastructure and other constituencies that made them less desirable. Ithaca was chosen because of its isolation and the paucity of the faithful living in the city. Beginning there would raise minimal resistance from the organization's own constituency. Virtually every church which still operates in Ithaca has already been deemed apostate."

"'Apostate' meaning?" He sought a clear definition of the term from someone proficient in its use.

"Denying or defying central principles of the Abrahamic tradition. To include tolerating, harboring, or exalting abortion or homosexuality, denying God's direct hand in man's creation, or disavowing the uniqueness of mankind. If even Muslims would correctly recognize it as apostate, it is."

"What does that mean? Disavowing the uniqueness of mankind?" Cassius rebutted. If she was going to bandy about these vague but ominous sounding terms, he was going to put her on the spot and make her define them.

"God created one Eden and fashioned one blessed child. Humankind. We alone in the universe are both sentient and blessed and are the stewards of the rest of creation."

The detective wrapped his mind around this. "Wow...so you don't think there's life anywhere else in the universe?"

Emily shook her head. "If there are other civilizations, which there is no evidence whatever for despite all the billions of dollars liberals have spent looking for them," she explained, "then these other civilizations will fall under our God-given stewardship."

He didn't recall this debate even emerging in his church. It never ceased to amaze what theological differences some people would hate each other for holding. Mankind couldn't even get to Mars, but here was a church was ready to destroy anyone who denied mankind's claim to the stars. He caught the waitress approaching with his check out of the corner of his eye. He raised his hand so Emily would pause. The waitress started at seeing her.

"I'm sorry, Ma'am! I didn't see you take a seat. Can I get you something?"

"No, it's okay," Emily reassured the girl. "The detective and I are leaving soon." The waitress left again with Cassius's twenty dollars in hand.

Detective McCrae took a moment to stare the woman down.

"All this stuff you're telling me is great. But it doesn't tell me what happened to Taryn Thomas. And it's not enough to get you protection. To get you some protection, you will need to show us evidence the Pillar of Flame is capable of violence and likely to target you specifically."

"I can't take you to Ms. Thomas. But I can show you proof the Pillar of Flame is capable of violence," she said.

"What proof?" he asked.

"The remains of a Nigerian national named Elphabia Wasilatu." Cassius's skin prickled at the name "Wasilatu." The woman saw the ripple in his expression. "I see you know that name. Then you know I'm for real."

He did not confirm or deny this. "I'll take you to the station, you can tell us more there. But one thing. Why did you leave the Pillar of Flame?"

For the first time, it was the woman's turn to look uncomfortable. "My reasons are my own. Suffice it to say I had to refuse the repeated advances of my superiors. I am not marrying off and making Christian children, and it wasn't going unnoticed. The combination of advances from my superiors and the turn in sentiment from 'hate the sin' to 'hate the sinner' made me feel at odds with the organization and with myself. I left it because I decided I could more effectively serve God elsewhere where my lifestyle choices are more accepted. But after Taryn's disappearance, I knew they would come for me. I've been staying with friends, but I can't keep making excuses, and I can't keep endangering my hosts. I need your help."

That story made sense. Alibi's was where Taryn had last been seen. She had left there with a woman with brown hair and a Midwestern accent and not been seen again, according to witnesses.

Cassius started to remember this testimony. Emily's hair had been bleached. And he realized now who her accent reminded him of: Tom Brokaw. He felt his world contract from grand philosophical revulsion at Emily's ideas to the careful cascade of one moment after another.

He schooled his expression back to one of neutrality. After three deep breaths, he stood. "Let's go. I'll take you to the station." He led her out to his car, and she followed behind, looking relaxed and smiling at the staff as they left. He was glad as he left that he had parked at the far corner of the lot. He led her to the passenger side of his car, and once they were screened from the restaurant windows, he drew his pistol and pointed it at her.

"You need to search me?" She raised her eyebrows. "Do you suspect me of a crime? Should I have been read my rights?"

"I am not asking you further questions. But I have a wife and kids. You might be innocent as a lamb but I will take precautions if only for their sake. Put your purse on the ground and your hands on the car roof," he directed. She lowered her purse, faced the car, put her hands on the roof, and spread her legs shoulder width apart without prompting.

"This one has been searched before," he concluded as he patted her down. He found nothing in any of her pockets except some loose change. Keeping his gun on her, he then tipped out her purse. The contents clattered to the asphalt. His eyes fetched on an oversized cell phone. It had a touchpad but was much thicker than his own phone.

"The iPhone is expensive. It's a new one. I hope you didn't break it," Emily said in irritation. Cassius ignored her and spread the purse items out with his foot. He saw nothing which looked dangerous. He breathed easier. He had been overreacting.

"Okay, I'm sorry for your phone and the inconvenience. You can put your things back in your purse." He put his pistol away as his adrenaline cooled in his veins. He had a witness, not a perpetrator here, he decided. He opened the passenger door for her and went around to the driver's side. A glance around the lot showed the search had drawn no attention.

He shut and locked the doors, saw that the woman had fastened her seat belt, and then pulled out his cell phone. He wanted to call the duty desk to tell them he was en route with a murder witness and they might need to call in a forensics team. It also occurred to him that he should call Nidya to say he'd be late, but his phone showed "no service."

He glanced across the parking lot through the glass at his dinner table. There, fifty feet away, he had gotten a five-bar signal. That was life with T-Mobile. He texted Nidya "Case Break. Home late. Love you. Kisses for the girls." The phone would transmit it as soon as he got a signal back, and then he'd call her from the station. She'd understand. She had for years.

He checked behind him, pulled out, and went his way back down Erie Boulevard toward the police station. Strip malls and big box stores flew by: Syracuse was shown in all its glorious dullness.

"Thank you, Detective," Emily told him. "I don't like to be searched, but I do feel safer already. Do you know what it's like, living on the run?"

"I'm doing my job, protecting and serving," deflected Cassius. "And I'm not promising we can or will protect you."

It occurred to him after a few minutes more of driving he had not yet heard the tone which would indicate his text message had been sent.

Rosie woke up. Nanny was there, sitting in the straight backed wicker

300

chair she had dumped her clothes on before bed. The old woman was reading through her half-circle glasses from a thin book. At first, the sight of her was so confusing Rosetta just stared. But then she recalled that, half asleep as she was, she was seeing more spirit world than usual. Nanny would fade to a presence if she woke all the way up. She resolved to treasure the in-betweenness, and watched in pleasure and comfort as Nanny licked her fingers and turned a page of the book without shifting her eyes a jot. Rosetta had seen her turn pages this way as the woman had kept watch over her brothers and sisters in the laboratory. Usually when one of them was dying.

"You're awake, child," said Nanny after a moment, eyes still fixed on the page. "Do not think I cannot see you because I do not look at you. You know this, don't you?"

"I love you, Nanny," Rosie said the most important thing first.

Nanny smiled and closed the book. She took off her glasses and wiggled her eyes a moment to refocus them.

"I love you too. My life was filled with sick children, all blameless, all deserving. But from among them you are my favorite," Nanny confessed.

"Do you like heaven?" She wondered if Nanny was visiting because she was tired of it.

Nanny explained. "It is so good this question has no meaning. It is. It fills you, and is the end of all suffering and the gentle reunion with God. Do not be concerned for me. I shall never want again."

That sounded wonderful. "I want to go to heaven."

"My dear, do not rush. God has hopes for you. Great hopes," she soothed. "And I do, too! Think what you want of God, but you had better not disappoint me!" she said with mock sternness.

The woman and the girl grinned at each other and broke into a mutual giggle. Nanny had always understood about God.

"David is nice to me," Rosie tried to reassure Nanny. "He cooks better than the laboratory."

"Be nice to him, too. He needs you, in his own way. Do not leave him," Nanny advised. "Now another thing, child."

Rosie looked Nanny in the eyes. This is what Nanny expected when she said "Now another thing, child."

"It may be someone may find my body. And if you have to see it, I wanted you to know I do not suffer."

She nodded. "I knew as soon as it happened," she said.

"I thought you might. But I am the Nanny. And the Nanny must make sure." Nanny stood and bent over the bed. The girl took the familiar hug and felt the brush of Nanny's bushy, curly hair against her cheek and neck.

"Go back to sleep," said Nanny, patting the pile of folded clothes as she replaced them on the wicker chair. At these words and tone, the girl felt lulled back into dreams. She was happy with the certainty that, at the end of her journey, she would be with Nanny.

Chapter 22

Disappearing Man

Faith scrolled through her email. The city building inspectors had forwarded her some fire safety concerns about another Victorian wood-frame home which had been subdivided into student apartments. In a perverse twisting of inspection logic, the building inspectors were allowed to fault houses for fire code issues, but if *she* found safety or construction code faults during a fire inspection, there wasn't much she could do about them. The upshot of this imbalance was the building inspectors made work for her to follow up on as they worked throughout the city, sometimes needless work, and she would have to sift through their rambling emails to pick out the faults. Still, it was valuable information to have, since any fire prevented was a financial win for the city, and it created a steady stream of re-inspections on her calendar for any dry spells in her work flow.

Her phone rang "Law and Order." She smiled. A phone call from Detective McCrae and a few laughs could be what she needed. She rolled her chair over to her jacket on its hook and took out her cell phone, then held it to her ear as she rolled back to the desk.

"Hey Cash!" she said.

"Is this Faith Haversham?" said a woman's voice. It sounded familiar, and had a tinge of a Buffalo accent.

She raised an eyebrow. Who had gotten ahold of Cassius's cell phone? "This is she. Who is calling?"

"Hi, Faith, this is Nidya McCrae," she said. On introducing herself, the woman sounded less formal than upset.

She pricked up her ears at this change in tone. "Oh, hi, Nidya! What can I do for you?"

"I was wondering...You will think I'm terrible for asking you this, but I wonder if you might know where my husband is."

She pondered the meaning of this question. "No, I don't. What's wrong?"

Anxiety filled Nidya's voice. "He hasn't come home. And this is awful of me, but I thought that...that since you spent so much time together during the investigation, and, and I found your number in his recent calls a couple of times. I was wondering if...if...you might know where I could find him. I want to talk to him," she explained. The woman sounded on the verge of tears.

"Oh, Nidya, I'm so sorry. No, it wasn't like that between us. Cassius is a good man. He never said anything to make me think he was unhappy."

"I know. I know he's good man. But he left me this note. It's his handwriting, but it's like nothing he has ever said to me. He said he was leaving me, and he needed a new life, and I would never find him...and awful things. We had our anniversary this week, and he never even indicated he was unhappy. When he didn't come home, I assumed he was working late, until I rang his cell phone and heard it ring in the study next to his note. And now, I don't know what to think. I'm so sorry I suspected you, it was wrong of me. But the girls are getting scared, and his department won't even let me fill out a missing person report for another sixteen hours, and I-"

302

Faith interrupted. "Nidya, it's okay. No offense taken. If you're worried, then I'm worried too."

Nidya was encouraged. "Oh, thank you. I've no right to expect it after what I've asked you."

She let the woman's implied messages roll off her. "Did he give some indication where he was going?"

"No. He said he was leaving, and not to try and find him, because no one would ever find him until he was ready to come back."

Faith frowned. The story didn't sound like her friend at all. The man had talked about his family regularly and with real affection. On the other hand, she'd heard of good and happy men running off before, many of them at about the detective's age. But on the other hand, as a detective, if anyone knew how to vanish and *not* be found, she suspected Cassius would. She could see Nidya had a long road ahead of her. Faith hoped that, because her own future partner would be a woman, she would never have to deal with the restlessness which affected men of a certain age.

"What will you do?" she prompted the other woman. "Is there someone up there who can help you?" Nidya's tearful response came all too soon.

"I don't know... If he left me, he's going to lose his pay and we won't get his pension. I won't be able to afford this house, and the school for the girls. And I can't...I can't understand the things he said in his note," Nidya sobbed.

Faith stayed on the phone and listened to Nidya's life fall apart.

Special Agent Bitters sat with his boss, the Hunter. He was almost always seated when he talked to the Hunter. His boss didn't stand around or walk much. The older man's heart condition made stairs or extended walks challenging. Nonetheless, this laboring heart kept alive what Bitters regarded as the greatest patriotic mind in America, the wellspring of the political movement which had crushed the liberals and surrenderists and had even made the man vice-president for four years.

Bitters supposed a lesser man would have regarded falling from the vice-presidency to director of domestic counter-terrorism as a demotion. But the depth of the Hunter's patriotism and zeal was such that the older man was at his desk sixteen hours a day, and did not go home, instead resting and showering in the dormitory which adjoined his office. The only time Bitters had ever seen Hunter with his family members was when they had come to the section Christmas party and Hunter's secretary had set up the food buffet on the director's own desk. Hunter dressed up like Santa Claus and bounced his grandchildren on his knee, but had never left his office.

The Hunter was staring at his computer screen. "New mission," he said, without looking up. Bitters took this as his cue to remove his notebook from the pocket of his dark suit, and fill the pocket again with his sunglasses. He held his pen at the ready.

"What do you know about the concept of peak oil?" Hunter squinted at him. Bitters recalled what he knew. "The idea accessible oil reserves will peak and then deplete, leaving the world with less and less energy for more and more people?"

"Yep. It's true. It's already happening. Fortunately, the fact has thus far eluded the majority of the peasants. We have a new mission to keep it that way as long as possible by silencing and suppressing peak oil's most radical proponents," Hunter said, leaning back. "Those who would oppose our government have begun to wield evidence of peak oil as a sign of the 'bankruptcy' of our current political system. This is a willful confusion propagated by unAmericans: peak oil threatens our economic system, not the legitimacy of constitutional America. Nonetheless, the exhaustion or limitation of energy supplies poses significant future hardship for most Americans, including some who matter. We've attempted to distract them from this by emphasizing the volumes of offshore oil discoveries, the potential of fusion power, the fascinating aspects of Hollywood starlets' fashion choices, and the like. Still, the facts of energy depletion are starting to shine through. To delay and dilute political upheaval which could threaten America, we need to disrupt the dialogue. That's where you come in.

"The president has determined proponents of apocalyptic models of oil depletion are working counter to the interests of the United States. There are plenty of government and industry models which suggest oil depletion will be gradual enough that we can usher in alternatives in time to prevent a cataclysm, at least in this country. But this can only happen if the political system remains unchallenged.

"Whether or not the apocalyptic models are scientifically supportable is not of interest to the president. If the scenarios of widespread poverty and starvation they generate are true, these effects are unavoidable. Advancing these models serves only to create upheaval and undermine national resolve at a crucial juncture. And if these models have even a modest chance of being untrue, advancing them to the public at the risk of causing upheaval and weakening national resolve is inexcusable scientific irresponsibility.

"Either way, the president has deemed a reasonable person would only advance theories of apocalyptic oil depletion in order to fearmonger in support of a domestic or foreign conspiracy of terror. In light of this, you and your information security team are authorized under the Patriot Act, as amended, to investigate and suppress proponents of apocalyptic oil depletion scenarios. The first of the domestic intelligence surveillance act warrants in pursuit of this should come down this week. Be ready."

"Check. I'll read up on this stuff. Any particular names I should expect to see come down? Give me some names and I can be ready to make the arrests as soon as I have the warrants."

"There will be some names. Chief among them will be a University of Maryland professor by the name of Archibald Stevens. He's tenured, and entrenched in his community. Disappearance will have to be impeccably thorough or another plausible reason for his departure or removal will have to be manufactured. If you need help with this one, I'm sure our friends in the oil industry could provide you a honey or an operative to take him out."

"Archibald Stevens – Peak Oil. Ask Texans for help," wrote Bitters. His notebook pages were full of the names of people who no longer troubled America. He loved this notebook. Someday, if security clearances would allow, he would use it to write a book.

Hunter leaned forward again, shed his suit jacket, stood, and hung it up. Bitters had learned this gesture was analogous to Mr. Rogers removing his sweater. Hunter's show for the day was starting.

"So, I've expanded your missions again. This means we'll have to expand the proportion of your personnel available for black operations. Who presently on your white team can you develop to become a member of your black team?"

Bitters furrowed his brow. His white team was the group of his agents who were only aware of the less sensitive of the Information Security Detachment's operations. The concept was that, over time, he could develop a sense for which of these agents had the necessary character and resolve to take part in black operations. He already knew which one he wanted to choose, but he also knew Hunter would not like his choice.

"Boss, I still think Angela DeMarco is the one," Bitters said.

Hunter sat back down, drew a deep breath, and fixed his baggy dark eyes on Bitters. Bitters recognized the man's searching look as one of serious consideration.

"I'm skeptical that girl has the grit for our work. But convince me. Tell me why DeMarco is a good choice."

Bitters had this argument prepared. "Two reasons: Lynndie England and intuitionism."

Hunter waved his hand for Bitters to continue.

"You remember from Abu Ghraib how we were able to distract the public by focusing on Lynndie England? According to the web search tallies, about seventy percent of the news coverage anyone ever read about Abu Ghraib wound up being those racy stories about Lynndie and her supervisor Graner. Like Lynndie, Angela has a face and a body America will hate to send to prison. We need a sacrificial lamb on the team. All our current guys are getting too valuable. If one of these ops goes south, we can hang DeMarco out to dry and make our getaway while the media circus focuses on her."

Hunter nodded. "You mean, *you* can make *your* getaway. Because I won't be implicated. Or if I am, you won't get far on your 'getaway'."

Bitter waved indifferently. He was aware of the risks of his chosen profession, but he was too old to care as much for his life as he did for his country. "Sure. If over time, DeMarco proves to be reliable and valuable, we can find a prettier and younger face to be our Lynndie England."

"Okay. Now, what's this about intuitionism? I don't remember anything special about her score."

"You know all of the Department of Homeland Security garrison recruits get a twenty-five question intuition test. DeMarco is a consistent seventeen."

Hunter shook his head. "I instituted those tests myself. But a score of seventeen is not so special. There are a couple dozen of those every year. Our recruitment goal is for twenty plus."

"That's it, boss. Most people who score twenty plus can't keep it up for whatever reason. The next time you test them, they bolo the test. Or maybe they can do it sometimes or not others for reasons we don't understand. The phases of the moon change, or they didn't have their coffee or some shit and they lose the ability.

"DeMarco is different. Since her score wasn't anything too special, and she was a female, she was assigned to the eavesdropping program instead of field operations. When she was working in internet search surveillance, she could connect the dots better than anyone. She could link together internet searches and IP addresses, even those which were masked and apparently unrelated. We began busting kiddie porners, socialists, bomb makers, greenpeacers, union agitators, and other miscreants right and left using her hunches. She was tested again and scored seventeen of twenty five. A year later, she scored seventeen of twenty five. Last month, she again got seventeen of twenty five."

"So her results are consistent and reproducible," granted Hunter. "But is a seventeen a useful degree of intuitionism?"

"In the aggregate, I think it will be. A typical score for an average person is a five, meaning they answer the questions correctly out of dumb luck. If you want eighty percent certainty an intuitionist's guess is correct, then you need a score of twenty. DeMarco, when she guesses about something, is right about two thirds of the time. It means you shouldn't make one decision based on her hunches, but if she helps you out with a lot of hunches over a long period of time, she'll tend to steer you right more often than wrong."

"Huh," said Hunter. "So you think this is more valuable than having a twenty on the team?"

Bitters shrugged. "Put a twenty on my team and I'll tell you. But every time we get one who is switched on for any length of time the spooks swoop in and take them away to do decryption work. Remember Clark? He was a twenty for us for about six days before the CIA came for him. Now he works in code breaking. DeMarco could be useful enough to use, but low rated enough for us to keep."

Hunter broke his stare at Bitters and turned to face his monitor instead. A few mouse clicks suggested Hunter might be checking an email or looking something up. Bitters was not fooled, however, by this apparent distraction. Ignoring others was how his boss thought. He waited, admiring the view of Arlington and the Potomac out the director's window.

"This sword has two edges," said the director at length. "What if she starts getting intuitions about things we don't want her to have intuitions about? We're in a dangerous business."

Bitters had his answer. "See, that's our advantage in this game. She doesn't know she's an intuitionist. The intuition tests she has gotten are only the routine annual retests all the recruits get. Her guesses are correct only two out of every three times or so, so she hasn't come to rely on them or trust them to a great degree. And if need be, I can set her up for failure to shake her confidence in her hunches or drag her through the dirt for a while when she makes a mistake to keep her confidence down. That's the beauty of women, boss. Their negative self-images only need occasional reinforcement. The rest of the time Hollywood and the fashion industry do that work for us."

Hunter lapsed into silence again, clicking his mouse only so often. "Be sure she never finds out she's an intuitionist," he ordered.

"She never will. The only other person I've discussed this with is you. To those who can't think, all her test scores will ever say is she's not good enough."

The mouse-clicking stopped. Outside Hunter's window, a wing of F-22s from Andrews Air Force Base passed over the Potomac to take stations as Washington's air intercept detachment. Bitters scarcely felt their rumble through the reinforced concrete and bulletproof glass of the director's office. His boss's own raspy breathing was louder.

"Okay, she's your selectee, then," decided Hunter. "If she starts to balk, dump her back to white team and we'll contrive to discharge her. If you're wrong about her, then you'll have to work your people harder to keep up with missions as they come in."

Bitters made no reply. Needless answers in situations like this reduced his boss's plausible deniability, one of the things he was charged with protecting. He was confident in his ability to shape DeMarco, or to pick up the slack if he had to dump her. Instead, he referred to his notebook.

"Sir, about the policeman from Bumfuck, New York who was sniffing after Taryn Thomas? We can't find him."

Hunter waved his hand dismissively. "Don't worry. You were too busy. I gave McCrae to the Rainmaker's people since he was getting too close to the Army of God for their taste anyway. He has been taken care of. It's good to have friends, isn't it?

"Now we've got to work out what sort of tech the Rainmaker's men used to blow up that barn or whatever. But the time will come for that. If nothing else, we can get the president to give Domini a contract and watch as they use whatever it is to burn up sand niggers." At this, Hunter enjoyed a long heartfelt laugh. Bitters

306

smiled too.

David watched Faith pick at her food. Rosie was waiting politely for the woman to finish before looking to be excused, but it was clear to him something was jamming his daughter's hunger circuits. He motioned that the girl could put her dishes in the sink, and she dropped to her feet and wandered into the kitchen. He watched over his shoulder as Rosie than went upstairs to her room. He wondered what the girl would be doing up there so soon after supper, but resolved to check on it later. He had to take care of his eldest first.

"What's on your mind?" he inquired. Faith spent another few moments selecting and eating a green bean before answering.

"Dad, did you ever think about leaving Mom?" she pried. His daughter's eyes were clear and hazel, like her mother's.

David shifted in his seat at the question. He and Constance had always taken great care to avoid arguing or fighting around their daughter, but she was old enough that she was ready for the truth.

"Our marriage wasn't a perfect one. There were difficult times. Both of us considered ending the marriage at one time or another. And I think everyone has idle fantasies of leaving their spouse when things get stressful. Why? You thinking of a divorce, Honey?"

She smirked at her father's dry humor. "Cassius ran out on Nidya. Left her a nastygram and his cell phone and took off. With no warning."

Mr. Haversham tried to process this news. On meeting the detective at Faith's award ceremony, he had been impressed by the younger man's demeanor and by his attention to his family. The story didn't match what he remembered.

"How do you feel about that?" he followed up after a moment.

"Horrible. Embarrassed. Angry for Nidya. She called me wondering if I'd seen him. She wondered if Cassius and I might have had an affair while we were working together, since he mentioned another woman in the note he left her. That was awkward. And she needed someone to talk to, so I listened. And...and I wonder. She built his life around him, moved to Syracuse for his career, gave up her own, had kids, and then he took off," she said with dismay.

He took a guess at what his daughter was feeling. "So you're wondering how if something like this can happen, how is it people can take a risk on each other?"

"Yeah. It's like, if Cassius and Nidya can split up, then what chance do I have? *They* had it all, career, kids, roots, everything."

David sighed. "You need your name. You need faith. Unlike God, people can be faithless. That risk is always there. You need to have some fundamental belief or hope in the goodness and trustworthiness of your partner. For some people, this doesn't work out, because the person doesn't turn out to be who you think they are, or you don't turn out to be the person you thought you were."

At his last statement, his daughter stiffened, wide-eyed.

"Got to go, Dad," she apologized after a moment. "Forgot something at the office. It's got to be done by tomorrow."

He eyed his daughter's half-finished supper and wondered at the sudden change of subject. "Let me put that in a travel box for you. You ought to eat some more of it." He took her plate, scooped an extra pork chop and green beans into a plastic freezer box, and brought it to his daughter as she was standing in the doorway donning her uniform jacket.

"Thanks, Dad," she said, giving him a kiss before ducking out the door.

"You're the best. Don't wait up."

She pulled the door closed behind her. David stood at the door and watched her bustle out to her car and drive off. Contrary to her reassurances, he did worry. He wasn't sure if it was the plain fear and surprise which had been on her face, the ample evidence she had become a workaholic, or her telling him not to worry which worried him. But he wondered what had so struck her she felt compelled to run out to her office late in the evening.

Faith's mind and heart felt like they were dancing a tango as she drove through town. Evening traffic was light, and she was well on her way to the office when her feelings started to coalesce into coherent thoughts. She had been thinking on her recent romantic disappointment with Taryn when her father's phrase "sometimes the person doesn't turn out to be who you think they are" had connected.

Her lover had disappeared while she was investigating the carriage house fire or something related to it. And then FBI agents Ingle and Foxworth had said she might be headed for trouble. And then Cassius had vanished while looking for the woman.

When she arrived at the headquarters, the only cars left on the headquarters lot were at the dispatcher's entrance. Even Chief Bauer's car was gone. She unlocked the main doors, relocked them behind her, and headed quickly to her office, where she opened up a pleasantly fast and responsive web browser on the new computer Ingle and Foxworth had bought for her.

She googled Taryn Thomas, something she supposed she might have done before sleeping with the woman. At first, she was shocked to find the search returned a Wikipedia page listing a "Taryn Thomas" as a porn starlet. While such a job would match the journalist's flirtatious ways, a look at the woman's picture and bio ruled out any possibility this was the same woman. Further down, more links connected the woman to articles from the Ithaca Times online edition, most of them about local crimes, fires, or major events like the Dalai Lama's visit.

After scrolling down, Faith saw links to books, published through e-book vendors. One was called "The Terrible Swift Sword: Three Centuries of American Christofascism," and the other "Domini: Corporation or Christian Crusade?" She clicked through to read the book jackets.

"*Taryn Thomas is a graduate of Cornell University with a bachelor's degree in history. She lives in Ithaca, New York, where she works as a journalist for the Ithaca Times and other local periodicals. She enjoys gothic music, snowboarding, and the company of her three cats, Hussey, Adams, and Doktor Avalanche...*"

"Bingo," she thought, "That's the right girl." Taryn's books were priced six dollars apiece, so she downloaded them while she ran searches on Cassius McCrae. After sorting through three or four men with the name, she narrowed in on links to the correct man. She learned that, as she had heard, he had resolved three cases and been featured all three times on *Cold Case*. Everything else on Google matched what she already knew. The record showed he was a policeman, had experience in homicide investigation, had numerous awards, lived and went to church in Syracuse, and had done two tours in Iraq as a criminal investigations division agent. There were no pictures of him with unknown women, no scandals or brutality complaints, not even an embarrassing school yearbook picture.

When at last Taryn second book finished downloading, she flipped to the index and scanned it for any references to the Army of God. Her eyes widened as she read about the organization. Its history included hostage-taking, kidnapping, arson, and threats against abortion doctors, gay bars, and government and private facilities involved in stem-cell research and genetic engineering.

"The Army of God arrests in South Carolina uncovered weapons, body armor, and explosives listed with federal authorities as stolen from Domini corporation's North Carolina training facilities, and two of those arrested were current or former Domini security employees. However, Domini's executives deny any links to the Army of God, stating one of the two former employees found at the site had been fired from his job at Domini for 'extremist views.' Domini pointed out that Rainer Iseli, Domini's CEO and owner, is Catholic, and while he does not support abortion and homosexuality, he also does not underwrite evangelical fundamentalism.

"Though Army of God activities have increased since Market Garden and the organization has taken credit for a dozen killings and burnings of 'apostate' churches in the northeast and in southern California, no further arrests have been made. The increasing sophistication in their attacks and their getaways point to the Army of God as a serious emerging threat, though their status on the FBI's watch list of terrorist organizations remains unchanged."

Faith felt all her hairs prick up. Cassius had told her about the Army of God, but he hadn't told her how successful they had been. And Taryn's book was two years old. She suspected they had achieved much more in the meantime. She wondered why she hadn't heard of this group on the news or radio.

She tried to interrupt her panic cycle. She had no proof the Army of God had kidnapped the journalist or driven her into hiding. Likewise, she had no link between Detective McCrae's apparent abandonment of his family and the Army of God. *"I could be overreacting,"* she reasoned. *"Or maybe Taryn did get into trouble, but Cassius left Nidya. And even if they did, there's no proof they could follow the trail back to me. Rosie's foster parent isn't mentioned in any of the official reports. There's no proof my family is in any danger. I can't get crazy here."*

Despite her logic, the headquarters around her went from feeling like a safe yet private place to a network of darkened hallways and blind corners which could be filled with lurking "Army of God" fanatics. She wanted to enclose herself in four familiar walls. She downloaded <u>The Terrible Swift Sword</u> to her thumb drive, picked up her unopened box of supper, shut off the lights, and left.

When she arrived home, Rosie and her father were faced off across the checker barrel. Her father was glad for the distraction from another checkers rout. "That was quick. I didn't even have to wait up. Did you work whatever it was out?"

Faith opened her mouth. "Yeah, it's okay. I was...kind of overreacting." She wanted to tell him the whole story, but she knew if she did so, he might begin to worry as she was. Without any real sign of a connection between Taryn's disappearance and Cassius's, there wasn't any sense in doing so. She'd lay low, let the carriage house fire fade into the past, and go back to her life, which was busy enough.

She took her thumb drive upstairs to plug into her e-reader. She could lay low but still finish reading Taryn's book.

Chapter 23

Resonance

David was growing tired of the *Nature* magazine. It had some pictures, but was full of text which was too complicated to read, and without Connie to unravel the occasional fifty-dollar word, he didn't feel inclined to try too hard. He felt surprise at the odd things which made him miss his wife. He wondered if Hildegard could explain the words to him, and then reconsidered. The woman was not a placeholder for Connie, and it would be wrong to ask her to fill that role instead of consulting a dictionary or settling for the pictures and captions he could absorb unaided. Besides, English wasn't even her native language, and he wasn't about to concede to a foreigner her mastery of his language was greater than his own. If only because she would tease him mercilessly thereafter.

He read a few more photo captions, and then put down the magazine and surveyed the office. The professor's office was not what he had envisioned and had sometimes seen at the university after the stray cigarette or lab accident required a fireman's intervention. Even so, he recalled it had been years since he'd had to fight fires on the campus. Cornell's own life safety service and their fire prevention program had all but eliminated calls for outside help for routine fires. The university had done a good job, he had to admit.

This professor's office was cleaner than any he had seen before. The bookshelves which walled and divided the room were not filled with books, but with a combination of books, DVDs and thin, metal-edged rectangles like picture frames of some kind. The desk was clear, holding just a photo of what he assumed were the professor's family members, but featured three flat-panel monitors, one for the professor's computer and two facing the guest chairs. The few open expanses of wall were covered with posters showing the anatomy of the brain with various cut-outs and layers. One poster was titled "What is an MRI?" and explained the workings of magnetic resonance imaging with simple terms and diagrams.

After a moment, he heard a knock at the office door. The clock over the door read four thirty, the time he had been set to meet Dr. Jacobs, and the assistant who had ushered him in had assured him the professor was aware of his appointment. But he wondered why the professor would knock at his own door. He stood to answer the door but it opened, and Hildegard poked her face in.

"Good day!" she said, looking pleased.

"Hello!" said David. He smirked. Think of the devil, he observed, and she might come. The woman of his desire crossed the room and sat in the chair beside his. He sat down again, wishing her chair was closer to his, but he remembered she wished to keep their relationship invisible to her peers. So he settled back and enjoyed a whiff of her gingery perfume. Her scarf was scarlet today.

"Any sign of our host?" she inquired, looking at her silver watch-bracelet.

"The assistant said he was coming. Didn't say much about when, though."

Hildegard's mind wandered toward their next date, just as his was. "So, how does this Friday look? I could make supper if money is tight."

David smiled at the question. He didn't want to wait until Friday. Now that she was in the room he wanted to follow her home, to follow her to her couch, and to enjoy the merry twinkle he'd see in her eye. He opened his mouth to give some voice to this impulse, but at her question the office door opened.

In came a harried-looking slender man. If his hair was long, it would have been wild, but cut close as it was his curls suggested disarray without being out of line.

"Mr. Haversham, Mrs. Haversham, sorry I'm late," he apologized. "I'm Ren Jacobs." He shook the doctor's hand, trying to find a delicate way to point out the professor was not his wife. He was getting tired of the mistake, more so now because they were trying to avoid precisely that appearance.

Hildegard handled it. "I'm sorry. I'm not Mrs. Haversham, I'm Professor Teschke from the linguistics department. The chair."

Dr. Jacobs stuttered his surprise. "Oh, so sorry, Dr...."

"Teschke," she repeated.

"Ah, I apologize. But my aide explained you were the subject's guardians."

"I'm her legal guardian, as is my daughter, who is at work and isn't coming." explained David. "Dr. Teschke was the one who helped arrange for these tests. Your assistant mistook Dr. Teschke for my daughter."

"I spoke to your department head at the last heads' meeting," said Dr. Teschke. "He was helpful and suggested I might attend the meeting if Mr. Haversham agreed. He did."

"Okay," said Dr. Jacobs, "That decision was made over my head." David recognized the younger man's accent as being from Brooklyn. The doctor set down a stack of metal frames he was carrying, which he saw held large photo images in negative. "Mr. Haversham, whatever my department head may have wanted for this meeting, Dr. Teschke's presence does create an issue of medical privacy. I am going to discuss the details of your foster daughter's neurology and its probable impacts on her mental state. You have to give me permission to discuss this in front of her." He sat in his desk chair, folded his hands, and waited for Mr. Haversham to respond.

David glimpsed Hildegard's face. Her expression was flat, which meant she was hiding some disappointment or displeasure.

"Sure," he answered. "Her department is helping us understand Rosie's speech problems. She should see this, too."

"Alright, then," agreed Dr. Jacobs. "Before I begin, I need to explain something about the images I will show you. I also need to warn you in advance I will have many questions about the girl's behavior. I'm hopeful you'll clarify for me as much as I do for you." He worked on his keyboard for a bit, and in a moment, both flat screens lit up, showing two different oval images David guessed were cross-sections of human brains.

"Do you mind if I record this meeting?" Dr. Jacobs asked. "It would help me recall the answers to the questions without having to call and ask you questions again in the future."

Mr. Haversham again checked with Hildegard, who nodded. "No problem, Doctor," he agreed.

"Great, thank you. I'm of the keyboard generation, you know, my handwritten notes are slow and painful," Dr. Jacobs said sheepishly. "Plus, I'm a doctor, so no one can ever read them afterwards anyway." If the doctor intended this to be a joke, no one else laughed.

David waited for the doctor to produce a recording device, but he did not. The younger man focused his attention back on the computer. He guessed the desktop computer would be doing the audio recording as well as the displays. "This should be straightforward at first, then get more complicated," Dr. Jacobs said. "So, let me begin with these images. To your left is an image of a typical human brain involved in quiet thought, eyes closed, at rest, after fifteen minutes.

The subject in this case was evaluated as being within observed normal human activity ranges. Most human brains we have studied have this pattern with eyes closed in thought. With these MRI scans, brighter and whiter regions indicate areas of greater activity. You can see that in the normal brain, activity is distributed in both hemispheres and there are few regions of distinct brightness.

"To your right is an image taken from a Tibetan Buddhist monk at meditation for fifteen minutes. Notice the distinct difference in brain activity. The monk's left hemisphere is much more active than his right hemisphere. In addition to the different levels of activity, there are organic differences between the monk and our sample American. The Rinpoche's brain has larger and denser structures. His hippocampus, orbito-frontal cortex, thalamus, pineal gland and the inferior temporal gyrus, are all enlarged and denser." Blue circles flashed on the two images in tandem, drawing David's attention to the differences between them.

He could see the indicated areas on the monk's images were indeed larger and had fewer void spaces and a brighter gray color than the normal sample. The distribution of active areas was larger and brighter for the monk. The doctor continued. "It's unclear if these differences and enlargements stem from his lifetime of meditation, or if he was born with these differences which in turn drew him to meditation and his monastic lifestyle. There is growing evidence, however, that the more one practices a mental task, the more the brain grows and rewires itself to do that task efficiently. If this is true, it could explain the differences in the monk's brain. And this is the assumption I'll start from when I discuss your daughter's case.

"The Rinpoche shows some hallmark differences typical of experienced meditators. While the sample of such meditators is still too small to derive reliable statistical studies, examination of the small sample we do have shows his image is fairly typical. All the enlarged regions are more active. His left hemisphere is more active than his right. And his pineal gland is extremely active, where in our typical American's sample it is quiet.

"While meditating, monks tend to report happiness, or outright joy. Many monks report after years of meditation, this sense of joy fades, but is replaced with a profound sense of being connected to everyone in the world, and an understanding that everything in the world is morally significant. Tibetan Buddhists are reported to be gentle and pacifistic, and capable of facing the grimmest affronts without violence or anger. They also have very low rates of suicide and mental illness. Again, whether these facts stem from these changes, or are the result of their theological training, is unclear. Similarly, Zen Buddhist monks, while not strict pacifists, are able to perform complex tasks with no interference from their own emotions even in the most trying situations. Any questions so far?"

David shook his head. Hildegard shrugged. The doctor continued.

"Now this," he said, holding up one of the framed images he had carried in and sticking it magnetically to a white light panel behind his desk, "Is part of a series of images of your foster daughter's brain. They were done on the same grayscale as the other images. There may be some differences in apparent activity brightness because these are on my light panel and the others are on the computer screens, but they should be comparable.

"This is your daughter in quiet thought, eyes closed, after fifteen minutes. Notice how its pattern and structures more closely resemble those of the Tibetan monk. The same structures are enlarged and denser. And the same ones are more active. But it doesn't stop there.

"The difference in activity levels in these regions of your daughter's brain are greater compared to those of the monk than the monk's are to our typical sample. In other words, she appears to be meditating at a level much higher than the monk. It's remarkable, as the Rinpoche we have imaged here estimated he had spent over forty-three thousand hours at meditation thus far in his monastic life. That's more than five years, twenty-four seven, *spent meditating*. But your foster daughter is estimated to be twelve years old. Based on the changes we see in the monk, your daughter would have to have meditated for eleven of her twelve years of age. It doesn't leave much time for eating, sleeping, playing, or learning languages. It doesn't leave much time for anything."

"Wow," marvelled David.

"*Kaum zu glauben,*" muttered Hildegard.

"Sounds impossible, doesn't it? I think I have an explanation," said Dr. Jacobs. "This is your daughter's brain while drawing pictures in the activity lab." The doctor snatched a fresh film from the stack and put it in place on the light board.

"We see increased activity in the visual cortex, that's not unusual in visual art activities. This other pattern suggests she is recalling long-term memories, also not unusual in someone drawing something from memory. But also active are the hippocampus, the pineal, the orbito-frontal complex-"

"The same ones involved in meditation," David observed.

The doctor nodded, and changed to a new film. "You're dead on. One could always argue drawing is a form of meditation. So check this film out. This is your foster daughter dancing in the activity center. The activity was, erm, spontaneous, we don't normally have people dance with that many delicate sensors wired to their head. We had asked her to listen to music, and she-"

"I know. She does that from time to time," David reassured the doctor. Dr. Jacobs looked relieved.

"Good, this was to be one of my questions. Anyway, we see in this image increased activity we might expect in the motor cortex associated with movement, balance, and proprioception. But in addition, we see that same activity cluster associated with meditation, even while engaged in complex motion."

"What's proprioception?" Hildegard wondered.

The doctor was undeterred by the question. "Yes, please do stop me if I'm using terms you don't understand. Proprioception is your ability to sense where your body parts are in relationship to each other. It's the sense which lets you close your eyes but still touch your nose with your finger without poking yourself in the eye. Try it."

Hildegard closed her eyes and, without apparent difficulty, reached up and touched her nose.

"See, that's proprioception. It's universal in higher vertebrates. Even mice and blue whales have it."

David wondered how the doctors had administered a proprioception test to a blue whale, but didn't ask. He was afraid the question might lead him to a depressing use of his tax dollars.

"Here we are again," said the doctor, pointing to the images. "Guess which other parts of your daughter's brain are fully active?"

"The meditation ones?" David guessed.

"Check, and next." He slapped another image on the light panel. "We got this image while your daughter went to pee in the activity lab bathroom. See anything familiar?"

"The meditation pattern?" he observed.

"Yeah, ok, so here is the real kicker. This one is the image of your daughter's brain while she was asleep in the lab. It was only a catnap, not deep

REM, but-"

"The same ones," Mr. Haversham concluded.

"Judging by this, your daughter is meditating in her sleep. What this suggests to me is her meditative mental state is neither deliberate nor voluntary. She may be unable switch off these parts of her brain. That might explain how she has apparent meditation-induced neuronal change equivalent to her age. She may have been meditating since she was born. Or even before she was born. There's a lot of mental activity which goes on the in womb. She may, in effect, be 'shut in' to a meditation-like state." He put down the films, sat back, tapped his chin with the forefingers of both hands as if smoothing a beard which wasn't there, and drew a long sigh. "So, all in all, this is a fascinating case. We've never seen anything like it, and neither have my colleagues in Madison, where most of these MRI studies took place. If you don't have any questions, I'd like to ask *you* some questions about your foster daughter."

David reflected on Rosie for a moment. She had become the joy of his life. He had attributed it to her good character, and to her spiritual nature, and it disturbed him to think this personality might be a 'condition' rather than a reflection of her choices and will. But this depressing prospect didn't make the doctor's questions any less valuable in understanding her.

"Go ahead."

"How would you describe your foster daughter?"

"She's the most even-tempered and happy child I've ever encountered. I'm taken with her," David admitted.

"Would you describe her intelligence as appropriate to her age?" the doctor asked.

"In some things. Other things she doesn't ever learn."

"What are the things she is good at?"

"Dancing. Drawing. And judging other people's emotions."

"So, you'd describe her as having empathy?"

"Yes. Much more than is typical for a child. Come to think of it, much more than is typical for most adults I know. Maybe....Maybe all of the adults I know."

"That's not all," added Hildegard. "She's a prodigal polyglot. She either knows or learns languages at great speed. We've already confirmed she can read more than fifteen languages."

The doctor was intrigued. "I'm not a linguist, so forgive me when I ask how rare this ability is. I'm terrible with languages, I even flunked Hebrew."

Dr. Teschke rolled her eyes up and reflected. "I've been a linguist all my life. And I've heard of a handful of people who know that many languages, but none of them were twelve years old. I'd say her talent is unique."

"Fascinating," said the doctor. "It suggests another test. I'd love to do some images of her brain when she's being exposed to a novel language. Any other special talents I should be aware of?"

David shook his head. The professor added nothing.

The doctor then picked again at his non-existent beard and hesitated. "And what would you describe her as bad at? I don't mean to be rude, but we'd like an impression if you can give us one."

"She hates math. According to the tutors she's good at some of it. But she doesn't want to pay it any attention."

"So, would you guess it's an issue of math ability, or ability to focus?"

"I'm not sure. She can focus on drawing or dancing," explained the foster father. "It's more like she finds it unimportant. Things she focuses on she's great at, but you have to return her attention to math, and when she gives it her

314

attention, she's either correct all the time or none of the time."

"So, types of math are easy for her, and others hard, but all of it boring?"

"That's it."

"Anything else?" The doctor added.

Hildegard was looking at David as if she were waiting to say something. He wondered what it was. "Go ahead," he invited her.

"For all the languages she reads or understands, she only speaks one," she said.

"Oh, of course!" he thought. There was that limitation, the one which complicated and colored his life with Rosie so pervasively he'd even forgotten to mention it!

"By speak, you mean what?" the doctor prompted. The linguist frowned at the question, as if it should be obvious.

"By that I mean she will only produce speech of any kind in one special language. An obscure language at that."

"Is her speech phonetically normal? Does she show any signs of deficits or difficulty speaking?"

"It's not only normal, but better than normal. I can't judge it because I don't speak the language, but when we have found other speakers of her language they describe her as fluent, with no accent, a large vocabulary and a subtle sense of humor."

"Huh," mused Dr. Jacobs. "And this inability to speak other languages, what do you think causes it?"

Hildegard and David traded looks with each other before he answered. "We were hoping you could tell us. If we knew we'd already be working on it."

Dr. Jacobs looked surprised at this expectation. "I'm not a neurolinguist, or even a linguist, I'm a neuroanatomist. Are you aware of any like cases or conditions which cause this?" Dr. Jacobs questioned the professor.

She handled the question with confidence. "It's not uncommon for children who suffer severe trauma or grave disability to develop a pathological language, that is, a language only the child and their caregivers understand. But in this case, the language she speaks is a real, existing language, so we know she can learn and formulate in shared languages. Thus far, all we've been able to conclude is her attachment to using this language is pathological. If you didn't see any organic issues which might explain it, I guess we'd have to consider it a functional speech pathology."

"Wow. This is...cool," said the doctor. Dr. Jacob's fascination with Rosie's deficits struck her foster father as morbid, but he said nothing. The doctor leaned forward on his desk and cupped his hands together.

"Mr. Haversham, your daughter's case is so unusual I think it would be child's play to find some funds to conduct further tests. Heck, the grants to study your daughter could write themselves. She would likely be a seminal case in neuroanatomy for decades, if not centuries, like Phineas Gage. I'm not kidding. I could make a phone call and get Oliver Sachs in here."

David didn't know who Oliver Sachs or Phineas Gage were, but he assumed they were important neuro-anatomists. "Sure, I suppose if her case would be useful to science, she'd want to do it. She loves to help people. I'd have to ask her, though."

"She's of an age where you can consent on her behalf," the doctor noted.

Mr. Haversham hesitated. He didn't want to explain Rosie was a guest brought to him by God, and her consent was necessary for this reason. He supposed that the doctor was an atheist, like Hildegard was, and this explanation would sound crazy, so he simplified it.

"Trust me, trying to get the child to do something she doesn't want to do is more than you want to take on. It's more than I can take on. I've already got a pacemaker," David said, patting his chest. Dr. Jacob nodded at this.

"Let me know. If you're willing to cooperate, I think your daughter would generate international interest in parts of the scientific community. And she's so young. A longitudinal study of her as she matures could tell us a lot about the role of different parts of the brain in thought and emotion."

"I'll ask her," David repeated.

"I don't think you have much to worry about, Doctor," the professor reassured him. "The girl has shown great patience with my department's tests. I can't see her saying no to yours. Mr. Haversham is trying to be a respectful foster parent."

"Ah, good, good. Do either of you have more questions of me?"

"Would your studies involve more of these MRIs?" he asked.

"Yes," said Dr. Jacobs.

"Are there any side effects from these tests?" he drilled deeper.

"Not that we're aware of. If she has kidney problems of any kind, there will be certain MRI tests we cannot perform, but if her kidneys are normal, we should be able to repeat these tests many times with no harm. In addition to being one of the most useful imaging methods, MRIs are the safest known. But not all the tests we could do would be MRI tests. We'd discuss each type of testing method with you, and her, before attempting them."

David felt better about the prospects of the test. He wanted to be able to explain the risks to Rosie. He took another moment to think of more questions, and couldn't. "I guess that's all I had." He turned his attention to Hildegard. She did have a question.

"Is it safe to assume neuroanatomists know the parts of the brain associated with language use and development?"

"We know what parts we *think* are involved. But that's why testing Rosie could be so illuminating. She has a special talent for it."

"Might these areas be overdeveloped like her meditation parts?" she speculated.

"That's a good question," the doctor said. "I didn't bother to make a comparison, as these parts weren't active during our imaging." He pawed through the stack of images on the desk, holding them up to the ceiling lamp to check them. "Uh-huh. Huh. Curious," the man muttered. "I can't say definitively, because I didn't select these images for how well they show Broca's area and Wernicke's area, and there is no sign of activation during our tests. But what I can see of these areas is more dense and vascularized than either our American control or the monk. Still, we did capture images of her whole brain, so I can go back and look again without the need for doing more scans."

"If you could do so, the results might be interesting for the speech pathologist working on this case," said the professor. "Call me or email me with them. If it's okay with Mr. Haversham."

"It is," said David. "To my mind, you're one of her doctors, Hildegard."

At this, Dr. Teschke raised her eyebrows at him, as if to say "caught you." He realized with chagrin he'd used her first name in front of one of her peers.

"I will," said Dr. Jacobs, glancing between the two of them. "Anything else?"

They both shook their heads. Dr. Jacobs then stood, and they followed him to his office door. He shook hands with them as he walked them down the corridor and out of his department.

"I've seen a lot of caretakers for people with neurological differences," recalled Dr. Jacobs, walking down the hallway. "It's obvious it takes special qualities to do it, I'm not sure I have those qualities myself." He offered David a handshake. "If there is anything I can study or do which might help you day to day, don't hesitate to call back. When I have some more testing proposals, I'll let Dr. Teschke know and we can discuss them together."

"That's fine," he agreed.

Dr. Jacob shook Hildegard's hand. "It's nice to meet someone with enough interdisciplinary perspective to bring this case to our attention. I think we specialists often malign the liberal arts, and you're a case in point."

The linguist laughed. "I'm afraid in the liberal arts, I'm regarded as a specialist. But you flatter me," she said. With that farewell, they left the doctor together and walked to the stairwell.

"So, I'll call about Friday night," said David.

"Use my cell phone. I don't need my assistants answering or listening in on a personal call," she said.

He decided to probe her reasoning. "Sure you're not ashamed of me? Sounds like you're hiding me."

The professor scolded him. "I can accept that other adults will learn about us. But as long as I can delay it being a subject of conversation with my assistants, I will."

The firefighter smiled at his lover's use of the word adult. Whether someone was an adult or not changed the older one became. He decided to test her. "How old is your oldest assistant? Thirty? Thirty-five?"

"A stripling. With charming naiveté," she laughed at him. They came to the bottom of the stairs.

"So, I walk from here. Good to see you again," she said.

"I'll see you tomorrow afternoon, when I bring Rosie," he reminded the professor.

"No, you won't, I have a meeting. Shawn and maybe Akiko will be there." answered Hildegard. She held out her hand, raising it at arm's length before her hips and shoulders. "It's old-fashioned. But if you want to make me feel good and traditional, you can kiss my hand."

David grinned at this. He had a mental image of Errol Flynn kneeling to kiss a renaissance lady's hand. His knees protested at the idea, but he could at least go halfway. He stepped forward, raised her hands to his lips, and kissed her knuckles.

"There. Boo-boo all better, sweetie?" he cracked at her. She laughed.

"Condescend to me at your peril." She withdrew her hand. "But let's get together Friday. You know, to give you a chance to improve on your performance. I'll even cook something."

David assented with a smile. "Practice does make perfect."

Vincent sat down at his desk. A steaming cup of tea was waiting, alongside a pair of Amerikaner pastries on a plate. The sounds of Sharrah's efficiency filtered in from the outer office. He could make out occasional clinks of dishes, the opening and shutting of the kitchenette refrigerator, and the sound of her typing as she began sifting through the morning's voicemail messages. The voicemail alone was no small job. With the recent addition of his Hong Kong office, the sun never set on Vincent Foster and Associates. His assistant's perspective and ability to summarize kept the enterprise from overwhelming him.

He took a bite of the pastry and unlocked his computer. His inbox wasn't "full" in the sense most executives he rubbed elbows with complained of. He had only eight messages. And he would be able to answer each one without worrying about nuisances like "shareholders," "regulators," and "public relations themes." After the recent touch-and-go about his cattle ranches, his laboratory heads and associates were now encrypting sensitive messages and sending them directly to him. An unexpected benefit was he could focus on these technical items first thing in the morning while Sharrah sorted out the current day's business correspondence. He was out of touch with some of his contacts as a result, but in the time following the decision, he felt much more in touch with the progress in his research. And research, after all, was the point of his operation.

He scanned the subject lines of the messages. Then he stopped, mid-chew, rubbed his eyes, and stared again at the subject line. It was a message from Dr. Jacobs, his MRI expert in the United States.

"Case #490 films and images."

He gulped the pastry in his mouth, took a quick but deep sip of his tea, and complimented Dr. Jacobs before he even opened the message. "Clever boy. However did you find her?" he said aloud. He opened the letter.

"Sir,

"Attached find images and videos of fMRI studies of prepubescent female presented at my laboratory whose description and anatomical specifics match those you forwarded on case #490 in anticipation of her initial appointment at my laboratory. Subject was presented in care of state-appointed foster parent and a university colleague intrigued by the girl's linguistic talents.

"490's foster parent has been cagey about the details, but has related thus far the subject was discovered at scene of fire not far from my university. The conclusion of local authorities was she was the target of arson, but there is no media coverage which explains how she became lost. Suspect concerns for the child's welfare or public scrutiny may have caused the case to be handled so discreetly it would require skill and resources outside my circle to divine what occurred there. However, I will forward any details I might learn in passing.

"Subject was presented with speech pathology of unknown cause, speaking only an obscure and artificial language. This matches the original symptoms you described when sending her for testing at my laboratory, but I am unable to judge if her condition has worsened or improved in the intervening time.

"In any case, I conducted not only the tests the foster parent requested but the full battery you had initially requested of me. I now consider this contract closed and will take receipt of your funds which I had held pending this girl's rediscovery. Emphasize that, whatever disabilities the child manifests, a publishable study of her unusual neurology could be a seminal work in the field of human modification. My images and videos come with full narrations of my conjectures and suggestions for further study.

"Thinking you might have further interest in more studies, I have indicated to foster parent that I might be able to receive 'grants' to continue my studies to elucidate her case. He was receptive. All that remains, then, is for you and I to come to understanding about publication rights, protection of your trade secrets, and the division of laboratory costs, and I will present the foster parent with a series of proposals.

"Must indicate, however, the subject is generating significant interest at Cornell, a school of not inconsiderable talent and resources. If you declined, and another party came forward with a request and funding to study this child, I would be hard-pressed, both ethically and politically, to turn them away.

"Await your reply.

"Yours,
"Renee"

Vincent thought. Renee Jacobs was one of the best. For Rosetta's brain to have ignited this kind of interest from him his findings must be dramatic. The man had seen every other case worth seeing in his field. So Dr. Foster was sure the slides and videos would be worthwhile to him and his research, but he put his curiosity about them aside for now.

What concerned him most was what Renee had said about interest in Rosetta from others. While his industrial processes had no rivals, the science he did was only one or two steps ahead of the cutting edge of human genome research. If the girl attracted too much attention, someone was bound to notice her eyes, her nose, and her GI tract contained cells of a non-human origin. And this would lead to more inquiries about her origins, which might in turn lead to the discovery her human genome had also been modified. And when this happened, "feeding frenzy" would be an understatement for the scientific melee that would follow.

Vincent righted his glasses with a fingertip, leaned on one elbow, and swiveled his chair to stare out his office windows at the tranquility and order of the street. Change was inevitable, he supposed, though it was ironic it would come as he was beginning to envision retirement, and beginning his search for a successor who could continue his quiet work. Instead, he guessed, he would now have to find the successor who could lead his enterprise through turbulent times.

He considered his other options. In frank conversations with Jean-Paul, his attorney had sometimes mentioned that in business and science the best solutions were not legal solutions. Dr. Foster agreed with this in part. He had a lot of money and materiel to move and a lot of people who were experts at moving it quietly, and not necessarily legally, for him. But he had always disdained means which were destructive or violent. And even if he were willing to use violence, he didn't see how even well-placed bullets could extricate him from the present situation. In fact, if the girl was killed, her body would be more exposed to the scientific inquiry of third parties, not less.

He would have to go public. It had always been a question of when, but "when" had grown a whole lot closer to "now." Indeed, it might be "now" as in "right now." He had to think about it.

It dawned on him he might have been wise to find a reliable PR firm before this juncture, but he had always envisioned the ultimate disclosure of his work to be a gradual process, not a rushed one. Thus, he'd always been able to justify delaying taking on such a firm and their associated cost and liabilities. And now his hesitation might be about to cost him. He was in the position of needing a good spokesperson and not having one he could trust.

He reviewed his resources and his situation. If he went to a big PR firm with his story, there was a chance it would be leaked. On the other hand, if he waited until after the story broke, chance would determine the initial "spin" the story would be given, and the initial spin could be crucial. He balanced one risk against another.

He swiveled back to his computer screen and consulted his address book for former clients who might be able to make a recommendation for him. There was that Oscar winning actress! But no, she was an airhead and her two "PR firms," as it were, were made firm by silicon. There were more than a few legislators, but they were not the best ones to rely upon. When it was revealed he had helped them with their children, they wouldn't want to be seen to have had any further dealings with him. There was the head of that Wall Street bank, but he had enough problems at the moment. Vincent pondered. Whom could he trust, when it came down to it?

Sharrah walked in front of his office door, humming a happy tune. She came in, smiled at Dr. Foster's stare, and presented him with her daily notebook page of phone numbers and summarized messages.

"Here are today's calls," she said. "Do you have anything you need me to do today? I'll be walking to the cleaners with some of my clothes, so if you need me to take yours along-"

"Didn't you mention you were on the debate team at Burn Hall? They had a fine reputation," he recalled.

The woman was miffed at being stopped mid-sentence. Then she gave him a quizzical look. "Yes, but-"

"Did you do well?" Vincent continued.

Sharrah was pleased to recall this. "I got some first prizes. I would have been captain if I was a boy, but the school had just gone co-ed and they weren't yet ready for me, I think."

"Excellent!" he said, feeling relieved. "Then I may need to temporarily expand on your already considerable responsibilities."

She sat in her gilded chair. "Please explain."

"I have a tricky problem, a matter of public relations, or of 'spin,' if you will. Now, I plan to hire a proper public relations firm for it, but the matter is so sensitive I don't dare hire a firm which might leak the information before-"

Vincent absorbed Sharrah's expression. Keen interest sculpted the woman's face.

"Got you hooked, have I?" he said after a moment.

"I'm more than happy to handle your dry cleaning and make your lunch, but I have thought for a long time I would like to be more involved and helpful." As Sharrah said this, she leaned forward and, with a wink, took his second pastry. "Now go on, Vincent."

Chapter 24

An Unusual Soup

David stood for a few moments outside Hildegard's door. He had chosen not to use the elevator and instead be manly and climb the five stories of stairs in the apartment building, leaving him breathless and sweaty. He didn't want the woman to see him this way, and the corridor was empty of anyone who might find it strange to find an old man propped up against the wall with a bottle of wine and box of chocolates. So it was as good a place as any to recover.

"Pride goeth before the fall," he recited once his breath returned. He gathered his thoughts and knocked.

Dr. Teschke answered after a moment, and Mr. Haversham was struck by her beauty. She wore a heather gray shirt chased with green flowers and embroidery and a green skirt, which contrasted with her usual modern and cosmopolitan dress. He stammered his appreciation as she accepted the wine and coat.

The smell was as striking. He smelled pork, chicken, and paprika, and his mouth watered.

"Smells divine!" he said.

"Thank you! I do have some culinary skills. And it's nearly ready for the table," she said. David saw the table was already set with plates and bowls. "And thank you for the wine! I'm not sure it will be a good match tonight, but we can save it for another time." She put the chocolates and wine into one of her many glass-fronted cabinets.

He wondered how long they'd be on display there, and felt crestfallen. He'd spent some time with the shop clerk at the wine store picking out a German wine he hoped would please her. The clerk had described the wine as a "delicate Riesling," however, and he had to admit the hearty smells coming from the kitchen would overpower a delicate wine. So he contented himself with anticipation of whatever it was she was cooking, and hoped that whenever she did drink the wine, she would appreciate it.

"You're flushed!" she said. "Are you feeling well?"

The firefighter felt chagrin. She'd noticed.

"I took the stairs is all."

"Hmmm..." she said significantly. David braced for more criticism, but it never came. When she emerged from the kitchen with a steaming pot in her hands, he pushed out his chair to help her, but she motioned him back to his seat. "It's nothing, allow me. Rest."

After two more trips she was done. Once she sat and took her own first bite, David started on the first plate she had set before him. It was a sweet onion salad in a reddish curry sauce and a sweet apple flavor.

"You look...traditional," he commented. "Is this also a traditional German dish?"

"Yes...no, not exactly," she said. She didn't clarify. "Have you heard anything more about your daughter's MRI results?"

"They're asking for two more days of testing this month, including one this coming Monday I'm hoping you can come to with me. They'll be 'biogeographic tests' or something that should tell me what country she's from. Dr. Jacobs is very interested in Rosie."

Hildegard shrugged. "It's understandable. I'm interested too."

"It's all new to me. I've lived in this town more than sixty years and I've only encountered interested and helpful university professors in the last few months," David explained. "Not to mention lovely ones."

She said nothing while she ladled him a bowl of a reddish orange soup with floating yellowish cubes in it. This was the dish which smelled of paprika.

He lifted his first spoonful and enjoyed it. The cubes had a firm texture, suggesting they were part of a root. "What is this?"

"Rutabaga soup. If it's too spicy, you don't have to eat it."

"No, it's great. I guess....I guess I thought of German food as sausage and sauerkraut and pork and beer. All nice, but not exactly a vegetable soup and onion salad."

"This isn't mainstream German food," Dr. Teschke explained. "I grew up in East Germany."

Mr. Haversham tried to wrap his mind around this bit of the professor's past. It was tough for him to believe, for as practical and down-to-earth as she was, she'd been raised a communist. But maybe she'd gotten over it. "Oh, is eastern German food different from western German food?"

She shook her head. "The regional cuisines of the states of Germany are all different, but they share common ingredients and flavors. This is 'East German' cooking in the sense that it is the food which was prepared while East Germany was part of the Soviet bloc. It has influences from Hungary, Russia, and Poland. It's the food I grew up with."

David smiled. "So it's what your mother used to make?"

The professor shook her head. "My mother was a university professor like myself. She worked and seldom cooked. My family ate most of our meals at state cafeterias. Many housing units didn't even have kitchens, so I got used to this food. There were about three hundred state-approved recipes for the state kitchens which made use of spices and foods common in the Soviet bloc. Like McDonald's here, one could travel anywhere in the country yet get familiar food at the state kitchens. Since East Germany and its state kitchens are gone, most modern Germans, east or west, would not recognize this food anymore. But it still makes me feel at home."

He nodded his appreciation. "Even if it's communist food, it's good."

She grinned. "The way to a man's ideology is through his stomach, is it? After a few more meals I'll have you in the proletarian vanguard, yes?"

David shook his head. "Don't think so. I went to war against communism in Viet Nam. But I like the soup." He finished the bowl. "I liked Vietnamese food, too. Except for the stuff made with dogs and cats in it. What was it like growing up in a communist country?"

"What was it like? It was....different. More egalitarian, more orderly, creative in some ways, yet conformist in others. We had to improvise many things, and share more things, and spend time together as a society in cafeterias, buses, and trains. It's not like here where every family can teach their children at home, eat at home, and travel in their own cars. But if I was willing to work, trade, or improvise, I could leave home for a week, want for nothing, and fear nothing. I could travel by bus, stay in youth shelters, and eat in state kitchens. If my family hadn't gone political, I might have had a happy childhood."

"What happened?"

Hildegard stared into her half-empty bowl. "My father was a leading member of an alternative political party, the Christian Democratic party. Unlike

322

other communist countries, East Germany had more than one state-approved party. But in the 80s, he started breaking from what was politically acceptable and my family was persecuted. And my name didn't help."

"Your name? What's so special about it? It sounds German to me."

Her eyebrows rose. "Yes, it's a traditional German name, like Ludwig or even...Adolf. That was the problem. In East Germany, traditional German culture was out of favor. Children were given short modern German names or Polish or Russian sounding names. My best friends, for example, were named Ilse and Katje and Nastassia. My name smacked of old, capitalist, fascist Germany. Likewise, my father's religion earned us no favor."

"Ah. You got teased, then?"

"I think 'bullied' would be a better term. Sometimes I think the bullying of children, not the actions of the secret police, was half the reason I was so happy to move to West Germany."

David considered her story. "What was your father's religion? I didn't think communist countries allowed religion."

"It wasn't banned. But it was treated with suspicion by many as a servant of fascism. Including myself."

He popped the question he had long avoided. "You're not religious?" He suspected this already, but he hoped the question would net him an explanation for her atheism.

She shook her head. "Everything I've seen in this world, good or evil, has been made by men. Even before my father went political, I thought his obsession with an imaginary God and His stupid rules to be foolish. 'God' was to me the equivalent to the state's 'Proletariat': another invisible authority who promulgated senseless rules for life. But the gulf between us on the subject grew wider when I was...mistreated for his political stances I did not share, and continued to be mistreated after his imprisonment and death. Not only did I not have religion, but I resented the effect his religiosity had on my life.

"Looking back, I see my father was a good man if a bad father. He worked for justice and freedom, and he paid for it with his life, so I cannot fault him. I admire him and recognize my anger with him for what it was: pain and girlish pride. But now, in my own life, I leave other people to enjoy their religions and quietly enjoy my atheism."

"Your dad sounds like my kind of guy," David said.

"Yes, I suspect you would have gotten along," Hildegard said regretfully. "So, onto the main course." She went into the kitchen and he soon heard the clatter of what sounded like a large casserole dish.

"What is it called?" he called after her.

"*Wuerzefleisch*," she answered.

He grimaced. "I'll be happy to eat it," he said. "But don't ask me to pronounce it."

"I won't. It would pain me to hear you try," she shot back from the kitchen. "Just let it nourish you for tonight's activities."

David had never before been to the veterinary research tower on Cornell's campus. It had been built after the university's own Life Safety department had taken over complete responsibility for fire safety on the campus, and his department had only rarely responded to the veterinary school. He marveled that the veterinary research tower, which had been built since his middle age, could now be out of date. There was an enormous and modern brick and glass wing to the building he presumed was more contemporary, but the tower itself screamed early eighties. Bare concrete, lots of brown glass, rounded corners and stairs, and asphalt tiles were the rule on the inside. He stopped and gawked curiously, which caused Hildegard to look impatient while she waited for the elevator.

"I don't know why they didn't want me to bring Rosie," he said after rejoining her.

"Please," she countered. "Few adults understand genetics well. Asking a girl to come sit through a genetics counseling session would be like inviting her to a linguists' conference. I'm sure she would find it dull and be restless. Imagine if we'd made her sit through the MRI analysis."

David wasn't so sure. Living with the girl was giving him the impression that, however uneven and unusual her mental faculties, Rosie understood most of what was said around her. What made people assume she was stupid or simple was that she reacted to it differently and, in any case, could not articulate her thoughts aloud. But he did not contradict the professor. "Thank goodness Shawn agreed to do a session with her. Finding a sitter on this short notice would have been tricky."

"Glad my department could be of service once again," she chimed. "And the time will be put to sterling academic use, I'm sure."

"Dancing in your office again?" he laughed. Hildegard's surprised expression suggested to David he hadn't been supposed to know about it. At length she smiled.

"Whatever it takes to get her to talk. The pursuit of knowledge requires some flexibility."

Mr. Haversham smirked. Dr. Teschke was plenty flexible, he knew, particularly at the hips. As the elevator doors closed behind them, he envisioned pinning her to the wall of the elevator with a passionate kiss. But he kept his hands in his pockets, mindful that on campus she preferred to keep her private life private.

After long moments of lustful contemplation, the elevator doors opened for them. Unlike the foyer of the tower, the upper floors were stark, contemporary, and practical. The level was nothing more than a corridor of swirled white linoleum tile flanked by beige walls. Following posted signs to the "Center for Vertebrate Genomics," they walked by laboratory after laboratory, and white-coated young men and women gawked at the couple as curiously as the couple did at them.

At length they came to a room labeled "CVG-Conference Room." David stood back to let the woman in first.

When he came in behind her after a last glance down the corridor to remember the way to the elevator, she was already shaking hands with the conference room's occupants. A short, bearded man with silver hair shook his hands.

"Hello hello! I'm Hammond Kuhese, professor for bioinformatics and physical anthropology. And the lady here," he nodded at his colleague, "is Dr. Katherine Phelps, an expert in vertebrate genomics." The smallish woman seemed shy and nervous, but shook hands firmly.

When the greetings were done, David and Hildegard took the open seats at the table. "So, what's this about? I didn't know Rosie was being studied by an anthropologist." Dr. Phelps withdrew slightly at his glance, but Dr. Kuhese was ready with an explanation.

"I can explain. Dr. Jacobs from the human neurodynamics lab referred a genetic sample to me of your daughter, Rosetta. Before I begin, however, I want to be clear. Rosetta is your foster or adopted daughter, is that right?"

324

"Yes."

"Good, because if she was your genetic daughter I would ask permission to take a DNA sample from you."

David looked to Dr. Teschke. She seemed curious but not repelled by the comment. He crossed his arms and faced the anthropologist again. "Why?"

"First let me make sure of something. You did consent to allow Dr. Jacobs to take a genetic sample from Rosetta to aid in identifying her country or region of origin, did you not?"

In a rush, David remembered giving the doctor's office permission to do so during one of the MRI exam visits. It had made sense at the time. The idea that Dr. Kuhese's questions related to the simple test put him at ease. It had involved only one of the techs swabbing the inside of Rosie's mouth with a large q-tip.

"I did."

Dr. Kuhese rubbed his palms in relief. "Good. Okay. I'm an expert on genomic ethnography. I specialize in a study of the distribution of certain genes in different human ethnic groups."

"Ah, I see. So you interpret those test results."

"Yes. And Cornell asks me to ensure all such genomic test results are presented professionally and accurately. There's a lot of misrepresentation and quackery in genomic ethnography. The university, however, holds itself to a higher standard, as do I. My colleagues joke that I suck all the certainty out of any biogeographical test. Commercial biogeographic testing services, on the other hand, skip over the subtleties and limitations of these tests in order to leave the customer with certainty and a sense of belonging to an ethnic group. Their science is secondary to the identity they are selling. And Rosetta's case is so unusual, I decided to do this final counseling myself rather than leave it to my assistants."

"Okay. So what does Dr. Phelps do?"

"I asked her along for her technical expertise. While I study the distribution of genes in human populations, I am not an expert per se on genetics and the mechanics of changes to a genome. That's where she comes in."

"Your daughter is fascinating," Dr. Phelps said. If her tone was meant to reassure him, however, it did not. Instead David felt some impending dread. Rosie was being "fascinating" again.

The professors both noticed his grimace at the word "fascinating." "Go on," he prompted them after an uncomfortable pause.

Dr. Kuhese punched a button on a projector sitting on the desk, and then stood up to dim the lights before standing beside the image being projected on the wall. The projector displayed a world map with arrows flowing out of Africa into all parts of the world.

"This is a simplification of what's called a mitochondrial DNA map. Mitochondria are small organelles which live within every human cell. However, they have their own genes which are separate from the genes of the larger cell. The cell's genes get mixed with every generation, but the mitochondrial DNA does not. It stays 'pure,' as it were. Every child inherits his or her mother's mitochondrial DNA. Thus this mitochondrial DNA changes slowly over time and is similar even amongst people we would consider distantly or even wholly unrelated. Through studying patterns in this 'mtDNA' all over the world, we are able to say what region a person's mtDNA was most common in over the larger part of history. Modern transportation and migrations mean mtDNA cannot say for sure where an individual person comes from or what their modern 'nationality' is, but it can tell you a great deal about their ancestry.

"Now, I don't want to offend your religious sensibilities, Mr. Haversham. If you don't believe in human evolution, that's fine. But I should still explain the best scholarship today indicates *Homo sapiens* forebears evolved in and migrated out of Africa to the other parts of the world. This map reflects what mtDNA indicates about how this migration occurred. For example, most white Americans today came to America over the Atlantic from Europe within the last four hundred years. For all intents and purposes, most white Americans belong to one of the seven subgroups of 'European' mtDNA."

"That makes sense," David said after taking a moment to follow Dr. Kuhese's laser pointer spot out of Africa, through Europe, and along a dashed arrow on the map to north America.

Dr. Kuhese was reassured. "Rosie's mtDNA is of a well-known but broadly distributed line, called line M." The professor then pointed to the map. "Based on the distribution of line M, we can say her matrilineal ancestors traveled out of Africa and into the middle east, the Indian subcontinent, and Polynesia to Australia. This is a huge area. But for most of history, the vast majority of people with Rosie's mtDNA type have resided in the Indian subcontinent. Though the middle east has been settled since ancient times, it was sparsely populated for most of history, and the same could be said for Polynesia and pre-colonial Australia.

"Okay. So she is from India?"

"No. We don't know she's Indian. That's the pitfall in people's interpretation of these tests," Dr. Kuhese said firmly. "Through modern migration, people of all different mtDNA types live all over the world. There are families from India in the United States, for example, who have lived here for five or six generations. She could be a fourth generation American. All the test tells us is her maternal ancestors lived in the Middle East, India, or Polynesia for most of human history, not where they lived in recent history."

David nodded his head. "I get it. Nationality is distinct form ethnic origin."

"And of all places, in North America is this disconnect common," Dr. Kuhese confirmed. "But for all this complexity, the mtDNA test is the easy part. From here on it gets complicated, and this is where Dr. Phelps comes in."

Dr. Phelps now spoke. She had a quiet voice, but unlike her nervous greeting, she sounded confident when speaking on her subject matter. "Mr. Haversham, you may have gone to school or college in a time when genetics was less well understood than today. So please do not be afraid to stop me if I use terms which are unfamiliar."

"No worries," said David, not wanting to pop the woman's apparent bubble of confidence.

"I'm an expert on vertebrate genomics. I study the genes of any animal with a spine, including humans and mammals, but also including fish and reptiles. But since the human genome is the most extensively studied vertebrate genome, I'm familiar with it. Cornell's biggest expert on human genomics, however, is in Washington at the moment, and I want to be clear I'm not representing myself as having his level of expertise."

"Got it. You were the best person available. That's fine." David acknowledged.

"When we use a person's DNA, instead of their mtDNA, to try and tell where they are from, we look for specific sequences of information, or markers, which we recognize. By cataloging variations in these markers, and how changes in these markers both occur and combine, we can get a rough idea of a person's ethnic group. Today this is even being used in law enforcement to help get an idea of a witness or suspect's ethnic group from their DNA. This typing grows more exact as the number of DNA samples in each database increases. Ironically,

326

though, it's becoming less and less relevant as more people marry between ethnic groups and create children with mixed heritage. But at present this method is the best we have, and it works well.

"Often when we run these tests, the person agrees with the results based on what they know about their family's genealogy. But from time to time these tests produce results which don't match what a person knows about their ancestry. This may be because sample sizes of some ethnic groups are small, and because in any ethnic group someone's father may not always have been who they were thought to be. So sometimes unusual genes occur in any group that may have come from an ancient traveler who fathered or mothered a child in a region far from where they were born.

"To give you an example, Shakespeare's play Othello tells the story of a black man living in Italy during the renaissance who married a white woman. If such marriages did occur, there could be Italians today, even white looking Italians, living in the United States who had some unusual African gene markers. If they took our tests, they might be confused if we tell them they are part African. And if we told the police to look for a black person based on those markers, we would be sending them barking up the wrong tree and investigating innocent people. That's why these tests have to be used carefully. That's why we're taking the time to talk to you this way."

"Alright. But what do these tests tell us about Rosie then? Does she have unusual combinations? Is she part Chinese or part native American or something?"

The two professors looked at each other. They decided through dueling eyeballs that Dr. Phelps would continue.

"Mr. Haversham, what's both remarkable and frustrating about your daughter's tests is they tell us nothing about her ethnic background. Her pattern of gene markers matches no known ethnic group. For some of the markers, she has entirely new 'colors' of the markers we've never seen before. Other markers she doesn't even have at all. As far as the test results are concerned, she is an ethnic group of one."

"Oh," said David, feeling crestfallen. Here he had been hoping modern science would produce something concrete. "How does that happen?"

Dr. Phelp's expression softened with sympathy. "There are a number of ways it might happen. For example, she might be of extremely mixed heritage. Imagine a middle eastern sailor who settled in South Africa and married a black woman. Then imagine during the British and Dutch colonizations of South Africa his descendants married or bred through these groups. Then imagine his further descendants bred again with a man or woman brought as a servant by British colonists from India. Then imagine a child of this marriage again became a sailor and married a Chinese woman from Taiwan. Such people do exist. It's not that there is anything wrong with them, but their heritage is too jumbled to identify. They become 'pure mutts,' as we sometimes say about dog breeds.

"Or she might be a normal representative of a small ethnic group which hasn't been widely sampled yet. Remote communities, particularly mountain communities, in many parts of the world have distinct gene pools and have yet to be sampled and included in our database.

"But based on the distribution of markers, I don't believe this is the case. Isolated ethnic groups may have unusual patterns of known markers, and from time to time they have a marker type which is unique. But every human we've studied always has certain markers, and no human studied has as many missing or unique markers as your daughter. In fact, the two sequenced Neanderthal genomes on record have more markers in common with modern humans than those of your daughter. These tests would not even classify your daughter *Homo sapiens.*"

David wrapped his mind around this. "So...what should I get from this? She's not human?"

Dr. Kuhese interrupted. "That's a poor way to put it, Katherine. Mr. Haversham, whether or not someone is human is a philosophical question. What Dr. Phelps is *trying* to say is your daughter's genes are so rare some ancient human ancestors or parallel branches of the human tree look more closely related to modern humans than your daughter. But that's a statistical result, not a philosophical judgment. If your daughter looks like human and walks like a human, then she's human."

Dr. Phelps put her hands together and closed her mouth as Dr. Kuhese explained this, and her brow furrowed in apparent restraint. The firefighter marveled that Rosie was causing smart people such heartburn.

Finally, Dr. Phelps continued. "Mr. Haversham, does your daughter suffer from disabilities, deformities, or unusual disease?"

He nodded. "Yes. Not a deformity, but she has disabilities."

"Are they of a sort which might prevent her from conceiving and raising children? Because such disabilities cannot be inherited and are usually a result of genetic damage to the mother's egg cell."

Hildegard shrugged to David, so he went on to form the answer. "It's...hard to say. She's not old enough to know yet."

"One possibility is Rosie's unusual genes are the product of widespread genetic damage. If we put her unfamiliar gene markers together with we know about the Indian subcontinent, this explanation becomes plausible. We know there have been a number of industrial accidents within our lifetime in India which released large quantities of mutagens, that is, chemicals which change genes, into the environment. Rosie may be a child so damaged by those mutagens her genes no longer resemble those of her healthy mother and father. If it's true, though, then it's a miracle she's even alive, given the degree of change we see in her genome. Even small changes to a fetus's genes can cause them to die during pregnancy. Either they don't develop or the mother's body rejects them and miscarries.

"Alright," David supposed, given the number of industrial accidents worldwide, such children were bound to occur. And if Rosie's father or mother had been exposed to radiation from a weapon which could turn concrete to glass, it could explain a great deal.

"There is a last explanation, but it's the least likely of all by far," Dr. Phelps began.

"For the record, Mr. Haversham, I regard this as science fiction," interrupted Dr. Kuhese. Plainly he knew what Dr. Phelps would say. "I wouldn't even raise this possibility, Katherine. It's not...intellectually responsible."

"What's that?" David asked.

Professor Phelps sighed. "It's not as far out as Dr. Kuhese thinks, but, ethically speaking, it ought to be. A wide open field in genomics is gene therapy. There are two kinds of this therapy. The first is negative therapy, which focuses on curing genetic diseases by changing the genes of existing people. The other is positive therapy, which attempts to create or recreate desirable traits in future children by altering the genes of a sperm or egg cell. The technology to change a person's DNA is well understood. What isn't understood is how to predict how changes to a person's DNA will play out in the human being who grows from the altered DNA. And like I said, human genetics is so sensitive even small genetic abnormalities cause enormous problems during pregnancy.

"All attempts thus far to genetically engineer humans already living have led to cancers or caused more problems than they solved. Most governments have banned this kind of research for all kinds of reasons. But an irresponsible scientist could, theoretically, genetically engineer a human and try to manipulate the child's genes to produce a certain set of traits. There are rumors such attempts are already underway in countries which have not banned the practice or do not have a strong enough government to enforce laws against such things."

Dr. Kuhese pushed back into the conversation. "This kind of manipulation would result in a miscarriage or a very disabled child. Not enough is known about how genes become traits, like fair hair or brown eyes, that anyone could tinker with DNA and have a snowball's chance in hell of getting what they wanted from it. I would rest easy, Mr. Haversham. Your daughter is not gene-manipulated."

David thought on this. He had met some disabled people in his time, and Rosie wasn't bad off compared to the worst he'd seen. "It does sound unlikely. She's not *that* disabled."

"Yes it is. It's extremely unlikely," said Dr. Phelps. "I only mention it because I wanted to be complete when discussing these things with you." She sounded relieved to have the idea understood but dismissed.

Mr. Haversham reflected on what he'd been told. "So, what I get from this is the test can't tell me anything."

"No, that's not so," said Dr. Kuhese. "We can say without doubt her mitochondrial DNA is type M. This means that, more than likely, her maternal ancestors resided on the Indian subcontinent, the middle east, or Polynesia. But where within this area she might have come from, due to her unique set of SNPs and other markers, we cannot say."

"I'm sorry if this explanation was less than helpful," said Dr. Phelps. "I have done my best. The media often presents our science as more advanced than it is and this can inflate people's expectations. There's a great deal we don't yet know."

David saw the distress on the two scholars' faces. "Listen. It's okay. Some days I'd like to have some clue, some certainty, so if she ever looks at me one day and says, 'I want to find my mom and dad,' we have somewhere to start. I want to be of use to her. But day to day, it wouldn't make much difference. She's living with me, this is Ithaca, and her skin tone makes no difference to anyone. Thanks for trying, but don't feel bad. The real challenges I have are clothes on her back, food on my table, and getting her to do her homework."

Hildegard was nodding in agreement as he said this, and his words cheered the two academics. He signed some forms allowing an "Institutional Review Board" to decide if the university would retain her information for more study if new promising techniques were found, and allowing her information to be entered into a biogeographical database.

Dr. Hammond had a last thing to add. "If she ever does ask to find her family, bear in mind our knowledge is still growing. Two, or five, or ten years from now we may be able to tell you much more than we can today. Don't hesitate to try again in the future."

"I won't," said David. "Thank you for your time!"

He and Hildegard walked down the gleaming lab corridor to the elevator.

"You were quiet," he said.

"I confess...For historical reasons, I find genetics to be an unpleasant subject. In East Germany, when I was young, it was illegal to even teach Mendelian genetics. The Soviets had enshrined Lysenkoism, another genetic theory, in our textbooks since they deemed it more compatible with communist ideology. And to even study genetic ethnography is risky. It could lead to a resurgence of ideas which are – how do you say – better off dead?"

"Ah," said David. "I think I see where you're coming from. But this is America."

Katherine was taken aback by Hammond's ferocity. He was flushed and stuttering, his voice raised so loud as to be uncomfortable even across the conference table.

"Katherine....I...I wish you hadn't even raised the subject. It's farcical!"

"Hammond, listen to me. I'm the technical expert here. I'm telling you, I make alterations to the DNA of lower vertebrates every day! My lab will do it hundreds of times this year! It's not as far out as it sounds. Four, five, years ago I might have agreed with you, but the truth is all that keeps people in my field from wading out into human gene manipulation is the ethical implications of it. I'm sorry but we can't hide from the public behind the shield of 'not possible' anymore because it's becoming possible."

"Even if it were possible now, the child is what? Twelve? Thirteen? For it to be true in her case that means the gene manipulation would have taken place more than a decade ago. Was it possible then?"

Katherine sobered. "No. No, I don't think it was."

Her colleague relaxed at her admission. "I'm sorry. I got upset. I'm- it's Occam's razor, Kathy. The girl's condition can be explained by chemical injury without inventing a mad scientist who altered her genome. And now, thanks to you flouting a basic principle of logic, there is a member of the public at large who has been told by a tenured Cornell professor that his foster daughter might have had her genes manipulated."

Katherine kept her temper steady. She doubted Hammond would speak this way to her male counterparts, but resolved not to inject gender issues into their disagreement. "I stand by what I said. There's not much difference between surmising her genes might be intentionally manipulated and surmising a mutagen did enough damage to her genome to make it so unique yet left her viable enough to live. One possibility may be more palatable to the public than the other but both explanations are vanishingly unlikely events. If I could find more markers on her genome I recognized, I'd dismiss *both* possibilities out of hand."

Hammond mopped his brow. "Even so. Talking about the possibility of it, especially on the thinnest of probabilities, risks everything. Can you imagine the outcry against genomics if it was ever believed or even proven some nutjob was tinkering with the human genome? My nightmare is I'll be on some talk show someday saying 'it can't be done,' and then the next day some teenager will win a science fair for doing it."

Katherine empathized. "The science *is* at this tipping point *now*. I know you feel like the last thing you need is a 'scientifically responsible' person coming out and saying humans are being gene manipulated. But I'm on your team. I'm trying to tell you the time where we can make categorical denials about the existence of eugenic human gene manipulation is ending. It's bad enough what you have to go through because of the ideological divisions on this subject. Don't put your hard-earned credibility at further risk by lagging behind on the state of the science, too.

"We need to put our heads together and think of a way to talk to the public about this. This is where the humanities come in. This is where anthropology and you come in. This is where cooperation and peer review and consensus come in. This kind of thing is what this university was made to do. There can be a rational

330

discussion of this. We can choose to hide, or we can choose to shine."

She reached out and touched his arm. "I'm not the enemy. The crazies are out there, lurking with their pitchforks and torches. Some of us will fall but we've got to work together. The truth is always on the side of good science ethically done. Even Galileo won in the end."

Hammond's breath now returned to him. He mopped his brow. "You're right. I've got to pull myself together. There is only one good: knowledge."

"There is only one evil: ignorance." Katherine finished for him.

Chapter 25

Bright Futures

The streetlights on Morgartenstrasse were the only things visible through the glass. Sharrah rarely saw nighttime in the office since under normal circumstances Vincent and she both stopped working at four o'clock sharp, which got her out of the office before nightfall on all but the shortest winter days in Zurich. But for the last three days, they both had worked harder and later to craft Dr. Foster's public announcement of his gene therapy offerings.

She shook her head to reawaken herself. The smell of the expensive Sumatran coffee the doctor had asked her to brew teased her nose. She was not a fan of coffee, but she was so tired she considered asking for a moment to brew her own cup to replace her tea.

Ms. Bassi read her latest draft aloud. *"Vincent Foster Associates is pleased to make available to the general public a range of new and exclusive recombinant gene therapies and positive genetic engineering techniques. Through our proprietary splicing technologies and phenotyping research, prospective parents can now protect their children from inheritable diseases and ensure they have the physical and intellectual characteristics needed to compete in the global economy's challenging and uncertain future. And since many techniques alter not somatic cells but a family's germline, a discriminating parent's investment in their child's health and competitiveness will benefit even their grandchildren's generation and beyond."*

Dr. Foster nodded to her and took a sip of his coffee. "That's it. It hits all the notes I wanted to sound. What parent, and hence what voter and what customer, wouldn't want to protect their children from inheritable diseases and ensure their future success? Protecting and advancing one's children are two of the obsessions of humanity. Natural selection has made them universal. By phrasing our message this way, we ensure every parent, worldwide, is viscerally interested in what I have to offer."

Sharrah's doubts clamored disagreement. "I'm sure it could be better put, sir, but we've read and edited this text so many times in the last two days I can scarcely think about it anymore. I recommend we put it aside, wait a few days, and come back to it. Perhaps we'll have some better wording then."

Vincent waved her objection away. "Perfection can be the enemy of excellence. It may be you can't think of a better way to word this because it's worded excellently."

Ms. Bassi shook her head and leaned her forehead on her palm, staring down at the text she rested on the arm of her chair. In fatigue and frustration, she let her eyes unfocus, and then wander in search of relief along the carved wood and embroidered floral patterns which covered her chair arm. "I'm sure it can be better," she worried again after noticing her mind had wandered.

"Maybe so. But can it be made better within the time we have available? Probably not," said the doctor. "Go on. Read the next paragraph."

She picked up her head and read off the paper. *"In order to protect the privacy of previous clients and our industrial secrets, Vincent Foster Associates will not offer testimonials or video footage of our existing clients unless those clients volunteer to come forward. However, we invite prospective clients to review our new papers in future juried journals and to pose splicing challenges in non-human vertebrates and seed crops to verify our claims."*

The doctor was pleased. "Straightforward and true. I'm looking forward to the puzzles people will bring us. What results will they want as proof? Rice which grows in deserts? Lab rats that can do calculus? For decades I've been making up all the puzzles and solving them. Let's see what my peers or even Mr. and Ms. John Q. Smith can throw at me." His hazel eyes glittered with excitement. "Why, I'm half tempted to call the labs and tell them to start inventing some eye-popping organisms for the sheer joy of it."

Sharrah didn't share his exuberance, though Dr. Foster had been clear about his love for this paragraph since they'd first drafted it. Her eyes searched the text like a frustrated raptor, floating in circles looking for the errors they knew were there but could not yet find.

It occurred to her as she scanned the page that Vincent's enthusiasm was the result of vanity, the first vice she had seen in her employer. He didn't wear fancy clothes, he didn't buy famous paintings, he didn't act like he was Allah's gift to women and, so far as she knew, he didn't even own a personal car. But he was vain about his science. She supposed if she was the worldwide best at something, she'd get vain about it too, doubly so if she had to keep her mastery secret for years. So she carried on.

"Third paragraph, Vincent?"

"Yes, please."

"Vincent Foster Associates is based worldwide and serves a discriminating clientele in private venues. Submit both press and genetic counseling inquiries at our enterprise website at www.fostersfuturegenome.sci. Please fill out our inquiry forms fully. Incomplete inquiries will not be addressed."

"It sounds snobbish, but while my potential market is every husband and wife on the planet, my realistic market is a tiny percentage of those couples. What I do is so expensive as yet only the richest of the rich could afford it, so I have to be snobby for now."

Sharrah challenged this point. "Won't this medicine be universally available one day, sir?"

The doctor looked surprised at the question. "Certainly! Why wouldn't it be? I can't make it so yet, because it's horribly expensive. But what could be more important than one day ensuring every child born is healthy, talented, and wanted as they are? What better way into the future? What better way to universal peace and prosperity? What better way to repay the....investors who gave me my starting science and starting capital?"

She felt some relief at this. She didn't know who Vincent's initial investors were and didn't feel any allegiance to them. But during the three days of working the text over and over, she had reflected on what she actually knew about the man's business. She had then begun to wonder if he was as noble to all as he was to her, and if her work for him was serving the world or the richest slice of it. But here he was, enthusiastically foreseeing the universality of his technology.

Ms. Bassi indulged her skepticism through one more question. "Then why not distribute the technology, sir, if you're not trying to make money from it?" she challenged him.

The doctor sobered. "My dear, that would be foolish. First, the technology is young and one or two more decades of high investment will make it more reliable, safe, and exact. When one deals in human flesh, the more inexact the science, the more cruel the error. And second, the potential for the abuse of this technology is catastrophic. Think for a minute what the governments of the world would do with the tools to customize human beings. The same governments which today lie, suppress, and invade over the backs of their citizens would love to engineer both their soldiers and their citizens to achieve greater efficiencies. Whatever cynicism one might have about the private sector, I don't see corporations invading large countries with tanks and jackbooted thugs. Best to keep the genetic engineering to the private sector for a while."

Sharrah thought over this. She hadn't anticipated the potential abuses of the technology, but now that Vincent had pointed them out, they were frightening and obvious.

"But it's beside the point," the man continued. "The decision to universalize the technology will be made by someone else in any case. Someone younger. By the time the technology has, I'll be dead or in my dotage." His eyes fixed on hers as he said this. The look made her uncomfortable, and she didn't know how to reply.

She devised a polite escape from the grip of the stare. "So, you'll read this announcement yourself, sir?"

"Yes. At the iGem conference in London. I'll be presenting a paper there and judging a competition. It's the perfect venue. It's private enough I shan't be mobbed, yet attended by enough of my peers who know I don't joke about such things. It will get the proper amount of attention from the best people. Even Dr. Ventner will be there. I can hardly wait to see his face. He's smarter than I am, no doubt about it, but he hasn't had someone trounce him in a decade or so and it needs doing." The older man thumped his desk in glee at the prospect.

Sharrah shook her head to hear friend's vanity. "Was there anything you would like to add or take away, sir? So far I have no notes on this draft. It stands untouched." As she said these words, she felt fatigue overtake her. A glance at the clock showed it was four in the morning. Here she was, drooping, but her aged employer couldn't contain his energy.

Vincent paused, quiet and serious at the question. "No. Nothing to add or take away." After a moment, though, he reconsidered. "Read it to me again. From the top, as it were."

She read it again. The doctor listened with his eyes closed, one hand still on his coffee cup, the other pressed to his temple. When she finished, he opened his eyes.

His voice was quiet. "You have a gift. Whatever your estimates of yourself may be, there's no doubt in my mind you have penned one of the most important announcements in the history of mankind. The moon landing was nothing compared to this."

Sharrah took in the three short paragraphs. Together they amounted to a third of the page. To her, they did not vibrate with history, morality, or philosophy. They were plain words which formed a snobbish advertisement.

"If you say so, sir."

"I do." Vincent rose from his chair. "And I've got reason to know. The moon landing was a parlor trick, a mere extrapolation of technology from the V2 and the U-boat," he said with assurance. Then he gaped at the clock. "I've kept you up late, dear. Give me the text on a USB drive and email me a second copy, then go rest. You've done important work without complaint."

She rose gratefully. "Thank you. I am tired. But how about you? Are you sure you'll be ready to travel tomorrow?"

Vincent stared at her. "You booked my train ride yourself, a private cabin if you did as we discussed. Those cabins have beds. I'll have plenty of time to sleep on the train to London. If I can even bring myself to do so. I'm buzzing with excitement!"

Sharrah remembered the train reservation. "You're right. Shall I stay and see you to the train station?"

The doctor's expression reminded her of the calmness and confidence of her father in Pakistan, even to the moment the Taliban led him away. "No. Though I pretend sometimes to be helpless so as to luxuriate in your attentions, I am capable of packing my own bag and calling my own cab. Sleep, my dear. And thank you," he said. He crossed from behind his desk, put a gentle palm under her elbow, and started guiding her to the door of his office. "You have a bright future."

Angela DeMarco was perusing the birthday wishes streaming at her from her family through Facebook when the official inbox tone chimed. The cheerful video from her mother and sister had taken the edge off her grumpy resentment that, though it was a Saturday *and* her birthday, she was not only working, but the duty officer for the information security detachment.

Her inclination to ignore the tone was counterbalanced by its melody. The mail program was playing the "Republican Victory March." It was the urgent tone which indicated the message was a hot one from the biometric surveillance camera section. She cursed. As the number of biometric cameras grew, these messages came in more and more often. Nonetheless, it was her team's job to sort through the alerts, and she was the agent on duty.

She sipped her coffee as she read the alert.

FAST Biometric Detention Alert:
Detainee: Ms. Desiree L. Jefferson, female, African, age 31.
Biometric check term: "Islam will destroy America."
Measured response: 77% positive, full smile with full pulse and partial eye corroboration.
Scanner Model and Mode: WECU model 3, 1/40th of a second visual exposure.
Detention Site: Reagan National Airport, Arlington, VA, TSA resolution center 1."

Angela grunted another curse. If the detention had occurred in any other city, then all she would have needed to do was catalog the message and forward it to a DHS field office. The field office would then dispatch either a DHS or FBI agent to interview the suspect. But, since this detention had happened in Washington on the Information Security Detachment's home beat, as the agent on duty, she would have to do the interview. She had been hoping to take the pager to the barracks gym and get a workout, but she guessed this case would take the rest of her afternoon.

She made a note in her officer's log. "Contacted re biometric detention DCA. En route 1441." She then checked her pistol and badge, hung her photo ID around her neck, snatched a handful of chocolates from the section candy dish, and went to the parking lot to take a car to Reagan National Airport.

"Heading out, Special Agent?" asked the Charge of Quarters officer as she passed the bulletproof glass enclosure before the main doors.

"TSA hold," she explained. She jerked a thumb over her shoulder toward the information security office wing. "It's at Reagan. I have to do it myself. I'll be taking car four."

The clean cut man looked down at his desk. "Check, Special Agent.

Logging you out at 1446 to car four." When he was done making his notes, he pushed a button. With a hydraulic thunk, the steel bolts in the glass doors to the barracks main entrance released and swung open, and she walked through them and turned to the fleet parking lot.

She was tempted as she left the barracks to stop at McDonald's or somewhere to grab a bite to eat. But she resisted the temptation. First, she didn't want to explain, if someone happened to check the record, why it took her forty-five minutes rather than thirty to drive the five miles to Reagan National. And second, she didn't want to work off a McDonald's burger on the treadmill in the gym, especially one she had eaten because she was bored. So she unwrapped one of the chocolate kisses from the candy bowl and drove to the TSA resolution center.

The resolution center was inside a converted maintenance hangar at the airport. It had interrogation rooms, holding cells and billets, and an armory for the TSA officers and DHS troops who secured the airport and the many VIP travelers that frequented it. Its sheet metal walls and concrete floor made it uncomfortable in heat or cold, but it was better than the tent city the TSA had originally had to decamp in after the Market Garden attack.

She parked her unmarked car in front of the unmarked hangar and walked in. She held up her photo badge to the DHS duty desk inside the door, and after a flash of the laser scanning her card and eye, she was ushered through to the detention area.

She recognized the TSA station chief, Will Hartman, as she approached.

"Agent DeMarco," he smiled. "Follow me to interrogation room two."

"Who'd you catch?" she asked as she followed. The man might have details the report had not.

Hartman clicked his tongue with pride. "African American female, early thirties. Got a big old grin on her kisser when we flashed 'Islam' at her from a departures monitor screen."

"Did you search her?"

Hartman nodded. "Yep. All bags and body cavities searched. She had nothing dangerous. Just liquids in permissible volumes, no razors or metal grooming tools, an interesting piercing, and a couple of romance novels. The most unusual thing we found was this." He handed Angela a copy of "Mother Jones" magazine. Angela flipped it over as Hartman opened the interrogation room door. The cover story featured an article on "America's Disappeared."

"Oh ho! Mother Jones! I hadn't confiscated one of this month's issues yet!" Angela said as she entered the interrogation room and dropped into one of the plush investigator's chairs. She picked up the magazine and started paging through to the cover article.

"Yeah, I thought it might interest you," said Hartman with satisfaction. "Should I bring her in?"

"Sure," said Angela. "Any time you're ready."

Hartman left the square sheet metal room, and Angela read the article on 'America's Disappeared.' The first few pages of the article featured a photo gallery of those people the unAmericans who wrote the magazine designated as "vanished under political circumstances." The sheer number of faces startled her, but when she reasoned about it, she was able to put it in perspective. A certain number of biometric detentions would become long-term detentions, and those could happen at any airport, rail or bus station, or even major bridge tollways. Add to it arrest from information security violations like illicit web browsing or teaching of classified subject matter or scientific theories, and she supposed the number of people detained would get large. Besides, with local police and state police in certain states empowered to act against terrorists and criminals, there was no telling how many of the 'disappeared' had never entered the federal system at all but been handled by state authorities.

She lingered on a picture of a woman. It was a face she recognized. Was it an actress? She read the subtitle and grimaced. It wasn't an actress, but a popular disco revival singer. She wasn't surprised, she had heard the woman was writing unpatriotic songs. She supposed it had only been a matter of time before someone had picked the woman up. If it had been the government who'd picked her up, soon Angela would get the order to delete the woman's songs from her iPod.

After a few minutes a DHS guard pushed open the door, and Hartman brought the woman in by a tether to her wrist shackles. From the snot on the woman's face and her bright orange jumpsuit, she guessed the physical searches had been done swiftly and firmly, if not gently.

"Sit, please," she motioned the woman to a steel shop stool across the table from her. In the silence, the sheet metal walls made her voice sound tinny. She hated the effect. She would have to speak from her stomach so as to make her voice more baritone and compensate for it.

Once the fearful woman had been seated, Angela went back to her reading. After a moment, Hartman took a seat beside her, saying nothing and projecting the same patience. Timing was everything in interrogation, she knew. If she asked questions of the woman right away, the woman would get the idea her time was important, or that Angela was working against some time limit. So it wasn't until she had finished the article, and started another one, that Angela offered her first question.

"Do you know why you're here, Ms. Jefferson?" she inquired at length.

"No!" The woman complained. "And I don't even know what I'm charged with! And I don't see where you all get off....searching me like that!"

Angela didn't respond. She read the second article, something about a petition to introduce a multiparty political system because the Democrats had failed to offer Americans alternatives. It was another liberal pipedream. They imagined if they split into more political parties more liberal voters would somehow emerge from the woodwork to vote for them. In fact, the majority of Americans hated liberals. She'd seen a poll to that effect in the *Washington Post*.

"It'll go easier for you if you come clean with me. If I can't determine the nature of the threat you pose to national security, I'll have to make other arrangements to satisfy the interest of national security. Those arrangements often include a free ticket to Cuba."

The woman's chin quavered. "But...but I was going to visit my mother in Pensacola!"

Angela began reading a third article. "Yeah, the 9/11 terrorists were all going to 'visit family,' too." The next article discussed the spring fashions out of Paris. It was interesting. Late 1930s European fashions were back in, and some of the stuff the models were posing in did look hot. When she was done, she put the magazine down.

"Do you always read unpatriotic magazines?" Angela folded her fingers together across the magazine.

"It's not illegal," Ms. Jefferson sniffed.

"No, it's not. Freedom of the press is guaranteed. But it's unpatriotic. And the courts have determined possession of a magazine or newspaper which does not bear the 'Patriotic Publishers Association' stamp, while not illegal, can be considered an element of reasonable suspicion. I'm a reasonable person. And your possession of this magazine gives me the suspicion you hate America. Do you hate America, Ms. Jefferson?"

Angela abandoned her detachment to look straight into the woman's eyes. They were red from rubbing, and the woman shivered in the air-conditioned chill. Angela took a moment to look the woman over, seeing no signs of bruising or bleeding. So Hartman had been playing by the rules. That was good. If she saw signs Hartman was taking liberties with female detainees, she'd have to do something.

"No, I don't hate America," Ms. Jefferson said.

"Let me explain your situation. Our biometric cameras caught you smiling at the message 'Islam will destroy America' we displayed on a departures terminal. Your heartbeat also accelerated after we presented the message. Can you explain to me why you were smiling? Did you find the message 'Islam will destroy America' funny? Or did it make you happy for some reason?"

"I don't remember the message! I never saw that message! I must have been laughing at something else!" Ms. Jefferson protested.

"The message was displayed for a full fortieth of a second," Angela explained. "And you clearly smiled."

"I don't remember seeing it!" The woman protested.

"So you don't remember seeing this message. Do you remember thinking it? Do you remember thinking 'Islam will destroy America'?"

"No!" The woman protested.

"So you have no memory of thinking it?" Angela arched her eyebrow.

"No, I never thought it, either!" The woman countered.

"Then why did you happen to smile at that particular time, Ms. Jefferson?"

"I...I think I was thinking about my little sister. She always makes me laugh. I'm going to see her in Pensacola."

"So you have a little sister?" Angela investigated. Ms. Jefferson nodded, perhaps relieved to have a question she could answer with 'yes.'"

"Do you want your sister to be safe?" she persisted. Ms. Jefferson nodded again.

Angela came to her point. "So you understand why it's important for us to ask questions when we find someone smiling at the message 'Islam will destroy America.'"

Ms. Jefferson gave no reply.

"Okay, Ms. Jefferson. I've explained to you our concern over your choice of what messages you find amusing or happy, and I've discussed with you the issues your possession of this magazine raises. Since you are unable to supply any explanation or show any contrition for your actions, I will go check your file. Will I find anything in it? If you tell me now what I might find in it, I can argue you're being cooperative and truthful about something."

The woman shivered in her chair. "I...I had a DUI in college."

"Anything else? Foreign boyfriends? Family members in prison? Homosexuality? Socialist politics? Strange religion?"

"I had a cousin picked up. Something about selling methamphetamine. My family is Baptist."

"Alright. Anything else?"

Ms. Jefferson shook her head. Angela turned to Hartman. "Get her something. She's freezing." She then stood up and left the interrogation room.

Once outside she went to the computer terminals in the Resolution Center's operation room and signed into the consolidated domestic surveillance database suite.

At first blush, Ms. Jefferson was in the clear. Her account of her criminal record checked out. She did have a DUI, and only a DUI, on her record, as she had

338

said. Likewise, one of her cousins had gone to prison for sale of methamphetamine. And a search of her border crossing records showed she had no history of foreign travel to Islamic or Socialist states. The most controversial places she had visited were Cancun and Hawaii.

Likewise, Angela read in the church attendance database that Ms. Jefferson was, as she claimed, a Baptist. She had even gone to church regularly, missing only two Sundays out of the last hundred and four. But a blinking field in the database flashed "The Progressive National Baptist Conference is a recusant church – click for details."

Angela had seen the word "recusant" before, but didn't understand what it meant. She clicked, and the link explained it.

"Recusant churches are churches whose leadership has not endorsed the ecumenical 'Affirmation of Christian Origin' under the 'American Restoration Act.' To qualify as a patriotic church, synagogue, mosque, or fraternity, a church of any faith must affirm:

1)   the founders of the United States were Christians;

2)   the United States is a majority Christian nation;

3)   the United States Constitution and the Federal Government it forms are the product of a divine inspiration, and their authority supersedes that of any worldly church or religious hierarchy.

"First amendment protections bar the federal government from establishing any one church as a state religion. Likewise, the Constitution prohibits any level of government from administering a religious test to anyone seeking government employment or political office. Officers thus may not penalize members of recusant churches. Attendance at a recusant church may not be considered an element of probable cause or reasonable suspicion when making arrests or questioning the public. However, attendance at a patriotic church may be a mitigating factor. An officer may find and introduce into evidence a suspect's dutiful attendance to a patriotic church. The officer may then use this fact to offset other factors which might otherwise have led the officer to conclude the suspect had committed a crime."

Angela was not churchgoing herself anymore, and most of the explanation was so much mumbo-jumbo to her. But what it meant in practical terms was Ms. Jefferson's attendance at a "recusant" church could not be held against her when Angela decided if she had probable cause to arrest the woman. She moved on to Ms. Jefferson's political records.

Here Angela frowned at what she read. Ms. Jefferson had, during the Obama campaigns, been a field manager for Blue State Digital, the communications firm which had managed the campaign's distributed communications. She had also voted for Obama both times. That meant the woman was both a liberal and skilled with distributed messaging systems like Twitter.

She sat back, and pinched her upper lip between her teeth, worrying a piece of chapped skin there. Working for Blue State Digital was not a crime, in and of itself. Neither was voting for Obama. For whatever reason, the majority of voters had voted for Obama both times. But the woman's working record gave Angela a suspicion Ms. Jefferson had unAmerican sentiments. The real question was not "is working for Blue State Digital a crime?" but, when combined with the "Mother Jones" magazine, her cousin with a criminal history, and Ms. Jefferson's inexplicable reaction to the phrase "Islam will destroy America," did working for Blue State Digital create a pattern which would cause a reasonable person to suspect Ms. Jefferson was involved with a foreign or domestic conspiracy to commit terror or undermine national resolve?

She reviewed Ms. Jefferson's file again, looking for mitigating factors. Other than her regular church attendance, which she was barred from considering because Ms. Jefferson's church was recusant, there were none. The facts left Angela balanced. The woman's clean criminal record and apparent honesty were offset by her political leanings and her proficiency with a dangerous technology.

"Hard decisions are why you get paid the big bucks," she recalled, echoing what she knew Special Agent Bitters would say if he was standing over her shoulder. "The government trusts you. So if you can't decide from the facts, go with your gut." Angela closed her eyes to begin a "gut check." She would have to go with her instincts on this call.

After a few minutes of reflection, she logged out of the database, motioned to the operations officer to indicate the terminal was again free, and returned to the interrogation room. Hartman was still there, sipping coffee and flipping through the "Mother Jones" magazine. Ms. Jefferson sat with her arms clamped to the desktop by a padlock looped through her manacle wire. The only concession to her comfort was a black and gold shawl hung over her jumpsuit. But at least Hartmann had listened to Angela's request to get the woman some warmer clothes.

Angela felt some butterflies in her stomach as she prepared to speak. She always felt some, even though she had done this a dozen times and Ms. Jefferson was less belligerent than other unAmericans she had dealt with. She took her seat across from the woman and nudged Hartman with her elbow. Hartman put down the magazine and cleared his throat.

Agent DeMarco began. "Ms. Desiree Jefferson, despite your unexplained biometric responses, your possession of an unpatriotic periodical, the criminal record of your larger family, and your previous work for Blue State Digital, I find I do not have a reasonable suspicion you are party to a foreign or domestic conspiracy against the United States."

The woman looked relieved, and opened her mouth as if to say something, but Angela continued. "Had I formed this suspicion, you would have been transported to the National Security Evaluation Barracks in Guantanamo Bay, Cuba. There the totality of circumstances would have been examined by a Domestic or Foreign Security Tribunal and a disposition chosen for you which would have satisfied the needs of national security. Such an evaluation period would have complicated your travel and future employment."

Angela was pleased with how smoothly the words flowed off her tongue. Between reading all the memos and arrest scripts she could find and watching her boss Bitters at work, she felt she was getting some flair for the delivery. But instead of cowering or looking chastened, Ms. Jefferson began to cry. It was a pitiful, mewling bawl. It made Angela want to slap her. And it made her angry because she had spent most of twenty minutes fact checking and soul searching to let her off, so what cause did the woman have to be upset? But since she had found Ms. Jefferson was guilty of nothing, slapping the woman was now off the table as one of her options. Angela waited.

"I was going to visit my Momma-" the woman blubbered. Angela's temper snapped.

"I'm letting you off, so shut it," she told the woman. "And I suggest that, in the future, if you can't learn not to smile at inappropriate times, then maybe you shouldn't smile at all. Do that and you'll save both of us a lot of trouble!"

The woman agreed emphatically, eyes squinted shut in tears. Angela took a deep breath and continued. "Officer Hartman will return you your clothes and belongings and bring you back to your airline terminal. Negotiating your onward travel, should you have missed your flight during this brief detention, is a matter between you and the airline. One nation, indivisible."

"One nation, indivisible," blurted the woman. Tears were rolling down her face again. The woman's odd responses to Angela's restoration of her liberty made her wonder if Hartman or his people hadn't taken some "liberty" with her. If the possibility ever became impossible to ignore, she'd give Hartman his own trip to Cuba.

She didn't let this thinking intrude on her interaction with the older man. "Thanks for your vigilance. Send her on her way. I've made a note in her record so if she pops up again she'll get a free Caribbean vacation from Uncle Sam."

"Righto, Special Agent. Thanks for your quick response," Hartman said. "I want to have the cell open for the next one. Not that I mind handcuffing these insects to the steam pipes outside, but surrenderists might complain."

"I'm on duty until eleven tonight if you get any more," Angela said grimly. She picked up the "Mother Jones" and walked out. If she was quick and the night was quiet, she thought, she could get back to the barracks, get an early supper at the chow hall, and get in her workout before the end of her shift.

The duty officer popped open the doors for Angela before she even got to the intercom and pressed the button. They swung open, showing her the worn grey edges of the inch-and-a-half-thick Lexan which formed the clear panes, and she stopped to present her ID. The RFID tag sounded a chime as she waved it, and the duty officer waved at her. "Forgot to say it earlier, but happy birthday, Special Agent."

"Oh. Thanks!" she replied, cheered by the man's friendliness. She continued through the foyer to the information security wing, keyed in her passcode, and re-entered her office.

She blinked in surprise. The collection of cubicles, long tables, and video conferencing suite were hung with bright streamers and balloons, and the room was filled with her like-aged coworkers. On the center of the conference table was a white sheetcake with an American flag and a large "Happy 21st" and "America is Safer Because of You!" frosted into it.

"Happy Birthday Angie!" they all shouted.

Angela laughed in surprise. "Hey guys! Wow, thank you for all this!" Her friend Bella rushed up to give her a hug.

"Now we're both twenty-one! Let's go get smashed and meet some Georgetown boys!" she said.

"Hey, what's wrong with us homeland security boys?" bantered Phillip, styling in the new sneakers and athletic clothes he saved his pay for. Angela had long known Phillip had an unrequited interest in Bella.

"You guys are alright. But a girl needs a change every now and again," Bella tittered. Angela grinned at this. She had a steady boyfriend, but her friend Bella had sampled the skills of many of their co-workers. Angela hugged her back. "You know I can't go out. I'm on duty. But we can go out Sunday night."

"Pish!" snorted Bella, looking crestfallen. "Sunday night is a bore! None of the bars will be open."

"Thanks for another year of good work," Angela heard Special Agent Bitters say from behind her. She turned, startled. Bitters often crept up behind her in ways which unnerved her, but since he never did anything scary, she was learning to accept it.

"Hey, sir!" she said. She saw that beside her boss, back to the wall, stood Agent Spinoza, a hulking Mexican older agent who, while smiling, was still somehow out of place among birthday streamers and chatter. "Wait, how did you guys know I'd be gone to set this up? I was only gone ninety minutes."

Bitters took her under his arm. "We told Hartman to pick up some civvy who stuck out too much. He called us before he filed his report. We had everything ready to go." Bitters swiveled her toward the sheet cake. "I've been staring at this cake for ninety minutes now, and I'm ready for a piece. You going to cut it or what?" he demanded jovially.

Despite Bitter's friendly tone and her friends chattering around her, Angela felt her insides curdle. The woman she had been poised to send to Gitmo forty-five minutes before had been chosen in part to distract her so a surprise party could be thrown in her honor.

"Whew. Well, I made the right decision..." she decided. She smiled again to erase her expression, since Bella and Phillip were looking at her in alarm. Bitters handed her the cake knife.

"Spin volunteered to take the rest of your shift, DeMarco," he told her. "Go on and start cutting, and then go have some fun. You're only twenty-one once."

Angela felt her hand shake on the knife. But the task of cutting the cake focused her, and soon she was lifting out squares of chocolate cake onto paper plates and handing them out to her smiling comrades.

As she handed the slice to Spinoza, the mountain of a man slipped her a twenty and a one dollar bill. "*Para tequila,*" he explained.

"Thank you, Spin!" She gave the enormous man a hug the best she could. "I could use some tequila!"

Spinoza patted her awkwardly on the back. She sensed the big man was uncomfortable with the hug, so she let him go and cut a square of the cake for Bitters.

"Here you go, sir."

Bitters studied her face before taking the cake. When at last he accepted it, he grinned. "You've got a bright future, kid."

Angela reached into her breast pocket for her sunglasses. They were oversized aviators, like the ones Bitters wore. She put them on with a flourish.

"Future's so bright, I've got to wear shades. Sir," she quipped.

Bitters laughed. "That's the spirit. While we're talking about the future, do some homework on this guy. Archibald Stevens, a geology professor at University of Maryland. You'll be arresting him next week. But enjoy your party first."

Angela felt a thrill as she translated words into expectation. "Oh, boy, a field op!"

Bitters nodded. "You've earned the chance. Put America first, and more will follow."

Chapter 26

Can't'cha Smell that Smell?

David got down from his truck when it was clear Rosie had not noticed him parked outside the school. She stood alone away from the small groups of other children waiting for their buses. He walked across the grass divide between the parking area and the bus loop. She spotted him as he was partway across and came dashing up, her backpack and her computer bag making her run lopsided. A teacher's aide came running after her, but the woman relented when she saw him and released the girl with a wave.

"Hey sweetie! We have to go straight to the university so Shawn can download stuff from your computer. Then we should stop at the grocery. Did you have a good day at school?" he asked as they turned back toward the truck.

Rosie shrugged.

"Where's Rod?" David wondered about her usual playmate. He picked her up from school every so often, and when he did, he found her playing with Rodney Falver while she waited for the bus. The son and grandson of Ithaca firefighters, sickly Rodney had a speech impairment and diabetes, and the two were in the same speech therapy group. He guessed that they were both teased by the other children so they kept each other's company.

Rosetta looked upset, but only shrugged in response to that question too.

"You can explain it in the car while we drive," he suggested. And once they were underway the girl unpacked her computer and beginning to type.

"Rodney is angry at me. I told him he smelled," LIDIA's voice explained.

David glanced at Rosie, but she was focused on the keyboard. "Why did you tell him he smelled bad? That's kind of mean. Were you angry at him?" He hadn't seen her ever do something spiteful, so her story puzzled him.

"No. He smelled bad, so I told him so," LIDIA continued. "And he got angry with me. Even when I said I wasn't joking."

Mr. Haversham shook his head at this. For as sensitive and caring a child as the girl was, she often had to discover the hard way what hurt people's feelings.

"Did you tell him that in front of other people?"

Rosie nodded. A moment later LIDIA explained. "I told him in class. I had to sit next to him."

David reflected for a moment about how to explain the manners that were second nature to him. "Honey, in this country, if someone smells bad, you're not supposed to say anything about it. It's even better to pretend not to notice. If the person is your friend, and you're worried about how they smell or afraid they'll embarrass themselves, then when you're alone, you can try to tell them politely. But you shouldn't say that in front of other people."

"It was true! And then Susanne came and told him it wasn't, and he went and sat with Susanne all day. It wasn't a good smell. It was a smell that made me worry about him. He smelled like Devon."

He frowned. "Devon was your brother in the laboratory, right?"

"Yes," answered LIDIA's voice. "He had the bed next to mine."

He continued to confirm his memory of the translation of her interview with the esperantist. "He is the one who died of sugar in his blood?"

"Yes."

David thought of the Falvers. He knew the eldest Falver well enough that he could talk about Rodney with him without making a stir.

"Are you sure he smells like Devon?" he pressed her.

"Yes," LIDIA repeated.

"What did he smell like? Describe it."

"Sweet but not good. Like bad apple juice," Rosie computer voice droned.

"That does sound ketonic," David decided. "Alright then. I'll talk to Rodney's grandfather about it. But in the future, remember that we don't talk about how people smell in public. It's embarrassing and even your friends will get mad at you if you do it."

"But it's true," the electronic voice protested without emphasis. "I'm worried about him."

"The fact that it's true doesn't make it okay to say something mean in public. If you need to say something like that you say it gently when it's you and the other person."

When he got a look at her at the next light, she was still wilted by unhappiness. "In any case Chocolate will be glad to see you. I'm sure he'd appreciate a nice long walk," he suggested.

At the mention of the dog, Rosie found her smile.

Bitters sat alone in the Hunter's office. The afternoon view of autumn on the Potomac was striking without his boss between him and the glass wall to obscure much of it. Motor yachts and crew teams were visible on the river behind the enormous metal statue of the Iwo Jima memorial. Behind it the Washington Monument and capitol dome shone in the clear sun. Enough white cloud hung in the sky to ornament the blueness of it. The view made him long to be outside, on the move, out and about, but increasingly the Hunter's assignments for him had him hanging around the headquarters.

The Hunter emerged into his office from the attached dormitory, short of breath, and tightened his tie. Bitters assumed it was his heart condition until his secretary emerged from the dormitory a moment later. She exchanged nods with Bitters before retiring to the outer room.

"Didn't expect you here so quick," the Hunter explained breathlessly.

"I can go if you have unfinished business," Bitters volunteered.

"Nope. Besides, this can't wait," the Hunter stated. "A huge information security mission got dropped in our lap this weekend. I've spent the first half of today in meetings about it. The president is concerned."

Bitters tried to recall any news he'd heard over the weekend that would worry the president. He couldn't. But the new war was on. He supposed a mass casualty event or some slip-up in media cooperation could quickly give the president heartburn. But he hadn't heard anything.

"You don't know about it, or if you do, I need you to shoot the person who told you," explained the Hunter.

"Oh. That kind of job," grunted Bitters. "Must be hot."

"Story is, some Swiss doctor announced at a major gene tech conference in London this weekend that he's gene-engineering humans."

"Is it true?" Bitters asked. "I thought that was supposed to be next to impossible."

"So did I. So did all the experts we had on tap. I was all set to blow it off as more European self- aggrandizement, but we got confirmation from highly placed sources that this guy is for real. In fact, he's already gene-engineered the children of some important people, people who would prefer to have that fact kept private," the Hunter elaborated.

"Uh-huh."

"Their privacy is particularly important given that the tea party types are certain to get worked up on this subject. Apparently, if you're a biblical sort of conservative, engineering humans is 'tampering with the machinery of God' and 'undermining the fundamental equality of all mankind.' I myself was unaware that conservatism admitted of myths like the 'fundamental equality of all mankind.' But these Bible types are making various demands for a response to this doctor's work. They range from an invasion of Switzerland to shut the guy down to hunting down and killing or sterilizing any gene-engineered humans who might be present in the United States. Their argument goes that we're waging a war to stop the spread of nuclear weapons and Islam but letting some European tear up the sanctity of the human genome."

"Sounds straightforward. I mean the kill or sterilize thing. Invading Switzerland, not so much," Bitters commented.

Hunters squinted at Bitters and drummed his fingertips. "Both are out of the question. First, Switzerland gets a pass from invasions because it manages the retirement funds of anyone who matters. Second, there's too much potential in genetic engineering to let these Bible-thumpers have their way on this issue. Abortion? Sure. Gays? Who the hell cares? Warning stickers on biology textbooks? Whatever. But *this* subject touches on national security. It doesn't take a rocket scientist to understand that if this tech is out there, the Chinese and the Russians will both make military and labor application of it. We can do the same, or we can be left behind."

"Oh," Bitters mused. "So, we're not talking just blonde-hair-blue-eyes kind of gene alterations here."

"We're not sure yet," said the Hunter. "But even if we are at the moment, down the road there will be military and labor applications for this stuff, so we have to stop the Christian crusade on this now. Truth is, a showdown on this subject with the Bible-types has been a while in coming. The timing could be better, since we owe the last election to their votes and support. But in the grand scheme of things, I'd sooner lose the next election and come back to power in bed with socialists than forsake the application of this technology in the national interest."

Bitters left the estimation of political necessity to his boss. "It sounds important. But where do I fit in?"

"A compromise has been proposed at the RNC's political bureau. It would allow the Centers for Disease Control to test for and take control of any genetically engineered children and quarantine them. Everyone gets to be happy this way. The prince and his people get their 'ban' on genetic engineering, we get our military tech, and the friends of the president get to keep their pedigreed wonder-kiddies when the CDC fails to identify those kids as gene-altered, provided Mommy and Daddy behave themselves. But we need to keep this story out of the public eye so that public discontent does not derail this process of compromise. The patriotic media understands that some period is needed for the wheels of government to spin up and has agreed not to cover the story or feature foreign journalism on the subject for a few weeks. Your job is to take care of any unAmericans who might not be so considerate of the realities of governance."

"Alright. I'll get on it," said Bitters.

"I'm not talking only media here," Hunter said. "There are legislators, some powerful, who will try to pursue this."

Bitters considered. "Hmmm."

"Indeed. Move on journalists or private citizens on your own. But any legislative terminations will have to be coordinated with the intelligence community and the secret service. One shot, one kill, like you did with congresswoman Spears. We can't afford another muffed job like what happened with Giffords."

"Can do," Bitters said. Giffords was the last assassination he had left to a "lone gunman." They were too unstable to be reliable. Virtually everyone Lohner had struck with a bullet had died *except* Giffords. Bitters decided he would pull the trigger to make sure it got done.

"This is your new top priority. With luck, it will only be an issue for a few weeks. After that spin control should have a way to play this to the public that prevents any upheaval and we can go back to business as usual."

"How about the peak oil thing? Last night DeMarco helped me pick up that Archibald Stevens guy you wanted us to nab. Took me some time but he's locked up down at Walter Reed."

"Back burner," Hunter responded. "If our team doesn't get control of the debate on gene engineering a priceless opportunity will be lost. Let Archibald cool his heels until you have time and manpower."

Bitters sorted through the work. He had a lot on his plate, but it was clear to him that he was to make the plate empty if that's what it took to get this done.

"Got it, sir. We'll start right away."

"You'd better not start any later," the Hunter said. "Get out there and manufacture me some silence."

Once through the door with Rosie after school, David jabbed a button and played back the recorded phone messages while he carried his groceries into the kitchen. The girl trotted on his heels with her own two bags.

"Hey Chief," said the middle Falver's voice from the phone. "My dad passed on your message. I wanted to let you know we followed up with Rod. We tested him as soon as we got your message. Your girl was spot on. He was ketonic. We've changed his insulin dose and got him a doctor's appointment. He should be okay now.

"I've explained about ketones and the smell thing to Rodney. I think he'll make up with Rosie when we send him back to school in a couple of days. Sharp nose on that girl. Tell her thank you for me."

David looked back to Rosie to be sure she had understood the message. Her face beaming from behind the bags of groceries she carried said it all.

Chapter 27

In the Spotlight

Come Tuesday morning, Sharrah settled into her desk, wondering what, if anything, would change about being Vincent's executive assistant after his press conference the Sunday prior. The weekend had been so busy she hadn't had much of a chance to think about the changes it might make in her tranquil job of assuring the doctor's privacy and keeping track of his communication. Dr. Foster had returned by train early Monday, but Monday had been so frantic and busy she hadn't had time for reflection and scarcely any to sit down at her desk.

Once her computer was booting up and scanning itself, she started her boss's favorite morning tea blend. Then she went into his office and opened the blinds enough to let in slices of the morning sunshine through discreet slits, and reached into the decorative vases to pull out and inspect the jamming devices. Their batteries tested three-fourths strength, and she decided that they had another two days of operation left, provided Vincent didn't work through the night. If he did, she'd have to remember to change the batteries tomorrow morning. She then cleared the previous night's coffee service and took it to the kitchenette to clean and empty it and prepare the doctor's breakfast.

The bakery delivered at its usual time, and she shared pleasantries and her halting German with Ute, the gray-haired delivery lady who had rung the doorbell. Sharrah admired how the older woman handled the hills and rises with her heavy basket of baked goods on a bicycle. She had then stopped to chat with one of her neighbors, a middle-aged woman named Seville. Seville made no comments about the news, so she guessed Vincent's press conference had not made a big splash at all.

She then stooped to pick up the newspaper left at the doorway and walked back past her apartment door and up the stairs to the office floor. She was halfway back up to the office, and already looking forward to her breakfast from the bakery bag, when she was stopped by another ring at the doorbell. Curious if Ute had rung again, she walked back down the stairs and opened the door.

At the door was a man, about Ms. Bassi's own age, with shoulder length dirty blonde hair, a curious vest with lots of pockets, and a strong smell of cigarette smoke on him. He carried a rectangular bag and a camera.

"*Can I help you, sir?*" she asked in German. It was one of the few phrases she had used so often that it rolled off her tongue.

"*I was hoping for a moment to speak with Dr. Foster about his amazing discoveries. Is he in?*"

"*The doctor is not taking new patients at the moment. If you leave me a phone number or an email address, I can give you a list of his colleagues whom he recommends. Or you can fill out an online application and join our waiting list.*"

"*Oh, I'm not a patient.*" The young man laughed again. "*I'm Udo Gensch, science writer for the Neue Zuercher Zeitung.*"

Sharrah felt surprise and anxiety pass through the pit of her stomach. She and Vincent had discussed how to deal with any inquiries by telephone, and drafted standard email messages she could use to reply to press requests by email.

But they had not discussed a press visit in person, especially not one so soon after the press conference.

She was torn. Her defensive inclination was to take the man's card and request that he come back later. But she felt that might be rude since the person had taken the trouble to call in person, and if her boss was getting noticed by the media, she didn't want to start him off on the wrong foot with the first reporter through the door. This would be doubly unwise since the NZZ was the chief local newspaper. In fact, it was the very newspaper she was holding in her hand by its yellow plastic rain cover.

Ms. Bassi stammered her attempt at a reply, and the man interrupted her thoughts. "Would it be easier if we spoke in English?"

"Yes, that would be easier for me. Forgive me, I am new in Switzerland."

"It makes nothing. It will be good practice for me," the man admitted. She couldn't help but notice the handsome perfect teeth that ornamented his broad round face. Perfect teeth had been a rarity in Pakistan, her own were somewhat crooked, but this man's were striking.

Sharrah began again, deciding to stall for time. "Dr. Foster and I had not discussed how he wished to deal with press inquiries in person. We expected telephonic or electronic inquiries. I can take your card and contact you later today when we have discussed it?"

"Could I wait for him?" The man persisted. "I understand if he's busy, but I would love to have some material for tomorrow's paper, so if by waiting he could give me a few minutes, I'd be happy to do so."

His question put her back into her conundrum. She either had to ask him to go and be rude, or invite him in and risk angering her boss. She thought about it. She'd rarely seen Vincent get either angry or rude. And when he was dissatisfied with one of her choices, he was straightforward and gentle. These thoughts or rationalizations, as well as the reporter's hopeful brown eyes, evaporated her resistance. She would take whatever correction Vincent needed to give her and err on the side of being hospitable. It would be an opportunity to practice receiving guests.

"I suppose you could wait, but this does not mean he will want to speak to you, so you may be wasting your time," she explained.

"Do you expect him soon?"

"Yes," said Sharrah. "He's punctual."

"Then I'll wait, thank you," he said. When she gave no response, he shifted toward the stairway. "May I come in?"

"Yes, but you must leave your bag," she pointed. "No cameras, cell phones, or recording devices or anything that can hide them. Pen and paper only."

"Here?" He said, looking around the stoop of the row house. "My camera is expensive."

"You could leave it in your car," she suggested.

"Umm, I came with my bike." Udo replied, motioning toward a large blue bicycle with wire side baskets and NZZ placards on its side. "I live uphill a couple of kilometers."

Ms. Bassi paused, then solved the problem. "You can leave it in my apartment."

The journalist looked surprised. "Oh, is it nearby?"

Sharrah nodded. "Yes, it's here." She stepped aside, motioning Udo into the stairwell, and then opened the doorway of her apartment a crack. The writer stepped forward as if he was going into the apartment while he packed the camera away, but she stopped him. "Just your bag, if you please." She held out her hand, and the man hung his bag on her fingers by its strap. She passed the bag through her doorway, closed her apartment door, and locked it.

She smiled at him, trying to dispel the awkwardness of requiring his bag. "Our office is upstairs. If you wish to be welcome here again, you will not publish our address or describe our office in any detail. Nor will you mention me or describe me. As far as Zurich knows, I don't exist. I value my privacy."

"Umm, sure," the man replied as he followed her up the stairs. "So you live here and work here too?"

"Yes. May I ask how you found us?" One of Sharrah's acts the last week had been to go outside and remove the small brass sign that read "Vincent Foster Associates" from the front of the building and sterilize their website of any address information.

Udo shrugged. "The telephone directory? You're listed under fertility doctors, though I saw your website doesn't list this office."

"Ah, yes," she said. She supposed there wasn't much she could do about removing their address from a phone book which had already been published. But the number of people worldwide with access to an actual paper Zurich telephone directory was small. When they reached the upstairs landing, she motioned him into her reception area and vestibule.

Udo followed her as he went through into the kitchenette to put down the bakery bag. She paused awkwardly, and decided she would have to find a place for him to sit else he would follow her about like a puppy while she finished the morning preparations.

"Should I sit somewhere?" The man grasped the problem.

"That's the awkward part. Dr. Foster's patients never wait to see him. Dr. Foster only sees patients by appointment, so the only proper chairs other than mine are in his office. But I can't let you wait for him in his office." She put her hands on her hips, and hemmed. At the end of the kitchenette were two stools.

"Should I sit there?" Udo motioned to the stools. Sharrah thought better of it. She had to keep the man where she could see him. She didn't want him planting listening devices or snooping around.

"If you would be so kind as to take a stool and come sit with me in the reception, that would be best." She stepped aside and let him grab a stool, and then led him out to her desk. With a gesture, she stationed him in a corner to one side of her desk and he positioned the stool and sat.

"The doctor is unprepared for fame," the journalist laughed at their situation. "Or unused to guests."

She smiled woodenly at his joke as she spotted the blinking voicemail counter. Twenty-six messages! It was five times the usual number for a morning. She masked her surprise. "I guess he is. Would you like some coffee?"

"Yes, thanks, I was up all night preparing the story on the doctor's announcement," the writer confided.

"Ah, that's ironic. We were up all night twice last week preparing the announcement." Sharrah laughed companionably. She figured the best way to keep him under control was to make him feel welcome.

She went back to the kitchenette, placed the fresh pastries on the service tray, and filled the carafe from the flash coffee maker. She poured a side cup for herself and one for Udo. She brought the man his cup.

The writer accepted it and sniffed the vapor. "Yes, that's not surprising. I often wonder if public relations people spend more time crafting an announcement or press release than the sum of their readers spend reading them. Dr. Foster's is sure to be the exception, since it will be widely read, but I think people spend too much time preparing press releases instead of letting newspapermen write more interesting articles for them. That is our job, after all."

Sharrah put a cynical lilt in her voice. "If newspapermen learned to ask the right questions, public relations people wouldn't have to write articles for them." She turned as she heard his laugh and a clink as he returned his cup to the saucer.

She took her seat at her desk and smiled innocently. "Everything in order?" she checked.

"Yes, *ahem*, yes." The reporter cleared his throat. "You have a dry wit."

She focused on her keyboard. "Live for years in a burqa with self-satisfied twits of men telling you what to do, and you'll have a dry wit, too."

"Ah," her guest considered. "May I ask where you are from?"

"Pakistan. Dr. Foster rescued me from the Taliban."

Udo raised his eyebrows at this while he took his next sip of coffee.

"You must be grateful to him."

"Very," she answered.

"And you live here. And work for him."

"Yes." She decided to let him piece together those facts. Together they should banish any hope she might be induced to provide him a 'scoop' story for money.

The writer changed the subject. "Your English is excellent. It sounds British."

"I attended British boarding schools in Pakistan. And I had two years at the university, but the Taliban closed it to women my third year. Your English is good, too," she noted.

"The fine swiss education system. I'm afraid it's better even than my French. Ask a Bavarian, and he'll tell you my English is even better than my German!"

At this, it was Sharrah's turn to laugh. She had been in Switzerland long enough to realize that the French, German, and Italian parts were always at odds over preserving their linguistic heritage through the schools, and that Germans and Austrians regarded Swiss German as unintelligible.

Udo continued. "My English is only this good because I have to go to scientific conferences and read scientific papers, which are always in English."

"Ah, that explains it," she nodded. Then she looked back at the blinking voicemail counter. "If you'll excuse me, Mr. Gensch, I should begin to listen to this morning's voicemail while we wait. I expect the doctor soon and I need to be ready. It's my job."

"By all means," Udo demurred. He got out his own notebook and pen from a large pocket on the side of his khaki pants and began to make notes. Sharrah started up her computer, connected her telephone headset, and began to screen the voicemail.

Within a few moments she realized they had a problem. While some calls were from the accountants and other offices, a number were from Dr. Foster's patients, anxious that the press attention he was drawing might draw attention to them, too. She sorted through them, taking down phone numbers and extensions.

Toward the end of the list, she got other calls, including some that introduced themselves as staff members of senators or congressmen. Vincent had anticipated some of these. She skipped through them to come back to them later. First priority were the patients, then the other offices, then the media, and last of all, politicians.

As she was typing she caught the sound of the journalist flipping to a fresh page in his notebook. What on earth could he be writing about that he had already covered a page of notes? She reviewed their conversations for what she had said that could warrant a page of notes. She decided to remind him of her wish for

350

confidentiality before he left.

After what was too short a time, she heard the tone from the security alarm that indicated that the front door had been opened with a key. She perked up. "That would be Dr. Foster."

"Alarm system. Snappy," said Udo. He folded over to a clean page in his notebook and sat up straighter on the stool as faint footsteps sounded from the stairwell.

"Yes, and complicated. But I can get that part to work," she joked.

"Electronics," the man laughed. "I have to get my, how do you say, *Neffe*, to work my computer."

"*Nephew*," Sharrah supplied the English word. "I'm not so lucky. My tech-savvy nieces are all in Pakistan with their skills rotting," she lamented.

"Then I'll lend you my *nephew* some time. He fixes my camera, even. And he works for chocolates and pats on the back," Udo smirked, "You won't find cheaper."

They were both still chuckling as Dr. Foster entered. Ms. Bassi saw a look of surprise flash across his face upon seeing someone already in his office. But he hung up his coat and cap as normal in the vestibule and was calm when he came to her desk.

"Good morning, sir," she said, trying not to betray any concern about the guest.

"Good morning! Company already, I see?"

"This fellow was sniffing around the stoop when I brought in the pastries and milk, and he followed me in," she explained with a smile. "He's the science writer for the *Neue Zuercher Zeitung*."

"Good of you to bring him in! Only a fool spurns his local paper," the doctor commended her. He then turned to Udo. "Pleased to meet you, Mr. Gensch. I appreciated your literate and calm coverage of the Marburg virus outbreak last month." He offered his hand. "It's rare to find a science writer for a newspaper who does more than dress up a Reuter's story and call it research. It's also refreshing to find a reporter who doesn't spend time trying to turn science stories into hysteria."

Udo's eyes widened in surprise and pleasure, and he stood, brushed his hand on his slacks, and shook hands. "Uh, thank you, *Herr Doktor*. An honor, I hope I'm not imposing. And that I'm not getting your charming assistant," he nodded to Sharrah, "in any trouble."

"Not at all," Vincent replied, "Let me attend to the morning's business before we talk. I am, first and foremost, a doctor, and I must give first shrift to my patients and laboratories." Vincent took the paper from Ms. Bassi's desk. "Would thirty minutes of interview suffice?"

Udo looked as though he'd been handed a present. "Why, yes, that would be...*perfekt*."

Sharrah spoke up at this point, trying to interject routine into all this upheaval of her employer's morning. "Your breakfast is on your desk, sir. I have a summary of the first part of the evening's voicemail messages in your inbox. And your privacy is, umm, assured," she said. She saw comprehension flash across his features. He remembered the code phrase for the jamming devices.

"Excellent. Thank you for bringing order to my chaos."

"My pleasure and duty, sir," Sharrah nodded. She took from this compliment that he was satisfied with her handling of the situation.

"It may be an hour or so," Vincent warned the writer.

"Take your time, sir. You're the hottest story in science today. You can make me wait," he answered.

The doctor laughed, shook his head, entered his office, and closed the door, leaving Ms. Bassi and the reporter together again in silence. At this, she began flashing forward through the voicemails again. Now that she had screened the patient and lab messages, she could now start on the press and politicians summary.

After a moment, the man cleared his throat and caught Sharrah's eye. She paused the voicemail, irked by the interruption.

"Yes?"

"This is the office of Dr. *Vincent S. Foster*?"

The question puzzled her. "Yes."

"How strange," Udo shook his head and flipped backwards through his notebook.

"What's strange?" said Sharrah.

"I was expecting him to be older. Much older."

"Why?" she asked, out of a mix of interest and politeness.

"He's listed in the medical registry as having his medical degree from Harvard in 1934 and again from Berlin in 1938. If he went straight to medical school from college, that would mean he was born in 1908. Yes, here it is, in my notes. I thought it was remarkable that a man his age would still be working, much less making important discoveries."

Ms. Bassi paused at this news. "Must be a mistake," she dismissed it.

"Must be," said Udo. "I'll clarify it." He began writing in his notebook again. "By the way, may I smoke?"

"Thank you for asking, but please don't," she said without looking up. That was one thing she would refuse him without remorse. When she was sure he was finished speaking to her, Ms. Bassi began slogging through the voicemail once again, typing as fast as she could.

Later that day, after Udo's interview was complete and Dr. Foster was working over his lunch, Sharrah got the warning tone in her headset that a phone call was incoming. She saved the text file she was working on, opened a phone message shell on her computer, and pushed the "receive call" button.

"Vincent Foster and Associates, can I help you?"

"Yes, I'd like to speak to Dr. Foster, please." The voice was older, confident, and had an unfamiliar drawling accent to his English.

"Who is calling, please?" She prepared to fill in the "caller" field on the computer. She noticed that the poppies on her desk vase were drooping. She'd have to remember to replace them.

The voice at the other end paused before continuing. "Senator Warren Sprague. I'm head of the Senate Life Sciences Committee. I'd like to talk to him in person about his experiments."

"Ah, a politician," she recognized. "One moment, sir, I'll check to see if the Doctor is free. Could you hold?"

"I'll hold," said the man, in a tone that suggested he would rather not.

Sharrah switched lines and paged Vincent.

"Yes?" he picked up.

"A Senator Warren Sprague wants to speak with you, sir. He's chairman of a 'life sciences' committee."

"Hmmm..." said Vincent. "Is that Sprague spelled S-P-R-A-G-U-E"?

"Yes."

"Stall for me while I Google him. I think I know that name, but I want to

352

be sure."

"Can do," she switched lines back to the caller. "Are you there, Mr. Sprague?"

"Yes," said the man.

"You said you were a Senator, sir? Is that the correct title?" Sharrah typed quickly and loudly, so that she was sure the caller could hear.

"That's right, Miss."

"What country, sir?" she inquired innocently.

At this, there was a long pause, and when the man spoke again, he sounded irritated.

"Miss, is this a joke?"

"Sir, Dr. Foster does business in many countries, states, and provinces, many of which have a senate. No disrespect, but I need you to be more specific."

"Okay, Miss, Senator Warren Sprague of the *United States* Senate."

"Very good, sir. What number can I call you back at if we are disconnected?"

"That's my business, Miss. If you're finished with this bullshit, I'd like to talk to doctor now."

Sharrah frowned at the screen. Who was this man talking to her this way? She didn't have to put up with his rudeness. "I'll thank you not to be vulgar, sir. Please hold."

She cut him off and paged Vincent again. He connected.

"He's an American. And he's irritable."

"Yes, I checked him out. He's the sort of politician we discussed."

"Should I take a message, then?" she prompted him after a moment.

"No, I'll talk to him. But let him wait while we chat a moment."

"Go ahead."

"Can you stay on the line while we talk? I want you to hear what we are up against."

"I can do that. But if he has a security device on his end, it will show that a third line is up."

"Then come into my office once you have connected him. I'll put him on speaker so you can listen."

"Will do."

"Okay, give him about three more minutes to hold, then connect him and come in."

Sharrah reconnected the senator. "Senator Sprague?"

"Yes?" The man sounded refreshed to hear his title.

"You're in luck, the doctor is finishing up with some patients. Hold on for another few minutes and I'll put you through."

"Okay, Miss, three minutes is all you get."

She grimaced and held his call again. She had always heard tell that the United States was a country where men treated women well. She wouldn't have guessed it based on this call. Maybe it was propaganda.

"Three minutes or you do what, you pretentious American fool? Fire me? Or will you drone bomb me because you don't like my attitude?" Ms. Bassi said aloud to the closed phone line.

She heard Vincent chuckle from his office. In a moment, he called out, "Put him on."

She opened the line again. "Senator Sprague? The doctor will take your call now."

"Good. Put me through," he said.

"Connecting now." She pushed the transfer button, disconnected her

353

headset, and got up.

As she tiptoed into Vincent's office and quietly closed the door, she heard the doctor begin the conversation, sounding artificially pleased and flattered. "Good day, Senator. How can I help you?"

"Am I on speaker phone?" the senator growled.

"Yes, Senator. I'm an old man, and a handset causes static in my hearing aids. We could talk by email if you'd prefer. I could assure you doctor/patient confidentiality concerning whatever fertility issues we discuss." Sharrah could see a smirk turning the corners of her boss's mouth.

The senator paused, sounding irritated. "I guess I'll talk on speaker phone. But I'm not calling for your treatments."

"That's good, Senator, because I'm not taking new patients. I was afraid I would have to refer you and the young lady to one of my colleagues. Embarrassing, but there is only one Dr. Foster to go around."

There was another hesitation. "Are you playing games with me, Foster?"

"Not at all. I would never waste your time and taxpayer dollars on levity or pleasantries." The doctor gave Ms. Bassi a wink, and she covered her mouth, afraid she would laugh aloud. "Shall we get to business, Senator?"

"I will. I'm asking for senate hearings on your cloning enterprise."

"Cloning, Senator?"

"Whatever that stuff is you do. Recombinant in-vitro exogenesis or whatever. Don't make me put a staffer on to translate, you know what I'm talking about, and it would be a waste of taxpayer dollars."

"*Maybe* I do, Senator." Vincent sat down and leaned back. "I'll have my assistant send your staffer an information paper so you can use the correct scientific terms when you talk to the media. So we at least start on a level playing field."

"Bury that snooty European attitude. I'll use the words that suit my angle. We have laws against that sort of gene tinkering in America, and you're breaking them."

"Hmmm. How inconvenient for American science. I guess the rest of the world will have to do your science for you."

"It's thanks toAmerican science that you all aren't speaking German or Russian every day."

Vincent was laughing as he stood again, shaking his head to Sharrah before he turned to face the window. "You'll have to forgive me, Senator, but I speak German every day as it is. So I guess American science has let me down. But I wouldn't be the first person so disappointed."

"Okay, Foster, laugh all you want. But this is no joke. The human genome is a creation of God, and should only be altered by acts of divinely inspired love. We don't know the details, but our experts are saying your methods must entail trial and error, and as a result human suffering and abortions on a massive scale. So you can play God, but unless you can prove to me and my colleagues that your methods are humane and protect the sanctity of the human genome, you can plan on us shutting you down."

"Ah, there it is. So often American crassness hides subtle and complex moral reasoning. I'm impressed, Senator. Based on your Congressional Quarterly tables, I'd mistaken you for being yet another unschooled demagogue."

"Yale, class of '65," said the senator. "Unschool that."

"Harvard, class of '34," said Vincent. Sharrah felt her eyebrows go up in surprise. Udo's information had been correct. "And you'll forgive me, but the rolls of Yale graduates do contain some names that, shall we say, fail to impress with their intellectual weight."

At this the senator laughed. "Kerry and Obama were no standouts. I agree."

"Those aren't the names that came to my mind, Senator, but let's not be dilatory. Did you call me to tell me that I'm the spawn of hell, or did you have a request or demand I could fulfill?"

"Now I'm starting to like you, Foster. You can come to the bottom line," the senator sounded pleased. "I want you to come to my hearings."

The doctor paused. "Are you sure that's wise, Senator? Shouldn't you stage some kangaroo hearings where you can bring in camera-shy nerds and control the spin rather than let me verbally and technically flog you and your peers?"

"Call me a glutton for punishment. I think your highbrow technocratic slop will flop in publicized hearings. So I'll bet some political capital on it. What's at stake here is God's creation and the fundamental equality of all men, and the American public will see it my way and write me a check when I'm done with you in hearings. But are you in, or do I have to freeze assets and write subpoenas?"

Vincent's face had grown stony, and his eyes focused far beyond the wall behind Sharrah. "A fascinating offer."

The Senator agreed. "I thought so, which is why I stayed on the line while your uppity raghead secretary put me on hold. Is that a yes?"

At this, Ms. Bassi gaped in anger. She couldn't believe what she had heard. After all those months of dodging the fatwa, this man had lumped her in with the Taliban. She felt the urge to shout, but didn't know what to say. Her boss raised his hand to hush her.

When Vincent replied, his voice was relaxed and assured. "Since we're so friendly and on a last-name basis now, Sprague, I'll make you a counter-offer. Call your lads-in-blue and try to write subpoenas and freeze my assets. When you've deduced that I foresaw you coming twenty years ago and you can't touch me, give your spooks another bit of homework. Call my Executive Assistant back by name, give her your opinion of what she has been through, and apologize to her for your racial slur. Then I'll be happy to discuss the hearings and share my best scientific and ethical reasoning with the American people."

"What the fuck kind of bullshit answer is that, Foster?" Senator Sprague blurted.

The doctor opened his mouth like he had something comparably forceful to say, but he recovered his coolness. He poised his finger over the phone for a half second. "I'll thank you not to be vulgar, Senator. Good day."

There was a click over the speaker, and the senator was disconnected.

After a second of silence, Sharrah stamped her foot in fury, remembering the Karachi rooms full of brave women wanting to learn to read, to control their fertility, and study science and business. Then she remembered two of them hanging from a soccer goalpost while she was forced to watch.

Vincent sat down hard in his chair and stared into the distance.

"I'm sorry you had to hear that," he said hoarsely. "Racism is one of the greatest blights of the human spirit. I was a racist, too, when I was younger. It took me half a century to outgrow it. Forgive him."

"Fuck him," she said without thinking. She tried to think of something else to add to it, but after reflection she could find nothing that bore repeating so well as "fuck him."

The doctor stood. Through the blur of her tearing eyes, she saw him raise the blinds, and the bright sunlight prismed into a flash that made him a silhouette.

"Take the rest of the day off. Do whatever comforts you. Find a technique to counter this insult. I fear that as long as we have dealings with Americans, you will bear it again."

Sharrah wiped her eyes and waited for her breathing to become regular. "Thank you," she said, getting up. The idea of putting on leather, getting on her motorcycle, and driving in any direction into green hills had great appeal. She turned to the door, to avoid crying more in front of her employer.

"Don't thank me," said Vincent behind her. "Forgive me."

Early Thursday morning was warm for the fall. Udo pedaled more easily so as to prevent overheating and sweating. He didn't want to arrive at his office sweaty if he didn't have to. His bicycle and its baskets were too overburdened with papers for him to reach a speed that would cool him. So he had to be content with a plodding sub-sweat speed as he continued his paper route through downtown Zurich.

He had taken these morning paper routes for the NZZ for a few reasons. For one, it got him some exercise. While the Wiedikon and Stauffacher areas of Zurich were not hilly, it was still a workout to ride the heavy, over-engineered NZZ bicycle laden with newspapers. The delivery routes also made him some money, which was always helpful. Competition from online media meant that the NZZ was hard pressed to stay in business, and even though his writing got compliments and awards, his expense account and pay had been frozen for some years. Arguably, he rode the routes so that for about fifteen days a year he could afford to attend scientific conferences elsewhere in Europe.

These first two reasons made sense, he had to concede each morning when he got out of bed before five so he could deliver the papers on the way to work. Still, the sense they made was easier to concede during the spring and summer months. In the winter, Udo had to supplement these reasons by asserting that delivering papers was a proof of his manliness. These same winters, after all, were the ones that had stopped the Roman legions in their tracks. This idea that he was continually testing his manliness also helped console him when one of his contemporaries drove by, safe and warm in the expensive cars Udo had never be able to afford.

He'd had to make up the absurd but appealing "test of manliness" theory because the first version of the third reason he had for taking the paper routes hadn't worked out. He had, in his naiveté, imagined that taking the paper route would put him in touch with the NZZ's subscribers and earn him more name and face recognition. This was the dumbest idea he'd ever had. Most newspaper subscribers paid online or directly from their giro-accounts because they didn't want to talk to anyone in the morning. And all of them were either asleep or hurrying to work when he delivered. None were interested, when they emerged bleary-eyed for their commute, in chatting with an obscure journalist. He could count on one hand the number of subscribers he had gotten to know by name working his routes.

The dismal failure of this original reason three had been accented two days before by an irony. He delivered Dr. Vincent Foster's newspapers but had not met the man, or his fascinating and beautiful assistant who now haunted his daydreams, until the doctor's press release. This fact galled him particularly when he rode onto Morgartenstrasse and began tossing papers. His fourth toss on the south side of the street would be for Dr. Foster and Sharrah.

He made the toss, landing the paper at the top of the stoop with an artful arc that bespoke his twenty-four months of experience at paper delivery. Once he reached the banks of the canal he doubled back and lined up for toss number five, only to swerve dangerously close to a parked Alfa-Romeo when a spectacle of beauty unfolded before him.

Ms. Bassi herself had darted across the street about half a block ahead of him, wearing sweatpants, a sports top, and a bandanna wrapped around her head. While the outfit was not as skimpy or immodest as he'd seen bouncing along on one or another beauty of Zurich, it still brought a bright smile to his face. His current speed would bring him alongside the woman in a few moments.

He savored those moments. He considered riding past her and saying nothing, thereby demonstrating his work ethic and athleticism. But such a display of his fitness would go unnoticed if she didn't recognize him. Or the approach might even work against him if she saw it was him and was miffed that he didn't speak to her. So he settled for a cheerful *"Hallo Sharrah!"* and a wave as he passed.

"Hallo, Udo!" she called back. He looked back to look at her and wave again, but this caused him to steer the overloaded bicycle into the curb and tip his bundled newspapers out onto the ground.

"That was sure slick," he muttered with chagrin. Sharrah jogged to a stop beside him, and began helping him collect all the spilled newspapers.

"So, you keep a paper route? I thought your bicycle was a special bicycle for reporters," she asked.

"I have two routes. Hence the excess of newspapers I flung all over the sidewalk. I deliver around here and more around the Stauffacher trolley stop. I then take the trolley into the office and then the bicycle back home in the evenings." Not for the first time he felt embarrassed by his humble means. "This paper route pays for my pathetic and ill-paying hobby as a journalist. It's an unnatural obsession, journalism. If I could afford it, I'd see a shrink to talk me out of it and into something sensible. Like banking."

The woman tittered at his joke. "Do you know Ute? She delivers our morning pastries, also by bicycle."

Udo shook his head. "No, but maybe I should get to know her in case she takes a spill like this one. They keep the sidewalks here clean enough to eat off of. I might be able to supplement my breakfasts."

Sharrah's amusement showed as she reached for another fallen paper. He jammed the papers tighter in the basket to make room for it, and to increase the coefficient of friction so they'd be less apt to fly out again. *"The physics graduate runs a paper route,"* he grinned wryly when he found himself using the term "coefficient of friction" in his internal narrative.

"So, you're a runner?" he said to cover the gap in the conversation.

"Only now starting," she explained as she scooped up loose newspapers. "I used to be fit in school and university, when I played field hockey. But I'm coming up on my green belt test in Kung Fu in eight weeks, and I'll have to fight for an hour for that, so I want to be in good shape."

"Ah," Udo said, sizing up the woman up again. He absorbed the notion that she was a martial artist on top of being exotic and pretty, smart, even more multilingual than he, and working for a man who was fabulously wealthy and kept her in a gilt nest. For a moment, the fact of her martial arts training fell as the straw that had broken the back of his already labored self-esteem.

To the rescue of his flagging ego came reason three, version two, for why he delivered papers. *"Go on,"* he prompted. *"As a brave paper-deliveryman of fine Helvetian stock, you brave the winters that frostbit Caesar's legions. Ask her."*

Sharrah was still smiling at him and shaking her head when she handed him the last loose newspaper.

"Sharrah, are you doing anything tonight?" he asked.

She tilted her head, and Udo admired the opalescent ends of the hair pins that kept her enormous roll of hair squeezed under her bandanna. "French homework, I expect."

He felt still more of his confidence fade away at this. Either she was so uninterested in him that conjugating with verbs appealed to her more, or she was a touch bookish. *"Carry on, be indomitable in your pursuit of rejection,"* he thought. *"Remember brave Helico!"*

"How about Friday night?" He waited for her reaction, watching for signs that she was concocting an excuse or was disappointed that he didn't take a hint from her first rejection.

A long second was followed by a question. "What do you have in mind?"

Udo was stunned by this reply. She hadn't rejected him outright. His odds had seemed so long with Sharrah he hadn't planned for success. Here she was, asking for his plan for their date with apparent curiosity, and he had no plan.

He turned his lack of preparation to his advantage. "Umm, I'm flexible. There's always the classic dinner-and-music, or dinner-and-moonlit-walk. I could even settle for dinner-and-watching-you-eat. I'm not proud. Or rich, even. As a matter of fact, I'm just this side of broke and groveling."

To his further surprise, she blushed. "Thank you. I'd like that. But I'll have to ask Dr. Foster first."

The writer's soaring hopes began a meteoric dive toward the Swiss plateau. "I'm sorry, I didn't realize your relationship with him was like that. How silly of me."

"Oh, no, it isn't!" she protested. "No, I'm...I'm not his lady-in-waiting. It's that you're a reporter, and we're careful about our publicity and secrets, so I would want to ask him. He's done so much for me. I know you don't understand, but I feel duty bound."

Udo took out one of his business cards. "Call me when you've made your decision."

She waved it away. "I have your business card from Tuesday."

"In case you've lost it," he offered it again.

"I'm an executive assistant. I don't *lose* business cards," she refused it again. "I *will* call you, no matter which answer he gives me. We'll have to see each other again so it makes sense to be considerate of one another."

He tucked his card away again. "I hope you're not playing with this humble reporter's heart," he replied. "I could write a scathing critique of you in the science section, you know. It could humiliate you if, by chance, someone in Zurich ever opened the science section."

"No, I'm not playing games. Did you know you're the first person to ask me on a date since I came to Zurich?" she replied. "I think...I think it's my head scarf."

The man found this hard to believe. "Really? Then I'm benefiting fabulously from my peers' lack of ambition," he replied. "If you bless me with a date, maybe they'll learn more courage and begin beating a path to your door. And later when you've married a handsome and sensitive international financier with more money than God, you can look back and say 'it was my date with Udo that started it all!'"

She laughed, a fond, full lipped laugh which made him relax. "Alright. Now deliver your papers. The city is waiting, and I need to get my run in and get to work on time."

Udo smiled back at her, ran beside his bike to get it some speed, and then swept up onto it. "I'll see you Friday!" He called out to her.

358

He pushed the pedals hard as he rode away to his second route. He had been concerned with getting to work sweaty, but now, he realized, he was more concerned with trimming another half-kilo of belly fat in the next thirty-six hours.

Chapter 28

How to Say "Sorry"

Sharrah worked on one of Vincent's responses so hard that she was chewing on the end of her pen in a way that would have mortified her had her boss been around to see it. But he had left for one of his walks.

The letter was meant to reassure his clientele that their identities would remain as safe as Dr. Foster could make them, and announce that he was still open for business regardless of the many threats made by politicians worldwide. Clients were still proving reluctant to begin or continue their business with him. In particular the North American clients were uneasy. She supposed she understood this. Vincent had played for her a sample of a *Voice of America* broadcast the day before which was vicious in its attacks on gene modification and its users.

She paused for a second. Part of what made the doctor such an earnest and comforting person to talk to was his informality. He had a way of becoming familiar without becoming rude or presumptuous that she wanted to capture in this letter, but she couldn't reproduce it.

After another quarter hour of attempts, she decided that this characteristic of her employer emerged from his manner and language in ways that could not be imitated. She had started to rewrite the message in a more formal tone when the security system relayed a buzz at her doorbell. In alarm, she reviewed Vincent's calendar. She saw that it was indeed empty for the afternoon, as she had remembered it, and relaxed.

She opened the security camera window on her computer screen. The caller was a gray-haired man in black suit with a strangely styled broad-brimmed cap that curled upward to the left and right.

"Vincent Foster Associates. Can I help you?" She asked into the microphone.

"Good afternoon, Miss," said the man to the camera. "I'd like to speak to Sharrah Bassi. If she's available." The man's English had another accent she remembered as an American one, but it didn't give her the chills of fear that the drawling American accent did.

"This is she," she said with curiosity. Other than Ute the pastry lady and, more recently, Udo, no one ever rang for her. "What's your business?"

The man held the hat to his chest in a gesture that struck her as both strange and non-threatening. "Ma'am, I believe the United States Senate owes you an apology. I'm here to make that apology."

Sharrah froze for a moment in surprise. She struggled for something to say in reply. She could think of nothing, however. So she pressed the "unlock" button on the security camera window. "Second floor please, sir. Mind the first stairwell step. It's uneven."

"Thank you, miss," said the man with a wave of his hat. He stepped off-screen.

She looked around the office in a rush for anything that might not be presentable. First, she hid the pen cap she had disfigured by chewing it. Then, she reached into her drawer and tied on a yellow headscarf she kept there in case

Vincent ever had a Muslim client who might be put off by her bare-headedness. Then she spun her coffee cup so that it showed the flag of the former Islamic Republic of Pakistan. She was headed to open the office door when the doorknob turned and the gentleman stepped in, his hat still in hand.

"Good day," she said. She didn't know the western protocol for greeting someone who'd come asking after her. She supposed it would be a good idea to treat him as she would someone who'd come to see the doctor, since that could be the only reason. "Can I take your hat and coat, sir?"

The man ignored her request. "Madame Bassi, I assume?"

"Yes, I am she. And you are?"

"Senate Majority Leader Cuspis Brownell."

Sharrah blinked. If she understood that title, it made the visitor one of the most important legislators of the United States. And here he was in Vincent's office, hat in hand, and she hadn't the faintest idea what protocol was appropriate. She vacillated between embarrassment and suspicion.

"I'm sorry, sir. Had the doctor told me you were coming I'd be prepared to receive you-"

"I'm not here to see the doctor," explained the senator. "I'm sure if the good doctor wants to talk to me, he can find me, and I won't refuse him. I was here to do something more important."

"Do...do you have an entourage? Security? Photographers?" She peeked down the stairwell. It was empty.

"No, Ma'am, I don't. An apology made first in front of a camera is no apology at all. It's grandstanding," answered the senator.

"Can I offer you a seat?" she stammered. She would have to take him into the doctor's office to offer him one, she realized, but she was sure her boss would be displeased if he came back to find her making the senator stand in the hall.

"A chair would be a blessing. I walked in from the train station with a GPS. I couldn't read your bus schedules. Shameful of me, I know, I've never taken the time to learn another language."

Sharrah ushered him into Vincent's office. He sat down stiffly. He was not an unfit man, and his weathered face and hands suggested to her that he had done some hard labor for some, or most, of his life.

"Tea? Coffee?" She continued her protocol list for guests.

The man shook his head with a chuckle. "Ms. Bassi, I'd be very obliged if you'd sit down. I do have a plane to catch up in Stuttgart this evening. I'm sure your tea would be fine, but I have the sense if I don't stop you you'll spend the whole afternoon being polite to me and I won't have time to say what needs to be said."

Ms. Bassi took her cue and sat, looking at the man, his black suit, and his wrinkled face and gray eyes.

"Thank you," he said, leaning back. "This is a beautiful office, and chair," he said, admiring the room. "This would be British Raj style, wouldn't it?"

Sharrah smiled at the compliment. "Yes. Since Dr. Foster is English by birth, when he charged me with decorating his office, I chose a style that would combine his heritage with mine. Thank you for noticing!"

Senator Brownell seemed pleased with his guess. "You see a lot of fancy places as a Senator. I guess that despite myself I'm learning something about culture." He faced the puzzled secretary. "So, this brings me back to you, Ma'am. I had many occasions to visit Pakistan during our wars in Afghanistan and Iraq. Before the fall, mind you. I am against any negotiation with the Pakistani Taliban in power there now. If I'm not mistaken, your father was the education minister, wasn't he?"

Ms. Bassi nodded. "Until the fall," she replied. The Senator's information was good.

"And your mother was a school teacher?"

"Until my eldest brother was born, yes." The Senator's information was *very* good. She hadn't even known her mother was a schoolteacher until she uncovered an old photo album in a closet. Her mother had only taught for a few years and never spoken of working outside the home.

"But now I understand that one of our Senators, Mr. Warren Sprague of Florida," the senator harrumphed with disdain, "referred to you in a vulgar, ignorant, and bigoted way. I don't know *exactly* the words he used, since he was mumbling like a guilty schoolboy when I asked him to repeat them. Since he was acting that way, I made him sit in a corner for a good long time. If I get back to the U.S. and find he's not still in that corner, he'll get a paddling he'll remember. I shouldn't have to be a schoolmaster to grown men, but politics in America is more like primary school than you might guess."

Sharrah smiled at the mental image of Senator Sprague in a corner with a dunce cone on his head.

Senator Brownell continued. "Now, since you come from a family of educators, I'm sure you know that sometimes the best way to teach misguided children the right way to do a thing is to do as an example. So that's what I'm here to do." He leaned toward her in his chair.

"Ms. Bassi, the things Senator Sprague said to you were unworthy of the gracious and Christian character of the American people, and I apologize to you on their behalf. The vast majority of Americans, and of our soldiers, are aware of the courage and character of the Pakistani people in their search for peace and democracy. If Mr. Sprague comes to me for an endorsement for his next term, you can be sure he won't get it. I am convinced that the first requirement of a Senator, especially a Republican in my senate, is that he or she be a gentlemen or a lady. There are too many fine and capable Americans to choose from to accept a lower standard."

Sharrah's head was spinning. Was she getting a heartfelt apology? And what did it mean?

"What part of the United States are you from?" she wondered after a moment.

"The great state of Iowa," he said. She remembered from geography classes that Iowa was in the American Midwest and lay along the Mississippi river. She pictured it as green wet delta buzzing with mosquitoes like Bangladesh.

"I don't think I've ever met, or even heard of, an American like you," she replied. "Thank you for your apology, Senator." She felt the need to dry her eyes, but had to settle for blinking, instead.

The senator shrugged. "I think the only place in the United States my ideas would be out of the ordinary is in Washington, DC, itself. Stop into any church on the roadside and Americans would treat you as I do."

Sharrah felt her eyes grow wetter. She stood to look for some tissue when the senator produced a plastic packet of them from his coat pocket. She accepted them and sat back down, now able to let tears run. The Senator sat quietly until she composed herself.

"Now, there may still be some good both for the United States and Pakistan that could come from Mr. Sprague's outburst. I would be honored, Ma'am, if you would share with me the story of your journey from Pakistan to Zurich. It could prove to be a useful story for me to know when I discuss with my colleagues the support due to the remains of the secular Pakistani government or immigration policies surrounding Pakistanis seeking refuge within our borders."

Sharrah reflected on this. Telling the story would make her more tired than hearing the senator's apology had. At the same time the idea that her story might find some sympathy from this important American, and help some of her countrymen find asylum in the west, made it a moral imperative that she tell it.

She began. She found it easier to speak when she kept her eyes focused on a vase behind the senator; looking into his patient eyes only made her feel more emotional. From time to time he would harrumph, or ask for an explanation of Pakistani or Islamic customs. And when at last she was done, the senator was solemn.

"Ma'am, with the exception of our soldiers and emergency services, few Americans ever risk as much for their freedom or their countrymen as you have for yours. I also apologize for the fate of your family. It remains a blot on America's honor that we let Pakistan fall when so many of your people, if not your intelligence services, stood with us in our hours of need. Now, I'm just a man, and just one Senator, so I can't fix all that was done wrong, and neither can I apologize to everyone who deserves our apology. But I can do my part, and with the gift of your story, I am sure I will be able to do it better."

Sharrah nodded. The Senator again paused. As she finished her reflections and felt ready to continue the conversation, the senator stood.

"Thank you for your time and your patience with my institution." When she stood as well, he reached into his pocket and pulled out a visiting card. "If you need to reach me, this is the number to my personal aide, rather than my front desk. I can't do things that are illegal or not in the interests of the United States, of course. But if you can think of a favor I can do you that would balance the insult you've received from my senate, call and let me know. My aide is Nancy. She'll take care of you."

Ms. Bassi walked to her desk and inserted the card into its own page in her card album. "Can I call you a taxi, Senator? A person such as you ought not to be walking alone."

The senator waved off her concern. "I'll find my way. This is an interesting city, and it's a refreshing change to be able to walk without a security detail dogging my every step as though I'm made of cut crystal. It's not Tehran out there. I'll walk back to the train station and ride back to Stuttgart to join the rest of the legislative delegation."

Sharrah followed the senator to the door, wondering what parting protocol would dictate of her. The Senator turned as they came to the door, and again held his hat to his chest. She didn't wait for him to phrase his goodbye.

"May the peace of God be upon you, Senator," she said, extending her hand.

The man smiled, shaking her hand. "Thank you, Madame Bassi. I'd welcome some peace, I truly would. May your mother and father, and your students, rest easy in Heaven."

"God willing," she replied as he stepped out through the door and began his careful climb down the stairs.

"You need to find this guy!" Hunter heard himself bellow at the head of the legislative delegation's security detail. But these words were automatic: his mind was already miles ahead of his outrage. The likelihood that the Secret Service had lost track of Senator Brownell by accident was small. There were simply too many ways to track him: his GPS token, his cell phone, and the flesh-embedded IR chips worn as keys to his various doors and offices were just a start.

So the senator had either been kidnapped by those sophisticated enough both to snatch him out from under the eyes of his escorts and to defeat electronic tracking methods, or the senator himself had dodged his own security detail. The feeble excuses of the field agent went straight into Hunter's mental wastebasket as his subconscious branched through possibilities.

"At this point we have to assume the senator has been kidnapped. Centralize and secure the rest of the legislative delegation in such a way that doesn't tip off the Germans that something is up. We don't need their help, and we certainly don't want their media tipped off. But we have to account for Brownell. Call if anything changes, or in another sixty minutes if nothing does," he barked. He put the phone down and frowned.

Morning sunlight from the glass wall behind him had heated his shoulders, and he adjusted a dial on his desk to polarize the glass. As the light dimmed and he cooled he considered what he knew about Senator Brownell. The man was a Johnny-come-lately to the Senate, having spent most of his life as an industrial farmer. Despite his short political career, the Senate had selected him its leader after his second term, over the protests of some of the very agri-businesses that had put him in the Senate in the first place. The man's technical knowledge of agriculture and botany had caused him to vote in ways inconveniently different from lawyers on issues of gene-manipulated crops and livestock. But since his votes had not prevented agribusiness from getting what it needed and the rest of his votes had been on-message, Brownell's name had otherwise never come to Hunter's attention in his meetings with the President.

He absently spun his Rolodex, watching names flip by. Perhaps Brownell's high office had made him a target of some terrorist group. Such a kidnapping would put egg on Hunter's face, since he had no warning of the threat. But this was unlikely, and its unlikeliness made Hunter dwell on the other possibility. Why would a Senator at the peak of his political power and favor with his party give his security detail the slip? What was he up to?

He supposed it could be as simple as Senator Brownell being in the mood for someone spicier, or more masculine, then Mrs. Brownell. He delved into the files on the legislator and found that the senator was newly a widower, and that thus far his security detail had not recorded any new romantic interests. That was sad, he concluded. A man ought to have interests, powerful men more so. *"How many of these ideologues drink deep of power without fucking whatever they can put their hands on?"* he wondered. *"Kind of pathetic. And unnatural."*

Whatever the senator's reason for disappearing, Hunter supposed that if the senator re-appeared that evening with an innocent smile and a lame apology, a follow up with the CIA would be warranted. Either it would give him dirt on the man he could later turn into leverage, or it could give him insight into the senator's allies and ambitions. Maybe it would even turn up something unAmerican. One never knew.

"Legislators," he grunted. "Running around like they own the place." He picked up the phone to dial the President.

Vincent listened to Sharrah's excited retelling of the senator's visit when he returned to the office. The story impressed him. Not only had she handled the visit with apparent poise, but the gentleman had tamed her recent anti-American fervor. When his assistant finished both her story and her pacing and come back to the present enough that she had taken his cane and hat for him and gone to her desk, he pondered the meaning of the visit.

Senator Brownell may have felt an apology was due Ms. Bassi, and he may genuinely have been interested in her story as an example of what moderate Muslims had suffered at the hands of the Taliban. But the politician could have apologized in many ways. He could have invited Sharrah to the US, or agreed to apologize to her in front of al Jazeera, or even brought her some award and had her feted publicly. But he hadn't done any of those things that would have showcased his virtue to the world. He had, instead, done what Dr. Foster had asked Warren Sprague to do, and done so to the letter, and discreetly. Vincent saw a message in this. Cuspis Brownell shared some of his own expectations about how cricket ought to be played, and had signaled with the apology that he was ready on the pitch. Overall, the doctor thought the senator's visit a subtle piece of work.

He did not share this thinking with Sharrah. If she believed that the politician had made this gesture to mend fences with her, he would not disillusion her. In this respect, a lifetime of nihilism had taught him compassion. If someone had a myth that made them happy and harmed no one else, it was the epitome of cruelty to take that myth away. The senseless and brutal truth that life as it was lived today was all about power was more than capable of introducing *itself* to the uninitiated. He sensed that the woman treasured the apology, and he would let her treasure it. She had endured enough.

Instead he examined the opportunity the senator's visit presented. Someday he would have to take his case for genetic engineering to the American people in any case. Warren Sprague was a sophist git whose political career was about to be cut short, but this Cuspis Brownell person might be a gentleman enough, and open-minded enough, to be worth his trouble. He did wish he'd come home sooner from his walk, since he would have liked to have met the man and formed his own impression. But, he supposed, he could always call the senator and get an impression over the phone.

He resolved to trust Sharrah's instincts about the man. She hadn't let him down yet. "What is your opinion?" he called out, "Is it your impression that Senator Brownell is a good man?"

His assistant answered quickly. "I don't think he and I would agree about everything, but he acts like a man with principles."

Vincent was encouraged by her description of Senator Brownell. Principles were the key thing. One could negotiate with a man with principles. If a man had things that were important enough to be principles, that meant he also had things that were unimportant enough that he would make concessions on them. And in this gray area of concessions to one another, Dr. Foster and Senator Brownell might find room enough to say what they needed to say but still have space to listen. He would sound the senator out, he resolved. And if Brownell was the right man, he would hire a public relations firm and set a date for a hearing.

"You're a lucky lady. You may be the only Pakistani alive who's heard an American apologize."

Sharrah mulled over this. "Is it that rare? He was comfortable doing it. He was troubled to have to do it, but not hesitant to do so."

Vincent nodded. "It's rare in my experience. But maybe I'm mistaken. I've been wrong in my stereotypes before."

Rosie walked down Buffalo Street in the afternoon. The steep slope pushed her along, and Chocolate tugged on the leash. Between the two forces she felt as light as a feather, and this added to her sense of freedom. This was the first time David had allowed her to walk Chocolate alone. For patient weeks before now, he had walked with her each time she went out with Chocolate. He might, she considered, have been willing to let her go alone sooner if she had reacted differently to the leash.

The leash and collar had seemed absurd when her foster father put them on the dog. After all, Chocolate belonged to himself. Hanging tags of metal around his neck to proclaim ownership was just rude. Chocolate had chosen to come to their house, and he would choose when to leave. At first she wanted no part of the leash, and every chance she got, she would unclip it and Chocolate would scamper off. This made the man upset, which was even stranger and more childish the more times it occurred because Chocolate *always* came back. Rosie had thought a few repetitions of this would suffice to illustrate to him the true nature of his relationship to the dog, but he just hadn't learned. She let herself roll her eyes at the memory because no one else on the street was close enough to see her be rude.

She had tested the theory that the leash being attached to the dog was the important part of leash custom by simply dropping the leash when he handed it to her. Again, however, her foster father had grown frustrated and scolded her. So she had first concluded that he was fixated on control, possession, and ownership of Chocolate. On one afternoon the week before, she had just felt she had enough, and partway down Buffalo Street she had stamped her feet, refused to go another step treating the dog like this, and thrown herself onto a bench.

After a few moments of impasse, David had started to explain things. First he said that Chocolate had to stay on the leash so that he didn't run into the street and get hit by a car. *That* was a bald-faced "rationalization" if she'd ever heard one. Chocolate had grown up, and even covered the miles between the park at which they'd found him and their home, without getting hit by a car. Why would he run in front of a car now? Even now, as they walked together, Chocolate showed no interest in the street. He acted as if anything in it were not even there. If a dog appeared on the other side of the street for him to look at, he behaved as if the road formed a glass wall. He would look at the dog, sniff, listen to the other dog's barks, but not take a step toward the street.

She had continued her passive resistance, sitting on the bench beside the sidewalk and pouting, until David had elaborated a better reason. There was a law, he explained, that dogs had to be on leashes. If Chocolate didn't have a leash, and that leash didn't stay attached to the person, people called "animal control" would come and take Chocolate away. He explained that he knew dogs ought to be free, and that he had often let the other dog he had, long ago, off his leash. But he insisted that it couldn't be done in the city because of the law.

She had examined this idea. If by putting the leash on, Chocolate was allowed to be closer to free than he would be if the "animal control" people came and took him away, then the leash *was* a way to improve his condition. But this did not explain *why* animal control would come and take him away, or *why* the law existed at all. She had finished the walk, and then made use of LIDIA to approach him with these questions. That was when he had told her the most breathtakingly bizarre story of all, one which said far more about the people of this kingdom than anything else she had read or deduced. One of the drawbacks of the LIDIA computer, she had found, was that the discussions it enabled revealed how many of David's strange behaviors had no logical reason behind them.

According to her foster father, the leash law was based on what could only be described as a myth known as "liability." According to this myth, things only happened when people did or failed to do them. An even stranger concept was

366

that every piece of land, and every animal in it, was owned by a human. Anything that an animal did, or that happened on a piece of land, was thus the responsibility of the person who "owned" the land or the animal. If an animal did something that a person didn't like, or something happened on "someone else's" land that a visitor to it didn't like, the upset person would sue the "owner" of the animal or land. As a result, the owner would have to pay money. For example, if Rosie herself dropped the leash, and Chocolate ran off and bit someone, David would have to pay, because he "owned," or was "responsible for," both her and Chocolate. She had been shocked to learn through this conversation that the man now "owned" her until she was eighteen years old. If she "belonged" to any third party, she belonged to Nanny, but she had always felt as though she owned herself. She was sure this was what God and Gabriel thought too.

Rosie had never heard a more logic-defying or atheistic idea in her life. Pretending that people caused everything to happen denied God's role in the world. For example, the gorges throughout the city of Ithaca had been there when the town had been settled, she had read. Who did people in this kingdom suppose had "caused" these gorges to be? What poor person had been chosen to be liable if someone fell or jumped into one, and why? Likewise, she had read in the Ithaca Times that there were deer which ran in the streets and were sometimes hit by cars. Who owned the deer? Could someone come forward and sue for the deer and get money for the deer to go to the doctor? That would be nice for the deer, she supposed. But if the accident seemed like the "deer's fault" (as if deer wanted to wreck cars with their bodies), who got sued for owning the deer that caused the wreck? It seemed silly to just not be able to admit that some things happen that no one intends, and some things belonged to no one. Animals and people were obvious categories of things that weren't ownable.

Still, the myth at least explained David's attachment to the leash, and his insistence that she use it without fail. She understood that his money was not unlimited, and since it was what they used to eat and travel, it made sense to conserve it by following the strange rules rather than give it away by flouting them. So now she used the leash, and her choice to compromise had made a positive difference for both her and Chocolate. Any time she didn't want to be in the house, she could just put Chocolate on his leash and walk out, whereas before her foster father always refused to let her walk around alone. And Chocolate no longer had to wait to poop until the man was rested and ready to walk.

Buffalo Street had leveled out as she had walked and daydreamed, and Rosie came to DeWitt City Park. It was crowded with people and signs saying "Occupy Ithaca," and "Bring Home the Disappeared." She wanted to talk to the people with the signs. Ithaca hardly seemed empty, but rather, well occupied by the people who lived there. Was there an empty part to the city somewhere that these people wanted to occupy and live in? Curiosity tugged her toward the people and their signs. But David had explicitly said she was not to talk to them, or any "dirty hippies," whatever those were.

She also wanted to continue down Buffalo Street, deeper into the city. She was sure that somewhere down the street, perhaps just out of sight, were the buffalo for which the street was named. Maybe it was a pen of live buffalo, or perhaps just a statue of one creature. But as she had promised to avoid dirty hippies, she had promised to walk no further than this park. So, after staring down the street for a while, looking for a clue as to the buffalo's whereabouts, she turned herself around and began to walk back toward David's house. The way to defeat temptation, she knew, was to avoid it.

She thought of the buffalo that lived along the street somewhere and the problem of ownership and liability. Who owned the buffalo, if there were any?

367

And how did "animal control" deal with the enormous beasts if they misbehaved?

She had an epiphany as Chocolate paid his fifth fire hydrant a visit. The role of "animal control" people, it occurred to her, was not just to take away animals from people who didn't control them. It was also to cover up the gaping hole in the myth of liability by snatching away and killing animals that didn't agree to live with people and be owned. David owned her now. What would happen to her, she wondered, if she didn't agree to be owned? Would "kid control" come and snatch her? Would someone sue David? Would she be killed?

She decided not to ponder these unpleasant questions. She didn't know the answer, and trying to deduce the rules that might be applied to her from a system of such nonsensical reasoning was a fool's errand. Her conclusions could only be wrong. So instead she enjoyed watching people and Chocolate's companionship. He smelled like satisfaction at the moment, which resonated with how she felt. The day was as perfect as only God could make things. Sunlight warmed her skin. Beautiful new red and purple leaves ornamented the green trees or even lay on the sidewalk for her to pick up and examine. And in the distance she could hear the bells of the ice cream truck which would, later that afternoon, even drive onto DeWitt Terrace.

Once she had started up the slope of the hill again, a wet breeze reached her over the rooftops of the lower city. Then Chocolate stopped and raised his nose to smell. She sniffed too. On the breeze, she could smell fried potatoes, roast apples, rain, car exhaust, and spilled liquor. She guessed the breeze was coming to her from off the area called the Commons, which had many restaurants. But a second later she smelled what had Chocolate's attention. It was a musky smell, strong and organic, definitely an animal. The animal had to be close because the smell was coming from downwind. Chocolate began tugging on the leash and, despite the fact that they were headed uphill, she began to run so as to give Chocolate the slack he needed to discover the animal.

Chocolate veered left and dashed off into the tall grass and overgrown forsythia at the corner of a side street. Rosie at once began to drag on the leash, reluctant to plunge at speed into the grass when she could not see where she was putting her feet. Together, at half speed, they came under the spreading branches of a colorful grand maple and saw what they smelled.

At the base of the tree, trying very hard to look like the rock beside it, was a small gray creature with beady eyes. As they stepped closer, it grunted, and rolled its face into the space between the rock and the tree trunk. The movement turned the animal's back from undifferentiated grayness into a phalanx of spines.

"Ho! Histriko!" she recoiled in alarm. Though the animal was much smaller and had different colors than the porcupines she had seen inside the laboratory grounds, the wall of quills it presented left no mistake as to its pedigree. Rosie recalled sitting with her brother Lionel as a nurse had been forced to pull some quills all the way *through* her brother's fingers since they were barbed and would not travel backwards and out. Spectacular amounts of blood had flowed, such that other children had begun to gather and stare and had to be shooed away. Lionel had cried horribly, and all Rosie could do was clench his other hand and hug him. She was not about to repeat her brother's experience. She felt a safer distance would be one or two steps further from the animal.

Chocolate, however, had the idea that closer inspection was due. She stepped one way, and he tugged in the other. In a gesture that surprised both her and the dog, she yanked on the leash.

The force of the jerk lifted Chocolate off of his scrabbling front paws and turned him around. The dog's reproachful look, as well as her own dismay at the gesture, made her feel terrible. But she was not about to let Chocolate fill his nose

368

with quills. She tugged some more, then put her hips into it and pulled, and the dog reluctantly left the animal behind. She stopped a few paces away, and glanced back in time to see the porcupine waddle into the shady garden of the nearest house. She contemplated going to the front door and warning the occupants they had a porcupine, but the thought of trying to explain the situation with hand gestures and stuttering dissuaded her. She prayed that no pain emerged from the interaction between porcupine and people, and with another tug on the leash, started back uphill toward Dewitt Terrace.

In a moment Chocolate was walking, snuffling, and wagging his tail in excitement at this or that smell as if nothing had happened, but Rosie felt wretched. Not just because she made horrible use of the leash, but for all her scolding of David for trying to control the dog with the leash, she had just done so as well. It was irony, she concluded, and irony was a sure sign of a divine hand at work. God had been trying to show her she was being smug, judgmental, and self-assured with David. *"Message received,"* she acknowledged to the God in the world around her.

As she mulled her use of the leash, she had another epiphany. The leash was not just an instrument of control, but a kind of language. Chocolate had pulled on the leash to say they needed to run to see the porcupine, and she had pulled it to say he should beware of that animal. The leash had been first a means of communication, and only secondarily a means of control. In contrast, *people* always waited for her to *talk*, and were dissatisfied when she didn't, as if there were no other way to communicate.

She saw in this God's wisdom in sending Chocolate as her friend. First, like her, Chocolate could smell things and didn't think smelling was weird or rude. And like her, he wanted to touch things, rather than just stare at things without touching like David or Faith. But most importantly, he didn't care that she didn't talk, or if she used a funny language. He was happy just to use the language of the leash.

She took a moment to be thankful for Chocolate. When they at last came to their house, instead of going inside, she sat down on the long, cool, concrete steps under the great maples. Chocolate sat beside her, and licked her. She unsnapped the leash and let him sit. After a few moments, she reached over and picked up one of the waiting green felt-covered balls, and threw it. He bounded away and fetched it. She threw it again. She decided she would make up for her yank on the leash with a bit of this game he never tired of.

Chocolate smelled the rain before she did and abandoned the ball game to sit under the porch, where he stared at her expectantly. Soon, she smelled it, too, but she felt no need to move. Whenever it rained David made her go inside, so she had never properly experienced a rainstorm in this new kingdom. She listened to the hiss and patter of the raindrops, and the rumble of afternoon thunder, as the storm came up the hill. She looked up. The canopy of maple leaves above her, which earlier in the summer would not let one drop through for five minutes, now had holes in it as well as new colors. A colder rain than she had expected started falling onto her face and shoulders. But she remained sitting, fascinated by this kaleidoscope of swaying green and colored leaves interspersed with patches of purple rain clouds and blue sky.

"Thank you," she prayed again to God, both for this display, and for his afternoon lesson in humility. As the rain soaked her shirt and chilled her legs, she wondered how to apologize to David for all the challenges she had posed him. It wasn't that she wasn't right, most of the time, but her foster father had dealt with a lot, for much of the time without her even being able to explain herself.

She heard a porch window come open behind her. "Jeeper's whiskers, girl, get out of the rain!" her foster father called out. Despite the moment of gratitude to him she had just had, she felt her eyes roll again up toward heaven. She took a deep breath, stood, and smiled to think about the many forms of love.

Chapter 29

The Sweet Fruit of Paradise

Udo walked back with Sharrah to her apartment after their date. It had been a delightful meal. They had gone to a cafe set in the cellar of an old government building in Zurich. It served what the writer had assured her was some of the most traditional Swiss food available. What she had ordered had turned out to be three courses of melted cheese baths with different items to swirl in it with long forks. He had also chosen a white wine from Germany that was excellent. She suspected she was no judge of wine, having had so little wine in her life, but this wine she had liked better than the others. Or it could be that the man's company and enthusiasm had made it better.

Still it was clear that the writer, despite his travels to many countries in Europe as a journalist, had a narrow view of the world. Other countries to him were nothing more than different collections of airports, rail stations, languages, and restaurants. He assumed that everyone was like him, which was charming, humanistic, and safe within Europe, but it meant he was puzzled, or even uncomprehending, when she tried to explain customs of Pakistan and things she had noticed about Europeans.

He had also refrained from smoking all night. She appreciated that. She considered as they walked through the streets what she should do. She felt relaxed, energetic, and even lustful, and the writer's slender frame, longish hair, and laugh made him look good to her now. But the last man she had lain with was a British exchange student a couple of weeks before the Talibani putsch in Pakistan. She knew that Europeans were casual, and often direct, about sex, but Udo was older than her other lovers, and also Swiss and not British, so she hesitated to apply her experiences to him.

When they finally came to the stoop of the office row house, she stopped at the few steps up to door of Dr. Foster's office and her apartment, stepping around the "*Zuercher Zeitung*" bicycle the newspaperman had chained to the handrail.

"Thank you so much," she said. "I would never have expected a fancy restaurant beneath a government building. I guess I look for sidewalk cafe tables when I search for a restaurant."

Udo shrugged. "I've lived in Zurich my whole life, but the town still surprises me from time to time. I'll share what I know." He smiled at her, his hair and chubby cheeks adding abundant charm.

He kept smiling, but said nothing helpful. She fumbled for something to say, and, discovering she didn't know what she wanted to say, fumbled again to sort out her feelings.

On the one hand, she was ashamed to be standing on her doorstep, alone, contemplating bringing indoors a man whom she had only recently met, and by any decent standard, had barely courted her.

On the other hand, he was charming, he was funny, and she was enjoying the evening and didn't want it to end yet, which alone could be enough reason to invite him in.

And she felt desire. She was surprised to find that she felt so much desire, since day to day she didn't feel it at all. But now that Udo was here, on her doorstep, she did feel the need, clearly and explicitly.

She let go of her doubts and said what she wanted to say. "Would you like to come in? Get your bags and see the 'forbidden apartment?'" He laughed at her joke, a bit shyly, and by way of an answer stepped up to the bottom of the stairs.

"Sure, if you are comfortable with this. May I smoke before I go in?"

Sharrah felt lust turn to dismay. There was no way she could kiss him if he was going to smoke. She didn't know what tobacco addiction was like, but she supposed after as much restraint as he'd shown for the evening, he desperately wanted to smoke.

She felt disappointment pool in her stomach. But then an idea came. She would test the strength of his addiction. She blushed already as she decided to do it.

"Relax," she thought. "This is the west. No one is watching, and no one would care if they were. This night belongs to me and my heart, not to disapproving old men and the sharia."

She stepped up onto the second step to better equalize her height to Udo's. "If you must smoke, do so. But before you do..." And she pulled him close and reached up with her lips.

As she did so, she felt her burst of confidence crumble, and she couldn't complete this kiss. What if this is not what he wanted? What if she was being too forward, even for the west? What if he did not even desire her?

The man's lips on hers soon banished all her worries. They kissed for a long time, and she savored the smells and sensations, of white wine, of a chocolate desert, and even the faint and somehow now less offensive smell of tobacco on his clothes. As they kissed, however, his hands slid from her neck, to her shoulders, and then to her back... Her pleasure stopped.

Sharrah stepped backward, and within a second had replaced her confused look with what she hoped was decisiveness. "What did I feel? Why did I stop?" she wondered.

Udo, however, did not look dismayed. She couldn't say what he was feeling, but his look was anything but that of one who felt put off. He stepped forward again, but she raised a hand to stop him.

"Since I can't bear to kiss men who have just smoked, I wanted that," she said with a grin. She began fishing for her keys in her jacket pocket, found them, and walked up the stairs, leaving the writer behind her at the bottom step. "Go ahead and smoke now, if that's what will satisfy you," she sighed. "I know how important it is to some people."

She heard him come up behind her as she slid her key into the lock. He pressed up against her. "Only a fool would choose tobacco when presented with such a sweet alternative," he said. At this, she felt his hand on the small of her back again, and she flinched away instinctively. She opened the door and stepped inside the stairwell, putting space between them, disarmed the alarm, and then started work on her apartment door.

Udo stepped into the stairwell too, and she saw his fair skin was flushed pink at the cheeks. Her face felt hot and she was sure she was similarly flushed. She only hoped it didn't look as obvious on her as it did on him. To her dismay, she recalled that years in a burqa and followed by two years in an office she rarely left had made her pale enough to show it easily. But then, she supposed her kiss had been unambiguous enough that a flush on her face would hardly be giving her intent away.

Sharrah worked her key into her apartment lock but fumbled the attempt as the man began kissing the side of her neck. She moaned and trembled, but then

372

remembered the security camera in the stairwell behind her, which would be recording as long as it sensed heat in the stairwell. And she suspected the two of them were creating more than enough heat. It was usually she who reviewed the security recording files, but she'd hate for Dr. Foster to take an interest at an awkward time. She focused though the pleasure she was feeling and turned the lock successfully.

She popped her door open and motioned Udo in, shutting the door behind him. They both blinked for a moment as the motion-sensing lights flickered on, and then her guest took in the apartment.

The furnishings of her apartment were not Pakistani, even though a Pakistani style was precisely the way she had furnished her employer's office. For her own space, she had made a choice to go for a European furniture style, and she had chosen one called "Bauhaus." It had clean, curvy lines and forms that suggested the purpose of the furniture. Bauhaus items were also expensive, so her apartment was sparely furnished as yet.

She supposed Bauhaus put European men at ease, because after spying the chairs, Udo sat on one in precisely the opposite way that its curves would suggest one ought to. Sharrah smirked and considered sitting down with him to resume their kiss, but remembered to play the hostess.

"Would you like a cup of coffee? Tea?"

The man's jaw hung slack as he admired some of her wall art, a series of prints by Hassan Musa. "A glass of water would be fine."

"Okay," she tossed him a tilted smile as she went to her kitchen. He seemed too struck by the art to notice.

She brought water with a touch of lemon juice in a curvy glass that echoed the lines of the furniture. The man appreciated the shape of the glass before drinking, and once he had drunk, put the glass down on a side table. She sipped from her own matching glass as she watched him, and then, giving in to an impulse, walked over to his seat. She put down her glass beside his, and then slid it over until the curves of both glasses matched and nestled into each other. She looked at Udo significantly, and a moment later joined him in his abuse of the furniture design by straddling the width of the chair. In a moment, she locked both her hands into the collar of his jacket and kissed him. One of his hands fell to her neck, and another reached into the crook of her knee and pulled her leg up, drawing their hips close together.

"This is more like it," she thought, "This is mutual desire, openly expressed. This is how it should be." She moved one hand down to his belt and took a good grip. She felt the leather fold in her grip, and caressed the metal studs in it with her thumb.

Udo chose that moment, however, to withdraw. He moved the hand from her neck to her shoulder and pushed her back ever so lightly. Even this tiny movement, though, was enough to pop her surge of confidence.

"What is it?" she asked, dismayed.

"You're amazing. But I think once you get moving, you won't stop. And I'm not in a hurry."

Sharrah pulled away from him the rest of the way. Examining her feelings, she shifted and sat next to him, hip to hip. The position did not feel sexual, but somehow still intimate. It reminded her, for a moment, of sitting beside her friend Durnave.

"That's okay, you don't have to be." She let a long, cleansing breath out. "But I like the way you touch me." She half expected the man to shrink away, but he did not. She was amazed that she could be so direct and in control. In Pakistan, lovemaking and courtship were a game of flourish, deception, and teasing that

373

lead only to a marriage before sex. Udo had neither expectation.

"How would you like me to touch you?" he countered.

"Whatever way you like, I guess. Or not at all if you don't like. However your desire leads you. Part of what I like so much is to see what desire causes you to do."

The writer paused. "This is awkward."

"Am I being rude? Making you feel bad?" Sharrah checked herself. Was it possible that she was too forward for western men?

"No, it's that...normally women sort of slide into this. Emotion leads you to it, or alcohol and hormones."

She smirked. "I'd be more desirable if I were drunk?"

"No, not exactly."

"I'd be more desirable if *you* were drunk?" She raised an eyebrow at him. She didn't know how her guest meant what he was saying, but she felt sure she'd be offended if he answered "yes" to that question.

"No, no, I find you attractive enough to desire you stone sober, even in the first moment I met you."

They sat side by side on the chair in silence and contemplated their awkwardness. Then Ms. Bassi hatched her plan.

"I'll tell you what. We'll play a game, then. I have some western clothes I have bought, but I am too afraid to wear them because once I got them home they struck me as too immodest to go to work in. Work is all I do."

"Okay," Udo said.

"I'll go put them on, and you give me your opinion of them. And if I'm pretty enough, you will find yourself in the mood to touch me. And if you do not, I will still have your opinion of the dresses, and you will have been useful."

"I'm a poor judge of fashion," he protested. And her glance at his worn leather coat, scarf, and faded blue jeans suggested he was being honest. "But okay."

"Wait here," Sharrah said. She stood, crossed the room, and pushed open her bedroom door. She left it open as she began taking off her clothes, being sure to toss this or that piece into Udo's line of sight. She turned to her closet and regarded what she had hanging there.

She had about half a dozen black, navy blue, or gray skirts and jackets or pants and jacket combinations. She also had a selection of scarves, and a few western ties. These she had all worn to work and they had occasioned no comment from Dr. Foster.

She had another skirt/jacket combination which, while the sales girl had said it was appropriate for the workplace, the doctor had suggested was not the "best match" for his office. It was a jacket with a much wider V in the front, a black shirt with thin straps that held things only as high as her breasts, and a skirt that came up over her knees, with no stockings. She started tugging this on, and slid into the high-heeled shoes that had come with it.

She walked out, keeping one hand on her hip as she had seen models do in movies. Udo appraised the dress, sipping from his glass of water.

"Nice. A cocktail dress."

Sharrah tilted her head at him. "Is it sexy?"

"*Sehr,*" he said definitively.

"The saleswoman said this was appropriate for business meetings, but Dr. Foster did not like it."

"Umm, I agree with the Doctor. Whether that would be appropriate for a meeting would depend on whether you were to be stared at and admired so people could be jealous of the doctor, or if you were going to say something and

374

participate. Because people might desire you while you wore it, but they would not take you seriously in it. I would save it for a party or evening occasion the doctor was invited to. It would be most appropriate then."

Sharrah reflected on what he said. "Thank you, that does help me." She walked out, trying to show some thigh as she left, and searched her closet again.

"I bought this dress because I love it, it was so beautiful. But the skirt is so tight at the knees I can't walk in it. And each time I think about wearing it out I stop at the door because I imagine men thinking evil thoughts about me."

"Let's see it," said Udo. "Maybe I'll think evil thoughts, too."

She put it on. It was a gold silk dress, long and slender, that hung to cover her ankles but was slit on the sides up to her knee. It had bell cuffed sleeves and a high, smooth collar like she had seen Chinese and Japanese royalty wear in movies, and it was embroidered all over with white birds with red tufts on their heads. The saleswoman had said it was Korean. She knew nothing about Korea, but assumed it was like China.

She let her hair down, and picked up the gold silk flower ornament that had come with it and tied it into her hair. It took a while, but, looking in the mirror, she was pleased with it.

The man's response was what she had hoped for. His jaw went slack, and then he laughed and shook his head.

"I can't believe I'm in the apartment of a woman this beautiful," he said. She smirked at him.

"Do you want to touch me now?"

"Yes!" said Udo, putting down his glass as if he were about to stand.

"Too bad," she said, with a careless toss of her hair. "I've got another thing to try on."

Despite her refusal, she heard him get up and follow her to her bedroom. She rounded on him once she saw him in her bedroom mirror.

"No, I don't want you to see me naked."

Puzzlement overtook her suitor. "Isn't that part of a romp?"

"Being naked is part of a romp. Being seen naked isn't. This is what light switches are for."

He closed with her and wrapped his arms around her. As they embraced, he slid a hand over her back. She felt it slide along the silk, then over her scars. She was suddenly self-conscious. When she felt his hands starting on the buttons in the small of her back, she clapped her hands to turn off the light.

With the light off, her self-consciousness eased. She began kissing him, the tongue kissing she had learned from British boys, and Udo held her tight. She backed up toward her bed, and they fell onto it. She blew his tumbling hair out of her face and laughed.

As her dress started to come off, though, he stopped again and seemed uncomfortable.

"What is it?" she bridled.

"I...don't mean to be rude, but I can feel these ridges along your back. Are they scars?"

Sharrah felt her heart skip a beat. She barely dared to breathe. He'd found them so quickly. And now there was no running from the truth. "Yes, they are."

"They're...They're huge. There are so many." She felt Udo trace them with his hands, along her bare back and then over the silk of the dress.

"Don't look at them. They are so ugly. Imagine me as you saw me, with the dress on." She felt desperate not to let this moment to slip away.

The journalist, however, could not drop the line of questioning. "What happened? Was it a car accident? A motorcycle accident?"

Sharrah exhaled slowly and sought patience. She had feared the scars would make her unattractive. Instead they had made the man curious and upset. She supposed there was no way she could have anticipated this. Udo was the first man to feel them.

"No, I don't want to talk about it," she said.

At this, he stepped back, and their passionate embrace was broken.

"Let me see," he said.

"They are ugly. They make me self-conscious," she protested.

"I want to see them," he insisted.

Ms. Bassi paused for a moment. She had lost her lustful mood. Udo's persistence was rude and bizarre. She had been going to show him the beautiful parts of her, but here he was focused on the ugliest. Nonetheless, here they were.

"I suppose I can get his opinion of scars. Like the dresses." She unsnapped things, let her dress drop all the way to the floor, and turned her back to Udo. Then she clapped her hands twice, and the full lighting in the room came back on. She watched Udo's reaction in the mirrored doors of her closet.

She knew how her scars looked, or thought she did. She could only catch glimpses of them in mirrors. They were purple, thick, and often had flaking skin on them.

"Mein Gott," he said. "Do they hurt?"

"They are mostly numb, but they itch now and then. Sometimes they itch so much I'll take my clothes off and rub my back on a wall, or a rug," she said.

She felt a vague pressure trace a line on her back. She guessed he was touching one of the scars, and then saw in the mirror that he had extended a hand to her back.

"How did you get these?" The inevitable question arrived.

She hadn't wanted to talk about it. She wasn't a museum, she was a woman! But he had already asked the question, and her passion was already cooled.

"I was whipped. As punishment," she said.

He sat down heavily on her bed, eyes focused on the wall. *"Barbaren,"* she heard him condemn.

"The wounds were not the worst part. The whip they used was dirty, it carried a disease. I was sick for many days, and there were no antibiotics, so I had these scars. They were the worst days of my life. I prayed to die. Had I not had a good friend with me, I would have."

"Who did this to you?"

"My brothers," she answered matter-of-factly. She faced him, naked except for her shoes and the dress around one ankle. She stepped out of it. From the look on his face, she could tell a romp was the last thing on his mind, now, too.

"So, you have satisfied your curiosity, now?" While he worked on a reply, she knelt and unbuckled her shoes. "The Taliban are not only news reports to you any more, are they?" She reached for her bathrobe, tied it on, and slid her toes into her waiting slippers.

"How would a brother whip a sister like this?"

"My eldest brother was Taliban. And if he hadn't done it, to show the mullahs he could control me, the Taliban would have killed me. Or so he said. And I believe him, because the Taliban killed other women who did the same things I did. In my brother's twisted way, I suppose it was an act of love."

"What did you do?"

"I taught sex education, sex disease prevention, breast cancer self-examination, and birth control," she explained. "The Taliban had banned it, but I taught it anyway. Dr. Foster sent me the materials, and the birth control devices and supplies. Eventually, he smuggled me out the way he smuggled these things in."

Udo said nothing. His eyes were on a point on the bedroom wall. "The Taliban must be evil, evil men."

"No more or less evil then western armies and horrible things they do," rebutted Sharrah, surprised to be defending the Taliban. "When western drones do airstrikes on weddings and schools to kill a handful of Hamas or al-Qaeda fighters, that is not brutality?" she challenged.

When the westerner stammered, she saw her opportunity to drive her point home. "Yes, the scars are ugly. They remind me of how my own brother betrayed our family, and our democracy, a democracy built from blood and labor and the best intentions of millions. The scars break my heart. I don't like to talk about them. I am careful to pick clothes which cover my back and thighs. I was hoping you would not notice them.

"But now that you have seen the scars of one side of the war, go seek out the scars of the other side. Do not choose sides so easily. War savages everyone."

Udo gave her a strange and searching look. "They make you beautiful."

The statement stunned her. "You're mad," she decided.

"I know many beautiful women. I've even known some I think were brave, and withstood some awful things. But I know only one woman who withstood such things for the sake of other women. Other people. Those scars spell courage in the language of the heart. You can cover them, but I will remember them, and they will make you more beautiful no matter what you wear over them."

Sharrah said nothing. She didn't know what to say. She didn't feel brave. The women who had stayed in Pakistan with their children, their good husbands or bad ones, they were brave. In contrast, she had run from danger, and she felt her cowardice and shame every time she read of the Taliban's abuses in Pakistan. Whenever she reflected on it, she came to the conclusion that she ought to have died for her beliefs, and that her current life of luxury had been ill gained by her lack of character.

"Stop talking. You have no idea what you're saying." She turned to her mirror, saw past her tubby and scarred reflection playing dress-up in these fancy clothes, and recalled the only picture she had seen that made her look beautiful. It was one of her as young girl with a spray of jasmine flowers in her hair. And that child was long gone.

She heard Udo stand up behind her, and felt his hands on her. She shook them off. "I'm no longer in the mood for this. I'm sorry."

"I'm not in the mood for this, either," said Udo. "But I'll make you another offer."

"I'm listening."

"Your scars are dry. That may be why they itch so much. I'll put lotion on them."

Sharrah stopped to consider. Her first reaction was to reject the idea, but after a moment, she thought it sounded pleasant.

"On my stove I have almond oil. It will smell nice. Bring that." With that she removed her bathrobe and lay face down on her bed, scooping her long hair carefully off her back.

Her suitor left, clattered around in her kitchen, and reappeared with a small green bottle.

"I cannot read the label," he apologized, "but this smells like almonds."

She sniffed the air and caught a whiff of almonds. "That is the correct bottle. The language on the bottle is Urdu, the official language of Pakistan before the Taliban. Now the official language is Arabic, the language of the Koran."

"Will I run it out?" said Udo, looking at the small bottle. "There's not much here. Maybe you should save it for cooking."

"Use it," she insisted. "The smell reminds me of something."

The writer was good to his word, and better. He worked the oil into her scars, and the itching, which she had learned to ignore, all but vanished. Then he took handfuls of the oil and began rubbing her shoulders, stretching her muscles, and sliding his hands sensually along her back.

After many sighs, she fell into a happy warm sleep.

Despite her happy start, that night Sharrah returned in her dreams to the whipping.

Sharrah was cleaning up from a woman's circle meeting in the family compound. She had just done her 'basic sex' class. It focused on teaching marriageable or newly married girls the outward signs and other symptoms of common venereal diseases, how to use condoms, and alternative sex acts women might offer so as to avoid becoming pregnant or sick. With other groups this conversation had gotten awkward at times, but with this group of young women from her neighborhood, the conversation had been relaxed and even bawdy.

It had been nice to have the house full. With her parents gone, her brothers living at militia and Taliban quarters throughout the city, and her sister married, she was the only one who still lived here. After her last encounter the Taliban's local morality patrol made it clear she was being watched and was not free to travel as she wished, so she had begun inviting women in need of her services and advice into the compound. It kept her out of sight of the mullahs and made constructive use of the space. She knew her mother and father would have approved.

She gathered up some stray saucers and spoons and began rinsing them in the sink and stacking them in the drying rack. Then she rolled up her teaching flip charts and posters, slid them into their cardboard tubes, collapsed her easels, and replaced all of it in hiding places in wardrobes or under her parents' old bed in their unused bedroom. She reset cushions on the sofas and carpets, and pushed the television cart back into the corner that had held the easel.

Sharrah was drying cups and saucers when a knock came at the door. She heard her name called, and the voice sounded familiar.

"Who is it?" She called.

"Fahad," she heard the answer. It was her eldest brother. "Open the door. We have family business."

She opened the door and welcomed her brother formally. After all, she could not refuse him. She was not married, and under the Taliban law, her eldest living male relative was both her chaperone and the holder of all her property.

He barely returned the greeting and walked over to the couch, jaw tense. Behind him she saw her youngest brother, Danial, whom she'd often babysat when he was younger. Danial was her favorite. He looked nervous, and his aversion of his eyes told her that this visit from Fahad was not for happy reasons.

"May I bring you tea, brother?" She asked Fahad in the high register of Urdu. Fahad was vain, she knew, and she figured obeisance was the best way to take the edge off of whatever harm he had come to do.

"Yes, bring me tea. But dispense with the court and camp. You'll curse me before I leave here, else I have not done my job."

She bowed and went to get some of the hot tea she had saved from the tea party. She set it back on the gas burner until it steamed, and carried it on a tray to her brothers. In the living area, she decanted it into the family china cups and stood while her brothers drank.

"It's good," said Danial.

"Indeed it is," agreed Fahad. "You have many skills that will make you a good wife, if anyone will have you at your age and with your western taint."

Sharrah felt her backbone begin to stiffen, and knew she was headed for trouble. "That 'taint' is called education. I respect you, and I welcome you in the house of our father as you are my sponsor. But I am not tainted."

Fahad motioned the tea tray away. "Take it away and come sit. I don't have much to say, but I know you will have so much back talk it would be cruel to make you stand until we are done. I will show you grace before I teach you the place you have forgotten."

She did as she was told, though her heart was roaring in anger. Fahad had gone from obnoxious to insufferable as he advanced within the Taliban. She wanted to say something that would project her disgust with him, and with his forsaking of everything their parents had stood for.

She sat in a padded chair across from him, gathering up her skirt as she did so.

"When they came for father, and for you, I told you that if you wanted to live, you would have to do what I say. The only reason you are not already dead, or a mullah's junior-most wife, is because I vouched for you, that you could be reformed."

Sharrah nodded. "I recall this."

"Your actions make a mockery of my guardianship. Still, you travel alone to visit women and advise them to try sinful western practices and medicine."

"Reproductive health counseling is not sinful, Fahad, except for the narrowest of minds. Teaching women to identify venereal diseases on their husbands is not against the Koran. And if so many men were not whore-mongers or adulterers, women wouldn't need to know these things."

Fahad paid no mind to her logic, as if she had said "you're right, big brother, punish me." He focused instead on what he had wanted to hear. "So you do not deny teaching these things?"

"I do not. You would have these women sick?"

Fahad rejoined quickly. "No, I would *not* want these women sick. But what I do not want more is to watch you hung at the soccer stadium, which is what would be happening to you tonight had I not intervened on your behalf. Men who come home with these diseases have lost the true teaching and need the instruction and leadership of the Taliban. Their sin is no trifle. But you teaching women to forget their place, and not to submit as the Sharia dictates a woman should, is no trifle either. And the mullahs will not ignore it."

Sharrah glared at him. "You exaggerate for the sake of taking me to task. I don't teach them not to submit, except as a last resort. We talk about alternatives they can use to please the men and protect themselves."

Fahad reacted as though she had missed the point. "You do not believe me? You do not believe the mullahs are angered? Then hold your meeting again next week. See how many of the women you taught tonight are dead by then. See how many others are too afraid to come. You will sip tea alone. You and your flip charts."

She felt her blood freeze at the mention of flip charts. She wondered if her teaching had been overheard through a window on the street. She was always careful to run both the radio and the TV and close the window shutters.

Fahad continued. "I am here, instead of the morality police, because I made a promise to the mullahs that I would bring you to heel. I told them it was my responsibility to my family and the memory of my pious mother."

Sharrah burst out in anger. "Mother died because of you! It broke her heart when they took father, and it broke it twice that you helped them!"

Fahad was nonplussed. "Her devotion to my father despite his western ways shows that she was a much better Muslim than he ever was. If he hadn't spent his career shutting down every madrasah he could find like some panting western lackey he wouldn't have visited death upon his family. May Allah smile upon our mother."

She clenched her fists at his words, but resolved to stop contradicting him. Arguing would prolong this nonsense.

"So, what do you want me to do?"

Fahad sighed. "Remove your shirt and bra, and hold out your hands."

She gaped at her brother. She would not remove her clothes in front of a man in plain light.

"Never! What outrage is this?" she shouted.

"This is no outrage. This is brotherly love," said Fahad from his seat on the couch.

"It's perversion! We are kin, yet you would see me naked?"

"Perversion? Was it perversion with those British schoolboys? Who never knew you, held no care for our family, and only wanted to run their hands across you? Was that perversion? Or did the perversion start when you gave yourself to them? In any case, your protest of honor is faint, sister. Faint indeed, as a comfort girl to the spoiled brats of the west."

Sharrah's ears burned. She glanced at Danial for some support, but her younger brother looked grave.

"Please, sister, do as he says," her youngest brother said. "This for your own sake."

"Oh, Danial. Not you, too. Not my little bear."

"I only wish to see you live," Danial's answer was sincere and loving, as he had always been to her. The realization chilled her. Her elder brother would do violence to her, her younger would obey him, and both would believe it was best. She was now not sure which of the men frightened her more.

Fahad stood. Danial stood with him.

"Don't touch me! Don't touch me, Fahad!" she shouted at him, standing up and retreating across the living room.

"Shout as loud as you like," Fahad said, stepping toward her. In a blur he had planted a fist in her stomach, bending her double. He then pushed her to the floor.

She wanted to shout more, to scream, but she couldn't catch a breath. Her stomach felt like the fist was still lodged there. Fahad, showing the muscle his time in the militia had put on him, grabbed her arm and dragged her like a sack of rice to a radiator pipe in the corner of the living room. He then hauled her whimpering to her knees, and locked a pair of handcuffs around the pipe to her wrist with Danial's help. Danial unbuttoned her blouse and lifted it off her back, over her head, and onto her arms.

"Danial, don't let him," she pleaded.

"Please, make it quick. Do as he says," Danial implored with equal sincerity. She kicked and lashed out at the both of them and they withdrew. Danial backed away into a tea table, and one of her mother's rare china cups and saucers slid and shattered on the floor.

Sharrah's breath returned. She used it, her only weapon. She hoped the neighbors would hear, and this would shame her brother. "What perversion is this, Fahad? Will you rape your own sister? Is this the law of the Taliban?"

"The law of the Taliban is the Sharia, the Hadith, and the Holy Koran. You will learn to obey all of them," said Fahad. Behind her, she heard something long and sinuous uncoil with a creaking of leather. She twisted on the handcuffs and gaped at the long, brown, coiled whip. The kind used on camels.

"A whip? You'll whip your own sister?"

"Rather than see you hang, yes." Fahad shook the coils out of it. "Turn your back. I don't want to hit your face."

"Hit it! Mark it! Let everyone who sees me know the monster my brother is!" She spat at him. "Let everyone see what the Taliban makes a brother do!"

Fahad gave his order to Danial. "Hold her legs." Danial grabbed her ankles, pulling them out from under her. Stretched between her ankles and the handcuffs, she could no longer twist. Danial rolled her to face the floor and held her feet down.

She screamed before she even heard the crack. The first stroke of whip on her back was like nothing she'd ever felt.

"You monkey!" She cursed Fahad with words she had thought but never dared use. "You're a monkey, now, you do the dances the mullahs teach you!"

Fahad said nothing to this. She cried out despite her resolve with his second stroke.

"Monkey!" she shouted. "You forsake everything to do their whim! Fling more dung on our parents' graves!"

His next lash was harder, and all she could do was wail in reply. "Louder," said Fahad. "Prove to those who listen in the street, in this neighborhood, that I will do what it takes both to honor the law and to protect my family. I do not fear any judgment but Allah's."

With that, he landed the fourth stroke, and Sharrah broke. She cursed herself, but she could do no more than weep. "Monkey Fahad."

There were ten strokes in all, but after the fifth, she scarcely felt them. They were the prolonging of a vicious absurdity. She only knew they were over when she felt Danial release her ankles and leave her lying on the cool tile floor.

Fahad had one last thing to say. "You put me in this position. Each time you anger the mullahs, they will exact a higher price in return for your life. I will pay these prices, because you are my family. But there may come a time when *you* no longer wish to pay these prices. I pray that time is soon. For both of us."

With that, she heard a slap as the whip hit the floor behind her, and her brothers walked out and left her chained to the radiator pipe.

She struggled to get her hands from the cuffs, but their metal edges cut her. She twisted and saw rivulets of her own blood on the floor. The sight brought on new sobs, not of pain, but of fear. She was bleeding! How could she stop it with her hands chained?

"Help!" She screamed. "Help, my neighbors! My brothers have left me chained, and I am bleeding!"

She repeated her pleas, but for a long time, no one came. At some point she either fainted or fell asleep, and when she awoke, she was in the arms of Durnave, one of the other women in the circle that came to her classes.

Durnave was struggling to put a key in the handcuff lock. Her hands were shaking.

"Your brothers left this key with my husband. He came to help you, but returned to send me because you were undressed. The prudish coward." Durnave said.

One question overrode Sharrah's thoughts. She asked it of Durnave even as the woman focused on freeing her. "Oh, they even make my family into monsters. How can I stay? How can I stay in Pakistan?"

"Hush about them. In this moment, think of yourself." Durnave fit the key in the lock, opened the cuff, and Sharrah's left hand began to tingle as full blood flow resumed. She sat up, then gasped in pain as the curve of her spine stretched open the wounds on her back.

Durnave hissed to see what Sharrah could only feel. "We've got to get you to a hospital." The woman nudged her wide-eyed daughter, who was watching and trembling. "Go get hot water, girl. And don't forget this sight. This is what men will do to you when they come to believe they are gods."

The girl scampered off, returning with a plastic mixing bowl of hot water from the teakettle and a first aid kit from under the sink. She left these with her mother and dashed away again.

Durnave swabbed the wounds on her back with the water and studied them. Her neighbor opened the first aid kit, but closed it again without taking anything out. "This is for kitchen cuts. Where do you have cloth? Lots of cloth? We will get blood on it."

"In the kitchen, the cabinet below the cutting board, there is a linen tablecloth. It was my mother's, but it is old and stained already."

Durnave shouted instructions to her daughter, and Sharrah heard the thump of doors and the clatter of china from her kitchen. The girl returned with the tablecloth and a teacup that rattled on its saucer as her hands shook. She handed the tablecloth to her mother, and then passed the teacup to Ms. Bassi. She took it with difficulty since her blouse was still hanging on her arms.

"Thank you," she said, willfully projecting calm. "You are being brave."

The girl said nothing but stared as the older woman drank. Durnave waited for her to finish the cup while she ripped the tablecloth into strips. Then she wadded them up. After Sharrah had put down her teacup amongst the blood smears and china fragments on the tile floor, Durnave packed the cloth into her wounds and wrapped the wadding tight to her body with longer strips.

"I am not in danger, am I?" Sharrah worried after a moment. She knew Durnave had taken many Red Crescent classes on first aid so as to take better care of her four children and late mother-in-law.

"I have done what I can, but you still bleed, and there is much broken skin. We must go. Can you walk?"

She stood up. Her legs and feet were cramped, but she shuffled around until they worked loose, and then raised her arms over her head and shook her blouse and burqa down over her body. She grit her teeth as the cloth dragged over the bandages across her back and legs. She was glad she could not see them.

"Let's go."

It was a couple of miles to the hospital. Durnave got them some help by flagging down a man returning from the market with a wheelbarrow who agreed to push Sharrah to the hospital for a few dinars. Once she arrived, she was taken to the women's emergency room, and Durnave and her daughter waited with her and went with her to the exam room.

The nurses hissed and wailed when they lifted her burqa, but immediately set about to cleaning her wounds. In a moment, a woman doctor was shown into the room. She faced her back to the older woman, and heard the doctor inhale sharply. "Was this done with a whip?"

"Yes," she and Durnave nodded.

The doctor sucked in her breath again. "Was it punishment from the Taliban?"

Durnave said nothing. Perhaps she feared that if she said yes, the doctor would not help them if it were so. So Sharrah answered. "Yes, Doctor. Punishment for teaching contraception and venereal disease prevention."

382

"Oh, you are *that* Bassi. The fools," the old woman growled. She scrubbed her hands at a sink with a harsh yellow soap, and a few moments later, Sharrah began wincing as the woman peeled back some bandages and started prodding her wounds. "Fools to whip a woman for a man's sin."

When the doctor was done with her exam, she stepped into Ms. Bassi's line of vision while the nurses scrubbed the wounds with gauze. "These will take many weeks, even months, to heal. If they were not so wide, so deep, I would stitch them together. But these will have to fill in. They will make large scars. Ugly ones. I can cover them with some liquid plastic bandage, if you can afford this, but this will not last long. You will need to recover them with bandages when it wears off. Change the bandages daily, boil them for ten minutes, and dry them in the sun for two days before re-using them."

"Yes, Ma'am," Sharrah acknowledged, imagining doing these things. They sounded manageable.

But the doctor was not done. "The worst is yet to come. If this is like others I have seen, the whip used was a camel whip. The mullahs and barbarians from the western regions use these whips on camels they know are sick, and then they send them to Karachi for use on women who disobey. If your whip was one of these, in a few days you will have camel or cattle brucellosis. High fevers. Much joint pain. I am out of antibiotics for this. You must...bear it." She drew a heavy sigh and patted the younger woman's hand. "Be strong."

Durnave sat back, aghast. Then she set her face. "You will stay with me. My husband can sleep on the couch for tolerating this Talibani nonsense. You will stay, and rest. We will be well together."

Sharrah looked at Durnave. She had always found the woman blustery and overdramatic, but now she was developing new respect for her.

"Thank you." She embraced her, but Durnave was too careful of her back to return it.

After a receiving a bag of yellowish fluid through an IV, she felt able to walk home. She and Durnave and Durnave's daughter held hands all the way.

"I never want a man," said the girl.

Durnave laughed. "You say that now."

"I never want a man," the girl repeated.

"Well, you'll get one. So pray to Allah for good luck," Durnave replied.

Sharrah didn't know what to think. Men had pushed her around, and the British boys at her prep school had teased her and deceived her and made her feel inferior for being Pakistani. But she'd never experienced anything like this. She had known that this happened, she'd seen enough of it in the first few weeks of Taliban rule. But she had never guessed her own brothers would do something like this. To her. Had they all gone mad? Had they forgotten they'd grown up under the same roof, with the same parents, laughing at the same jokes, playing chess and Nintendo and kicking each other under the table?

Sharrah knew then she had to leave Pakistan. She felt guilty thinking it, knowing that women like Durnave would feel betrayed or abandoned. But she couldn't face what had become of her family.

Sharrah awoke face down in Durnave's bed, covered with sweat and all but naked. She opened her eyes, but was careful not to move anything else. The doctor had been right. Fevers had set in, and the joint pain that came with them was as bad as the stroke of a whip. Only these strokes never stopped. Even walking to the bathroom made her wail, and Durnave had begun to bring her a chamber pot rather than put her through the torment.

The sound that had awakened her repeated itself. Someone was banging on Durnave's door, and shouting. She couldn't make out what they were saying.

"My husband is not home," she heard Durnave reply, "and I do not open this home to strange men, especially not at this hour."

"We have come for Sharrah Bassi. We have orders from the mullah," came the voice through the door.

"She is sick, and not dressed. Does your mullah order you to arrest a sick woman, not your kin, who is not clothed? Oh, you must be brave men indeed to be chosen for this duty!"

There was silence outside the door. "I will ignore your mockery, woman, since some of what you say is in keeping with the Sharia. But you will dress Ms. Bassi and bring her. And you will come with her, to be her chaperone."

"And leave my daughters alone in this house? I think not. Come when my husband is here, then I will open my doors. What sort of woman do you take me for?"

Again there was a pause. "It is awkward. We wish to respect the home of a good man and a pious woman. But do as I say, or we shall have to come in and make it as the mullah has said."

Sharrah turned over despite the pain. "Durnave!" she called. "Don't risk your daughters. Help me! I will go."

At once Durnave was in the room, her anguish plain on her face. "I cannot refuse them or they will break in. Then who knows what will happen?"

"Don't refuse them," she replied. "Your children come first. Help me up."

Durnave helped to lift her friend upright on the bed, and Sharrah moaned as she bent her knees to put her feet on the floor. She couldn't stand it anymore. She knew it was the morality police at the door, and that once she stepped outside, the worst and even worse than that could happen. But she didn't care. She was ready.

Durnave gathered up Sharrah's clothes and helped her dress. She tried to stand, but the pain in her knees and ankles stopped her before she could rise out of the bed.

The two women exchanged a glance, and then with a synchronicity born of many joint trips to the bathroom, Durnave lifted as Sharrah pushed herself to her feet. She wailed with the pain, and felt the burqa Durnave had pulled over her shoulders slide over her bandages and slap her in the back of her calves. She then shuffled a few steps forward, bending her knees as little as possible.

Durnave stood anxiously in front of her friend, waiting to steady her. "What will become of you?" she whispered.

"Take heart. If now is my time, I know what I am dying for. What more can they do to me?"

Durnave said nothing, but wiped angry tears from her face. She gathered up the other woman's veil and pinned it across her face. The sick woman was grateful for this kindness. It meant she didn't have to raise her aching arms. Durnave then put on her own veil, and opened the door to her home.

Outside the door stood two bearded Talibani, with turbans from the western provinces about their heads. The mullah, Sharrah noted, had sent trusted troops. These were not fresh converts from the Karachi streets, but the scarred Waziri footsoldiers who had driven the Pakistani secular army back to their strongholds on the Indian border. Wherever she was going, the mullah was making sure that she got there.

"Sharrah Bassi?" The shorter of the two men asked.

"That is I," she answered.

The two men regarded her with no expression. "You will accompany us to the soccer stadium," they answered.

Behind her veil, Ms. Bassi grimaced. The soccer stadium was kilometers away. And the streets were not level. The trip would be grueling at her present shuffle. If the Talibani were even prepared to let her shuffle.

The guards motioned to Durnave. "You will come. Bring your daughters if you must."

They heard another voice. "I will watch your daughters." Everyone turned, and there in the street was a lone woman. Sharrah recognized the voice behind the veil as that of Durnave's aunt, who lived two houses down.

"What are you doing alone in the street?" The Talibani asked.

"I am coming to care for my grand-nieces, young man. Or would you like to bring the girls to where you are going? Would it be something you wished on your own blameless daughters, to see what it is you do at the soccer stadium?"

The Talibani reflected. "No, you are right, I would not, grandmother. But you should not be in the street alone. You could only be making mischief, and if not, only mischief could befall you. Keep the Sharia, and your life will be righteous and safe."

"I am old. Even if I were up to mischief, what man would make mischief with me? I care for my family. It is my duty."

The Talibani deferred. "As you say, grandmother." He stepped back to give the older woman space to enter Durnave's home.

Durnave's aunt gripped Sharrah's arm as she passed. She could only see the woman's eye for a second as she leaned forward to whisper to her. "Your father would be proud. So would your mother."

Ms. Bassi felt an unbidden tear drop from her eye, but it vanished into her veil before it could be seen. The older woman stepped into Durnave's house. Durnave stepped out of the doorway with a glance at her aunt, and allowed the door to be shut behind her.

"We go," Sharrah decided. She began to shuffle toward the soccer stadium. She had a long way to go. But then, she reflected, all this madness would be over. The thought helped her move forward.

"Your brother sent this," said the Talibani behind her. She shifted around in place, careful not to move her neck, until the saw the wheelbarrow the Talibani was indicating. With Durnave's hands for support, she sat down into it. She bit her tongue when she felt like crying out. She would minimize her frailty in front of these men.

One of the Talibani pushed the wheelbarrow as Durnave walked beside it, whispering occasional comforts to her. The other soldier had unslung his AK-47 and held it at the ready, vigilant for anyone coming to rescue Sharrah, or anyone who might be violating the Taliban's night orders.

Every bump in the exposed cobbles and the pitted asphalt of her decaying street hurt, but it was still far better than walking. Her brother had either had a moment of contrition, or had been more aware than she that it would impossible for her to walk to the soccer stadium in her present condition.

She wondered how much experience her brother had in these estimations. What did he do for the Taliban now? He had been a small unit commander, she knew, and the troops he organized had helped the Taliban seize Karachi. But she had never learned what he did for the Taliban now. She hadn't wanted to know.

Her mind wandered. It was night, and the streets were quiet, far quieter than she had ever experienced them. The moon was waxing, and the light allowed her to see details hidden in the daytime by the traffic in the streets. There were blocked drainage ditches. Broken street work and curbs were all over. The surface of the sidewalks, and the carved wooden doors of shuttered stores, had acquired a dingy grayness from the fires people had begun to set in desperation to dispose of their trash.

Her neighborhood had been a good one before the putsch. It was upper middle class, but her family had been wealthier still than that. Her mother had married up when she married her father, but her father had been impressed by her mother's clan and brought his money to their neighborhood, as his own family was all but gone. Sharrah had no illusions. She had a privileged life, good medicine, and good schools. And she had used all of her time since, which she figured was now about to end, to better the lives of others. She felt some pride, reduced though she was to this tearful lump. She had spent her life in a way that left her with no regrets.

The stars twinkled overhead, and the wheelbarrow steadily creaked.

"It is a beautiful night," she commented to Durnave.

"Yes," answered Durnave. Her friend was humoring her, she decided, injecting false casualness into her veil-muffled voice.

"*She suspects, as I do, that I go to hang now,*" thought Sharrah. "*She will have to watch.*"

The two Talibani said nothing. After a while, the men switched jobs, and the one who had been pushing the cart drew his AK-47 before the other one slung his. They peered vigilantly into the night, paying the two women no mind in the process, as if their load were a cartload of ammunition or rice.

The wheelbarrow journey began again, causing the woman to grit her teeth. After another ten minutes, they rounded a corner and Sharrah could see downhill into the soccer stadium. Some of the lights were on, she saw. She always wondered what it would be like to stand down on that soccer field, on the turf in front of the lights. She guessed she would find out.

The slope of the road to the soccer stadium increased their pace, and it was not long before the Talibani was straining to keep the cart from rolling away from him. As the hill leveled out, they came to the chain link fence that surrounded the stadium. The armed Talibani moved forward and opened the gate. The wheelbarrow lurched forward again, and after passing by the ticket boxes and under some of the bleacher seating, traveled across a smooth carpet of astro-turf. It was a welcome change. The cart ceased its creaking, and the bumps that gave Sharrah so much pain stopped. The turf was gray in the moonlight, but at the far end, it was bright green under the white beams of a single panel of stadium lights.

The lights likewise lit up the white steel goal rectangle. As she noticed this, she and Durnave both sucked in their breaths. Hanging from nooses on the rectangle were still, burqa-clad forms, their calves and feet swollen. Beside them was an empty noose hung low. Sharrah wanted to look away at first, but did not. She would meet her fate head on.

"You are not shameful," she told to the spirits of the dead women. "Whatever you did, if it was a crime or not, you did not deserve this. This could never be the will of the compassionate, the merciful. I will join you now."

She saw movement to her left and shifted her eyes toward it to avoid turning her head. Walking across the lit area of the astro-turf that they were now entering themselves was her brother, Fahad.

"*Has it come to this? Is he here to be my hangman? So be it,*" she concluded. She looked back to the hanged corpses.

Beside her, Durnave began to wail, letting loose her anger and her fear. But Sharrah felt only calm. She kept her eyes on the unidentifiable hanged women as the Talibani guards set the wheelbarrow down. They walked away as Fahad arrived at the wagon, and posted themselves at the edge of the soccer field, still in earshot, but far enough off for some privacy.

After long moments of silent contemplation, Fahad spoke.

"Do you know who these women are?"

"Martyrs," she answered. "Women sainted by this mockery you call Islam."

"No," said Fahad, "They are your students. Husna Ranyal, Malika Bhadiar, and Yaida Pannun."

At the pronouncement of the names, Durnave wailed again. Sharrah winced in regret. Husna and Yaida had both been younger than twenty, recently married off to Taliban soldiers, and Malika Bhadiar had two children from a husband known as a whore-keeper. But she did not blame herself. The women who came understood that their attendance was risky, but not knowing the medicine and the signs of venereal diseases was risky too. To accept the guilt for the death of her brave students would be playing the Taliban's game.

Besides, she decided, she needn't feel guilty. She was about to share their fate.

As if he somehow sensed the solace she was taking in this thought, Fahad turned to her. "You will not hang today. The lashes on your back and fevers you feel are your warning. But the memory of this moment, this is your punishment. Remember it, these mothers and wives and daughters who died for the sins you taught them."

Ms. Bassi drew a breath to speak, but had to hack out a wet cough before replying. "I did not kill these women. And neither did Allah take the hands of your men and make them kill. You killed them, and your mullahs killed them. Live with your choices!" Sharrah snapped. "If you're man enough."

Despite the venom she had tried to give her voice, her brother was quick to answer. "The sad thing about your bravado is that it is noble. You have high motivations, even admirable ones. But the westerners have made you their pawn. Why do you feel such allegiance to their ways? What have they given us with their "assistance" and their crusades and 'administrations?' They arm the corrupt spawn of Saud, enrich the warlords who grow the opium the Taliban had all but stamped out, prop up godless dictators like Musharraf and Mubarak, lock us up in the ghettos of Palestine, and call drone strikes on weddings. Then they complain of *our* barbarism and lecture *us* on 'democracy' and 'tolerance.'

"And with this treatment of your Muslim brothers and sisters, they buy such allegiance and devotion from you? Such devotion that you send young women to their death with the grotesque western sexual culture on their lips?"

Fahad's rant gave Sharrah not a moment's pause. "I owe the west and their corruption nothing. But corruption is not western only. Even Muslim tyrants are corrupt. Look at the impurity the Wahhabi wrought by bringing Saud to the throne. What I owe to anyone is the knowledge of basic womens' health. Recall, Fahad, that I almost died before the Taliban putsch from a cancer that was only detected because I had taken a class and gotten a simple blood test. And I was only cured by those western doctors who arrived a few weeks later to help after the earthquake. Without those things, the cancer would have spread and I would already be dead.

"Medicine gave me every day I have had since then. Medicine is not a thing of the west. It is a gift from Allah that allows us to care for one another. And it is medicine I will share. If you can't tolerate it, you should hang me now and save yourself more humiliation, because I'm not going to stop."

Fahad looked on the corpses for a long while, giving no answer. Sharrah felt her skin burn, and then began to shiver so uncontrollably her teeth rattled aloud. She wondered if her fever was overtaking her, and if she would now die where she sat, having been spared a hanging. But after a moment she was able clench her teeth, and she resolved to make no sound that would betray her suffering to her brother's satisfaction.

At length, her tall, bearded, grim brother drew a breath. She could see in his eyes and nose the same determination and intellect which had trounced her at chess during their childhood. "Mother always said we were alike," Fahad replied. "Together we could choose not to fail her this way." Without another word, he walked back the way he had come. As he departed, the two Talibani guards returned to the wheelbarrow.

"We will wait here," one of the guards announced, "until they take these women down to bury them before sundown. It is the Mullah's order that you remain, and watch, Ms. Bassi. Your friend may escort you to the bathroom, you may have water to drink, but you will remain."

"It is well. I will remain with my sisters until they are buried," she agreed.

"And I will stay with mine until she is buried," Durnave added defiantly. Her friend was impossibly small and frail in front of the soldiers, but not intimidated. Sharrah was once again grateful to have a friend in the midst of this madness, no matter how hard she was to predict or understand. At the same time, she felt shame knowing that if given the chance she would not stay but flee Pakistan and leave Durnave behind.

Rather than express any outrage or discontent at the women's replies, the Talibani nodded gravely to them and each other. After a moment, the shorter one spoke up, his graying beard and scars lending his few words gravity.

"You both missed your calling as soldiers when Allah made you into women."

Sharrah sat up in her bed in Zurich with the Taliban guardsman's words still ringing in her ears. She shook a tangled mat of her hair out of her face, noticing that it was stuck together by something. She pulled the tangle back in front of her face to untangle it, and as she did so she discovered her hair was saturated with almond oil. The smell reminded her profoundly of her mother's kitchen.

"Udo. Udo brought me to bed," she recalled. *"Such a lovely backrub."*

She sat up. Her gold silk dress lay on the floor in a heap beside her panties and the matching dress shoes. She reached into her hair and removed the silk flower that was still there but crumpled from having been slept on. The empty almond oil bottle was on her nightstand. There were no mens' clothes, no long blonde hairs on her pillow, and no sounds from the rest of her apartment.

She checked her clock. It was half an hour before the alarm, so it was no use trying to go back to sleep. She decided to get up and use the time to clean up the mess her failed attempt at western debauchery had created. She stood, strapped on the bathrobe over her now itch-free scars, rehung her gold dress and its accessories, and walked barefoot into her living room.

Udo was not even asleep on one of her comfy Bauhaus chairs. He was gone. Even the water glasses were gone from the table beside the chair. A glance in the kitchen told her he had carried these into the sink.

One the side table beside where the glasses had stood was a plastic box, the disposable acrylic kind. She picked it up and read its label. *"Marzipan Fruechten,"* the label read, and inside the box she saw marzipan candies molded into the shapes of fruit. A sniff at the box filled her nose with another almond flavor, this one sweeter than the oil and including traces of honey and cinnamon.

She picked up the note Udo had left beneath the box, scrawled on the back of a subscription payment ticket for the *"Neue Zuercher Zeitung."*

"Sharrah!

"I don't believe that I have ever met as remarkable a woman as you.
"I ran out to get this from an overnight store before I left. They are maybe not the best but I hope the flavor of them carries you back again to whatever happier place it was that smelled of almonds.
"I left your keys on the hook beside the door.

"Your Udo."

She pried open the box of marzipan, selected a piece shaped like an apple, and took a bite.

In a moment the smell pulled her back, and she remembered sitting in her mother's kitchen at a dining table. She had on the dark school uniform she had worn in Form II, and she kicked her dangling feet under the kitchen table. She had jasmine flowers in her hair that her mother had tied there for the class pictures they had that day. And her father was in the kitchen corner, with his camera, about to snap the family picture she had left behind in Karachi but never forgotten. It showed her with her jasmine flowers, her mother with cookie sheet of those unforgettable almonds, and matching smiles on both their faces.

The scene unfolded into the picture. Her mother offered her some fresh honey-roasted almonds from a cookie sheet. Sharrah beamed as she smelled them, the words "thank you, momma!" forming on her lips when her mother vanished before she could say it.

And then she was back in her living room in Zurich, standing alone in a bathrobe with a marzipan in one hand and a plastic box of eleven more of them clutched to her breast with the other. She laughed, and cried, and chewed, and cried, and eventually dropped to her knees and left the candy box on the floor.

When she had finished the one apple-shaped piece, she sobbed like she hadn't even done at the double funeral for her parents. She had been so mindful of all the Taliban around her, of the dangers of grieving too loudly for her father, the educator and the heretic, and her mother, the source of all the grace in her life.

"I made it, momma," she whispered in Urdu. *"I'm free."*

Chapter 30

Apologists

Sharrah sat on the Hallwylplatz. The trees were now partly bare, and yellow pear leaves swirled in the gusts that crossed the park. The barbecuing crew had returned for a final appearance of the year, and the pleasant tang of the barbecue sauce still teased her nose and tongue. Since Vincent was lost in thought, she picked up a copy of the *NZZ* a previous visitor had left on the bench and began reading it.

The headline article read *"Iranian president-in-exile visits EU Parliament, reiterates Holocaust denials."* Because it involved the Iranian president, she stopped to read it. Normally, she would have paged to the sports section to see the news about the world cup or cricket, or to see if Udo had written a new science article she could flirt with him about later.

Sharrah had thirty months of German behind her and no dictionary at hand to translate difficult words or pick out subtle biases in wording, and so the headline article proved challenging to read. But it recounted how the Iranian president-in-exile was denouncing the United States' ongoing invasion of his country and accusing the United States of uncritically underwriting Israel's claims with force.

"American parents," the paper quoted the president as saying, "are sacrificing their sons and daughters in the name of two Israeli fairy tales. The first that the peaceful Iranian people seek nuclear weapons, and the second is that the Arab world will undertake an Israeli genocide. This second claim is the most hurtful, even if one agrees that a genocide of the Jews ever occurred at all, it assumes that Iranians, a modern and civilized people, would do something considered barbarous even by Europeans who, historically speaking, are latecomers to tolerance and civilization. Throw off the blinders of the lies you call 'history' and look around you!"

She nodded at the president's remarks. They made sense. It infuriated her that the west always railed on about "peace" and "tolerance" and "democracy" in condemning Islamic countries when its own history up until the Second World War was one of bloodshed, colonialism, and conquest. Even its present was tainted by the barbarities that ensured its supply of oil. The proof of western cruelty and ambition could be seen in the arbitrary borders, colonial names, and languages written on any globe. Middle easterners had kept to themselves, but European elites had conquered, enslaved, parceled, and colonized the entire world in an attempt to remake it in their own image. South America, North America, Africa, and eastern Asia were all colonies of Europeans.

Her employer interrupted her thoughts, leaning over her shoulder to look at the paper. "Iranian president running his mouth again, is he?"

She sighed. "Yes. I don't like him much, but he makes some good points every now and again.

This remark drew Vincent's complete attention. "I wouldn't have guessed that you'd support his stances. But tell me, what do you agree with him on?"

"The whole Holocaust myth for one. It's shocking to me that people believe it."

A shadow passed over the man's face. She felt alarm at his expression, and braced for anger, something which Vincent had never directed at her before. But instead of shouting, he calmly formed another question.

"Why does it seem to you that the story of the Jewish genocide is a myth?"

Sharrah struggled to compose her argument in the face of his flash of emotion. But she managed. "Look at how many Jews there are all over the world. There are enormous numbers of them, everywhere you look. If there had been a real Jewish genocide, then where did all the Jews in New York City come from? And where did the Jewish soldiers come from who overthrew the Palestinian government to create Israel? There are too many of them, and they are too powerful, for genocide to be the real story," she explained. "Besides, the Europeans love the Jews. Anytime someone says anything critical of Israel they get called anti-Semitic. Germany even arrests people for being anti-Semitic. If the Europeans hate Jews, how do you explain that?

"Besides, look at these people. Do these look like murderers to you? They'll arrest a person for kicking a dog, something one does every day in Karachi. I can believe that in the 19th century, before they were democracies, they would let their governments kill foreigners if they couldn't see what was happening. But do you think that in the 20th century they'd let anyone kill six million people in front of their own eyes? These claims don't match what I see. They are not even close."

Vincent leaned away from her on the bench and his gaze flew out over the rooftops. "What if I told you that I had been there? That I had seen genocide myself? What if I'd been a part of it?"

"You? I could never believe that." Sharrah did some quick math in her head, and then dismissed it. Udo's information about his age had to be wrong. "Besides, you're too young! Even if you were alive when it happened, you can't have been more than a baby."

Vincent did not reply immediately. He kept staring into the distance. It made her nervous. She was afraid she might have created a permanent distance between her and benefactor.

At length he spoke, his features softened. "We've been working too hard since I put out that press release. And we'll be working even harder, you especially, once the hearings in the United States begin. And you've been in Europe too long to have only seen Zurich. We should take a trip. Let you see some culture and some history at a go. And I know the place."

The change of subject made Sharrah feel better. "That sounds wonderful! Where shall we go?"

"A village called Weimar," he smiled at her. "It's historic and home of some of Europe's finest poets. If you memorize some Schiller when we're there you'll impress your German teacher, I'm sure of it."

The thought of seeing her German teacher's face light up was a pleasant one. Sharrah admired the younger woman, who was always chipper and determined no matter how stubborn her students' accents proved. "Let's do it!"

"We'll leave next week. I'll make the travel plans myself, you focus on clearing a few days of my calendar."

David looked up from his copy of the Ithaca Journal when he heard footsteps on his porch. Expecting to see the mailman, he was surprised to find instead a young woman wearing a suit and tie.

"Hello, sir, are you-," she glanced at her clipboard, "Mr. David Haversham?"

"That's me. What can I do for you?" He adjusted his glasses on his nose so he could see the woman over them.

"I'm Paige Willis from Tompkins County GOP. I'm here as part of our voter registration drive. We're trying to make sure all voters understand the recent changes to the election laws." The woman extended her hand for a shake but did not come close enough that he could take it without standing up. So, stifling a groan prompted by his stiff back, he stood and shook it.

Once the shake was complete the woman held the clipboard between them. "New federal election regulations have changed who can vote in federal legislative and presidential elections. We want to determine who in your household may be eligible to vote under the new system and ensure they are registered prior to the upcoming general election. Do you have a few moments to answer some questions?"

David reflected. "I registered when I renewed my driver's license last year."

"Yeah, I understand," said Paige, tilting her head and adding a sympathetic tone. "The changes have a lot of people confused. Because of the rampant voter fraud in democrat-controlled states, under the new regulations, you cannot register for a general election through your DMV or post office anymore and your existing registrations are invalid. You have to register through offices of the Democratic or Republican parties or through a private election attorney. Now, are you renting or leasing this home, or do you own it?"

"I own it," said David, puzzled by the question.

"Does anyone else live with you?"

"My foster daughter, who's at school at the moment, and my daughter, who's at work."

"Do either of them have an ownership stake of thirty three percent or greater in this or any other property in the county?" The girl asked, making a deft series of check marks on a voter registration card.

"No, I'm the sole owner of this house, and it's the only land we own. My wife willed the house to me, on the understanding that I would will it to our daughter."

"But your daughter does not yet hold an ownership stake in your home?"

"Nope."

Paige pursed her lips. "Then that makes it easy. Under the new system, you're the only one in your home eligible to vote in the federal election!"

David blinked. "What?"

"The Voting Reform Act that took effect on the 1st of January this year made many changes to our outdated electoral system. In order to be eligible to vote in federal elections, a person must own a thirty-three percent or greater interest in a residential, commercial, industrial, or eligible church property in the election district where they register."

"So my daughter can't vote?"

Ms. Willis began writing on the card. "Sure! She can vote in state and local elections, or she can obtain a thirty-three percent interest in a qualifying property any day before election day!" She finished writing on the card she had marked, then folded and tore it along a perforation. "Do you want to register as a Democrat or a Republican this time around, sir? Don't worry, I won't be upset if you register as a Democrat."

"I, umm... register as an independent."

"I'm sorry, sir. 'Independent,' isn't a political party. If you wish to participate in the general federal election, you have two choices. You can register with the eligible political party of your choice. The party will then validate your property ownership and voter eligibility at their expense and invite you to vote in their primary elections. Or you can opt out of identifying as Republican or Democrat. But then you'll be shut out of the primaries. You'll also have to pay a processing fee to one or the other of the parties or a private election attorney to verify your property ownership, identity, and citizenship before you can vote in the general elections."

"Okay. Can I register with the conservative party?"

"They've merged with the county GOP to increase our electoral chances. We appreciate their support."

"How about..." David grit his teeth suggesting it, "The Socialist Workers Party?"

"Parties whose organizing principles are antithetical to the republican system of government cannot participate in federal elections. You could still vote for the Socialist Workers Party on the state or local level, though."

These rules gave him pause. "When did these changes happen?"

"The changes are part of the Voting Reform Act, which was passed as a part of the repeal of the 14th amendment. Thanks to the changes, illegal immigrants and others with no stake in their community will be barred from voting, returning control of America to real Americans." The fluidity with which the visitor recited this made it clear she had done it many times. "Did you want to pick a party, sir? If you prefer to register as independent I can take cash, check, or credit card and validate you through our party office."

David frowned. "I guess I'll pay you. Put me down as independent."

"That'll be forty dollars. Cash, check, credit, or debit?"

"Cash," he said, reaching for his wallet. He passed the girl the twenties, signed where she pointed, and received a stiff manila paper card in return.

"Sir, this is your receipt. Here at the top is my name and Federal Elections Commission number, and at the bottom the amount and date you paid and my notary stamp mark. If you haven't received either your voter registration card or your explanation of ineligibility within fourteen days, please contact the county GOP. If we determine that you are ineligible to vote, but you feel you are eligible, you do have the right to take your receipt and explanation of ineligibility to another political party's office. If they do their own investigation and deem you eligible, they will bill us instead of you and you won't pay a dime for the second attempt!"

David scratched his head. "You know, it's been a while since I read the Constitution. But I thought poll taxes were illegal."

Paige smiled. "I'm sorry I wasn't clear enough about that. The charges aren't a tax, they're a fee the law permits us to levy to cover the expense of determining your eligibility. You're free to go to another party and see if they'll do it for less for you. But I'd stick with us Republicans! Our price is competitive and it'd be a shame if you showed up on election day and couldn't vote because some surrenderist muffed your eligibility check."

The retired firefighter examined the receipt. It seemed official enough, but for some reason he couldn't dispel the anxiety that the girl might be running a scam.

Now that she had his money, Paige began to hurry. "Here's my card. If anyone else in your household decides to try and register, give me a call and I'll come running! Our prices are good and everyone benefits when everyone who's eligible participates in the election!"

"Yeah. Will do," answered David. "Have a good day!"

"One nation, indivisible!" the young woman chimed as she darted off his porch.

Sharrah opened the rental car door rather than wait for Vincent to come around and open it for her. The drive from Weimar had been long. She had spent the last twenty minutes staring out the window into the amazing forest. Trees, one after another, grew so close together that she couldn't take them all in as they paraded by her, each clad in pine green or gold autumn leaves. She'd seen forests only either as green blurs from trains or as green patches on Google maps. Being inside one, so close that one could see individual leaves, and so deep that in any direction one turned one would see a tree trunk, was a novelty to her. The signs along the road all referred to *"KZ Buchenwald."* The name *Buchenwald*, she had determined, meant "beech forest," though she didn't know enough about trees to determine if these were beech trees. "KZ" was another inscrutable German acronym whose meaning might or might not ever become apparent.

Weimar had been nice enough, though far more people had stared at her headscarf than had done so in Zurich, so she didn't feel as comfortable. Vincent had known the town well, and been able to tell her so much about all the ornate buildings and the paintings in the museums. But after two days of dusty museums and a long teasing ride through the forest, she was ready for a walk, curious to go touch the leaves and stones and mossy trunks she'd been feasting her eyes on.

The doctor motioned for her to follow, and she crossed behind the car to walk beside him. They walked together in silence, but to her dismay, Sharrah saw they weren't heading into the forest. They were instead walking toward some fenced in buildings.

"No walk in the woods?" she felt disappointed.

"No, not today," he said.

"Then what are we here to see?" She wondered what could so interesting that it would make them walk by a forest.

"A memorial. It happens to also be a former workplace of mine. From the war," he said.

She studied the fence ahead. It had guard towers at either end, and in the middle of the fence was a great wrought-iron gate. As they drew closer, she could read the words worked into the gate. It read *"Jedem das Seine,"* which she translated to "to each what they deserve."

Vincent began to walk more slowly, and to look around as if expecting to see someone. When they squeezed through the gate door together, she kept this close distance to him, feeling more and more uncomfortable as they went.

Once a fair distance past the gate, he stopped. Without looking at her, he explained the place. "This is the concentration camp Buchenwald. This was my last place of duty with the German SS."

Sharrah scanned the open space. "What did you do here?" For some reason, she asked the question in a hush.

"This whole open area used to be filled with wooden and stone prisoner barracks. I provided medical care for prisoners and analyzed the results of medical tests performed on the prisoners. By the end of the war, I spent most of my time in the quarantine area of the camp, trying to triage sick prisoners and control epidemics. I was evacuated when allied forces grew near the camp, and I had to leave many patients behind, certain to die. And I also spent some time in that building," he pointed to a brick building with an oversized chimney, "the crematorium. Autopsies on experimental subjects were...part of my duties."

Sharrah shivered. She felt her eyes grow wide, and she stared at Vincent, trying to see in his face, in his jovial and gracious ways, the kind of man that

394

would work in a prison camp.

"I visited this place last in the early 1990's, after East Germany and West Germany were reunited. At the time, each of these buildings had historical displays which were, on the whole, accurate. Since the plaques were created by the communists, they did overlook that after the war the Soviets used this place to exterminate Germans who opposed the communist occupation. But I daresay some of them the communists killed here may have deserved it. Possibly I deserved it too. I like to think that I have changed, but change is easier than redemption.

"In any case, look around. Visit the displays until you've satisfied yourself. If, when you return, you still believe the Jewish genocide was a fairy tale, and that Europeans are incapable of such things, there's no more I can do to educate you."

Sharrah felt small, and somehow she felt less certain of her opinions of the jewish genocide. "You...you won't walk with me?" She wanted Vincent to come with her, she realized. Coldness radiated off the empty gravel field, and the emptiness seemed full of gravity.

"This is a place best experienced alone, for me, and for you," her boss answered. "If you need me, go over there," he pointed to a ring of stones and concrete blocks on the ground. "There's a tree stump there. If I'm not standing there when you arrive, I'll come to meet you from wherever I am when I look back to see you."

Sharrah felt her decision gel. "But I don't *want* to see this place."

The man's eyes flashed, and his voice was firm. "You've said you don't believe in the Holocaust, and I did not challenge you. All I am asking is that you look at this evidence and decide for yourself."

Reluctantly, Sharrah nodded. She had seen this determination in him before when he had confronted the American senator on the phone. She looked around, picked out the largest looking building, a beige two-story building at the lowest point on the sloped land, and began her walk across the sea of gray gravel.

Vincent stared down at the remnants of the Goethe oak. The decaying wooden stump was surrounded by stray leaves that had blown in during the autumn and with stones left as signs by visitors. Whether they left the stones in honor of the great poet, the tree, or to the tens of thousands who had died on this piece of ground, he was not sure. He supposed that in a sense it didn't matter. Appreciation and understanding of the poet had died on this ground along with the German dissenters, the Jews, the Poles, the Americans, the Russians, and the countless others who had fallen here alongside the tree.

When Dr. Foster had started work in the camp, the huge oak had still been alive, grand and shady. The SS guards who had been there since the camp's erection had told him that this was, indeed, the same oak which his favorite poet, Goethe, had often rested under to meditate and write poems. During his tenure at the camp, he had often taken the time to stand or sit beside it, using the tree and a small volume of Goethe's works as a refuge from the growing voices of his own discontent. When an allied bombing run on the nearby armaments factories had killed the tree, he had only been briefly angry. He later came to understand the tree's death as foreshadowing of the future. Like other good things in German culture, it was being destroyed and forgotten because of its not-quite-accidental proximity to the grotesque excesses of Nazism. He had continued to visit the tree, leaves or no, until he was evacuated. He had expected to die before the tree's ashen bulk ever crumbled.

Instead, here he was, still alive, and the huge tree itself was reduced to the few inches of dried wood ensconced in concrete.

He surveyed the camp. The crematorium, the prisoner's canteen, and the storage warehouse still stood, but he felt no urge to visit them. They were familiar enough. He cast a brief glance at the excavations that revealed the quarantine area he had overseen as one of his duties, but there was not enough there to be worth visiting either.

Ghastly recollections of the camp stormed through his head. There were Frau Koch's lampshades of human skin Vincent had seen in her love nest after her man, the commandant, had been arrested for pushing even the SS's limits of morality. Then there was the long week he had been charged by Gerhard Rose to sit awake with a stopwatch in the camp infirmary. His mission had been to time how long it took each of a row of Polish prisoners with 10%, 20%, 30%, 40%, and 50% levels of exposure to a new compound of white phosphorous to die from their untreated burns. Then there had been the endless, and unrealistic, demands for autopsies of deceased test subjects. Dr. Foster had been unable to keep pace with the cascade of corpses, and Dr. Rose had begun piling the bodies for him beside the crematorium door. Before the new commandant had put an end to it, Vincent had done sixty-one days of straight autopsies.

Self-loathing, he reminded himself, availed him, and mankind, nothing. Like forgetting, self-loathing was weakness. It was a way of denying that every day of his life he could chose to do good or evil anew. And for many years since he had left here, he had chosen to do good, and to expand the knowledge the experiments here had produced until they benefited all mankind.

He looked around again. Far across the compound, he saw Sharrah emerge from the door of the crematorium. She began walking toward him. He did not have much time left on these grounds.

He wondered if the young woman would pass this impromptu test. Was she a person who, when confronted with evidence, could change her beliefs, or would she rationalize away what she had seen as tricks, or exaggerations, or exceptions? Her assertion that the Holocaust was a hoax had shaken his confidence in her and her readiness for a new role in his organization.

One thing that had surprised him about her willingness to deny the Holocaust was that she was a witness to unspeakable evils done in the name of an ideology. If she could believe what she had seen with her own eyes, why was the Holocaust in turn so hard to believe in?

Part of it, he supposed, might be the nature of the evil. The evil she had seen had been selective and personalized. If her accounts were true, then some of the violence had been staged for her benefit. Still, each killing she had seen was in response to an action each person murdered had undertaken. The victims had attended womens' medicine classes, refused their husbands' advances, or challenged the Sharia laws. And while there had been no shortage of personalized evil in the second world war, in contrast to Sharrah's experience, much of the violence of that period had been against classes of people. In that war, millions had been rounded up because of their faith, ethnicity, or ideology and exterminated or worked to death without concern for their individual conduct.

On the other hand, he supposed her understanding of one sort of violence would serve as a stepping stone to her understanding of another. It might, in the end, aid her understanding of it as much as it had at first contributed to her denial.

He glanced over his shoulder again. Sharrah had stopped to read some plaques, but was closer to him, looking distressed and solemn. He had little time left to just his memories and the stump. He was sure this visit to this tree would be his last. He reached into his jacket and pulled out a small volume. Its leather cover cracked and flaked under his fingers. He opened it to the bookmark ribbon, a red strip of silk long since gone brown with the oils of his hands and time.

He reflected on small snatches of the good memories from this place. There was the simple comradeship he had shared with one of SS guards, also a Goethe reader, who would join him here under the oak's boughs in the dead of winter to read verses with him. Though the triviality of their arguments amidst these ruins of morality troubled him in retrospect, he still smiled to remember their debates over whether the German or the English versions of the poems were better. He had shared his last pack of cigarettes here with the resigned and gaunt Polish doctor selected from amongst the prisoners to help him run the quarantine area. And there had been the ample, and final, harvest of acorns from under the tree. Desperate to ease their misery, he had detailed some British prisoners to rake up the acorns from under the tree. The guards had laughed to see it. *"He cares about that tree more than himself,"* they said. But after night had fallen, Vincent had his countrymen shell, boil, and grind the acorns to make acorn flour they could add to their ration of vegetable soup for a few days. By doing so, he and the tree might even have saved some lives. So some good things, few but dear to him, had happened on this spot. And when he died the memory of them would be lost to history.

He spoke to the old tree's stump. *"It wasn't your fault, old one,"* he acknowledged in German. He looked down to the volume of <u>Goethe for Englishmen</u> and read aloud from the poem there, "The Dance of Death."

> *The warden looks down at the hour of midnight*
> *On the tombs that lie scattered below*
> *The moon fills the place with her silvery light*
> *The yard like daylight seems to glow*
> *Then see! First one grave, and then others open wide*
> *And women and men stepping out of them are spied*
> *In shrouds both white and trailing.*
>
> *In haste for the sport soon their ankles they twitch*
> *And whirl 'round in dances so gay*
> *The young and the old, and the poor and the rich*
> *But the shrouds cling and stand in their way*
> *And as modesty means naught on this midnight clear*
> *The dancers shake themselves free, and the rags soon appear*
> *Scattered on tombs in confusion...*

The poem reminded him of the bizarre nighttime assemblies of the living dead that had been routine while he was at Buchenwald. The camp guards would wake him when they discovered a prisoner in the camp out of his bunk. Vincent would then go the highest watchtower and join the guards there to observe, in case a guard was injured and medical attention was needed during the following action. Then the guards, invisible in their coal black and gray uniforms, would then blow whistles and shout. The prisoners, stick figures in white in the moonlight, would then dash from their barracks and mill about before finding a formation. Some prisoners would trip or collapse from exhaustion during this mad dash and not arise again, lying limp like rags cast on the ground. Then the guards would begin, name by name, a roll call that would last for hours, and intermittently more rags would drift to the ground.

He wondered, not for the first time, if this poem "Dance of Death" was not proof that Goethe had some vision of the macabre dance that would surround his beloved oak tree decades after he died. He closed the book when he finished the poem, and replaced it in his pocket. Sharrah came to a stop beside him, and put her hands to the knot of her white headscarf uncomfortably. She stood for a long time, looking down at the stump and reading the bronze plaque that described its significance to the following generations.

"I'm sorry I doubted you. I believe now," she said after a time. She put her hand on his shoulder. "Thank you for the truth."

His mood did not allow him happiness, but he nonetheless felt some elation at her announcement. For one, it meant that his involvement in what happened here had not caused her to loathe him as he had feared it might. But more importantly, history had passed from one generation to another, and one culture to another. He supposed that in all the grim truth and sadness of this place, if there was an honest joy to be had, he had now experienced it.

Chapter 31

The Kindness of Strangers

Sharrah stirred her tea in its gold-trimmed bone china cup. Her table at the sidewalk cafe outside the Bauhaus museum overlooked the Goethe and Schiller memorial and Germany's national opera house, gleaming in all its Bauhaus glory. Still, her enjoyment of the artisanal skill that had produced the tea, the sculpted metal table, the opera and memorial, and even the cobblestone roadways that lay under it all, was dampened by her memory of the displays in the concentration camp. She tried to let the warmth of the tea rise through the silver spoon and reanimate her. This did not work, but she did feel some relief when she at last raised the cup to her lips to drink.

"I have to leave you tomorrow," Vincent said from beyond the edge of her vision. "Early, before you awaken." She turned to face him.

"Why? Has something come up? A medical emergency for one of our clients?"

The doctor frowned. "You recall when you and I began to work on my press announcement to go public with my work, I told you that certain people would oppose my work so vehemently they might hunt me down? And that others would desire my cooperation so badly they might do the same?"

Sharrah nodded. She had thought the concerns exaggerated, but now reconsidered this. Her benefactor had not supposed that her fears were exaggerated when she had refused to go with him into the Pakistani restaurant he had found.

"There is some evidence now that certain parties have begun to do this. So I think it's best if I spend the last few weeks or months before the hearing in Washington traveling so that I will be difficult to find. I do not want to be intercepted before I can discuss my science in that most public venue."

"Where will you go?" she wondered.

Dr. Foster hemmed. "It's best that I don't tell you. What you don't know can't be coerced from you should they approach you in Zurich."

Sharrah felt the pit of her stomach tingle. The reality that she might once more be beginning a life of danger and vigilance gave her a sick sensation, especially now that her naive trust in the "civilized" character of Europeans had been yanked out from under her. But she did not betray this moment of misgivings to him.

"I'll keep my own itinerary, and I'll have to mask my IP and email addresses while traveling," the man added. "You and I will still communicate, but even you cannot know where I am at any time."

Sharrah hoped the training she had given Vincent on operating his encrypted modem had stuck in the older man's mind. She supposed his freedom now might depend on his ability to use it.

"We should rehearse the use of that special modem before you depart."

"Thank you, but I kept the manual and think I remember your instructions. However, before I go, I have some questions for you," he began. Sharrah sensed from his voice that they were coming to an issue of importance.

"Yes? Ask away."

"There is a chance I will be intercepted, either before the hearings or thereafter, and may not be able to return to my position as head of the organization."

She contemplated this possibility. "If so, I will support whomever you name in your place," she said.

"Yes, I expect you will. Because the person I would like to name to run things in the event of my absence would be you."

Sharrah put down her teacup and stared. "Is it frailty, sentimentality, or madness that has led him to this choice?" she wondered.

"I'm hardly qualified-" she began.

"That's right. You're unqualified. You're not a lawyer, a financier, a doctor, or an executive. You're a woman who has been driven from her home, whipped for her beliefs, lived with the kindness and cruelty of others, and kept her compass throughout. And you are also someone who can change her opinion when presented with cold, hard facts. You are, in one of those delicious contradictions of life, unqualified yet perfect for the job."

"I-" she stammered. He cut across her.

"There will be no discussion, only a decision," the doctor insisted. "Will you do it?"

"If you wish, Vincent," she replied, feeling overwhelmed by his demand.

The doctor relaxed and gave a satisfied smile. "You won't be alone at the top," he said reassuringly. "Jean-Paul is prepared to advise you as corporate counsel. Mr. Chahine from the Beirut office is prepared to advise you on finances. And Dr. Ling from the Hong Kong lab will be your technical advisor. I have no doubt if you heed them and do your best, you cannot fail.

"Now listen to what I am saying. I'm saying heed them, not defer to them. I am choosing you for your unique characteristic: the moral compass your experiences have given you. If, as you become familiar with the organization, you find something that you think needs to change, either for the organization to survive or remain an ethical operation, change it. I charge you to do this. The worst that can happen is that I will return someday, thank you for doing me this favor, and change your decisions back."

Sharrah did not feel that that was the worst that could happen by any stretch of the imagination. But she held her misgivings in. She would do her best to repay her employer's confidence in her with her own confidence in his judgment.

The waitress stepped into the lull to take their dinner order. Sharrah felt as though all she wanted was another cup of tea, but given Dr. Foster's impeccable taste in restaurants, she knew she was certain to regret her restraint when Vincent's meal arrived. So she ordered "lamb medallions in cognac-crème sauce" and then picked up her tea to savor the heat from the rest of it.

"How shall we begin?" she asked the doctor.

"I think it's best if we treat my kidnapping as an eventual certainty. This being the case, it makes sense to start building your rapport with the leaders of the different operations and laboratories. Eventually, you should even visit them, but not now. All eyes will shift to you once they cannot find me, and if you visited laboratories you might be drawing attention to them. In the meantime, I would like you to start receiving and replying to all my correspondence, even the more technical messages, so that if I am snatched, everyone is already familiar with you."

She nodded at this. "Sensible," she said. "But this may reduce the amount of time I have to attend to other things."

The doctor seemed unconcerned. "Not having to attend to me in person

400

should leave you with more time. But, we may need to explore hiring more staff for Zurich. Particularly as your experience increases, it makes no sense whatever to have you vacuuming or answering phones. Welcome to the ranks of the international executives. Someone will be along to collect your soul shortly."

The last comment puzzled Sharrah, but since Vincent was grinning, she supposed it must have been a joke. She tried to smile in response. "I hope not. Isn't my soul what you're promoting me for?"

"Precisely!" he said. "But that doesn't mean that someone won't come for it. Trust me in this!"

She drank the remainder of the tea. "I'll be on the lookout," she commented. "By the way, if I'm now an executive, do I have to change the way I dress?"

"The change might fall into the range of things that you should discuss with a fashion consultant. I can only get away with wearing my unfashionably British things because I am not only an executive, but a sole owner, so I'm allowed to be eccentric. As an employee, your dress should be professional and conservative, but not include any dresses or even skirts. Again, though, consult an expert on this. Zurich should be full of tailors and such willing to advise you."

"The United States Secretary of State wears dresses," she scowled at Vincent's restriction. She did have some dresses she liked and wanted to wear again.

"Yes, but she is but a harlot-in-chief for a decadent and bankrupted empire. *You* represent a discreet, forward thinking, and profitable business. Dress accordingly."

Sharrah absorbed this while she watched over the square, and noticed that young couples in splendid clothes had begun converging on the national opera house. As if it was taking flight from the responsibilities her employer was shoving at her, her mind wandered. She wondered what it would be like to have grown up, young and carefree, in a place like Weimar, familiar with art and culture, surrounded by forest, with no morality police in sight. She envied the young couples, arm-in-arm in suits and black dresses with clutch purses, and laughter on their lips. She envisioned walking here with Udo at some day in the future, when her executive pay and independence allowed such things.

Dr. Foster was quiet for a while, thoughtfully letting Sharrah savor her daydream. "Before I go, I have a gift for you," he said.

She recognized this moment. When she realized she would have to live on the run in Pakistan unless she could find a way out of the country, she had given two friends final gifts on the assumption she would be caught.

From his jacket pocket, the man produced two letter sized recycled brown envelopes. He handed her the first.

"This contains some bank account information. I've set up a trust fund for you. You and your descendants should be able to live off the interest of it if you leave the principal to grow."

Sharrah took it, but then puzzled at his words. "But I won't have any descendants. You did the operation yourself."

Vincent looked unsurprised by her protest. "Which brings me to my second envelope," he passed it to her across the table. "You may open it now if you like."

She did so. Inside was a USB Drive folded into a number of paper records and technical printouts which she did not understand. She focused on the one cover letter, reading:

"To whom it may concern;

The data contained on this disk, selected printouts of which accompany this letter, should prove with legal certainty the maternity of Sharrah Bassi..."

She stopped, her heart pounding.

"Vincent," she said. "Glory be to Allah..."

"Yes, my dear, you already have a daughter. By now she is twelve years old. Jean-Paul can help introduce you to her, if you like. Duplicates of this data are in safekeeping with the Capetown and Hong Kong laboratories in case these are taken from you. If the authorities do come for me, ultimately they will come to the office and seize all documents that they find, even in your apartment, so I would keep these copies in a safe place outside the office."

Sharrah was still gaping at the paper "How did I have a daughter?"

The doctor raised his palm. "It's actually not too hard to explain. Do you remember in Karachi, before the surgery, the documents we had you sign?"

Thinking back, she vaguely remembered signing many papers. At the time she had been in terrific pain, and bleeding heavily, and she wasn't sure she'd paid enough attention to them. And she was sure she hadn't given these papers a moment's thought since. The surgery had returned her life to her, if not her fertility, and she had been busy living it. She nodded mutely.

At her nod, Vincent continued. "One of those papers you signed authorized me to use any tissue we removed from you for any scientific purpose. At the time you were no one special to me, clinical as I was. I had your ovaries frozen like everyone else's, and stored for use at the laboratories."

At the word frozen, Sharrah felt a chill come over her like a wave. The doctor carried on, and his mild British accent and voice began to sound somehow sinister, like a fraud. Her knees began to feel weak and shake, even though she was sitting. She raised her hands to her face, as though putting her palms to her cheeks could stop the words from reaching her ears.

Oblivious, or unable to stop his confession, the man continued. "For purposes of anonymity, I don't keep identifying information on the ovae and sperm I bank. It's not useful for any reason, and Jean-Paul advised against doing so for legal reasons back when I started the collection. But when the senator called, and I knew the way things were headed, I decided to find your ovaries. As a gift. All it took was a few strands of your hair taken from your desk chair for DNA comparison. You FedExed them to the lab the next day with the outgoing mail yourself."

"Oh, no," Sharrah said.

"As it turned out, in the course of things, we had already used most of your ovae for experiments, and much of what remained had been touched by cancer. So initially I despaired of being able to give you this gift. But against all the cruel odds of my trial and error experiments, I discovered that not only did some of your eggs remain in the unused tissues, but one of the children we had created from other eggs had survived. She's remarkable, with great mental gifts, though like so many of my experiments she has certain disabilities that will prevent her from leading a normal life.

"But I hope that you won't hold these against her. These flaws are my fault, a product of my blind tinkering with the machinery of God. Hold them against me."

Sharrah felt as if the ground had fallen out beneath her stomach and her guts and heart were drifting in free fall. As they had when her own brother had come home from the mullah's house to whip her. As they had at the hangings in the soccer stadiums. Her shaking hand rattled the teacup against the saucer as she tried to pick it back up, and she set it back down.

Her employer kept on, though the thoughts roaring through her head were all but drowning him out now. "You could even disregard this child and start anew. A handful of your viable eggs might remain in your frozen ovaries. Select a sperm donor, and call the laboratory, and you can have more children. Exogenically, without any gene manipulation this time and without all the bother of preg-"

"Vincent, please, I need to think!" she burst out, her hand on her temples, the other clutching the envelopes.

"Of course. Forgive me." The man waited, transformed from a voice booming with impossibilities to the patient presence she was more used to. With silence upon her, and the wind blowing through the turning leaves, she stilled her thoughts, listening to see which one of them re-emerged as the most important.

The waitress hovered, drawn by her cry. She saw that guests from other tables were staring at her. "*Is everything in order, my Lady?*" she inquired in crisp high German.

"*Yes, everything is in order,*" Sharrah answered. "*It was only a surprise. It's a personal matter. I'm sorry if I've disturbed anyone.*"

She feared at first that her German was too accented for the waitress, but the woman's answer showed otherwise. "*If you need something, give the word,*" said the waitress, giving the doctor a reproachful look as she withdrew.

Sharrah drew a deep breath and formed what she wanted to say. Anger was chasing away her surprise and shock, and it soon coalesced from a whirlwind into words, like had happened so often on the Burn Hall debate team.

"The first thing I need to say is that you are a monster. You did all these things with the sham of consent taken while I was in pain and barely able to think. I can't tell you how it feels to know that the motherhood that I feared was gone forever has instead been taken and then twisted this way."

"Granted," said Vincent, without resistance. "I have been a monster, for decades. I am one of the last great monsters of a monstrous century. Today was a reminder to me of that."

Sharrah ignored him. "What's worse is that I was your partner in this. I pretended I understood what you were doing when you explained it to me, piece by piece. Some of your ethics were strange to me, but you had saved my life, and been so kind to me, and given me this home, that I resolved to help you anyway. I put those doubts out of my mind, until now, when you made it...so personal."

"Yes," said the doctor. "Things which are merely unethical to the observer feel much different to the victim. And that's why I need you. I have done this so long, and so single-mindedly, that I'm beginning to doubt that my judgment will do this organization any good in the future. Ethics evolve, but I fear I cannot evolve any further. I've done a lot of evolution in this lifetime."

Sharrah tried to understand him, but found she could not silence her anger to even acknowledge his contrition. "If you're going, go. Go now. I just... I just need you to go. I can't think. I don't know what to do," she felt her chest tightening. "I don't even know if I can breathe."

Vincent looked worried and crestfallen. "I'm sorry. I've done so much harm in my life. I thought by doing this, I could undo some harm, undo a great loss."

She elaborated on her request since the man had made no move to leave. "We can finish this by email. I am not leaving you. I will not abandon you. You did not abandon me. But right now I need to be alone. Go or I will."

Looking crushed, the old man withdrew, turned on his heel, and walked away. He paused to whisper an explanation to the waitress, who nodded and made notes. Sharrah had never seen emotion so plain on the doctor's face, but she was sure that at the moment, she didn't care. His feelings were the least of her problems.

"*Jedem das Seine*," she cursed after him in anger.

She picked up the letter the doctor had left with her, read it, and reread it with incredulity. She had a daughter, already twelve years old, living in the United States, in New York. The attachments that came with it charted her date of birth, her sperm and ovae donor numbers, and a photograph of a black-haired toddler in a hospital or child care clinic of some kind. At the back of the stack was a more recent photograph of a shyly smiling black-haired girl with Sharrah's mother's rounded nose. The face brought her another mix of emotions, and finally, tears.

Vincent had need of her services, she knew now. If it hadn't been obvious to him how wrong and unnatural what he was doing was when he created a child from her tissue, she shuddered to think what else she would find in his labs when she cleaned house. And she would clean house if she had the chance, she decided. She would fully enact her ethical sense. It was what he had asked for.

The lamb medallions arrived, along with a second cup of tea that she hadn't ordered and a stack of paper napkins. She picked one up and dabbed her eyes, grateful again for the kindness of strangers.

"*Danke*," she thanked the waitress. The woman retreated again.

The lamb medallions were cool by the time she put down the photograph of the girl with a giddying realization. At the bottom of the photograph of her daughter was the note "Case #490". She wondered about the number. Did it mean that, somewhere, Vincent had four hundred and eighty-nine other children?

She picked up the warm cup of tea and cradled it in her hands.

Epilogue

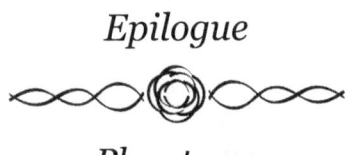

Phantoms

Rainer Iseli stood in the jet's gangway and waited to disembark. For all the comforts of the aircraft, the thirteen hour flight from Addis Ababa to the New Dominion Training Center had left him restless and coiled like a spring. Victoria, his stewardess and an old friend from many trans-Pacific flights during the wars in Iraq and Afghanistan, gave him a smirk as they stood by the door. "The local time is nine-oh-four in the morning, Mr. Iseli. Thank you for flying Greentree Airways."

Rainer grinned. He had once owned Greentree Airways, and still had a large interest in it, so he appreciated Victoria's unspoken irony. "Thanks for another smooth ride, Vickie. I slept like a baby."

A tone sounded, and a light over the door blinked on as the whine of the jet's engines began to spin down. She reached forward and spun the latch wheels, and once they heard the bump of the runway steps hitting the side of the plane, she opened the door and stood aside for him to walk through. "My pleasure, sir," she said as he departed.

The wet, warm air reached his nose immediately and carried with it the nostalgic smells of peat, still water, and pine needles. At the bottom of the runway stairs stood two men he wanted to see, and one man whose presence he would have to tolerate.

"Hey hey, my brothers! I didn't expect to see you here!" he shouted over the engine as he came quickly down the ramp. He threw an arm up on the waiting shoulders of Clive and Owen. The two men had been with him in the Special Forces. "Are you my bodyguards for this trip?"

"Sure enough," said Owen, as the two men returned his clasp, all but crushing him. Rainer was not a small man, but Clive and Owen were two rugged behemoths, and he knew from memory that either man could pick him up off his feet easily. He felt the edges of their body armor and weapons under their suit jackets, and rapped Clive's paneled chest with his knuckle. "Geared and ready, huh?"

The third man spoke up. "I figured 'who better to guard him,' right? After all, you're paying us for our best. May as well have your old friends."

"And you gave me your best," Rainer beamed. Though he still served on the board of Domini, he no longer owned it, and so he made a practice of paying for his security escorts from the company. This helped to reinforce the fact to Domini's endless critics that he was no longer in charge of the company. "You didn't have to come here to see me, Joseph, I'm sure you've got better things to do."

Joseph put his hands in his pockets. "Like I'll let you land here and just wander around. Besides, if you were just 'passing through' you would have touched down at Reagan National and already be swapping spit with the Secretary of State at the Forrestal Building. So I've lined up a few things. Our new APC just beat Blackwater's Grizzly to be the US Army's MRAP III. If you can take the time, I'd love to show you the progress on both it and the dirigible drone." Joseph's suggestion hung in the air, waiting for Rainer to either jump back into Domini's business, or by refusing, refresh Joseph's anointment as the new president and CEO.

Mr. Iseli considered this choice carefully. He had moved to Addis Ababa precisely to avoid being involved in corporate management. He wanted to spend time on the Somali project, his ministry, and his kids. Between his military service and the grand adventures of Domini in the wars in Iraq and Afghanistan, Judith and he had agreed he'd spent enough of his life playing with guns and bombs. But his curiosity rose at the thought of the novel technology. Undecided, he left it to Clive and Owen to make the decision.

"What do you guys think? Are Joe's toys worth seeing?" As Green Berets both men had been proficient users of cutting edge technologies, and he knew they would be good judges. To his surprise and guilty pleasure, both men nodded. "The APC is what it is. But the drone is cool shit, no question," Clive rumbled.

Rainer looked back to the plane. Vickie was halfway down with his bags. He knew they would be taken to wherever he would sleep that night. So he turned to Joseph. "Okay, you proud father, I'll come coo at your babies. Show me."

Joseph grinned with pleasure. He pointed his former boss toward a hangar about two hundred yards away and then walked alongside him. Rainer would have expected a car to meet them on the long tarmac, but the man seemed to be leading him on foot.

"How are Judith and the kids?" Joseph asked conversationally once the engine noise had fallen off enough that shouting wasn't necessary.

"Prospering, thank the Lord," he answered. "How are you and yours?"

"Adjusting. Mississipi has a lot of charms," Joseph said casually. Rainer noticed how little he was saying to the man, and how little the man volunteered in return. *"Strange how we play these games,"* he lamented. *"We're co-religionists, comrades-in-arms, all leaders in this great crusade to restore the Kingdom of God. We should have brotherly love, not this cagey back and forth."* He pondered what to say next, but Joseph continued first.

"How's that Somali project running?"

"Pirate attacks around the cape are down ninety two percent versus project start. I call that near total success."

Joseph cast him a glance and grinned. "Paying Muslims to kill Muslims on a dime. It's win-win for Jesus. And America."

Rainer frowned at this. He recognized this tone, the conspiratorial "us and them" voice, and the celebration of the death of unbelievers. He wanted to scold Joseph, but he stopped himself. He had helped foster this anti-Islamic culture in Domini, when he had been younger and had more zeal and less wisdom. To scold Joseph would be hypocritical. Instead, he should minister to him. Ministry was his new calling.

He phrased his reply carefully. "Some of our Somali operatives have already converted. And others are Ethiopian, and their families were Christian back when ours were still clutching pagan idols around campfires in Europe. So I don't see it that way, Joe. I like to think that inside every Muslim is a Christian trying to get out. "

This time Clive chimed in, his words reflecting that he had not grasped this new tone. "Split their chest with a bullet and you'll be *really* helping the Christian get out." At this, the other three men sniggered, but it died off rapidly when they realized that Rainer wasn't joining in. Mr. Iseli again subdued his desire to criticize the men, or to lecture them on the virtues of the Muslims he had come to know and respect in his new home. He would preach with his example, he decided, rather than lecture men he knew were stubborn but capable of changing if they decided they wanted to. So he changed the subject.

"I need to know about this Vincent Foster. Have we found him?"

"No, he has gone to ground, sir," answered Joseph. "But I've got our whole European intel section on the hunt for him.

"Anything unusual in his movements?"

Joseph shook his head. "From what we can tell, not up until the day he disappeared. Our investigation shows that he travels between Lebanon, West Africa, Brazil, Hong Kong, and Zurich, staying a couple of weeks, sometimes a month, in each place. He came back to Zurich as normal, traveled to London to make that announcement, and then flew back to Zurich for a couple of months. But last weekend, out of the blue, he paid cash for train tickets to Leipzig with his executive assistant and just vanished."

"We have a lead on any of his confidants?"

"Just his executive assistant, a woman by the name of Sharrah Bassi. She's his only employee in Switzerland, and a Muslim, though not a strict one."

"Try reaching out to her then," Rainer suggested. "My experience has shown me that many Muslims will cooperate if the right incentive can be found."

"I'll show you her file, but I wouldn't bet on that working with this one. She...she's a strange bird, and the evidence points to strong personal loyalty to this Foster character."

"Strong personal loyalty? Like yours, Joseph?" he wanted to ask, but didn't. *"Jesus gave Judas a chance to prove his faith, I should give Joe his,"* he reminded himself. So he continued past his doubts about Joseph. "Well, if Foster has gone to ground, then he knows we're watching him. So you're not giving anything away if we approach his assistant and she refuses us. I don't see what we have to lose. Just make the effort: even if she doesn't come over, we may learn something of use later."

For a moment only the whine of the jet and the tramp of their shoes on the asphalt could be heard. It was Joseph's turn, it seemed, to take time and think out his replies. "You may be the 'rainmaker,' but I make the calls now. And my call on that woman is no dice. Intel says she's very loyal. As near as we can tell, that is her only virtue in Foster's organization. She has no leadership experience, no finance background, no science, and no law. So why else would he have left her in charge?"

"Fine," Rainer answered. "I've got some old friends I need to visit in Belgrade anyway. They still have issues in the Presovo valley, and I'm the global go-to guy on the 'Muslim question.' Give *me* her file and I'll fly home via Zurich and Belgrade. We can change this world person to person, Joe. That's what the Lord did."

Joseph said nothing to this, choosing instead to fume to himself. The silence continued until Clive spoke up. "What brings you back to the US of A, boss?"

"Godlessness," Rainer replied. "The leviathan of sin, hypocrisy, and greed that sits astride this nation."

"Um, Hollywood?" Clive hazarded.

Mr. Iseli shook his head. "No. Congress. I have horses in my stables in Addis Ababa with more fear of the Lord than our congressmen. The Congress thinks, now that we brought them their victory, they can blow us off and blame Democrats for their own inaction. But Christ's believers demand their due. Someone must show these men the light. I am here to take my turn."

This answer, too, netted silence. Rainer reflected that the awesome and ancient Christianity he had encountered in Ethiopia, and his studies in Jerusalem, had informed his faith a great deal and made him a believer in ministry where he had before only believed in action. Some awkwardness was to be expected, then, when he rejoined his fellow crusaders who still thought only of war.

They were two-thirds of the way to the hangar when Rainer broke the silence he had made. "So tell me about this 'blimp drone.' How is it different than the reconnaissance blimp drones we used in Iraq?"

"Actually, sir, I've prepared a demonstration. We can do it before we go inside, if you're ready."

"Go ahead."

Clive and Owen traded looks and grinned. "You'll love this one, boss," Owen said conspiratorially. Clive sniggered.

Joseph nodded. "Here, take a look at this schematic while I call the pilot." Rainer took the tablet computer and perused it. The CEO put a finger to his earpiece. "Phantom Demo, this is Numero Uno. Are you on station?"

"Roger sir, on station, demo target in sight," the pilot's voice came back faintly.

"Approach and engage, Phantom Demo."

Rainer turned away from the hangar and scanned the sky over the airfield. "Where should I look?"

"You'll see it. Presently," said Joseph. And a second later, Mr. Iseli felt himself grasped by the waist and shoulders and lifted into the air. He gave a startled curse and looked up to find that he was hanging beneath a small cylindrical blimp. Waldos held his waist and shoulders, and his feet kicked futilely. He stopped struggling and relaxed. When he looked down, he was already thirty feet off the ground and hovering.

Joseph shouted up to him. "You remember, during the Iraq war we were given that non-competitive contract to develop a remote extraction drone that could silently enter an area and recover a casualty or evacuate an operative?"

"I remember," Rainer replied, controlling his voice to betray no fear.

"Well, the funding got cut in 2009," said Joseph. "But I took the project back out of the mothballs. In the meantime, engagement software had improved enough that I figured 'why settle for just grabbing people who *want* to fly away?' And the Phantom Lift drone was borne. It was hovering just beyond the crest of the hangar roof, waiting for my signal, and you didn't hear it. Powered by batteries and Dyson-style prop fans, this baby can sneak up on a target and carry it off. No shots fired, barely any motor sound, and it can fly nap of the earth the whole way so it's nearly undetectable on radar. Fill it with hydrogen instead of the current helium and inflate the auxiliary lift buoys, and it can carry away a medium-sized car."

Rainer alternated glances between the ground and the drone. Terror and fascination alternated through him, too, but not necessarily at the same rate.

Joseph took no notice of his distress. "She tops out at atmospheric heights: she can go as high as a weather balloon if needed. So depending on what you've picked up and why, you can fly low and put it down gently, or fly high and, well, study your cargo's maximum descent velocity. This thing can be a guardian angel, or witness to regrettable tragedy."

"I don't doubt it," said Rainer. "Put me down, Joe."

With just the barest of hesitations, the drone descended, setting him back on his feet so softly as to scarcely bend his knees. The padded waldos released, and the drone silently lifted away again. It made no more noise than a window air conditioner as it turned away and floated through the hangar doors.

Rainer watched the drone. He was not Joseph's biggest fan, but he did not banish the frank admiration on his features. This machine looked like a masterpiece, so he would give the man the credit he was due.

"Has she been field tested yet?" Rainer checked.

"Twice. She did two operations in support of the Charge of Joshua. Worked like a dream, even in built up areas."

Mr. Iseli smiled at this. He knew he shouldn't: the Charge of Joshua operation was one of the ideas he had dissented over. But the drone opened up new possibilities he never would have envisioned at the time. Despite himself, he felt his attitude changing.

Credits

No story is wholly original. Artists borrow inspiration from other sources they encounter. I'd like to acknowledge my sources of inspiration. If there are many, it's because I'm a fraction of the artist of each of them and needed that many crutches. I hope that by listing them I can share with the curious reader the joy in their works.

My literary inspirations included:

The Gift, translations of Hafiz by Daniel Ladinsky

Franz Kafka: Amerika and The Trial

Bertolt Brecht: The Caucasian Chalk Circle and *If Sharks were People*

Gunter Grass: The Tin Drum

Yevgeny Zamyatin: We

Musical inspirations that sparked the writing process and chased away writer's block were:

E.S. Posthumous: *Unearthed*

Beloved World Music Ensemble: *Beloved*

Rob Dougan: *Furious Angels*

Pierce Pettis: *When I Grow Up*

and finally

Tangerine Dream: *Poland, Pergamon,* and *Destination Berlin*

My thanks to Russell Bridge for his artwork, and for the confidence in me to do the artwork on percentage.

Thanks also goes to Jeffrey Anbinder. Jeffrey read my first draft of the book and loved it so well, despite all my typos, that he submitted over four hundred corrections and notes to me, making the book better for every reader that followed him. As an independent writer I could not afford a professional editor, but thanks to Jeff you probably wouldn't know it.

More thanks to Doris Rubruck who, on her own time, translated portions of the book drafts into German for her friends to read. She was my first fan, and her enthusiasm gave me the courage to continue writing.

From "Her Folded Wings..."

...At the top of the laboratory wall, Suliya and Sharrah were greeted by a large muscled man with an AK-47. But despite his size and potential menace, the man merely gave Suliya a fond smile and Sharrah a nod. Apparently he had assumed she was one of the nannies or governesses.

"Good afternoon, Mistress Suliya," his bass voice rumbled.

"Hello, Edward. It is a beautiful day, isn't it?" said the girl blithely.

"Yes indeed," replied the guard, though the faded colors of his fatigues and the sweat rings under his arms and collar showed that he spent many such "beautiful days" in the hot sun. "Have you come to speak with the butterflies again?"

"Yes, I will show Madame Bassi how I do it."

At the name "Bassi" the guard started and straightened himself. "It is an honor to meet you, Madame," he said.

"Thank you, Edward, for helping to take care of these children," Sharrah answered his formality with praise and his name, as her internet courses on leadership techniques had taught her to do.

"Thank the Emir, whose large heart gives me this honorable duty of protecting the meek," replied Edward even more formally. "I am not afraid to fight, of course, but it is good to help children."

She nodded in reply and followed anxiously after Suliya, who was now using her white cane to tap her way out onto a concrete walkway atop the wall that was scarcely two feet wide. But once she found its beginning, she reached out and grasped the chain that hung to her left and walked along it quickly. She marveled at the girl's confidence on a catwalk she couldn't even see, and wondered how often she had come here before. She guessed from the guard's lack of concern that the child's visits were regular.

After a moment Suliya stopped and turned to face out from the compound, sweeping her blind gaze across the vast sea of grass and shrubs that rolled away to the horizon.

"No one ever believes me when I tell them I can change my smell. At least, not the first time I tell them. So I will show you," she said. She raised her arms to the horizontal and closed her twitching eyes. And then she simply stood there.

Sharrah watched, puzzled. She sniffed the air for some new smell, but detected nothing. After a moment, however, an enormous butterfly came and alighted on the back of the girl's left hand. The butterfly had brown and orange wings with spots and stripes that matched the colors of Suliya's own robe and head scarf. She was dazzled by its beauty.

"We are different from you," Suliya said abruptly. "All the children here. Aren't we?"

Sharrah was taken aback by the demanding tone of the girl's question, and also by the fact that she was right about something she should have no way of knowing. None of the children knew they were experiments, or at least, that's what she had been led to believe.

"I'm not sure what you mean," she asked as she recovered herself. "Of course you're different. That's why you're here. But you're still people, like Edward and like me, so that's why we take care of you."

"You're afraid. So that means you're probably lying," reported Suliya.

"All the children here, we smell similar. And all the grown-ups and doctors and guards, they smell similar, but different from the children. Even you. You smell like Rosetta, but not in the way we smell like Rosetta. So we are not the same, and even you and Rosetta are not the same."

Sharrah found an answer. *"Maybe the guards and the doctors and nannies smell different because they are older. There are smells people give off as they get older. Pheromones."*

"Yes, I used to think that might explain it after I learned about pheromones in biology lessons," answered Suliyah. *"But there are differences. They say that people cannot consciously smell pheromones or change them, but I can do both. And last month I had my first cycle, and I still smell different from you. I still smell like the children, and not like the grownups. So I have a different answer.*

"We have pheromones that you do not. We can control how we smell, and you cannot." As Suliya spoke, two more of the orange and brown butterflies landed on her, one on her headscarf and other on her hip. And when Sharrah looked down off the wall, she gasped. Gathered there like a tiger-striped dustdevil was a swarm of the same butterflies that were slowly rising higher and higher. After a few more seconds, Suliyah was covered with the insects, glimmering in the sun and languidly opening and closing their wings. Though Ms. Bassi found the sight frightening, Suliya did not move or show any surprise or concern at this.

"We are different," Suliya repeated. *"We are not like you. And that is why we all live here. Isn't it? Are we all that there are? Or are there more of us in other places?"*

Sharrah said nothing. Suliya was exactly right: she had worked out with her mind and nose something none of the adults who surrounded her knew or had probably ever imagined. And with her nose she could even guess that she was hiding something. After a moment of silence, the girl bent a hand back to her face and stroked a butterfly that had landed on her cheek.

"They feel so beautiful," she said. *"I wish I could see how pretty they are. And I want to go to the places they come from. I want to be free. Once I thought if I could call enough butterflies, they would pick me up and carry me away over this wall. I wish they could."*

As Sharrah listened to Suliya's ramblings, she felt both pity and fear. Pity for the girl who simply wanted the same freedom as anyone her age, and fear of the bitterness in the child's voice and keenness in her insights. Even if Suliya did not share her suspicions about her differences with the other children, how could the laboratory hope to keep secret from these children what their own senses told them was true? They grew older every day: one day, in groups or one by one like Suliya, they would all know.

She watched, speechless, as a single butterfly lifted back off of Suliya's shoulder and fluttered away.

About the Author

Martin Sparks makes his living as an anti-Christ, a title he shares with other, better known, anti-Christs such as Barack Obama, Dubya, Mick Jagger, Chaz Bono, and Javier Solana. He is also a shameless namedropper. When not penning texts designed to fragment the Republic, advance corporate greed, and damn millions of souls to purgatory, he lives a quiet life in a suburban home in an upstate northern outside-the-beltway bedroom community of the twin cities of Sodom and Gamorrah.

Martin enjoys the company of his lovely wife and personable tortoiseshell cat, as well as bingo and automatic weapons target practice at the local Gay Socialist Muslim Elitist Unstable Swinging Veterans of Foreign Operations Other than War Post. His previous works include electoral speeches and ghostwritten "autobiographies" of congressional and presidential candidates (almost certainly including ones you voted for), numerous divisive internet memes, and a guide to the cultivation of sectarianism he co-authored with his great uncle Screwtape. After the Rapture, he looks forward to world domination, throwing a wild party for seventy-two virgins who all leave unsatisfied, and a quiet retirement filled with tea.